THE OB

Also by Freda Warrington from Earthlight

The Amber Citadel
The Sapphire Throne

Books One and Two of The Jewelfire Trilogy

THE OBSIDIAN TOWER

Freda Warrington

EARTHLIGHT
SIMON & SCHUSTER

London • New York • Sydney • Tokyo • Singapore • Toronto • Dublin

A VIACOM COMPANY

First published in Great Britain by Earthlight, 2001
An imprint of Simon & Schuster UK Ltd
A Viacom Company

Copyright © Freda Warrington, 2001

This book is copyright under the Berne Convention
No reproduction without permission
® and © 1998 Simon and Scuster Inc. All rights reserved
Earthlight & Design is a registered trademark of
Simon & Schuster Inc.

The right of Freda Warrington to be identified as author
of this work has been asserted by her in accordance with
sections 77 and 78 of the Copyright, Designs and Patents Act, 1988.

1 3 5 7 9 10 8 6 4 2

Simon & Schuster UK Ltd
Africa House
64–78 Kingsway
London WC2B 6AH

Simon & Schuster Australia
Sydney

A CIP catalogue record for this book is available
from the British Library

ISBN 0-7434-1607-4

This book is a work of fiction. Names, characters, places and
incidents are either products of the author's imagination or
are used fictitiously. Any resemblance to actual people living
or dead, events or locales is entirely coincidental.

Typeset by Palimpsest Book Production Limited,
Polmont, Stirlingshire

Printed and bound in Great Britain by
Omnia Books Limited, Glasgow

Contents

One: The Darkest Day 1
Two: Vaurgroth the Merciful 27
Three: Breaking the Circle 43
Four: The Order of Calathvahn 77
Five: Trust and Mistrust 103
Six: Jthery 121
Seven: Orb of Clear Sight 145
Eight: Webs of Fire 169
Nine: Dark Mirror 191
Ten: Blood and Rose Moon 217
Eleven: Paths into Twilight 243
Twelve: Crusaders of Q'elethrios 271
Thirteen: The Ruby Plains 291
Fourteen: The Wolf Mage 319
Fifteen: Lord Sunstone 351
Sixteen: Ink in the Skin 375
Seventeen: The Turquoise Court 395
Eighteen: Defiance 423
Nineteen: Forest God and Dragonfly 443
Twenty: Falthorn's Shadow 475
Twenty-one: The Dark Spire 501
Twenty-two: The Eye of the Sun 529
Twenty-three: Reunion 553
Twenty-four: Beyond the Almandine Vale 593
Twenty-five: Heliodor and Obsidian 643
Twenty-six: Blood Sunset 679

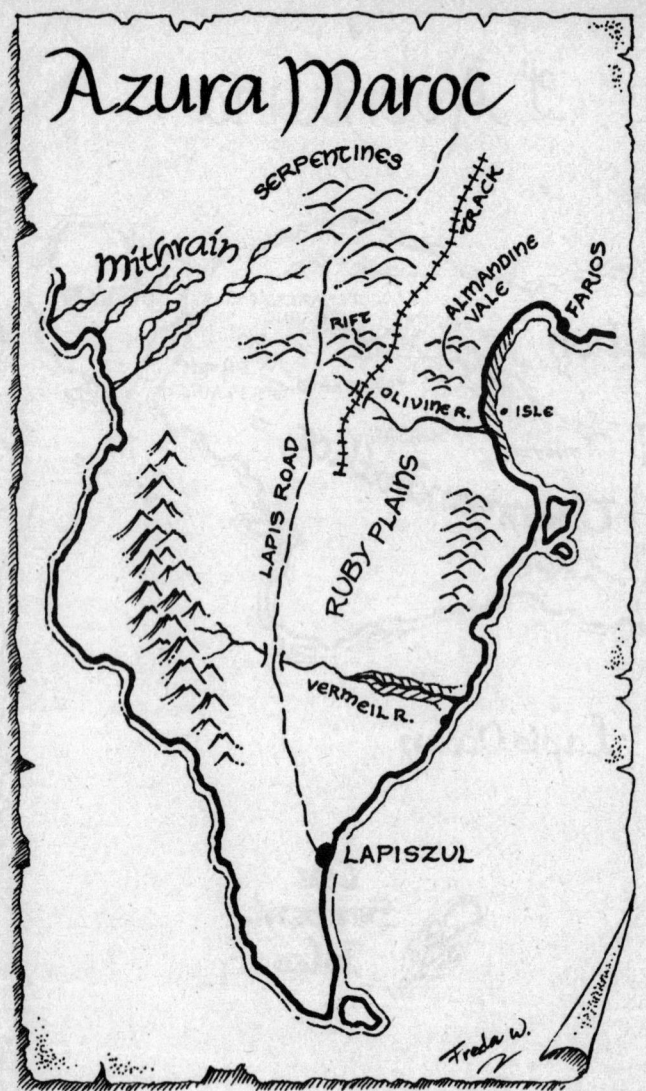

The Jewelfire Trilogy
The Amber Citadel, The Sapphire Throne
and *The Obsidian Tower*
is dedicated with love to

Justina Robson

Beloved friend and star of Silver Screen

Chapter One. The Darkest Day

Jthery fell asleep, waiting for Falthorn. Lying on the bank of a sapphire pool with one hand trailing in the water, he dreamed of Aventuria.

He saw a Seer in a darkened hut, leaning over a disc of crystal; and in that crystal another scene unfolded. An empress of dragon-hawks flying steadily against a bleak mountainscape, her long scaly head pointed forward, her leathery wings outstretched. All of the world was held in her eye. Visions within visions.

Jthery gasped with the thrill of falling. Now he flew with her. The sky was a vast upturned cauldron. Birds tumbled across the boiling clouds, flung by storms. Only the dragon-hawk's flight was steady. The whole of the Nine Realms lay stretched out below. Down there in the darkness of forests and hills, plains and cities, he saw wave on wave of living creatures fleeing in terror.

Pursuing them came the Devourers.

First the *ghelim*, mimicking dra'a'ks but more terrible by far, erupting from the clouds with venom in their claws and cruel intelligence in their eyes. Then the Bhahdradomen troops in soft-moving, unstoppable lines, wielding weapons that cracked with lethal lightning. And last came the *graukhim* herds to suck the very sap of life out of the land.

Far below, Jthery saw the lakes of Mithrain, the beloved lakes of his own realm, glittering in the misted night. He yearned towards them. Only to see that their shores were already clustered with Devourers, with *graukhim* plunging their muzzles in the sacred waters. They would not stop drinking until they had drunk every lake dry.

He groaned. A gigantic black tower came roaring up out of the ground, into the sky, flinging Jthery-as-dragon-hawk into a tumbling spiral.

Falling, he screamed.

He jerked awake. Verdanholm, the realm of the Aelyr, lay serenely around him, all blue-green foliage and moist shadows. Its tranquillity felt sinister.

His hand had gone numb, trailing in the water. Sitting up, he cradled it and rubbed the chilly white flesh, feeling that it didn't even belong to him. The pool was like black sapphire, inscrutable. Where was Falthorn?

Fear pulsed through him. Shall I wait? Jthery thought. Shall I trust him? Or should I flee? The nightmare coloured everything. Jthery couldn't shake off the terror that it wasn't a dream but a vision of reality; and that if it was real, Falthorn was intimately entwined with it. No, he thought. No. Falthorn would never do anything to harm Aventuria . . . would he?

As if in answer, the pool became alive with elementals whispering warnings. Jthery sat transfixed by the blue-black, dancing shadows. Then they were gone and the water was still, empty, silent as death.

The poet Saphaeyender woke and stared at the ceiling, knowing at once that something was hideously wrong. He recalled a restless, wine-blurred night, punctuated by a feverish ecstasy that was mostly an attempt to hide from reality; but mainly dry-mouthed anxiety and fitful sleep. It took him a moment to remember why he'd got drunk. Then he did, and his heart lurched into the heavy rhythm of dread.

Everything looked as usual. Winter sunlight fell through the lattices, dappling the marble walls. Surely he'd dreamed the horror. For as long as he stayed in bed, he could convince himself that the world had returned to normal.

The young man who lay beside him stirred and pushed back the ivory sheets. His resemblance to Lynden wasn't obvious; this youth had yellow hair and blue eyes and he was a typical Parionian, well-spoken and pampered. And yet, his face and innocence and eagerness to please reminded Saphaeyender painfully of Lynden.

Damn, he thought. So much for my resolution not to take advantage of another acolyte . . .

Seeing the poet awake, the youth blinked and his angelic face clouded. 'Sir?'

'Goddess's sake, Eander, don't call me sir.'

'It's difficult, since I work for you.'

'Difficult, when you're in bed with me? Use my name.'

'Saphaeyender, then.' His eyelids fell. 'Is it . . . are they . . . ?'

Saphaeyender said nothing. Gravely he ran his hand over Eander's smooth white shoulder, his muscled chest and narrow hips. He thought, I'm terrified. This boy, and my staff, and my actors . . . they all rely on me. How am I to protect them? I could barely protect them from Garnelys; how in Nepheter's name am I supposed to protect them from *this*?

'I am hoping it was all a bad dream,' he said at last. 'I trust you're not as badly hung over as I am?'

'I'm fine. You drank more than I did.' Eander frowned. 'You're not regretting last night, are you?'

Saphaeyender touched the young man's cheekbone, thinking of Lynden again. 'I only regret the ones I never had. I don't think I could have got through last night without you here. Thank you for that. Whatever we find today, at least we've had the solace of pleasure.'

Eander laughed uneasily. 'You're talking as if we're going to be executed.'

'Who knows?' Saphaeyender took a breath, threw back the sheets, and placed his feet on the cold marble tiles.

'What are you doing?' Fear in Eander's voice.

'Just looking.'

Saphaeyender walked across the bedchamber to the row of windows that overlooked the street. The central and right-hand ones were obscured by the trees around the walls of his villa, but the left-hand window gave a clear view onto the pale road snaking down Temple Hill. He pulled the shutters back. The glass panes were clear but treacly with imperfections; the shapes outside were dark and vague. Dry-mouthed, he opened the window.

The street was deserted. That was unnatural. On a normal day there was always traffic between the city and the Temple of Nepheter. But this morning, no priestesses in pale yellow, no citizens in their pleated robes standing gossiping in the pleasant shade of the trees, no horses, no carriages or merchants' carts rattling by.

Eander came to stand silently beside him, one hand on his shoulder. The light was grey, the air motionless. Against the gloom three figures came into view. Roughly human in shape, clearly not human at all. Scaly skin stretched over skull faces, high vulturine shoulders, strangely-jointed limbs. They wore tunics of some thin leathery stuff that shifted colour constantly to blend with the background. Around their thin straight waists were belts, hung with weapons of oily grey metal. Their aura of confident menace was as tangible as heat.

Saphaeyender's throat contracted with a fear that he couldn't control. Like a nightmare, it bypassed all reason. Eander's fingers became a vice.

'We didn't dream it,' Saphaeyender whispered.

A few days ago, the Bhahdradomen clustering around the city had been pitiful refugees. Yesterday they had changed. Something had happened to make them throw off their helpless disguise and swell with strength.

'Are the doors locked?' asked Eander.

'Yes, but do you think that will keep them out?'

One of the Bhahdradomen soldiers looked up and saw them. It met the poet's gaze with deep-set whiteless eyes. Saphaeyender froze. The thing spoke, in Paranian so guttural he could barely understand it.

'You have nothing to fear, citizen. Vaurgroth is a merciful

master. Stay in your home until you hear the bell. Parione is under control.'

'Nothing to fear?' Saphaeyender mouthed. He would have slammed the window shut, but at that moment the soldier's attention jerked away as something thudded into its ribs. The Bhahdradomen hissed in anger. Someone had thrown a stone at it.

And then another. The patrol was caught in a deluge of rocks and arrows. One of the Bhahdradomen fell, only to rise again, dragging an arrow from the scaly flesh of his arm as if removing nothing worse than a bee-sting.

Drawing their alien weapons, the three plunged into the garden from which the attack had come. It was thick with evergreens, with arkh-woods and other species that kept their foliage in winter. Saphaeyender watched, paralysed. The rain of missiles ceased. He saw shrubs thrashing, heard muffled voices. The patrol emerged empty-handed. Then their officer drew some kind of crossbow, a deformity of grey metal, and calmly fired up into the branches of a tree.

There was a shout, a fall of leaves. A human dropped at the invaders' feet.

They seized him, dragged him up by the scruff of his neck. It was a man, thirty or older, in a threadbare green tunic and breeches, an old uniform of Garnelys's day.

The man was screaming in pain and terror. The missile, whatever it was, had pierced his thigh, leaving a dark hole in fabric and flesh. Eander pressed his head against Saphaeyender's shoulder, shuddering.

'Vaurgroth is a benevolent conqueror,' rasped the Bhahdradomen officer, loud and furious. It looked around as if addressing all the humans who might be watching unseen from villas and gardens along the hill. 'He has taken the city peacefully. Do not try to resist him.'

'You filth!' the man roared. 'There'll be no peace until we've driven every one of you back to the pit you came from!'

'Vaurgroth is kind,' said the Bhahdradomen. Now he extended a long thin weapon like a fencing foil and pressed it to the man's face. 'Master of Light loves those who love him. But if you defy us . . .'

The blade crackled with green lightning. Red blisters appeared where it touched the man's skin. He screamed. Even from yards away, Saphaeyender could see the scarlet bubbling of flesh. The stench of hot metal and blood filled his head.

He slammed the window shut. He and Eander sat huddled on the bed, clutching each other as an eternal five minutes crawled past. At last the screams stopped. They uncurled and sat without looking at each other. Only trying to breathe.

'Brutes,' Eander said faintly. Then, as Saphaeyender stood up, 'Where are you going?'

'Out. The Citadel bell is ringing, can't you hear it?'

'What?' The blue eyes stared up at him, desperate. 'No, you mustn't!'

'I must,' the poet replied. 'I need to know how this happened.'

Darkness lay on the Amber Citadel.

Tanthe sat on a couch beside Auriel with her feet drawn up and her arms round her knees, watching Helan pace round and round their luxurious prison.

Queen Helananthe of the Nine Realms of Aventuria; Queen no longer. Her strong-boned, rosy face had turned white as paper and her honey hair drooped in disarray as she paced, paced. She hadn't rested all night. Now it was light outside, Tanthe noticed, but the grey glow hadn't penetrated the windows. For all the lamps and candles blazing around the chamber, none of it could push back the darkness.

'How did this happen?' Helan's voice was hoarse. 'Tell me, Eldareth. The Aelyr despise the Bhahdradomen – yet now, Falthorn's in league with Vaurgroth? How?'

'It's not that simple,' Eldareth replied grimly. He looked at Tanthe but she felt numb, had nothing to say. 'I wouldn't say they were in league, as such. Falthorn made a treaty with Vaurgroth, in which Aventuria was the ultimate bargaining counter.'

As Eldareth spoke, Auriel's hand crept onto Tanthe's and his fingers folded tight round hers. At least Falthorn hadn't taken Auriel away with him. That was something.

After the confrontation in the Sun Chamber, Vaurgroth's henchmen brought them to this suite of chambers and, thankfully, removed their chains. There were worse places to be locked up. The walls were panelled with azurite and malachite, the furnishings gilded with silverleaf and padded with oyster satin. Velvety rugs of green and blue lay on tiles of silver marble. Yet still a prison, in a Citadel now occupied by enemies.

They'd barely slept. Yet it was only now, in the cheerless morning, that they'd begun to talk freely and make sense of the disaster. Since they were all exhausted and in shock, Tanthe wasn't sure they were making sense of anything.

The dry bones of fact remained. Lord Falthorn of the Valahyr had manoeuvred Helan into giving up the Sapphire Throne to Vaurgroth.

Her humiliation had been unbearable to witness. And yet, thought Tanthe, by giving in she saved all our lives.

'It's as Falthorn told us,' Eldareth went on. 'Verdanholm has been under attack from the Bhahdradomen for aeons, even while they were quiet on Earth. Falthorn vowed to free his realm from them, once and for all. Apparently he found Vaurgroth amenable to a bargain; if they would cease their attacks on Verdanholm, Falthorn would deliver Aventuria into their hands in exchange.'

Helan paused, leaning on a table with braced arms. She'd thrown off her regal gemmed robe. The under-robe of violet satin was dark with sweat around her armpits. Everyone was watching her, gauging her reaction to Eldareth's words. Mawrdreth, her husband, sat taut and silent on the edge of a chair, his face pallid beneath the dusk of his skin. Elrill, Lord of the Shaelahyr, leaned back in another chair with his long white hands resting on the arms. His face was a snow-sculpture, but his eyes were as bright as an arctic ocean.

'And this he has done without effort, just as if he were snatching a toy from an infant!' said Helan. 'Why did I not see it coming, when all the warnings were there?'

Tanthe shifted uncomfortably. Excruciating to witness Helananthe's pain. No-one knew how to help her.

'I wouldn't say he did it without effort,' Tanthe said, her voice thick.

Helan turned to her. She looked dreadful; face grey, eyes glittering. 'What?'

'Falthorn didn't do this without effort,' Tanthe repeated, untangling her limbs and sitting up straight. 'He's worked towards it for years. He showed me how the Eaters were attacking Verdanholm, which he said is a more liquid and unstable realm than Earth. Not with weapons or armies. Somehow, they were sucking energy itself out of the realm. It's been going on for aeons, he said; the Aelyr trying to recreate the fabric of Verdanholm as fast as the Eaters consumed it. Only now the Eaters were winning. I wasn't close enough to see exactly what they were doing, but where they'd been, there was nothing. I don't mean bare earth, I mean *nothing*.'

Helan was shocked into silence by this. Tanthe added, 'That's why saving Verdanholm is all Falthorn cares about.'

'Has he sent you to be his advocate?'

Helan spoke so sharply that Tanthe flinched. 'Of course not! I'm only saying that he's clever and driven and it wasn't your fault!'

'And would I do the same? Sell Verdanholm in order to free the Earth?' She resumed her pacing, dragging her fingers through her hair. 'I don't think I could be that cold. That's the difference between us. That's why he outwitted me.'

'Us,' Mawrdreth put in. 'He outwitted all of us.'

Eldareth looked icily at the younger man. Tanthe could only imagine what he'd felt when he discovered that Helan had married the handsome Thand'rathian nobleman in his absence. The atmosphere between the two men made the darkness even more oppressive. She wanted to sleep. She felt too wretched to care about any of it any more.

Elrill said, 'It's infuriating to admit that, despite being fully aware of Lord Falthorn's devious nature, we still fell into his trap. Valahyr!' he added with contempt.

'I know this wasn't your fault. Falthorn had it all planned; you just happened to be there when he chose to carry it out.' Helan took a deep breath, held it, let it go. She looked exhausted. 'By the way, Tanthe, your child?' She pushed a curly tangle of hair off her forehead. 'I'm so sorry, I've been so preoccupied I didn't even think to ask. Did you ever find it?'

Tanthe's throat tightened. She looked at Auriel, her Aelyr brother. It had been his child too; one that Falthorn had tricked them into making, then stolen for his own uses. He looked back at her, his lovely face shadowed with pain. Her throat was so tight she couldn't speak for a while.

'No,' she said, when the spasm eased. 'Auriel said he thinks it was a boy. Falthorn was evasive, wouldn't tell me where it was. He seems convinced the baby has some amazing power, the potential to be a great *roth*-mage. He implied that he was going to . . .'

'What?' Helan said more gently.

'Give the child to the Bhahdradomen.'

There were quiet gasps in the room. Now they were all looking at Tanthe. She was finding it hard to breathe; Auriel put his arm round her, pressed his lips to her hair.

'Why?'

Tanthe took deep breaths. She wasn't only thinking

about the infant, but her sister Ysomir, who was imprisoned elsewhere in the Citadel, at the shape-shifters' mercy. 'Falthorn has the Basilisks, so he holds the balance of power. The Bhahdradomen don't like that. So to appease them he'll give them the magical child, a kind of hostage to keep them sweet and stop them breaking the agreement. But they won't dare harm the child, so he claims, because if they did it might destroy them.'

'Destroy them? How?'

'I've no idea. But then, how can we trust anything Falthorn says? He might have been lying through his teeth.'

'So you've no idea where the child is now? Auriel?'

He shook his head. 'None,' he said, very quietly.

'It's no good asking Auriel anything,' Tanthe said bitterly. 'He's completely terrified of Falthorn and I know how he feels. Our uncle has wonderful ways of torturing you, when he can't get what he wants.'

'Press harder next time,' said Eldareth. He caught Tanthe's eye and they shared a moment of perverse amusement. Helan looked quizzically at Eldareth. 'Tanthe jumped on Falthorn and tried to strangle him,' he explained.

'A brave attempt,' said Elrill.

Tanthe gave a wan smile, closing her eyes as a grim fist of memory struck her. She couldn't bring herself to tell them how Falthorn had punished her for the attack. She shuddered, and Auriel squeezed her arm. He knew.

'I'm sorry, Helan,' Eldareth sighed, stretching his long limbs. His angular, weather-beaten face was pale with despair, his fine black hair escaping from the thong that bound it on the nape of his neck. 'Our quest to Verdanholm was a monumental failure all round.'

Tanthe thought bleakly, And Rufryd's quest to Vexor? He's still there, stranded, thousands of miles away. I don't even know if he's alive. Gods, why was I so cold to him when we said goodbye? He was trying to be friends again and all I could do was cold-shoulder him. Even if he can't forgive me, I would give anything to see him again. Ymmi's off in some remote part of the Citadel I'll never reach. I can't help either of them.

'Oh, yes, I suppose Falthorn has worked hard,' Helan was saying. 'He stole the Basilisks from under our feet, the only weapons that kept us truly safe from the Bhahdradomen. He abducted my mother and brother then presented me with a choice. Give up my throne to the Bhahdradomen, or watch my family being tortured to death! No choice at all. But what have I done? Saved two people, only to throw thousands of others into despair and death? Broken the Xauroma!'

'Helan.' Mawrdreth rose and took her arm. 'Don't. We should rest.'

'How can I rest?' she said fiercely. 'The Amber Citadel is full of Bhahdradomen! I can feel them, like webs in the air. Can't you taste the *gauroth*? It tastes like iron, like blood. Every citizen in Parione must have that taste in their mouth this morning – and I have let this happen!'

'No,' said Eldareth. 'The city was already full of them, waiting for Vaurgroth to arrive. The palace guards were already disabled, all of your councillors and staff ensorcelled. If you hadn't given up the throne they would have taken it by force.'

'This way, they squeezed every possible drop of humiliation out of me.'

Eldareth answered, 'This way, at least we're still alive.'

'For how long?' said Tanthe. She got up and went to the double doors that led out of the suite. They were locked, and she knew that Bhahdradomen guards stood outside. She could *feel* them. Their aura was a physical vibration that sapped the body and infected the mind, distorting reality into nightmare.

The situation seemed utterly surreal. She'd been there in the Sun Chamber when the dreadful elite of the Bhahdradomen had appeared and quietly taken over. She knew how Falthorn had worked hand-in-glove with them to strip away Aventuria's defences. She had witnessed the way they'd destroyed the Queen with the simplest of threats. *Give us the Throne or watch your mother and brother be tortured.* Checkmate.

She'd watched Vaurgroth slide his thin frame onto the Sapphire Throne, clasping its arms with spindly fingers. King and conqueror. She remembered with distaste how serene Vaurgroth had seemed on Helananthe's throne, how perfectly at home and joyful.

'Ancestor is merciful,' he had said, insisting that no-one would be harmed, that life would simply go on as it always had, give or take a few small differences.

How could they believe any of it?

Eldareth said, 'Helan, Lord Mawrdreth – forgive me, *King* Mawrdreth – is right. We need to rest.'

His reference to her husband was barbed. Mawrdreth looked levelly at Eldareth, his slanting green eyes narrow. His expression gave little away; Tanthe couldn't tell whether he resented Eldareth, or felt magnanimous towards him. 'King no longer, it appears,' he said quietly.

'I can't rest,' said Helan.

'What does the stupid throne matter anyway?' Tanthe exclaimed. 'You're still *our* Queen! You can't abdicate from that, ever!'

The others voiced their agreement, even Elrill. Helan sat down suddenly on the arm of a chair, her hands covering her face.

The lock gave a loud *clunk*, making them all start. Tanthe sprang away like a spooked cat as the tall doors swung open. A party of Bhahdradomen glided in, their bare clawed feet rustling drily on the floor. As she retreated behind Elrill's chair, Auriel came to her side and pressed one arm around her. She wished to all the gods she could fight this wretched net of fear the Devourers cast; grotesque as they were, it was out of all proportion to their physical appearance.

There were three of the elite – Vaurgroth's closest

counsellor-mages – including the ancient pale one, Rhazagramen. Flanking them were six officers, menacing figures uniformed in layers of leathery membrane, green and black. Behind them, a handful of lower-ranked guards in plain, shadowy tunics. The lower ones had opaque skins, with lichen-like mottling of grey or greyish green. The higher ones had a translucent quality, pearly light shining through the very bones of the skulls and throbbing in their vessels.

All of them looked confident, impassive, terrifying.

'You will come with us now,' said Rhazagramen, pointing a white scorpion of a hand at the Queen.

Immediately, Eldareth and Mawrdreth and Elrill gathered protectively around her. Tanthe felt sick. 'You're taking her nowhere,' said Eldareth.

Rhazagramen's tiny mouth tightened with contempt. 'How did such rabbits ever pose any threat to *domenim*? Did not Vaurgroth the Merciful assure you that you have nothing to fear? How dare you doubt his word? The ex-Queen is required to address her citizens.'

'What?' said Helan, on her feet again.

'You shall be instructed what to say, don't worry,' said Rhazagramen in his metallic, perfect Paranian. 'And the rest of you may come too, to witness your ex-Queen's last moment of glory.'

None of them moved. They stood petrified. There was a hiss of dark weapons being drawn from belts, and the air thickened with static. One of the guards lashed out with what appeared to be a whip. The long steel-grey snake split the very air in front of them with a deafening crack and a flash of sour green lightning.

Tanthe felt something worse than fire on her skin. A pulse of hideous radiation, pure lethal *gauroth*. Her mouth went bone-dry.

'Don't make us herd you like *graukhim*,' Rhazagramen said sweetly into the silence that followed. He raised a clawed hand. 'Move!'

* * *

The street outside the villa was quiet, the graceful marble houses oddly luminous. A wind rose, making the trees dance wildly against the sky.

Saphaeyender and Eander began to walk the curving avenue that led from Temple Hill towards the Amber Citadel. They made a striking sight in pearl-grey cloaks embroidered with jet and silver; the tall, unmistakable figure of the playwright with his white-streaked black hair flowing, and the blond young man at his side. His apprentice, working and living with his mentor while he learned the crafts of the theatre.

Saphaeyender hadn't meant them to become lovers, but it had been all too predictable. Secretly he feared that Tanthe might be dead by now. At best, he'd given up hope of her ever coming back to him, and he was bad at being alone.

On impulse he had grabbed an ebony cane that concealed a thin sword. It was only a prop from an old play, and probably wouldn't harm anyone, but it made him feel safer.

Further down the hill there were a few men and women standing about on the street, talking uneasily to one another. They watched him pass, but said nothing. The air was a mass of dark tension. The whole of Parione lay under a trembling, breathing silence.

A few yards on, they saw the first of them.

They almost walked into the creature, it was so hard to see. Saphaeyender snatched Eander out of its way just in time. The Bhahdradomen's long tunic blended with the pale greys of the street. Its feet were bare, long and gnarled with clawed toes. A belt encircled its thin waist, hung with the strange, sinister implements that were beginning to be too familiar. A whip, a black rod like a cosh, some form of crossbow made of gnarled metal.

The creature's hood was pushed back, revealing a yellowish head dappled with darker hues. Its features were human in arrangement but unnervingly alien, like a skull pinched from yellow clay. Deep holes for eyes; then, as a glint of light caught them, small deepset orbs shone in the sockets, proud and replete with power.

It made no move towards the two men, only stared at them. But the stare said everything. *We are here.*

The invader's aura filled Saphaeyender's mind with thoughts of dying landscapes, skeletal trees, despair. Eander let out a gasp.

'Come on,' said Saphaeyender, pulling him onwards. 'Don't look at them.'

Further on, there were Bhahdradomen everywhere. They were changed utterly from the miserable refugees they had appeared to be only the day before. Hunched, passive figures in rags no longer. It was as if they had physically grown. Now they walked with their heads high and the gleam of victory in their pond-deep eyes.

'Where have they come from?' Eander whispered. 'How has this happened?'

'They were already here, waiting for a source of power. And now the source has arrived.'

The disaster had been looming for weeks, presaged by wild storms and oppressive skies that pressed down on Parione's rooftops. Yesterday there had come a moment when Saphaeyender simply *knew*. It was in the air, a whispering web of nightmare, tangible as smoke. He'd looked out of his window and seen a group of Bhahdradomen refugees in the street below, physically changing like moths bursting out of pupa-cases. Raising their faces to drink in their new power.

It didn't take a *roth*-mage to sense the change. Everyone in the city had known.

The summoning bell rang insistently. Closer to the Amber Citadel, the streets were full of people. There were citizens in fashionable pale robes or embroidered, boned silks, merchants in cloaks of every hue, artisans in their work clothes. He sensed panic, simmering chaos. Overnight their city had been taken by stealth, and no one understood how.

There was a constant clamour of voices, punctuated with yells of impotent rage.

The citizens were furious but terrified. That had always been the shape-changers' power, Saphaeyender knew from history books. Their very nature was inimical to humans. Now it seemed they could shape and intensify the effect of that aura, emanating webs of fear to stifle their enemies' courage and sap their energy.

Lines of Bhahdradomen stood on the fringes of the human crowds, watching. When one did move, though, it sliced between the humans like a dra'a'k through air. They simply fell out of its path in panic.

As they entered the square, Saphaeyender saw three of his actors coming towards him, all flying silk, dishevelled hair and ashen faces. He thought sadly, If only they could be this convincing on stage! Sharm was the elegant matriarch of his company, Evender her younger lover, Saliole the extravagantly-mannered father-figure.

'Saph, my dear fellow,' said Saliole, his usual rich enunciation fragmented by fear. 'We've been trying to find you all morning. Dyon's prick, what a day is this.' He shook his grey head. 'What a day.'

'And we thought one little battle against Garnelys was the end of the world,' Saphaeyender said aridly.

'What are we going to do?'

Saphaeyender stabbed the marble flagstones with the base of his cane. 'Why does everyone expect me to have the answer to that question?'

'I meant *Arkenfell*,' said Saliole. 'We're right in the middle of rehearsals. Shall the performance go ahead?'

Saphaeyender gaped at his old friend. 'Are you mad? I've just seen a man tortured to death almost on my doorstep! How can you think of performing plays, under these circumstances? Thank you for giving me something to laugh about, on a day I thought it was impossible. Incomprehensible disaster falls on us, and still you care more about your career! Will the Bhahdradomen make as appreciative an audience as humans, I wonder?'

Sharm retorted, 'It's all we have to keep us sane! The hope that life might continue in some semblance of normality!'

He groaned. 'Yes, of course. I'm sorry. I ceased to be sane quite some time ago. However, yes. Let us go on working. It might give us the illusion of hope, at least.'

A thin dark line cleaved the air between them. Sharm lurched backwards, almost retching with fear. A shapeshifter stood there, wielding a thin blade, uttering some incomprehensible threat.

'I think it wants us to move on,' said Saphaeyender, backing away. 'Come to my house later.'

Leaving them, he forged his way through the crowd, with Eander hurrying to keep up. The Amber Citadel rose before them, golden tiers encircling the crown of the palace. They were approaching the main gate of the Citadel across the broad square that lay before it. The tolling came from a bell tower on the right-hand side of the square; a summons to the people of Parione.

As Saphaeyender came close to the Citadel wall, the crowd thinned suddenly. A long chain of warriors stood along the base of the wall, as still as basking lizards in their chameleon tunics, *gauroth* weapons hanging at their sides. Their aura made an unseen but effective barrier that kept the humans back by twenty feet or more.

In front of the great gate itself stood a cluster of Bhahdradomen of a different order. The looked incongruous against the gold filigree and lapis extravagance above them. These were not camouflaged, but imposing in layers of tissue-thin green and black membrane. Saphaeyender stared at their skull-like faces and turned faint.

The empty strip of marble that lay between him and them looked like an abyss. Drawing a deep breath, he set out. He glanced to either side as he went and saw people staring at him; a man – a celebrity, no less – doing what they dared not. This was the strangest audience he had ever had.

'Saphaeyender, what are you doing?' Eander hissed, following and clutching his arm. 'You can't mean to approach them!'

He walked on across the empty space that divided the citizens from the shape-changers. Eander went too, hiding behind him. 'Great Goddess, what are *those*?'

Saphaeyender looked up. All along the top of the wall were perched great flying beasts, with leathery wings, long skulls, tiny watchful eyes.

'*Ghelim*,' said Saphaeyender.

'What?' Eander gasped.

'Bhahdradomen in a different shape. Flying ones, as if they aren't bad enough on two feet.'

The Bhahdradomen officers watched his approach. They seemed to be grinning.

Saphaeyender went up to one who stood little ahead of the others, as if he were in charge. This being's face was like charred wood, ash-grey patched with soot, with a high skull and long, vertical lines around the slit that passed for its mouth. There was a scent of metal around them, a reek of badly cured leather. Saphaeyender's head span, but he mustered all his acting skills to hide his revulsion.

'I wish to enter the Citadel,' he said.

The being gazed at him from red eyes. He could feel Eander trembling against him.

'Do you not speak Paranian?' the poet said sharply.

'I speak it,' said the being. Its voice, too, creaked like old wood around the language that was strange to it.

'Then would you please step aside? I wish to enter the Citadel and you are standing in my way.'

A ripple passed through the shape-changers; grim amusement.

'No human is permitted to enter the Citadel,' said the commander.

'Since when?'

'As of yesterday. Day One of our deliverance by the Master of Light.'

Saphaeyender took this in. He felt ill. It was not so much a shock as the confirmation of his worst fears. 'Then what has happened—' His voice nearly failed. 'What has happened to the humans already in the Citadel?'

'This is not your concern. Move away from the gate.'

He eyed the *ghelim*, perched restlessly on the wall high above the gate. He looked at the Bhahdradomen's weapons and his stomach turned. Arguing with them would doubtless get him – and worse, Eander – killed.

'Please,' he said softly. 'There is someone inside whom I visit regularly. A prisoner called Ysomir. I must know how she is. I have a visitor's pass that allows me free access to the innermost circle. I have this.'

He drew out a rald, a grass-green coin of high value. The officer looked at it with disdain. 'What is that?'

'It's money.'

'We have no need of it.'

'You might, if you are planning to stay in Parione.'

'Under the new administration, such human trinkets will be outlawed. Move away from the gate.'

Eander's fingers were digging into his arm, a silent plea to obey. Saphaeyender was growing desperate.

'I'm a friend of the Queen.' His usual confident tone sounded lame to his own ears. 'She has always allowed me free access to the Citadel.'

'Aventuria no longer has a Queen,' the Bhahdradomen replied flatly.

Dread rose in him. It struck him that if they did let him in, he might never come out again. 'What's happened to her? Where is she?'

The thin lips flattened. 'This is no concern of yours.'

'It is most definitely my concern. She's my friend. I wish to see her.'

'Who are you?' The red eyes were suddenly too interested.

'Saphaeyender.' He felt Eander's hand tighten, warning him not to tell them, but he had nothing to hide. 'The writer. Surely you've heard of me?'

'No. Whatever status you enjoyed is gone,' the creature said softly. 'No human is permitted to enter the Citadel. Move away.'

The aura of malice was growing unbearable, but he couldn't give up yet. 'Are they still alive . . . the people inside?'

'There is nothing to be afraid of.' The long ashen head tilted to one side. 'Vaurgroth the Chosen is a gentle liberator. If you wish to see your Queen, I suggest that you wait in the square with your *domenim.*'

'My what?'

'Your people. I forgot that our terms are not familiar to you. They soon will be.'

The officer took what appeared to be a whip from his belt and poked Saphaeyender in the shoulder with the handle. Saphaeyender felt a leaden thump that sent him reeling back several paces. It was only when he straightened up that it started to hurt, a throb of fire that turned his whole arm numb.

White-faced, Eander dragged him away, back into the ragged edge of the crowd.

Saphaeyender was speechless with pain for a minute or two. All he could do was stand there rubbing at his shoulder while, around him, men and women, young and old, clung to each other in disbelief, cried out protests, asked each other over and again the questions that had no answer. *'Where did they come from? How have they done this? Weren't they defeated, exiled centuries ago? Why didn't the Amber Citadel defend us?'*

'No soldiers,' Saphaeyender said when the pain finally eased its grip.

Eander frowned. 'What do you mean?'

'Well, where is Helananthe's army? The Citadel guards? Who tried to stop this?'

A man standing next to him overheard and said gruffly, 'Lord Saphaeyender? There's some of them over there.'

Saphaeyender turned. The tolling of the bell was making his ears hurt. At the base of the slim bell tower was a small group of soldiers – a mixture of palace and city guards – surrounded by Bhahdradomen. The human guards stood limply, staring ahead with vacant eyes, making no attempt to resist as their weapons were taken from them.

'A bloodless coup,' Saphaeyender murmured. 'Gods, oh gods . . .' A wave of horror swept over him and he thought for a moment he was going to collapse. Eander held onto him and the moment passed.

'Sir, are you all right?' the young man said anxiously.

His voice cracked as he answered. 'Please stop calling me sir. As all right as I can be, considering Parione's woken up to the darkest day in history.'

The bell ceased ringing abruptly. In the sudden hush, people were looking up at the wall above the gate. There was a balcony up there, a platform behind the parapet from which the monarch would address her subjects on special occasions. Figures were moving upon it, coming to the wall to look down on the crowd.

It was hard to see from this distance, but Saphaeyender picked out a handful of familiar outlines, courtiers and aides from the royal court. Small jolt of relief. The Eaters hadn't slaughtered everyone, then. He picked out his old friend Eldareth, and the imposing figure of Mawrdreth . . . and was that Tanthe? He willed her to come forward but she hung too far back so he couldn't be sure the dark hair was hers.

He also saw at least a dozen Bhahdradomen up there on the royal balcony, standing easily as if they owned it. These creatures were of a higher order again. Elaborate robes of black, ivory and crimson, pale skulls rising from heavy collars, staffs gripped in their misshapen hands. They carried themselves with a look of complete power and authority.

One of these shape-shifters came to the front of the balcony. He was a wizened creature like an old, wise mage. He raised his head, looked searchingly over the crowd, and began to speak.

'Good citizens of Parione.' His thin voice cut clearly through the air. 'I am Rhazagramen, chief aide and counsellor to our Master of Light, Chosen of the Ancestor, Vaurgroth of the Fire. Vaurgroth the Merciful extends his greetings and goodwill to you, the people of Aventuria. Blessings of the Ancestor be upon you.'

Murmurs of bewilderment greeted this statement. The crowd waited for him to continue.

'You are no doubt confused by this change to the order of things. Let me reassure you that none of you has anything to fear. There has been a restoration of balance, a deliverance, by the grace of our Ancestor, from darkness into light. Rejoice!'

A ululation broke from the Bhahdradomen in the square. The humans remained deathly silent. Saphaeyender's arm tightened round Eander's shoulders, and his mouth was arid.

As the wailing died away, Rhazagramen went on, 'Yet you will accept this reassurance more readily from one who is known to you.'

He turned, and a woman appeared on the balcony, ushered forward by Rhazagramen's cronies.

Helananthe.

Cries went up from the crowd. The Queen came slowly, hesitantly, to the parapet and stood there for a few moments, looking out at the crowd. Her golden hair was loose on the shoulders of a simple jade-green gown. She carried herself with dignity but her face was colourless and she appeared half-paralysed with shock and exhaustion.

Saphaeyender stared at her, willing her to meet his eyes. She didn't see him.

'Good citizens,' she began, her voice clear but husky with emotion. 'I, who was once Queen of the Nine Realms, stand before you, Queen no longer. The last obligation I lay upon you, in the name of the love there has always been between monarch and people, is that you accept this change. I had no choice. If you would live, *you* have no choice. I am the only one from whom you will accept this truth, I know, therefore I come in person to tell you. I had no course of action but to give up the throne. Vaurgroth of the Fire sits upon the Sapphire Throne in my place.'

The uproar of dismay and anger was ear-shattering. Helananthe was still speaking, but no one could hear her. She went on trying until at last, in a lull, she cried out, 'Not for my sake, but for the sake of my mother Ghiseyma whom you all love, for my brother the young Prince Veny and for my friends, let there be no acts of violence or resistance. Co-operate with the Bhahdradomen and we shall all live in peace!'

The wave of protest swelled. Helananthe turned away in a posture of despair. She half-collapsed, and was helped out of sight by Mawrdreth and Eldareth.

Saphaeyender stared at the place where she'd been, outraged for her sake. It had clearly been a statement written by the victors. Being forced to make it must have broken her heart.

Rhazagramen came to the parapet again.

'As you have seen, no harm has come to your royal family. We have simply deposed them, as once they deposed us. No harm will come to any of you, as long as—'

From out of the crowd, an arrow flew at Rhazagramen. It missed, clattering off the stone just below him, but the wizened face soured in fury. Bhahdradomen guards were in the crowd at once. People were screaming, falling over themselves to get out of the way. The shape-changers surrounded a woman who stood with the bow still poised in her hands. Saphaeyender caught glimpses of her between the shifting sea of heads. A mature woman with a flow of silver hair, a senior member of the printers' guild from her leather tabard . . . He put a hand to his mouth. He knew her. Had many a raging argument with her over the typesetting of his plays because she always knew best . . .

She froze as the Bhahdradomen encircled her. Then the fear in her face turned into a grimace.

'Never,' she snarled, drawing another arrow to the string.

Before she could let fly, several whips snaked out and encircled her chest and waist. There was a crack of lurid fire. Her hands flew up and she jerked and juddered as if in a fit. Then she fell with blood flying out of her mouth.

The stench of burned flesh and ozone crept into Saphaeyender's nostrils. Everyone nearby stood horrified. Other small pockets of rebellion on the fringes were being dealt with in the same brutal manner. The crowd milled, pushed this way and that by panic. Saphaeyender was shoved around with the rest, doing his best to protect Eander, who was just as hopelessly trying to shield him.

The Bhahdradomen strode along the edges, lashing them with lightning and pain, driving them towards the centre, until at last the mass of people stood pressed together, degraded and overwhelmed.

'If you have quite finished?' said Rhazagramen, his voice soaked in contempt. Two more of the elite flanked him now; one a steel-grey, deadly figure as thin as a sword. 'Follow the example of your ex-Queen. Our Lord of Light wishes humans and *domenim* to co-exist in peace. Do not mistake Vaurgroth; he comes not as conqueror but as liberator. Love him as he loves you and you will reap rewards of joy beyond your imagining.'

'He's going to love us to death at this rate,' muttered Eander.

'Go,' Rhazagramen went on. 'Disperse. Return to your homes and go about your everyday business. Attend your temples. For as long as you co-operate with us, you have nothing to fear.'

Stunned and wretched, the crowd began to move. Some

stampeded out of the square. Others wandered aimlessly, weeping or merely staring, as if they had lost their minds to disbelief. Saphaeyender remained where he was, hoping for another glimpse of Helananthe, Eldareth . . . Tanthe. They were gone. Everyone had left the balcony and the sinister *ghelim* were moving in to take up positions along the parapet.

'What are we going to do?' said Eander. He was weeping and trying to hide it, smearing the tears off his cheeks.

'I don't know,' said Saphaeyender.

'How can you be so calm?'

'I'm not. But given a choice between descending into hysterics and having a stiff drink, I know which I favour. Come on, dear friend. Let's go home.'

At the bottom of Temple Hill, a patrol of ten Bhahdradomen stepped out in front of them. The leader drew a short black rod from his belt and they watched in alarm as it extended to three times its length, producing a thin vicious blade that hummed with latent *roth*. As the patrol surrounded them, Saphaeyender felt his palm turn moist around the cane, a pathetic stage sword useless against such weapons. Fear swamped him.

He was aware of Eander trembling, his breathing quick and shallow with dread. The tip of the weapon danced near Saphaeyender's face. Where it passed, his skin tingled as if pricked by pins.

'What do you want?' he managed at last.

The leader grinned. 'We wish to see your play. We look forward to it. All that humans do, we wish to partake also. You shall welcome us?'

His mouth dropped open. 'Y— yes. Best seats in the house.'

The creature retracted the blade and the patrol parted to let Saphaeyender and his companion pass. The corridor they made was so narrow that, as they edged through, they couldn't avoid touching the shape-changers. Saphaeyender flinched as he felt the lick of *gauroth* and the hot, butterfly-flutter of their hands brushing his body.

They were laughing. Lapping up their disgust. Mocking them.

All around them, *ghelim* wheeled in the air and perched on rooftops, flexing their claws, watching.

Chapter Two. Vaurgroth the Merciful

Alone in her cell, Ysomir felt the world end.

The voices of the dead cried out inside her skull. She shot to her feet and pressed her hand over her ears, as if that could keep out the clamour. Strange *roth*-energies crawled over her skin, presaging a dire change, cataclysm.

Later, she would discover that her flash of terror coincided with Helananthe surrendering the Sapphire Throne to Vaurgroth. All she knew in this moment was that something unutterable had happened. In panic, she ran to the door and hammered frantically on it, shouting for the warder to come.

Someone came.

The face that met hers through the grille, however, was not the familiar female one she'd expected. It was not even human. Instead Ysomir found herself looking into the soft milky features and the wet black eyes she'd prayed never to see again.

She stared at the face and it stared back. Then it smiled. Its inky eyes seemed to caress her.

In a breath, her safe little world was wrenched inside out. She knew what had happened. All the *ethroths* inside her wailed warnings. Her mind recoiled but her physical form held steady, out of long habit.

'Where's the warder?' she said at last. Her voice came out faint but level. At least her door was locked.

'The warder isn't coming,' said the Bhahdradomen. And it opened the door and came in.

Ysomir started back as the slight figure came gliding towards her. She'd assumed the door was locked . . . but no, of late her kindly warders had only locked her in at night, because they knew that she would never try to escape.

She shouted the warder's name. No-one came. The silence echoed.

'Don't you remember me?' the Bhahdradomen said gently, its head on one side.

'Laphaeome,' she said. Her voice was dry. She seemed to have lost the habit of expressing emotion. Could he see her terror? Or did he only see a self-contained woman, who looked more startled than petrified?

'Ah, you remember. Call me Zhoaah, though. It is my true name. There is no more need for artifice.'

Zhoaah came towards her, his feet shuffling unseen beneath the edge of his robe. Strange robe, made of what looked like fine, scaly white skin, with panels of black and moss-green hanging from the shoulders, and a blood-red ruff standing up around the neck, like the crest of a lizard. She didn't remember him dressing so strangely. He'd always worn a plain hooded robe before . . . posing as something he wasn't.

'Why are you here?' Zhoaah asked.

Her breath felt cold in her throat. 'I – I killed Garnelys.'

'Are you awaiting sentence of death?'

'No,' she said, 'no. The Queen commuted my sentence to life imprisonment.'

'I see. A suitable punishment for regicide . . . do you think?'

She was taking small, slow steps back, but he crept forward with her. His eyes seemed to spill into her mind, holding her like strings of tar. 'I do think,' she said firmly.

'Do you mean that you are content to be here, Ysomir?'

'Perfectly. I deserve it. I accept it. Why are you here?'

Zhoaah shook his head. He was quietly tormenting her, feeding on her pain. 'Poor Ysomir, cut off from all contact with the outside world, with no means of knowing what is going on outside these walls. Something may have happened, but then again it may not.'

'I know it has.'

She took another step back, found the edge of her low bed pressing into her calves. The Bhahdradomen asked intently, 'How did you kill him?'

'I stabbed him – no, it's none of your business! I don't want you here. I am not forced to receive any visitors I don't want! Please go!'

'It is wicked of me to tease you,' Zhoaah said lightly. 'I always liked you, Ysomir. Yes, you are right; everything has changed. We are in charge now.'

Her mouth opened in pain. 'How?'

'The details are not important. You played your part.'

'I killed him for nothing, then!' she gasped. 'I thought that if only I killed Garnelys, all the evil would end!'

'Well, that depends what you would term "evil". His reign ended. Ours began.'

Her reserve was crumbling, and he knew it. When he reached out and took her hands, she couldn't stop him. His touch felt light until she tried to pull free, then his fourteen thin fingers became barbs in her flesh. 'I admired the old King. A shame you killed him. Describe it to me.'

'No!' she cried, shocked.

Zhoaah started laughing. 'It's all right, you don't have to. I was there.'

'What?'

'You never saw me, but I was there. I saw all that you did. Impressive display of passion. Seventeen wounds with a fruit knife, and enough blood to drown a small dog.'

Ysomir trembled. There was a tight ball in her chest; she couldn't swallow, could hardly breathe. 'What do you want?'

Zhoaah's pallid face creased in concern. 'What do *you* want?' he asked softly, for all the world like an anxious friend.

'To be left alone,' she said. 'I want my door locked, and no-one to come in but the warders I know, and my sister.'

'This is not much of an ambition, Ysomir.'

'If it's to be judged by the difficulty of achieving it, it's a very great ambition indeed!'

'Ohh,' breathed Zhoaah, letting go of her hands. 'Sharp. I had really forgotten how much I like you. We used to get on quite well, didn't we?'

'Are you referring to the way you used to sit and talk to me, distract me, tell me that everything was for the best – when you knew full well that Garnelys was torturing people in the other room?' To her dismay, Ysomir felt tears welling onto her cheeks. Zhoaah always seemed to needle his way right into her. She had no idea how he did it.

'It was too great a burden for you to bear. I was concerned for you then, as I am now. You are . . . how shall I put it . . . now in the custody of the Bhahdradomen, rather than that of the Queen.'

A dozen appalling thoughts occurred to her. 'What's happened to the Queen? Is she dead?'

'No. She's alive and well. Simply disempowered.'

'And my sister – Tanthe? Have you heard anything of her?'

'When I came in you were terrified of me. Now you are appealing to me for news and reassurance. See how easy it is to trust me? I believe your sister is with the ex-Queen, and quite well also.'

'Are you telling me the truth?'

'I've no reason to lie. Perhaps I can bring her to you.'

She had been distant from reality for too long. Now it crept slowly upon her. She pressed one hand to her collarbone. 'But the Bhahdradomen have taken over . . . *all* of Aventuria?'

'It's begun.'

'I had nightmares about this,' she whispered. 'All my life. The Xauroma dead. Everything dead.'

She still couldn't cry. Instead a terrible ache germinated inside her and grew upwards through her chest and throat, choking her until she nearly fell. Zhoaah caught her. His sinuous pale arms wound tight around her and from his thin, sexless body came what felt like compassion; and she thought how strange it was that his embrace felt *comforting*.

'You are not alone. I am here now,' Zhoaah said softly. 'Shall I visit you often?'

Helananthe stood in the great doorway to the Sun Chamber. Once, the atmosphere had been vibrant and joyful, but now it was leaden. Webby curtains had been strung across the stained-glass windows, obliterating their glory. Even the sparkle of gold light in the amber panelling was dead. A brooding heaviness lay on the Chamber. The air buzzed with intense energies.

The intentions and desires of a hostile race were knotted thickly around the edifice that had been her home. She couldn't bear it. She felt the very stones of the Citadel vibrating with the anguish of the *xauroth* sphere. Somewhere deep beneath her feet the sphere rotated like thunder, expressing the Earth's misery.

At the far end, the Sapphire Throne stood on its dais as it had for centuries; but it was her throne no longer. Instead the usurper sat in it, his gaze welded to hers, reeling her towards him. The shining floor lay between them like a frozen sea.

Bhahdradomen guards and mages stood on every side, watching her. Under their impassive scrutiny, Helan began the long walk towards the throne. She felt the pressure of their will upon her, dark claws digging into her mind. Surely they had hearts that pumped blood, nerves branching through their limbs, *something* that made them not wholly alien ... but she couldn't see it. They were dry creatures of cartilage with plasma oozing beneath the wrinkled membrane of their flesh, unknowable minds behind their deep, shrewd eyes.

Helan had come to Vaurgroth alone, refusing to admit any fear. If she appeared tough and dignified to their eyes, it was only that shock had encased her like armour. She'd become incapable of emotion. If the tiniest chink of passion should slip through, she feared she would collapse into madness.

Some days had passed since the Bhahdradomen leader had seized the Sapphire Throne from her. She was puzzled that he hadn't executed her; apparently he preferred to prolong the agony. She'd been petitioning Rhazagramen and his other minions for days to speak to Vaurgroth. Now, unexpectedly, he'd summoned her.

Vaurgroth. Master of Light, Chosen of the Ancestor . . . oh, and all the other grandiose titles they showered upon him. It turned her stomach sour with loathing.

He was a pale figure, shrouded in scarlet. The domed head was patterned with a red web; a tattoo or a bizarre birthmark, she wasn't sure. A rope of chalk-white hair hung from the centre of the web, twisted with dark gems. He had thin sharp features, not ugly . . . but not human. His eyes, like his complexion, were changeable and now they were solid black, as if they were all pupil, great light-gathering pits that saw everything.

Vaurgroth was smiling.

Helan shuddered. How dare he smile! If he'd sat there glowering, preening at his victory and her downfall, it would have been easier to accept. Instead he looked utterly relaxed, as if his sitting there was the natural order of things.

'Lady Helananthe,' he said.

She stopped, five feet from the dais. He was poised on her throne, nine broad marble steps above her, looking down. She had the impression that a column of power surrounded him, flickering with tiny forks of lightning, as if he had a psychic form much greater than his physical body. This power repulsed her, suffocated her, dragged on her like chains. All the Bhahdradomen had this aura in some degree, but Vaurgroth carried it like a personal storm.

At his feet sat a strange creature resembling a hound, but

covered in greenish-gold scales. It, too, watched her with Bhahdradomen eyes.

She was unarmed. Attacking Vaurgroth, even with bare hands, would get her killed on the spot . . . yet if she'd had that intention, his aura would have drained her of the will to try.

Four of his counsellors stood on the steps, two on either side. They smiled too, but said nothing. Rhazagramen. Zhoaah, the quiet one who'd corrupted Garnelys. Uryzht, a gnarled beige creature with a long, wolfish face. Naghrur, whose steel demeanour was almost more alarming than Vaurgroth's. They had been there when she'd had to stand on the balcony above the gate and admit her failure to protect the Nine Realms.

'How good of you to come.' Vaurgroth seemed to shed sentient wisps of *roth* that swirled about the floor, crawled into the corners, skittered over the walls like disembodied hands . . .

Helananthe shook her head. She felt faint. She was hallucinating.

'Lord Vaurgroth,' she said. Her throat was stiff, her voice dry. 'Thank you for agreeing to see me.'

'I sent for you.' His tone implied that her own petitions had nothing to do with it. 'Are you comfortable?' he asked, leaning forward a little. 'In your quarters, I mean? Have you and your companions everything that you need?'

She was stunned. Her mouth fell open, but all that came out was, 'Ah . . .' She swallowed hard, collected herself. 'Yes, in a material sense we are perfectly comfortable.'

His voice had a rich music that made the hairs rise on the back of her neck. 'If there's anything you need, you have only to let my *bharu'grothrim* or *vagharim* know.'

'Excuse me, I don't know these terms.'

Patiently, he waved an oddly shaped hand at Zhoaah and his companions. 'My mage-counsellors, *bharu'grothrim*.' The hand moved to indicate the darkly clad guards. '*Vagharim*, my elite warriors. As I was saying; if you require particular foods, new clothing . . . after all, human needs are not so very different to our own. We are not so very different at all. Whatever your requirements, my *domenim* are at your disposal.'

Helan forced herself to meet his eyes. 'Why are you doing this?'

'Being kind to you?' Vaurgroth said matter-of-factly.

'Showing us a semblance of courtesy. It's condescending of you to treat me like a guest in my own palace. I suppose it's part of my humiliation?'

'No. We wish you no harm. I have allowed you to stay in your home and I am concerned for your welfare.'

She moistened her dry lips. 'You could have ripped our hearts out where we stood, as you did to Lord Poel. Instead you let us live. I don't understand.'

Vaurgroth rose. He came down the steps towards her, stopping on the third one up so that his eyes were on a level with hers. She noticed his feet were not bare but encased in red leather with long spikes at the toes and heels. She was taller than him, but couldn't shake off the impression that he was towering over her.

'Do you think I am a monster?' he asked with a slight frown.

'You've taken the Nine Realms from me. Your *bharu'grothrim* destroyed my grandfather and caused a war. You still hold my mother and brother under threat of torture.'

'No. They were under threat, but since you made the right decision, they are living as comfortably as you are.'

'But still your prisoners! I haven't been allowed to see them. And you slew Lord Poel in front of me.' The image reeled across her mind. Vaurgroth's fingers diving through the man's breastbone, Poel tumbling wide-eyed from the dais, the crack of his skull hitting the marble. 'This hardly inspires faith in your good nature, my lord.'

When Vaurgroth paused he was as still as the pseudo-hound beside him. He hardly seemed a living creature at all until he spoke. 'I didn't call you here for an argument, my lady. There is nothing to argue about. We have come out of exile and taken back what is ours, that's all. You can rail against the situation all you wish, but since you can't change it, I can afford to take a lenient attitude towards you. It would be rash of me not to confine you and your companions. However, I don't fear you. Why then should I need to kill you?'

'I see.' Helan gave a bitter smile. 'Your clemency is a demonstration of your confidence.'

Vaurgroth looked mildly exasperated. If he was acting, he was very good at it. 'You asked for an explanation. Since Ancestor is merciful, so am I. I bear no ill-will towards you, nor towards humans in general. This is the beginning of the new age. The time for malice is over.'

'Does this mean you will let my mother and brother go?' she said.

'I'm considering their release, yes,' he said, his manner so easy that he left her gaping. With a couple of graceful steps he was back on the Sapphire Throne again, looking down at her. Raw anguish to see him there. 'First, there are other matters to discuss. Our arrival has been a shock to the citizens of Parione.'

'You're the master of understatement, too,' she said grimly.

Vaurgroth appeared amused. 'They seem convinced that they're going to be tortured, enslaved, and slaughtered, that we are about to inflict all manner of atrocities on them.'

'Haven't you already started?' She couldn't keep her voice steady. 'The last time the Bhadradomen ruled Aventuria, terrible things happened. We've had only two hundred and fifty-odd years of freedom!'

Vaurgroth blinked. 'Don't let us dispute the meaning of the term "freedom", my lady. This is not the past. Things will be different this time.'

'In what way?'

'I wish them to understand.' He leaned forward, his

spidery hands dangling over the arms of the throne. His tone was fatherly. 'I wish *you* to understand that there is nothing to fear. Humans and Bhahdradomen can co-exist peacefully side by side, can they not?'

Helan stared at him. Her eyes burned and her jaw was solid with tension. 'I don't think it has ever been tried. I don't see how it is possible.'

'There has been some difficulty in the city and the surrounding countryside. People forming defiant little bands against us, and suffering for it.'

She said nothing. In one way she was glad to hear they were fighting back. In another she despaired. Under Vaurgroth, the Bhahdradomen were deadly.

'Yes, they're dying for nothing,' he said, speaking her thoughts. 'There is no need for your citizens to panic. As Theosopher Rhazagramen tried to inform them, they can go on with their daily lives as if nothing has changed.'

'How? Are you asking them to accept what has happened? To tolerate it? Impossible!'

'They will, though,' said Vaurgroth. 'They must.'

'Never.'

'Then what will they do instead? Form their little bands of rebels and try to drive us out? Now that will get them killed, for certain. What a waste. There's no need for it.'

'I can't stop them,' said Helan. 'I have no influence over them. I gave the last of it away when I stood on that balcony! If that's why you called me here, you've made a mistake. They know I gave you the Sapphire Throne. They won't listen to a word I say.'

She was uncomfortably aware of the eyes of the *bharu'grothrim* upon her in the gloom, their cruelly amused expressions. Their *gauroth* tasted like metal dust on her tongue.

'You misunderstand. I'm not asking you to command them. Just to lead by example. To promote our message of reassurance.'

'You're asking me to be your mouthpiece?'

He leaned over her, eyes gleaming with a dark and deadly eagerness. 'You're wrong to say they won't listen to you. I need you to show them that they won't be harmed as long as they accept me. More than that. They will come to realise that if they love me, as my own *domenim* do, I can open a realm of joy to them that they have never imagined!'

His head dropped back. She saw crescents of white under his eyelids. She stared at him in astonishment, thinking that he was not only power-crazed but insane.

'You imagine they can *love* you?' she said.

He raised his head and looked serenely at her. 'It is not so incredible. They will, once they stop resisting and see what Ancestor can offer them. They will be happy. You can help them achieve that.'

'You want me to encourage them to adore *you*? I, who was their Queen?'

'It would be helpful if we worked together in this, yes,' said Vaurgroth. 'Surely you want to help your own people into the light?'

'This is unbelievable.'

'I am serious.' His manner became confidential, sincere. Behind the ghastly weight of his power he had an awful charm. 'Let me put it another way. They don't assume you "gave" me the throne. They give you the benefit of the doubt and believe you were forced. Perhaps they are angry with you, but they still love you. They worry about your fate and want to be where you are. They will attend to you. You don't even need to speak. You can show them by example.'

'Show them what?'

'The way we can live together.'

'I don't think so.'

'But you will be saving their lives. You want to preserve their lives, don't you?'

'You hold their lives over me as blackmail!'

He disregarded her remark. 'What day do they normally go to their temples?'

Helan was startled. 'They go whenever they feel like it, but the big formal ceremonies are on Firstday, which we also call Leafmonday.'

'The day after tomorrow. Good. All citizens shall attend the Temple of Nepheter on that day. We shall let it be known that their devotions will take place in the presence of their former Queen.'

She shivered from head to foot. 'Do you think I want to be seen in public, after the way I've failed them? They'll hang me!'

'Of course they won't.'

'I can't face them. Don't you see how ashamed I am?'

'You have no reason for shame.' His tone was consoling; he sounded like a priest. 'Your presence will reassure them that they're safe, and free to live in a way that will be pleasant to them.'

'Pleasant?'

'We are not monsters,' he said. 'You can't still think that, now we've talked? You've spoken freely to me. Surely your opinion of me has altered? Tell me honestly.'

Helan paused. Stiffly she began, 'I think you are a very clever man—'

'*Domenim*. Not man. *Domen*, if you would prefer to shorten it, as we often do.'

'*Domen*, then. Very clever to understand humans as well as you seem to.'

'Now you're the one being condescending. The Bhahdra-domen are not fools. Still, I take it as a compliment.'

'We never thought you were fools,' she said. 'You're too devious for me. I can't see why you'd allow our temple gatherings to continue unless you stood to gain from it.'

'Can't believe I wish your citizens any good?' He sat back in the blue-jewelled throne. He smiled but it was as if an ice-veil fell over him. His intimate manner was gone; she sensed he'd lost patience and wanted the meeting to end. 'Would you have preferred me to issue promises of torment and slaughter?'

'It would have been . . . more predictable.'

'I am not predictable,' said Vaurgroth. 'Is there anything else you wish to discuss?'

'Yes. I would like to see my mother and brother.'

'Of course. Naghrur will arrange it.'

'Thank you,' she said, taken aback he'd agreed so easily. All part of wrong-footing her, no doubt.

'Anything else?'

Ysomir flashed into her mind. Despite the fact she had slain Garnelys, Helan felt concerned for the young woman's welfare. She was human, and stranded in the prison quarter . . . yet if the Bhahdradomen hadn't found her, the last thing Helan wanted was to draw Vaurgroth's attention to Ysomir's existence.

'I do not want to go to the temple,' she said, quietly and firmly.

'You must.'

The force that radiated from him crushed her. Strange patches of light moved under his skin. His dog-like *ghelim* stared at her with the glassy eyes of a dead sea-creature. What a weird conceit, she thought, to shape one of your fellow *domenim* into a pet . . . It seemed insane. She felt she'd stepped into an incomprehensible, terrifying dream.

'Our business is concluded,' Vaurgroth said brusquely. 'My *vagharim* will accompany you and your friends to temple on Leafmonday. I sense, however, that you will be eager to go of your own accord.'

'Why?'

'Because you feel a sense of duty to those who were your subjects,' Vaurgroth answered with a razor-cold smile. 'You would not let them destroy themselves.'

Every time there was a knock at his door, Saphaeyender nearly leapt out of his skin. The invaders had begun to commandeer houses all over Parione. Soldiers and civilian *domenim* alike would simply walk in, and if the inhabitants objected they would be killed. If they didn't, they were allowed to stay; but what human could bear to live in such close proximity to the shape-changers? Thus they ended up abandoning their own homes. It had happened to Saliole, who had moved in with Sharm and Evender. Saphaeyender feared it was only a matter of time before it happened to him.

He feared for his staff: Eander, and the two couples who had kept house and garden for him for years. If one of them went to answer the door he no longer left them to it but went with them, a knife hidden in his robe, fully prepared to die defending his household. So far, the visits had been false alarms. Usually it was a member of his theatre company, rushing over his threshold to pour out their distress at some new atrocity.

Bhahdradomen strutted the streets of Parione as if they owned them. A pall of despair and disbelief lay on the city. At least they kept their *graukhim* out of the city itself, but the cattle-like beasts roamed freely around the outskirts, ravaging the green slopes of the Serpentines, devouring the vineyards that lay to the south, chewing the buds off the trees so that spring would never come and autumn would bear no fruit.

His beautiful villa had begun to feel like a besieged and defenceless refuge.

The actors still assembled in the small theatre on Amber Street to rehearse, but their hearts weren't in it. They were edgy, starting at every sound. Much of rehearsal time was lost to endless complaining about the Eaters. Sometimes a couple of Bhahdradomen would enter the theatre and watch them, standing motionless as if embalmed. They said nothing, did nothing, only filled Saphaeyender and his friends with dread as they stumbled through their lines.

'Look at us,' he said to Eander as they lay in bed together. 'Too craven even to plot resistance.'

'We've seen what happened to the few brave souls who tried it,' Eander replied unsteadily. 'I don't want to be killed by that revolting power they have.'

'*Gauroth*. That's the correct term for it.'

The young man shuddered. 'Even the word makes me feel sick.'

'Quite. So what chance have we? The invaders are full of *gauroth*, garlanded with deadly weapons. And the sad truth is that, even after the trouble with Garnelys and the civil war, the folk of Parione are still at heart good-natured, peaceable and hopeless at defending themselves. Our lives have been too easy.'

Eander uttered a noise of disgust. '"Go about your everyday business," that wizened turd Rhazagramen said. He must have known full well it was impossible.'

Saphaeyender hated to leave his home in case, returning, he found it infested. One day, as he and Eander came home from rehearsal, he thought his nightmare had come true. There was a soldier climbing the steps to his front door. *Yrim*, the ordinary soldiers were called; this *yrim* appeared to be an officer, with grey gems clustered on the shoulders of his tunic.

Saphaeyender's heart nearly failed. He gripped Eander's elbow with his left hand; his right was on the knife-hilt. He strode up to the *yrim* and looked into its expressionless stone-grey face. 'What do you want?'

'All citizens are required to attend their usual worship at the Temple of Nepheter,' the creature said mildly. 'Inform your household.'

'What?'

'All citizens are required—'

'I heard what you said, but I don't understand.'

'All citizens,' said the patient voice, soft as cobwebs, 'are encouraged to attend their usual devotions. Vaurgroth of the Light is a gentle master, by Ancestor's grace. It is his desire that you go to your temple, freely and without fear.'

In complete amazement, Saphaeyender watched the *yrim* continue up the hill towards the next house.

Eventually Eander said, 'What the hell is going on?'

Saphaeyender gazed across the treetops at the sight he loathed but couldn't avoid. It was always there, haunting him. The stump of the unfinished Heliodor Tower, Garnelys's loathsome legacy, brooding atop the hill where the beloved Old Royal Theatre had once stood.

The yellow marble of its walls was turning paler, as if bleached by the weather to the colour of bone. As he watched, he heard a low, disturbing vibration that seemed to come from the tower itself. A heat-haze whirled above it, flickering. It wasn't the first time he'd observed such phenomena around it. Vaurgroth had secret business there; a portal to Vexor, they said, if not something worse. No human could set foot near the tower to investigate, however, for it was guarded by Bhahdradomen troops. Their shields of *gauroth* dazzled those who dared to approach with blood-soaked visions of madness.

'Whatever it is,' Saphaeyender said at last, 'I think it is something much greater and much worse than the Bhahdradomen simply wanting revenge.'

Chapter Three. Breaking the Circle

Helan found her mother and brother being held in another guest suite on the same wide, curving corridor as her own chambers. She was startled, as the *vagharim* officer unlocked the door, to realise her mother had only been a minute's walk away all the time. Once these suites had been reserved for visiting nobles from the Nine Realms. She'd never dreamed they would become prison cells.

Princess Ghiseyma was resplendent in a dark-blue gown, her grey hair swept up in stiff waves and held with opal clasps. Her months of imprisonment by Falthorn didn't seem to have harmed her. Her face, with its strong nose, pointed chin, intelligent eyes, was still handsome, her carriage proud. She rushed forward to hug her daughter.

'My dear. Oh gods, Helan, I am so sorry . . .'

'What have you to be sorry for, dearest?' Helan clasped her mother, trying not to cry. Over her shoulder, she saw her brother coming towards her with a look of wary surprise.

'Stupidly getting ourselves kidnapped by the Valahyr. Truly, we never heard a thing, we didn't know what was happening until we were halfway to Verdanholm.'

'I bit Ostarial's hand,' Veny said fiercely.

He made no move to embrace his sister. Prince Venirryen was a tall, good-looking boy with straight brown hair. Helan noted that he looked much older than his eleven years.

'Well done, you,' she said.

Veny showed no pleasure at her praise. Instead he turned disdainfully away from her. Then she knew that his harsh words in the Sun Chamber had not been said in the heat of the moment after all. He asked, 'When are they going to let us out of here?'

'I don't know. I am trying.'

'You are not trying hard enough, in any respect,' he said, turning to glare at her with angry blue eyes. 'First we're prisoners of Falthorn. You give up the throne, *our* throne, to save us – yet here we are, still prisoners! Captives of the Bhahdradomen now!'

Helan hardly knew what to say to him. 'I think Vaurgroth will release you, now he's got me instead. Are they treating you properly? You look well.'

'Oh, we are quite well,' Ghiseyma said briskly. 'The Valahyr treated us reasonably, if you overlook them drugging us with some noxious potion on occasion, not to mention transporting us back to Earth in a cage. *This* lot don't come near us, except to bring us food.'

'Good. They kept their agreement, then.'

'What agreement?' demanded Veny.

'Not to torture you.' Helan spoke emphatically, meeting his eyes. 'Do you understand? I gave up the Sapphire Throne in exchange for the shape-changers' promise not to torture you *and our mother* to death.'

Veny's red mouth was sulky. 'We're still prisoners. They can torture us when they like, really. How are you going to stop them?'

Helan groaned. 'But they haven't. What should I have done instead?'

'If I'd been King, I would have fought them.' His voice rose with passion, 'I would have died on the Sapphire Throne before I let them take it!'

He folded his arms and turned away. Helan gazed hopelessly at his proud, narrow back. 'That's easy for you to say, when you didn't have to take that decision,' she said quietly. To herself she added, Perhaps being tortured might have done you some good! She bit her tongue. She didn't want to descend to the same immature, black-and-white level as Veny.

Ghiseyma said, 'We must appeal to the Mediators to decide our fate. The Bhahdradomen cannot deny us that!'

'Oh, they can,' Helan said through her teeth. 'They accepted the intervention of the Mediators only in defeat, if you think about it. Recently they've made plain their utter contempt for the mediation of a neutral party. The last Mediator who tried to help us – my poor friend Rathroem – the Eaters murdered. Now I doubt the Mediators would intervene even if we begged them.'

Her mother looked stricken. 'Is there nothing we can do?'

Helan slipped a hand through her arm and spoke quietly so her brother wouldn't hear. 'I'll petition Vaurgroth to have you released. He didn't seem completely unreasonable. He said he'd consider it.'

Ghiseyma sighed and patted her hand. 'Thank you, dear, but what would it achieve? Where should we go? In or out of the Citadel, I'll still have the same concerns. How to protect Veny. How to help you. How we are going to live under these dreadful, dreadful creatures. I'm glad, now, that your poor father didn't survive to see this day.'

In the doorway, the *vagharim* said, 'Lady Helananthe, your permitted visiting time is over.'

'I've hardly been here five minutes!' Helan snapped. 'Please wait!'

Ghiseyma smiled tiredly. 'You begin to get used to them, don't you? Enough that you're not afraid to answer them back, at least.'

'Don't do anything too rashly courageous, will you, Mum? I know you.'

'Oh no, tempted as I am, I obey them to keep Veny safe.'

'I don't need keeping safe!' The boy strode furiously up to them. 'If I'd been King . . .' Tears shone and spilled from his eyes. With a moan Helan reached out and hugged him. He didn't resist.

'Veny, I'm sorry. I know you think I let everyone down.

You're probably right. Blame me if you must, but don't blame yourself; you're a child, not a king. There's nothing you could have done.'

'I shall soon be a man,' he said, pulling out of her embrace. Despite the tear-trails on his face, he had a certain dignity. She smiled at him, but his mouth was still trembling.

The *vagharim* took an impatient step towards them. 'You'd better go,' said Ghiseyma.

'I'll visit you as often as they let me.' Helan hesitated. 'Mum, do you think I did the wrong thing? Surrendering, to save you?'

'You did the only thing you could.' Ghiseyma said firmly. She raised her chin and her eyes were grave. 'For Veny. However, if it had been only me under threat, I would have said, "Fight. Damn the consequences. I would rather be tortured than know my daughter gave in to them." I might have felt, like Veny, that it was better for us all to die in the Sun Chamber defending Aventuria, than to surrender and live on in this disgrace.'

While they waited for Helan to return, Tanthe and the others talked. It was partly to distract themselves from their anxiety, partly to feel they were taking action of some kind.

Their situation had stopped Tanthe being even slightly nervous of Mawrdreth. She liked him. He might be King, and the son of a duke, but he had no airs and graces. Eldareth's antipathy towards him was simple jealousy. He'd loved Helan but hesitated to marry her; come back to find her unexpectedly married to Mawrdreth instead. Tanthe felt for Eldareth, but she couldn't blame Helan. Mawrdreth was a formidable and highly attractive man, tall and bronze-skinned, with high cheekbones and fierce leaf-green eyes. His long umber hair reminded her of Rufryd ... though Rufryd's had more red in it. Perhaps the Thand'rathian style – a single long plait bound with leather thongs – would have suited him, too.

She tried to stop thinking about Rufryd.

Auriel sat cross-legged on the floor, listening but saying nothing. He doesn't belong here, Tanthe thought sadly. Neither does Elrill. None of them looked more out of place than the Shaelahyr lord, who was like a snow-sculpture with his long face and fall of ice-white hair. Of them all, though, he seemed the calmest.

'There must be a way to escape,' said Mawrdreth.

'Yet we must be realistic about our chances,' Eldareth countered drily.

Tanthe pulled a face at him, which he ignored. He was playing up his role as wise old campaigner to make Mawrdreth look hot-headed. The game was getting on her nerves.

She looked at Elrill. 'Could you call the Zampherai again? Get us out of here, like they got Eld out of Fortress Arabeth?'

Elrill met her gaze. His eyes were as startlingly blue-violet as ever but she suddenly noticed the lines of strain around them. 'We could as easily break through a window ourselves. We'd still be faced with a sheer drop down the walls, with the outer circles of the Citadel to break through, and Bhahdradomen swarming everywhere. Eldareth is wise. We need to fathom Vaurgroth's intentions before we can lay plans.'

Tanthe stared through a leaded window on the far side of the room. Beyond, she saw the sandy bulk of the inner wall, circling the central palace. Inside that wall lay staff quarters and workrooms, stables and stores . . . and prison cells.

'My sister's trapped up there,' she said. 'I don't know how I'm going to get her out.'

Eldareth squeezed her hand. 'The Eaters must have a weakness. We need to find it.'

'Weakness be damned,' said Mawrdreth. 'If I only had the Thand'rathian army at my disposal now! I'd like to see the Eaters stand against them.'

'Dreams will get us nowhere.'

'Eld!' Tanthe said through her teeth.

'One of us has to be realistic,' he replied coolly.

'There is something we can do, at least,' said Elrill. 'We can keep ourselves physically fit. We can train in the Shaelahyr arts; Tanthe, you grew quite proficient while you were in Silverholm and you should keep in practice, even if we have to use chair legs for swords.' He fixed her with an intense, serious look. 'And since not two but three among us are Aelyr, there are other gifts we may develop between us.'

Tanthe shivered. She still felt human. It was the first time Elrill had acknowledged her Aelyr side in an open rather than grudging way. 'Forgiven us our Valahyr blood, have you?'

He smiled. 'If you'll forgive the length of time it takes me to trust someone. You and Auriel and I must work together now.'

When Helan was brought back to the chamber, her waiting friends rushed to greet her with profound relief and expressions of concern. She hadn't realised how the meeting had drained her until they told her how pale she looked.

'I'm quite all right,' she insisted, releasing a long breath as she dropped onto a couch. She felt too heart-sick to answer the inevitable questions, but there was no avoiding it. Mawrdreth brought her a glass of wine and sat beside her.

'So, you saw Vaurgroth?' Eldareth said. She nodded.

'Well?' said Tanthe. 'What was he like?'

'You've all seen him,' said Helan.

'Yes, and he scared the fuck out of us.' Tanthe frowned. 'We were worried he was torturing you, or something. I can't imagine him doing anything else.'

'He didn't torture me. We talked. He wasn't unpleasant as such, more . . . avuncular. I don't know how else to describe him.' She shivered. 'Patronising. Yet talkative, and polite.'

'Polite?' Mawrdreth said in disgust.

'What did he say?' asked Eldareth.

'Simple message. The Bhahdradomen are here and we must accept it. He seems to think he can use me to facilitate this process. Encourage people to behave themselves by setting a good example.'

'That's obscene!' Mawrdreth said hotly. He looked furious; she hadn't seen him so angry since he'd first marched into the Sun Chamber with his sister to demand Thanmandrathor's independence. It was terrible to see him, a fiery energetic man, confined to these few chambers.

'But he holds their lives over me,' Helan answered quietly. 'If people accept Vaurgroth's regime, they'll be allowed to live. If they rebel, they'll die.'

'So there are people out there trying?' said Tanthe.

'Better to be dead than live under this evil!' said Mawrdreth. He strode away to a window and stood with his back to them, rigid with unspent energy and frustration. Helan looked at his proud lean form, the bronze plait hanging between his shoulder-blades. She wished she had some hope to offer him.

'I don't agree,' she said. 'Alive, people have hope. Dead, there's sod-all we can do about anything.'

He turned on her. 'So, you'll just give in to his demands?'

If he wanted an argument, she hadn't the energy to oblige. Vaurgroth had drained all the fight out of her. 'He's right. If I still have enough influence to stir people up to rebellion, it follows that I can do the opposite.'

'What will you do?' asked Tanthe.

Helan paused. 'Vaurgroth suggests that it is possible for both races to co-exist peacefully. He wishes no harm to humans, as long as we obey.'

'Ridiculous!' said Mawrdreth. 'We can't subjugate ourselves to him.'

'But we're in no position to defy him! Perhaps he means

it. He's allowing humans to continue their usual temple devotions. He's insisting that I make an appearance at the Temple of Nepheter.'

Cries of surprise. 'Do you want to go?' Eldareth asked.

'The prospect horrifies me.' She shook her head vehemently. 'Do you think I want all those people I betrayed staring at me? The last thing I want is to be seen in public! Still, maybe it would be for the best. If it would give them some form of reassurance, my feelings don't matter.'

Mawrdreth said in a low voice, 'The citizens are not fools, Helan. Vaurgroth's motives are purely evil. We cannot go on forever giving in to him.'

'The trouble is,' Eldareth said, facing Mawrdreth with folded arms, 'it doesn't help us to understand the Bhahdradomen by assuming they are "purely evil".'

'They are. History proves it!'

'Don't you realise, they think *we* are evil! It's not wickedness that's prompted them to conquer us, it's the need to survive. Also anger, and the desire to avenge two and a half centuries of exile, yes. But mainly, the urge to survive. Perhaps Vaurgroth truly believes that if he's easy on us, he'll gain our co-operation.'

'But Eld,' said Tanthe, 'they're keeping people quiet through fear, not kindness. They can call themselves "merciful" until they're blue in the face; no-one will ever care, or believe it.'

'I know,' said Eldareth. 'And the fact that they're trying to secure their own future – rather than merely to make our lives a misery – makes them all the more dangerous.'

'Stop!' Helan said suddenly. Her ears were echoing with the anguished spinning of the *xauroth* sphere. No-one else could hear it, not even Mawrdreth; it was the monarch's burden. 'Stop. No more of this. I need to think.' She put up her hand as Mawrdreth began to follow her. 'Alone.'

Helan shut herself in the bed-chamber and lay down for a time on the satin cover of the bed. She stared up at the canopy, sewn with a repeating pattern of royal symbols, gold on blue. The Tree of Life, superimposed on the eight-spoked Wheel of Rebirth. The symbol seemed empty. Broken beneath the clawed feet of the Devourers.

She couldn't sleep. After a while, she heard a door opening out in the main chamber, voices. She sat upright in alarm. Then someone knocked at the door and came in softly.

'Helan?'

It was Eldareth, bearing a tray of food. 'That was only food arriving,' he said. 'There is chicken, a salad of rice and another of goat's cheese and olives. Tea, wine and cakes.'

She felt a brief hunger pang. Then a thought occurred to her and her appetite fled. 'I can't eat.'

Frowning, he set the tray on a cabinet and sat on the bed beside her. 'You never lose your appetite.'

'How are the kitchen staff faring with the Bhahdradomen everywhere? What's happening to my staff, all my aides and counsellors?'

'Well, the kitchen staff are obviously alive and well, at least,' Eldareth said, biting into a chicken leg. 'I doubt the Bhahdradomen know how to cook like this.'

'They could be poisoning us.'

'If they wanted to kill us, they have instant methods. They've no need for subterfuge, since they're in charge.'

And I am the monarch who surrendered that control to them. She didn't say it aloud. The burden of responsibility lay so heavy on her that she could hardly move or speak under it.

'Start with some tea, at least,' said Eldareth. He poured her a cup from the silver pot and passed it to her, his large bony hand brushing hers. 'We've had no chance to talk.'

He looked no different; the creases around his grey eyes were a little deeper perhaps. She'd never noticed the Thand'rathian in his face before but now – familiar with Mawrdreth's face – she saw it, in the long nose and high cheekbones and the slight slant of his eyes. But he had the pale, rugged complexion and dark hair of Torith Mir. 'I'm so sorry, Eld. You come back from a quest that could have cost your life, and find me married to Mawrdreth. I wanted a chance to explain, not for you to find out like that.'

He exhaled. He offered her a piece of chicken from his fork and she took it, chewing slowly. It tasted like old books. 'It was a shock,' he said gravely. 'No more than I deserved, though. I had no right to hope you might have forgiven me.'

'No, you hadn't.'

He gave her a forkful of rice. 'At least you didn't marry Serpeth.'

'I don't know why I even considered it. I wonder if Serpeth's house was full of Bhahdradomen when he arrived home? Anyway, Mawrdreth is a good man. He'll be a good King – gods, what am I saying? He *would* have been . . .'

'He's a handsome young man. Not a ravaged old adventurer.'

'Eld, what are you implying? Yes, we're lovers. It's not just a marriage of convenience. I thought it would be, but I was wrong.'

'Oh.' Eldareth turned slightly away, ceased feeding her. 'Does he know about me?'

'Yes, I told him. He would only have heard it from someone else. I didn't tell him you refused to be my King, though. Only that it was over between us.'

'Is it?'

'Oh, Eld,' she said, touching his wrist. 'I think it's been over for quite some time, don't you?'

His eyes shone. She hoped he wasn't going to weep; he rarely did, but she couldn't have stood it. 'I didn't want it to be. I only said that I didn't want the throne, never that I didn't want *you*.'

'But I *am* the throne. Or I was. You couldn't take one and not the other.'

'I'm sorry,' he said heavily. 'Foolish of me to think . . .'

'You thought we could still be lovers, while I was married

to a man I didn't care for? Perhaps that would have been possible with Serpeth. Not with Mawrdreth.'

'I take that to mean you love each other.' He poured himself a goblet of wine, and drank deeply from it.

'Don't sound so disgusted. I didn't think he'd desire me, but he does.'

Eldareth nearly choked on his wine. 'Not desire you?'

'I'm hardly a beauty, am I? I can do a fair passing impression of a horsewoman, a warrior or even a monarch, but I'm never going to inspire poetry.'

'Rubbish! I take it Mawrdreth has had no more success than I ever had at persuading you otherwise, then?'

She smiled. Hard as this conversation was, it gave the illusion that everything was back to normal. Just her and Eldareth, talking. 'Well, he is very enthusiastic at trying to convince me. Sorry. But I do love him. Can't help it.'

'And do you still love me?'

'Of course I do. I'll always love you, Eld. You're my dearest friend. The last thing I want is to lose your friendship.'

'You haven't,' he said, not looking at her. 'Well, so be it. It's almost the greatest regret of my life, that I let you down.'

'Almost?'

Fumbling in a pocket of his breeches, he produced a folded and dog-eared piece of paper. 'Here. It's rather the worse for wear, but still in one piece.'

'What's this?'

'This is a letter I wrote to you, when I was in prison.'

'You were in *prison*? Where? Why?'

'It was in Torith Mir. I never told you, but I'm a wanted man there. I wrote this while I was awaiting execution. The letter will explain why I could never have been your King.'

Helan read the letter in complete astonishment. In all the confusion that followed the seizure of the palace, she hadn't had time to find out the full story of Eldareth's journey. She read it a second time, then let the letter fall into her lap and stared at him, open-mouthed.

'Is this really true?'

'I should have told you. I couldn't. But yes, there it is. My father was a jealous and unbalanced man who killed my mother in front of me for daring to leave him, then killed my younger brother who was trying to defend her. And so I fought and killed him. And since his cronies caught me with the sword red in my hand, I was accused of slaughtering all three. I escaped, and have been fleeing ever since . . . But when we went back into Torith Mir, I was arrested. And I was ready to die for what I did. It was a relief, to stop fleeing at last.'

'Gods, Eld. If only you had told me years ago, I could have placed you under some kind of royal protection.'

'It wouldn't have changed anything.'

She read aloud from the letter. '"That is why I cannot be King. I cannot watch over Aventuria while my loved ones' faces hang in the way, screaming and dying in front of me. Even my father's. For I loved my father, too, despite all he did. Hated him, yet loved him." Eld, this is terrible. If only you'd told me!'

'I couldn't. It's still hard to say his name. Mordraken. He was a jewel-mage of some kind, a favourite of Drathnen. That's why they were so keen to execute me; I'd killed Viceroy Drathnen's best friend. I think that I, too, should have been a jewel-mage, like my mother, if only my father hadn't utterly tainted the possibility. But after him, I could never be a mage, any more than I could be a king.'

'The shadows you talk about . . . are they still with you?'

'Less substantial than they were. I think that by facing my fate, yet escaping with my life, I left the darkest of them behind in Torith Mir.'

'But still . . . ?'

'Couldn't be King, even if it wasn't too late.'

'I understand,' she said after a few moments. 'I understand, Eld. I'm sorry I put you under such pressure. And I forgive you, if it's forgiveness you need.'

He barely moved, but she felt and saw twenty years of tension drain out of him. 'Thank you. Dearest Helan.'

She read out the last line. '"All the love I gave you will stay with you always, and . . ." What came after the "and"?'

'Wishes for your happiness. I was interrupted by rescuers in the form of Elrill, Tanthe and some Zampherai friends. Alas, there is no such easy escape for us now.'

She clutched his wrist. 'If ever, if *ever* I get my hands on Drathnen—'

Eldareth pressed his hand over hers and grinned. 'Would that we had so little to worry about.'

'If you find another lover, dear, I'll try not to mind.'

'Thanks,' he said through his teeth, 'but that's the last thing I'm interested in, just at present.'

'Still friends, aren't we?'

'Yes. Neither of us ever needs to question that, surely?'

'Then please stop needling poor Mawrdreth. It's not his fault. He's had a wretched time, being married to me. Forced to spend nights poring over huge books of law, or crouched in underground chambers trying to translate arcane information that might, just might have saved us from—'

Grief ambushed her. She fell silent, waiting until she could speak again without falling apart.

'If you blame yourself, how much more do we?' said Eldareth. 'We should have sabotaged Falthorn's plans. We failed.'

'What are we going to do?'

'Do you ever ask Mawrdreth that question?'

'No, because I'm supposed to know what I'm doing. Fuck!'

'Eat something, before I finish it all myself,' he said,

putting the tray on her lap. 'And let us all go to the temple. It may be our only chance to escape.'

Tanthe was used to freedom, action; she couldn't bear rattling round these few rooms with no hope of escape, no news of Ysomir. She daren't let herself think that this might be the end, that they'd never escape, just fade and die here while the Bhahdradomen swarmed over Aventuria.

It was hard for them all. Despite their efforts, they got on each other's nerves. She suspected that only Elrill's insistence on long training sessions each day prevented them from killing each other.

Auriel alone managed to avoid all their arguments. His face serene within the rippling autumn-red fall of his hair, he walked about like a living golden statue, as if he was not really there but in some shadowy glade of Verdanholm.

'How come you're so calm?' Tanthe asked him one afternoon, curling up beside him on a window seat. He was wearing a long-sleeved blue robe; she couldn't get used to seeing him in human garments. 'Do you think all this has nothing to do with you?'

'No, I don't think that,' he said, moving up to make room for her. From the window she could see part of the innermost wall. *Yrim* were moving about on the battlements. 'As Elrill says, it won't change anything to get angry.'

'Don't quote Elrill at me! Aren't you scared? Because I am fucking terrified.'

He pressed his hand on hers. In Verdanholm they'd been passionate lovers. Now she wasn't sure where they stood with each other. Their first passion for each other had been tainted by her discovery, later, that Falthorn had manipulated them into producing the magical child he'd wanted. On her second visit to Verdanholm they'd made love again, if only to exorcise Falthorn's influence. Since returning to Earth, though, it was as if a translucent barrier had fallen between them.

Tanthe wasn't sure why. She still found Auriel alluring.

He still looked at her with affectionate eyes. Yet they didn't really know each other. Perhaps it was a natural separation, as they accepted each other as brother and sister rather than lovers. Neither had rejected the other; it was something unspoken.

'Tanthe, I've been through the worst fear I can believe possible. I lived with it for years.'

'Falthorn,' she said. 'I know. What he did to me—'

'I'm sorry it happened to you. What he did to you once, he has done to me dozens of times, until I forgot what it was like *not* to jump in terror every time he came near me.'

'I know, love,' she said, stroking his arm.

'But look; Falthorn isn't here.' Auriel smiled and his lovely face lit up for a moment. She rarely saw him smile. 'That's why I'm calm. I'm in a place where Falthorn isn't.'

Tanthe smiled back. 'Fair enough.'

'I wonder why he left me, though? Is he still in the Amber Citadel? Has he gone home?'

'I don't know,' said Tanthe. 'Helan said he wasn't there when she saw Vaurgroth.'

'Falthorn never does anything without a reason,' Auriel said bitterly. 'He's still trying to trap our parents, or something.'

'I don't see why. He's got everything he wants, hasn't he? Maybe he doesn't need us any more. He's discarded us.'

'I hope so. He's got Jthery, though.'

'Yes, well, Jthery was a bloody idiot, falling for Falthorn's dubious charms. He deserves it.'

'No-one deserves the *ezht*, Tanthe.' He stretched, pulling his fingers through his hair. She looked at his lithe body and felt a ghost of lust . . . then realised she had no energy or will to do anything about it. The Bhahdradomen had even taken that. Or was it that, beautiful as Auriel was, he had a passivity about him that did not attract her?

She groaned silently. Too confusing. Better they were just brother and sister. Even though they had a child . . . somewhere.

'Elrill has helped me a lot,' he said, as if to himself. 'I'm not sure what it is he wants the three of us to do together, though . . .'

'Don't look so worried about it. It's probably just group sex.'

He was amused by that, to her relief.

'It will be good to go the temple,' she said. 'I can't believe they're letting us. Apparently they think that if they let us carry on with our customs, we'll accept their rule more easily.'

'That won't work, surely.'

'No, but you're missing the point. They don't realise how much strength our rites give us.'

Auriel's eyes sparked. 'What sort of strength?'

'I don't mean magical powers. I mean inner strength, the feeling that we are all part of a great circle. Just saying the chants. *I am goddess. I am god. The circle is unbroken*.' She caught a quick breath of optimism, the first she'd felt since this had happened. 'I know you don't believe the same things, Auriel, but it will help us all. Including you.'

'Strength. I'd like to know how that feels.'

'If the circle is unbroken,' Tanthe said softly, 'the Bhahdradomen can never break through it. Never.'

Now her eyes were fixed on the Temple of Nepheter as they climbed towards it. She tried to ignore the crowd, to stop herself searching fruitlessly for a glimpse of Ysomir or Saphaeyender. The sky was clear, the day chilly and fine, as if the world had forgotten that it had been wrenched inside out. The pale golden dome looked as it always had, an exuberant paean to life. Sunlight poured lusciously over it, gilding the pale walls, flashing on the jewellery of the citizens who walked in loose procession towards it.

She'd never seen such a turn-out. The street that snaked uphill to the temple was seething. There was an atmosphere of trembling hope that perhaps life under the Bhahdradomen could be bearable after all.

Auriel was at her side, Eldareth and Elrill behind them, Mawrdreth and Helananthe in front. Auriel hadn't wanted to come but she'd made him; she was afraid that if he stayed behind, he might vanish. It was a relief to be outside, but she could see no chance of escape. It was too public. A heavy escort of *vagharim* surrounded their party. *Yrim* kept a subtle profile on the edges of the crowd, but they were still there, watching.

Heads turned as people realised their ex-monarch was walking among them. Astonishment rippled through the procession and some fell aside to watch her pass, at least until the Bhahdradomen moved them on again.

Helananthe – Queen no longer – walked like a woman being taken to her execution.

All eyes were on her, but she looked at no-one. She walked with careful dignity, statuesque in a stiff gown of creamy-yellow with an over-robe of russet silk. Her hair hung loose in honey waves. Tanthe thought she looked like a sorrowing goddess. Her movements were minimal, her eyes blank. Occasionally, over the past few days, Tanthe had seen a dreadful fire in them. That look always chilled her to the core. Too much of the time, though, Helan's eyes were empty.

She noticed that Auriel kept glancing around. His long hair on the sapphire fabric of his robe shone garnet-red. 'What are you looking for?'

'The Valahyr,' he said.

She tucked her arm through his. He clamped her wrist against his ribs and she realised how tense he was. 'You're not worried Falthorn's going to turn up and take you away?'

He didn't answer, just gave her a dark look. 'Don't,' she said. 'He's gone. I wouldn't let him take you, anyway.'

That was a foolish promise; no-one could stop Falthorn doing anything. Not even Vaurgroth, she suspected. Auriel only gave a grim smile. 'Who is Nepheter, anyway?' he said.

'Oh, Auriel!'

'Well, how should I know? The Valahyr told me hardly anything about Earth. They don't talk about humans much.'

'Don't consider us that important, I suppose,' said Tanthe.

'They don't think about you at all.'

'Oh.' She exhaled, shaking her head. 'That stung. Charming. Well, since you aren't as well-educated as you could be, my dear; Nepheter is the patron goddess of Parione. She especially favours poets, artists, all the finer things in life. Her consort, Dyonis –' she pointed to one of the statues that flanked the doors of the temple, a perfect youth in white marble – 'represents vigour, loyalty, athleticism, love, sex, pleasure, joy; everything that's good about life, really.'

'I see.'

'No, you don't,' said Tanthe. 'It's complicated. Nepheter is only one aspect of the Great Goddess, the Goddess in her youth. The Maiden. Now in her Mother form she's called Bronia here. There's a Temple of Bronia on Pearl Street, but they tend not to worship her separately – only on special, personal occasions, births and that. Otherwise, she's partly merged with Nepheter, and partly merged with Nuth. In Sepheret, where I come from, the Mother is our main goddess, only we call her Breyid. She doesn't just represent motherhood, but the fertility of the fields, our responsibility to nurture the earth. What it means to be an adult, not that I've ever felt like one.' Tanthe grinned. Auriel was looking sideways at her, bemused. 'Breyid's consort is Anthar, who is equivalent to Dyonis, only ours is a god of forests and animals. He appears as a stag to the Deirlanders, and a fox to the Eisilians – who, by the way, portray their goddess as a snake, the symbol of wisdom. Now, in Mithrain they call her Eshte of the Lake. In Thanmandrathor, she's Q'enartre of the Lightning. I think Q'enartre embodies all three aspects in one, but I'd have to look it up to be sure. Are you following this?'

'Almost.'

'Our Breyid also has a maiden aspect, called Nephenie; she's the same goddess as Nepheter, only our Nephenie is more of a huntress than a poet. So after Maiden and Mother comes the Goddess in her Crone aspect. Our version is called Mahaa. She's a wise woman, a healer, but she's also the goddess of death, winter and rebirth. The watcher of the gates. In Parione they call her Nuth. Nuth is the same as Mahaa, and yet she isn't.' Tanthe's voice fell. 'Nuth is the one, *the* Great Goddess, the Creatrix, the blackness at the beginning and the end. Nuth is bloody scary. That's why her temple is stuck down by the river and hardly anyone goes there. But her priestesses are the most powerful in Aventuria. I've met a couple of them; if anyone could scare the Eaters, they could.'

'What's frightening about them? Are they like . . . Falthorn?'

'No, no. They're good people. It's because they're realistic. They always tell you the truth, however much it hurts. They make you tell *yourself* the truth. Most people don't enjoy that. Nuth is death, but that doesn't make her bad. She's also life. She makes death bearable; you came out of her cauldron and you go back into it. Or her womb, or her raven wings, depending on your preferred metaphor. That's what they say, anyway.'

'And the god, Dyonis?' said Auriel. 'Does he have different aspects?'

'Not in the same way. Dyonis and Anthar are vigorous, joyful gods, but Anuth is a sort of shadowy figure, a male reflection of Nuth. Anyway, the story is that the god loves the goddess in the spring, and impregnates her with himself. Then in the autumn he dies. He spills his blood as a sacrifice to save the land. In the winter the goddess mourns alone, until she gives birth to him again at Hollynight. The god is reborn, the sun is reborn, green shoots come up, baby birds hatch, everyone celebrates. He grows up and becomes her lover again . . .'

Auriel looked amused and bewildered. 'Gods can die?'

'It's symbolic,' she said. 'It's about the cycle of the year ... You don't have that in Verdanholm, do you? The gods and goddesses represent us, or what we could be. They're about the sweetness of life, or sometimes the misery of it. They're about reality.'

'This seems a very complicated way to represent reality,' said Auriel.

'I know, it's wonderful, isn't it?'

'I think I'm glad the Aelyr have no gods. I hope Nepheter doesn't strike me down for not believing in her.'

'She's not that sort of goddess. Just copy what the rest of us do. It's not hard.'

They were at the temple, climbing the steps to the wide, light portico. The doors stood open, revealing an interior flooded with sunlight and packed with a shifting mass of celebrants. Tanthe felt a pang of emotion as they entered. A painful reminder of the last time she'd been in here with Saphaeyender, free and unsuspecting.

The temple was round, the seats arranged in circular tiers around the central altar, the dome shedding light high above. The *vagharim* escorted Helan's party to the special area reserved for nobles, a railed segment with padding on the stone benches. Helan sat in front with Mawrdreth and Eldareth. Tanthe, Auriel and Elrill settled themselves on the bench behind. They were quite high up and there were no public seats in front of them, so Tanthe had a clear view of the whole temple. The air was fragrant with flowery incense.

Everyone's attention was fixed on Helananthe. She moved as if in a dream, a waxen figure drained of life by shock, rarely speaking even to Mawrdreth. Tanthe dreaded to think what she must be feeling. She was the monarch who had given up her throne to the Bhahdradomen, and now stood vulnerable before the people she felt she'd betrayed.

Tanthe's gaze roamed over the crowd. She saw the priests and priestesses in pale greens and yellows, waiting tensely for the congregation to settle. Usually they were joyful, greeting people with laughter and jokes. Now their faces were white with anxiety. She also saw some familiar black robes, striped with red and white.

'Look, the priestesses of Nuth are here too!' she whispered to Auriel. Helan frowned at her. Tanthe fell quiet. She saw Ariolne and Rouna, then recognised a few faces from the palace. There was Lord Derione in the front row, and some members of the Sun Chamber Council . . . not dead, after all.

Derione's eyes were fixed on the Queen. Tanthe hardly knew him, but she knew Helan trusted him; he was a quiet, stolid man of middle years, with the thick blond hair of his Noreyan descent. Suddenly he left his seat, walked swiftly across the central area past the altar, and ran up the steps to the royal tiers. The *vagharim* guards watched him, yet made no move to stop him.

'Your majesty!' he whispered, kneeling in front of Helan and weeping openly.

'Derione.' She leaned forward and hugged him, then sat back, gripping his hands. 'Thank all the gods you're alive! I didn't know what had happened to you.'

'We've all been expelled from the Amber Citadel, ma'am.'

'All?'

'Palace staff, courtiers, guards, all members of the Sun Council. Only a skeletal household staff were kept, enough to service the Citadel.'

'And us,' she said.

He shook his head despairingly, tears dripping down his cheeks. 'Ma'am, you are hostages to ensure the peace,' he said.

'I know,' she said softly. 'That's why they haven't killed us. We're more use to them alive. Sit beside me, Derione.' She glanced at the Bhahdradomen guards but they were only watching. 'Do people still care enough about me to preserve my life by not rebelling? Don't they know what I did?'

'Ma'am, of course they care! Whatever happened, they know that you were forced, manoeuvred, threatened, overwhelmed—'

'Have you been reading dictionaries to pass the time?'

'Ma'am,' Derione said helplessly. 'They don't blame you.'

'I blame myself.'

'I was there. You had no choice!'

'Perhaps I had a choice to fight, and die, and not be used as a lever against my own people. That is what my mother and brother say I should have done. What's happening in the city? We've heard nothing.'

'People are terrified,' he answered. 'They're looking to you for reassurance.'

Helan didn't answer. Tanthe leaned forward and touched Derione's shoulder.

'Lord Derione, do you know what's happened to my sister Ysomir? Was she released or is she still . . . ?'

Helananthe turned and gave Tanthe a glacial look. It had been her decision to imprison Ysomir; every time Tanthe was reminded, she came close to hating the Queen. She drew back, but Helan's demeanour softened. 'I'm sorry, Tanthe. I never foresaw her being stranded there. I feared that if I mentioned her to Vaurgroth, it might put her in worse danger.'

Tanthe gaped at her. Derione said quietly, 'I've heard nothing of her, anyway. I'm sorry.'

There was activity below them. The tall doors were closing. Music sprang up; flutes piped and the priestesses sang the traditional song of welcome. Their joy sounded forced. Tanthe was acutely aware of their escorts, standing silent and reptilian on either side. All around the circumference of the temple, on the walkway behind the highest tier, stood similar, more discreet figures. These had grey-white cloaks, hoods hiding their faces, no weapons visible. There were *yrim*, too, dotted here and there on the steps and by the doors. She shivered.

The temple was crammed. The altar was ablaze with the tiny candles, overflowing with offerings of winter fruits and flowers.

Helananthe let out a small sigh. 'I hoped my mother and brother might be here.'

'Make another request to see them,' said Mawrdreth. He made to take her hand but she pulled away.

'Don't touch me. I don't want them to see any weakness in me.'

'Helan,' said Eldareth, 'they aren't judging you. If you cry, they'll only love you the more for it.'

'I don't want their pity, either,' she said quietly.

Tanthe shifted uneasily. She felt out of place, intruding on the Queen's misery. What on earth am I doing, she thought, sitting on the royal tier, with everyone staring up here and wondering who the hell I am?

'Not faring so well?' whispered Eldareth, moving back to sit between her and Elrill.

'I can't believe this,' Tanthe said under her breath. 'I keep thinking I'll wake up and it won't have happened.'

'My thoughts exactly,' said Eldareth, pressing her hand.

The high priestess of Nepheter was speaking. Her voice, usually strong, was hesitant. 'In the name of Nepheter and Dyonis, we welcome you to this our celebration of . . . life. For as we are all children of the Goddess . . .' The priestess paused, glancing at a cloaked shape-changer standing a few yards from her. 'We join together in the circle, noble and merchant, artist and artisan . . .'

Then Tanthe saw him.

Saphaeyender.

She snatched a breath, would have leapt out of her seat if Eldareth hadn't restrained her. It was all she could do not to call his name. But he'd seen her. He looked as if he'd been staring at her and Eldareth for the last ten minutes, trying to get their attention. He was on the far side of the temple, about four rows back from the altar, with his household staff around him and a blond man she didn't recognise.

Some of his actors were there as well. He had quite an entourage, as usual.

They stared at each other. It was all they could do.

'This day, this notable day,' the priestess went on, stammering, 'our sister, Good Mother Ariolne of Nuth, will lead us on our trance journey to meet the Goddess.'

'Trance?' whispered Auriel.

'Just close your eyes and visualise what the priestess is describing,' said Tanthe. 'It's usually a walk through a forest to a cave where Nepheter is waiting, that sort of thing. She may give you a gift, or a message. It's nothing to be afraid of.'

'I can't do it,' Auriel said anxiously.

'Don't, then. Just close your eyes. Shh.'

The temple fell silent. Ariolne stepped to the altar, a powerful hawk-faced woman in black. Her strong, deep voice rang. 'Let your breathing become deep and slow. Let your mind become quiet. Let us now feel the energy that we share, the light that surrounds us and keeps us safe in our journey . . .'

Lulled by her voice, Tanthe closed her eyes and tried to relax. For a few moments she floated – then, abruptly, she knew why Auriel had refused join in. As soon as she began to slip into trance, a ghastly flashback jolted her. Her eyes flew open. She had been on the edge of the *ezht*, the nightmarish non-world to which Falthorn had sent her as punishment for attacking him. Sweat broke out on her palms. She fought to control the fear.

She took a breath and tried again. *No, no.* The darkness was still there, waiting. Whether it was the *ezht* itself or only a memory, she didn't want to know. She was shaking. Around her, everyone sat with closed eyes, hands resting loosely on their knees, travelling to meet their Goddess. 'You find yourself standing between two great trees at the edge of a vast forest,' said Ariolne's voice, hypnotic. 'The forest is beautiful, with shafts of sunlight falling through the trees. Smell the earth, feel the healing warmth of the sun. A stream runs past on your left-hand side and you begin to follow it.'

This isn't fair, Tanthe thought. I'm not going to be cut off from this by that bastard Falthorn! Again she closed her eyes, pushed the darkness away, forced herself with all her will to see the sunlit forest instead.

The trance lay deep on the worshippers. Tanthe felt the energy they were raising, a golden fire scintillating in the air. She hoped the Bhahdradomen found it disturbing. 'You are following the stream. Birds sing in the branches. Hares run along the path before you; they are her sacred animals, showing you the way . . .'

The voice stopped. There was a pause, then it began again, so low and soft that it took Tanthe a few seconds to realise that someone different was speaking. 'Where the path bends you see a temple in the shape of a tall black tower. You enter and you are surrounded by utter blackness. Stop here a moment. Rest. It is a friendly darkness and you are safe, held in the hands that hold the entire universe. Shed everything that you have ever known into the darkness. All your experiences, all your beliefs . . . let them go, let them go. You stand in the darkness washed, cleansed, innocent, naked . . .'

The image of nothingness was making Tanthe uneasy. She felt the *ezht* creeping in again and she shifted in her seat, unable to open her eyes. The voice droned on and on, mesmeric.

'Alone. Abandoned. Feel your utter aloneness, experience the purity of your essential darkness. You are nothing. Feel your despair.'

Around the temple, people moaned. Tanthe felt she was falling helpless down the black throat of a well.

'And then a light begins to appear. A spark in the darkness at first, it grows brighter and brighter. It is the most beautiful light you have ever seen. You yearn towards it.' The voice rose, growing more intense. 'The light fills your hands, it pours over you. You are filled with joy. All the veils have been torn away, all the shadow-screens of false gods who kept you from the light are gone. Now He shines before you, the one true light of the universe, He from whom we all came . . .'

'No,' Tanthe mouthed. She struggled to open her eyes, couldn't move, as if she was stranded in a hypnagogic state.

In her trance, she saw the light. It was oval, with a core of red fire. For a split second she was suffused with awe and a feeling of bliss, as if some drug had washed all her cares away.

'*No!*'

The denial came soundlessly from her own mouth. Her eyes came open; feeling rushed back into her limbs. Dizzily, she stared down at the altar and saw who was speaking.

Rhazagramen. His hood was back and she recognised his pearly, wizened face, his precise, human-sounding voice. A couple of his colleagues stood with him, ones who'd been with Vaurgroth when he invaded the palace. Ariolne had been dragged to one side and was being held between two *yrim*. All the priests and priestesses had been herded into a loose group by the Bhahdradomen, threatened by *gauroth* weapons, though most were plainly in trance. A handful of citizens, like Tanthe, had their eyes open and were staring in consternation at the scene; but the vast majority were deep in visualisation, lost.

'He that came before all else,' said Rhazagramen. 'The Ancestor.'

Someone shouted, 'Don't look at the light! It's false!'

It was Ariolne. She struggled with the soldiers, falling as one of them struck her with the butt of his whip. Tanthe leapt to her feet, only to be pressed back into her seat by the leaden hand of a *vargharim*. One or two others were shouting, but it was too late. All that reached the worshippers was Rhazagramen's voice.

Tanthe looked round at her companions. Auriel's eyes were open and he looked horrified. Elrill was fully alert, observing. Eldareth was sitting forward, head on one hand. Urgently she shook his arm. He looked round and she saw, in relief, that he'd abandoned the dream-journey as well.

Helananthe, Mawrdreth and Derione, however, were sitting with lowered eyelids and slack mouths. Tanthe leaned forward, but Eldareth held her arm.

'Careful. They need to be brought out of it gently,' he said.

'There isn't time.' As discreetly as possible, she pinched the arms of the King and Queen. 'Helan! Stop visualising. The light's gone. Come out of it, come out!'

Helan and Mawrdreth both started and groggily opened their eyes. Neither seemed able to speak. Derione, though, wasn't responding at all to Eldareth's efforts. He gave up, whispering, 'Sit still until it's over. The guards are watching.'

As Rhazagramen went on, something new began to happen. People were moaning, crying out. The voices of the objectors were drowned as those in trance began to sway and ululate.

'Look upon the Light of the Ancestor. Feel its beauty and its fire. Let the light pour down its merciful healing upon you, take the blessing of the Ancestor into your soul. For He is merciful. He is the mighty Ancestor of His Chosen ones, but fear not! He fosters His human children as His own. He brings the lost ones into the fold. Submit yourselves to His light, surrender yourselves to the ecstasy of His presence!'

People were screaming, rising from their seats, waving their hands above their heads as if saluting the sun. Tanthe and her friends watched, aghast. Three feet in front of her, Derione was doing the same. Crying out he rose, swayed, dropped full-length onto the floor as if in a fit. There he lay, slack-faced and laughing.

'This is what we have brought you. Power. Ecstasy. Truth. Relish it!'

The worshippers weren't crying out in pain but in ecstasy,

Tanthe saw. She'd nearly been drawn into it herself, felt one touch of seductive bliss before she pulled out.

From Derione, she looked across the temple and saw, in horror, the same thing happening to Saphaeyender. He was swaying, long arms moving gracefully above his head, face contorted in an expression that she'd only previously seen when they'd been in the throes of sex.

Tanthe couldn't stay silent. At the top of her lungs she screamed, 'Saphaeyender!'

And her voice reached him. She saw him stop, snapping out of the trance like a sleep-walker waking up bewildered. He sank down onto the bench, one hand pressed to his forehead, the other groping out to shake the blond youth beside him.

The temple was in uproar. Rhazagramen did not end the trance properly, as Ariolne would have done, by walking them gently out of it and grounding them back in reality. Instead, having worked them to fever-pitch, he dropped them. Once their cries drowned out his words he stopped and merely stood at the altar, grinning at his cronies, waiting for the hysteria to subside. Presently the white-cloaked Bhahdradomen began to move among the crowd, administering drinks of water and helping them back onto the seats. The sight of people staggering like drunks made Tanthe feel sick. Some were laughing; others looked stunned. She sat numb, helpless to do anything but observe.

Tears ran down her face. She felt a monstrous, invisible cloud gathering, suffocating the last of their hopes.

'They're all mad,' Auriel said, very low.

The scene went on for fifteen, twenty minutes. Helan and Mawrdreth, both pale, helped Derione back onto his seat where he sat shaking his head and murmuring, 'He was there. It was beautiful. We've been wrong, our eyes have been closed. Didn't you see Him?'

The others didn't answer. Eventually Rhazagramen raised his arms and silence fell again.

'Ancestor has manifested here today.' His tone of choked pride sounded false to Tanthe. 'The One. The First. Our progenitor, the god of gods, the only true god. He has revealed His light to you today. He has poured His mercy upon you, outcast humans! Have you not felt the ecstasy of his presence?'

There were scattered calls of affirmation. Tanthe saw scores of flushed, slack faces; they looked like people who'd won a race, or had astonishing sex. All else had quit their minds but a sense of blissful triumph.

Rhazagramen's voice softened. 'Will you look a little more kindly upon us after this? This is why Vaurgroth came here. Not to conquer, not to enslave. Only to deliver you into the bliss of Ancestor's light. This has been a remarkable day. A day of new friendship and understanding between us.'

A woman shouted, 'He's a bloody liar! *Liar!*'

It was the high priestess of Nepheter. She tried to rush between the *yrim* but there was a crack of greenish lightning and she fell.

Helan gasped and covered her mouth with her hands. Tanthe clutched Auriel's arm.

'See, even your ex-Queen is here to show the way into the light,' Rhazagramen continued smoothly. 'Follow her example. Give yourselves to the Ancestor as sweetly as she gave us the reins of the Nine Realms, and you will know this joy forever.'

Mawrdreth was trying to comfort Helan. Derione said, 'Ma'am, don't grieve. We've been shown something wonderful here today. Everything will be well.'

'Shut up,' Tanthe whispered fiercely. 'Don't you get it? You've been hypnotised! They can't take everyone in!'

'If you didn't see the light, I pity you.'

Mawrdreth leaned across and grabbed Derione's arm. 'If you don't get out of here *now*,' he growled, 'I am going to break your neck.' Seeing that Mawrdreth was serious, Derione leapt up and hurried away. The *vagharim* let him go.

Eldareth put his head in his hands. Elrill merely looked on, shaking his head grimly.

'Well, it seems the Eaters have thoroughly ambushed you here today,' he said drily. 'Perhaps now you understand the absolute folly of all religious belief?'

Helan rose suddenly to her feet. She looked across the temple, eyes afire. 'Rhazagramen *is* a liar!' she cried, her voice ringing with anguish. 'Don't listen to their lies! I gave up the throne under pressure of deceit, force and threats to my family and it is the greatest regret of my life. I have broken the Xauroma. Now the covenant is broken, the Earth is wild! Keep faith with our Great Goddess and you may save yourselves. Turn away from Her and you turn away from the land itself. There'll be no-one to protect the Earth so she will protect herself! In fire, flood and storm she'll destroy everything!'

The congregation was transfixed. Even the Bhahdradomen seemed paralysed.

'Blame me for this,' the Queen said fiercely. 'Blame me. I would offer my life-blood to remake the Xauroma.' She ripped down the edge of her bodice, baring her chest almost to the nipples. 'If you think I deserve death for my mistake, kill me now. Only I adjure you; do not turn to this false light for comfort. Stay on the hard, thorny way of Nuth and save Aventuria. In return I give you my life. Take it!'

No-one moved. Her head fell back, hair wild. There was an endless, frozen pause; still no-one took up the offer. Then her eyes rolled back in her head, two white sickle-moons, and she collapsed.

Inside the Heliodor Tower, the darkness was chill and heavy with the odour of stone, thick with the tang of *gauroth*. Nine *bharu'grothrim* walked silently through the darkness, bearing their precious burdens from the temple.

Gulzhur moved with them. Vaurgroth stood like a flame in the shadows, ready to receive their gifts.

The unfinished interior resembled an immense chimney with rough-hewn walls, open to the night sky. Trails of ghost-light swirled in the air. The earth floor had been paved and the walls encrusted with power-drenched stones; magnificent mineral specimens that the *bharu'grothrim* found best attuned for storing *roth*, or entering the *ezht*. Oily lumps of haematite and bournonite, blendes veined with metals, clusters of smoky quartz, shining black slabs of obsidian.

Vaurgroth was a pillar of fire. White as snow, red as blood. Behind him, in the centre of the tower, the gateways to other realms were tall flat shadows, inactive.

'Come to me, faithful ones,' he said in their own language. The sound rolled off the walls like the booming voice of a god. 'Show me the *roth*-stones. Place them in a circle in our midst.'

One by one his elite offered up their gifts for approval. Gulzhur's was a huge quartz crystal, brown as old blood, tingling and burning his palms with its energy. Vaurgroth pressed his fingers to it and gave an *ahhh* of pleasure.

'The quality is excellent,' he said. His approval poured a hot balm of relief over Gulzhur's ego. Vaurgroth displeased was a formidable prospect. Even veteran mages like Gulzhur and Rhazagramen sought to keep him happy at all times.

As he placed his crystal with the other eight, the ring of stones began to glow. The whole tower shuddered, throbbed, uttered ghostly moans. *Gauroth* saturated the very atmosphere. There was plenty for all; they could gorge on it until it leaked from their pores like blood.

Gulzhur took his place beside Zhoaah, who looked sideways at him and smiled. Gulzhur allowed himself a sour grin in return. He looked around the circle. Rhazagramen was beside Vaurgroth as always, then Tzumezht with his long charred-ash face, and Uryzht the beige scholar. On Vaurgroth's left stood Naghrur, his chief of security.

Naghrur was unusually tall for a Bhahdradomen, almost six feet in height and razor-thin, with a polished-steel look about him. His skin was smooth, his eyes pale as glass, his movements precise. He had the look, Gulzhur thought, of a *bharu'grothrim* who appreciated pain as humans appreciated poetry or wine.

Bharamezht, next to Naghrur, was formidable in a more physical way, a great dark bull of a *domen*. He had something of *graukhim* about him, as if he'd sacrificed some of his intellect to muscular bulk. We can never have both, Gulzhur thought disdainfully. A menacing commander he might be, but only glorified *yrim*.

Vaurgroth, Rhazagramen and Zhoaah considered themselves *neshrim*; *domenim* who'd shaped themselves to pass as human, when necessary. They were poor specimens compared to Rhuaaku, though. He was the true adept. He'd given himself a willowy form, smooth gold-tinted skin, even moved his joints to the human position. He looked so convincing that Gulzhur regarded him with a mixture of admiration and revulsion.

Between Rhuaaku and Bharamezht stood the least human-looking of them all. Grahzamen, a grey, webby creature with a beaked face, like some strange bird. *Aghramen*, a drinker of pure energy.

'Today was splendid,' said Vaurgroth.

'Ah, great Master, you should have been there!' said Zhoaah. 'It was miraculous.'

'Zhoaah, I *was* there,' Vaurgroth said with a smile. 'A bystander in a white cloak. I saw everything. It was a triumph.'

'Even the ex-Queen surpassed herself with that ... performance,' said Rhazagramen. Murmurs of laughter.

'I hope the cynics among you will now admit I was right.' Vaurgroth cast his narrow gaze over them, lighting on Gulzhur. 'There is more than one way to raise *gauroth*. Any intense human emotion produces energy; it doesn't have to be pain. Enabler?'

'I'm old-fashioned,' said Gulzhur. 'I trust the older methods. I've always found that anguish produces the most fiery results. Violence, bloodshed, torture, grief. However, Lord of Light, I must concede your methods are a triumph.'

Vaurgroth beamed. 'Fear has its place in keeping the humans docile, but it's not the whole story. How much more effective it is to control them with ecstasy instead. The benefits are unrivalled. In one sweep we control them, reward them and teach them. And we absorb their energy.'

'If they dispute about it, that only makes us stronger,' Rhazagramen put in.

'By all means slay the ones who cause too much trouble, but don't think of killing them en masse,' Vaurgroth said with his most paternal smile. 'There's no need. Humans are of more use to us alive, dwelling alongside us as part of our system. To fulfil that role they must give themselves to the Ancestor. And they want to, that's obvious. They thirst to know Him.'

'Ancestor be praised,' said Rhazagramen.

'Praised,' the others echoed. And Gulzhur kept his guilty secret, that he didn't believe in the Ancestor; not with Vaurgroth's passion, anyway. What did it matter, when the Master of Light had brought them so much? Gods might not exist, but this power was real enough.

Vaurgroth dropped his head back so that the long white rope of hair almost touched the floor. Energy leapt from the crystals at his command. Bronze and green ribbons of light went swirling into him and out again, filling all of them, reaching tendrils all through the city to invigorate his warriors; reaching through the *ezht*, regardless of space and time to touch every Bhahdradomen with the fire of the Ancestor.

Vaurgroth reached out to either side. The circle of *bharu'grothrim* joined as one. *Gauroth* coursed like a river of flame through them, blazing, overwhelming; agony and exhilaration mixed. Gulzhur's mouth stretched in a soundless laugh.

'Give this *roth* to the tower!' Vaurgroth cried. 'For this is but a shadow of the True Tower. We light the shadow with our will, we make it a beacon to call the truth! For the truth shall be made manifest. It is coming closer. Closer!'

And the Heliodor Tower shone and thundered in the night.

Chapter Four. The Order of Calathvahn

Rufryd came back to awareness very slowly.

He couldn't recall any sudden leap to consciousness; only a long, tedious journey of days. Unending nights trapped in a cocoon of fever, body frozen and head burning, coughs ripping like saws through his chest . . . blurred days spent staring at cobweb walls, with no understanding of where he was, or why. He could make no sense of his surroundings. It was a distorted place, a near-dark tunnel or cave . . . sometimes patterned with dapples of dusty light like a deserted temple. Wherever he was he felt part of it, a growth of bone or stone that was slowly wearing away until it would break from its mooring and tumble into darkness.

Periods of oblivion were interspersed with strangely clear dreams in which he saw himself from the outside. A tiny figure being carried over a thrashing ocean in the claws of a gigantic dra'a'k . . . A man left for dead beneath the smoky cone of a dark, squat tower while grotesque figures swarmed around him in a weird victory dance. He floated, looking down at his own pallid face on a pillow, unknown figures bending over him. He felt no anxiety, only an urge to sever the cord that held him and drift into the gentle black wings of Nuth.

Rufryd swallowed hard. He was awake. His fever-dreams receded as if they had happened to someone else. He knew that he'd been here for a long time, that he'd been conscious many times before . . . but this was the first time he'd been self-aware.

His throat was rusty, his body cold and limp. The ceiling was a low vault of stone. This was no great tunnel or cave-maw after all, just a small oddly-shaped cell with basic furniture and a hard pallet for a bed. He wasn't alone, but that was no surprise; part of his mind had been aware of a presence beside him all night.

A sopping rag was pressed to his mouth. He sucked the moisture out greedily, feeling it flow in a delicious icy thread down his throat.

'Your fever's down at last,' said a soft voice.

The figure kneeling beside the pallet was a slim man of thirty or so with a long face and cropped grey hair. He wore a white tabard over a long-sleeved grey robe. His face was beatific, the pale-green eyes radiant with compassion. And he was familiar. Rufryd had a dim awareness that this man had been watching over him for days.

'Umnh,' Rufryd attempted. His tongue was nerveless with disuse.

'What is that, brother?'

He tried again, enunciating painfully. 'You're human.'

'Yes,' the man agreed. 'It is a burden I carry joyfully. More water.'

This time he held a cup to Rufryd's lips. The coldness of the fluid made Rufryd dizzy, but eased his rusted throat. 'I'm out of Vexor, then,' he rasped. 'So good to see a human face. Seen nothing but Bhahdradomen since . . . Who got me out?'

The man's expression darkened. 'Don't tire yourself. Lie back.' His accent was strange, similar to the Thand'rathian Rufryd had grown used to, but lacking their music.

'No. S'all right.' Rufryd managed to prop himself on one elbow, although the exertion made him feel faint. He looked around the little chamber of beige stone, seeing how it tapered at one end into a shadowy alcove that his febrile mind had turned into a cave. It was gloomy but clean. A stove burned in one corner and oiled cloth hung over a small, high window in the wall facing the side of his pallet. Rufryd heard a winter gale howling outside.

'How long have I been ill?'

'A good many days. We thought we'd lost you, a time or two.'

'Are we in Thanmandrathor?' he asked, stifling a cough.

'You could say that.' The man turned away and busied himself at a small table with an assortment of vessels and medicine phials. Measuring drops of a tincture into a tumbler, he diluted it with hot water from a pot simmering on the stove, then brought it to the patient. Rufryd drank it convulsively, welcoming its heat and herbal pungency.

His nurse smiled. 'If you can drink that, you are feeling better. It will help you regain your strength. I'll bring you some broth later. My name is Herex.'

Memory stirred. 'Herex . . . Yes, I know, though I don't know how.'

'I've told you before. You have been very ill, Rufryd. You had a high fever when you came to us, and the affliction settled on your lungs.'

'How d'you know my name?'

'Your companion told us.'

Rufryd frowned. 'Companion?'

'The young *domenim*, Vetru.'

At that name, his heart sank. He lay back on the hard mattress, shivering. Herex went to the stove again, filled a stone bottle with hot water and pushed a stopper into it. Without a word, he wrapped the bottle in a blanket and slid it under the covers beside Rufryd.

The sudden heat made him shiver all the more. Then the heat crept into him and he curled around it, staring at the ceiling vault, trying to remember what had happened.

Fragments fell into place . . . except for the last few days. He groaned. All of it seemed like a dream now. Every single thing that had happened, a dream. He couldn't believe he was still alive.

'Did Vetru bring me here?' he said after a time. 'Wherever "here" is.'

'Yes, Vetru brought you to us. Or rather, we found

him out on the hills, seeking help. We call this place Calathvahn.'

'What's that? A town, a village?'

Herex shook his head. 'We are a community. Quite isolated here, and self-sufficient. It's unlikely you will have heard of us.'

'You say Vetru brought me.' Rufryd took a deep breath. His lungs hurt. He looked down at his body under the thick blanket, saw that his once-muscular limbs were skinnier than he remembered. His hair had been cut short, and they seemed to have shaved and washed him. 'But – unless there were ships I don't know about – I don't see how he could have got me out of Vexor.'

'He didn't,' Herex said ruefully. 'You are still in Vexor, Rufryd.'

He'd suspected, known in his heart, yet the confirmation hurled misery through him. 'I asked if this was Thanmandrathor and you said yes! You lied!'

'I didn't lie. Vexor is an island belonging to Thanmandrathor; not a separate realm. Don't distress yourself.'

Rufryd lay back, his heart thudding with exertion. He wasn't afraid; only disappointed, resigned, worn out with false hope and illness. He clutched the warm stone bottle to him. Stared at Herex until his eyes watered.

'*Neshrim*,' he whispered.

Herex's eyes were kind, and wholly human-looking. The few *neshrim* Rufryd had seen – Bhahdradomen who had altered their forms to imitate humans – were never quite perfect; their eyes always gave them away.

'Does that disturb you?' Herex asked. 'Vetru led us to understand that you have lived among the Bhahdradomen for some time. That you have become quite attached to each other, although he is *neshrim* himself.'

'I shouldn't take too much notice of anything Vetru says,' Rufryd said dully. 'He's hardly more than a hatchling. I haven't been here long enough to get used to it all, so yes, it's a shock.'

Herex smiled. 'I see.'

'You're the best one I've seen, though,' Rufryd added. 'I can't tell at all. You've got the eyes right, the mannerisms and everything. It's remarkable.'

Herex gave a soft laugh. 'Thank you, but I must confess. I am in fact human. We are all human here. A burden we carry joyfully.'

That was the second time he'd used that phrase. Rufryd sat up, propped himself against a pillow and gazed at him in astonishment. 'Humans living in Vexor? That's impossible.'

'Not impossible, since obviously we are here.'

'I don't get it.'

The green eyes cooled. 'You speak strangely. I heard that you came from Parione.'

'A lot further away than that. Sepheret.'

That ruffled Herex's composure at last. 'Well, you have travelled far, Rufryd of Sepheret. There are humans in Vexor, and this is not for you to "get", nor for us to explain.'

'I wasn't trying to be offensive,' Rufryd said evenly. 'Mind you, I usually manage it even when I'm not trying. But we've never heard of any humans here!' His chest spasmed into a coughing fit.

'It's not that we don't wish to talk to you, nor that you are unwelcome here,' Herex said, giving him sips of water and supporting him until the fit subsided. 'But I would be doing no service to your health if I kept you talking about things that can wait until you are well. Besides, it isn't my place to speak of it.'

'Do the Bhahdradomen know you're here?'

'Of course.'

'And they haven't . . .'

Herex shook his head. 'Enough questions. Rest now.'

A wave of exhaustion pulled Rufryd down into the bed's embrace. He was safe and alive, and too tired to care about anything else. It would be enough to sleep.

'How long did you say I've been here?'

'Let me see . . . twenty-seven days, I think.'

'That long! Goddess, I don't believe it!'

Herex's small mouth pursed. 'And it will take you as long again to regain your health. You have been dangerously ill.' He leaned over Rufryd, a pale and soothing presence, still as cool water. 'If not for Vetru, you would have died.' He smiled, eyes dancing with amusement. 'Consider that; a Bhahdradomen saved your life.'

Rufryd slept for a time, then ate a bowl of broth, dragged himself with Herex's help to the privy that lay off the corridor outside his room, slept again.

When he woke, it was light outside and he knew he was better.

The oily curtain had been tied back. He lay in the hard narrow bed, staring at the white sky through the window. Although he felt limp and drained it was a pleasant feeling; all sensations of illness had faded. The pain behind his eyes, the fits of shivering, the bands of iron around his chest and throat, the hideous unreality of delirium; all were gone. He felt normal. He wasn't going to die after all. It might take him a long time to recover; but whatever grim infection Vexor had inflicted on him, his young strong body had fought it off.

The aged grey door opened, and Herex came in with a tray. Even the bland scent of porridge made Rufryd's appetite leap in anticipation. Another figure came in behind Herex, almost treading on the hem of his robe in his haste. As soon as they were clear of the door, he darted to Rufryd's bedside.

'Herex said you are well. They let me come to you.'

It was Vetru, the young Bhahdradomen who'd been his guide across Vexor. Rufryd regarded him with dismay – as he might regard a boisterous, unpredictable puppy – and also with a grudging trace of relief.

Vetru was dressed like Herex, grey robe with a white

tabard over it, but the soft cloth bunched over the unhuman angles of his joints as he moved. He was shorter than Rufryd, a scrawny figure, all gangling legs and arms. Rufryd had never seen an Eater who was more than skin-draped bone.

The most disturbing thing about Vetru, though, was that he had begun to look like Rufryd. Brownish hair had sprouted from his scalp. His undefined features had strengthened; there was a suggestion of cheekbones, a stronger nose. Even a flush of pink in the grey-green skin. But the change was imperfect; he was still so plainly Bhahdradomen that the effect was grotesque. Rufryd couldn't see it without cringing.

'You haven't stopped, have you?' Rufryd said.

'What?' said Vetru, perching on the end of the pallet as Herex placed the tray on Rufryd's lap.

'Trying to look like me.'

'I am not trying,' Vetru said in his careful Paranian. 'I am not help it.'

'You mean, "I can't help it."'

Vetru nodded enthusiastically, staring at Rufryd with dark, unfathomable eyes. 'I cannot help it,' he said.

Rufryd couldn't answer. He focused all his attention on breakfast; some kind of grain cooked to a grey mass, which didn't taste as bad as it looked. He was pleased to find it sweetened with honey. Herex was feeding the stove, setting water to boil for another herbal brew.

Rufryd was famished, yet he'd been so long without solid food that his stomach cramped after a few mouthfuls. He set down the wooden spoon and said, 'You had better learn to help it, Vetru. You are *domen*, not *neshrim*. Have you looked in a mirror? You're not even very good at it.'

Vetru looked devastated. 'I get better.'

'No, I don't want you to get better at it! I want you to go back to the way you were!'

For an awful moment, Rufryd thought he was going to cry – if his kind were capable of tears. Herex turned and said, mildly reproving, 'Must you speak to him like that? He's a child! A child to whom you owe your life. Don't you see that his change is the greatest compliment he can pay you?'

Rufryd exhaled grimly. The other two looked at him as if more sad than angry. Eventually he sighed again and said, 'Well, I'm sorry, Vetru. I don't see it as a compliment, I just find it very disturbing. I don't know how to make you understand, but I do. That's why I was angry. But we'll let it rest for now, all right?'

'All right,' Vetru said sulkily.

'Herex said you saved my life.'

The young *domen* brightened a little. 'You were sick. *Domenim* in Zhahgrament would not help. I carry you here.'

'*Carried* me? I must weigh twice as much as you, even half-starved.'

'I carry you,' Vetru repeated firmly. 'Bhahdradomen are strong.'

That was true, Rufryd thought, remembering. They were small beings, rarely more than five and a half feet tall, but it was as if they were made of wire and leather, tough and hard to kill. And the ones that had changed shape – imprinted at hatching to become *ghelim* or *graukhim* – were even worse, bristling with claws or bloated with stolen energy. Strange, strange creatures . . .

And swarming now across Aventuria.

The hammer of memory fell on him. He pressed his knuckles into his forehead, groaning to himself, thinking, Goddess and god, I failed. Failed. Why didn't bloody Vetru leave me to die!

It seemed a decade ago that he'd been in Parione, raging at everything and everyone because his brother Lynden was dead and his lover Tanthe had rejected him. In that bitter, reckless frame of mind he'd volunteered for a suicidal quest; to travel across Thanmandrathor to Vexor on Helananthe's behalf.

On the way he had lost his companions in a flood, continued alone until the ancient dra'a'k, Akarata, had made the last, hopeless part of the journey possible. Carrying him in her claws she'd flown him across the Vexat Straits; and after that there was no going back. He'd travelled across the starved island of Vexor into the heart of the Bhahdradomen, mingled with them, even found friends of a sort among them. At last, ill from lack of food – and from the shape-changers' continual, unintentional sapping of his life-energy – he'd come to Zhahgrament, the stronghold of their leader, Vaurgroth of the grandiose titles.

Unfortunate that Helan should send him on a diplomatic mission, when he was the least diplomatic person in the world. As a spy, though, he hadn't been bad.

Except that he'd come too late. Too late for negotiation or treaty, subterfuge or sabotage. He'd found the Bhahdradomen already fully armed, afire with zeal and ready to invade Aventuria. Vaurgroth and his elite had received the tardy ambassador, made sport of him, then thrown him back onto the street to die.

Bhahdradomen were poison to humans. Poison to everything.

The last thing Rufryd remembered was lying on the roadside beneath Vaurgroth's smoky tower, watching a mass of unhuman forms writhing in an eerie victory dance. He must already have been in the grip of illness, some stray infection against which he'd had no defence. He didn't know whether the scene had been an hallucination, born of nascent fever, but it had been vivid. Cobwebs of light breaking over the dancers, making them look like moths cracking their way out of cocoons.

'You died on the road, or they killed you,' Vetru said. 'So I took you away.'

'Did you know about Calathvahn? That there were humans here?'

'Some *domenim* told me of it, yes.'

'Is it far from Zhahgrament?'

'Far,' said Vetru.

Herex put it, 'It is almost thirty miles east and south of Zhahgrament. A long way for a hatchling to carry you and keep you alive.'

Rufryd tried, but couldn't remember a thing. He let the image sink in. Vetru hauling him like a corpse, or at best helping him stagger along like a drunk, for mile on mile of Vexor's barren plains. A Bhahdradomen hatchling who'd fulfilled his duty to guide him to Vaurgroth's lair; who had every reason to desert a dying human and go back to his *tzcement*. Yet he hadn't.

'Vetru,' he began helplessly. 'Thank you. I don't know what else to say. I don't know why you did it, but I'm grateful.' That was the wrong word. He wasn't grateful to be alive as such; but he was stunned and moved.

'I think you are better with humans. They make you well.'

'Weren't you afraid they might hurt you?'

Vetru frowned. 'I never think of that. I only think of you.'

'Oh, gods.' Rufryd leaned back on the pillow, pushing his hands through his hair. 'What have I done to deserve you?'

Herex stood over him, hands folded. 'Rufryd, you should know that Vetru was never in any danger from us. We live peacefully alongside the Bhahdradomen, and have done for many years.'

'Without killing each other?'

'We leave them alone. They leave us alone. We have sympathy for them.'

'Well, you know something?' Rufryd put the tray aside and swung his feet onto the floor. Today he was going to begin the process of getting fit again, however unsteady the first steps. He felt the possibility of a new life, flowing up from the cold flagstones. 'So do I. I can see that they've been starving half to death on this island. Unfortunately, it seems their leaders have decided to solve the problem by launching a full-scale attack on Aventuria. Goddess knows what state I'll find my friends in when I go back!'

Herex helped him to stand up, but faintness rushed through him and he had to sit down again. 'Rufryd, I don't think you will be going anywhere for quite some time. Be at peace. You've done all you can; and you are welcome among us, for as long as you wish to stay. Indeed, we'd be happy for you to make your home among us.'

Rufryd was tempted.

The days went by, and each day he made a little more progress; was able to walk further, bathe himself, eat more. Herex brought him a grey robe and a white tabard – with some undergarments for warmth – and then he looked as if he belonged. It was like living in the Temple of Nuth again. They insisted on keeping his hair trimmed short, but he didn't care about that. Women had called him handsome, even beautiful, but he'd never been vain. Arrogant, perhaps, but not vain.

In the corridor beyond his small cell he found a line of similar sleeping chambers. Outside was a maze of long, low, cloistered buildings, arranged around courtyards as some of the Bhahdradomen *tzcements* had been. But these courtyards contained gardens; plain, functional plots full of root vegetables or chicken-coops, thick with the scent of wet soil and rotting vegetation, but still, tiny pockets of life and fertility.

Vexor was not utterly flat after all, Rufryd noticed. The community nestled in a ring of low hills, which were as barren as the rest of Vexor and mottled with the dull hues of lichen like Bhahdradomen skin. Winter clouds massed above them and cold salty winds blew unhindered from the sea; but the settlement itself was a small oasis of life.

There were about six hundred humans here, Herex told him. They lived quiet contemplative lives. What they contemplated, Rufryd wasn't sure; as a stranger, the building that housed the temple and archives was placed out of bounds to him. He didn't care. He had no real curiosity at present. They were good-natured, they gave him food and they left him alone; he couldn't ask for more.

He felt that his illness had cleansed him. All his anger and pain had been bleached out. He felt like a blank page, with no questions to be asked, no desires at all. He didn't bother asking Herex what these people were doing here; it might have spoiled his sense of miracle, that he'd found humans in this Goddess-forsaken land at all.

They all had the same calm, sweet quality as Herex. Their serenity amazed him. It was the sort of peace he'd hoped to find in the Temple of Nuth, but which had eluded him. Could he find it here, in this tiny refuge in the land of the Bhahdradomen, of all places?

The more he thought about it, the less point there seemed in returning to the mainland. First, he'd been so ill. Second, there seemed no way to do it; no bridges, no boats. Third, what would he find there?

He wondered if the people of Calathvahn were an order like the Mediators, peaceful folk who devoted themselves to the study of *roth* and wisdom, who took no side in war. He had heard descriptions of the college on the Serpent Isles and this seemed similar. It lacked the lush setting, the hot weather and the warmth of terracotta tiles underfoot, yet it had the air of simplicity and dedication that he'd imagined.

Crossing Vexor, he'd nearly starved on indigestible Bhahdradomen meat and the few grains and berries and evil-tasting fish with which they supplemented their limited diet. Here the food was still sparse, but better. There were vegetables from the gardens, small pale eggs, grain that they managed to cultivate in the valley without *graukhim* tearing it to destruction. Often there was stringy chicken, or fish caught from a nearby river, and fresh winter berries. No milk or cheese, but at least what they had was edible. Rufryd got used to feeling hungry all the time. The prospect of spending his life gardening did not worry him, either; it would be like being back in Riverwynde again. Full circle.

Yet something was wrong here. It was only on the seventh day, when he was well enough to eat in the refectory for the first time, that he realised what it was.

'There are no women here,' he whispered to Herex, who was sitting beside him.

'Mn.' Herex had his mouth full, and seemed to use this to avoid answering his remark.

'Do they eat separately, for some reason? Can't stand the men's table manners?'

'Rufryd,' Herex said, low and serious. 'Calathvahn is an all-male order. There have never been women here, and there never will be.'

'What?' Rufryd stared at him, uncomprehending. 'That's a bit weird, isn't it? Why would you exclude women? How can you get on, without any priestesses?'

'Please, lower your voice.' Herex dabbed his mouth with a napkin. Other men nearby were glancing at them. 'We have no need of women here.'

'Oh, I see.' Rufryd grimaced.

'I don't think you do.'

Rufryd sensed he'd touched a nerve. He went on, smiling but serious. 'Herex, you have been amazingly kind to me and I'm forever grateful. Whatever goes on here is fine by me and none of my business. All acts of love are sacred to the Goddess. But I can't join in. I want to get that clear, should the subject ever arise. For some strange reason, I'm only interested in sleeping with women.'

Herex's face lengthened into a mask of shock. There was even a touch of colour in his cheeks. Rufryd, amused to see his serenity punctured, realised he hadn't quite outgrown his own malicious streak.

'You are quite wrong,' Herex said crisply. 'We do not have any form of physical relationship with each other.'

'Oh, come on.'

Herex seemed mortally offended. 'We do not! Whatever makes you suggest such a thing? We are a celibate order.'

It was a word Rufryd had never heard before. An odd, academic-sounding word that the elite of Parione might use. 'What in Hellaxis does "celibate" mean?'

'It means that we do not indulge in such acts.'

'You don't have sex?' Rufryd said at normal volume, ensuring that everyone at the table looked at him. He couldn't understand why they were shocked. Half of him was enjoying the fact that he'd disturbed them; the other half was completely astonished. 'Why not?'

'Because we . . . Isn't it self-evident? To rise above the grotesqueness of human urges!'

Herex stopped, visibly recollecting himself. Rufryd gaped at him. 'Why would you think sex is grotesque? That sounds like the sort of thing Rhazagramen said to me. I'm completely confused. I shouldn't have asked, obviously.'

'No, no,' Herex said, calm again. 'Rufryd, you come from the mainland. We can't expect you to understand overnight. It's entirely my fault for not saying anything.'

Another man came up behind them and leaned down, resting a hand on each of their shoulders. 'Is everything well here, Herex? I sensed a disturbance.'

Rufryd had noticed the man on the far side of the refectory, but hadn't realised he was heading towards them. He was tall and broad, the weight of his hands hinting at powerful muscles beneath the shapeless sleeves of his robe. Rufryd looked up at him and saw a large head with close-cropped iron-grey hair, powerful black eyebrows arched over sharp green eyes, a humorous mouth. He had a Thand'rathian look about him – high cheekbones, slanting eyes – but his skin was paler, his jaw and neck wide and powerful. He looked good-tempered but formidable.

Herex shot to his feet, almost tipping his stool over. 'Quite well, Father,' he said, dipping his head in respect. 'My apologies.'

'This is our guest, I take it?'

'Yes, this is Rufryd of Sepheret. Rufryd, this is Father Arax Vahan, the head of our order.'

Rufryd stood up more slowly, and nodded. He loathed making the right noises to people in authority, even priests. 'I'm glad to meet you, good Father.'

Arax Vahan smiled and clasped his right hand warmly. 'We are glad to have you here. I was told you have been very ill. Alas, Vexor is unkind to newcomers, at least until they have acclimatised. I trust you are recovered?'

'Not fully, but I'm much better. Thanks.'

'Our way of doing things is unfamiliar to you, of course.' The green eyes were jade-pale and probing.

'I only wondered why there were no women here.' Rufryd spoke lightly, trying not to provoke another alarming response. 'If I spoke out of turn, I'll shut up.'

Herex said, 'As I was just saying, it's my fault for not explaining.'

'No, no,' said Arax Vahan. 'You acted correctly, Herex. He is our guest. We have nothing to explain. When he is ready to understand, he'll let us know.'

Rufryd felt vaguely intimidated. He didn't know whether to sit down again, excuse himself from their company, or declare that he had no curiosity whatsoever. The Father spoke again, saving him from making the decision.

'I understand you came as an ambassador from Parione?'

He nodded. 'There were meant to be four of us. I was the only one who made it. Completely wasted journey, as it turned out.'

'Surely not. You're clearly a very brave young man, to cross Vexor alone.'

'If I'd known Calathvahn was here, it might have made things a bit easier.'

'Well, you are here now,' Arax Vahan said with a broad smile. 'And very welcome. Finish your meal; make yourself at home among us. And when you are ready, not merely to ask questions but to consider the answers, don't impose on poor Herex. Ask him to bring you to me.' The Father began to turn away. 'I am always here.'

'I might not be, though,' Rufryd said suddenly.

Arax Vahan turned back to him. 'What do you mean?'

'I may want to leave, when I've got my strength back.'

The leader smiled reprovingly. 'Rufryd, there is nowhere for you to go. Everything you need is here.' He came forward, clasped Rufryd's shoulder and looked into his eyes with a warmth so intense it took his breath away. 'You've arrived here at such an exciting time, it must be divinely ordained. Live with us, understand us, then you will see how it's possible to shed your old life and find peace. You'll wonder how you could ever have considered going back.'

Shed my old life, Rufryd thought, hoeing up the stumps of winter vegetables. Why not?

Why the fuck not?

Whatever happened, it seemed he was stuck here. In his weak state of health, trying to travel would probably kill him. And if by some miracle he found a means of crossing the Vexat Straits, there would be hundreds of miles of travel ahead, even to reach Tasqabad. His conscience gnawed at him to go back, fight the Bhahdradomen; but then he thought, Why do I think it's my responsibility to save the world? To go and get myself killed trying? I've done my bit. I'm tired.

He saw the tranquillity of the men here, and envied them. He didn't care what they believed, as long as they didn't pressure him to share it. All he knew was that they bristled a little if he happened to curse in the name of a god or goddess. He could live with that.

He'd never felt at ease in Parione, with its heated villas and piped water and bountiful, delectable food. Here it was simple, like Riverwynde, though harsher; there were no grassy meadows filled with herds of sheep, and wood was so scarce that even simple fires could not be taken for granted. But the austerity of it felt right.

'You will stay here?' Vetru asked him. He'd already asked several times, having worked out that Rufryd never gave him the same answer twice.

'It looks like it,' Rufryd said. 'Will you pick up a fork and do some work, instead of flapping around like a headless chicken?'

'I thought you would leave again,' Vetru said, sounding disappointed.

'Why?'

'I would go with you. See land that is not all sucked dry.'

Rufryd leaned on his hoe. 'You don't have to stay with me. You're free to go back to your *tzcement*, or follow Vaurgroth in his glorious campaign. I'd go soon, if I were you, before the whole of Aventuria's sucked dry.'

He wasn't sure Vetru understood everything he said, but the hatchling had proved a fast learner. 'I want to stay with you,' he said stubbornly.

Rufryd had grown exasperated with Vetru's clinginess. He'd wasted precious energy trying to make him sleep in a different cell, and not follow him around all the time, to no avail. Now he just tried to ignore him.

'What for?' he exclaimed.

'I don't know,' said Vetru.

'If I went back among humans on the mainland with you in tow, they'd kill you! I've seen it happen!'

'I don't know!' Vetru repeated angrily. 'But I was sent with you. Must stay with you.'

Rufryd gave a sigh. 'Fine, then stay. You're not that much trouble. But these people aren't your *domenim*.'

'Yes, they are,' Vetru answered. 'They like Bhahdradomen.' And he looked a tiny bit more human, a tiny bit more like Rufryd, than he had the day before.

Winter lingered, wet and miserable. Rufryd gave himself to the daily round of gardening, cooking and cleaning that sustained Calathvahn and felt himself absorbing some of the order's serenity at last. If it hadn't been for the foul-smelling smokes that sometimes drifted across from Zhahgrament, he could have forgotten he was in Vexor at all.

Arax Vahan spoke to him frequently, but the conversations were only of everyday matters. Rufryd sensed the Father was weighing up his answers, so the more he probed, the more taciturn Rufryd became. He didn't want to know their secrets or join their devotions. He just wanted to be left alone.

He had been there some time before it struck him that they hadn't celebrated any festivals. Had he missed Hollynight while he was ill? How far off was Breyid's Day – or Maid's Day, as they called it in Paranios – when the first shoots poked through the soil? He'd seen no calendars, heard no talk of the changing of the seasons. Strange, when it had been a full-time obsession in Riverwynde.

He thought he knew why. Herex and the others had been instructed to tell him nothing unless he asked, but it wasn't hard to work out, from odd remarks they dropped and the ease with which he managed to embarrass them on occasion. And the more clearly it dawned on him, the less he wanted to know their reasons.

Why else did the Bhahdradomen tolerate them here?

'You have settled in well,' Arax Vahan said, looming suddenly beside Rufryd as he was putting implements away after his day's work. It was growing dark, and Lily Moon was rising full behind smoky streaks of cloud. 'You seem content among us. Is this the case?'

'Pretty much,' Rufryd said. He went on with what he was doing – propping forks and spades in the tool-room, then backing out and latching the door – refusing to show the Father any deference. The priests and priestesses of Nuth had hated deference, he recalled. 'Yes, I'm content.'

'Come, stroll with me about the gardens for a while. We can take supper later. Show me what preparations are being made for planting.'

'Digging, mostly,' Rufryd said under his breath.

Side by side they wandered from courtyard to courtyard, with Lily Moon rising above them, Rose Moon large and low on the horizon. The rest of the Order had gone into the refectory, so the cloisters were deserted. 'You're not fully content, I fear,' Arax Vahan said. 'What is lacking? Tell me.'

Rufryd shrugged. 'I can't get used to not seeing any female faces around, that's all.'

'Ah, still troubled by the urges of your body. That can be a great difficulty.'

'What?' said Rufryd, folding his arms. He frowned, but Arax Vahan walked placidly on like a ship in sail. 'Did I say, "I wish there were women here so I could have sex with them"?'

'You didn't have to.'

Rufryd was getting annoyed. He tried to remember Akarata's wisdom; not to react, just to listen and observe. It wasn't so easy. 'I'm sorry, good Father, but I don't see what you're getting at. Yes, I like sex, and if there were women here it would be nice if one of them fancied me enough to join in. I don't see wanting that as a "trouble" or a "difficulty". But that isn't what I meant. I just meant that it's normal for them to be there, and I miss them.'

'Yes,' Arax Vahan said knowingly. 'You will, at first.'

'What do you mean, at first?'

'You have to learn a new way of thinking. My child, it takes weeks, months, perhaps years of hard work to appreciate the beauty of our life here. The purity of being free from all lust, all desire, all pain.'

'Pain?' Rufryd was brought up short by memories.

'You have suffered a good deal of it, I sense.'

'Enough.'

'Much of it caused by women . . . Am I right?'

Rufryd paused; tightness had seized his throat and he couldn't speak. 'Yes, you'd be right.'

'You can tell me of them,' Arax Vahan said gently. 'You don't have to, but I think it might help you to speak.'

For the first time, Rufryd felt the man's warmth and wisdom as a physical presence. He could talk to him after all; it was safe. 'Well, it was Tanthe, mainly. I loved her all my life and I couldn't believe my luck when she eventually loved me back. But the moment she met this great hero of hers, this bloody poet she was besotted with, she couldn't drop me fast enough. And then – you'll hardly believe this – she left him too but instead of coming back to me, she went off and had an affair with . . .' He wasn't sure how to describe Auriel, so he kept it simple. 'She had an affair with her brother.'

'They are instruments of faithless lust,' said the Father, without a hint of surprise.

'I didn't think I could love anyone else, but there was this woman . . . she was . . .' He thought better of mentioning Branq'elin's name. 'Someone I met on the way to Vexor. I nearly fell in love with her. I think I did, in a way, but it was all a mess because I had to come to Vexor and I couldn't let myself . . .'

'And you still think about them both?'

'Constantly.'

'And this is the hold they have on you. Barbs in your flesh, rending you, chaining you to the earth when your spirit should be free to fly.'

Rufryd considered this. 'That's a bit harsh. The only times I've ever really been happy were with them.'

'But what are a few moments of false ecstasy, compared with the constant bliss of peace? Are you not more content here? Can't you see an end to pain and striving?'

'Well . . . yes.'

'That's why there are no women here,' said Arax Vahan.

'Maybe you're right. It was more sheer bloody misery than anything. I'd love to forget them and not care any more.'

'We have no relationship with anything or anyone but the light of spirit. It's the only path. Come, I want to show you something. I believe you are ready.'

He led Rufryd down a cloister and opened a door into a dark corridor. This was one of the places Herex had told him was out of bounds. The air was intensely cold. Somewhere out of sight a light burned and he was reminded of the Temple of Nuth, where he'd lived for a while to lick the wounds that had nevertheless remained raw. He caught the same sepulchral smell of old stone, an odour he found disturbing and exciting at the same time.

Arax Vahan led him along the bends of the corridor and through another door. They came out into a wide dark space with a high roof. Rufryd thought it was circular, like most of the temples he knew; then, looking more closely, he counted ten flat walls. And the seats weren't arranged in circles but in straight lines all facing one way. There was an altar at the front, a block of stone with a large censer burning upon it. Flames danced, filling the darkness with blacker shadows.

Above their heads, though, was colour. High up in each of the ten walls was a stained-glass window of detail and workmanship he hadn't seen since leaving the Amber Citadel. He studied them in surprise. The last of the twilight gleamed through the glass in a subtle array of hues; leaf-greens and autumn colours, greys and purples, accents of blood-red and sapphire blue.

'Feel free to look around,' said Arax Vahan. 'Take your time.'

'These are beautiful,' Rufryd said. 'I never expected to find anything like this on Vexor. Where were they made?'

The Father didn't answer. 'You will notice something interesting about the windows.'

Nine of the scenes were similar. Each showed a figure on a landscape, the detail beautifully painted on the glass. In each, the figure was dying; slain by a sword or pierced by an arrow, consumed by fire or lightning. Each expiring figure had one hand outstretched and a jewel resting in the palm like an offering.

Rufryd looked at each one, his mouth turning dry. 'The dying figures are all Bhahdradomen,' he said. 'The artist has made them look almost beautiful.'

'And the jewels?'

'They represent the Nine Realms, I assume. The amethyst would represent Mithrain, Torith Mir is a black diamond, the red and green one . . . that's tourmaline, for Eisilion. Sapphire for Sepheret, almandine for Paranios, emerald for Noreya. Azura Maroc is turquoise, Thanmandrathor topaz, and Deirland . . . an opal.'

'I'm impressed by your knowledge. Yes, the jewels symbolise the realms.'

'So . . . it shows the Bhahdradomen trying to take the Nine Realms and failing?' Rufryd looked up at the tenth window, above the altar. It showed another landscape, all in textures of clear glass, shades of silver and grey. Against this bleak vista rose a tower that soared from a broad base to a slender tip. A jet-black spire, standing impervious and uncompromising against a pearly sky. 'What's that, Father?'

'That is the Obsidian Tower.'

'I've never heard of it.'

'No, that doesn't surprise me.'

Rufryd turned and found Arax Vahan looking hard and meaningfully at him. He shivered, not with cold but with the feeling that some immense revelation was gathering, a secret composed of pure white light about to burst from the Father's mouth.

'Are you prepared to shed your beliefs and look at life in a different way?'

'I suppose so,' said Rufryd. 'I have no beliefs anyway, so what have I got to lose?'

'Do you know who it is we worship here?'

'I have an idea. I might be wrong.'

'Speak it,' said the Father. 'Don't be afraid. You're a novice among us, we won't be angry if you're mistaken.'

Rufryd took a deep breath. 'Well, from things I've overheard, which I probably shouldn't have heard, I got the impression you follow the same god as the Bhahdradomen. The Ancestor?'

Arax Vahan's eyes were steady. 'Yes. We worship the Ancestor.'

Rufryd gave a quiet gasp of shock, too subtle, he hoped, for the Father to notice. He'd suspected, but to hear it stated as baldly as that . . .

'Why?'

'It's not what you are used to, I know. You have been brought up with your goddesses and gods, your worship of all that is fecund and sexual . . .' For a moment, there was plain revulsion in the Father's voice. 'But don't judge us. Put aside your preconceptions and consider what I have to say.'

'I'm listening,' said Rufryd.

'Human life,' Arax Vahan said heavily. He moved behind the altar and turned, so that the light from the censer flame flooded his compelling face. 'All human life is misery, is it not? Our bodies are imperfect, fragile things, bags of waste matter, breeding grounds for every foul plague, victims of the sick desires born from their imperfection. We are cut in half, male and female; yet our attempts to rejoin, to find the wholeness we have lost, are doomed to failure. In these frantic joinings we lose all dignity. All that is left in the aftermath is heartbreak, misery; and then more humans, spewed from the loins of females like frogspawn, more sacks of waste to perpetuate this wretchedness for eternity.'

Horrible as the words were, their mournful passion carried Rufryd along. They made him recall his unhappiness as a child – his mother's death, his father's indifference – and Lynden's pointless death. The anguish of losing Tanthe. Leaving Branq'elin. The ghastliness of the illness he'd barely survived, and now this grinding existence on a plug of land that could barely support life. But nowhere else to go, after the shape-shifters' invasion of the land he'd probably never see again.

Grey depression sank over him in layer on smoky layer. He might have wept, but he was too numb. He sank down on a seat, mouth open, and remained there, paralysed.

'Our Order was founded longer ago than you might think, when survivors of the Grey Plague fled here from Thanmandrathor and Azura Maroc. We cannot imagine the horrors they saw, though we feel the echo of it down the centuries. They realised that they had to find an entirely different way of viewing the world, in order to make sense of it. And out of the darkness came the light of revelation, like white light bursting from the tip of the Obsidian Tower. Human life is a mistake.'

'A mistake?' Rufryd said faintly.

'There is an ineffable light that we call the Ancestor. Our true selves came from Him and they can return to Him. He created the Bhahdradomen, His Chosen ones. But the light had a shadow, an enemy, a jealous and intemperate deity who sought to prove herself equal to the light by creating beings of her own. She was no more than a demon, you might say, and her creation was flawed. Humans.'

'What demon?'

'You call her Nuth.'

Rufryd's chin came up. 'You're telling me our Goddess is a jealous demon who . . .'

'I'm sorry, but it is the truth. It's there in the revelation of our founders. History proves it. Before the Grey Plague the world was decadent, a cess-pit of foolishness, lust and quarrels. Ancestor sent the Plague to sweep the land clear of humans; then He sent His Chosen, the Bhahdradomen, to replace them.'

'But we're still here. We drove them out.'

'Yes, and that's the pity of it. It wasn't time for the struggle to end – but now, the time has come. Ancestor's age has dawned. The foul sub-creation of Nuth will be swept away. The Chosen will reign. Those windows show the nine Bhahdradomen martyrs, cruelly cut down as they tried to deliver the Nine Realms to the Ancestor. They were cut down, yet they will rise again.'

Rufryd was remembering Rhazagramen's sneering words, *'You are split in half and you couple in grotesque attempts to merge yourselves. You make religion of your imperfection – your goddesses, your gods – trying to sanctify your repellent existence. You have no idea how we despise you, your maleness and femaleness, your revolting urges ... The Bhahdradomen are perfect. We are made in the image of the Ancestor, whole and self-contained. You are like things cut in half, striving to be joined.'*

'This is the worst thing I've ever heard,' Rufryd said. 'You're human, but wishing your own deaths on yourselves?'

Arax Vahan came to him, but instead of sitting beside him, knelt on the floor and clasped Rufryd's hands. Rufryd started, but couldn't release himself from the Father's warm, powerful grip. 'Dear son, it *is* terrible. Life is terrible; you know that for yourself. But there is hope. We can leave behind these wretched bodies and return to the light, where there is eternal bliss and peace.

'Even the other races have some small glimpse of the light. Your people call it the Summerland of the Goddess. The Aelyr call it the Jewelfire. Both are deluded. Only the Bhahdradomen truly understand it, for they came from the Ancestor, perfect and complete; that light is the presence of the Ancestor, where only the Chosen may dwell.' He gripped Rufryd's hands harder, gave them a little shake. His eyes with their strong brows were overwhelming. 'Yet there is good news, Rufryd. We can join the Chosen.'

'Can we?'

'Look at the Obsidian Tower,' said Arax Vahan, full of passion. 'It is their symbol of hope and renewal. A darkness that must be climbed, endured, in order to reach the light. It's our symbol too; we look at it every day as we call upon the Ancestor to guide us. This is the first stage; to discard the females who chain us to the Earth. To divorce ourselves from all earthly pleasures and pains. To become complete unto ourselves. To loosen the spirit from the body, so that it is ready to fly into the light.'

'And then what?' Rufryd said. His lips were dry, the blood rushing in his ears.

'As the Chosen move across the face of the Earth, all other life shall be cast out into the darkness of Nuth, which they deserve. But we, the Order of Calathvahn, shall go with our brothers the Bhahdradomen into the light. For we lucky few have cast off the vile chains of our birth and become Chosen. And so can you, Rufryd.'

He sat stunned, staring at that perfect, slender tower pointing up to the light. It seemed to promise everything. Arax Vahan's voice was a warm power, promising relief from suffering and eternal peace. It made perfect sense. Something collapsed inside him and it was as if his soul flew free like a blue-dove, striving towards the Tower. Perfect sense . . .

'We want you to be with us, Rufryd,' said the power, echoing. 'Who else has ever wanted you, or cared for you? But we care. We want you to share this joy. Stay with us, dear son. Be a warrior in our crusade.'

Chapter Five. Trust and Mistrust

'Helan?' said someone. 'Can you hear me?'

Leaf-green lightning flickered round the edge of her vision. She saw the Earth raging, groaning. Saw the red heart of the earth energy – the eternal flame that she was sworn to protect – blazing lime-white, an uncontrolled fire. Heard the voices of a million ancestors whispering in accusation, *'The Xauroma is broken. Now chaos shall reign!'*

'Helan!'

She opened her eyes. She was back in the Amber Citadel. The faces of her friends shimmered above her, and behind them the blue satin drapes of her bed and the azurite panelling of the walls. She couldn't see clearly. She couldn't find her voice, even to cry out her despair; all she could hear was the stone-cold silence of the *xauroth* sphere and she knew that, deep below in its underground chamber, it had stopped spinning. It lay dark as a boulder in her mind's eye; opaque, cold, lifeless.

'She's coming round. Thank the gods.' She realised it was Eldareth whose voice had reached her. Mawrdreth's hand was warm on her forehead, his green eyes looking bleakly into hers. There was a stranger there too, a small round woman with dark skin and raven hair.

'It's over,' Helan gasped. 'My fault.'

'Hush, you're safe.' said Eldareth. 'You've been unconscious for hours. Do you remember collapsing in the temple?'

She swallowed. 'I remember.'

'The guards brought us back,' said Tanthe. Her face was a creamy cloud in a frame of glossy dark hair, her eyes bright aquamarines. 'They found a healer in the palace kitchens. Considerate of them.'

The healer gave a ghost of a smile. Her face was marked with strain. 'I'm Lahjaya, ma'am,' she said with a soft accent. 'I can find nothing wrong with you, except that you are exhausted.' Her black eyes looked into Helan's, full of concern. 'It's no wonder. I'm going to prescribe you a special infusion of honey and certain herbs; I'll go back to the kitchens to prepare it.' Fear flickered across her face; she would have to brave the Devourer-filled corridors again. 'It will strengthen you. So will a decent meal.'

'Thank you,' Helan said, struggling to smile. She wanted the healer to know she was grateful for her courage.

When Lahjaya had gone, Tanthe said, 'What happened, Helan?'

'I . . . I felt it die.' She thought they would know what she meant.

'What?' Tanthe frowned. 'Our belief? Not me. They couldn't fool everyone.'

Helan stared at her; at the concerned faces of Eldareth, Elrill, Auriel. How could they not *know*? She remembered the knife-thrust of despair that had made her fall, the terrible whirl of visions that followed. She couldn't articulate any of it. Simply couldn't understand how they'd not shared the wrenching loss.

After a pause, Mawrdreth spoke. 'I think she means the Xauroma.'

The word went through her like a knife. 'Mawrdreth?' she whispered.

'I felt it too.'

Her husband's face was bloodless under the bronze sheen. She grasped the hand that rested on her head, pulled it against her heart. He leaned down and embraced her. There was nothing to say, no words to express the grief they felt. She and Mawrdreth remained there, clinging to each other, oblivious to the others.

'Er . . . what do you mean?' said Tanthe.

Mawrdreth let Helan back onto the pillows, where she lay numb. She heard him answering Tanthe's question as if they were in another room. 'Ever since Garnelys began this vile train of events, the Xauroma's been under strain. And now it's torn, blown away like rotten silk. I doubt that I suffered as Helan did – but I was initiated, so I felt it.'

'It's a covenant,' Tanthe said intently. 'How can you feel a covenant break?'

'Don't you understand?' Mawrdreth said, turning on her. 'It's more than a mere promise, it is the covenant between monarch and land, a bond, an energy—'

'A flow of intention,' said Elrill.

'Yes, exactly so. And that intention creates energy, *xauroth*. It has a life and reality of its own. The great *xauroth* sphere, the indicator of its health, has stopped turning. The energy's gone.'

Tanthe nodded. 'I needed you to explain, that's all. My sister always claimed she could feel the Xauroma, but everyone else thought she was strange. I should've paid more attention to her.'

'My fault,' Helan said, her voice cracking.

'No, it isn't,' said Tanthe, leaning over her.

'I gave the Sapphire Throne—'

'That's not when it happened! Garnelys started this, not you!'

'And I struggled to hold the sides of the chasm together but they slipped away from me at last, there in the temple, when I listened to Rhazagramen's words and – for however few seconds – believed what he was saying.'

'And this means – what?'

Eldareth said, 'Tanthe, let her rest.'

'No,' said Helan, reaching out to touch her arm. 'You all deserve to know. I failed the land. It's as if a green arc of light shielded Aventuria, but my efforts to keep it bright came to nothing. All the storms and strange weather we've had of late? That was the Earth herself, screaming warnings. Now she lies unprotected, prey to the Devourers' hunger.'

'So, make the promise again!'

'Tanthe, I can't. I'm no longer the monarch. It's over.'

'No,' said Tanthe, her eyes bright with tears. 'You offered your life. No-one took it. Doesn't that tell you something? They still need you!'

'We will remake the covenant,' said Mawrdreth. 'All is not lost.'

'All *is* lost. I wasn't strong enough.' Her voice was failing.

'You did all you could!'

'All that I could do,' she replied woodenly, 'was not enough.'

'You are still the Queen in our eyes!'

'To what end? The land itself chooses who shall be monarch, who is strong enough to make and keep such promises. Now I am un-chosen. It's over.'

'Don't talk in this way!' Mawrdreth said, close to breaking down. 'The Earth accepted you! The Xauroma will be remade!'

Absently, she reached out to stroke his hair. 'It has happened so in the past, I believe. But if it is remade, it will not be by me.'

'You mustn't give up!' he cried. 'This isn't your fault. You made the only choices you could. Vaurgroth has done this, not you!'

'And I should have been strong enough to stop him, and was not.'

Her despair silenced them. She had no hope to offer; and she knew, then, that she was going to turn her face to the wall and die. They knew it, too, if only they'd stop denying it. In the silence, the sound of the door opening rang like a crack of thunder.

'That's Lahjaya coming back,' said Eldareth. He was wrong.

Into the bed-chamber came Rhazagramen and another of Vaurgroth's elite, the most sinister *bharu'grothrim* of all. He was a steel-grey creature, sharp as a surgeon's knife. He came in with short, precise strides and stood looking at them from eyes that were chips of ice.

Torturer, Helan thought. Even through her numbness she felt a further shrivelling of her soul. His aura infiltrated the room like an odourless poison.

Rhazagramen, wizened as he was, shone with repellent power. He wore robes of scaly leather, white and black, with a ruff of blood-red feathers. Behind him, the tall grey one stood silent and intimidating.

'This is Protector Naghrur,' said Rhazagramen. 'Greatlord Vaurgroth, Master of Light, has instructed us to inform you that he was disappointed with your performance in the temple.'

'Our . . . *performance*?' Eldareth said in disgust.

Rhazagramen regarded him with chilling disdain. 'You did not appear to experience the ecstasy of the Ancestor with the intensity Vaurgroth would wish to see. Lady Helananthe, you achieved nothing with your outburst except to look foolish and make yourself ill. Still, there must be no repeat of such histrionics.'

They all stared at him. He folded his pearly hands in front of him and waited.

'We're not fools,' said Mawrdreth. 'Nor are we Bhahdradomen. We do not and cannot worship your Ancestor.'

'That's unfortunate. I suggest that, next time, you try harder. You will enjoy it. You saw how many of your citizens gave themselves into the spirit of it.'

'Next time?' Tanthe gasped. 'You don't expect us to do that again?'

'There will be meetings every day from now on, in every temple in the city. There will be penalties for non-attendance, but great rewards for those who go. The royal party shall attend under *vagharim* escort at least once a week.'

Helan couldn't answer. Each time she thought the nightmare could get no worse, she slid a little further into the pit.

'You fooled them once,' said Eldareth. 'You won't do it again.'

'You are wrong,' Rhazagramen said silkily. 'It becomes contagious, such worship. It becomes irresistible. You must not deny your people Ancestor's light. It's vital that they see their ex-king and ex-queen entering fully into the new faith.'

'I can't,' said Helan.

The red eyes met hers, round and piercing like a snake's. 'You should not have fought me.'

'We didn't need to fight,' said Helan. 'The light was seductive, but we all saw it for what it was. A poisonous illusion. That won't change.'

Rhazagramen gave a tiny smile. 'Try to understand what I'm saying. We don't care what your feelings are on the matter. In future you must all *appear* to be experiencing the ecstasy.'

'I don't think so,' said Eldareth. 'You can't make us.'

Naghrur spoke. His voice, too, was a razor; a caressing whisper, gentle, precise and reasonable. 'We still hold the Princess Ghiseyma and the Prince Venirryen.'

She shot upright, leapt to her feet although her head swam with dizziness.

'You bastards! I've kept my bargain with regard to them! You cannot keep using them against me, over and over again!'

'We can do precisely as we like,' Naghrur said softly. He turned, his long form bent slightly forward as he walked to the door, like a schoolmaster striding from one lesson to the next. Rhazagramen swept out with him, turning to grin at them with tiny pointed teeth.

'Next time, abandon yourselves to the Ancestor – or sit and contemplate the juxtaposition of Protector Naghrur, red-hot needles, and your mother's eyes.'

* * *

'Sir?' Eander said nervously. 'Saph, I mean?'

Still struggling to use my name, Saphaeyender thought with a sigh. It didn't seem to matter any more. It was difficult to know what did matter.

The living area was shadowy, shutters drawn, lamplight dappling the marble walls. The young man came hesitantly towards him, stopped, then sat down on the couch with an arm's length of space between them. They sat for several minutes without touching or looking at each other.

Eventually Saphaeyender spoke. 'Didn't you experience it, Eander? You haven't said anything. You still seem your normal self.'

Eander's eyes were wide in the gloom. 'I didn't go into the visualisation.'

'Then you're lucky.'

'No. I never do. I'm not very good at it, so I gave up trying a long time ago. I just listen to the words.'

Saphaeyender expelled a soul-heavy groan. 'Well, I wish that I, too, had just listened to the words. I must have looked ridiculous, as foolish as all the other idiots.'

Another silence. Eander leaned forward, resting his wrists on his bony knees. 'I wasn't thinking that you looked foolish, Saph. I was only worried. Terrified. What – what was it you saw?'

'A light.' Saphaeyender tipped his head back, remembering. 'A white light, shaped like an oval . . . no, an egg. An egg-shaped light with a red flame in the centre. And it seemed as if this light was pouring down an ineffable radiance that held the answers to every question and the balm for every pain ever suffered by humankind.'

'No. I can't imagine it.'

'Have you never had too much to drink, or taken a tincture of some interesting herb, and had the blissful sense of being at one with the universe?'

'Er . . . well, yes. A few glasses of your Marocian red have that effect on me.'

'It was like that, only a thousand times more profound. I thought that I was basking in the light of a supreme, benevolent truth. It was the most wonderful feeling I've ever had.'

Saphaeyender leapt up and strode around the room, tugging angrily at the leaves of ferns and palms. He felt disgusted with himself, so repulsed that he wanted to scour his skin, cut himself open to expel the pollution.

'"Give yourself to the Ancestor",' he growled, completing his circuit of the room and thrusting his face into Eander's. 'Goddess help me, I nearly did!'

The young man drew back, alarmed. 'It's all right. You didn't.'

'You don't understand!' Saphaeyender said, straightening up. 'I was *that* close! My mind was gone! Then I heard Tanthe scream my name. I came back to my senses to see the complete ugliness of what had nearly happened to me! What was happening all around us!'

'But what was it?' Eander said, looking ill.

'A form of hysteria. A kind of drug. This "light" leads nowhere but down a long dark tunnel with no end.'

He sank down onto the couch again. Eander said, 'You're frightening me.'

'I'm sorry. But we all should be frightened. I'm revolted at myself for being sucked in so easily . . . and yet, I want to feel that ecstasy again. Oh, I won't,' he said hurriedly, seeing his lover's horrified expression. 'I'll never let it touch me again. But the desire is there. There are hundreds, thousands of people in this city who were not jerked out of the trance soon enough to see its falsity. And they will go back to the temple. They will want to drink the Ancestor as if he was honeyed milk of poppies pouring onto their tongues.'

'So you're saying we're fucked.'

Saphaeyender burst out laughing. 'Yes, my dear, that's exactly what we are. Fucked. Isn't this nice? The Bhahdradomen don't have to stir their tired bones to raise a sword against us, when they can turn us into slavering idiots instead.'

'They can't make everyone fall for it. We didn't.'

'Why do you think I closed all the shutters? I don't want to hear them fighting in the streets.'

'Fighting?'

'Think of the consequences. Those who hold true to the Goddess will set themselves against the Ancestor-worshippers, who will be equally fervent. Human against human. And the Bhahdradomen know it! They planned it!'

Eander reached out, caressing Saphaeyender's shoulder with an unsteady hand. 'What are we going to do?'

Saphaeyender dropped his head back, breathing out his despair. 'I think that I want to go to sleep, and never wake up.'

In the days that followed, Ysomir saw no-one but Zhoaah. He brought her food three times a day, and the food was the same as it always had been; so she guessed that human staff were still working in the Citadel kitchens. But no-one else came to see her. Not Tanthe, not Saphaeyender, not even the Queen.

Locked in her peaceful cell, she had felt safe from the outside world. Even Helananthe, with her endless questions, had only pestered her for half an hour at a time. Now, though, the nightmare had walked freely into her refuge. She realised there was no safety anywhere.

For a time, she was certain that the warders – who had looked after her so kindly – were dead. Then, as the shock faded and her thoughts cleared, she realised that they couldn't be. Relief made her almost elated. When Zhoaah brought her supper, he noticed.

'You smiled when I came in,' he said, making his slow, soft way towards her. He set the tray down on the small table where she spent her waking hours, writing, thinking or dreaming. 'You smiled.'

'It wasn't for you,' she said. She lifted the white cloth covering the tray and looked at the food, a bowl of spiced vegetables, soft grainy bread, white cheese with a yellow crust. Her stomach groaned with hunger, but she could never eat until he'd left. Usually the hot dishes were stone-cold by then.

'Wasn't it?' he said. 'Then what?'

He sat on the other chair, facing her across the table. Soft unformed face as white as the cheese, eyes like tar, long fingers rustling like hoary twigs on the table top. She wasn't as frightened of him as she used to be. Uneasy, but not afraid; she'd almost grown used to his whispering, insinuating presence.

'You know I asked you what had happened to my warders?'

'And I told you. They were expelled from the Citadel. There was no need for them to be here. You didn't believe me.'

'Well, I believe you now.'

Zhoaah's eyes were rapt upon her. He reminded her of the portraits of monarchs in the palace, whose eyes followed you round the room. He watched her constantly. 'Why? Because you cannot smell their bodies mouldering in the corridor?'

'No. Because none of their *ethroths* came into me.'

'Indeed?' Zhoaah leaned back in the chair, studying her. After a pause, he said, 'Please don't let me stop you eating your meal. I haven't spat in it.'

Her eyes widened. She frowned, but Zhoaah only laughed soundlessly. 'Our saliva is quite poisonous to humans; were you aware of that?'

'No,' she said flatly. 'Perhaps ours is to you.'

'There's a thought. We had better resist any temptation to kiss each other. But I want to talk to you, and there's no need for you to sit there hungry.'

Hesitantly she took the white cloth from the tray, spread it on her lap, and began to eat. The vegetable dish was already lukewarm, but at least the tea was hot and plentiful.

'Would you like something?' Ysomir said, amused at herself for feeling the need to be polite. 'Bread, cheese? There will be plenty, I never eat a great deal.'

'No, thank you,' said Zhoaah. 'Most of your food is quite disagreeable to us.'

'I suppose you drink blood.'

His flat lips widened in amusement. 'No. But I am glad to find you in better spirits, if you will forgive the pun.'

'You know what I mean by *ethroth*, then.'

'Naturally. A disembodied energy. One that may be released when someone dies, perhaps. *Roth* of spirit, dreams, ghosts.'

She nodded. She needed to share her relief with someone. 'If any of the warders had been killed, I would have felt their *ethroths* leaving, or coming into me. But I didn't; I felt nothing! So I'm certain they're still alive.'

'And you know I didn't lie to you, at last.'

She met his eyes, felt a shiver of unease that she was so close to trusting him. 'I suppose so.'

'So, you have a propensity to gather the *ethroths* of the dead? That is highly unusual among humans, isn't it? Unusual for any race.'

Ysomir shrugged. 'So I've been told. But people have always told me I'm strange.'

'Do they stay, the spirits?'

'Some do. It's hard to tell with the ones that are quiet. The first was a friend of mine, Serenis. The second was Lynden.' She smiled sadly. 'I don't mind them staying; they speak to me in my sleep, sometimes I can even touch them ... but the others I wish I could be rid of.'

'Others? Are there many?'

'I'm not sure. There is Garnelys, of course. I couldn't avoid his *ethroth*, it went into me through the dagger, and it went so deep inside me I don't know how to force him out. He doesn't speak to me, thank Goddess, but he speaks *through* me sometimes.'

'Interesting.'

'No, it isn't. It's horrible. I don't want him. And as for the others, there might be dozens. Maharoth is one.'

'King Maharoth ... he who fought us on the Silver Plains?'

She gave a quick nod. 'A lot of them are vague. I don't know who they are, and they don't tell me. I think one might be Calabethron.'

'The *roth*-mage Calabethron?'

'I can't be sure. Perhaps all those who have ever walked in the Amber Citadel have attached themselves to me; I don't know why.'

'Is this ... painful?'

'Not really. It frightens me when they speak without warning. Otherwise I ignore them, except for Lynden and Serenis, of course. The worst thing was that Helananthe wouldn't stop questioning me about it. That upset me more than the *ethroths* themselves. Mostly they are quiet. I don't even know they're there. Anyway, that's how I knew the warders were safe; I didn't feel them die.'

Zhoaah regarded her for a time. 'I'm glad you feel you can talk to me about this.'

'I have no-one else to talk to. No-one living, anyway.'

'Perhaps I can bring someone to see you.'

Her heart leapt. 'Tanthe?'

'I can't promise, but we'll see. This is a great burden for you to bear alone. I always saw something special in you, Ysomir, something different. I want to help you.'

She frowned, wary again. 'Why?'

Zhoaah leaned forward and stroked her hand, his skin dry as bark against hers. 'I told you, my dear. Because I like you.'

Inside the Heliodor Tower, the darkness glowed with coppery snakes of *gauroth* crawling over the walls, spectral flashes of light. Gulzhur breathed in the invigorating metallic scent of power, harvested from the unfettered pain and chaotic emotions of humans. He admired the odourless bluish flicker of *anaroth*, summoned from certain crystals in specific arrangements to open the old gateways between one realm and another.

The two parties met. Greatlord Vaurgroth with his *bharu'grothrim* and their attendant *vagharim*. Lord Falthorn and his Valahyr. Gulzhur found their black- and indigo-draped elegance distasteful.

Falthorn and Vaurgroth approached each other and clasped hands, for all the world like two humans who shared a deep friendship. Only their eyes belied their physical warmth. Gulzhur noted that Falthorn's gaze was as shrewd, watchful and cautious as Vaurgroth's. The two leaders danced around each other like scorpions.

'I trust you enjoyed your stay in our land?' said Vaurgroth.

'We've had a most interesting excursion into the countryside,' said Falthorn. 'I'm impressed by how swiftly you've made Paranios your own.'

'I am sorry to bid you farewell,' said Vaurgroth. 'Our partnership has been fruitful.'

'And long may it remain so,' said Falthorn without expression.

'We have worked well together, indeed.'

'And the agreement between us will hold true.' Falthorn's words were both a challenge and a statement.

'All my *aghramen* that were in Verdanholm have been withdrawn,' Vaurgroth said softly. 'Here is Grahzamen, their Empowerer, to set your mind at rest.' Grahzamen stood proud and unmoving, like a frozen cobweb. Falthorn regarded him with naked loathing, which all the *bharu'grothrim* politely pretended not to notice.

'All are now here on Earth,' said Grahzamen in his moth-wing whisper. 'We have relinquished all claim to the Aelyr realm.'

Falthorn smiled, veiling his hatred. 'No race but the Aelyr

ever had any claim upon Verdanholm; however, let it pass. We hold the Basilisks of Calabethron. The humans have no defence against you. Thus you have nothing to fear.'

'You hold the Basilisks, indeed,' Vaurgroth said lightly. 'Though it would be better for both sides, would it not, if they were to be placed in neutral hands?'

'Whose hands can you mean? You've made it plain you won't work with the Mediators, so they have turned their backs on us.'

'I meant a stronghold, held equally by Valahyr and Bhahdradomen.'

'That was not the agreement. You've nothing to fear, since the Basilisks are already in neutral hands with us. Safe hands.'

Vaurgroth stared into Falthorn's face. Master of Light was smiling, but his eyes were pinpoints of red fire. Gulzhur shifted. How dare the Valahyr lord suggest Vaurgroth was afraid of anything! He felt like tearing Falthorn's smug head from his shoulders. Unfortunately, the dance of diplomacy must be left to Vaurgroth.

'None safer, I am sure,' Vaurgroth said. 'However, the continued existence of such dangerous weapons is a threat to us all.'

'They are peace-bonded. We are sworn never to use them against the Bhahdradomen,' Falthorn replied smoothly. 'Not for as long as the Bhahdradomen keep their agreement.'

'We do not break our agreements.' Vaurgroth's politeness stretched wire-thin.

'I am in no doubt of it.'

'However, what if the weapons were stolen?'

Falthorn affected shock. 'I don't understand. You cannot be suggesting that *your* people might attempt to steal them?'

'Of course not. I am suggesting that *someone* might. Humans, for example.'

'That would be impossible. They are too well hidden.'

'Still,' Vaurgroth persisted, 'the risk may be small, but it exists. As long as the weapons exist, there is a danger, however tiny, that they might fall into the wrong hands.'

Gulzhur grimaced. The weapons were already in the wrong hands, in their view. Hideous engines that had destroyed the Bhahdradomen on the Silver Plains; such things should not be permitted to exist. For another race – human or Aelyr – to hold them was obscene, intolerable.

Vaurgroth went on, 'It might be better for all concerned if the Basilisks were revealed and destroyed.'

'That, my friend, is a splendid idea.' Falthorn nodded warmly. His eyes remained discs of ice. 'However, what then would discourage the Bhahdradomen from making another attack upon my realm?'

'Do you not trust us?' Vaurgroth said thinly.

'I trust *you*, my dear friend. But there might be renegades, those who would take their chance . . .'

Gulzhur's shoulders rose. Vaurgroth's aura crackled with red sparks of fury, but his voice remained level. 'There are no renegades. I have full control of my *domenim*. We think and act as one great mind. We are of the Ancestor, and He moves through us.'

'I didn't mean to offend you. However, you must accept my assurance that the weapons are secure, and will remain so.'

'Your assurance is accepted,' said Vaurgroth.

'Good.'

'For now. This matter will be discussed again.'

Falthorn was finding it hard to control his exasperation, Gulzhur noticed with pleasure. 'Greatlord Vaurgroth, you hold hostages against me. What more can I give you?'

Master of Light's eyes glinted. 'You speak of Tanthe and Auriel?'

'They are my niece and nephew.'

'I'm yet to be convinced that you place any value upon

them. This is the first time you have mentioned them to me.'

'Well, I am surprised that you are not more perceptive.' The Valahyr lord turned away as if deep in thought. Then he turned back to Vaurgroth, opening his hands as if conceding to the self-evidently superior being. 'You are right, of course. We hold the weapons only to ensure peace, not to threaten you. In due course, if the agreement holds, let them be destroyed.'

The *bharu'grothrim* murmured their satisfaction. 'There, you learn to be as clear-sighted as us,' said Vaurgroth. 'This is progress.'

Falthorn gave a thin, sardonic laugh. An evanescent cone of blue light was shimmering in the centre of the Tower. The *rothanamir* that would take Falthorn and his entourage back to Verdanholm.

'I appreciate the compliment,' Falthorn said, inclining his head. 'Alas, if you were as clear-sighted as you believe, you would see beyond the Basilisks to other, greater threats.'

'What threats?'

'Don't imagine that with the Basilisks destroyed, Verdanholm will be naked. Nothing is static. A new weapon has been created, greater by far; a living, breathing creature beside which the old Basilisks are as dangerous as pins.'

'A living weapon?' Vaurgroth breathed. 'A *roth*-mage?'

'Greater than you can imagine. Greater than either of us. Impossible to destroy, unless you want to destroy your entire race in a blaze of Jewelfire. Nurtured by my loving care. So you really should be setting your sights higher than the Basilisks, my lord; they will be the least of your worries.'

Vaurgroth gave a tolerant laugh. 'It's good of you to entertain us with these preposterous stories, but you are persuading no-one.'

'That's all right,' Falthorn said lightly. 'I am bluffing; I am your trusted friend. Either way, you have nothing to fear, have you?'

He turned away in a swirl of black and silver, led his entourage into the light, vanished. Gulzhur bristled, growling deep in his throat. Vaurgroth went on staring at the portal until the light diminished to nothing.

'He's lying!' said Gulzhur in their own language. 'He's invented this new threat on the spur of the moment to confuse us!'

'Perhaps,' said Vaurgroth thoughtfully. 'Perhaps not. One thing he said that is true; we have nothing to fear from him.'

Gulzhur spat yellow venom on the place where Falthorn had stood. 'So let us take the Basilisks, and take Verdanholm.'

'Patience,' said Vaurgroth, his face serene. He looked magnificent. The taint of the Aelyr was forgotten. He came forward and touched each of them in turn, overwhelming as a god, expanding even Gulzhur's dry soul with something close to love.

'Gulzhur, Enabler, great veteran of many skills, master of my *ghelim*. Prefigurer Tzumezht, blessed for rallying the common *domenim*. Uryzht, Enlightener, soon to relieve even the ignorance of humans. Bharamezht, Thunderer, leader of my armies. Shadower Rhuaaku, my delight; deployer of my *neshrim*, supreme deceiver. Ah, Protector Naghrur. Most ruthless one, you are my left hand, as you, Theosopher Rhazagramen, are my right. Grahzamen, Empowerer, drinker of subtle energies; your time will come again. And Facilitator Zhoaah, slipping like oil between the realms of *domenim* and human alike; especially blessed are you for creating the Tower.' From each of them Vaurgroth drank a little *roth*, and gave a little back; a fiery, profound exchange. Falthorn's posturing seemed laughable. It was nothing, gone, forgotten. Only this was real.

'Some of you must leave me soon and go out into the Nine Realms, there to consolidate our power,' said Vaurgroth. Light spiralled round him. 'Go in peace, and in absolute confidence of our power. I am the fount, and the fount is endless. All will be as Ancestor wills it.'

Chapter Six. Jthery

Jthery haunted the house and garden for days, waiting for Falthorn to return.

He climbed the ridge of the hill, as he had many times, and stood gazing at the portal that led back to Earth. It appeared as a column of kingfisher light between a circle of stones, unearthly and resonant. He hesitated there, and the Aelyr who guarded it – slender, dark-haired and eldritch in their midnight garments – stood looking coolly back at him.

'Can we help you, friend?' one of them called at last.

'I wondered . . .'

'I'm sorry.' Their smooth, gold-sheened faces seemed to mock him. 'Of our gallant cousin there is still no sign.'

'Strange that you're so ignorant of your cousin's activities,' Jthery retorted.

He returned their cool stares, trying to make a decision. He had tried to be friendly to the Valahyr – Falthorn's family – but they had not reciprocated. Instead they seemed to look down upon him from a great height, dismissing him as nothing because he was human. He kept his dignity by showing them equal disdain, but he was only too aware of being the outsider. Not safe here.

Verdanholm was a realm of wonders, with rolling landscapes, blue-green forests, azure skies in which stars clustered like snowdrifts. The house was a proud, airy mansion of living wood, silver and palest gold, a floating structure that seemed not built but tethered to the hillside. Gardens clasped its flank, descending in tiers, rich with foliage and mossy streams. The perfect faerie realm. Devoid of Falthorn's presence, though, Verdanholm's beauty seemed to Jthery not inspiring but coldly alien. His sleep was plagued by vivid nightmares. The waters here were not friendly, but deathly silent or full of whispered warnings.

Falthorn had gone to Aventuria, asking Jthery to wait for him. Jthery suspected that something terrible was happening there. Didn't want to believe it.

He'd known what a risk it was, trusting Falthorn. Hadn't he taken Princess Ghiseyma and her son hostage? Hadn't he pretended to treat Eldareth, Tanthe and Elrill as guests, only to imprison them? Then tried to smooth it all over, telling Jthery, 'Trust me. I may do things that appear unacceptable, even cruel, on the surface – but all I do is for the greater good.'

Jthery had been too deeply infatuated with the Valahyr leader to heed Tanthe's warnings. All he could do now was to give Falthorn the benefit of the doubt. But the longer Falthorn was away, the more powerful those doubts became.

The house and gardens lay behind him. On the hill in front was the *rothanamir*, the shimmering portal through which Falthorn and the others had vanished. He couldn't be sure – hoped with all his heart he'd been mistaken – but he thought he'd seen what appeared to be Bhahdradomen against the light, clasping hands with Falthorn.

Jthery went closer. Turquoise boulders marked the portal's perimeter. The Valahyr men and women stood guard between the stones, forbidding in their cloaks of black and violet, watching him from cool grey eyes. He couldn't stand waiting any longer. He must know what was happening on Earth, whatever the consequences.

'Where are you going?' said one of the Valahyr, moving in front of him. It was Nialorn, a willowy young male; he knew most of them now, by name if not to speak to. Nialorn flourished a long staff tipped with a sharp silver point.

'I'm going back to Earth to find Falthorn.'

'No, you're not,' said the woman beside him, Tiana. She drew her sword, a curved blade that gleamed darkly with jewels. Their faces were lovely but cold, as if cast from palest gold metal. Statues of gold and ebony, they appeared, with their flowing dark hair and garments.

Jthery wasn't overly brave, but he was angry. 'How are you going to stop me, unless you cut me down?'

'No-one is going to cut you down, Lord Jthery,' Nialorn said mildly. 'But we have instructions to let no one through the *rothanamir* without direct instruction from Falthorn. And he's ordered you to stay here. You know that.'

'Besides, the portal isn't active,' said Tiana. 'The door is there, but locked. If you tried, nothing would happen. Or you might end up trapped on the grey paths between realms. Falthorn wouldn't be pleased with us, if we let such a thing happen to you.'

Other Valahyr were gathering around them, forming a dark wall. Frustrated, Jthery saw that he would never break through them. To disobey Falthorn, fight with the Valahyr – for what? To leap into the unknown, or even if he succeeded, to incur Falthorn's fury on the other side?

'You can sheath your swords,' Jthery said, low and angry. 'But Falthorn has not *ordered* me to do anything. I am his friend, not his pet dog.'

They laughed at him. Laughed. He turned in a whirl of grey silk and strode away, their mirth abrading his ears. Shivers of unease ran through him. He broke into a run, pushing blindly through the red-leaved trees towards the house, angling upwards to the meadows that lay above.

It had been simple. He'd come here to help Tanthe, Eldareth and Elrill find Ghiseyma and Veny, and to seek redress for the way Falthorn had misused Tanthe. Jthery had only wanted to help Helan, his beloved cousin; so he told himself. His real reasons were stranger and deeper. So strange he didn't even understand them himself.

He was idealistic. He'd felt the need to embark on a quest on Aventuria's behalf. Eshte herself, Mithrain's Goddess of the Waters, had appeared to him and set him on this path. The quest had never been an end in itself. All the time he'd been looking for some unknown goal of his own.

And then he'd met Falthorn, and known that *this* was what he'd been seeking.

The Valahyr leader had overwhelmed Jthery with his aura of power and mystery, his own pure idealism. 'Be on my side,' he'd told Jthery. 'Your friends misunderstand me. Although my actions may appear strange and cruel, they are all for the good. I act to preserve Verdanholm, just as you act to preserve Mithrain. We want the same things, don't we, you and I? Be my companion and you shall discover such wonders . . .'

Jthery had fallen.

'He's using you,' Tanthe had said flatly. He kept hearing her words, and those of his goddess, Eshte: *'Beware, Jthery. There are different kinds of love waiting for you. One is true, the other is false and lethal. The wisdom to know the difference lies only within you . . . so tread carefully and wisely, for your choices may save or doom us all.'*

Jthery didn't feel wise. He was terrified that he'd already made the lethal choice.

Out of breath, he vaulted over a gate of polished branches and into the meadow where the horses they'd brought from Earth grazed. Here was a spring bubbling into a wide clear pool; the stones on the bottom were blue as ink.

Jthery knelt on the bank and plunged his hands into the chill water, beseeching his goddess to manifest herself. Brought up among the lakes of Mithrain, water was his element, but the energies were strange in Verdanholm. He couldn't always touch them. It was as if the elementals had turned their backs on him, their silence intimating, *No. Your choice is wrong.*

'Eshte, please,' he whispered, raising one wet hand to the carved amethyst fish that hung at his throat, her gift to him. With all his strength he concentrated on attuning with the water. 'Am I doing the wrong thing? Is it too late? Tell me and I'll leave here, I'll do anything for you.'

The sudden vibration in the water startled him. Tiny

fish darted from between the stones to cluster round his fingers. He felt ripples racing around his hand, elementals. A column of mist rose from the surface and a pair of clear violet eyes regarded him.

'It is not for us to tell you how to act,' came her bubbling voice inside his head. *'Unless the judgement is your own, it is worthless. We are at the mercy of the powers that rack the realms. We look to you for salvation; unless you gain the wisdom to choose rightly, we are lost.'*

Jthery took his hands out of the water and sat back on his haunches, groaning. Gods, the disaster of adoring the one person everyone else painted as a villain. Again she'd turned it back to him, with the same message. His decision, his responsibility.

Only one answer. 'I must stand by the choice I've made,' he said to himself. 'I'll wait for Falthorn. I will not judge him until I've had a chance to speak to him.'

A horse snorted, making him jump. Jthery looked up and saw his grey gelding Heron standing over him, head lowered towards him in friendly curiosity. The other horses – Tanthe's bay mare Redbird, Elrill's white Nefri and Eldareth's chestnut Gany – went on grazing obliviously.

Jthery stood up, resting one hand on Heron's shoulder. From here he could see over the hedge and along the hill to the *rothanamir*. As he watched he saw the column of light strengthen suddenly, the aqua turning to an intense peacock. It thickened, streaks of light whirling around it.

Jthery's heart leapt. The portal was active. That must mean Falthorn was coming back.

Panic seized him. He had no idea where it came from. He'd made the calm decision to wait – yet the reality of Falthorn's arrival filled him not with joy but with an unexpected, devastating fire of blind terror.

He vaulted onto Heron's high, muscular back. Urging the horse with his legs, he turned him by pressing a hand on the side of his neck. Now he was galloping towards the flower-starred hedge . . . clearing it . . . riding across the corner of the garden, leaping the little streams. And now he was out on the open hillside. Heron ran eagerly, thrilled to be stretching his legs.

Jthery had no idea where he was going. All he knew was that he must escape. Silver-green grass rushed past, studded with boulders of lapis blue. Purple hills shouldered up in the distance. The landscape looked vast and yet fragile, like a painting. Its perspectives were strange. He was lost, lost. The only place he knew here was Falthorn's house . . . but he had an image of the other Aelyr race, the Fhelethyr, with whom they'd travelled for a while until the Valahyr caught up with them.

Ten or fifteen minutes into his flight, with Heron tiring but keeping up a steady hand-gallop, Jthery heard a second set of hoof-beats. Someone was pursuing him.

His heart jolted with alarm. He turned to see a figure on a horse, swiftly gaining on him. The horse was ice-white; its rider, also bareback, was dark, with flying black hair and raven cloak. Nefri, bearing Falthorn.

Panicking, Jthery urged Heron on. The gelding tried hard, but Nefri had always been faster. Falthorn caught up effortlessly.

'Jthery, where are you going?' he called.

'I'm not your prisoner!'

Falthorn urged Nefri ahead then swung in front of Heron, forcing him to a halt. The grey dug his hooves in and tossed his head, almost causing Jthery to lose his seat. Both horses danced to a standstill. Jthery righted himself, gripping the mane and breathing hard. Falthorn was there and real, in all his powerful beauty, with white jewels sparkling on the shoulders of his cloak between the wild skeins of hair.

'Who said you were my prisoner?' he said, more exasperated than angry. 'Don't be foolish. Where in Verdanholm are you planning to go?'

'I don't know. Back to the Fhelethyr.'

'They can't shield you from me,' Falthorn said coldly.

He was a great shadow, looming, inescapable. 'Wherever you last saw them – even if you could find it – they'll be long gone. Be sensible, my friend. You've nowhere to go, except back to the house with me.'

Jthery's panic began to subside, leaving him drained. Some visceral instinct beyond reason had made him flee and he felt foolish, shaken. He lowered his head and his long red-gold hair swung forward, half-hiding his face. Smiling gravely, Falthorn turned Nefri back in the direction of the house. Heron followed with no urging from his rider.

'So what's the matter?' Falthorn asked. 'Why were you suddenly fleeing from me?'

'I don't know.' He put his shoulders back, gathering what was left of his dignity. 'No, I do know. I panicked because I'm afraid . . . afraid that Tanthe was right about you.'

'In what regard?'

Jthery swallowed hard. His mouth was dry. 'She said you were going to give Aventuria to the Bhahdradomen.'

A steel-cold pause. 'I wish you would talk to me, instead of listening to rumours.'

'I saw you with them, just before you went through the *rothanamir*,' Jthery said defiantly. 'Some Bhahdradomen came out of the portal, and you shook hands with them.'

Falthorn was silent for a time. His face was carved marble, but his eyes shone with complex, terrifying emotions that Jthery couldn't hope to fathom. 'I have never told you a lie. I only said that you would see me do strange things that no one would understand. I asked you to trust me. I thought that you did.'

'I want to,' said Jthery, calmer now but hating the way he felt. Angry with Falthorn. Wanting him. Fearing him. 'But I must know what you did on Earth. I've a right to know!'

'And so you have, Jthery,' said Falthorn. 'Since you won't take me at my word; come. I'll show you.'

When the house came in sight again, Falthorn rode

straight past. He went up onto the broad back of the hill where the column of *rothanamir* light still shone. For a heart-stopping moment, Jthery thought that Falthorn was going to take him through the portal. He saw Nialorn and the others grinning as they passed, but no new arrivals.

'You didn't bring Tanthe and the others back with you?'

'No. They stayed in Parione. They're as safe as you are, so don't worry about them.'

Falthorn continued along the ridge, down into a valley and up onto a higher peak two or three miles further on. Here he eased Nefri to a halt and dismounted. Jthery slipped down from Heron's back and stood uneasily beside him. The horses began to graze, unconcerned; Jthery envied their indifference to everything but food.

Falthorn took a spyglass from a leather holder on his belt, raised it to his right eye and studied the horizon for a few minutes. His expression brightened. Presently, smiling, he passed the spyglass to Jthery and said, 'Tell me what you see.'

He saw the deep mysterious valleys of Verdanholm, sheened with amethyst, silver-green and fire-red. Bluffs of sparkling white quartz rising from sea-green forests. The sun, moving like a giant apricot lamp across the unearthly sky.

'The landscape,' said Jthery. 'What am I supposed to see?'

'The horizon. What do you see there?'

There were lavender hills blending into a perfect sapphire sky. 'Just hills.'

'Just hills. Exactly.'

'I don't understand.'

Falthorn placed his hand on the spyglass and pulled it from Jthery's grasp. 'Didn't Tanthe tell you what she saw? Since you set such store by her words, you must ask her sometime. If you had looked a few days ago, you would have seen a grey cloud there. Look closer, and you'd have seen that it wasn't a cloud but a wound, an abyss. A place where Bhahdradomen *aghramen* were consuming the very fabric of Verdanholm itself. Now they are gone and Verdanholm is safe. They kept their side of the bargain – for indeed, I gave them no choice.'

'So, you've saved Verdanholm,' Jthery said hoarsely, folding his arms. 'That's what the Valahyr were all saying, while you were away. "Falthorn is our saviour."'

'Even the Fhelethyr and the other *eretrue* admit it. They owe me their lives. There will be no more war in Verdanholm as long as they accept it. I have given Verdanholm back her future.'

'But to do it . . . you gave the Earth to the Bhahdradomen,' said Jthery. 'Is that true?'

Falthorn sighed. 'In a manner of speaking.'

'You gave them the Nine Realms? Gave them *my* realm, Mithrain?'

Jthery didn't want to hear the answer. He could feel despair filling him from the very roots of his soul. He felt that if he let his anguish burst from his throat, the groan would fill the whole world and go on forever.

Falthorn caught his shoulders, held him. His face was fierce, his eyes two violet suns. 'Listen to me, Jthery,' he said intently. 'That is how it appears but it is only a feint, a masque—'

'Then do explain to me the difference between appearance and reality!' Jthery spat.

'You must believe that the last thing I wish is any harm to the Earth. Yes, I had to seem to give the Bhahdradomen what they wanted. Your friends will suffer for a while, it's true, but they are strong, are they not?'

'Oh yes. Stronger than you know.'

'Then do not fear for them. This is not the end of the plan. And I still hold power over the Eaters; I hold the weapons that could destroy them, if they break any part of the agreement. If there'd been any other way . . .' Falthorn's eyes glittered with emotion. 'The one thing I could not do was to stand by and watch my own realm destroyed. I'd rather be called ruthless and every evil name under the moons, than allow Verdanholm to fall to such a fate.'

Jthery stared at him. He almost hated Falthorn for the power he had over him. For his radiance and absolute confidence, for the way he made Jthery desire him yet kept him at arm's length. 'I know. I know your love of Verdanholm is sincere.'

'Desperate measures are born of love,' Falthorn said more gently. 'As long as the Eaters think they've got their own way, they'll treat the Earth fairly. Aventuria may be in a degree of turmoil for a time, but history is full of turmoil. However, that's why I asked you to stay here. So that you would be safe.'

Jthery laughed. The Valahyr's beauty and closeness overwhelmed him. Thorns of anger and desire snagged him. 'So my safety means something to you?'

'Of course.' Falthorn shook his head, black hair winging about his shoulders. 'I thought that went without saying.'

'It didn't,' Jthery said flatly, glaring into his eyes. 'I thought we shared certain feelings. Yet you've been like ice, you've barely touched me. Nothing but talk. All I can conclude is that you are taking advantage of my feelings – which I wish to the Goddess I did not have – while using me for some other purpose entirely!'

'You're very young to be so cynical,' Falthorn said quietly. He stroked Jthery's face, tracing the line of one high cheekbone. 'Has it not occurred to you that I have been quite busy? That I wanted to wait until peace was accomplished, the better to savour your company? I thought this was understood.'

'Well, it wasn't,' Jthery said, flushing. He tried to pull free of Falthorn's grip.

'You complain that I haven't touched you.' Falthorn's tone was soft but not pleasant. Jthery was becoming more and more frightened of him. The fear was horrible, yet thrilling. 'Is this a more pressing complaint than the one about Aventuria?'

'Let me go.'

Falthorn only held him tighter. His mouth was close to Jthery's now. 'The truth is, desire is a thousand times more powerful than idealism, isn't it? You are only angry with me for being cold. You don't care what I do, as long as we are lovers.'

'If you would treat me like a lover and not like an idiot,' Jthery growled. The grip hurt. Jthery was breathing hard, terrified and furious and aroused.

Falthorn smiled. 'You want me to touch you, beloved? All right.' He slid one arm around Jthery's waist, hooked his legs from under him and bore him down to the ground.

It was not rape; not quite, though perhaps it would have been if Jthery had tried to stop him. The Valahyr pushed Jthery down into the long silver grass. He pinned him there as he tore off most of Jthery's clothes and his own; then he descended on Jthery and bit him all over his neck, shoulders and chest.

It was as much a struggle as an act of lust. Falthorn's long golden limbs straining against Jthery's pale ones. Their hair mingling, black and blond. The scent of horses still on their bodies mixing with the spice of Valahyr perfumes, Falthorn's beauty and strangeness overpowering him. Terror, confusion, ecstasy. *Not like this*, Jthery thought, but he couldn't stop.

Yet there was a moment, in the purely physical striving, when something strange began to happen. Jthery's mind seemed to flip into a different plane. He saw a field of a wondrous pale gold colour, and a pulsing point of light moving closer and closer . . .

The tension grew unbearable. He felt the seed spill from him, exquisite release; and with that the vision ended. He actually began to reach out after the vision, but instead his hand found the angle of Falthorn's shoulder. They lay tangled, exhausted, not looking at each other.

After a minute, the Valahyr lord pushed himself up on one elbow and looked down at Jthery. His eyes, now, were sad. 'I've hurt you.'

Jthery felt sore all over. Looking down at his chest, he saw bruises, some of them bleeding. 'I'll heal.'

'I'm sorry. I was angry with you for doubting me. I should not have done this; I should have realised you've not had much experience . . .'

'Hardly any,' Jthery said thinly. 'I thought you'd be gentler than that.'

'You seemed to enjoy it.'

'Well . . . that's not the point, is it?'

'Forgive me,' Falthorn said, stroking him. 'You are beautiful, Jthery. I asked you to stay with me because I want you, nothing less than that. It was never my intention to hurt or confuse you. Please forgive me.'

He gathered Jthery in his arms and hugged him. Jthery returned the embrace, eyes closed, heart torn. 'Come, we'll go back to the house,' Falthorn added. 'You need to rest; so do I. We'll find some salve for these bruises. And we'll talk.'

'Are you always so passionate?' Jthery asked.

'Always.' Falthorn smiled. Jthery was lost again.

'You know you said the Eaters would treat the Earth fairly?' he said, as they retrieved their scattered garments. 'Is that true?'

'Of course,' Falthorn answered. 'The Eaters themselves realise there's nothing to gain by ravaging Aventuria and destroying the human race. Vaurgroth's not a complete idiot.'

Jthery stared at him. Perhaps Falthorn was a tough-minded hero, or perhaps he was a devious villain; perhaps both. Either way, Jthery could not turn off his feelings. Staying with the Valahyr was going to be strange, hard and terrible, but he knew now that he had no choice.

'I know it was a horrible decision to take, but I had

no choice,' the Valahyr added. 'You do see that? I'll do anything to set your mind at rest.'

'That's thoughtful,' Jthery said softly. 'You should know that just because you are stronger than me, and very good at scaring the hell out of me, it won't stop me asking questions.'

'Scared of me, my Lord of Mithrain?' grinned Falthorn, clasping his hand. 'Ask whatever you want. I need you to understand that I'm not evil, and I'm not siding with the Bhahdradomen. Come home, and I'll tell you everything.'

As the days went by, Mawrdreth watched Helan in growing concern. She seemed unable to rest; even at night she would rise and wander around their bed-chamber like a ghost. Her eyes were lustreless. She was losing weight; she who never lost her appetite, whether for food or for life itself. She retained her dignity, showed no signs of self-pity; only seemed further and further beyond the reach of comfort.

It was the collapse of the Xauroma that had done this, Mawrdreth knew. Losing the Sapphire Throne she could bear; but to know that her binding covenant with the land was broken, the very promise that sanctified her monarchy, was killing her. It was as if her spirit, being part of the Xauroma, had died with it.

Mawrdreth had tried everything to help her. Eventually he'd run out of words and ideas. All he could do was watch her. It was killing him, too.

After the hideous debacle in the temple, Helan had requested another audience with Vaurgroth. She'd been refused. Since then, she'd sunk deeper into depression. She refused to see anyone but Mawrdreth; not even Eldareth. Every day, when Mawrdreth went into the main chamber, the others would clamour to know how the Queen was, but he had no good news for them.

'You look dreadful,' Tanthe told him one morning. It was about a month into their captivity. She'd come close

to crying when he told her that Helan was still no better.
'Bet you wish you'd stayed in Thanmandrathor.'

Mawrdreth knew she was joking, but he wasn't in the mood for it. 'No,' he said fiercely. 'I could never wish that. Everything I've endured, I'd gladly endure again to be with Helan. The only thing I cannot bear is to see her like this!'

'Sorry, Mawr,' she said, flinching. 'The next insensitive thing I say, just kick me through the window.'

He sighed. 'Forgive my ill-temper, Tanthe. It's hard to be calm in these circumstances. Can I speak to you for a few minutes?'

'Of course.' She looked surprised, but led him to the recessed window seat, away from the others. There she sat with her feet drawn up, her slim athletic form folded and her arms round her knees. She was a beauty, Mawrdreth observed, with her shiny mass of dark hair and the intense green-blue jewels of her eyes; he could believe she had Aelyr blood. Her frankness was attractive, yet she also had an elusive quality. More to her than met the eye. Not that he felt any desire for her; he loved Helan, couldn't think of anyone else. In other circumstances he might have felt differently. Now, though, he only noticed her qualities with detached interest. And he liked her, cared for her as he did his sister. She was very easy to like. 'What is it?'

He said, 'You spend a lot of time with Auriel and Elrill. I wondered . . .'

She bit her lip and blinked at him. 'Elrill is trying to train us in certain mental disciplines. Meditation, and trying to raise a bit of *roth* energy between us.'

'How is it going?'

'Not that well, really. Auriel hates it.'

'Why?'

'Because of something Falthorn did to us. He sent us into this awful non-place called the *ezht*, and when we try to meditate, it sort of brings it back. It's like having a nightmare every time you drop off to sleep; you get scared of sleeping. Not very pleasant. Elrill's trying to get us over it. Why d'you ask?'

'I didn't mean to be intrusive,' Mawrdreth said. 'I only wondered if what you were doing might help Helan.'

Tanthe was silent, chewing her lower lip. 'Oh, Mawr, this is awful for you, isn't it? I'll ask Elrill. I doubt it, though. Really, we're trying to develop this Valahyr skill between us. Unfortunately, none of us has a clue what we're doing, not even Elrill. He's Shaelahyr; they don't tend to play mind-tricks like the Valahyr do. So we're all in the dark.'

Mawrdreth nodded. 'It was just a thought. A straw to clutch at.'

'Don't you give up as well, will you?'

'No, but I keep thinking about Branq'elin. What's happening to her? Have the Bhahdradomen invaded Thanmandrathor, or is our realm still free? There's so much to brood on, and I can't talk to Helan about it now.'

'You can talk to me,' Tanthe said, touching his arm. 'Not much consolation, I know. I can't talk to Auriel about Rufryd, either.'

'But talking is fruitless, when we have no power to act! This cannot go on!' He struck the seat with his fist, rose to his feet and walked away. He didn't mean to be rude to Tanthe; he was simply on fire with frustration.

There was the soft tap of a Bhahdradomen finger on the door.

'Lunch is early,' said Eldareth on the far side of the chamber. Mawrdreth's heart sank. It only heralded another hour spent trying to persuade Helan to eat while she paced and paced, until his own appetite vanished too.

It wasn't the *yrim* who usually brought their meals. Instead, two of Vaurgroth's elite glided into the room, flanked by six of their own *vagharim*. The tiny mage Rhazagramen and the fawn-skinned Uryzht, with his elongated, wolfish face.

Tanthe joined Eldareth and Mawrdreth; Elrill and Auriel came from a side-chamber. Instinctively they clustered together. No-one spoke, but the atmosphere thickened with dread.

'Ah, Lord Mawrdreth,' said Rhazagramen in his wiry tone, 'there is a matter I wish to discuss with you. If you would be so good as to accompany us . . .'

The others closed protectively around Mawrdreth. 'Why?' said Eldareth.

Rhazagramen turned briefly to him with a slit of a smile. 'I did not, I believe, address you. Lord Eldareth. It's Lord Mawrdreth we want.'

'Are you taking me to Vaurgroth?' Mawrdreth asked. 'Why?'

'Because the Queen asked to see him and was refused. I am happy to act on her behalf, and I will gladly go with her, but I cannot allow you to disregard her authority. If anyone is to see Vaurgroth, it should be her.'

'I am given to understand that your ex-Queen is ill.'

'Our *Queen*,' Mawrdreth said pointedly, 'is suffering a malady more of the soul than the body.'

'Nevertheless, it is you to whom we wish to speak.'

'What's happening?' said Helan's voice from the far corner of the chamber. She was in the doorway to the bedroom, looking dreadful; face colourless, eyes smudged with purple, hair lustreless with neglect.

Mawrdreth groaned to himself. The Bhahdradomen were too clever. Whatever they wanted, they realised they'd get no joy out of her; she was too far gone even to fear them any more. Whereas he – fit, strong and angry – was more likely to yield rewards.

'Nothing to concern you, my lady,' said Uryzht. His voice was dry and nasal. 'There's a small matter on which we require your husband. He'll be returned safely – if he co-operates.'

'No,' she said. 'Mawrdreth, don't go!'

He had no choice. If he put up a fight, he would only get his companions hurt or killed. And it might be a drastic overreaction.

'It's just an interview, Hel,' he said calmly. 'Don't worry.'

He went with them, striding along the corridor with two *vagharim* behind him, another two in front of him, Rhazagramen and Uryzht leading the way. They'd had six guards originally. Where were the other two? Outside with the regular guards at the door – or still inside the chamber with his friends? Mawrdreth felt grim with anxiety.

Uryzht appeared a dry, scholarly individual, driven and humourless. Most of the Bhahdradomen were easily amused – especially by human suffering – but Uryzht's manner was as arid as his sand-coloured flesh. There was something soul-sapping, deadly about him. Rhazagramen, by contrast – despite his apparent great age – was quick-moving and full of energy. He made Mawrdreth think of a nasty little white terrier.

'Are you taking me to Vaurgroth?' he asked again.

'No,' said Rhazagramen, glancing over his shoulder. 'Why do you ask?'

Mawrdreth stood a foot taller than the slim figure of Theosopher Rhazagramen, yet he felt vulnerable. The *bharu'grothrim's* attention was like an invisible hand pinching some vital nerve inside him, turning his limbs numb and useless.

'Her majesty Queen Helananthe requested an audience with Vaurgroth and was refused. This is unacceptable. We insist on seeing him.'

Rhazagramen smiled. 'Plainly it is hard for you to accept the fact that neither you nor your wife are in any position to insist on anything.'

'Vaurgroth must see us. He can't refuse.'

'I suggest you learn to use his titles, Greatlord Vaurgroth of the Fire, Master of Light, Chosen of the Ancestor. Of course he can refuse to see you. He has.'

'I am the King,' he stated with all the conviction he could muster. The words sounded hollow. He'd hardly occupied the Sapphire Throne long enough to come to terms with the idea.

'You, my lord, are nothing,' Rhazagramen said thinly. 'You and your wife may consider yourselves ordinary citizens, and lucky to be alive. I am tiring of this conversation.'

Mawrdreth was shaking with fury, but he held back. There was nothing he could do, short of flying at Rhazagramen with bare hands. That would demonstrate nothing but his own powerlessness.

'That's unfortunate, because this conversation isn't over yet,' he said. 'If I am just an "ordinary citizen", why do you need me now?'

They passed down several wide staircases as they talked, and long corridors panelled with amber and blond marble. Rhazagramen fell into step beside him, his face sour. 'I am Vaurgroth's right hand,' he said. 'Whatever your complaint, you can address it to me. I suggest you do so while you still have the chance.'

Mawrdreth understood the implication. Soon even Vaurgroth's underlings would be too aggrandized to speak to them.

'Our complaint concerns the atrocities in the Temple of Nepheter. You've lied and deceived us. You told us we could continue our normal worship, only to violate our rituals with this alien god of yours!'

'Your complaint is noted,' Rhazagramen said flatly. 'Many of your citizens feel differently. They are daily receiving revelations which they would not see as any cause for complaint. Rather, they might be angry that the truth had been kept from them until now.'

'Truth? We know what you're doing,' Mawrdreth retorted. 'Turning our people into mindless slaves! It's monstrous!'

The Theosopher's whole form seemed to shiver. Mawrdreth realised that beneath his cool mask he was furious, dripping hatred like venom. 'But we *are* monsters. This is what we do. You wouldn't expect anything less, would you?'

Mawrdreth was speechless. As the mage leaned in towards him, he caught the fungal mustiness of his body, mixed with the metallic tang of *gauroth*. 'Which of our races is the more monstrous, in truth?' Rhazagramen went on. 'Humans, who tried to render us extinct then exiled the survivors to starvation – this is hardly the behaviour of blameless lambs! Yet compare our own civility in the face of such provocation.'

'What civility?'

'You have witnessed the clean efficiency of our coup. We achieved it peacefully, with minimal bloodshed. Could humans claim as much, the last time they pitted themselves against us?'

'You're playing with words,' Mawrdreth said. 'You took the Sapphire Throne with threats of torture. There's bloodshed every time some brave soul tries to defy you.' He felt disgusted. There was nothing he could say to pierce the armour of Rhazagramen's smugness.

'However you would view it, I say again, you are lucky to be alive. Take that message back to your wife. Our coup was peaceful, merciful, and necessary. You have nothing to fear – as long as you accept what is. Accept us, and you will find great Vaurgroth the gentlest of rulers, Ancestor the most merciful of gods.'

Mawrdreth fell silent. He couldn't fence verbally with this vile little mage, as an intellectual might have done. Between a father who could lecture interminably on the history of Thanmandrathor, and an older sister with a fiery personality, Mawrdreth had grown up the quiet one, his family's support. That made him a perfect foil for Helan. But without her . . . he felt inadequate to the task, with only brute courage to defend himself.

They were going deep into the Citadel. Here the stairs and passages were narrow, and there were no windows, only rows of oil-lamps along the wall, kept burning should the monarch ever pass this way. He knew exactly where they were. There was only one reason to come down here.

The shadows that lay on him deepened as he wondered what the Bhahdradomen knew, *how* they knew . . .

'Where are you taking me?' he asked.

'Surely you know your own Citadel, my lord,' Uryzht said flatly.

'I know it. But there's nothing for you here.'

'Indeed?' said Rhazagramen. 'We'll see.'

The door that led to the *xauroth* chamber was kept locked. Only the monarch was allowed to enter. Mawrdreth thought the journey would end here, but to his dismay, Uryzht produced the big silver key and they went in. A sloping, twisting corridor, and then a dome-shaped chamber built into the rock of the hill itself.

There had always been energy here; unearthly singing and a play of light. Now the place felt as dead as a cave. He'd expected it, but still it came as a sickening shock.

Filling the chamber, except for a narrow walkway around its circumference, was the *xauroth* sphere. Mawrdreth looked at it and his soul failed.

It was a great crystal, a gift from the Zampherai when the Citadel was first founded; a sphere sensitive to the *roth* of the Xauroma itself. It responded to the Earth's moods. A barometer, Helan had called it. It had no power or influence of its own; simply reflected the Xauroma's state of health.

Last time, he'd seen it rotating on the plinth that cupped it, smoky in colour but filled with flashes of light. Nursing the pain that Garnelys had inflicted on it, recovering, fighting.

Now it was dead.

There was no movement or sound. The sphere lay grey-brown and opaque like a great boulder that had been carried and deposited there by a long-vanished glacier. A sculpture of a huge sightless eye.

He forgot that the Bhahdradomen were there. He put his hand out towards it but couldn't bring himself to touch it. *Helan knew about this*. Without seeing it physically, she knew. This was why she'd sunk into despair. If she couldn't heal it, no-one could.

'My lord?' Uryzht's voice made him start. 'Theosopher wishes us to proceed to the lower levels.'

'What lower levels?' Mawrdreth said, looking sideways at the dry vulpine face.

'We know about the underground chambers,' Rhazagramen's voice came from somewhere around the curve of the sphere. 'And what's in them. Pretending ignorance won't help.'

Uryzht touched Mawrdreth in the back with the point of one finger; a cattle-herder prodding a stubborn beast. It hurt, a spiteful needle. With folded arms, Mawrdreth walked a few paces round the wall until Rhazagramen was in sight again. 'Whatever you think you know, you're wasting your time. You won't find your way down there.'

'Which is why you are here.' One of the *vagharim* held a lamp, while Rhazagramen leaned down to the flagstones, searching.

'I can't help you,' said Mawrdreth.

'I think you will find that you can.'

'There is no way in, without special keys. I don't possess them, nor do I know where they are kept.'

'Ah!' Rhazagramen's exclamation cut across Mawrdreth as if he hadn't even been listening. He had something in his hand, an object like a black mushroom with multiple stalks. Now he was marrying it into a set of holes in the flagstone. There was a *clunk* as he pressed it home. 'Uryzht, *vagharim*!'

He stood back while the others hurried to lift the flagstone. It opened to reveal a vertical passage into the rock. Spiral stairs vanished down into the darkness.

Mawrdreth was stricken. *Rhazagramen had the keys.* Only the monarch was allowed to possess and use them, and she'd kept them well-hidden in her chambers . . . not well enough. The Bhahdradomen must have ransacked the royal chambers to find them . . . or perhaps sensed their *roth,* as rats sniffed out food.

'You see, the keys are not the problem. I have the one for the chest, as well. Yes, we know about the chest and its contents. Shall we?'

Rhazagramen waved his hand at the stairwell. Mawrdreth had gone down there many times with Helan, never dreaming that the knowledge they'd gained would be used against them. In the chest, deep below, were slabs of semi-precious minerals. The scripts carved on them could only be read and understood by initiates; the King and Queen themselves.

'There's nothing down there that will make sense to you,' said Mawrdreth.

'That's why we need you,' Rhazagramen answered with thin patience. 'We know that you can read the slabs. You shall translate for us.'

'No, I can't.' He was alarmed and angry, trying not to show it. 'The conditions are wrong. You have no idea what you are doing.'

'Still something missing?'

'Yes.'

'This?'

Mawrdreth turned, and saw that Uryzht was holding Helan's sceptre of office. It was a staff with an orb of clear rock crystal set on top. The Orb of Clear Sight. He stared at the usurpers in outrage. 'Thieves. You Goddess-forsaken thieves!'

'You are going to help us, so stop wasting time,' Rhazagramen said irritably. Mawrdreth felt the wiry, many-fingered hands of the guards closing on his arms, the point of a weapon burning through his clothes.

They were asking him to reveal the secrets of the Xauroma, and more; details of the Basilisks of Calabethron and how they'd been deployed to defeat the Bhahdradomen on the Silver Plains. There was a wealth of knowledge there that the Devourers could use against humans. They might learn how to defend themselves against such weapons, perhaps to build worse ones of their own. And there might be more.

Knowledge that he and Helan hadn't touched on. As her King and consort, he was sworn to secrecy.

In that moment, Mawdreth resigned himself to dying. He would die before he gave one word of those secrets away.

'There's a human saying, "You can take a horse to water..."'

'"But you can't make him *think*,"' Rhazagramen finished crisply. 'Are you refusing to help us?'

'You can drag me wherever you wish, using force. You can't make me do your bidding once we're there. Not even with torture.'

'I am not going to torture you, my lord,' Rhazagramen said tiredly.

Mawrdreth said nothing. The Bhahdradomen looked at him with narrow red eyes. 'Your friends, however...'

'You Goddess-forsaken bastard,' Mawrdreth said, low and furious. 'Q'enartre strike you dead. Don't you dare threaten them! You cowards!'

'Well, let us see if you are brave enough to hold firm while we practise our subtle arts upon one of them. Uryzht?'

The beige one disappeared round the curve of the sphere. There were soft sounds; footsteps, someone struggling. A moment later Uryzht reappeared. Behind him came the missing *vagharim* and between them a rigid figure, jerking against their hands, her eyes bright with indignation and terror.

Tanthe.

Chapter Seven. Orb of Clear Sight

Saphaeyender locked himself in his study, lit a lamp and poured a large glass of Marocian red. Seating himself at his desk, he stared at the little statue of Nepheter in her alcove on the opposite wall. Nepheter, goddess of Parione; muse of poets and artists. She had always been a soothing, inspiring presence in Saphaeyender's life.

The wine was good, burning away the sick feeling in his stomach. He'd been trying for days, weeks, to forget the scene in the temple but wherever he went, whatever he did, it was there; bursting across the inner eye like the memory of a bad, frenetic play.

He couldn't stop thinking about the ghastly ecstasy he'd experienced. How it had hurt to resist the Ancestor, how blissful it had felt to surrender . . . opening his arms to let in the light . . . *'Yes, come into me, Ancestor. I am yours.'*

He shuddered with shame. He couldn't believe it had happened. He cringed, recalling Tanthe's shocked face on the other side of the temple. What must she think of him now?

She'd saved him from it, his name ringing from her lips like a slap across the face. Shaken him out of the trance before he was too far gone.

The feeling had faded, leaving him cold with self-disgust. What in the Nine Realms had come over him? It was as if he'd swallowed a drug that removed all inhibition and self-control. Only afterwards, when the drug faded, did he see what a fool he'd made of himself . . . how false and illusory was that feeling of ecstasy.

Hideous. Humiliating. But he hadn't been the only one. He hadn't been to the temple since, but he'd seen people emerging on other occasions, moving through the crowd with slack mouths and shining eyes, still lost in their vision. Those who hadn't been affected – or had dragged themselves out of it – were at a loss to help those who'd fallen. It was horrifying, as if half the population had gone mad at once. It was all going as he'd predicted. Ancestor-worshippers and Goddess-worshippers screaming at each other on the street. Terror among those who wouldn't give up the old beliefs. Refugees streaming out of the city, made homeless by the Eaters, or simply too frightened to stay.

'Good lady, forgive me,' he whispered to the statue. 'What are they doing, turning us away from you?'

Making mindless slaves for the Devourers.

The glass creaked in his hand, he was holding it so tightly. He put it down before he lacerated his fingers and lost the wine. Picking up a quill, he dipped it in ink, slid a sheet of fresh paper towards him and wrote hurriedly for a few minutes. Notes for a play. The temple scene was shaping itself into a script, a satire to highlight the seductive dangers of religious delusion . . .

It was the first serious thing he'd written since the fall of Garnelys.

He stopped and stared at what he'd written in disbelief. Goddess, he was working! A fine thread of excitement went through him. It might be possible. Some good might come out of this.

Someone tapped urgently on the door. Saphaeyender started, nearly knocking his glass over. Putting down his quill with a sigh, he called, 'Come in!'

It was Eander. His gentle face was bleached with anxiety, and his hands were shaking. 'Saph, I'm sorry. There's someone here to see you. Some of *them.*'

'Bhahdradomen?' Saphaeyender said, sitting taut on the edge of the chair. He glanced at the window, estimating his chances of leaping through it and fleeing. Pointless. 'I told you not to answer the door on your own!'

'I know, but – I thought it would be Saliole or someone, at this time of night . . .'

'What do they want?'

'I don't know. They were very insistent. I tried to tell them you weren't receiving visitors but I couldn't seem to turn them away. You can't say no to them.'

'I've heard rumours that you can't say no to anyone.' Saphaeyender patted him on the shoulder, but his companion was in no mood to be teased. 'It's all right, Eander. Go and wait in my chamber – or the kitchen, if you prefer company. I'll see them.'

Eander's blue eyes flashed anxiety. 'Alone?'

'My dear, if they are going to do something hideous to me, I'd rather be their only victim.'

'Saph!' Tears sprang into his eyes.

'Oh, don't worry. Go. They only seem to kill humans who attack them, and I'm not about to do anything that brave.'

He saw Eander down the pillared corridor that led to the staff quarters, then went into the main living area. The shutters had been closed against the night and lamps were burning on low tables, turning the marble walls to creamy gold. Stepping through the soft shadows of lattice screens and tall plants, Saphaeyender couldn't see them at first; the only sound he could hear was the music of the fountain in the courtyard. But there was a scent, like musty earth threaded with fungus. A darkness shimmering on the air, sucking out his vitality.

Then he saw them. There were four of them, clustered beneath his potted fig trees, blending with the dappled shadows. Two were in uniforms of dark-green stuff like ragged snake-skin, and armed with the usual array of vile weapons. The other two were of Vaurgroth's elite. One was an ashen figure, like a charred tree, with deep lines in his grey, sour face. The other was the most frightening Devourer Saphaeyender had ever seen.

He was tall, blade-thin and clinical as polished steel.

He looked like an administrator who would insist on fanatical attention to detail, and torture you with the same passionless precision.

'My lord Saphaeyender?' he said. 'Forgive the intrusion. It is good of you to see us. I am Protector Naghrur and this is Prefigurer Tzumezht, of the Amber Citadel.'

Saphaeyender had an urge to strike him for that outrageous claim. Of the Amber Citadel, indeed! 'Lord Protector, Lord Prefigurer,' he said tonelessly. *Lord* was a courtesy title afforded to anyone whose status was unclear, sometimes with a hint of sarcasm. 'How may I help you?'

'You attended your temple recently.' Tzumezht's Paranian was harshly accented.

'Yes.' He suppressed a grimace, aware of Naghrur's glacial scrutiny.

'The new regime is heartened to see such an eminent citizen as yourself settling in so well.'

'Settling in?'

'Embracing the Ancestor so whole-heartedly.' Tzumezht nodded approvingly. 'It's the best way, the only way.'

Saphaeyender couldn't reply. He was sure they'd come to arrest him for not attending since. If he spoke his true feelings, the two henchmen might beat him half to death. He moistened his lips, wishing he could have got a lot more wine down his throat before this happened.

'You are a writer,' said Naghrur. His voice was clear and silken, pure as a finger singing on the wet edge of a wine glass.

'Sometimes.'

They didn't appear to understand self-deprecation. 'What do you mean, sometimes?' barked Tzumezht.

'I have also been an actor, a soldier, a lover, a general dogsbody and a shirker. But sometimes I write, it's true.'

'You are a poet,' Tzumezht insisted. 'You are a playwright.'

'Yes,' Saphaeyender agreed helplessly.

'You are the most highly renowned of the living writers.

You are feted in Parione and your name is legend through all Aventuria.'

'Thank you.' Uneasy, he folded his arms. 'My box office figures are impressive, it must be said.'

'Who publishes your work?' asked Tzumezht.

'What?' He gave a startled laugh.

'This work of yours is printed and distributed, is it not? By whom?'

'Er . . . You only have to look at the flyleaf of any of my work.'

'We have not personally seen any of your work,' said Naghrur. 'I doubt it would mean anything to us. Yet it is widely read by humans.'

'For that I have to thank Meritus & Heyma of Pearl Street.'

Naghrur nodded. 'Who also recently published a volume by a Lady Ysomir, detailing the last days of King Garnelys?'

'Yes,' he said, his hands tightening on his elbows. He couldn't see where this was leading. 'I took her manuscript to Meritus myself. What she had written was an extraordinary record by a first-hand witness. It helped people to understand what was happening inside the Amber Citadel in those terrible days. Which were, in retrospect, not as terrible as these.'

Steel sparks glinted in the Protector's eyes. 'Good. All copies of Lady Ysomir's books shall be withdrawn and destroyed. As shall any of your works with a political or religious content.'

'What?' Saphaeyender frowned. Outrage rushed through him. 'That is virtually all of them! Withdrawn, destroyed? *Why*?'

'You are not a fool,' Naghrur said thinly, 'even for a human. In these new times, it is not good for humans to be reminded of the old times. In your work, there is altogether too much celebration of goddesses and rutting gods, human life and sensuality. Ysomir's, on the other hand, is likely to stir up anti-Bhahdradomen prejudice.'

Saphaeyender wiped a hand over his forehead, laughing in disbelief. 'You are doing a fine job of that on your own without any help from us.'

Tzumezht grinned, apparently finding this funny. Naghrur's demeanour froze a little harder and Saphaeyender suspected those words had just consigned him to the Lord Protector's execution list. He swallowed and went on, 'Do you think that by withdrawing our work, people will forget their beliefs, forget that Garnelys's decline was stage-managed by the Bhahdradomen all along? You'll never find all the copies. Those books have been read by thousands! You'll never wipe people's memories.'

'True,' said Naghrur. 'But memories can be altered. New experiences can replace the old. Truth can replace lies.'

Saphaeyender went dizzy. He broke into a sweat, and Naghrur's hard, metal-grey face filled his whole vision. His legs gave way and he sank onto a couch. 'Your idea of the truth is not the same as ours.'

'Really?' said Tzumezht. 'Have you forgotten how it felt in the temple, to open yourself to the Ancestor? Now you are trying to fight it again. But you will never know true peace until you give yourself up to Him – and the same is true for each and every human in this land. *They must know the Ancestor*. Only then can they accept their place in the world.'

'So you've come round to apologise for burning my books,' Saphaeyender said roughly. 'That's most courteous of you. You needn't have taken the trouble.'

'You misunderstand,' said Tzumezht. 'The matter on which we came to see you is an important one. Crucial, indeed.'

Saphaeyender sat back, startled and wary. 'What do you mean?'

'You are highly honoured by our Lord of Light Vaurgroth,' said Naghrur. 'He has chosen you to work with us. He has sent us here to enlist your help.'

The writer stared at the two *bharu'grothrim*. 'With all due respect, how can you possibly expect me to help you? I don't understand.'

'I am the representative of the common *domenim*,' said Tzumezht. 'I speak for them. My interest is that truth and education shall be disseminated among them. Now my concerns extend to the common humans of Parione; that all have equal rights to correct information. My role is to make their lives fulfilling and valuable.'

'*What?*'

'Humans read your poems and watch your plays,' Naghrur said. 'You make them laugh and cry and wonder. You manipulate their reactions. They don't try to resist, because you have made them love you. You can make them see the truth.'

'More effectively than Rhazagramen?' he said sourly.

'There has been considerable resistance to the Ancestor, as we predicted. Some humans will prove stubborn. They are the ones we must reach.'

'*Reach?*'

'Vaurgroth intends you to write for him. New works, that praise the Bhahdradomen and make them see that our rule is the natural way of things. That the Ancestor is their only way forward. You can make them love Vaurgroth.'

As Naghrur spoke, without any evidence of irony, Saphaeyender gaped at him. He was close to retching or screaming, but all that came from his throat was a dry cough. 'You're asking me to write propaganda?'

'Not propaganda. The truth.'

'I won't do it.'

'You must.'

'But I can't. Even if I tried, it wouldn't be believed. My heart wouldn't be in it, you see.'

'This is nonsense,' said the smooth clear voice. 'A great writer can make any point of view convincing. And your heart *will* be in it, as soon as you give yourself fully to the Ancestor.'

'A wonderful new set of works by Saphaeyender,' added

Tzumezht with grotesque enthusiasm. 'It is just what my citizens need, to take their minds off their difficulties. You will be doing a great public service; you can't deny it to them.'

'I can't write,' he said desperately.

'What do you mean?' said Tzumezht.

'Ask anyone who knows me. I've written nothing for months. I – I lost someone I loved, and since then I cannot find any words.'

Naghrur looked irritated, and Saphaeyender began to feel a fear that turned his whole body to seething water. 'It is amazing what you can find, when there is no choice.'

'I suppose you are going to torture me, or something tedious of that nature.'

The *bharu'grothrim*'s face was a huge metal mask, with needles of ice for eyes. 'We know all your friends, my lord, and where they live. If you wish them to go on living, rather than to die slow and terrible deaths, you *will* write poems and plays for Vaurgroth. You will write exactly what we tell you.'

Mawrdreth looked at Tanthe, held between the two *vagharim*. He felt his rage fragmenting into bitter resignation. Her hands were bound in front of her with chains weighting her wrists, and a strip of white material had been wrapped tightly over her mouth. Her expression was strained with anger and fear.

They must have taken her just after him. Planned it all along.

'She won't be harmed, if you are good,' Rhazagramen said evenly. 'This way.'

Mawrdreth had no choice but to follow him down the long, deep throat of the stairwell. A guard walked behind and another in front of him; he could hear the deadly hum of their weapons. He'd heard them call the lightning-whips *tzirin*, a name he'd rather not have known. Uryzht was at the rear, bearing the Orb of Clear Sight.

Mawrdreth had never liked coming down into the recesses of the earth. He'd done it gladly for Helan. This was the first time he'd felt truly afraid.

They came at last into the low-ceilinged chamber that only the monarchs of Aventuria were meant to see. Lamps threw writhing shadows onto the stone walls and glinted on the marble lid of a chest, lying embedded in the floor. Only then did Mawrdreth realise that Tanthe was still up in the *xauroth* chamber with the other guards. He glanced back at the narrow fissure of the entrance, out of his mind with anxiety for her. If it had been Helan or Branq'elin, he couldn't have felt any worse.

Rhazagramen delved in a pouch on his belt and drew out the second key; a mushroom carved from amethyst, with multiple stalks, each a different length. Mawrdreth guessed he'd done this before, but found the slabs illegible. The thought sickened him. It was a violation, a cold-minded rape of the sacred sanctum.

As Rhazagramen stepped towards the chest, Mawrdreth put his head back and yelled, 'Andamanque!'

All the Bhahdradomen stared at him. He didn't know what possessed him to do it, perhaps it would only make things worse. But she came. Andamanque answered his call.

Lavender light shone in a crevice, and from it stepped the tiny, humped figure of the Keeper. She was a Zampherai, a creature less than two feet high with skin the colour of stone. Her race dwelled in the deep caves of earth, husbanding and mining the minerals that grew there in the dark. She was an ancient one of their kind, with straggling black hair and a robe of grey rags.

'Who disturbs the Keeper?' she said.

Rhazagramen, Uryzht and the others were motionless, staring at her. It was the first time Mawrdreth had seen them caught unawares.

'You,' she said, pointing a pewter finger at Mawrdreth. 'You did not take enough care. The Earth cries out in torment!'

'The Bhahdradomen want to know what's in the chest,' Mawrdreth said. He didn't know what else to say. The desperate situation was obvious.

'That is clear,' she said harshly. She stood regarding him from a beady silver eye, her face feral. 'Shall the secrets be revealed to the Devourers?'

'No!' said Mawrdreth. 'But how can I stop them? They're threatening a friend of mine!'

'Then you shall keep the secrets and both of you die, or give them up and both live. It is not my decision,' said the Keeper. 'It is yours, o King. Look at me; d'you think I can stop them? Do you think I am some Umbaroth with great powers? Not so. *You* are the guardian.'

'What is this creature?' said Rhazagramen.

'I am the Keeper,' said Andamanque, her voice echoing as if it came from a distance. 'A guide, not a guardian.' She angled her sharp finger at Rhazagramen's heart. 'But *you*, creatures of swamp-mud, I shall never guide. Break into the secrets if you can; then they might as well be broken open to the world! The Xauroma is sundered. Be warned, Eaters of life; the Earth herself will turn against you and spit you out!'

Rhazagramen's small pearly face contorted with anger. Uryzht was the first to react. Stepping forward, he swung the sceptre down onto her, like a boy aiming to break a rat's back with a stick. Metal hit stone with a resounding crunch. Mawrdreth sucked in a sore breath of horror – only to see that Andamanque had been too quick.

The sceptre struck bare rock and the crystal orb rattled in its mount. The Keeper had vanished. The lavender light was sucked back into the crevice, a moan echoed in the distance. The lamps wavered.

So, Mawrdreth thought, Uryzht has a hell of a vicious streak for a scholar. Even the quiet ones are fanatics.

When all was still again, Rhazagramen turned to Uryzht, the amethyst key clasped firmly in his spidery fingers.

'Foolish interruptions aside, shall we continue?'

Mawrdreth looked on helplessly as Rhazagramen bent down to the chest and pressed the key home into the lock. There was a familiar *crunch* as it clicked home. Then Uryzht leaned in and lifted the lid.

Yes, they'd done this before. The tablets of stone shone as if lit from underneath, layer on layer of translucent crystal like a deep mysterious pool. They must have lifted out the slabs and stood in sheer frustration – as he once had – when they realised they couldn't make out a word of it.

He wasn't sure quite what the Bhahdradomen stood to gain from the slabs, but he could guess. He and Helan hadn't finished the painstaking process of translating the cryptic language. But they'd found no shortage of dangerous information there; secrets about the War of the Silver Plains, the Basilisks . . .

'This is all we want of you,' said Rhazagramen, straightening up. 'Show us how to read the slabs.'

'We must have this knowledge,' Uryzht hissed. 'Knowledge.'

'I can't,' Mawrdreth said evenly. 'You know I can't.'

Rhazagramen looked at him for a moment, loathing naked in his wizened face. Uryzht called *'Vagharim!'* Moments later, Tanthe was dragged struggling into the little cave. Seeing her fear, he felt sick.

Tanthe was pale and her eyes glittered with fury. She shook her head at Mawrdreth, as if to say, 'Tell them nothing.' Sweat plastered dark strands of her hair to her forehead. He realised that he was sweating too, despite the cold. His only hope – Andamanque – was gone, and all he'd done was nearly get her killed.

'We thought it in bad taste to threaten your wife with torture, since she's indisposed,' said Rhazagramen, 'so we brought this one instead. I've forgotten its name . . . Tanthe, is that correct?'

Tanthe was struggling fruitlessly, making outraged noises in her throat, *mnnph mnnph*. Mawrdreth looked on in dread as Rhazagramen drew a short black rod from his belt.

The rod lengthened and hummed. Mawrdreth smelled *gauroth*, a foul mingling of hot metal and blood. That was their power, he knew. Not only to feed on emanations of pain, but to store and channel them into lethal bolts of fire or lightning.

Rhazagramen let the tip of the rod dance over Tanthe's face. She winced and pulled away. Thoughtfully, he brushed the tip over the contours of her cheeks, down over her neck and collarbone, as if idly teasing her. The tip drifted over her shoulders; then he suddenly brought it over her collarbone and dug it into the side of her throat.

Tanthe emitted a muffled scream and bent double. The guards pulled her upright again and she leaned back against the wall as if her legs would barely support her. A red weal came up on her throat. Sweat gleamed on her face.

Staring straight at Mawrdreth, she tried to say something; *mn-mn mmnn*! He understood her effort. 'Mawrdreth, don't!'

From the defiance in her eyes, he knew what she meant. Not, *don't let them do this to me*, but, *don't give in to them!* As brave as Branq'elin or Helan.

Rhazagramen tapped a light rhythm over her shoulder and down her breastbone, a delicate staccato trail that stopped just above her heart. Tanthe strained in her captors' hands, uttering a raw growl of agony. The sound faded to a rasp, then she appeared to pass out. The guards shoved her roughly back against the wall. It all happened so fast, he was still drawing breath to react.

'Stop!' he shouted. The other two *vagharim* seized his arms with a grip like steel rope.

Tanthe came round, her head rolling from side to side against the cave wall.

'I am toying with her,' said Rhazagramen, stroking the dark rod. 'Do you want to see what this *sten* can really do? It cuts.' Casually he flicked it across Tanthe's upper arm. 'It burns.' He touched it to her collarbone and she jerked, her eyes rolling up in their sockets. Another blister bubbled. 'It can stop a human heart.'

'Don't,' Mawrdreth said, low and hoarse.

'I can do this all day,' said Rhazagramen. 'It's all humans are good for; reservoirs of pain to quench our thirst. However, I don't have all day. The chest, if you will?'

'Yes, just stop,' Mawrdreth said desperately. 'Don't touch her again. There was never any need to touch her! You did that for the hell of it! Now leave her!'

Rhazagramen smiled and slipped the *sten* back into his belt. The guards let Mawrdreth go. Moving slowly, never taking his eyes off the *bharu'grothrim*, Mawrdreth bent down to the chest and lifted out the top slab, an oblong of pale gold crystal. Rhazagramen took it greedily. Mawrdreth watched him, no longer seeing him as an old, wise mage, but as what he was. A little sadist who thought that humans were the lowest form of life.

Uryzht pushed eagerly alongside his comrade. Their small eyes scanned the slab.

'The problem is to read it,' he said impatiently, turning it this way and that in the lamplight.

'There's a secret to it,' Mawrdreth said, trying to steady his breathing. It repulsed him to use their grandiose titles, but he forced himself. 'Lord Enlightener Uryzht, the Sceptre of Clear Sight must be placed to stand in a certain slot in the chest wall . . . If you will permit me?'

'I wish you would,' Uryzht said irritably. 'Your co-operation is overdue.'

Uryzht let him take the staff. Mawrdreth moved around the chest, so that he was facing them across it, and lifted the staff to guide the base of the shaft into its carved niche. As he slid it home, the orb began to glow red.

'Now, hold the slab to the light,' he said. 'As the light shines through, you will be able to read the script.'

Rhazagramen and Uryzht both moved forward, intent on the slab. He saw the familiar lines of light running along the carved letters. They both made noises of amazement, and said something to each other in their own language.

Mawrdreth still had his hands around the staff. He seized it out of its niche and swung it down on their necks, felling them both. He heard Rhazagramen's skull crack on the corner of the chest. He lay still, but Uryzht lurched up at once, groping for a weapon.

Mawrdreth stabbed the end of the staff through Uryzht's left eye socket, bursting the eyeball and piercing the soft matter of the brain.

His stomach heaved, but he ignored it and wrenched the sceptre free. All four guards were on him, pulling weapons from their belts. He swung the royal staff like an axe. The orb connected with the first one's head, knocking him sideways. Then Mawrdreth found himself fending off three crackling whip-like *tzirin* with the staff, knowing that if one touched him it would take him down. He felt shocks entering the staff, travelling painfully through his body, making his limbs jump, but he held on.

The only sure way to kill them was to pierce them through the eyes, he knew that. Wound them on the body and they just kept coming.

Tanthe was on her knees, crawling along behind him. He didn't see what she was doing, couldn't spare her a glance as he parried with the guards. One was trying a *sten* now, but couldn't reach past the length of the staff. A *tzirin* caught his wrist and he gasped.

Tanthe rose awkwardly to her feet beside him with Rhazagramen's *sten* clasped awkwardly between her chained hands. In the same motion, she thrust it straight into the abdomen of his attacker. There was a crackle, a stink of burned flesh. The guard collapsed with a squawk. He lay there writhing and trying to get up again.

Mawrdreth hefted the staff in one hand and took the *sten* from her in the other. He finished the guard who was down – pushing the rod-tip into his eye – without taking his attention from the others.

Meanwhile Tanthe was crouching again, wresting another weapon from Rhazagramen's collection. One of the *vagharim* dodged past Mawrdreth and went for her instead.

She spun, fast as a dancer, and kicked out, catching the guard across the side of the head so that his own momentum carried him to the floor. He landed across the chest, on top of Uryzht. Before he could rise, Mawrdreth turned and half-severed his head with the *sten*. The smell of singed Bhahdradomen flesh was oddly sweet.

Then there was only one guard left. He went down slowly and stubbornly, under many blows from the sceptre; but at last he went down, his skull misshapen like a cracked egg.

Gasping for breath, sick to his stomach, Mawrdreth fumbled to undo Tanthe's chains. They weren't locked, only bound tightly around her wrists. He quickly released her, and she pulled the gag off herself before he could touch it. She caught several deep breaths and rubbed at her crabbed wrists.

'Bastards,' she was the first thing she said. '*Bastards*.'

'Help me, quickly,' Mawrdreth said, already busy. Together they stripped every weapon they could find from the guards – five of the *tzirin*, six *sten*, and four ordinary short swords that must have been taken from the Citadel's own armoury. As he bent over the last guard, he heard breath come from its lips. It opened its eyes, lunged at him – and Tanthe was there, bringing a sword-edge down on his throat. In a crunch of cartilage, she half-severed its head.

'You *can* kill them,' she panted, pushing her hair off her forehead. 'They don't bleed much, do they? They look like they're never going to die.'

'Come on,' said Mawrdreth.

They hurried to the stairs. The winding ascent through the dank throat of the stairwell seemed painfully slow, even taking the steps two at a time. More *vagharim* might be in the chamber of the *xauroth* sphere; if so, he and Tanthe were ready. He carried the staff in one hand, and in the other one of the *sten*; a nasty, effective weapon, that could stab like a stiletto or kill with fire.

The chamber was deserted. The sphere lay dark and lifeless. Mawrdreth laid a hand on it briefly as he passed, a promise.

'If we go back into the palace, we'll be fucked,' Tanthe said succinctly.

'There's another way that Helan showed me. A secret way.'

He went round to the far side of the sphere and found the entrance to the small, secret passage that Garnelys had once used. Helan had meant to have it blocked off, but like so many other plans, there hadn't been time.

They climbed the second flight of narrow stone stairs – the dim glow of the Orb lighting their way – and came up at last into a little dark cell, a space hidden between the walls of the most ancient part of the Citadel. Tanthe had dropped behind. Mawrdreth paused to let her catch up. They were both breathing hard; the climb had been long.

'We'll rest in here for a few minutes; it should be safe.'

'Thank Breyid,' said Tanthe, leaning against a wall and slumping over to get her breath back.

'How are the wounds?'

'I'm all right,' she answered, straightening up. Her eyes squeezed shut with pain. 'Oh, Anthar's balls, it's sore. I've never felt anything like it. Like being dabbed with a red-hot poker.' She probed at a blister on her neck, and winced. In the Orb-light, it was livid crimson. 'I'm all right as long as I keep moving, and don't think about it.'

'Gods,' Mawrdreth breathed in horror at what had happened. What *might* have happened. 'I wish they'd tried it on me instead. Bloody cowards.'

'He was just playing, Mawr. I'm glad he didn't get serious.' She put her hand to her lips suddenly. Her eyes shone, but she mastered herself. 'Shit, I was so scared. Thanks – thanks for getting us out. That was the sort of mad thing Rufryd would have done.'

'I could have got us both killed, of course,' he said, with a quick grimace. 'It was as much thanks to you. You fight well. You're very fast.'

'I had a lot of practice, what with Garnelys,' she said. 'The Shaelahyr were good teachers.'

'Fighting with your hands chained together; *that* was the sort of mad thing Branq'elin would have done.'

'I'll take that as a compliment.' She gave a shaky smile. 'Now what are we going to do?'

'There's a way out of here to one of Garnelys's old chambers,' he said. 'Whether there will be Eaters in it, I don't know. They'll certainly be in the corridors outside.'

'No other way of escaping?' she said. 'Of course not, how could there be. And even if there was, we can't just flee without trying to rescue the others.'

'No. And this is our chance, our *only* chance.'

They looked at each other. There was pain in Tanthe's face, but her expression was perky, defiant and brave, like his sister. He knew she wouldn't let him down; he mustn't let her down, either.

He placed the sceptre in a niche in the stonework, hoping the Eaters wouldn't find it. It was the best hiding place he could find, in the circumstances. He looked sadly at its dented metalwork; the damage seemed to enhance its nobility, in a sad way. Then he hung the weapons in a bundle off a belt he'd taken from one of the guards and slung it over his shoulders, all except a sword and a *sten* each for him and Tanthe.

'D'you know the way back to our quarters?' she asked. 'I don't know the palace that well. Every time I come here, I get lost.'

'I don't have Helan's knowledge, but yes, I can find the way.'

'Come on, then.'

'You are courageous, Tanthe,' he said.

'No, Mawr,' she said. 'I am absolutely shit-scared. We are probably going to be dead within about half an hour;

and we have no choice at all but to go and meet it head-on.'

Tanthe hadn't lied. She was terrified, yet excited. It was like the time she and Rufryd and Lynden had set out after Ysomir; frightening, but a thousand times better than staying miserably at home. Or like going into the Battle of Hethlas Rim; at least that meant it would be over soon. And it had been over, once and for all, for poor Lynden.

The small chamber in the tower, which had once been a favourite haunt of Garnelys's, was empty. Tanthe shivered with relief. Perhaps the old King haunted it quite literally now. She was out of breath again from the twisting stairway that led up from the cell, and her burns throbbed in time with her pulse. Her chest and neck were on fire; all she could do was keep moving, try to ignore the pain. Now if the outer door was locked, they would be in even more of a mess.

Halfway across the chamber, she saw a pale grey cloak lying across a chair. She took two steps past it, stopped, and turned back to take it.

'What are you doing?' Mawdreth whispered.

'I've got an idea.' She swung the cloak onto her shoulders, pulled the hood deep over her head. It reached just to her feet. She was glad she'd stayed in the habit of wearing a shirt and breeches, rather than palace robes. 'You're too tall, and there's only the one cloak, so it will have to be me.'

A Bhahdradomen had worn this cloak; a fairly tall one, at that. She could smell the characteristic dry, fungal scent, not bad, but not pleasant either; rousing too many frightening memories.

Mawrdreth he shook his head. 'It will never work.'

'I used to act a bit, back in Riverwynde,' she said, as they reached the golden oak door. 'We'd put plays on, to celebrate the festivals. The villagers never took it seriously, like they were meant to, but still, I wasn't bad.'

Mawrdreth turned the handle. Every small noise seemed to reverberate. For all his care, the door opened with an alarming creak; but there was no-one outside. There was a short, broad passageway leading to another set of stairs.

'This will take us down from the tower and back into the main body of the palace,' Mawrdreth said softly.

'Let me go first.'

'No.'

'I must. I'll confuse them, buy us a bit more time.'

They met no-one on the stairs, nor in the confusing warren of chambers and narrow corridors that lay below the tower. Tanthe knew the invaders were using these rooms. Their scent hung in the air, thick as spores. The atmosphere was different. She felt it even more strongly as they came out into a broad gallery in the newer section of the palace. Instead of the air of golden, inspiring solemnity she remembered, there was a sense of something watchful, oppressive yet frenetically active, just out of sight. Spiders spinning.

They saw their first party of Bhahdradomen, crossing the end of the gallery. Mawrdreth pulled Tanthe into an alcove and they stood holding their breath. The *domenim* passed on without seeing them.

Several times they saw groups of *yrim* patrolling the corridors, and a couple of assistants to Vaurgroth's elite hurrying along on business of some kind. Each time, Tanthe and Mawrdreth were able to hide themselves in a niche, behind a door, or in the mouth of a narrow stairwell that only the human staff ever used. She was sure the Eaters must smell their sweat, but apparently they weren't as perceptive as she'd feared. Or else they weren't concentrating. Six Bhahdradomen lay dead in the underground chamber . . . how long would it take for them to be discovered and the alarm to be raised?

Their journey rushed past in a jagged blur until they reached the corridor that led back to their quarters. Here they paused, Mawrdreth looking as anxious as she felt. This was the most dangerous place of all, a wide, curving passageway with several junctures from which *yrim* might appear, and nowhere to hide. And Bhahdradomen definitely awaiting them at the end.

As they'd planned, Tanthe went first. Although she knew Mawrdreth was following, just out of sight round the curve of the passageway, she felt alone and vulnerable.

She pulled the hood deep over her face, kept her hands covered. She was too tall to pass for most Bhahdradomen, really, but if she hunched over she was more the right height and it meant the hem covered her boots. She tried to walk as they did; a sort of springing glide off the hocks, shoulders forward, head down a little. Hands firmly on the weapons beneath her cloak. She favoured the sword; knew where she was with a sword.

Presently she came in sight of the double doors to their chambers, an arch of polished oak as golden as the amber walls. *Vagharim* were standing guard. Her heart kicked. There were three, and they were so still at their post that she could believe they were taxidermy specimens, with unblinking glass eyes.

Hurry. She was only going to fool them for a moment.

She broke into a shuffling run, keeping her chin down. 'Humans!' she exclaimed in a rasp. 'They've broken free!' She pointed behind her, keeping her hand inside the wide sleeve. 'Quick, help us!'

The three guards jerked into life, scuttling down the corridor in Mawrdreth's direction. As soon as they were past her, she followed and took the hindmost one down from behind. Mawrdreth was waiting. The leading two died almost instantly, one with a sword through the eye, the other a *sten*. The last one uttered a shriek that seemed to echo all over the palace.

Tanthe raced back to the doors, put her sword to them and began trying to pry them open. Three seconds later, Mawrdreth was beside her, with the keys in his hand.

They were through the little ante-chamber and into the main room.

Inside, Eldareth, Elrill and Auriel stood gaping at them in amazement.

'Right,' said Tanthe, pushing the hood back. 'We're going to escape and we're going to do it *now*.'

'But what—' Eldareth began.

'No arguing. If we don't do it *right* now, there will be dozens of guards here and our only chance will be gone forever. Weapons . . .'

Mawrdreth gave her the bundle of stolen weapons and she distributed them. Meanwhile he vanished into his bed-chamber and emerged, a moment later, with a startled-looking Helan. She was pale, but Mawrdreth was clearly not going to tolerate any argument.

'Tanthe, what have you done?' said Eldareth. He and Elrill were active at once, helping her, their eyes keen with the relief of doing something at last.

'Mawrdreth and I have just killed three Eaters in the corridor. Oh, and another six in a cave, including Uryzht and Rhazagramen.'

'You've killed *Rhazagramen*? He's Vaurgroth's—'

'I know,' Tanthe said, feeling suddenly sick with dread. 'So we're really in trouble, aren't we? If we don't go right this minute . . .'

'This is mad,' Eldareth said, grinning fiercely. 'We haven't a hope.'

'Yes, we have,' answered Elrill. He was a calm ice-white presence, reassuring. 'Tanthe, Auriel, remember what we practised together? We have no proof that it will work on the Eaters, but we can try.'

That steadied her. 'One thing. I can't leave the Citadel without Ysomir. I don't care what the rest of you do, I must find her.'

'No,' said Helan, coming to her. Tanthe had doubted she would be well enough to make the attempt, but her eyes gleamed with desperate energy. 'If we're going to get out, we have to take the shortest route. We'd never make it to the prison section.'

Tanthe flared, 'Do you really still hate her so much, that you'd just leave her?'

'No, of course not!' Helan said, gripping her shoulders. 'I don't hate her, and if she was along the corridor, as my mother is, I'd say of course we'll take her. But she isn't. It's physically impossible to do it, even for you on your own. Believe me, you would not make it! If we're to have a chance, we can't even consider it. I won't let you.'

Tanthe knew she was right. She could have screamed with frustration. *What am I to do?* she thought. *Abandon my sister, or sacrifice my own life in a hopeless rescue attempt? I don't even know if Ymmi's still alive . . .*

Auriel was watching her, wide-eyed. 'Don't just stand there, take one of these weapons,' she snapped.

He looked paralysed. She was afraid his tenuous courage had failed him. Then to her astonishment, he reached inside a pocket and drew out two small, dull-grey knives.

'I have these,' he said.

'*Mnelir!*' Tanthe gasped. 'Did you take these from Falthorn?' He nodded sheepishly. 'Why didn't you tell me?'

'I didn't know how. There was no chance to use them, anyway.'

'Give one to me!' She swallowed. 'Sorry, Auriel. Please?'

'Helan,' Eldareth was saying softly, 'it may be a dreadful liability to take your mother and brother with us.'

'I don't care. I'm not going without them.'

Tanthe fumed silently at the injustice of rescuing Ghiseyma but not Ysomir. She could only hope there might be a chance later. Pushing her emotions aside, she waited impatiently as the others threw off cumbersome robes; glad now they'd all agreed to wear practical gear and boots underneath, just in case the chance of escape came.

Armed and ready, the six of them crept out into the passage. It was deserted. It had only taken a couple of minutes to leave the chamber so if the shape-changers had been alerted, they must be on their way. Tanthe observed the others' shock as they passed the three dead *vagharim*.

Moving lightly, they came in sight of another set of double doors on the left. Tanthe and Mawrdreth had passed these doors a few minutes ago and thought nothing of it. Now Helan seemed concerned.

'I don't understand,' she said. 'That's where Mother and Veny were. There were guards on these doors, as there were on ours. Something's wrong.'

'A trap?' suggested Eldareth.

Moving cautiously, looking up and down the corridor, listening hard for the slightest sound through the door, they edged towards the chamber. One of the double doors stood slightly ajar.

Elrill slid his sword through the gap, cautiously pushing back the door. Then with a rush he thrust it open fully and strode into the room, spinning to confront anyone who might be lurking behind it.

'No-one here,' he said.

'No-one?' said Helan, pushing in after him. They all entered, Eldareth last, closing the door behind them.

Tense, speaking only in faint rushed whispers, they made their way through one chamber after another, opening cupboard doors, prodding at the heavy folds of curtains. There were signs of the princess's recent occupation; a grey hair or two on a pillow, a cup with cold tea drying in the bottom, a book left open face-down like a fallen butterfly on the bedcover. Helan picked up a white shirt, discarded on a chair, that must have been her brother's.

Helan stood in the centre of the largest bedroom, a room made claustrophobic by the huge canopied bed, tall wardrobes of dark wood, drapes of thick midnight silk. She picked up the book and shook it – perhaps to see if a note would fall out – then threw it down again.

'Where are they?' she said, bewildered.

'They must have been moved,' said Eldareth.

Helan's face was bleak with shock. 'No-one informed me. Where would they have been taken, and why?'

'We've no way of finding out,' Eldareth said gravely. 'That being the case, we'll have to go without them.'

Tanthe grimaced. Now Helan must feel as bad as she did about Ymmi, but there was no satisfaction in knowing it, just more distress.

'Come on,' said Eldareth.

As he spoke, there were voices from the main chamber. Bhahdradomen voices, speaking their own language, then switching to Paranian.

Tanthe's heart felt as if it was trying to gallop out of her chest. They all looked at each other, their faces expressing helpless horror.

'They would not have been rash enough to come in here,' said the mild, sinister voice of Naghrur. Just the sound of his voice woke an intense response of fear. Tanthe's skin crawled; her wounds tingled and burned. 'They will have fled to a further part of the palace by now.'

'Perhaps,' said an older voice, hissing with malice. 'But I want every chamber searched.'

Tanthe thought she was going to pass out. She and Mawrdreth stared at each other. The voice, unmistakably, belonged to Rhazagramen.

'Every inch of the palace combed, Naghrur,' Rhazagramen continued. 'They'll suffer for Uryzht's death. Even more will they regret that they tried to kill me!'

Chapter Eight. Webs of Fire

Ysomir always knew when something was wrong. It was a difference in the air, like the resonance of faint sounds beyond the physical level of hearing. Something was changing, but the *ethroths* didn't enlighten her.

Zhoaah was late. When he arrived, she knew before he said anything that there was someone with him, waiting outside.

'I have brought a visitor to see you,' he said with a lipless smile.

'Tanthe?'

Before the name was out, she knew she'd made a mistake. Tanthe would have come straight in. Tanthe didn't emanate the magnetic waves of menace that began to buffet her.

'No.' Zhoaah sounded sad to have let her down. 'Someone else.'

The being that came into her cell was a column of thunderous crimson power, shot through with flashes of lightning. Darkest crimson, almost black on the outside, with a blazing scarlet core. Terrible red eyes stared at her from the centre of the column.

She cried out, backing away until she was pressed up against her writing table. An hallucination, a sudden nightmare. She could make no sense of what she was seeing, but it filled her with wildest terror.

'Ysomir?' said Zhoaah, holding her elbow. 'What's wrong? Please, this is no way to greet your visitor.'

He, too, was a hostile presence. She'd lost her mind. She wondered for a moment if she were dreaming and if so, could she wake herself up?

'What does it want?' she gasped.

'Ysomir,' Zhoaah said tightly. 'Please. What's the matter with you? You are highly honoured!'

She squeezed her eyes shut. When she dared to open them again, the thunder-column had gone. There was only a *domenim* dressed in a silver tunic of velvet-soft skin. The tunic had a long ragged collar, and each point of the collar had a small red stone. There was a blood-red crystal held on his forehead with a fillet of silver. His face was smooth and even more human-looking than Zhoaah's; the high white dome of his skull was tattooed with a scarlet web. From it came a white braid of hair, woven with arcane stones. His eyes were overwhelming; fiery, fatherly, terrifying.

At his side was an animal, a sort of hound covered in green-gold scales. It was grotesque and beautiful at the same time. It kept its muzzle raised, eyes fixed on its master.

The *domenim* regarded her and she stared back. Suddenly she realised where she'd seen that red crystal before. It was the circlet set with a large almandine that only the monarch wore.

'You can't wear that,' she said, before she could stop herself.

Zhoaah winced. 'My apologies, Master of Light,' he said, with a dipping motion. 'I don't know why she's behaving like this.'

'It's natural,' said the stranger. His voice was rich and melodic, somehow reassuring. 'She recognises me. Ysomir, come forward.'

Reluctantly, she peeled herself off the table-edge and took a couple of steps towards him. She couldn't see the power that swirled around him now, but she could still feel it. It was as strong as the force that held her to the ground, and it snapped little darts of pain at her.

'Do you know who I am?'

'Vaurgroth.'

'Greatlord Vaurgroth, Lord of Light,' Zhoaah put in quickly. 'Chosen of the Ancestor.'

'Never mind titles,' said Vaurgroth. 'She knows me. That's good enough.' He nodded. 'That's very good indeed. Don't be afraid, Ysomir. I've been looking forward to meeting you.'

The paradox was unbearable. His warm reassuring manner, and the terrible *gauroth* around him. He reached out his hand and she thought that if he touched her, she would die; but she didn't. The killing jolt of horror didn't come.

His hand on hers was hot and dry. His thumb pressed her palm, while the six fingers caressed the back of her hand. Unlike Zhoaah's fine digits, Vaurgroth's were thicker, with a hint of deformity about them; the last one not much more than a stump, the skin pink and papery like scar tissue. She had to swallow her distaste down hard.

'I don't know why everyone is so eager to talk to me,' she said coldly. The hound gave a jerk of its head. It was no animal; it had the same alien aura as its master.

Vaurgroth only smiled, and let her hand fall. He saw her looking at his pet, and said, 'We can change, Ysomir. We can all change.'

'Your hound is . . . Bhahdradomen?'

'You can tell. *Ghelim.*'

'Why?' she said.

'Why did he change his shape to please me? Why do I take pleasure in such a companion? Who can answer such mysteries? Humans love their pets, Ysomir. I thought you would understand that.'

'I never thought . . .'

'What? That we too are capable of love?'

She couldn't answer. Vaurgroth went on, 'But you are right. I should not be wearing this.'

He took the almandine off his head and slid it over his pet's narrow skull. The royal circlet hung crookedly on its neck. A dog collar.

Zhoaah made a hissing noise. She looked at him and

realised he was trying not to laugh. Her throat hurt and a laugh burst from her; she couldn't stop it and it wasn't amusement. This was horrific, not funny, like some bizarre pantomime, yet she had to let out that dry laugh of disbelief or go mad. Vaurgroth joined in and for a few moments they were all laughing like mad puppets. The shape-changed hound sat proudly with the sacred circlet of Aventuria round its neck, basking in the attention as an ordinary dog would have done; showing no sign of higher intelligence.

'A drink,' said Zhoaah at last. He produced a long thin flask of yellow metal, and poured a tiny quantity into each of three beakers. He handed one to Ysomir and she gazed suspiciously at the yellow liquid.

'Try it,' said Zhoaah. 'It won't poison you.'

'What is it?'

'Crushed *ghelim*,' said Vaurgroth. 'The distilled blood of a hundred *domenim*.'

'A liqueur made from fermented herbs, actually,' Zhoaah said confidentially. They stood teasing her, smiling at her, but their humour wasn't friendly. She remembered feeling like this years ago, when she'd been a small child and Rufryd had teased her in the same falsely smiling way. He'd changed, but her fear hadn't.

'To our Ancestor's glory,' said Vaurgroth.

She had no choice. Tensing her jaw she raised the beaker and swallowed the liquid in one gulp. It burned its way down, and didn't taste bad after all. Sour and hot, but palatable.

'You're meant to sip it,' Zhoaah said, smiling. 'It's in short supply, you know.'

She was afraid they would make her drink more, but apparently one toast was enough. Zhoaah put the beakers to one side.

Vaurgroth said, 'Facilitator has told me a lot about you.'

'Oh?'

When he turned his full attention on her, he was overwhelming. She sensed that he was only cruel when it was expedient, not for the sake of it. But he was ruthless. A fanatic, replete with the power he needed to stay in supreme control. Yet she saw thirst in his eyes. His authority was laced, she realised, with a desperate hunger to be loved.

The revelation shocked her. So, power wasn't enough for him. Vaurgroth thought he had a divine right to be adored.

'You're very interesting,' he said.

'Not really.'

'Do you know what I'm talking about?'

The red eyes slid into her. His hands were on her arms, his odd scent of iron and dust filling her head. 'I think so.'

'The *ethroths*, Ysomir. Show them to me.'

'No,' she gasped, trying to pull away from him. On the second jerk, she managed it. She drew a huge breath to yell, 'NO!'

Her voice was so loud it hurt her own ears. The hound rose to its feet. The two Bhahdradomen stared at her, apparently startled. She'd startled herself.

'I didn't mean to distress you,' Vaurgroth said gently. His eyes were steady. 'Be at ease. We won't make you do anything you don't want to.'

'I will never want to do this.'

'It's all right,' said Vaurgroth, as soothing as a human physician. 'When the time comes, you will be ready. And it won't hurt. You'll be free of the burden.'

With an ominous smile he turned and walked out, the rope of white hair swinging between his shoulders. His *ghelim* went with him. Zhoaah remained, and Ysomir turned on him.

'I thought you were my friend!'

'I am!' Zhoaah opened his hands apologetically, but his ink-black eyes were angry.

'I thought you were protecting me. Letting me stay here and keeping the others away from me.'

'Ysomir, no harm is going to come to you. You are a fascinating, singular individual. Vaurgroth is naturally interested, I couldn't hide your existence from him.'

'You're no better than the Queen!'

'You sound as if you had expected me, a mere *domenim*, to be *better* than your beloved ex-Queen? Extraordinary. I am . . . flattered, I think.'

'You Goddess-forsaken bastard!' she cried, throwing a book at him. He dodged and it hit the wall. 'All she wanted to do with me was use me. And you are the same!'

He came after her, trying to soothe her, but she evaded him.

'You told Vaurgroth about me! How could you? So he thinks I'm full of some weird power or knowledge, and he wants to suck it out of me? Hasn't he got enough?'

Zhoaah stopped chasing her. He stood very still, a wax figure with eyes of clotted blood, and she saw the stark lie of his friendship.

'I'll warn you now, he will come back and he will get what he wants. It will be easier if you don't fight him; I don't want you to be hurt. Sleep well, Ysomir.'

He left, closing the cell door behind him. It was beginning to get dark and she was shaking so badly she didn't think she could manage to light the lamps.

She sank down on the edge of her bed. There was no warder to call for help or company. She couldn't eat or sleep, write or rest; she felt unable to do anything but sit and watch the door, waiting for the pale shadow of Vaurgroth to come in and steal all she had left; take Serenis, take Lynden, perhaps even take the essence of Ysomir herself.

She sat for a while with her hands pressed between her knees, rocking. Then she reached beneath the mattress and drew out the *silvenroth* mirror Tanthe had given her. It was a disc of milky quartz, an Aelyr device. Her mother had a similar one back in Riverwynde. Ysomir had used it a few times; stared into the mirror until she sank into a trance, let her mind float into the *silvenroth* layers until Aynie answered. Then they could see and speak to each other.

In a way it made it harder for both of them. They never knew what to say, and one or other of them always wept. Ysomir stroked the edge of the mirror and thought, What's the point? Mum can't help me. All this will do is drive her out of her mind with worry, because until now she thought I was safe . . .

Still, I should tell her about the Bhahdradomen in Parione. It isn't fair not to warn her. And if she tells me they're in Riverwynde? Can I bear to know that?

She stared into the mirror and tried to concentrate. Her reflection turned dark, cloudy. Spinning into the cloud and there was nothing on the other side . . . . she jerked out of the trance in alarm. Whether the fault lay in her or in a disruption of the *roth* itself, the link wouldn't come.

Bereft, she paced the room, hugging herself. All colour had bled from the scene and the sandy walls were the grey of dust. Even the thought of writing held no comfort. She hadn't been this frightened since she'd first been taken from Riverwynde . . . or since her time with Garnelys. For the first time, she went to the door and tried the handle.

It was locked. She backed away and stood shivering. For months her cell had been her refuge; now, again, it was just a prison.

The Bhahdradomen worked their way through the room, opening wardrobes, peering under the bed, thrusting their *sten* into the thick folds of the curtains. Finally Naghrur said, 'Enough! They are not here.'

'Then where are they?' said Rhazagramen's voice from the doorway.

'I don't know, but not here.' The *vagharim* were leaving the room, but Naghrur remained where he was. Eldareth could see his gnarled feet from where he hung, arms straining and legs braced, flattened to the underside of the bed frame. The Bhahdradomen had glanced on the floor beneath the bed, but they hadn't looked up to check beneath the mattress.

'They could be on the far side of the palace by now! I was sure they would come for the princess and hatchling.'

'As was I,' said Naghrur's steel-silk voice. 'Which is why I had them moved.'

Eldareth was shaking with the exertion of holding himself in that position. Silently he willed them to leave.

'I'm far from convinced of the wisdom of that decision,' Rhazagramen said sourly.

'To send them to Torith Mir?' said Naghrur. Eldareth nearly dropped to the floor with shock. 'It is neutral territory. The Sapphire Throne was traded for their lives, and so their lives must be preserved.'

A dry sound of scorn came from Rhazagramen's throat. 'Their lives are worthless, in my view.'

'But Vaurgroth is an honourable *domen*. There is no point in making codes unless we abide by them.'

'Such a stickler for the rules, Protector. How much more gratifying to have taken the hot needles to them.'

'We are not here to enjoy ourselves,' Naghrur said icily. 'We're here to implement Vaurgroth's will. The human hostages have become a nuisance, an irrelevance. However, Master of Light wishes it to be seen that he's merciful. In Torith Mir they're out of harm's way.'

'The Queen's a spent force anyway,' Rhazagramen said, forgetting in his haste the ex. 'Still, she must be found, if Vaurgroth is not to dispatch us prematurely into Ancestor's presence. He won't be so merciful to us. Nor am I feeling merciful to those who almost split my skull open.' His tone became a threat. 'We *will* find them, or . . .'

'I will take responsibility for this,' Naghrur said softly.

'Yes,' Rhazagramen snapped. 'You will.'

Naghrur was on his way to the door, his feet making a dry whisper on the marble tiles. Eldareth hung on a few moments longer, sweating. He heard their voices fade, the closing of the outer door. Silence.

His arms were giving out. He let himself down, feet and backside first, then shoulders, rolled from under the bed and stood up. Above him, the faces of Helan and Mawrdreth appeared over the edge of the canopy. With groans and sighs, Tanthe and Elrill appeared from behind the curtains where they'd concealed themselves, not at floor level, but clinging to the curtain rail in the recess high above the Bhahdradomen's heads. And Auriel let himself down lightly from the top of the wardrobe, where he'd been curled up behind a high, ornate pediment. Helan and Mawrdreth climbed down from their perch and they gathered around Eldareth, exhaling their shock and relief.

'They didn't look too thoroughly,' Tanthe said, rubbing her left shoulder.

'Don't complain,' said Eldareth.

'They've taken Mother and Veny to Torith Mir,' said Helan. 'Did you hear?'

'Yes,' said Mawrdreth, 'and they said they'll be safe.'

'I can't believe it. What do they mean, Torith Mir is neutral?'

'We should have a talk about Torith Mir another time,' Eldareth said gravely. 'But for now, it's one less thing to worry about.' He peered round the door into the main chamber. 'All clear. Come on.'

'Where are we going?' asked Tanthe. 'We need a plan, or it's pointless!'

'I have an idea,' said Helan. There was some colour in her face, and she was behaving more like her old self, decisive and resolute. Her eyes, though, were emotionless. She looked, Eldareth thought with a heavy heart, like someone who was merely going through the motions. 'Along the corridor, there's a green and gold door narrower than the rest, that leads down to the staff quarters.'

'We passed it,' said Tanthe. 'We hid behind it.'

Elrill said, 'A hidden stairway? That may be the first place the Eaters will look.'

'It's not hidden,' said Helan. 'It's just a way for the staff to get to and from the main body of the palace. Let's hope that the Eaters have already looked there.'

'If not, it may be easier for us to take them on in a confined space,' said Eldareth. He felt a grim smile on his lips. 'Come on. Let's chance it.'

The curve of the corridor was empty. Tanthe went with a dry mouth, wondering how long they could spin out this adventure before the inevitable end. She was exhausted, functioning purely on nervous excitement, refusing to acknowledge the pain of her wounds or wonder what the Bhahdradomen would do when they caught them. It was like climbing a mountain; best not to look down.

The stairs behind the door were barely wide enough for two abreast. The stairwell was of plain sandy-gold stone, the unadorned fabric of the Citadel. It was a long way down to the staff quarters; the stairs turned, gave onto short corridors, ran downwards again. The way was lit by lamps, and windows here and there where the stairway met an outside wall. They went as quietly as they could, but their breathing and footfalls seemed loud in the silence. At every turn, other doors led into different parts of the palace. Tanthe watched each one, waiting for a party of Devourers to burst through. Not so long ago, she thought, these stairs must have been in constant use with the traffic of the palace. The quietness was ominous.

Mawrdreth and Helan went in front and Eldareth at the back. Tanthe was in the middle with Elrill beside her and Auriel just in front of them. She held the *mnelir* in her left hand and it glowed a little. Sudden heat would warn her of the Eaters.

'Remember what we practised,' said Elrill. 'Join with me.'

Auriel glanced round at them, his large eyes anxious. He hadn't enjoyed their meditation sessions but he had persisted. He gave Tanthe a faint smile of reassurance and she smiled back. She was proud of him for keeping so calm. As he'd said, nothing could frighten him as much as Falthorn had.

'Will it work on the Bhahdradomen?' she asked.

'I don't know,' said Elrill. 'We shall try.'

Tanthe made an effort to steady her breathing. It wasn't easy. They'd practised while sitting still and quiet, not while running down stairs with weapons in their hands. It was a strange feeling, letting her mind slip to a different level while all her senses remained alert for danger.

She felt the familiar sense of floating. She became aware of Elrill, not merely at her side, but as a white, cool presence pervading her mind and her vision. And Auriel flowed around her too; autumn-coloured, warm and gentle, nervous but with a core of nascent strength. They began to weave the web and she could *see* it; a net of white, red and indigo *roth*-fire, faintly overlaid on the air.

It flickered. It was full of holes, and as soon as they sealed one, another appeared. 'Keep your minds still,' said Elrill. 'Concentrate.'

'What are you doing?' asked Eldareth.

'Trying to confound our enemies. You will have to cover us; we can't do this and fight physically at the same time.'

'Well, if it doesn't work, Rill, you'd better shake it off and use those weapons,' Eldareth said shortly.

Tanthe was so preoccupied that she hardly registered the *mnelir* turning hot, the orb glowing. In the juncture of the stairs below them, a door opened.

An *yrim* stood looking up at them. He was fully armed but alone. Seeing them, he set his hand to his lightning-whip, opened his mouth to bark for his colleagues.

In that moment Elrill, Tanthe and Auriel acted as one to throw the net over him. He froze and stood blinking at them as if he had forgotten why he was there.

Tanthe felt a flicker of triumph. It was working. She poured her full concentration into the web as they began to creep past the *yrim*. The *mnelir* pulsed in her hand but she barely had the strength to hold it, let alone wield it.

Helan and Mawrdreth were on their way down the next flight of stairs, Tanthe and her companions passing the Devourer, when he began to stir. The web wasn't holding him. He was fighting it.

'Stop,' he said in a crow-like voice. He fell into his own language, Paranian apparently too much of a struggle, '*Manach ag urkhaliz . . .*'

Tanthe increased her efforts. Pain sang through her head. The web jumped wildly and she saw spots in front of her eyes. Through this snow she saw the *yrim* struggling forward and unfurling his weapon as if through treacle. Then Eldareth was there, striking out with his sword. The *tzirin* tangled with his blade and he gasped with pain.

'Eld!' hissed Tanthe. As he turned she threw the *mnelir* to him. It arced brightly through the air. The Eater stared at it with alarm. 'The heart!'

Eldareth caught the knife, turned and plunged it under the Eater's guard. The *yrim* convulsed over the blade, spilling pinkish-yellow plasma. With a rasp of anguish he collapsed. Eldareth stepped over him, quietly closed the door and pushed the body against it. That would obstruct anyone who tried to come through.

Quickly he wiped the blade and gave it back to her. They went on, more urgently now. They were almost at the lowest level of the palace.

'Now we know,' Elrill said presently. 'The web will slow them down, but not stop them.'

'Better than nothing,' said Auriel, 'but Elrill, I'm not sure I can sustain it much longer.'

'Neither can I,' said Tanthe. 'I didn't realise it would be so hard.' Her head ached. She felt it might burst if she didn't stop.

'Try a little longer.' Elrill was stern. 'We're no adepts, but we must try.'

Scents of cooking wafted to them, mingled with baking

bread, vegetables and the steamy dampness of laundry. The air became a blast of warmth. A short passageway ended in an arch, and beyond it lay the wide main room of the kitchen, with smaller rooms leading off through alcoves.

There was a fire in a large grate, long black stoves along one wall, a small forest of pans hanging above the preparation table in the centre. Men and women in blue tunics were working at the stoves. Others, in fancier robes of blue and gold, were sitting round the end of the table. Ten or eleven of them, young and old. Tanthe recognised some of the faces from the days of freedom; waiting staff and other palace attendants. There was a subdued air on the kitchen, not much conversation. Her eyes flicked around but she could see no Bhahdradomen.

As Helan's party entered, the staff nearest to them leapt to their feet in amazement. At once, Elrill flung the *roth*-web over them, stifling their exclamations. It worked more easily on humans. Tanthe felt that at once.

As soon as the staff were quiet, Elrill began gently to ease the net so that they could speak and move again. They looked bewildered. 'You all know me,' Helan said, striding forward. 'You must help us. Hide us from the shape-changers.'

The women and men looked stupefied. Some bowed and said, 'Your majesty.' Others looked less than awed to see her. With her senses enhanced by the web, Tanthe could perceive why; not that she could read their minds, simply that their body language became transparent to her. Some of them had been seduced to the Ancestor; others believed that Helan herself had betrayed them.

'Elrill,' she whispered. She began to concentrate the web on those individuals; he sensed what she was doing and helped. To silence the ones who were most likely to betray them, that was the crucial thing. The effort sent an arc of pain through her eyes, green and red fires fighting across her vision.

'I am still your servant,' said Helananthe, her voice thick.

'Whatever you've seen or heard, I have not gone to the shape-changers' side and never will. Some of you have known me all my life. I ask you humbly, help us; not for reward, but out of love.'

Tanthe heard the faint but distinct bark of a Bhahdradomen voice. 'They're coming,' she said.

The tableau broke. A small dark-haired woman in blue came rushing towards them from the stove. 'Come with me, ma'am, sire,' she said. 'I'll hide you.'

Tanthe realised it was the healer who'd come to them when Helan had collapsed.

Her head was whirling as the woman led them off to the right and into a large store-room. She couldn't see properly. The web was writhing, breaking up; she struggled to hold it, to weave her strands firmly with those of Elrill and Auriel.

Then for a second time they crouched in darkness and discomfort while *vagharim* and *yrim* raked through the kitchen and laundry and linen-rooms. Tanthe, half-suffocating under sacks of flour, felt the *mnelir*'s heat burning into her. She held the web until she sweated with the exertion; pushing it out over the humans who might betray them, out against the Bhahdradomen. *We are not here. You never saw us. This is the wrong place.*

Suddenly a sense of doom came over her. A grey despair that stopped her in her tracks and made her feel that only death would end this nightmare . . .

She realised what the feeling was. There was a Bhahdradomen standing very close to her; it was his aura she could feel. She peered hard through a thin part of the sacking and saw that it was Naghrur.

The sight of his scalpel-cold figure terrified her. She felt like rising from her hiding place and throwing herself at his feet. Just to get it over with.

She didn't. She sat tight. Pain gripped her head. She tried with all her strength to maintain the web but it was too much; in a shower of light-blobs it dissipated; she couldn't hold it any longer. She'd broken the circle with Elrill and Auriel, but they had been weakening too. Naghrur didn't seem to notice anything. He stood and watched as his guards made their search; yet they'd barely begun, it seemed, before he said, 'They are not in here. Continue in the laundry.'

The feeling passed. The *mnelir* lost its glow. A long time later – fifteen or twenty minutes – Tanthe heard the voice of the dark-haired woman again.

'They have gone, ma'am.'

From behind flour sacks, tubs of grain and beer barrels the six emerged, dust-covered and coughing. Tanthe feared for a moment that the healer herself had been pressured into betraying them; but no, she spoke the truth. Only humans crowded in the doorway of the store-room. The Bhahdradomen had gone.

Helan leaned on Mawrdreth. She looked ashen.

'Thank you for not giving us away. Thank you.'

They made their way back into the main kitchen, the staff parting to let them through. A boy brought glasses of water, which they drank gratefully. A handful of people went out into the passages, to keep watch for Bhahdradomen.

'If there are any here who are not loyal to you, ma'am, they know better than to act on those unworthy feelings,' said the healer, aiming her sharp words at the staff. She was about thirty, Tanthe guessed, small and plump with a round, intelligent face, her skin a beautiful dark-copper colour. Her hair, curling from beneath a blue kerchief, was black with ruby lights, her eyes midnight sapphires.

'Lahjaya,' Helan said.

'You remembered my name, ma'am.'

'Of course. We thank you for acting so swiftly to help us. How have the Bhahdradomen been treating you?'

'Quite well,' said an older woman who appeared to be in charge of the kitchen. 'They've been civilised enough. But it's not easy. Things have changed so much.'

There were murmurs of agreement.

'I know,' said Helan. Her eyes were glassy, her tone flat with despair. 'And I would give my life for none of this to have happened. The last thing I want is for any of you to be punished for sheltering us here. The sooner we are gone, the better; but I don't know how we are to escape, with three guarded walls to pass through. Perhaps if I gave myself up, in exchange for my companions' freedom . . .'

'No,' said Eldareth and Mawrdreth in unison.

Lahjaya shook her head vigorously. Her eyes glinted. 'Ma'am,' she said, lowering her voice, 'the palace staff are not held prisoner. Those of us who don't live in the palace are allowed to go home each night. We have passes. Let us choose six people who most resemble you physically, and you can leave in their place.'

Tanthe's heart looped in hope. 'But what will happen to them?'

'Nothing,' said the older woman. 'They can hide here tonight. Someone will bring their passes back in, and they'll leave as normal the night after.'

'D'you really think this will work?' said Tanthe. 'There's no one who looks like Elrill.'

A young man at the edge of the group cleared his throat. 'There's me,' he said. 'I know I look nothing like, but . . .'

He was lanky and gauche-looking with messy white-blond hair; a stark contrast to the elegant Shaelahyr. 'But the right height and nearly as pale,' said Eldareth.

'We all wear cloaks,' said Lahjaya. 'As often as not, we put up the hoods; shields us from the *yrim*, or at least, makes us feel better protected. They don't take much notice of us, anyway. Say we all look the same to them.'

A ripple of quiet laughter. Eldareth said, 'It's our only chance.'

'Then we'll do it,' said Helan.

The worst part was waiting until dark. They spent most of the day in the store-room, where they were at least able to eat and rest. Three times, guards came to the kitchens to ask if anything suspicious had been seen; but each time they went away without making another search.

Helan was silent and listless. Mawrdreth spent his time with her, his arm round her shoulders, letting her rest against him. Tanthe was afraid she'd done too much, made herself seriously ill. She felt none too great herself, exhausted from fighting all morning and weaving the web. Now as she relaxed, the wounds Rhazagramen had stroked onto her skin were burning with a vengeance. Lahjaya applied some salve, which helped. Auriel sat with her and stroked her hair. She managed to sleep briefly, until nightmares of Rhazagramen's face and the *ezht*, muddled together, made her start awake.

Eldareth and Elrill were talking softly. 'There's the Heliodor Tower,' said Elrill. 'We know the portal is inside, to take us back to Verdanholm. However . . .'

'The tower will be choked with guards,' Eldareth said. 'And even if we made it, Falthorn would bounce us straight back here again. No, we need allies.'

In the pause, Tanthe again broached the subject of rescuing Ysomir, only for Eldareth to look sadly at her and shake his head. 'I understand how you feel, but you've no idea where the kitchens are in relation to the prison, have you?'

'Actually, I do have an idea,' she said. 'And I know it's impossible. We're almost on the opposite side from it, aren't we? I just can't bear to think of leaving without even trying. It could be my one and only chance, ever.'

'If there was the slightest chance, we'd do it. But we have a possibility of freedom now and we can't risk it. You must be realistic, Tanthe.'

'I know!' She dug her nails into her palms, trying to ignore the stinging of blisters all across her throat and chest. She had to stomach her frustration. 'I know.'

Lahjaya prepared them each a bag of provisions, a pot of salve for Tanthe. At last the time came. A Bhahdradomen official arrived to give the staff permission to leave. By this time, six of the staff were concealed in a linen-room just off the laundry. Tanthe and the others stood ready, mingling with the other staff, dressed in long cloaks of blue, green or violet wool, with the hoods drawn up over their heads.

An outer door was unlocked, and they were filing out into the first courtyard. The night air was poignantly fresh and sweet.

Their passes were squares of carnelian, carved with insignia of the Amber Citadel – the Tree of Life on the eight-spoked Wheel – bound in silver and worn round the neck over their cloaks. At each gate, their passes were checked by taciturn *yrim* who spoke little Paranian. The gate and the long tunnel through the innermost wall; the second courtyard; gate and tunnel through the middle wall, the third courtyard; and at last the tall outer wall loomed above them, and the final gate. All the way, Tanthe's heart was drumming. The closer they came to freedom, the worse she felt to be leaving Ysomir behind. *Should I have defied the others and struck off on my own? Can't do the right thing, whatever I do.*

They were through. The last gate swung shut with a clang behind them. Tanthe stood there in the crowd in complete shock, unable to believe it. Surely someone would stop them . . . but the Bhahdradomen sentries only watched them with indifferent eyes. The staff moved away from the gate as one. Only when they were out of sight of the sentries did they go their separate ways.

'Now the difficult part,' Lahjaya said brightly. The others began to disperse, some whispering, 'Goddess go with you,' to Helan and her party as they went. Soon only the six were left, with Lahjaya and another woman.

'This way,' said Lahjaya, setting off at a remarkable pace for her stature.

'There's no need for you to come with us,' said Mawrdreth. 'You've done all we can ask.'

'Sire, you're not out of danger yet. We'll guide you to the edge of the city. South would be best; there are more gardens and wild parks that way, fewer roads where the Bhahdradomen are patrolling. The sooner you are clear of Parione the better.'

'That's true enough,' said Eldareth. 'We need somewhere to hide, but nowhere inside the city's going to be safe.'

'The passes may help, if we are challenged.' She indicated her companion. 'And Nerini must come with us in order to take the passes back once we reach the countryside.'

'I thought you were going to take them.'

Lahjaya's eyes were mouse-bright in the darkness. 'It is my feeling that I should come with you. If you will permit me, ma'am, sire . . . ?'

'You've been a true friend,' Helan said, 'but why do you want to come with us?'

They made their swift way along the edge of a tree-lined street, then slipped between two mansions to cut across the shadowed gardens. 'It's the only way I can truly help you. I can't see any other way to make it work. You will understand soon; I only ask that you trust me. And I don't want to go back to the Amber Citadel. Not until you go back, ma'am.'

Helan was silent for a few moments. Tanthe suspected she was close to tears. 'Well, you were in my employ, Lahjaya,' she said softly. 'If you wish to come with us, you're welcome.'

'Ma'am, had you decided where to go?'

'It's difficult. We don't know where the Bhahdradomen are, and where they are not.'

'Then, if you are undecided, I suggest that we go to Azura Maroc. That's where I come from.'

'I know, my dear. But why?'

'Because Azura Maroc is still free.'

They were three-quarters of the way across the city – Tanthe could see the black domes of the Temple of Nuth against the river – when Nerini took her leave of them. 'My home is near here,' she said. 'And I'm not fit to go much further; I'd hold you up. Lahjaya, please take care. Goddess go with you all.'

They took the Citadel passes from around their necks, gave them to Nerini, and said farewell with profound thanks. Now they had no alibi for prowling the city late at night. Several times they had seen *yrim* patrols, but managed to slip silently behind them.

Lahjaya led them down to the river, through a straggling wild woodland and across a narrow road to the paved bank. It was deserted here, the only light coming from Leaf Moon in a fat greenish crescent. When they set foot on the narrow wooden bridge, the far bank was clear. As soon as they set foot on the other side, though, an *yrim* stepped out to meet them.

'Stop,' he said, beginning to draw his *sten*. 'Disobeying curfew. You are arrested.'

The Eater found himself surrounded, with two glowing *mnelir* blades held to his throat; one in Tanthe's hand, the other in Elrill's. His pond-green eyes stretched with fear and all his inert self-containment vanished. '*Mnelim!*' he croaked. '*Nah, ashrach* . . . I beg you . . .'

The only time Tanthe had ever seen a shape-changer frightened was when confronted with these small Aelyr weapons. They contained an energy, *liroth*, that was somehow inimical to them. With three Aelyr standing around him, the orbs on the knife hilts glittering and the blades hot and shining against the tortoise-skin of his throat, he went to pieces.

'You never saw us,' said Eldareth.

'Go,' he gasped. 'I never saw you.'

'Kill him?' Elrill said quietly.

'No,' said Helan.

Eldareth added, 'Better they find a live *domenim* with no memory of seeing us, than a dead one to give us away.'

They let him go and he collapsed, a little heap of shadow by the mouth of the bridge.

'I think it's a risk to leave him alive,' said Elrill. They

walked away along a twisting lane that would lead them out into vineyard country.

'Maybe,' said Tanthe, 'but I've killed enough of them today. I can't do it again. The thought of it is sickening.'

Mawrdreth touched her shoulder-blade, letting her know he felt the same.

'We need horses,' said Helan after a time. 'It will take us forever to get anywhere on foot.'

Again Tanthe thought longingly of Redbird, her swift mare who had been left behind in Verdanholm. And that made her think of Jthery, and feel a spurt of anger that he was not here suffering with them. She wondered where Rufryd was now; what he was thinking, what he was doing. Goddess, just let him be alive, she thought.

'We need a safe place to rest and hide when daylight comes,' said Eldareth. 'Helan, I know what you're like for going on without complaining, long after you should have stopped.'

'I am fine,' she said, her jaw set. Tanthe knew she was lying. And she was beginning to feel faint herself, with tiredness and the fire of her wounds. Auriel was pale. Even Aelyr – true Aelyr, she didn't count herself – got tired and suffered pain, just as humans did. Even Elrill, the least Earthly of them.

'We shall have to stop soon,' said Eldareth.

'Please, let's try to go further,' Lahjaya said, worried. 'It's not safe yet.'

'It's not going to be safe, is it?' said Tanthe. She had a sudden uneasy feeling about this woman. Lahjaya had an agenda of her own, something she was keeping back.

They walked on, down through vineyards where the rolling hills offered few trees to shelter them. The first glow of dawn touched the distant hills of Paranios, revealing a landscape of ridges lying like interlaced hands; and marking the perfect velvet, the black gouges of *graukhim*-herds. Those stains would join up and cover the land.

'Don't look,' Lahjaya said. 'Don't weep about it. Let us keep on towards Azura Maroc.'

For some time, Tanthe had suspected there were shadows following them. She'd put it down to her own tiredness. It was only as the dawn brightened that those shadows closed in, and became solid figures in the half-light, thirty-strong and closing in from every direction. She was too tired to feel more than shocked resignation. Gods, to come this far only to be led into a trap . . .

'Give yourselves up,' came a voice from one of the shadows. 'Drop your weapons or die.'

Chapter Nine. Dark Mirror

Rufryd gazed up at the Obsidian Tower. Arax Vahan melted back into the shadows of the temple, leaving him alone to experience the revelation. Lily Moon shifted into the frame, shining through the crackled glass like a halo around the tip of the spire.

'The world was decadent,' came Arax Vahan's deep voice. 'Ancestor sent the Grey Plague to wipe out mankind, a warning. Then came the Bhahdradomen, a perfect lifeform. The message was clear. *"Be like us.* All of humankind shall be eliminated and replaced by the Chosen; the only way to save yourselves is to be like us. When the halved ones fall into darkness, you shall be borne up into the light." This is Ancestor's promise to his followers.'

What complete sense it made. Tanthe had caused him nothing but pain. How sweet it would be to feel whole in himself; to need no-one else, ever again. To find a different path . . . one that left all pain behind and led to utter peace. To bring this light to the chosen few in Aventuria before the rest were swept into the darkness they deserved. How seductive.

It made perfect sense – for ten seconds. Then his common sense kicked in and it all peeled back, the stitches ripping out of the tightly-sewn bundle of delusion.

He heard the voice of the old priestess Rouna, gravelly and matter of fact. 'Nuth doesn't give a fuck whether you believe in her or not. She just *is.*'

Rouna had never lied to him. Never fed him false hope or fantasy. Never said, 'Give yourself to this deity and forget everything you were before.' No, she would have called that running away.

And Nuth was real, Rufryd knew, because she was a word representing reality; the darkness at the beginning and end of time, the rain on the earth, the sweetness of love and the misery of loss. None of that was inferior, evil or mistaken, as the Order of Calathvahn would have him believe. He knew it, to the core of his bones.

And yet ... Arax Vahan was right. Reality could be difficult and cruel and unbearable. It would be so easy to turn his back on it and believe this instead. A safe harbour of light and serenity. A place from which he could revenge himself on all that had hurt him, without stooping to the petty emotion of vengefulness. Feeling clean and superior instead, as these people did ... content in self-delusion.

Arax Vahan is asking me to turn away from reality, he thought. To despise reality. I can't do it. Never to put my arms round Tanthe or Branq'elin again – even if they do tell me to get lost? Me, make some great divine crusade out of the fact that I'm a loser in love? Pathetic.

And yet ... Arax Vahan was so sure, while Rufryd wasn't sure of anything.

He turned with these doubts on his lips, only to stop when he saw the Father's expression. A shiver went through him. Arax Vahan's face was intense, warm and expectant. He was nodding a little in anticipation of Rufryd's response.

Rufryd realised that only the correct answer was required. The Father did not look as if anyone had ever said to him, 'I'll think about it,' or, 'This is crap.' The subject was not up for debate. He had to appear to swallow it, or ... he was certain something extremely unpleasant was going to happen.

'You are quiet,' said the Father. 'Herex and many of his brothers were on their knees weeping with joy at this point.'

'It's a lot to take in,' Rufryd said carefully. 'I'm ... stunned.'

Arax Vahan nodded, relaxing a little. 'But it makes sense to you?'

'It's incredible.' He meant it literally.

'You see the beauty of it. No-one can fail to see the beauty.'

'There's a lot to think about.'

'Of course. You need time to take it in. There's much to learn. Rufryd, I will just say this; Ancestor requires complete obedience. Obedience to Ancestor is complete freedom.'

He guided Rufryd away with a fatherly arm around his shoulders. Rufryd was glad to leave the temple. He suddenly felt breathless with the horror of how close he'd been to giving way. The thought of prostrating himself to any god – let alone that of their enemies – was disgusting. Completely against his nature. Yet he'd come so close to betraying himself . . . and he wasn't out of danger yet. To go along with their beliefs would in the end be the path of least resistance.

Then he could even believe it was all right that Lynden had died. It must have been Ancestor's Will.

'Father?' he said. They were walking from the cloister towards the refectory, although he didn't know how he would manage to eat. 'Has anyone ever . . . failed to see the light?'

Arax Vahan was thoughtful. 'In my many years here, only two have found the light too dazzling. They deserve our pity.'

'What happened to them?'

'For such unfortunates, there is a period of correction. If that fails, it is an act of mercy to cast them into the darkness.'

In the days that followed, Rufryd kept his head down. He copied the brothers' modes of speech, mannerisms and behaviour, and did everything within his power to become invisible. Arax Vahan seemed pleased with him. He took it for granted that Rufryd accepted the Ancestor. But Rufryd thought, If he had half a brain . . . or if I was him, I would be so suspicious . . .

Rufryd felt resentful. He saw the serenity of the brothers, and he'd wanted to be part of it. Now he knew he never could. Their contentment came from a belief he couldn't share.

Or could he? Perhaps if he pretended for long enough, it would seep into him.

As things were, he wished Arax Vahan had never told him about their beliefs. He could have gone on envying them in blissful ignorance. Now he couldn't look at any of them, especially Herex, without thinking, *They believe that human life is a horrible mistake that must be destroyed . . . and this makes them happy!*

Days and weeks and seasons were passing. Spring came slowly and hesitantly, with wild winds and downpours that turned the gardens into quagmires. At last the new shoots began to appear, even in this sterile plug of land, and bees left their hives to drink the nectar of tiny, short-lived flowers on the hills. The changes were marked only by which garden tasks fell due. Rufryd missed the celebration of the festivals; Breyid's Day, Estrae, Firethorn . . . The Father explained that such festivals were of the reviled Goddess. To connect themselves to the earth, when their aim was to detach themselves from it, was wrong.

They did have one strange celebration, about the time Estrae would have fallen. It involved a divine egg. The egg didn't represent new life and rebirth, as it did in Aventuria; instead it represented the First Egg, from which the first Bhahdradomen had hatched. Ancestor had created it, yet at the same time he somehow *was* that first hatchling . . . Rufryd didn't quite understand, but the brothers considered it a wonderful mystery.

Herex was constantly at his side, ever more talkative. Rufryd realised that Herex was teaching him, reinforcing the revelation they assumed he'd received. The Order became friendlier to him. They met his eyes instead of avoiding them, giving him warm, knowing looks, as if he were truly one of them now. At least they left Vetru alone. Hatched Bhahdradomen, they assumed he needed no revelations; which was ironic, as he seemed to be even more thoroughly clueless about the Ancestor than Rufryd had been.

He felt guilty for not being truthful. But he wanted a quiet life, couldn't face the endless arguing and intimidation that would follow if he expressed his doubts. So he became carefully neutral. Pushed Ancestor aside, pushed Nuth aside, tried to think about nothing.

One night he dreamed about Lynden.

They were sitting on the river bank near Riverwynde, with the green branches of a willow trailing over them. The colours were lusciously vivid; Rufryd had almost forgotten what colour was in Vexor.

'What are you doing?' said Lynden.

'I'm fishing, what does it look like?' said Rufryd.

'No, I mean, what do you think you are doing in that place?'

'I'm content there.'

'No, you're not!' Lynden exclaimed. He looked and sounded exactly as he had in life. Volatile, passionate, completely pure of heart. Everyone had loved him as strongly as they'd disliked Rufryd. 'You're hiding and you're being dishonest. You can't stay here.'

'Why not?'

'It's not you, Rufe. I know you. When are you going to be true to yourself?'

'This is as good as it gets, Lyn.'

'No it isn't! You've never been true to yourself. That's what's wrong with you! Or you start, and then you run away from it. How can you think about giving yourself up to this Ancestor? How can you doubt for one moment that we had it right?'

'I don't. You know that. But they're so convinced, there's no point in arguing.'

'There is no Ancestor,' Lynden said gently. 'I should know.'

'I can't tell them that.'

'You have to try. You can't give up love and being human. Tanthe loved you and she still does. I loved Saphaeyender as well as Ymmi – never as much as her, never – but still, I loved him. I know you don't want to believe it but it's true, and the important thing is this. *It wasn't wrong.*'

'Death seems to have given you a lot of opinions,' said Rufryd.

Lynden smiled. 'Love is everything, Rufe. It's what made us leave here in the first place, because I loved Ymmi and you loved me. It's everything. But these maniacs here, they want to destroy that. They despise women, because they don't want to be reminded that they're human. How insane is that? They want the human race to die. They're worse than the Bhahdradomen, do you hear me? Worse.'

'Lyn, don't, please,' Rufryd said. Panic tore at him.

'You know what you've found here, don't you?' said Lynden. 'Just look in the mirror!'

Rufryd woke up weeping. Vetru came fussing around him, wanting to know what was wrong, but Rufryd pushed him away and lay staring at the grey vault of the ceiling. It had been so real. Talking to his brother again – if only in a dream – was a thousand times more real than anything at Calathvahn.

Later that day he sat with Herex, scrubbing and peeling vegetables for the evening meal. Herex had always been easy company; Rufryd could talk to him as he couldn't to Arax Vahan.

Herex said, 'It's so wonderful that you are truly one of us now. You'll be ready to take permanent vows in a year, or less.' He spoke so warmly that Rufryd hadn't the heart to disabuse him.

'Can I ask what is probably a stupid question?' Rufryd said.

'No question is stupid.'

'Well, you're all men here, and cut off from the mainland. Unless you've only been here a few years, where do your new recruits come from?'

'Those who are called will find us, as you did, Rufryd.'

'No, come on, really.'

Herex gave his faint, cool smile. 'The Order has existed since the time of the Grey Plague. At that time, they must have thought the end of the world was coming. But when the world continued, they realised that they must plan and be ready for the eventual end. So they found ways for the Order to survive.

'The Order hasn't always been here, nor in a single place. Rufryd, this is a closely guarded secret, but we have a brother-Order in Thanmandrathor, a cove on the south coast. We have small ships that pass between Vexor and there, once or twice a year. They are concealed within a *tzcement* of Bhahdradomen who live there. It may surprise you to know that the Bhahdradomen are there quite legally.'

Herex seemed to expect him to be shocked, but Rufryd shrugged. 'Yes, I know about the *domenim* in the Nine Realms. The Treaty of the Silver Plains?'

Herex raised his eyebrows. 'Oh, you do know!'

'It's Aventuria's guiltiest and worst-kept secret.'

'Well, you are right, we need new recruits or our Order would have died out within sixty years of its founding. Our brother-Order finds the male infants we need and raises them to adulthood. Then – once they are ready to begin full training – we collect them.'

Rufryd watched him for a few moments, marvelling at his unruffled demeanour. 'You "find" male infants? I can't imagine many Thand'rathian mothers willingly giving up their children to you.'

At the word 'mothers', Herex winced, as if he preferred not to be reminded of where his fellow acolytes came from. 'You'd be surprised.'

'You don't kidnap them, do you? Steal them?'

Herex looked uncomfortable. 'There are always unwanted ones.'

'So unwanted their mothers would seek out a secret order hidden in a Bhahdradomen *tzcement*? Seems unlikely, doesn't it?'

'The brothers go out and search,' Herex answered.

'Is that how you came to be here?'

'No. I was a young man before I found the Order. I came from the very north of Thanmandrathor. My father was a fisherman, until the ocean swallowed him. Then my mother took one lover after another, with no care for my brother and me.'

'Maybe she was lonely.'

Herex's eyes were less serene than glacial. 'You see, Rufryd, how every manifestation of love betrays you? I loved my father, and he fell into the jaws of the ocean. Loved my mother, and she turned away from me. There was a girl I loved, and I looked for happiness in her; but all of it proved false. She deserted me for my brother. *My brother*.'

'Yeah, tough, isn't it? You were lucky it wasn't her own brother.'

Herex went on as if Rufryd hadn't spoken. 'So I killed them.'

'You *what*?'

'I look back and see a different person; I was distraught, mad, nothing like the man you see now. I killed them and then there was nothing to do but kill myself. The village rejected me and I wandered the path through the mountains in rags, demented, seeing nothing but the pure horror and misery that is life.'

'Anthar's prick and balls,' Rufryd said under his breath. 'I was angry with Tanthe sometimes but I would never, ever have dreamed of hurting her. You'd have to be out of your mind. You can't *possess* someone like that.'

'I was out of my mind,' Herex agreed. 'If a brother hadn't found me wandering on the road, I would have stumbled into a ravine and died. He saved me; he showed me that it wasn't *me* that was at fault, but life itself. Humans speak of the Bhahdradomen as hideous, but I came to admire them. They are complete unto themselves, they recognise no parents but the One. For human life is foul, is it not? It's full of lashes, and barbs, and brambles. We stumble about in the darkness. We think we are about to stand upright, only for the vines to drag us down and thorns to tear our flesh. Life is a dreadful, cruel, evil mistake, the jest of a demon. But we are the lucky ones, Rufryd.' He leaned over and clasped Rufryd's hands, his pale eyes shining with certainty. 'We have found the way out.'

'Yeah,' Rufryd breathed. Inwardly he recoiled, dismayed to the core of his soul. For all he'd thought he might be able to live with this dark philosophy, now he knew he couldn't, not if he dwelled here the rest of his life.

Then he understood Lynden's words, 'You know what you've found here, don't you? Look in the mirror!'

The revelation came, not while he stood gazing at the Obsidian Tower with Arax Vahan's voice resounding deep and mystical in his ears, but sitting in a kitchen with cold wet hands and a bowl of muddy turnips on his knee. The mirror was Herex. In him, Rufryd saw his own pain and bitterness, taken to the extreme. He'd left Parione in rage, bent on self-destruction. Every man here was the same, or trained from birth by their twisted elders to see the world in that way. Yet instead of healing, they justified and sanctified their bitterness, honed it into a belief system to be hurled as lightning against the whole world.

Life has destroyed us, so let us destroy life.

Rufryd knew then that he was destined to leave, sooner or later. It wasn't going to be easy. He was aware that the brothers watched each other closely all the time, both to monitor and to demonstrate their obedience. And now he was an acolyte, they watched him, too.

Cold dry summer was turning into miserable autumn.

Every day they spent two hours in the temple, sitting in rows on the hard seats while Arax Vahan instructed, praised, ranted, encouraged them to see visions of the Ancestor. Some of the brothers would go into ecstasies during these sessions, waving their hands, falling and foaming at the mouth. Although he suspected that some of these demonstrations were exaggerated, Rufryd took care not to see anything. It was struggle enough to stay awake.

Still the seductive simplicity of life and the difficulty of escaping held him here. There was nothing for him outside. He wondered if there were others who didn't really believe but went along with it for a peaceful life.

Then, one day in late autumn, the peace ended. The first of the Bhahdradomen arrived.

He saw them coming over the hills, and at first he thought the community was under attack. But Arax Vahan and some of the elder brothers went out to meet them, and it became clear that the Bhahdradomen were expected. The brothers were excited, not afraid.

The leaders were a similar type to Rhazagramen, self-important mages in robes of ivory and black; garments made from the skins of *graukhim*, Rufryd knew. For a day or two, Arax Vahan was seen with the leaders, walking in the courtyards, their heads bent in lengthy discussion. Rumours ran through Calathvahn that the long-awaited time had come. Preparations for the crusade were imminent.

With the mages came a number of elite warriors, *vagharim*, and ordinary soldiers, *yrim*. No civilian *domenim*, though; only military. They sat in circles on the hillside, as if forming roofless *tzcements*. Vetru kept disappearing; Rufryd soon found he'd taken to watching them, always from the cover of a rock at a safe distance.

'I've been thinking,' Rufryd said one afternoon, sitting down beside him. 'Wouldn't you be happier if you went back to your own kind? Back to Tsur?'

'No.'

'Come on, I can see the way you're watching them all the time,' he said gently. 'You want to be with them, don't you?'

He'd struck a nerve. 'I am only watching,' said Vetru, clasping his skinny legs. 'I can never go back now.'

'Why not?'

Vetru clasped himself harder, agitated. 'I am become *neshrim* without permission. They will not accept me! Only the great mages, *grothrim,* are allowed to become *neshrim.*'

He groaned. 'Great, so I've made you an outcast now?'

'Yes.'

'I didn't ask you to do this! You've done this to yourself, Vetru!'

'I stay with you,' Vetru said doggedly. 'I have nowhere else to go.'

'Fuck.' Rufryd exhaled in resignation. 'Well, don't get upset. If you can't go back, you can't. No-one's going to make you.'

Vetru curled his hands around Rufryd's arm. He looked up at him. 'I watch not because I want to go with them. I watch because . . .' He couldn't seem to find the words.

'You're interested? Fascinated? Scared?'

Vetru nodded keenly. 'Yes. But I stay with you. I belong with you.'

Some days later, a dozen human men – strangers – appeared quietly in the community and began to train the acolytes in physical fitness. Rufryd knew at once that they were being trained for battle. No-one spoke overtly of it but everyone seemed to understand. And their arrival meant something else; a ship must have come from Thanmandrathor.

Rufryd joined in. He didn't want to draw attention to himself by refusing. Besides, he was glad of the exercise and a chance to regain his fitness.

Still, the implications of the training were unutterably

sinister. It went on all winter, and all the time, the Bhahdradomen elite came and went. *Yrim* joined the sessions, teaching bizarre drills and fighting techniques with wooden sticks.

Which later made sense when the *vagharim* issued live weapons.

These were Bhahdradomen weapons, newly forged in the smokes of Zhahgrament, judging by their oily feel and the metallic tang they exuded. Rufryd had seen such things before but never touched them. The *sten* would extend at the flick of a wrist, making a multi-purpose blade to stab, cut and burn. The *tzirin* was a vile black whip that could stun or kill; he'd felt the lash of it himself when he'd first entered Vexor. Some spoke in hushed tones of the supreme weapon, *uzrat*, but whatever it was, it wasn't issued to them.

Rufryd hated the feel of the weapons. They felt like rubbery flesh and they seemed to writhe and tingle in the hand. Their smell set his teeth on edge. On the first day, one of the officers dismantled a couple to show how they worked. The handles were packed with discs of smoky crystal, sandwiched with layers of beaten metal foils; the *roth* in the crystal was their power source, generating an energy that was, so the *vagharim* claimed, virtually inexhaustible.

They were preparing for battle. A fever of joy and excitement pervaded Calathvahn.

As time passed, Rufryd looked back on the beginning of his stay with nostalgia. It had seemed a simple, peaceful refuge then. Now it was a peace-loving community no longer . . . perhaps never had been. Rufryd understood that they'd always been preparing for this. The final battle.

They were to form part of the Bhahdradomen push into eastern Thanmandrathor, a tiny human crusade fighting even more fanatically for the Ancestor than the Eaters themselves.

He pieced the story together from rumours. The first

Bhahdradomen invasion had gone straight to the heart of Aventuria; Vaurgroth had opened some kind of portal inside his grey citadel in Zhahgrament, which emerged directly into Parione. Rufryd had already guessed as much. He'd seen the whirling caldera, and witnessed the lines of *yrim* and *domenim* who entered the citadel but never emerged.

The second invasion would flow in from the eastern and southern Thanmandrathor. The two walls would eventually meet, crushing what was left of Thanmandrathor between them.

There would be *ghelim*, specially adapted and under the command of mages, that could fold time and appear from nowhere. The rest, including the humans, would take the physical route, by sea. Even the great *roth*-mage Vaurgroth had limitations; he couldn't open portals everywhere. So he needed human help, for the Bhahdradomen were not boat-builders.

Rufryd wasn't in the habit of torturing himself by wondering what was happening to his friends, but he thought about Tanthe all the time. He hoped she and Eldareth had made it to Verdanholm, and were safe there.

Every moment of the day, as he went through the motions of training, Rufryd knew he couldn't take part in this. Yet he was being swept along in it. He had no-one to confide in. They were all caught up in their little crusade, proud and single-minded.

'It is Ancestor's Will.' That was Arax Vahan's first, last and only opinion on the matter. Fighting with Ancestor's lightning in their hands and his fire on their brow, they would sweep the worshippers of Nuth into the darkness.

Late one evening Rufryd and Herex were on their knees, scrubbing the refectory floor. Vetru was with them, the only creature Rufryd actually trusted. Nothing said to Vetru was ever repeated. As they worked, Rufryd asked, 'Herex, do you really believe this is right?'

'What do you mean, brother?'

'Haven't you thought about it?' He tried to modulate his voice, so that Herex didn't see how strongly he felt. 'Haven't you ever had a tiny bit of doubt about what they expect us to do?'

'Never.' Herex used the same mild tone in which he might ask Rufryd to pass the salt. 'It's Ancestor's Will.'

'But we'll be attacking other humans. People who could be our friends or family. Killing them.' He stopped, remembering the story Herex had told him. 'Of course, that won't be anything new for you.'

Herex didn't react. 'I am ready for this. I am prepared. I know why the crusade is essential and I thought that you did too, Rufryd.'

'I do,' he said hurriedly, 'but I can't help thinking . . . It's against . . .' He was going to say, 'against the Goddess,' but he stopped himself. He was supposed to have renounced all his own goddesses and gods as demons.

'If you are having doubts, we had better pray together,' Herex said, clasping both his hands. 'Ask the Ancestor to set you back on the path to light.'

'No!' said Rufryd, pulling his hands free. 'No. You're right, brother, but I'd rather pray alone, if you don't mind.'

He fell asleep with Vetru beside him, entreating not the Ancestor but Nuth for guidance. He addressed her in her form as Q'enartre of the lightning, Thanmandrathor's goddess, willing her to wield her power against the invaders . . .

He was woken by Vetru crying out. A bulky shadow was standing over him. It was Arax Vahan, with a brother on either side of him, gazing down at Rufryd with a mixture of sorrow and grave disappointment. Vetru crouched in the corner, looking on in alarm.

'You are having doubts, I hear.'

Fear flashed through him. He knew at once that Herex must have reported their conversation. He sat up, horrified that Herex had betrayed him. Should have known better than to trust him.

'You dare to question Ancestor's Will?' Arax Vahan's face was murderous, the heavy black brows set in a judgemental block.

'That's not for me to do,' Rufryd said quietly. He couldn't bear to grovel to the leader, didn't want confront him either. This was the first time he'd felt truly afraid here.

'No, it is not. Rise from your bed, Rufryd. I am giving you the chance to set aside your doubts, to swear full devotion to the Ancestor, to the Order, and to me. I require your solemn oath that you will fight the coming crusade as a fully committed soldier of the light.'

Rufryd stood up in his thin night-robe and looked into the Father's eyes. He thought of Lynden. Arax Vahan waited.

Then Rufryd said, 'I'm sorry. I can't.'

'What?'

'I'm not going to fight for you. Your crusade is obscene, and I want no part of it.'

They dragged Rufryd along a narrow passage that ran behind the temple, opened a grille in the floor, and pushed him in.

He fell and landed heavily on rough stone. A grunt of pain burst from him. He lay winded for a time before he could move to check that nothing was broken; no, he was in one piece. He knew how to fall and he'd rolled with the impact, but he could feel a dozen bruises beginning to throb.

He looked up to see shadows leaning over the grille, a good twelve feet above him.

'There you stay until your path is corrected,' came Arax Vahan's voice. 'I suggest you throw yourself on Ancestor's mercy and receive redemption soon; for if you leave it too long, the Order will be gone, and there will be no one to release you. It would be a waste, indeed, if you starved there with no witness to your change of heart.'

The shadows withdrew. Rufryd was in a dank lightless

cell that stank of acidic rot. All he could see was the silhouette of the grille against the grey glimmer of the passage above. A hard wave of panic swept through him and he had to bite his lip to stop himself crying out for help. *No don't leave me I've changed my mind!*

It wasn't so much pride that stopped him, as the fact that his throat was frozen with fear. This is it, then, he thought. A 'period of correction'. Either I lie, and go off with them to slaughter my friends . . . or I die here.

He felt his way to a wall, and sank down against it, knees drawn up and his head in his hands. His eyes adjusted to the darkness and he made out a scattering of old, dusty straw, walls of rough stone, a bucket. His heart sank deeper.

No skeletons of previous occupants . . . then he noticed a strange bundle in the opposite corner, a thing of sticks and grey rags. In the gloom he could barely make it out. His mind turned it into different shapes, trying to make sense of it. For several seconds he held his breath in a state of embryonic horror, certain it was a corpse. He had to know. He crawled forward, eyes straining to make it out.

A couple of feet from it he realised, with a huge sigh of relief, that it was only a roll of moth-eaten bedding or clothing that some other wretched occupant of this cell had left behind. Perhaps he could use it, if there were no rats living in it. Look how well I've done for myself, Tanthe, he thought sourly. From the marble luxury of Ashtar's villa to this!

He put out his hand to the end of the bundle and gave it a tentative prod. His fingers found something hard.

The bundle stirred and groaned.

Rufryd found himself flattened against the far wall in a surge of primaeval horror, his hands pressed to the stone and sweat sheeting his back. His mouth was open, his breath juddering out. 'Oh Goddess, oh *shit* . . .'

Eyes straining, he looked on as the stick-thing heaved, trying and failing to raise itself, like a half-crushed insect.

Whatever it was, it wasn't human. Grunts stuttered from it, '*Ach . . . ma . . . ngh . . .*'

Not human grunts, he realised, but fragments of Bhahdradomen.

With an effort of will he peeled himself off the wall and inched towards it. The rags of its garment fell apart to reveal stick limbs like the legs of birds, the bones reed-thin under tightly-stretched scales. The hands moved feebly, clusters of straws. The head was tortoise-like, grey and cracked with age, the mouth gaping like a dying fish, the two small dark eyes that swivelled in Rufryd's direction dried up with ancient pain.

The odd fungal scent of the Bhahdradomen rose from its body, so faint and dry that it was barely there at all. Rufryd couldn't believe this thing was alive at all. It didn't seem to be asking for help . . . merely responding to his presence, unconscious of its nakedly wretched state.

He swallowed hard, ignoring the revulsion he felt. He knelt down and helped it to sit up.

The *domenim* crouched back against the wall, uttering soft chattering moans. It was the most pitiful thing Rufryd had ever seen. He put his fingers to his mouth and looked at it with tears stinging his eyes.

'*Achrag . . . urkalich . . .*' the creature said.

Rufryd asked, in the few words of Bhahdradomen he'd picked up from Vetru – and which he couldn't pronounce properly – if it could speak Paranian.

'A little,' it said. 'Long time.'

'How long have you been here?'

'Long time,' it repeated. 'You . . . why?'

'Why am I in here, you mean? Because I refused to go on telling lies. As long as I went on telling the lies, I was fine. But as soon as I stopped . . .'

'*Ach. Ach.*' The creature, Rufryd realised, was uttering a sort of laugh. It understood exactly what he'd said. The eyes, though vague and filmy with weakness, were fully intelligent.

'Why are you here?' Rufryd asked.

It opened and closed its mouth, struggling. 'Too long.'

'You've been here too long, or it would take too long to explain?'

'Yes.' A drop of yellowish rheum ran from its left eye. 'Both.'

'I'm Rufryd. Your name . . . title, I mean?'

'Aazhoth,' said the being.

Rufryd looked at him for a few moments, startled. 'Aazhoth?'

'It means in Paranian, I think, Moderator.'

'And is that a common title among *domenim*? Only the . . . I came to Vexor thinking that the leader of the Bhahdradomen was called Aazhoth. When I got here I was told Aazhoth had been replaced by Vaurgroth. But that Aazhoth is dead . . . isn't he?'

The creature was stirring, clutching at Rufryd with spidery fingers. 'As good as. He is here.'

Rufryd tried to pull away, his revulsion getting the better of him. 'Oh, Goddess. You *are* him? You've been here, all that time? Eight, nine years?'

'Ah, the time . . . that is meaningless. But yes, very long. That being – I will not use the great titles he gives himself – that being who overthrew me cast me in here to die.'

'How come you're still alive?'

'For us to die by starvation . . .' Aazhoth paused, his energy failing. 'Takes a very, very long time.'

Rufryd was silent. He couldn't find words to express his horror. Even in this hopeless state, Aazhoth had the remains of an air of authority about him, a dry wisdom that required no pity from anyone. Eventually Rufryd said, 'Otherwise you wouldn't have survived on Vexor for so long.'

'Quite so. You are a wise human, you understand. We were surviving, we could have survived, but for the pride and ambition of certain factions. There was no need – no need to make another war on the humans! They said I was weak, that I appease the humans instead of fighting them – but all I do was for us to survive! I never betrayed them.'

He clutched the edge of Rufryd's thin robe. 'I believe you. Don't upset yourself.'

'They said I betrayed them, but I never did. They didn't understand my methods. They were too impatient. Fools!'

Aazhoth sank back against the wall. He looked so brittle Rufryd feared the slightest impact would shatter him. 'I came to Vexor as the Queen's envoy,' he said softly. 'You were the leader I was expecting to see.'

'You have seen me,' Aazhoth said sourly. 'Much good it has done us. I lie here forgotten.'

'Not by me.'

'Well, well.' The fragile voice and fingers came clawing at him. 'Then I am glad that you found me, Rufryd of the humans. Lie with me in the darkness. I have much to tell you.'

Water enveloped Jthery and he floated, loving its chill and glitter of liquefied sapphires. He'd found this lake nestling in the hills a mile or two from Falthorn's house, sheltered by a curved finger of peacock-green forest, cupped by silvery hills with blocks of white quartz clustered on their peaks. He came here every day because he had endless time on his hands; Falthorn was so often busy, or away. Jthery tried not to mind, but he did.

Yet these times on his own were giving him other rewards. He'd brought himself in harmony with the water again simply by spending hours here, not questioning, not trying to summon Eshte. Just being there. He touched something deeper than the whisper of elementals or their cold silence. He felt the deep currents of the water itself, carrying vibration and mood from distant streams, rivers and seas. Lifeblood in the arteries of the realms.

He closed his eyes and felt the golden-yolk sun on his eyelids. His arms were outstretched, hair fanning out in the water. He heard the bubbling whisper of elementals in the water.

'You look like porcelain,' said a voice above him.

He started, going under as he tried to tip himself upright. Pushing back his wet hair he trod water and saw Falthorn on the bank, smiling at him.

'No, don't get out,' Falthorn said as Jthery struck towards him. 'I have a mind to join you.'

'It's cold,' said Jthery, pleased. He watched as Falthorn threw off his cloak and robe and boots, revealing a sculptural pale-gold body.

'I like the cold,' said Falthorn. And he ran to the edge and dived in.

'You should, you live in it,' Jthery muttered.

Falthorn surfaced and swam in circles round him, his hair polished black glass from the water. Then he pulled Jthery down, and under the water kissed him, silver bubbles exploding from their mouths. They surfaced and Jthery tried to pull him closer but Falthorn was gone, striking out towards the middle of the lake. Jthery followed.

'How did you find this place?' Falthorn said, treading water.

'Exploring. I've had plenty of time for it.'

'Good.' He seemed deliberately to miss the implication. 'I wanted you to explore.'

'Why?'

'Because you told me that you found it hard to communicate with your water elementals in Verdanholm. Yet our realms are connected. I believed that you needed time to find them again in your own way.'

Jthery stared at him in complete astonishment. Falthorn did this every time. Confounded him by reading his mind, or being several steps ahead, or making a lightning turn onto a different path. 'That's kind of you. I thought you were just ignoring me.'

'I would never ignore you,' he said softly. 'Well, has it helped? Tell me everything.'

'How did you know?' Jthery was both pleased and exasperated.

'I didn't. But I know you better than you realise.'

'I stopped trying to talk to them, that's all,' Jthery said. They swam slowly together, side by side. He wanted to talk about it, thrilled that Falthorn was interested. 'I listened, instead, to what I could hear in their silence. I let my mind go down into the spaces between the elementals, into the *roth* itself. I can feel all the different little currents and vibrations. I can pick a single strand and follow it to its source.'

'You can?' Falthorn's eyes met his, lashes glittering. He seemed genuinely surprised. 'That's wonderful. And can you . . . influence this *roth* at all?'

'I think so. A little. I'm trying.'

'Of course you can do it,' Falthorn said, touching his shoulder. 'I saw that the first time I met you. You have a glow.'

'Even though I'm only human?'

'What's this "only human" nonsense? Any race can throw up a *roth*-mage, Jey.'

The shortening of his name sent a thrill through Jthery. He smiled. 'I'm no *roth*-mage.'

'You're on your way.' Falthorn spoke matter-of-factly and Jthery, in a rush of amazement, knew it was true. *Oh, dear Eshte, I am!* 'All you needed was time to work.'

'I thought you'd teach me.'

'This is something I can't teach. My affinity is with the ether, the mind. All you need to know is inside you, and you are the only one who can unlock it. It was the same for me.'

'Was it?'

'That's why I recognised you.' In a sensual motion Falthorn turned onto his back, smiling. It wasn't like him to be affectionate or playful; Jthery wondered if he'd had good news of some sort. Whatever had brought it on, he was glad.

'The realms are connected through water,' said Jthery. 'Earth and Verdanholm. The rivers in one affect the rivers in the other. Tides there are felt by the tides here. I don't mean they share the same water, but it's as if they share a *roth* that flows between them.'

'You have learned a lot. What have you discovered from this?'

'This realm is calm. Earth isn't.'

'Well, we shall have to do something about that.'

Falthorn struck off across the lake. Jthery dived after him, caught up. 'It isn't over, is it?' he said, panting. 'You and what happened on Earth – it wasn't the end game!'

'Did I ever say it was? Of course it isn't. I'll race you!'

Falthorn struck out across the sapphire flat, making for the shore. Jthery was after him at once, gaining, overtaking. He was the more practised swimmer but Falthorn was strong, and Jthery reached the bank only an arm's length ahead. Falthorn caught his shoulder and tried to pull him back. They struggled, went under, found their feet and stood chest-deep in the water, out of breath and laughing, close now. Laughter faded and their arms were round each other, hands sliding down each other's flanks, desire hardening them against each other.

'I think we should warm up now,' said Falthorn.

They hoisted themselves up onto the bank and knelt on the velvet grass with diamond droplets running down their bodies. Jthery leaned forward to squeeze the water out of his hair. As he did so, Falthorn whispered, 'Oh, Jewelfire, I could believe the gods are real . . .' And his hands came softly over Jthery's shoulders, not pulling roughly at him but stroking him as he might a leopard, gentle, tentative and reverent.

It wasn't the first time they had made love, but it felt like it. The previous times had been brief and sometimes painful for Jthery, as if Falthorn were trying to keep tenderness at bay with bites and bruises. This time, for some reason, was different. Slow and golden and wordless. Instead of the nip of teeth, there was the mutual caress of tongues. Moisture drying on their bodies was replenished by the sweat of pleasure.

As the deep, red pulse of excitement swelled inside him, accelerating by tiny degrees, Jthery began to hallucinate.

He saw rain. Rain falling into an ocean, and all of it bathed in the wondrous silver light of imminent revelation. He saw two figures moving along a cliff-top, glazed with rain; Aelyr. It was clear in the graceful way they moved, their aura of formidable beauty, even in the downpour.

He saw an island in the ocean, and a lighthouse standing on it. The scene was imbued with all the wonder of physical sensation, Falthorn around him and over him and inside him. The unutterable, mystical significance of approaching orgasm. Jthery was a sea-bird, whirling high over the lighthouse. He saw two pale, beautiful faces; the man looked like Falthorn, the woman like Tanthe. Pale, deathly faces on the rain-soaked darkness.

He cried out. He was in ecstasy, yet terrified. He wheeled upwards and was flying hard towards the centre of a pure white fire. The word came, *Jewelfire*.

Through it all he never lost his vivid awareness of Falthorn; hot, golden, worshipping him with feverish passion. They writhed. They came in the same moment, a mutual release of emotion dissolving all the barriers that had stood between them. They were, for those exquisite moments, naked in the Jewelfire together.

It was over. They looked at each other, eyes wide, lips parted, the breath coming hard from their throats. A flash of recognition passed between them. It scared Jthery. He suspected that it scared Falthorn too.

Falthorn knew. He knew Jthery had experienced a vision. Perhaps he'd shared it.

Jthery raised a tentative hand to Falthorn's face and touched the strong cheekbone. 'Did you . . . ? I don't know what to say. I love you.'

Falthorn broke the eye contact. 'Get dressed,' he said.

'Now?' said Jthery, blinking. He felt heavy and dazed, too sated to move.

Falthorn pushed him away, lightly but decisively. 'Yes. We're going back to the house. I have work to do.'

His tone was clipped. The sensual tenderness was replaced by a business-like chill. Jthery recoiled. 'Falthorn? What's wrong?'

'Nothing.' He jumped up and pulled his robe on as if he couldn't escape fast enough. The look he gave his lover was almost a sneer. It cut Jthery to the heart.

'What have I done?'

'I don't have time for this. Dress. I'm not waiting for you.'

'For the gods' sake, why are you being like this? I thought—'

'What? That you were anything more than an amusing dalliance to me? You think you have some kind of hold upon me, Jthery? You presume too much.'

'What have I done wrong?' Jthery cried, leaping to his feet. 'What we just shared – how can you feel nothing about it?'

Falthorn's face was glacial. 'Don't assume you know me,' he hissed. 'Your body has its charms. Your skills interest me. More than that – you are a skinny little neophyte, there to serve my whims, less to me than Auriel. You will do well if you never, ever forget that.'

He strode away, hair flapping wet on the shoulders of his cloak. Jthery made no attempt to follow him. He just stared after him, his heart breaking. Then he sank down onto the velvet grass, clutching his head, unable to do anything but sit there shaking, staring.

Every day, a flask of water and a cake of grain was lowered to Rufryd, but the brother who brought it never asked if his 'period of correction' had worked yet. Once Rufryd called out, 'How long am I going to be here?' but the man didn't answer him.

He tried to share this meagre ration with Aazhoth, but the old *domen* refused it. The best Rufryd could do was moisten his mouth with water.

Aazhoth rambled almost incessantly, sometimes in his own language, sometimes in Paranian. Rufryd couldn't take it all in. But the kernel of it, in the end, he understood. And after a time he realised that Aazhoth was repeating the same things, over and over again. He'd sleep uncomfortably, and wake, and Aazhoth would still be talking.

This must be the punishment, Rufryd thought. Not to be locked in here, but to be locked in here with him. Yet he was patient, helping the *domen* to sit up or lie down as he wanted, holding him as coughs racked his bird-fragile frame, like a nurse tending a dying man. They're more like us than they're not, Rufryd thought.

Deep in the night, the old *domen* asked with sudden clarity, 'Do you think that we are evil?'

'I've met several of you who aren't,' said Rufryd. 'I don't think that, as a race, you're evil. But I think Vaurgroth is, and Arax Vahan definitely. If you use the word "dangerous" instead, it's a lot easier to answer. Yes, very, very dangerous.'

'Ah, this is not as it should have been. If they had only listened to me! Fools. Fools.'

'I suppose if they get what they want, to feast on Aventuria for several hundred years until it's all used up, they don't consider themselves fools at all.'

'Ah, but it's wrong. This is not what Ancestor intended. This is not what Ancestor *is!* They misuse his name for their own ends. They rant of the Obsidian Tower without ever understanding what it is! How can I make them see?'

'I don't think you can,' Rufryd said tiredly. He was exhausted from lack of food. The eye-watering stink of the bucket was constant, for no-one had come to empty it. Next time he used it, it would overflow . . . He wished Aazhoth would stop talking so he could go back to sleep.

'I can't, but you can,' Aazhoth said, so clear he sounded

human. 'Honesty in this place will bring you nothing but death. If you want to survive you must lie. Lie, and escape, and live to fight again. Will you do this?'

'Yes. You're right.'

'Swear on the First Egg!'

'I swear on the First Egg, and I swear on the womb of Nuth,' Rufryd said quietly. 'Try to rest now.'

Aazhoth died in the night. He died peacefully in Rufryd's arms, slipping into the *ezht* or wherever it was Bhahdradomen souls went, so quietly that Rufryd wasn't even sure when it had happened. A minute ago, an hour ago. The corpse was weightless. It was that, more than anything, that made Rufryd weep. He wept long and convulsively, not even sure what he was mourning.

Later, the silhouette of a head appeared over the grille and a familiar voice called, 'Rufryd? They wouldn't let me see you before. I'm frightened.'

'Don't be, Vetru,' he answered. 'Will you go and fetch Arax Vahan? Tell him I'm ready to come out and vow whatever the hell he wants.'

Chapter Ten. Blood and Rose Moon

Saphaeyender had made everything ready. He had dismissed all his staff with generous payments but without explanation; Eander had protested and wept, but Saphaeyender had been ruthless. He had locked the outer doors, extinguished all the lamps except for a couple of candles. In the dim bluish light he padded round the villa; his home for the past twenty years, the birthplace of his most famous plays and poems, scene of many a fraught rehearsal or riotous party. He was trying to catch an echo of those lost joyful days . . . but there was nothing. He felt nothing. The air was cold. The villa was dead to him.

All was over now. He wasn't used to being alone, hated it, but now it felt appropriate.

He picked up a candle and carried it into the bathroom of creamy marble, where he had already begun his preparations. From a faucet shaped like a statue of Dyonis bearing a shell, hot water gushed into the veined marble hollow of the bath. It was half-full, the room wreathed in stream.

He stood for a few moments looking into the water. Slowly he began to undress, pausing only to drink from the decanter of whisky that he had placed on the side of the bath. Serpent Isles, the best; still, he'd never liked it and winced at its taste.

Saphaeyender stepped into the bath and lowered himself with a deep sigh into the water. He hadn't eaten for days so the whisky hit fast. He was warm now, floating. The easy way, this, so he'd heard. Like falling asleep. How in character of me to take the easy way, he thought.

The Bhahdradomen meant to turn him into an obscene weapon. Such weapons must be destroyed.

From the side of the bath he picked up a razor and pressed it to his left forearm. Tears ran down his cheeks as he forced the blade into the tender skin; his jaw was clenched so hard it ached. Not easy at all. But he did it. Left then right . . . and the water was filling with the dark clouds of his life.

Ysomir watched the door of her cell as if waiting for her execution. She knew that Vaurgroth would come soon, and when he did, it would be the end of her. She didn't want to die. Still less did she want to be left alive, a withered thing with all the *ethroth* sucked out of her. For her own life-energy would go out with Lynden, she knew. And if it didn't, it would be like losing him twice.

She'd waited two or three days, not sleeping but losing track of time. Zhoaah had brought her food – making her start violently when she heard the key in the lock – but he hadn't spoken to her nor met her eyes. Perhaps he felt guilty.

She was terrified they'd come in the night, take her by surprise while she was sleeping. She was determined to stay awake. Under the mattress she'd tucked all her writing and the *silvenroth* mirror, in the hope that it wouldn't be discovered.

Yet she dropped off, and was jolted awake by the snap of the key, the creak of the hinges. It was dark. Zhoaah stood in the doorway, outlined by lamp-flicker from the passage outside. Usually he brought a tray, but this time his hands were empty.

'I'm sorry to have kept you waiting,' he said gently. For a moment she'd felt relief that Vaurgroth wasn't there. Then she realised, in alarm, that he wasn't alone; there were two Bhahdradomen guards behind him.

'Waiting for what?' she said.

'I've come to take you to Vaurgroth.'

'I thought he was coming here.'

'He's busy. A minor disturbance. He has asked me to take you to him.'

'I'm not going.' She backed up to the table, one hand groping behind her on the rough surface.

Zhoaah gave a quiet sigh. 'I feared you would make this difficult. Hence the *vagharim*. Please co-operate, my lady. I don't want you to be hurt.'

The guards moved into the room behind him, their mottled faces impassive. She felt their aura and her knees turned weak. Zhoaah came towards her, one hand outstretched as if trying to coax a nervous cat.

Ysomir felt the long hard shaft of her quill-pen under her fingers. She raised it and swept it in an arc towards Zhoaah's left eye.

The hard point pierced flesh. He cried out, doubling over with his hands to his face, the quill caught between his long thin fingers as he collapsed onto the bed.

The *vagharim* launched themselves at her. Ysomir caught her breath, bracing herself against the table for the inevitable pain, unconsciousness or death. Then something happened, beyond her control. She felt her spine arching, a tremendous heat and pressure gathering in her chest.

A wavering oval of light burst from her. It came from her mouth, her forehead, her heart, her very pores. It stood, moving and shimmering, between her and the guards. And as they came for her, it held them back. Phantom arms and legs writhed in the light, eerie cries echoed. There were two lashes of light, two shock-waves thumping the air, and the guards fell to the floor as if they'd been cut down by swords.

The mingled *ethroths* flew back to her, but they didn't re-enter. They surrounded her as a cloud of hazy light, shot through with flickers of gold, blue and green. Faces floated past hers then vanished into the light again; some she knew, some she didn't. She felt their strong, protective rage and her throat tightened.

There was Lynden. Lynden's face, sweet and brave as

she remembered it, but transparent like a reflection in a window. *No-one will touch or hurt you*, a voice whispered in her mind. *We are here. Go now!*

His urging electrified her. She looked at the open door of the cell. These four sandy walls had meant safety . . . outside was a huge, terrifying world. The thought of stepping out into it choked her with fear. Her vision of growing old here, safe in this dry little world with plain food and clean linens brought to her door, shafts of sunlight bathing the table where she would sit writing year after year, with visits from Tanthe and Saphaeyender to sustain her . . . all that was dust.

Even Helananthe's visits seemed preferable to the horror of stepping outside. But Ysomir knew she had to do it. Hold onto her courage, and change the future.

'What have you done?' said a rasping voice. She jumped. Zhoaah wasn't dead.

He stood glaring at her, a smudge of ink on his cheek as if a black tear had leaked from his eye. In the centre of the smudge, plasma oozed out. The quill had only pierced the bottom of the eye socket.

'Should have known, after the way you dealt with Garnelys, the old fire wasn't dead in you,' he said.

'Don't come near me,' she said. She was tense, controlled.

'I've no intention of it, believe me,' Zhoaah said quickly. He indicated the fallen guards. 'Did you know you could do this?'

'No,' she said, breathless. 'It wasn't me. It's the *ethroths*. They won't let anyone hurt me. Not you, not Vaurgroth.'

'Well, this changes things.' Zhoaah edged warily round her, staring at her inside the flickering cowl of light. He daren't come near her, and she felt, for the first time in her life, a wary but growing sense of power.

'I'm sorry I attacked you,' she said, and meant it. For some reason, she was relieved that Zhoaah wasn't dead. 'I had to.'

'You could have killed me,' he said thinly.

'I still could,' she said.

'Yes,' Zhoaah said faintly. 'Yes. Well, don't; I am not going to try anything, I assure you. Now what am I going to tell Vaurgroth?'

'I don't care what you tell him. I . . .' She swallowed hard, more afraid of her own intention than she was of any shape-changer. 'I have to leave now.'

'Leave?' He turned whiter, if that were possible. 'How do you think you are going to leave the Amber Citadel?'

'The same way I dealt with these guards.'

'Ah. So you are going to battle your way through three gates, leaving a mass of fallen *vagharim* in your wake? And not be noticed? My dear, you will end up with the whole of Vaurgroth's army pursuing you, and I don't think all the *ethroths* in the world will keep you safe forever, do you?'

Ysomir's eyes hardened. She felt the spirits stirring with anger, a small whirlwind around her and inside her. 'I'll find a way. I am going. It's what Lynden wants.'

Zhoaah stood looking at her as she began to walk to the door. She didn't have time to stand arguing with him. He didn't matter any more.

'Ysomir, I'll take you,' he said.

'What?'

'Put my cloak on.'

He passed her the grey garment at arm's length, as if afraid to touch her. She took it cautiously, anticipating the slippery feel of the skin from which most of their clothes were made. Instead it felt soft and weightless on her shoulders, woven of the finest wool.

'Pull up the hood and hide your hands in the sleeves. As long as I am with you, no-one will stop us.'

'Why are you doing this?' she asked.

He gave her an odd look, shrewd and wary with a trace of twisted affection. 'Ancestor knows. Perhaps I want to play dice with the future.'

She stepped out of the cell. There was a rushing sound

all around her. She realised it was the rushing of her own pulse. Zhoaah led her down the curved corridor past empty cells, unlocked the two great metal gates that separated the prison section from the rest. The innermost wall housed many rooms, passageways and offices but they seemed deserted, cleared of all their human inhabitants.

'What do you mean, play dice?' she said.

'Isn't it interesting, to have it in your power to change the future? You changed it, by killing Garnelys. Now I have the choice to let you go, or betray you on the way down. Which shall I do?'

'Stop tormenting me. I should know better than to trust you.'

'This, from a human who has just tried to pierce my brain with a quill?'

'It was a very small target,' she retorted.

Zhoaah's laugh echoed. Then he put his hand on her forearm and said, 'Hush. Don't talk, especially when we pass *yrim* or *vagharim*. Keep your head down.'

The further they went, the more anxious she felt. She'd left her refuge, and outside was enemy territory. At each gate, Ysomir kept her head lowered and let Zhoaah do the talking. No-one stopped them, or even tried; she saw the fearful deference with which they treated him; one of Vaurgroth's elite. Then she knew that she could control the *ethroth* entity that seethed within her. It hadn't attacked Zhoaah. As long as she wasn't threatened, it was quiescent.

Another gate opened, a tall side-gate with a narrow arch. Ysomir passed through and stood in the open end of the archway. She realised that she was one step away from the street. Free.

'Where will you go?' Zhoaah whispered, holding her back in the shadows.

'I don't know,' she breathed. She felt completely adrift. 'There's a friend who might help me . . .'

'Ah. Good. I can guess. By the way, don't bother trying to hide from me, my dear. Wherever you go I will find you.'

She shivered. 'Oh?'

'Don't be alarmed. I wish to keep a friendly eye on you, that's all.'

'Why don't you come with me now?' Even Zhoaah's company would be less alarming than going on alone.

'I have to go to back to Vaurgroth and concoct some story to explain your disappearance,' he said drily. 'I think I will tell him you are dead, having launched a near-fatal attack upon me. The *ethroths* themselves killed you, yes. They would have been useless to him.'

'Will he believe you?'

'He thinks his *bharu'grothrim* can do no wrong at present. I shall just have to hope he is too busy to view the body, since I can't produce it.'

That jogged her memory. 'Zhoaah, you said something about a disturbance?'

He gave his inscrutable, lipless smile. 'Ah, that. My dear, there was an escape of hostages last night. Your sister and the ex-Queen were among them.'

'Tanthe! Where are they?'

'If I knew that, they would have been recaptured by now. Go, quickly.'

He was withdrawing. A vague panic came over her; she wanted to keep him there. 'I don't know how to thank you.'

'Don't,' Zhoaah said, and shut the gate in her face.

She stood alone and trembling in the dark. She was on an obscure side of the Citadel, where the wall was flanked by grass and trees. She hardly knew Parione at all, having spent most of her time here inside the Amber Citadel. How was she to get her bearings and find her way to a house she'd never visited before?

Again she heard the whisper, *Don't fear, we'll guide you.* The resonance of Lynden inside her, all that was left of him.

Pulling the cloak tight around her, she began to hurry down Citadel Hill through the belt of trees. When her feet met the flags of the street, Rose Moon sailed full from behind a cloud to scatter her way with faint silver-pink light.

She realised that Zhoaah's motive in releasing her must have been more sinister than a secret affection for her. More likely he'd been afraid that she would kill Vaurgroth. Was it possible? If Vaurgroth had tried to carry out his plan, would the *ethroths* have leapt to her protection, perhaps sliced through his powers before he realised it? Yes, it could have happened.

She moaned. Fool, she told herself. I could have . . . No, who do I think I am? Zhoaah overestimates my power. All he's done is save my life.

Then another wave of dismay broke over her. She put her hand to her mouth, on the edge of a cry. *No, gods, no!*

She'd left Tanthe's gift, the *silvenroth* mirror, under the mattress in her cell.

Tears stung her eyes and she walked faster, almost running. There was nothing she could do. She'd left her diaries behind too, but that didn't matter; it had just been something to keep her sane. The *silvenroth* mirror, though, was precious and might have helped her; and she'd lost her only means to contact her mother. Too late now. No good crying over it.

Ysomir had never been to Saphaeyender's house but both he and Tanthe had described it to her and she knew that it stood on Temple Hill. On the way she saw several patrols of Bhahdradomen, but each time her instinct – or Lynden's – warned her to take cover. She was frightened, but the fear seemed to be outside her, like the moonlight, bathing everything.

Ascending the wide avenue that curved up the hill, keeping to the shadows of trees, she saw it; a long pearl-white villa nestling on the side of the hill, softened by exotic trees and vines. Ysomir looked around carefully for *yrim*, then ran until the foliage enfolded her. Breathing fast, she worked her way along the marble wall until she found a gate that led her into a courtyard garden.

The villa was in darkness, the doors locked. Ysomir made a circuit of the building, tapping frantically on every door she found, afraid to pound too hard in case a Bhahdradomen guard in the street heard her. No answer. At last she found a window shutter that gave under her hand, and she scrambled through the window into the dark room beyond.

Stillness ... she heard water running, thought it was a fountain, then realised it came from deeper inside the villa. She ran into a pillared corridor, saw the glimmer of candlelight spilling from a doorway. From the *ethroths* came moans of warning.

Ysomir ran towards the light, found herself in a bathroom. The first thing she saw was a lake of blood glistening on the tiles. Red gore was dripping over the side of the marble tub, soaking into a towel that lay with its edge in the lake. So much blood.

Her throat closed. Garnelys's death echoed in her memory and she thought, *Murder*.

The poet was lying in the water, eyes closed, head resting to one side. His long black hair floated. He looked as if he was simply relaxing, and might leap up in shock if she spoke. There was a statuette of Dyonis with water trickling from a carved shell, although the bath was already full and running into the overflow. The air was rank with whisky vapours.

The poet's pale body was veiled by the crimson smoke of the water. His wrists were folded over his heart and they were wet with the blood that was flowing over his chest into the water, dripping down one elbow onto the floor, pooling in the hollows of his throat.

A moan came from his lips. His hands slid down as if he'd fallen deeper into unconsciousness. There was so much blood she thought, *Dear Breyid, his throat is cut!*

'Saphaeyender?' she said.

No answer. His shoulder, just out of the water, felt cold to her touch. Shivering, she leaned over him and saw, through the film of blood on his throat, that there was no wound there. The fresh flow was all coming from his wrists. Then she knew for certain that he had done this himself.

The water was warm. He could not have been here long. She threw off her cloak. Glancing around, she grabbed two small towels and bound them firmly around his wrists. Then, doing her best to keep his hands clear of the water, she began to drag him up out of the bath. Her clothes became soaked with water and blood. He was a dead weight. She got his torso over the marble rim but couldn't lift him any further.

'Saphaeyender! Saphaeyender! What have you done?'

His eyelids fluttered and he groaned, breathing stale alcohol over her. His hair clung in dripping strings to his face and shoulders.

'Saph, help me,' she said urgently. 'Open your eyes. Stay awake!'

With an effort that strained every muscle in her body, she hauled him over the edge of the bath and onto the blood-slicked floor. He leaned back against the lip of the bath, head lolling. Ysomir hurried to tighten the towel binding on his wounds and to keep his wrists bent up to his shoulders. With her free hand she groped for a thick white towel and arranged it over his shoulders.

The bath seemed full of blood. Was there any left in his body?

He groaned again, but remained conscious, gazing at her with accusing, unfocused eyes. He needed a healer . . . but how could she get one to him? All she had was the folk knowledge imparted to her by her grandmother Helwyn.

'I don't think it's as bad as it looks,' she said shakily.

'Wha . . .' he slurred. 'What th' hell are you doing?'

'Trying to save your life.'

'Don' want saving,' he growled. 'Don't save me.'

'Shut up. Thank Goddess, I think the bleeding's almost stopped. I don't think you cut as deep as you could have done.'

'Must have done.' He clawed his hands as if to emphasise how much it had hurt. 'Must have done!'

'No, really. The cuts aren't that deep. This looks worse than it is. A small amount of blood goes a long way; I should know.'

'Leave me to die, damn it!'

The agony in his voice shocked her more than the blood. She shouted, 'If you really wanted to kill yourself, you should have cut your throat!' Then, without warning, she began to shake with sobs.

Saphaeyender stared at her, as if she had shocked him back to awareness. 'What the hell were you thinking?' she cried. 'How could you do this?'

There was a long pause. He said quietly, 'Where did you come from?'

'The Amber Citadel, of course.'

'How?'

'I'll tell you when you're feeling better.'

'How did you get in here?'

'Through a window.'

'How did you know I was . . .' He tipped his head towards the bathtub. 'You can't have known . . . can you?'

'I didn't,' she said through gritted teeth. 'Saph, you've got to help me. I can't lift you on my own. Lean on me, so I can get you into the bedroom.'

'Won' be any use to you there,' he said, leaning his whole weight on her as she helped him up, his hair dripping strands of water down her neck. And he laughed, but it was more like a sob.

In the morning, Saphaeyender found himself still alive. Weak, hungover and with a pounding headache, but nowhere near death. Black depression cloaked him.

Last night Ysomir had plied him with soup and heavily

honeyed tea. Now she was there again, sitting on the edge of his bed with a mug of some restorative beverage. To wake up with this sweet, golden creature looking down at him . . . perhaps there was some consolation for his failure, after all.

'How are you?' she asked.

'Alive, apparently. Can you bring me some tincture of willow for this headache?'

'You can't have any,' she said primly. 'It can thin the blood. That's the last thing you need at present.' Then she frowned. 'I must have learned more from Namane than I realised.'

'Namane . . . why does that name sound familiar?'

'She was a physician at the Amber Citadel. She looked after me when I was ill.'

'Ah.' He took the cup from her awkwardly; his wrists ached under the thick towel bandages. He sipped the liquid, which was pungent with healing herbs and syrupy with honey. Yet it was, at that moment, the best thing he had ever tasted.

'Garnelys killed her,' she went on matter-of-factly. 'She was the one he tortured to death in front of me.'

Saphaeyender nearly choked on the tea. 'You chose your moment to remind me of that.'

'Sorry,' said Ysomir. Then, softly, 'Oh Goddess . . .'

'What?'

'Nothing,' she said, composing herself.

He pressed her hand. 'Is her *ethroth* inside you too?'

She seemed embarrassed. 'I don't know. I never felt it before . . . but I seemed to know everything to do last night . . .'

'Common sense.'

'Perhaps.' They were silent for a minute or two. Then she asked bluntly, 'Why were you trying to kill yourself?'

Saphaeyender's eyes burned with unshed tears. He felt heavy with remorse and misery, and the reasons for which he'd done it had not gone away . . . but he lacked the impetus to try again. 'I don't know what I'm going to do.'

'Saph, tell me.'

'Two of Vaurgroth's elite came here, with guards. They commanded me to write propaganda for them.'

'But you didn't?'

'I started. Ymmi, I had to! It made me physically sick to do it,' he whispered. 'But I couldn't refuse. If I refused to co-operate, they were going to capture and torture my friends . . . perhaps that would have included you, I don't know. They were trying to turn me into a deadly weapon against my own people. There was only one way to destroy the weapon, and that was to kill myself. And now you have been kind enough to save my life, the problem is still there. Oh, Ysomir, much as I love you, I wish to all the gods you had come half an hour later, or not at all.'

She was staring at him, round-eyed. 'You're not going to try again, are you? You can't die, Saph. You mustn't! It's not the answer!'

'Isn't it?'

'Well, of course not!'

Her fervour distressed him; he had to make her see it was misplaced. 'Try to understand,' he said. 'I didn't do it in a fit of pique, or terror. I did it because I could see no other way to protect my friends . . . or, indeed, my reputation. D'you think I want to be remembered in history as a man who sang the praises of the enemy?'

'Of course not, but killing yourself isn't the answer. It's defeatist.'

'No, it was a clean and simple solution. Do you think it was an easy decision?'

'Saph,' she said quietly. 'Staying in my cell was a simple solution to the fears I couldn't face outside. How easy do you think it's been for me to leave? I'm still so frightened I can hardly stand up. But we have to try! Promise me you won't do it again.'

'It's all right,' he sighed. 'That promise is easy. Once was enough. But how did you find me? You can't have known, surely? No one knew.'

'I didn't. Lynden seemed to be guiding me here . . .' She spoke quickly, her eyes downcast.

'Lynden,' he echoed. 'And how did you escape the Amber Citadel?'

'That's a longer story. But Lynden helped me. I saw him. He was really there.'

Feverish colour burned in her cheeks. He frowned, his heart beating heavily. 'What do you mean, *really there*?'

'I know it sounds mad. I don't mean that he was alive again, Saph. But as an energy-form, just for those few minutes, when I really needed him – he was there.'

'Dyon's balls on a skewer,' Saphaeyender said under his breath.

'One of the Bhahdradomen let me out. The one called Zhoaah.'

Loss of blood had made him dizzy and tired. 'The one who designed the Tower? Looks like a little pale snake? Smiles a lot, in a demented sort of way?'

'Yes.'

'But he's as evil as the rest. Why would he suddenly help you?'

'I think he thought I was dangerous.'

He took her hand – clumsily, for his fingers were stiff – and looked gravely at her. 'Are you?'

Her smile was hesitant yet luminous. 'I hope so.'

'Does Zhoaah know you're here?'

'I don't know. If he does he won't give me away; he's told Vaurgroth I'm dead, so it's hardly in his interests to be found out.'

'Well, you can stay as long as you wish, but I don't know how I'm going to deal with Naghrur and Tzumezht. This is horrific. The situation's impossible.'

She frowned. 'You're not really sorry I saved you . . . are you?'

'At the risk of sounding ungrateful, all my problems

would have been over by now. But no. It was worth it, to wake up and find you watching over me.'

He smiled at her. She gazed back, then a look of guarded shock came into her lovely green-gold eyes and she said, 'Tanthe.'

'Ysomir, regardless of what everyone says about me, I am not embarking on a campaign to seduce you. Believe me, I am feeling much too tired even to think of it. You could be the beautiful daughter I never had. You are the dearest of friends.'

'I know that,' she said, looking steadily at him. 'I was going to tell you that I heard something about Tanthe last night. Zhoaah said that she and the Queen and the other hostages have escaped.'

He sat up, his head swimming. 'From the Citadel? How? Any idea where they've gone?'

She shook her head, distressed. Saphaeyender felt the fog of his depression fragmenting, shards of reality stabbing at him. It had been a blanket of comfort, giving up to despair and death. Ysomir was forcibly tearing it away.

The hush of the villa was shattered by the boom of fists on the front door.

They both started violently, and stared at one another. 'Who's that?' said Ysomir.

'Probably Sour-breath's cronies. They said they were coming for the first instalment of bullshit today.'

'Did you write it?'

'Yes. Then I burned it. My plan was that they came in to find ashes and a body. That would have been an impressive scene.'

'What will they do if you don't answer? Break in?'

Another thunderous knock. They clutched each other.

'I don't know.' His heart was thumping painfully.

'If it's Zhoaah, I could go and talk to him.'

'But it might be Naghrur. You truly don't want to talk to him. He's terrifying; I think he's worse than Sour-breath.'

They waited for the next knock, but there was silence.

Outside, a bird that had stopped singing when the visitor arrived began to chirp again.

'I'll go and look,' said Ysomir, rising.

'Don't!' he said, reaching after her. Too late. Trying to ignore the rush of faintness, he climbed out of bed and followed her.

Ysomir tiptoed through the villa, looking for movement beyond the lattice-work of the shutters. She peeped through a gap from which she could see the wide steps and the columns that flanked the main entrance. There was no-one there; but all her instincts screamed that someone was still outside, trying to find a way in.

She heard a footstep in the courtyard, just outside the window where she'd climbed in. The shutter moved. She caught her breath, summoned the *ethroths* inside her, reached out to grab the first object she could find – a wine decanter – and moved forward.

The shutter swung open to reveal the face of a handsome young man with yellow hair. Seeing her, he jumped, looking even more alarmed than she felt.

'Who are you?' Ysomir hissed.

'Who are *you*?' he said. He jumped lightly into the room, closed the shutter behind him, stood glaring at her. Her hand tightened on the heavy glass. Saphaeyender's voice from a doorway made her start.

'Eander,' he groaned, moving slowly towards them. He looked as white as the under-robe she'd dressed him in last night. 'What on Earth do you think you're doing? Didn't I tell you to go to your family, and not come back?'

'Saph, you have got to help me,' said the young man, rushing towards him. 'My mother's been arrested.' Before Saphaeyender could react, Eander stopped dead and exclaimed, 'Gods, what's happened to you? Why the bandages?'

Ysomir put down the decanter. The *ethroths* had barely

stirred. They seemed to know, if she didn't, that Eander wasn't dangerous.

'It's nothing,' Saphaeyender said coolly. The young man went to him, tried to lift his arm to look at his wrist, but the poet shook him off. 'This is terrible news about your mother, but what did you think I could do about it? You're not even supposed to be here.'

Eander flashed back, 'How in Dyon's name could you expect me to stay away? It was obvious you were going to do something stupid! We've all been worried sick about you!'

'As you can see, I am perfectly well,' Saphaeyender said flatly.

'You look terrible. And what's she doing here?'

'Saving me from myself, as usual. This is Ysomir, a friend I don't deserve; Ysomir, this is Eander, my . . . secretary.'

Eander seemed startled. 'Ysomir who . . . whom you used to visit in the, er . . . ? They released you?'

'In a manner of speaking,' she said.

He looked darkly at her. 'Did Saph do what I think he did?'

She couldn't answer him. Saphaeyender said quietly, 'Don't go in the bathroom. It's still quite a mess. She found me just in time.'

'You fucking idiot!' Eander yelled. 'How could you? Don't you ever think about anyone but yourself? Do you think you're the only person suffering? My mother has been arrested by the Eaters, and all you're upset about is me not obeying your orders!'

Saphaeyender drew back, looking stunned. 'You don't understand. I'm truly sorry about your mother. What happened?'

Eander took a shaky breath. 'They're starting to send people to the mines again.' His voice was hoarse. 'Mum was with a group protesting against it. There was no violence, they were just standing there peacefully, but *yrim* arrested them all. Goddess knows what will happen to her. If I can't turn to you for help, who is there?'

'This is awful,' Saphaeyender said, putting a hand on his shoulder. 'I'd help you if I could, but I'm in enough trouble with the Eaters as it is. You ought to go. I mean it. It's dangerous.'

'Why?'

'Because several of Sour-breath's *bharu'grothrim* will be here soon to collect the work they commissioned from me.'

It was obvious from Eander's expression that he hadn't known. 'You're working for them?'

'Not willingly. Not at all. I don't know what I'm going to say when they arrive, because I have nothing to show them. They may arrest me; if they find you here, they'll take you too.'

The young man's face turned paler. 'Then I'm staying to protect you.'

'Oh, beloved.' Saphaeyender briefly put his hands over his eyes. 'Stop being so heroic. You can't protect me. The only way I can protect you is to send you away. Hell. Cursed Hellaxis, if only . . .' He looked at Ysomir and shook his head. 'No, I'm sorry. You saved me and I'm still alive; so I have to find a different answer.'

'What time are they coming?' said Ysomir.

'I don't know,' Saphaeyender said. 'It could be any moment now.'

He sat down on a couch. Eander put his arms round Saphaeyender's neck, his golden head resting on the poet's black hair. So they are lovers, Ysomir observed, with only the faintest reaction. She wondered how Tanthe would feel if she knew; jealous, or accepting? Saphaeyender had often said he was lonely without Tanthe. Ysomir wasn't surprised, and didn't blame him.

She said, 'The only thing to do is leave, then.'

The two men looked at her. Eander said, 'The streets are swarming with *yrim*. It was a nightmare coming here. There's rumour of an escape from the Amber Citadel.'

Saphaeyender sighed. 'I don't want to leave. Which

is more courageous – to stay here and face the consequences, or to flee? What would Tanthe do? What would Rufryd do?'

'I expect they'd put on their toughest travelling clothes and run for it,' said Ysomir, 'not sit agonising about whether it's brave or not.'

'I have to go home, anyway,' said Eander. 'I can't leave my family in this situation. Why don't you come with me? The house is in the countryside, and it's huge.'

'Just run away?' said the poet, as if the idea had never occurred before.

'We'd better be long gone before Naghrur comes,' said Ysomir. 'We won't have the cover of darkness, though.'

'If you ask me, it's safer to go by day,' said Eander. 'They still let people move about more or less freely. If they catch you at night, though . . .'

'All right,' said the poet. 'We'll go now.' He stood up, closed his eyes and had to steady himself on Eander's shoulder.

'Are you sure you feel well enough?' Ysomir asked. 'You need a few days' rest, really.'

'I don't have that luxury,' he answered, meeting her eyes. 'I'll manage. Let's make ready, then, and hope there is plenty of good food in the kitchen.'

'Don't you know?'

'My staff banned me from going in there,' Saphaeyender said with a grimace. 'My chef didn't appreciate my helpful advice and interference with his recipes.'

The streets were swarming, as Eander had said, with humans and Bhahdradomen. It helped the three of them pass unnoticed, but Saphaeyender was transfixed by the colourful nightmare that swarmed around him. There were people walking in lines like dull-eyed conscripts, herded by *yrim*. Others stood watching, apparently horrified but not daring to intervene. He saw rows of citizens sitting along the sides of the roads with grimy clothes and empty faces.

He realised that these were the ones who'd been made homeless by the Bhahdradomen.

Saphaeyender recognised a man and woman standing at the edge of the crowd. They were concealed by cloaks but their bearing gave them away. Two of his actors, Sharm and Evender. 'What's happening here?' he asked.

Sharm started and looked round at him. Her powerful face was strained with fear; she looked five years older than the last time he'd seen her. 'They're taking people away to the mines again,' she answered, her voice flat. 'It's said they mean to continue building the Tower.'

Disgust gathered in Saphaeyender's chest. It was a full minute before he could speak again. He thought, If only I had died last night I need never have known this.

'They arrested some people who dared to protest,' said Evender.

'I know,' Eander whispered. 'My mother, for one.'

Sharm placed her hand on his shoulder. 'Oh, poor boy, I didn't know. It was a revolting spectacle; conscripts themselves shouting at the protestors, "It's Ancestor's Will," or some such nonsense.'

'You avoided the temple madness, then?' said Saphaeyender.

She made a noise of contempt. 'We'll never go again, unless they force us.'

'We have other news,' Evender said, not looking Saphaeyender in the face. 'Saliole died two days ago.'

'Oh,' Saphaeyender said, closing his eyes. Another blow. He felt the ground falling away beneath his feet. Saliole, one of his oldest friends. Saliole who'd been there from his earliest days; a veteran actor, still at the very height of his skills. 'Gods, how?'

'It was his heart,' Sharm said stiffly. 'He simply couldn't bear what has happened. You might say he died of a broken heart.'

For a time they stood in silence, watching the scene before them in a state of disbelief. Lines of glassy-eyed men and women being herded down the avenue, as if they went blissfully to serve the Ancestor. The murmuring crowd who watched but dared not act. The alien figures of the Bhahdradomen, with their gnarled spindly hands on the handles of their weapons, eyes that were both expressionless and menacing.

'We have got to stay together,' Saphaeyender said, when he could speak again. 'We must help each other. We must flee the city before the Devourers destroy us all.'

The other two gave him a look that could only be described as weary. 'Listen to yourself,' Evender said bitterly. 'You never gave one of your characters such a crass line to speak.'

'Well, this isn't a fucking play, is it?' Saphaeyender said crisply. 'We're off. You should come with us.'

'And go where?' said Sharm. 'Saph, we've done this before, fled from Garnelys and lived in hiding, then ended up in a wretched forest in the middle of a sweaty rabble army. I'm not going through that again.'

A thread of panic went through him. 'But we'll have a better chance of survival together. We can't let them destroy the company.'

'Oh, Saph. The heart went out of it the day the King betrayed us.'

'No. We can keep it alive. It's up to us. We need each other, damn it!'

Evender gave him a look that was regretful – almost pitying – yet impervious. 'We have families to think about. If we are going to die, let it be in the city, with our loved ones, not fleeing through some blasted forest in the middle of nowhere.'

'Are you refusing to help me?'

'My dear, I'm sorry,' said Sharm. 'But in these times, we must all help ourselves.'

Eander was pulling at his sleeve. 'Come away, Saph,' he said. 'We'll be taking the long way round to the house. We won't get there before dark, if you stand arguing.'

The red light of afternoon was fading towards evening. To avoid the main roads, Eander had brought them along a little-used track through woodland, heading south and west through the outskirts of Parione. Ysomir suspected he didn't know what he was doing, but she said nothing.

'Eander, are you lost?' Saphaeyender said eventually.

'No.'

'I thought your house was only an hour or two's walk from the city.'

'By the main road, yes.'

'It shouldn't be taking this long, even by the old Aelyr paths.'

'We've had to stop and rest every ten minutes, thanks to you letting half your blood out on the floor last night,' Eander said tightly. 'I am not lost!'

'Fine. Good.'

The twilight deepened, gemmed by Lily and Rose Moon. The path narrowed, with a high bank on their right and a drop to their left, no immediate tree cover. Another path joined theirs from the left. As they passed the fork, there was the guttural snap of an *yrim's* voice behind them.

'Stop!' Its Paranian was so thick they could barely make out the words, but the meaning was plain. 'Curfew-breakers! Stop!'

'Shit,' said Saphaeyender. He put his hand through Ysomir's arm and they started to run, Eander behind them.

'*Stop!*'

She glanced back. Through the spectral gloom, the dark figures of four *yrim* came running after them. Ysomir heard the crackle of their *roth*-weapons. A ball of fire streaked over their heads. She ducked. What was it, a fire-tipped arrow?

They were in full view of the Bhahdradomen and there was nowhere to shelter. Another missile flew past and struck the ground in front of them, sending up a gout

238

of blue fire. It emitted a pungent, metallic smell. No, not an arrow.

'Stop, or we'll be killed,' she said quickly. 'Get down on the ground, both of you!'

She pulled her arm free of Saph's and turned to face the Bhahdradomen. She saw their grotesque faces, the lethal energies spitting from their weapons. One of them aimed a bulky metal device as if it was a primed crossbow.

'Ysomir, no!' Eander cried. He pulled at her arm, agitated.

'Get down!' she repeated, but he didn't move.

'For fuck's sake, both of you—' Saphaeyender was dragging at him from the other side. Another missile sizzled towards them, a blue comet with a white tail, and Eander hit the ground with a cry.

Terror broke over her like a wall of white flame. She felt sweat prickling all over her, her breathing high and shallow as the energies built inside her. The *yrim* came on, angry and brutal and shouting. She stood her ground.

Then it happened. She felt something hurtling out of her, a force; an oval of *roth*-energy, birthing itself from her body and taking shape. It was a hot amber mist, flashing with gold and red fire. Inside it, a ghostly figure moved, wielding a sword of pure energy.

The Bhahdradomen saw it and hesitated. Then they came on, lashing out with *tzirin* whips, thrusting *sten* into the cloud of light.

Ysomir fell back, breathing hard. The soldiers' weapons cut through the *ethroth* as if through air, making no impression; she felt a tingle of pain. The cries of the dead echoed faintly within the cloud, like a battle heard from a great distance. Fireglow lit up the night. Her spectre swung his blade of light and two of the Bhahdradomen fell dead, uttering fearful shrieks. Spears of red energy gathered, flew, took the third *yrim* down.

The fourth dropped his *sten*, and fled.

Stillness. Ysomir crouched down to Eander, found him

alive and groaning. Saphaeyender was helping him to sit up. Her shield of light lost its brilliance but remained, clinging to her skin as soft as down.

'Are you badly hurt?'

'Shoulder,' he said, fingering the singed material of his cloak. 'It just grazed the bony bit. Burns like hell, but I'll be all right.'

'Come on, then. Quickly. Before the one that escaped comes back with reinforcements.'

She and Saphaeyender helped Eander his feet. He looked luminous in the twilight. Together they hurried on along the path. Her *ethroths* floated with them, a sheath of light in which, now and then, a face or a pair of hands or a whole figure would briefly appear.

'I didn't believe it until I saw it,' Saphaeyender said, his voice rough.

'You saw what happened?'

'Everything,' he said. 'I still can't believe it.'

'If that *yrim* goes back and tells them what happened, Vaurgroth will know it was me. He'll know Zhoaah lied. They'll come after us.'

'D'you want to go after him?'

'No,' she said. 'I don't think I can make the *ethroths* attack. I'm not sure I'd want to. They defend me, and that's enough.'

As soon as they could, they left the path and forged down into the cover of wild olives, ferns and arkhwoods that cloaked the slope. 'You're remarkable, Ysomir,' Saphaeyender said after a time. 'Are you going to make a habit of saving our lives once a day?'

'It wasn't me who saved you,' she answered.

Eander led them stumbling down the steep rocky slope, burrs gathering on their cloaks, twigs catching painfully at their hair. Saphaeyender made no reply, and she knew he understood what she meant, and couldn't speak.

It was Lynden who had soared out of her, taken shape and defended her. She'd seen him clearly. Wavering like a flame – with the guards visible through him – but still unmistakably Lynden. Perhaps Saphaeyender had recognised him too. If so, it wasn't the first time Lynden had saved his life, either.

Presently the oval of *roth* shrank, clinging as a luminescent sheen to her skin, then vanishing into her pores. She couldn't distinguish the personalities, they seemed all one mass; but she felt Lynden distinctly. He remained outside longer than the rest, as if watching for danger. Later, she felt him slip back inside her without a word. She wanted to cry then. For he was so real and yet he wasn't . . . she couldn't touch him, couldn't feel his body against hers. Never would again.

Saphaeyender said nothing. When the ground flattened out and they could move more easily, he reached out and took her hand. A dra'a'k sailed across Leaf Moon, a tiny black arrow, a danger sign. Hand in hand they fled into the darkness.

Chapter Eleven. Paths into Twilight

Figures moved out of the dawn with the soft creak of leather and metal, surrounding the Queen's party. There was a swish of swords being drawn. Tanthe's nerves were firing too hard to register fear. She'd passed beyond exhaustion a long time ago, her whole being alert and tingling from the stress of their escape.

She squeezed the rubbery handle of the *sten* beneath her palm and stood ready to draw the hated blade. She would have given anything to feel her lost Shaelahyr sword there instead.

'Drop your weapons!' said a deep female voice. 'Who goes there?'

'It's Lahjaya of the Citadel,' their guide answered quickly. 'Kereyn?'

'I can smell Devourer weapons.'

'It's all right. We're friends. These weapons are stolen.'

There was a suspended moment. Then one of the figures came forward and clasped hands with Lahjaya.

Eldareth murmured, 'Thank the gods,' but by then Tanthe knew that these soldiers were human. The metal swish of swords had given that away, even before she'd realised they had no fearful aura, no dark electricity. As dawn brightened she began to make them out.

'What is this?' said Mawrdreth. Helan stood silently beside him, her face expressionless, her eyes watchful.

'Resistance,' said Lahjaya. 'Kereyn, these people are more than friends. They've escaped from the Citadel. I helped to get them out. Now we need your help.'

'*More* than friends?' said Kereyn. She stepped forward.

Half-light revealed a stocky woman in her fifties with short grey hair. She looked powerful, weather-beaten and as impervious as granite. Around her stood twenty or so soldiers, a ragged assortment of men and women from different realms, their garments and breastplates so varied in style and worn out that they looked more like peasants than warriors. Outlaws ... yet it was with just such an army that Helananthe had taken the Citadel from her grandfather.

Kereyn looked carefully at each of them in turn. Auriel and Tanthe, Eldareth and Elrill, Helananthe and Mawrdreth. Her face remained stony but she became very still and chewed at her upper lip.

Suddenly she dropped to one knee in front of Helananthe. 'Your majesty,' she said.

All the other soldiers copied her. There was a frozen moment; Helan looked horrified. Finally she spoke stiffly. 'Please get up. There is no need for this.'

They rose. Kereyn said solemnly, 'Ma'am, it is an honour beyond words. We shall do everything in our power to protect you.'

Helan's eyes were dark. Tanthe had seen no light in them since she'd given up the Sapphire Throne. 'Who are you?' she said.

'Lady Kereyn of the House of Mivrin,' the older woman answered. Although she looked as rough as a farmer, her accent was the rounded, precise tone of an educated Parionian. 'I fought with Masketh in the rebellion against Garnelys. I was in that terrible battle in which he was killed. I fought for you, ma'am.'

Helan said nothing. Complex emotions stirred behind the mask of her face. Kereyn went on, 'That was a battle as much against the Bhahdradomen as against the King. We're still here, rebels in the forest, trying to protect our land against the Devourers.'

'You will doubtless be aware that I was forced to give up the Throne to them.' Helan's voice shook.

'We know that, ma'am,' Kereyn said, her gaze unwavering. 'You are still our Queen – and King. We're here to lay down our lives for you.'

'Nor for me,' Helan said faintly. 'For Aventuria.'

Mawrdreth said, 'Lahjaya advised us to make for Azura Maroc. If you can offer us protection on our way, it would be greatly appreciated.'

Kereyn nodded, but her face was grave. 'The Devourers haven't entered Azura Maroc yet – but the border's in turmoil. Still, we'll guide you and guard with all our strength. It's an honour, ma'am.'

'We're bound to be pursued,' said Eldareth.

Kereyn's weathered face lifted into smile, apparently relishing the prospect. 'Well, you must be the most wanted group of refugees in the Nine Realms. Come. It's getting light. We'll escort you to a hiding place where you can rest and eat. And we'll make plans.'

Kereyn and her band led Helan's party through a belt of thick woodland, across several streams where thick ferns grew, and brought them to a deep, narrow valley sheltered by trees. By now Tanthe had no idea where they were, and was too tired to care.

While a number of the rebels vanished into the trees to take up sentry positions, Tanthe, Lahjaya and the others sank gratefully onto the grass on the bank of a stream. Helan and Mawrdreth sat slightly apart as they shared food from their packs. Helan looked no better than she had in the Citadel; pallid, emotionless, her hair in rats' tails. Yet there was something indefatigable inside her.

'Are you okay?' Tanthe said, sitting down beside Auriel.

'This is all so strange,' he said, with a faint smile. 'I feel as if I shouldn't be here.'

'I'm glad you are. Not going through this, I mean, but with me.'

'I'm happy to be anywhere that Falthorn isn't.' His dark eyes became troubled. 'I'm just realising that I know absolutely nothing about the world. But I feel safe with you there, Fliyet.'

She smiled at the secret name, felt uneasy at the idea of having to protect him. Not his fault, but Auriel was hopelessly unworldly. 'We should rest while we can. I feel too wide awake to sleep.'

She did, though. When one of Kereyn's soldiers woke her for supper, it was dark again. She felt stiff and cold. The rebels couldn't build a fire in case it gave them away.

As they finished eating, Elrill quietly took Eldareth aside and spoke to him at the edge of the trees. Tanthe watched them, their figures outlined by a faint dusting of moonslight – Eldareth dark, Elrill pale as Lily Moon – but couldn't hear what they were saying. The discussion looked intense; the two men had known each other for years, Eldareth a frequent guest at Silverholm.

When the two came back, Elrill stood in front of Helananthe and bowed his head. 'Your majesty,' he said gravely.

She and Mawrdreth rose to their feet. 'Lord Elrill?' Tanthe and Auriel got up too. With a trace of foreboding, Tanthe knew what Elrill was going to say; so did Auriel, from the worried look he gave her.

'Alas, I must leave you,' said the Shaelahyr lord. 'I'm going north, back to Silverholm. I must know how my people are faring under the invasion. You understand, don't you, that my first duty is to them?'

'Oh,' said Helananthe, looking sad. 'Yes, Elrill, of course. I'm sorry to see you go. We all are. But I understand.'

'Thank you. Be assured that all the Shaelahyr can do to halt the invasion, we shall do. We are not, and never have been, of Falthorn's persuasion. We are your friends.'

'I know that,' Helan said, biting her lower lip. 'Thank you. For your friendship, and for everything you've done, thanks. Goddess go with you.'

Elrill bowed again, a brief graceful gesture, to each of them in turn. When he came to Auriel, he paused and said, 'If you wish to be among Aelyr again, my friend, you could come with me.'

Auriel hesitated. He appeared so torn that Tanthe feared he would go. Then his expression changed to an acid smile, 'That's good of you, Lord Elrill, and you've been a kind friend to me. But I have no desire to dwell among the Aelyr again. I wish to stay with my sister.'

'We are not the Valahyr – but as you will,' Elrill said, clasping his shoulder. He kissed Tanthe's hand, his ice-blue eyes meeting hers. 'I hope we will meet again.'

'Yes, I'll miss being chained to rocks, ignored and insulted,' she said.

He grinned. 'Am I still not forgiven?'

'Oh, just bugger off,' she said, trying to swallow the stone in her throat. 'Go safely, won't you?'

'Fare you well,' he said, turning away.

With a sense of emptiness she watched him leave. In seconds his bright cloak and hair had faded to grey and vanished, like an owl swallowed by the forest.

No one spoke for a time after he'd gone. There was a sense of loss, and nothing to say. They broke camp, and went on.

Vaurgroth's rage, on discovering the hostages had escaped, was incandescent. Even Gulzhur, Rhazagramen and Naghrur trembled. He didn't raise his voice; didn't need to. His displeasure dripped on them like burning oil. The quiet brooding waves of his fury shook the Sun Chamber itself. For a time, Gulzhur feared that the Master of Light would slay his *bharu'grothrim* en masse, as he'd slain the kitchen staff who'd finally had their perfidy tortured out of them.

After venting his wrath, however, Vaurgroth became calm again. He began to cast them as victims rather than incompetents. 'The death of Enlightener Uryzht is a bitter loss,' he said. 'You, my precious mages, have suffered at the hands of these wretched humans. Rhazagramen was injured. Zhoaah suffered a near-fatal attack by a deranged prisoner who, mercifully, died. This is a warning that even we, Ancestor's elite, must be ever-vigilant against these outbreaks of defiance.'

'I take full responsibility for the escape of the hostages,' said Naghrur, soft and icy. 'I must have missed the obvious.'

'Shouldering blame is a virtue,' said Vaurgroth. 'I value it in you, Protector.'

Gulzhur sneered. Dirt slid off Naghrur like rain from a shining steel knife. He could do no wrong.

'Go, make further searches of the city,' said Vaurgroth. 'Gulzhur, take your *ghelim* and hunt further afield.'

At that, Gulzhur gave a secret sigh of relief. How good it would be to travel alone, just him and the *ghelim* at his command. To pass unseen in his cloak of Bhahdradomen skin; soft as velvet, supple with endless infusions of *gauroth*, shifting texture and colour to match the terrain. To enjoy the screaming horror of humans when they glimpsed him; a ghost with a skull-head, a horror of bones slicked with translucent flesh and knotted veins. He couldn't wait to taste their fear.

It would be good to leave the Citadel. He hated human dwellings, steeped as they were in alien history and atmospheres. He could never love them, as Zhoaah did. Zhoaah was becoming all too obsessed with humans, in his opinion. Gulzhur missed the *tzcements* of Vexor, the simple life. In the back of his mind he longed for the bleak landscape of myth, Hellaxis, and the unattainable black spire of fulfilment, the Obsidian Tower. They would re-create that promised land in Aventuria.

'You were lucky to avoid punishment,' he whispered to Zhoaah as they left the Greatlord's presence.

'Not really,' said Zhoaah. Always that smug, secretive smile, as if he knew something Gulzhur didn't. 'So, we let him down . . .'

'*I* did not. This escape had nothing to do with me.'

'Still, we're all tainted with the possibility of failure,'

Zhoaah went on. 'Luck didn't come into it. He knows we'll scramble all the harder to please him in future. If he doesn't have faith in us, who can he trust? Destroying us would be as pointless as cutting off his own right hand because he'd dropped a cup.'

South of Parione, vineyards covered the flowing slopes. There were buds on the vine and even through the winter the greens of the landscape were saturated in the moist air. The sky boiled softly with purple clouds. Often a cold snap would bring frost and snow to the city but this year the weather had stayed unnaturally warm, with eerie winds and storms. Disturbance of the Earth. The landscape was unnaturally deserted, as if the winegrowers were huddling in their homes, or had fled, leaving the vines to run wild.

'How did you know about the resistance?' Tanthe asked Lahjaya as they trudged through a valley the next night.

'There's a network,' Lahjaya said in her velvety accent. 'I made friends with some of them when Garnelys first took us from our homes. Seems years ago now.'

'Are you coming all the way to Azura Maroc with us?'

'Of course! I've no desire to return to the Citadel kitchens, thank you. There are some there who can't be trusted.'

'People who got carried away in the temple, do you mean? Didn't it affect you?'

'Hah!' Lahjaya spat vehemently onto the ground, just missing Tanthe's boot. 'I don't give *that* for their stupid Ancestor! How could they be taken in?'

'It's something the Bhahdradomen do. They get inside your head. Most people weren't prepared and had no defence against it.'

'Well, I've no wish to stay around such sheep. I want to go home.' Her copper face and gleaming black eyes were serious.

'It looks a long way on the map,' Tanthe sighed, thinking wretchedly of Ysomir. How far apart they were, again.

'It is,' Lahjaya said gravely.

Lahjaya, although small, was fit and quick-moving. She struggled to keep up with the long strides of Mawrdreth and Eldareth, yet she never complained — not without making a joke of it. Tanthe liked her immensely. Even Helan, who'd seemed so ill, found astonishing reserves of physical energy. Her eyes, though, were stone.

On Kereyn's advice they avoided the great trade road that ran south to Lapiszul. Instead they kept to narrow valleys on the fringe of the vine country, where it was easier to pass unseen. They travelled mainly by night, and in the gloom of dawn and twilight. By day they took shelter in wooded valleys, with Kereyn's party to scout for danger. Her soldiers were well-practised. They'd been living wild, Kereyn explained, almost since Garnelys initiated his conscriptions.

The journey could have been worse. The nights were chilly but bearable, the days temperate. Sometimes wild skies raced above, with clouds spreading bands of shadow across the landscape, strange flickers in the west. Several times, ferocious electric storms forced them to take cover.

Where the vineyards gave way to farmland, the party halted to share provisions. They were sheltered by an overhanging rock in a high cleft, with olive groves and orchards spreading below them. Beyond, velvet green hills rolled into an amber sunset. Villages lay snug in the folds. Tanthe could believe, at this moment, that the nightmare of the invasion had never happened.

'We've a choice of routes to the border, ma'am,' Kereyn said. The stocky leader was sitting in a circle with Helan, Mawrdreth and Eldareth. Tanthe, Auriel and Lahjaya sat on the fringes, listening. Helan looked exhausted yet magnificent, her lion-coloured hair rippling back over her shoulders.

She said, 'Eld and I made many journeys and pored over many maps together, in happier days.' Eldareth smiled;

Mawrdreth didn't react. Tanthe wondered if he was ever jealous of Helan's past. He seemed too dignified to feel jealousy, unlike Rufryd.

'Well, there is the Lapis Road, which is the most obvious way. There's the coast, which I don't recommend, since it's tortuous and impassable in places. It would mean too many long detours inland.'

'Or we could sail,' said Helan. 'I've done that before, hired passage on a ship from Farios port.'

Kereyn was shaking her head. 'We've heard bad news. It's said that Farios is under Devourer control and they are letting no ships leave. They are going to ruin us, you know. Traders coming up from Maroc have been stopped on the border; refugees fleeing the other way are causing havoc. No farming, no trading; it doesn't take a Lapiszul thinker to work out the results.'

There was a heavy silence. 'How far have they got?' asked Mawrdreth.

'They're concentrated in Paranios, the heart. Our spies tell us they're creeping into Mithrain, Eisilion, western Thanmandrathor . . .'

'Tasqabad?'

'I don't know, sire, I'm sorry. It's said the Viceroy of Torith Mir has saved his neck by making some kind of treaty and declaring himself neutral.' She sounded disgusted. Helan and Eldareth exchanged a glance. 'Idiot. Treaties mean nothing to the Devourers. They only thing they know how to do is consume. They will creep and blacken every inch of the Nine Realms, given time; nothing we're doing looks likely to stop them.'

'You seem to know everything,' Helan said tiredly. 'More than I've been able to learn, cooped up in the Citadel.'

Kereyn drummed her strong fingers on her knees. 'Ma'am, I was an historian and archivist in Parione, until Garnelys began his tricks. I knew then that mad times were coming; but when my son – a respected teacher of history – was taken to work in the mines, I vowed to do anything it took to stop the madness. A man of learning, wasted on digging stone!'

'I'm sorry,' Helan said quietly.

'For many of us, our rebellion began by searching for conscripted loved ones. We formed a network to pass on information, and it grew, and is still growing. Now, more than ever, Goddess knows we need it.'

'Did you find your son?' Tanthe asked.

'I learned where and how he died,' Kereyn said flatly. She went on, cutting off their expressions of sympathy. 'Ma'am, d'you think that Parione fell without resistance, that the Devourers have it all their own way? It's not so. There's still a network of resistance across Paranios. The Bhahdradomen hoodwinked us into fighting each other, but now we're united against them. Our task may be impossible, but we'll not give up. It means everything to us that your majesties and your friends reach safety.'

'If Lapis Road is obvious,' said Eldareth, 'perhaps that's the route we should take? We know the way.'

'Yes, but the positions of the Devourer troops down there make it difficult. I suggest we go across country to the east of the road. It's hard going, but plenty of shelter.'

'Over the tail of the Serpentine Mountains?' said Eldareth.

'That will be our best hope.' Kereyn's tone wasn't encouraging.

'Is there any chance we could get horses on our way?' Tanthe put in.

'It's possible,' the leader said, tilting her iron-grey head to face Tanthe. 'Could make us too visible to pursuers, though. And there's too many of us to mount everyone. A horse for the Queen and King might be a possibility . . .'

'I don't need special treatment,' Helan said gently. 'I've lived as a warrior in the wilderness too. I was more myself there than I ever was as Queen.'

The great Lapis Road ran south and slightly west from Parione, along the edge of the forest of Lusahniah, crossing rivers, down through the rich farmland and flowery plans that lay east of the Serpentine Mountains, on past the high rocky areas where the quarries lay – yielding up their prized cream and golden marble to build the beautiful towns of Paranios – down through gentle hills and woodland until it curved around the tail of the Serpentines.

Kereyn's party took the harder, pathless way alongside it, ever watchful for *yrim*.

The endless grind of travelling began to depress Tanthe. The landscape was familiar – she'd travelled it before, going north – but not familiar enough for comfort. Maps of Aventuria had shown that Lapiszul was as far, if not further, than the distance from Riverwynde to Parione. It was almost as far as Rufryd had travelled to Vexor. *Perhaps I'll never see him, or Ymmi or Saph or Parione, again . . .* She tried to stop herself thinking it.

She was missing Rufryd painfully. She'd taken him for granted, even when he'd set off to Vexor; he'd always been there, infuriating sometimes, but enduring as a rock. He was as earthy and reliable as Auriel was fey. The possibility that he was dead became a creeping wave of agony. *Why did I let him go?*

They seemed to be crawling ant-slow across the unrolling hills. Several times they had to hide when an *yrim* patrol deviated from the Lapis Road. Shadows and folds in the land disguised the ravages of *graukhim*, making the wounds seem deceptively insignificant.

The farmland they crossed was deserted. Usually the farmers would be starting to plough and sow by now. Then, not far from the quarries of Napheneth, they ran straight into a herd of *graukhim*.

Dawn was breaking. Their route brought them onto the crest of a low ridge below which was a wide valley, unrolling in gentle folds. Once it had been beautiful. Now great trenches of black earth furrowed the green, and trees stood like skeletons, stripped bare of leaves, twigs, bark. Tanthe froze, clutching Auriel's arm. No-one spoke. Only

Kereyn and her comrades looked unsurprised, but their faces were grim.

'The Eaters have done this to the land?' Auriel asked under his breath.

Tanthe nodded. Her mouth was open, her spirit pressed flat by horror. The devastation she'd seen in the forest of Ardharkria had been shocking enough. She'd never imagined it on such a vast scale.

'It's spreading faster than we feared,' said Kereyn.

There were hundreds of tiny figures moving on the edges of the scars. Cattle-shaped beasts, not merely munching the green grass but tearing it up by the roots.

Two of Kereyn's men came running towards them from the east.

'Go back down the ridge, head west,' one of them panted. '*Graukhim* and herders everywhere. The copse where we were going to make camp is matchwood.'

They spent hours zigzagging to avoid Bhahdradomen and seek cover, while the morning grew ever brighter. Scouts reported a safe valley half a mile away. As they reached it, descending around a bluff, they came face to face with a group of Bhahdradomen herders.

Tanthe felt the familiar shudder of fear. The faces of the *domenim* were blotched like lichen and their eyes were expressionless; algae-choked ponds. Their garments were rags and they leaned on staffs of stripped wood. Behind them wandered a handful of their flesh-animals, bloated ruminants with pallid shaven skin, square crushing teeth, curved horns.

The *domenim* stared at the human party. The humans stared back.

Tanthe's head swam. She fingered the *mnelir*, felt its bright heat against her fingers. She was going to draw it, but Eldareth stayed her hand and said, 'No. We'll go past them quietly, and say nothing. Come on, walk to the side. Don't look at them, don't run.'

'He's right,' said Kereyn. Her face glistened with sweat.

'These peasant-types are generally harmless. They don't even speak Paranian. They're as frightened of us as we are of them.'

Moving in single file on the path, they picked their way further down into the valley and skirted around the Bhahdradomen party. It was like passing a pack of wild dogs, trying not to excite their attention. The Eaters watched them impassively for a while. When Tanthe looked back the last time, they had gone.

'So much for the secrecy of our journey,' said Mawrdreth.

'Not necessarily,' said Kereyn. 'This lot seem to have little contact with the military. They're not spies. Unless Eater troops actually come this way and ask, it's unlikely they'll give us away.'

'Can we rest now?' said Lahjaya.

'Not here,' said Tanthe. They were crossing a swathe of earth that the *graukhim* had apparently grazed some time ago. There was no way round it. A sour smell rose from it and the surface grains were webbed with some kind of grey fungus like cobwebs.

'Why not?' said Lahjaya. 'It's just soil, do us no harm.'

'Bad idea, believe me,' said Tanthe. 'The *graukhim* carry a parasite in their guts. The larvae get into the soil where they turn into adults and drag any food they can find underneath the surface; dead rabbits, unsuspecting sleepers. They lay eggs in you, then you get eaten from the inside out.'

'You're making this up!' Lahjaya gasped.

'Wish I was. It nearly happened to us in the forest of Ardharkria once.' Tanthe grimaced. 'Of course, you'd suffocate in the earth long before the egg-laying bit started.'

'An insect – pull a human under the soil?'

'Not on its own, obviously. They work in thousands, so many of them they make the earth boil. They dig it away underneath you, and down you go.'

'You have a very strange sense of humour,' Lahjaya said darkly.

'She's not joking,' said Kereyn. 'All this land will be infested with them soon. Witness how Vaurgroth exploits his peasants. The *graukhim* are Bhahdradomen too; did you know that?'

The others stared at her. Mawrdreth said, 'I'd heard. I didn't believe it.'

'No!' said Lahjaya. 'Just grotesque animals, we thought.'

'No, they're the same as their masters. Hatched from the same eggs, but changed. That's why they call them shape-changers, yes?'

Lahjaya looked stricken. 'You're telling me that they eat . . . each other? I think I am going to be sick.'

'Mind you, look how happily they are exploited,' Kereyn snorted. 'Like blasted ducks to water on our land.'

Over the next few days they passed one *graukhim* herd after another. Usually they managed to avoid the attention of the herders, but sometimes the beasts would raise their heads and watch them with dim intelligence. Their attention was disturbing. Tanthe couldn't stop herself wondering how much they knew. Did the change reduce their awareness to that of animals – or were they fully aware of being trapped in bovine bodies that were going to be slaughtered for meat? Were they afraid, or glad, or did their consciousness work at some level she couldn't even imagine? The thoughts spun cocoons of nightmare in her dreams.

The herd territory gave way at last to a stretch of undamaged plain. Somehow the contrast made the ruined area the more heart-breaking. Kereyn's scouts reported the plain free of Bhahdradomen so, by star-gemmed twilight, they began to cross towards the woodland on the far side.

Something glinted in the grass, a long sword-straight line that ran from the north and on towards the Serpentines in the south. Tanthe saw that it was a metal rail, with a twin running alongside it, the two joined by lengths of wood. Grass had grown over it. Eldareth kicked at one of the rails as they stepped over it.

'What is this?' Tanthe asked.

'Part of Garnelys's great project,' Eldareth said sourly. 'This is the line that runs down into Azura Maroc. He had great wagons running on these rails, pulled by teams of horses. Quicker way to get the conscripts to the mines.'

'Of course,' said Tanthe. 'Ymmi travelled in one. She told me all about it.'

'I travelled in one too,' said Lahjaya. 'It was rough, but better than walking.'

'Well, I hate to mention this,' said Kereyn, 'but the network informs us that the Devourers are clearing the line to the north. Looks like they have plans to use it again.'

Eldareth fell into step beside Tanthe and lowered his voice so only she could hear. 'Are your feet as painful as mine?'

'It's not my feet I'm worried about,' she said. 'If I hear one more bit of bad news I think I'll throw myself in the next river.'

He sighed. 'That was just by way of enquiring how you are.'

She was glad of his company. She'd always felt safe with Eldareth there. 'Oh, I'm all right. I wish we had horses. I never thought I could miss Redbird so much. I hope she's safe in Verdanholm, and Falthorn hasn't eaten her.'

Eldareth laughed. 'Wouldn't put it past him.'

'I don't know which is worse, sore feet or a sore backside,' Tanthe said. 'What are we doing, Eld? Is this journey going to be worth it?'

'It will be, if Azura Maroc is free, and willing to help us.'

'I can't stop thinking about the people I've left behind. I feel I've let everyone down.'

'You too, eh?'

'What?'

'Thinking it's up to you to save the whole world. We're all at it. We should relax a little and just do our best, don't you think?'

She smiled. 'And here am I, moaning about myself as usual. How are you?'

'As ever.' He gave an ironic smile.

'It can't be easy for you . . .' She tilted her head towards Helan and Mawrdreth.

'It's strange. I cannot get used to the fact that I can't simply talk to her, console her or kiss her. That this other man is always there.'

'In your place.'

'I must accept what is. I like Mawrdreth. He's a good man.'

'You're being very gracious.'

'I'm a very gracious person, Tanthe,' he responded, straight-faced.

'I miss Elrill, don't you? I really wish he hadn't gone.'

Eldareth fell silent. He was staring up at the sky. Alarmed, Tanthe looked up too and saw the silhouette against the violet sky. Clawed wings, long tail, razor-sharp primaeval head. Dra'a'k, or . . .

'*Ghelim!*' shouted Eldareth. 'Run!'

Everyone obeyed, sprinting hard into the edge of the trees. Tanthe was breathless, her heart pounding. As they gained cover, Auriel stood wide-eyed beside her, staring up at the sky.

The *ghelim* arrowed above the treetops. There was no way of telling whether it had seen them or not. It circled two or three times, then arrowed back the way it had come.

'Now the real trouble begins,' Eldareth said between his teeth.

They found a place to camp, deep in the most tangled part of the wood. Everyone was on edge. Kereyn sent out twice the number of scouts to keep watch. Auriel sought out Tanthe and they nestled together, wrapped in both their cloaks, but neither of them could sleep.

'There's a town near here called Nachillei, where we hid for a while,' she told him. 'Beautiful white town shaped like a horseshoe. Two old men hid us in their house. They were twins, Olmion and Olberyd, beautiful old men with long white hair.'

'What happened to them?' he asked.

'We don't know,' she said, saddened. 'Probably killed by Garnelys's troops. I hope they escaped.' Sighing, she turned her face into Auriel's shoulder. He stroked her hair.. 'Do you ever think about our child?' she whispered.

'Yes, of course.'

'Do you think we'll find him?'

She felt him breathe out, very softly, against her hair. 'I hope so. I would like to unweave every foul thing Falthorn did to us.'

'You can, Auriel,' she said. 'We wove the web with Elrill . . .'

'I don't think I could do it without him. It was his power, not mine. It's still too frightening, trances, dreams, anything that makes the *ezht* seem close . . .'

'Hey, don't think about it now. I'm here.' Her hands moved over his lean firm back. She'd missed touching his golden body and his lovely autumn-red hair. The next thing she knew they were kissing. He was aroused, hard against her, and it was the easiest thing in the world to let him slip inside her, sweet and inevitable. Barely moving and trying to make no sound, they pleasured each other.

It was the first time since they'd left Verdanholm. It seemed an age since she'd enjoyed this bliss. As she came, Tanthe hung suspended in white light, again feeling she was on the very edge of something profound, about to break through the veil to her Aelyr nature . . . only for it to slide out of her grasp into the purely physical spasms of release. Auriel gasped, spilling his own ecstasy into her.

Then they lay holding each other, heads touching, no words passing between them. Tanthe felt strange. Vaguely empty and awkward, as if it shouldn't have happened.

Auriel was so easy to love, too easy, but she knew now that her feelings were shifting towards protective tenderness. No fault of his own, but he wasn't strong enough to be all she needed. He clung to her because she was his sister, and the only warmth he knew.

'Tanthe,' he said, very faint. 'I love you, but . . . I don't think we should have done that.'

'That's easy to say afterwards.' She kissed his cheek.

'I can't explain.' He held her hand loosely against his chest.

'I can,' she sighed. She felt sad. 'I think it's that we've really started to see each other as brother and sister. And you'll only find your strength if I let you go.'

A laugh that was also a sigh. 'You know everything, Fliyet.'

'It's my curse. All I know now is that I'm falling asleep. Warm me. Don't feel bad about it.'

She dreamed that Olmion and Olberyd were talking to her. They were sitting cross-legged in front of her, their white hair flowing around them like living light.

'We walk the path of stars into the Jewelfire,' they said. 'The *ezht* is a blindfold. The danger is to walk in it forever and never see. There is no means to avoid the fear, you understand; you must go through it. Climb the darkness to reach the light. Jewelfire and Tower are opposites. Jewelfire and Tower are one. Without death there is not life. Be as Wrothryr and see the utter simplicity of it.'

Tanthe woke violently in a cold sweat. Eldareth was calling urgently to them. 'Come, time to break camp. There's danger.' Seeing her with Auriel, he gave a crooked grin. 'Hope you haven't used up all your energy. Hurry!'

They got to their feet, hurriedly fastening the laces of shirts and breeches, pulling on jackets and boots, settling weapons on their belts. Then they were on their way, pushing up a wooded slope, taking a narrow path through a copse of blue-thorn trees. There was a sinister atmosphere, slaty clouds massing above them, disturbing breezes stirring the branches.

Kereyn's soldiers were forging a path through the copse. Some of them set arrows to bowstrings. Helan, Mawrdreth and Lahjaya were running in a close line, swords in their hands.

'Eld,' said Tanthe, 'is it . . . ?'

He pointed up at the canopy. In patches of sky between the spiny leaves, she saw them. Wheeling high in the ether were reptilian shapes, leathery clawed wings outstretched on the wind currents. They kept circling, heads turning this way and that.

'You sure they're *ghelim*, not dra'a'ks?'

He gave her a grim look. 'Can't be too careful.'

Auriel said, 'Tanthe, the *mnelir*.'

She touched the knife in her pocket. It was warm. '*Ghelim*, all right,' she said. Her mouth went dry. 'Have they seen us?'

'Kereyn's trying to get us to a cave before they do,' said Eldareth.

The scars where Rhazagramen had tortured her suddenly began to burn. The crystal sphere on the *mnelir*'s pommel flashed heat and light, so bright she could see it through the material of her jacket.

Ghelim burst out of nowhere, feet above them. They were under the tree canopy, leathery wings buffeting the air between the close-spaced trunks. Three of them, uttering metallic screams, claws raking the air. Their fanged jaws clashed, dripping venom.

Cries from the humans. Chaos. Tanthe fumbled to draw a weapon. Then the first of the *ghelim* swooped and she felt the rasp of claws on her scalp, saw Auriel fall.

Ysomir sat on a window seat, looking out. Eander's house stood on the western side of Parione, high on a ridge overlooking open countryside. She could see meadows, a golden loop of river, a line of trees blue with distance. The scene was peaceful. She felt, for the first time, a twinge of joy at being free. On that side lay peace, perhaps an unimpeded path all the way back to Riverwynde, her home. Behind the house lay the city, terror and misery.

Saphaeyender came in and sat beside her. He said nothing for a few moments, but she felt no awkwardness, no need to speak. Finally he said, 'I learned a salutary lesson yesterday. For years I have considered myself to be the centre of the universe. Everyone flocked to do my bidding, everyone adored me. I thought it was my due.'

'It must be nice to have such a high opinion of yourself.'

'It was wonderful.' His lips tightened in a grin. 'I basked in it. They were moths around the great light and I thought it would always be so. I was the one for whom they'd always sacrifice everything, follow to the end of the realms. I never saw this coming.'

'I'm not saying a word.'

'You don't have to, Ymmi. And I'm not fishing for reassurance. I've been the victim of my own delusion, that's all. I'm no more important and valuable than anyone else in this land. Now I know. If I had died that night, I would at least have become a legend.'

'And I wouldn't have to listen to you complaining.'

He laughed. 'What a mercy that would have been. You always seem so tranquil. I envy that.'

'I'm not,' she said. 'It's a mask.'

'What are you thinking about?'

'I'm wondering where on earth Tanthe can have gone. Where *would* she go?'

'You know her better than I do,' he said. 'She was never predictable at the best of times. Besides, it wouldn't be her decision. If she's with the others, Helananthe would be making the decisions. Or Eldareth, knowing him.'

She gripped her elbows. 'I don't know what to do.'

'There is the chance that we might be safer to remain in hiding here, though, Nepheter knows, I am sick of hiding. Eander's family are good people, they'll let us stay.'

She raised her eyebrows. 'Do they know you've been sleeping with their son?'

'Gods, don't sound so prim.' He rubbed his eyes. 'I don't know, but probably best not to broadcast the fact, hmm?'

Ysomir smiled thinly. 'This will cost.'

As she spoke there was movement and voices outside the door. It opened, and in came Eander, looking dishevelled.

'She's back. They let her go,' he gasped.

Ysomir and Saphaeyender stood up. Behind Eander came his father, a lean man with brown and silver hair and a hawkish, worried face. He was supporting a tall golden-haired woman. It was clear where Eander's looks came from, but her bony face was gaunt, her eyes marked with purple shadow. There were weals on her cheek and collarbone. She looked dazed. Eander's two sisters came red-eyed into the room, fussing after her.

Her family helped her to a couch.

'Yes, they released me,' she said. Eander had told them his mother's name was Viananthe. 'Not out of mercy, but as a warning. I'm supposed to describe to you what an ordeal it was, how frightening they were, how much these wounds hurt.' She touched her cheek, wincing. 'However, I'll let you use your imaginations.'

Eander looked distraught. His sisters were crying.

Viananthe went on steadily, 'They warned me that if I am caught involved in any such action again, they will arrest not only me, but all of you, and there will be no further shows of mercy. We're all under suspicion. I'm sorry, my dears.'

Looking up, she caught Saphaeyender's eye. He exhaled

and glanced at Ysomir. 'In that case, we shall have to leave,' he said.

'Did I say that?' She sat forward, gently freeing herself from the hands of her son and daughters. 'Eander told me you were here. Lord Saphaeyender, Lady Ysomir, it's a great honour to have you as our guests.'

Eander's father looked at them. His face was as open and resolute as his wife's. 'Vi is right. We want you to stay.'

'You're too kind,' said Saph, looking genuinely embarrassed.

'It's not kindness, it's our duty to protect you. We'll hide you here for as long as necessary.'

Saphaeyender opened his hands helplessly. 'But if you're found harbouring us . . .'

'Who said I was going do what they told me?' retorted Viananthe. 'We'll be in trouble if we are *caught*. So let us not be caught.'

Claws slashed like long bony sickles. Sweet stink of blood-rotten breath exhaled all around her. Tanthe ducked, feeling the sharp pain of her hair ripped from her scalp. She drew her *mnelir* and thrust up.

The little knife shone like a diamond. The *ghelim* shrieked but flapped out of her reach. She glimpsed Eldareth and Helan battling, a female soldier falling to the blow of a great wing-strut.

Her breath coming hard and raw now, she drew the hated *tzirin*. Her attacker wheeled away. She saw Auriel on the ground, struggling to get up, blood on the side of his face. As he rose, the *ghelim* spun round in an arc as if balanced on one wing-tip, and swooped on him.

Tanthe lashed out with the whip. A crack of power split the air. The snake-like end wrapped itself round the *ghelim*'s neck and jerked taut, brought it crashing to the ground in a shower of twigs and thorns.

She leapt upon it and thrust the *mnelir* into its eye. In doing so she received a jolt of energy from the *tzirin* that flung her back onto the grass. She bruised her back on a tree root, cursed, dragged herself up, saw Kereyn fire a well-placed arrow and bring a second one down. The third vanished.

All went deathly quiet.

'Are you all right?' said Tanthe, helping Auriel. He looked shocked, but it was only a flesh wound on his temple. 'Put some of my salve on it. The wounds they make burn like hell.'

'Fuck,' said Auriel, who never swore. 'Even Falthorn never actually tried to kill me. Are you all right, Fliy?'

'Fine,' she growled, disentangling her weapons from the dead creature.

'You saved my life.'

'It's what we all have to do for each other. Don't make an issue of it.'

One of Kereyn's soldiers lay dead. They scraped a shallow grave, scattered leaves over her, commended her to Nuth's care. Shaken and grim, they went on.

From then on, the *ghelim* harassed them constantly. Sometimes they gave them the slip for a few days, hiding in caves or keeping to thick woodland. The shape-changed ones always found them again. Sometimes they tracked them from far above, lazy sentinels cruising on the air currents. Sometimes they exploded from thin air, engaging them in vicious battles that lost Kereyn another four soldiers. The party existed in a state of constant tension, punctuated by bursts of terror.

'It's obvious they're playing with us,' Eldareth said.

'Not necessarily,' said Helan. 'We've killed a few. They haven't been able to get at us properly. They're not having it all their own way.'

'Does Vaurgroth want us back alive?' asked Mawrdreth. 'That's the question. If he still thinks there are secrets that only we can reveal . . .'

Tanthe said, 'All I know is that they love creating pain and panic, because they get power out of it. So whoever's directing the *ghelim* is going to spin out our misery as long as possible.'

The weather grew warmer as they approached the border. They all grew used to blisters, aching limbs, sticky mouths. Tanthe was inured to the smell of sweat, her own and other people's. Kereyn had begged some extra garments for Helan's party from her sources – secret contacts in villages along the way – but Tanthe felt that however often she changed and rinsed the spare clothing in streams, she would never feel clean again.

One thing she couldn't get used to; always watching for the next attack. Knowing that at any moment a winged demon from nightmares could burst from the air and kill her, Auriel, or any of them. Endless anxiety wore them raw.

Then came the low, green, treeless hills that were the tail of the Serpentines. The border was only a mile or two ahead. They were too far from the Lapis Road to see it; here there were only plains, grazed by Maroc deer. If they were to cross the border, they had to leave the last of the trees and rocks behind . . . and *ghelim* were not going to respect any border.

Kereyn brought them to a vantage point on a hillside beneath a mass of granite. The border itself was marked only by a loose chain of man-made conical hills; there was one far to the east, another to the west. Between them, the plain rolled away, vast and majestic. In the early morning its colours flowed from jade into russet, then soft reds that became a purplish haze with distance. The sky above them was clear, but in front a wall of thunderous slate-blue cloud curved down behind the plain.

Something was moving down there, wisps of boiling smoke. Kereyn put a spyglass to her eye.

'What is it?' said Mawrdreth.

'Too far away to see clearly. I'll send a forward party.' Three soldiers set off down the hill at her command. Presently they reached the conical hill, and signalled all clear. Kereyn raised her arm; Helan and her companions began to run down the open hillside.

The sky above the conical hill shuddered. *Ghelim* burst from thin air. Screeching, they swooped upon the advance party.

The sky boomed with their wings. In a flurry of dark membrane, great hooked claws and snapping fangs they harried the three terrified soldiers. Tanthe looked up and back; more *ghelim* were coming from behind. They were dark sails hanging on the wind. Their long bony heads turned this way and that.

'Keep going,' Kereyn panted. She pointed at her besieged scouts. 'Help them.'

There was no cover. Helan's party ran in a close pack, with Kereyn's soldiers flanking them. Reaching the scouts they joined the struggle against the *ghelim*; shooting arrows, slashing out with *sten* and *tzirin*.

One huge saurian flung itself at Tanthe. Its screech deafened her. She saw its tiny, dead eyes fixed on her. She brought it down with her *roth*-whip but it thrashed, its great wings powerful enough to break a limb, its long jaws gaping. Panting for breath she stepped back from it, drew her *mnelir* and struck the hot blade at its eye socket. The blade sank in. One wing caught her a blow across her arm. But it struck just as it lost strength, saving her from anything worse than a bruise. It was just a rank heap of leather and scales.

The other *ghelim* reared up and away from them, joining those who were drifting along in lazy, inescapable pursuit. Kereyn's men and women stood panting, wide-eyed, wiping blood and sweat from their faces. 'Onwards,' Kereyn said. They stumbled on across a swathe of uneven ground, thick with low, heathery scrub. A couple of hundred yards on, she cursed.

There was a battle roiling in a fold of the plain in front of them. Hundreds of ragged human soldiers like Kereyn's, fighting desperately against a horde of *yrim*.

'Karmensis,' the leader said under her breath. She turned to Helan and Mawrdreth. 'Ma'am, sire, we're trapped. Whichever way we go the *ghelim* will follow. If we head straight for the battle, make our way around the right-hand edge of it, we might lose the *ghelim* in the confusion. What's your command?'

Helan and Mawrdreth looked at each other, faces grim and sweat streaked. Mawrdreth turned to Kereyn, his white teeth bared. 'Forward,' he said.

They all began to run, Kereyn's soldiers around them, Helan and Eldareth in the middle, Lahjaya, Tanthe and Auriel behind. Lahjaya was struggling heroically to keep up.

Like water the battle shifted. They tried to avoid it, instead found themselves passing through a corner of it. There was fighting ahead of them and to both sides. Bhahdradomen everywhere. They had another weapon, Tanthe saw, a two-handed device like an encased crossbow that shot tiny white-hot comets. In shock she watched two humans fall to the missiles, only yards away. There was a foul stench of *gauroth*. The air thrummed with cries and smoke.

Kereyn and Eldareth kept everyone in a tight band, now stopping, now rushing them on. The plain was rough, full of sharp little ridges and hollows.

The *ghelim* had swept up to a higher altitude and were circling, as if confused.

Then a line of *yrim* appeared over a rise in the ground to their right. Everything turned to chaos. The party began to break apart. Lahjaya couldn't keep up so Tanthe and Auriel slowed down to stay with her.

Tanthe saw them advancing, a loose dark line of shapeshifters. Their expressionless faces filled her with despair, their ancient eyes hypnotised her. She clutched her Aelyr knife.

The *mnelir* shone like a star. Auriel wielded the twin to hers and together they carved an arc of light that no Eater dared breach. In front she saw Eldareth, Mawrdreth and Helan battling, running, stopping now and then to strike out at *yrim* who challenged them, running on again.

Tanthe saw a clear path between her and Eldareth, though her vision was misted with smoke, sweat and stars of exertion bursting across her eyes. Spots of pain burned across her chest, the marks Rhazagramen had put on her.

Auriel, just in front of her, looked round and cried, 'Tanthe!'

A group of *yrim* was closing on them from behind. Even the *mnelir* could not defend them from the *gauroth*-bows.

'Run! Come on!' Eldareth shouted, holding out his arm to usher them on.

'What the hell does it look like I'm doing?' Tanthe mouthed to herself.

She glanced round, saw one of them raise his dark bow and aim it. As if time had slowed to a snail-crawl and her own perceptions expanded, she saw that the barrel was aimed straight at Lahjaya. She saw the tiny, vicious missile come flying out, a ball of blue fire with a long streak of light for a tail, and the only thought in her mind was to stop it hitting Lahjaya.

So Tanthe threw herself into its path.

She felt a coldness in her back, and suddenly found herself lying on the ground with Lahjaya beneath her. What made me fall? she thought. I wasn't hit . . . was I?

She couldn't breathe. For a few moments she watched the figures all around her in a deadly dance. Kereyn's soldiers were there, engaging the Bhahdradomen, right on the edge of the hollow. Tanthe watched without emotion, as if she were watching everything through a veil of glass at a great distance . . . then all she could hear was her own thundering heartbeat, and her sight went darker and darker . . . then nothing.

Chapter Twelve. Crusaders of Q'elethrios

Rufryd looked up and saw the great cliffs drifting ever nearer with the rise and fall of the sea. Hour by hour he watched it change from a line on the horizon to a towering wall, dwarfing the ship.

All the time he'd thought he never wanted to see Aventuria again, he'd been deceiving himself. As the coastline of Thanmandrathor drew closer, and the wind swept salt spray over him, he felt a sense of relief.

Dread, too.

The past months had been hellish. There were worse things than sitting in a stinking oubliette with a dying Bhahdradomen in his arms. As he endured day after day of relentless training, his comrades now spurning him as a traitor, he wished he'd died in the cell rather than made his wretched, lying vows to Arax Vahan.

Some of them, including Herex, had been forgiving, assuming that he was genuinely repentant. Rufryd found their condescension obnoxious. Others, though – including the officers – had continued to despise him. He was constantly watched. He behaved impeccably and tried to draw no attention to himself, but even so, some of them singled him out, calling him 'Goddess-lover' as if this was the greatest insult they could conceive.

At intervals, a few of them waited in dark corners and beat him until he was spitting blood. At the start he got in a few good blows against them. Later, he hardly bothered to defend himself; it was over quicker that way. Vetru would flee in abject terror when this happened, but he'd always be waiting afterwards to lament the unfairness of it, and salve his bruises.

If he was to escape, he had no option but to endure it.

He tried to be invisible, speaking to no-one but Vetru. Seasons passed. He was horrified to realised he'd been in Vexor for two and a half years. Then, in the middle of the cold dry summer, word came that their training was complete and that a ship was ready to take them to the mainland. The time had come for the Order to leave Calathvahn.

A handful of men remained behind, the old and the unfit, to tend the place. The rest – over five hundred – were on their way to bring the light of the Ancestor to the darkness of Thanmandrathor. Arax Vahan led them. Now he was not only their spiritual leader but their general.

Once they stepped on board ship, the atmosphere changed. The brothers had greater things to occupy their minds than Rufryd's sins. They were fired with zeal. Although self-discipline made them outwardly calm and certain, their eyes shone with ravenous joy. Arax Vahan strode the decks like a peacock with his lieutenant Ominyx at his side, all smiles, backslaps and inspiring platitudes.

Their mood was ominous, but as long as Rufryd ignored it, he found a kind of freedom on board ship. He was a good sailor, he discovered. Unlike some of the others, he suffered no sickness. He liked to get away from everyone and stand at the rail, watching the green waves. The easeful progress of the ship, the creak of the rigging and the cries of seabirds; all these were soothing.

Rufryd enjoyed the voyage, but Vetru hated it. He was miserable throughout. The ocean seemed to terrify him. He spent the whole voyage sitting in the centre of the deck, refusing to go below even when the winds howled and blasted salt spray over the prow. He huddled there at the point furthest from the rails, his long legs folded up beneath him, his arms wrapped around himself.

That was when Rufryd noticed that he'd stopped changing.

It was as if he'd reached a certain point of resemblance,

and stuck there. Whether it was out of respect for Rufryd's feelings, or because the voyage had taken all his energy, or because he lacked the *grothrim* skill to make a convincing change, Rufryd didn't ask or care to know. The result was disturbing. Vetru looked neither human nor truly Bhahdradomen, but an uneasy amalgam of the two. Not ugly, but grotesque enough to make humans look twice.

Rufryd felt sorry for him. After all he'd been through, Vetru was the only friend he'd found in Vexor.

The voyage took them, not across the Vexat Straits – which would have taken a few hours – but by a longer route, from the southernmost tip of Vexor to a place several hundred miles along Thanmandrathor's south coast. They had been aboard ship for seven days, alone on the bleak ocean, before the vessel turned in towards the shore.

The ship sailed the perilous gap between two high cliffs and into the calm waters of a small, secret cove. Above the dock rose a half-circle of pleated white limestone. As the ship was brought to its mooring place, Rufryd was surprised to see a crowd waiting on the quay to greet them.

A plank was lowered and the company began to disembark. He saw that the people waiting were all men and boys, with a number of children among them. How eager they looked; what was this excitement about? They greeted the arrivals with joy and warmth, and more than that; with a deference that bordered on fear. They bowed to Arax Vahan as they might to an arriving king.

Rufryd looked on, cold-eyed, keeping his face expressionless. He wondered if he had the same granite face and steady, crusading eyes as the others.

A group of Bhahdradomen hovered on the edges of the human crowd, looking suspicious rather than overjoyed to see the knights of Calathvahn. They were ordinary *domenim*, Rufryd noted, not the more elevated ranks of *yrim* or *grothrim*. He remembered Herex telling him that the brother-Order was concealed within a *tzcement* of

Bhahdradomen. He wondered what the *domenim* made of it. Vetru was looking at them, but said nothing.

'Glad to be on dry land again?' Rufryd asked him.

'Silence!' snapped a voice behind him. He looked round and saw Ominyx glaring at him. He was the most senior and vicious of Arax Vahan's officers. Rufryd knew, even thought it had always happened in the dark, that he was one of the regulars who'd beaten him up.

Five elders came forward to greet Arax Vahan and his party.

'Welcome to Q'elethrios, noble brother,' they said to each man in turn. Then came a long climb in procession up a steep path. Part of it was through a torchlit tunnel that pierced the rock itself.

The mouth brought them out onto a rugged stretch of rock, high above the sea and cupped by a half-circle of jagged limestone hills. The vista was bare, bleak and windswept. Rufryd saw low barracks the same pale grey as the surrounding rock, some of the buildings fused with the rock itself as it ran in jagged lines into the roots of the hills. It looked mysterious and cold; even more forbidding than Calathvahn itself.

Dread shivered through him again. He couldn't understand their joy, let alone share it. They are all sick, he thought. Look at the cold hunger in their eyes at the thought of invasion. Rampaging across the continent to bring their own form of Ancestor-worship, spreading hatred of their own mothers and sisters . . . don't they have the faintest idea of the reality of what they're doing? Out of their minds, every one of them.

It was unthinkable they'd succeed . . . or was it? He recalled how quickly the peaceful folk of Aventuria had fallen under Garnelys's spell when put in uniform and commanded to conscript their own countrymen.

It could happen, Rufryd thought, feeling as bleak and soulless as the landscape around him. It could happen, if we're not vigilant. Is this what the death of the Xauroma would mean? The end of respect for life. Instead, embracing this idea that life is foul and must be destroyed. Nuth help us, they believe it and they're going to make it come true.

And Rufryd was to be part of the fire, one of the elite knights of Calathvahn.

For the first time, they took Vetru away from him and made him go with the other Bhahdradomen. Vetru protested vigorously, until Rufryd managed to persuade him there was no point in arguing. The last thing he wanted was the hatchling following him into battle; although Vetru could hardly be described as a hatchling any more. At least he would be among his own people again.

The men slept for the next few nights on narrow mattresses, crammed into dark chilly barracks that smelled of damp stone, stale clothing, and the rank fishy scents of the seashore. Here was none of the tranquillity he'd found at Calathvahn. The men of Q'elethrios had a famished, dissatisfied air about them, frustration that they hadn't yet been admitted to the true heart of the Order. They served Calathvahn and yet weren't part of it. Rufryd sensed resentment, mingled with a ridiculous level of awe.

During the day they trained gently, enough to keep them supple but not enough to drain their strength. They cleaned their weapons; Rufryd handled the *sten* and *tzirin* with distaste, vowing not to use them. Some of the officers had been issued with *uzrat*, a vile type of bow that spat fire, but the ordinary men – including Rufryd – had prosaic crossbows. Mysteriously, they had let him keep his Shaelahyr sword. The Bhahdradomen had never taken it from him, seeming to fear it, and it hadn't occurred to the Order to confiscate it. He was grateful for that small concession, at least. He would have given anything to have a good longbow again.

There was a day of rest. Tomorrow, Arax Vahan announced, the crusade would begin.

'You'd think we were a legion of gods, not gardeners,' Rufryd said to Herex, who'd come to sit on the edge of his mattress.

'Well, we come as emissaries of the god,' said Herex, seeming to think that this was droll. Rufryd winced inwardly. 'Brother, tomorrow we ride into battle. Are you prepared?'

'Has Arax Vahan asked you to come and give me a pep talk?'

'He needs to know that everyone is with him, mind, heart and soul.'

'I made my vows,' Rufryd said, looking steadily at Herex until he dropped his gaze.

'Forgive me. I had to make sure.'

'He's made you an officer, hasn't he? Congratulations.'

Herex smiled proudly. 'I have received that honour. It's more because I can ride a horse than anything.'

'So, you must know what the plan is?'

'No more than Arax Vahan has told us all. We take certain strategic towns and villages, creating a stronghold from which to move north and west, joining with the Bhahdradomen legions as we go.'

'And then?'

'We take Tasqabad, of course.'

The next morning, as they rose before dawn, Rufryd felt none of the fearful excitement he'd experienced before the battle of Hethlas Rim. He felt nothing. This didn't seem real. His comrades were as happy as children, with no apparent grasp of what they were actually going into. Their joy induced a sensation of dread in his stomach, but he felt distant from it. None of this was anything to do with him.

In the cold twilight they set forth.

The commanders, officers and standard-bearers of the Order had been mounted on horses; big, muscular, high-stepping Thand'rathian destriers, ranging from golden dun to dark brown in colour. They made a magnificent sight, the foot-soldiers in their austere grey uniforms with white tabards over their breastplates, marching in precise step, the outriders bearing fluttering banners. The banners were plain white, to represent the light of the Ancestor. A human conceit, Rufryd guessed. He'd never seen the Bhahdradomen themselves flaunting any kind of flag.

He had no idea what they would face at the end of their march. The landscape was rugged, with twisted conifers clinging to heaps of grey rock. The day was dry and warm. He imagined a fortressed town, a great army of Thand'rathians riding out to face them, with their plaited hair and fierce green eyes, bronze cloaks flowing over their earth-green garments, spears in their hands. What would he do? He couldn't fight against people who had recently been his friends . . . but neither could he switch sides. He was wearing the uniform of Calathvahn. If he tried it, one side or the other would kill him. And he didn't want to die.

Fear broke through his detachment at last. Excitement sent trickles of sweat over his skin, energy thudding through his body.

Suddenly Arax Vahan stood up in his stirrups, turning to shout back at them, 'Behold our first conquest! Mrenth! Let us take this nest of Goddess-worshippers for the Ancestor!'

No great town, no fortress in sight.

Mrenth was just a village.

As they drew closer, Rufryd saw the puzzled villagers emerging from their small ochre-washed houses to watch the approaching legion. They could easily have belonged in his home village, Riverwynde. They looked different, with their tall frames clad in loose clothes of green and brown, their long hair the colour of corn or chestnuts, but in other respects they were just the same; peacefully going about their everyday business. There were children among them, men and women with babes in their arms.

The crowd grew thicker. Rufryd heard their shouts of puzzlement.

The Order must have made a terrifying sight.

A phalanx of marching men armed with Bhahdradomen weapons, outriders with their dazzling flags, harsh-faced officers, all bearing down relentlessly. Rufryd's throat turned gritty with tension. He waited for Arax Vahan to slow down and stop, to give them a chance to surrender.

Instead, the leader raised his fist, his *sten* held aloft. Green lightning crackled on its tip. 'Give them no quarter. Show them no mercy. Man, woman, child; slay them! For the glory of the Ancestor, send them into the darkness!' His voice rose to a scream above the rising battle-cry. '*For the Ancestor!*'

'Oh, Anthar's horns, no,' Rufryd said under his breath, just as the surge began. Arax Vahan uttered a raucous, '*Aahhh!*' The cry spread until the air shuddered with it. Rufryd was caught up in the charge, swept along by his fellows on either side. There was a thunder of hooves and pounding boots. No turning back.

The Order burst upon the village. People scattered in terror. The tight-packed ranks loosened and Rufryd saw, in every direction, people screaming and running and soldiers bringing them down with *sten* and *tzirin* even as they tried to flee.

It was as if the villagers' fear and flight provoked the Order to collective madness. Cold discipline flashed into blood-lust. A man ran at Ominyx, hands raised in supplication, screaming for them to stop. The officer's *sten* fell, cleaving his skull in two. The man went down beneath his horse's hooves and Ominyx surged on, yelling.

Rufryd saw a woman fleeing for the safety of her house, only to be shot down on her doorstep. She fell with blood pouring from her back. Beside her body a small child stood wailing until a brother strode up to it. For a moment Rufryd thought he was going to whisk it out of harm's way. Instead he swung his blade and the little head went flying from the neck, as easily as an apple struck from a tree.

Time stopped. Rufryd stood unable to breathe, while all around him the world fragmented in blood-red chaos.

Cold panic rushed through him. He'd die before he would join in this massacre. And he'd always known it would be like this, and tried to deny it.

He dodged to the right and ran along a dirt path between rows of dwellings. Two young girls fled before him in terror. They didn't know he had no intention of harming them. Breathless, they ran themselves to a dead end against the wall of a house and stood there, hanging onto each other in uncomprehending fear.

Rufryd looked wildly for a way through. An officer rode alongside him, and rapped him on the arm with his *tzirin*. It was Ominyx.

'Shoot them,' he barked.

'Go fuck yourself,' said Rufryd.

Ominyx's face turned red with fury. 'Shoot them, Goddess-lover!' he snarled. 'Shoot them, or I will!'

'Right.' Rufryd raised and armed his crossbow. The girls clutched each other, crying out.

Calmly, he turned and shot, instead, the officer. With a look of outraged disbelief, Ominyx clutched the wound and tumbled from his golden horse. Rufryd seized the reins and swung up into the saddle.

He turned the horse and urged it on, riding straight past the frightened girls, jumping a fence and crossing a garden, threading his way between the cottages, through the mad and bloody chaos that raged around him. The Shaelahyr sword was in his hand. He killed two or three of the Order as he went – perhaps saving a life or two, he didn't stop to make sure – and then his comrades began to notice what he was doing. It was over. Reaching the last straggle of dwellings, he urged the horse into a flat-out gallop and kept going.

He kept low on the black mane and heard the hiss of

two or three *uzrat* missiles passing close. Then he rounded the curve of a hill, and was free.

It was dark and he'd ridden miles before he dared to stop. The horse was trembling, its head down and sides heaving. Finding a thick-boled tree on the edge of a dip, he tethered the horse, dried the sweat off its coat as best he could with his shirt, then settled down inside the hollow trunk to rest. The landscape around him was rugged, with outcrops of striated grey rock, high tors and solitary pines gnarled into fantastic shapes. At least there were plenty of clear streams to drink from. One meandered past his hiding place.

Rufryd was shaking. He hadn't planned to run away, hadn't planned anything at all. But, in the end, it was the only thing he could have done. He dropped his head onto his knees and let himself weep. This was where it led, the delicious white fire of faith. To the cruel and pointless slaughter of those who did not, and never could, share that belief. He sat there, shaking, until the soreness that racked his body and heart became one great ache of exhaustion, pulling him down into sleep.

Something touched him.

He woke violently, his hand wielding his sword before he was even fully conscious.

'Don't harm me!' said a small voice. 'It's me, only me.'

The half-human face of Vetru was staring at him out of the gloom.

'Anthar's prick, Vetru, you scared the hell out of me! How did you find me?'

'I was with you all day. I followed the Order into battle, and followed you when you rode away. When I lost sight of you, I followed the horse's trail and droppings.'

'Gods. You're quite the scout, aren't you? Come in out of the wind, there's plenty of room.'

Vetru squeezed into the hollow and sat down on the

soft peaty floor. To his own surprise, Rufryd was glad to see him.

'Did anyone else follow me?' Rufryd asked.

'I don't think so. I saw no-one. Too busy in the battle.'

'That was no battle, Vetru,' he said in disgust. 'It was a massacre. They think they're such heroes; oh, very brave taking on defenceless farmers and their children! Nothing but bloody cowards.'

'Why *did* they kill people in that village?' Vetru asked, sincerely puzzled.

'I don't know,' said Rufryd. He dropped his head and covered it with his hands, too drained to cry any more, but shuddering uncontrollably.

'Are you ill? Are you having a fit?'

'No.' He raised his head. 'It's despair. Haven't you ever felt it?'

'I don't know,' said Vetru. He looked so worried that Rufryd felt sympathy for him. 'Why did the Order kill them?'

'Arax Vahan is mad. They all are.'

'Why?'

'They've got an idea in their heads which is false, but they've become so obsessed with it they think it's real . . . I can't answer you, Vetru. It's a kind of delusion. They think they are so superior and special that everyone who's different deserves to die.'

Vetru asked hesitantly, 'Do those souls go into the light of the Ancestor?'

'They might, but I doubt it. The Order weren't doing them any favours. Their idea is to sweep all the Goddess-worshippers into the darkness, as they see it. If this spreads, we'll all be forced to worship the Ancestor or die.' He shook his head. 'I had no idea such a small group of men could be so dangerous.'

'What is wrong with worshipping Ancestor?'

'Gods, Vetru. Where do I start? What if there is no Ancestor?'

'But there is!' he said fiercely.

'Come on, Vetru, you can't be this innocent. You know that this isn't what your own people believe.'

'Isn't it?'

'No. Aazhoth explained it to me.' Vetru was the only one he'd told about his encounter with Aazhoth. 'The Ancestor who is revered by the Bhahdradomen is literally that; the first one, the first *domen* who came from the First Egg. The parent of their race, the *symbolic* parent. And they know it's only a symbol. The Ancestor is their identity. Not a god.'

'Not a white light who tells them what to do?'

Rufryd put his arm round Vetru's thin shoulders. 'All your ancestors are personified as a single, wise ancestor. It's the way they show respect for their own origins. You know this, don't you?'

'I was very young when I left my *tzcement*,' Vetru said quietly. 'It's hard to remember.'

'It's two and a half years ago.' *Gods, so long.* 'So you're five and a half years old now?'

'Yes.'

'When do *domen* reach adulthood?'

Vetru thought about this. 'There is no set time from hatching. Some are fixed in form and mind very young. Others go on changing in form and mind all their lives. But that's not to say that *graukhim* are adults sooner, or the great adepts are hatchlings longer.'

Rufryd sighed. 'You can't explain it in human terms, of course. I should have known better. I'm just trying to find out if you understand what I'm telling you.'

'I understand,' Vetru said, as sharply as any adolescent challenged on his intellectual ability. 'I said that I don't remember, not that I don't understand!'

'All right, sorry. The point is that this idea of the Ancestor as a blazing white light, a god who insists you do this or that on his behalf, is a new one. It's come from the Order of Calathvahn, from humans. Obviously Vaurgroth's found it expedient to take it up himself. *But it's not the Bhahdradomen's original belief.'*

'They've stolen it. Changed it.'

'Yes. To suit themselves. To fit this vile philosophy they've developed.'

'I thought they were good.' Vetru's eyes were dark, glimmering with a spark Rufryd had never seen there before. 'They saved your life. But today I see them kill human hatchlings. That is wrong. That is wrong.'

Rufryd paused. 'Vetru, why didn't you stay with the *domenim* in Q'elethrios?'

The creature stared at the ground. 'They don't like me for being part *neshrim*. They didn't want me. I heard them say many bad things, lies . . .'

'I'm sorry to hear that. But whose side are you on?'

The deep gaze met his. 'What do you mean?'

'You're Bhahdradomen. When I travelled through your land, your people were full of Vaurgroth, what a wonderful leader he was and how he was going to lead them out of exile. The Order are fighting for Vaurgroth. So are you still on his side?'

Vetru drew back, his mottled half-human face sour with confusion. He looked suddenly, desperately troubled. 'I don't know. I heard things, such stories . . .'

'What stories?'

'Nothing. Lies. I don't know.'

'Because if you support Vaurgroth, I can't take you with me where I'm going. You'd have to be on my side. Side of the humans, of the Queen of the Nine Realms, of the Goddess. You'd have to renounce your own *domenim*. Even betray them. Are you willing to do that?'

'This is not fair!' Vetru gasped.

'Isn't it?' Rufryd said harshly. 'You must decide. Go back to your people if you want. But if you want to come one step further with me, you must be on my side. Which is it to be?'

* * *

Later, it occurred to Rufryd that Vetru could have knifed him in his sleep. He'd given enough provocation to a confused young member of an enemy race. Vetru could easily have turned, in hurt and anger, and destroyed his tormentor. But he didn't. He was still there in the drizzly dawn, waiting patiently for Rufryd to wake, ready to greet him with fresh water and nuts and berries he'd collected.

He was still at Rufryd's side, a journey of many long, arduous days later, when Rufryd reached his destination. They had travelled north from the coast of Thanmandrathor into its heart, through jagged hills, stretches of bleak green and gold moorland, eerie pine forests. Here and there he'd seen signs of Bhahdradomen activity; a few *yrim* in their strange outfits of snake-fine skin, standing guard on desolate roads, a stretch of downland with the mark of *graukhim* on it. On two consecutive nights, he and Vetru rested in villages that appeared to have been deserted. But as yet there was no sign of a full-scale invasion.

That was coming on behind him, he feared. He'd ridden hard, swapping one tired horse for a fresh one whenever he could persuade a farmer to help him. Even with Vetru in the saddle behind him, they'd made good progress; Vetru was light, and Thand'rathian horses were strong. The progress of an army, although inexorable, would be much slower.

Nearer to Tasqabad, there was heavy military activity – all Thand'rathian, he was relieved to see. When they reached the edge of the town, soldiers were everywhere in their garb of bronze and green. Rufryd rode among them with a sense of relief. The town was free, and guarded. No one stopped him; he'd acquired a dark cloak with hood for Vetru, and no one looked twice at the apparently human figure perched behind him

His heart lifted as the town rose before him, drenched in the silver-gold light of sunset trying to break through the rain. The meadows and orchards that lay around it were intensely green. The painted houses glowed softly ochre, ivory and blue, their overhanging eaves and shuttered windows seeming to gaze down at him with warm but quizzical expressions. And there at the centre, raised up on its wooded hill, was Tasqabad Hall itself. He had missed the great stone hall with its timber pillars. It was the only place that had ever felt like home to him.

As he rode up the path that led between wide lawns to the front door, guards came and stopped him. He recognised many of them. As soon as he explained who he was, they saluted him and offered to take his horse to the stables.

'I'll take her myself, if you don't mind,' Rufryd answered. 'I know the way. Is, er, the Duchess well?'

'She is well,' a female soldier answered sombrely. 'I'll tell her you're here, sir.'

'No, don't,' Rufryd said. 'I'd prefer to surprise her.'

Once he was in the courtyard at the back of the hall, he led his horse into a loose box and pulled Vetru in as well. 'I want you to stay here and keep out of sight.'

'Why?' said Vetru, putting seven spindly, wood-dark fingers to the edge of his hood.

'And leave your blasted hood up!'

'But I am faithful to you. I have served you well. My Paranian is good. Are you ashamed of your friend?'

'Oh, gods, Vetru. Of course I'm not. Trust me on this, it's for your own protection.'

'Why?'

'Fuck,' Rufryd said under his breath. 'I know how these people feel about the Eaters. They found one living here once. He'd been here for years – just a slightly odd boy, they thought – but when they found out, they murdered him. Didn't stop to ask questions, just set on him as if he was a rat. Mind you, he was trying to poison the Duke – but that wasn't why they killed him.'

Vetru's eyes swam with guarded fear. Rufryd added, 'If they'd stopped to question him, they might have discovered why he was poisoning the Duke. Did Vaurgroth plant him here years ago, or what? But now they'll never know. They killed him out of a reflex of horror, like someone might stamp on a spider. And if they find another *domen* in their household, it will be ten times worse. That's why I want you to stay here, all right?'

Vetru nodded, mute. They are really not that different to us, Rufryd thought. With a sigh, he left the stable and crossed the darkening courtyard to the kitchen door.

He remembered his way through the house and soon found his way to the main hall, where the household gathered for meals. How strange it felt to be here again, after so long away. He felt his spirits lifting; if not to actual pleasure, at least to calmness.

He'd missed the meal, it seemed, but there were still a few folk dotted around the hall at the long tables. The air was smoky golden with candles and firelight, stone columns rising up into the darkness of the high ceiling, banners fluttering above the great fireplace. Hounds lay curled on the hearth. All was as he remembered it. He moved through the light, the scents of woodsmoke and animals, candlewax and food and the stone of the building itself, drafts of cold and warm air, looking for Branq'elin. There was no sign of her at the round table where she and her family used to sit.

Yet there were three figures seated at the table, talking over goblets of wine. The woman had unmistakable, bright copper-red hair. Rufryd stopped and stared at them, his heart quickening. He hadn't expected to see them, hadn't even dared to hope they might be here, but there they were.

Dawn, Mirias, and Con.

He'd feared they were dead. Last time he'd seen them, they were being carried off by a flood, and he'd gone to Vexor alone. He had found Con, injured, and left him at a farm to recover – but the boy must have found his way back. Not really a boy any more, Rufryd corrected himself. He must be eighteen by now, and he looked older. Tall and straight and handsome with his long umber hair tied back, still lean but more muscular now. Painful experience was etched in his fine face and dark green eyes.

Dawn and Mirias had their backs to him. Con was the first to see Rufryd. He said nothing, just froze as if he couldn't believe his eyes.

Rufryd walked slowly up to the table, not knowing what to say. He stood there a good few seconds before Dawn realised that Con was no longer attending to her but staring over her shoulder. Then she turned and saw him.

'Hello,' said Rufryd.

'Oh, my Goddess!' Dawn leapt up and flung her arms round him. 'You've been gone for – how many seasons? – and all you can say is hello?'

'How does, "Hello, I'm glad you're not dead," sound?'

She was laughing and crying at the same time. Rufryd was too choked up to do either. The others came to him, Con clasping his hands, too awkward to give him an actual embrace. Even Mirias – with whom Rufryd had often quarrelled – gave him a heartfelt hug with pure joy in his expression.

'You didn't drown,' Rufryd said as they drew him to the table, sat him down and gave him an overflowing goblet of wine.

'No, we didn't,' said Dawn. 'It seems so long ago now.'

'We fetched up a long, long way downstream and would have died, if some kindly shepherds hadn't spotted us and dragged us out,' said Mirias. 'We were in bad shape. We were both half-drowned; I broke my arm, and we were both ill with coughs and fevers for weeks afterwards. Lost the horses, poor sods.'

'I'm so sorry, Rufe,' Dawn added. 'You must have thought we'd abandoned you. But it was all we could do to drag ourselves back here, let alone find you and go to Vexor.'

'You – abandoned me?' He grinned. 'There was me thinking it was the other way round.'

'Con told us how you saved him. You're quite the hero, Rufe.'

'To Con, anyway,' Mirias said with a smirk.

Con reddened. 'I would have done anything to go to Vexor with you, Rufryd. But I knew Akarata had taken you, and I had no idea how to find you. So I came back here.'

'You did the right thing. You didn't miss anything, believe me.'

'How was Vexor?' Dawn asked.

'Grim.' Rufryd pulled a face. 'It did its damnedest to kill me, but I'm still here, Goddess knows how.'

Mirias's expression was grave. 'What's the news?'

'Bad,' said Rufryd. 'Invasion on its way. You look as if you already know that.'

'They've taken Parione, and we know they're in the south,' Dawn said quietly. 'It's only ever been a matter of time.'

'Look, do you mind if I tell you about it later?' he said, standing up. 'I ought to tell her ladyship first. Where is she?'

Suddenly they were all grinning at him. 'In her rooms,' said Dawn. 'She really will be pleased to see you.'

Rufryd found Branq'elin, not in the room she used to have, but in the chambers that had formerly been her father's. She'd become Duchess of Thanmandrathor on her father's death, a short time before he'd gone to Vexor. Of course, he should have realised that she'd be in the ducal chambers now.

Her attendants, knowing him, were persuaded to let him go in without being announced. He knocked lightly, and the door opened onto a large state room, with tapestries on the stone wall, thick white candles burning on floor sconces. Branq'elin was seated at a desk of dark wood, holding flat a long scroll of parchment as she read it. She looked just the same; slender in a simple dress of green velvet, gold thread plaited through the rich brown of her hair. Her face with its high cheekbones and narrow chin was intent, serious. As she looked up, though, her eyes startled him. He'd forgotten they were such a bright green; lynx eyes.

She didn't appear to recognise him for a moment. Then her mouth fell open and her sombre expression transformed.

'Rufryd, oh Q'enartre, I don't believe it,' she said. 'Oh, gods, I thought you were dead.'

She came to meet him, not in a rush but gracefully, intently, putting her arms around him and her head on his shoulder and holding him so tight he could hardly breathe. Rufryd's hands slid onto her shoulderblades. Her body felt deliciously warm under the velvet and her scent was wonderful, her skin lightly perfumed with oils. He hadn't expected this, hadn't been sure what sort of reception she would give him, but this pushed him to a perilous knife-edge between tears and simple lust.

'How are you?' he said, managing to master both impulses.

'Besieged. I'm well, or I would be, if my realm were not in such peril. And you?'

'Better, now I'm here.'

'I missed you.'

'Did you? I've got nothing but bad news, Bran, I'm sorry. Dreadful news.'

'Don't tell me yet. Let me be happy for a minute.'

As they held each other he heard a strange, small voice from another room. Looking up he saw, over her shoulder, another door standing open to a bed-chamber. Inside was a large cot and in it a little girl standing up, holding onto the bars. Hopeless as he was at telling babies' ages, he guessed she was somewhere between one and two.

'Hello, who's this?' he said.

'Oh.' Branq'elin broke the embrace, took his hand and led him into the other room. The child, who had messy brown hair and chestnut eyes, stared up at him warily, unsure whether to smile or burst into tears. 'This is Annuin.'

'I didn't think a Duchess's duties included baby-sitting,' he said. 'Who does she belong to?'

Branq'elin cleared her throat. 'She's mine, Rufryd. That's why she's in my chambers. She's mine. Named after my mother.'

'Oh, hell,' he said softly, letting go of her hand. 'I had no idea. You've gone and got handfasted or something, and here am I thinking we might . . . Damn. I'm sorry.'

'Rufryd,' Branq'elin said with a gentle, exasperated sigh. 'Look at her. How many men in this house have brown eyes like that? Just one, and I'm looking at him.'

'Gods, you are joking,' he said. He stepped backwards and sat down on the edge of the bed. In the rush of shock and tiredness, he felt he might actually keel over. The child gave him a tentative grin, revealing a row of small, perfect white teeth. She was pretty. And she looked startlingly familiar. She had Bran's sharp chin, but rest of her face was his.

'I'm not, my dear.' There was a hint of a smile on Branq'elin's face. 'She's yours.'

Chapter Thirteen. The Ruby Plains

Eldareth saw Tanthe fall.

Auriel flung himself to his knees beside her, seemingly unaware of the white comets hissing past him. The *yrim* who'd attacked her were turning away, engaged by Kereyn's soldiers. Eldareth saw a couple of them cut down, but their line held.

He ran back towards Tanthe, scanning the battlefield. The crack of *roth*-fires left pungent smokes drifting across the plain, and through the grey layers he saw human soldiers in desperate conflict with Bhahdradomen. The humans fought fiercely in tight-packed lines. There seemed to be far fewer of the shape-changers and they moved in loose, random formation, appearing to float; slow, silent, unstoppable as death.

'Eldareth!' It was Helan's voice, far ahead. The party was fragmented. He knew they'd be lost if they didn't regroup. Ignoring her shout he dropped to his knees with one hand on Auriel's shoulder. The young Aelyr was shaking with misery as he eased Tanthe to one side. Lahjaya struggled out from beneath her, panting but unhurt.

'She can't be dead,' Auriel whispered.

'Stay low!' Eldareth said, jerking Lahjaya down beside him as she tried to rise. There was a horrible wound in Tanthe's upper back, a few inches below her left shoulder. A red-black hole surrounded by cyanosed flesh. The fabric of her jacket was burned black around it and an iron smell of blood and *gauroth* emanated from the wound.

'What happened?' Lahjaya asked, voice trembling. 'One moment I was running, the next she threw me down like a sack of rocks hitting me.'

'She's been shot,' said Eldareth. 'Took the missile that was aimed at you.'

'Oh, Lady of Tears,' Lahjaya breathed. Then, mastering herself, she pressed two fingers under Tanthe's jaw. 'I cannot find her pulse.'

'We can't leave her,' said Auriel.

'We're not going to,' Eldareth replied.

The line of *yrim*, outfaced by Kereyn's troop, was retreating from the attack. The battle shifted. Ahead, small struggles were won or lost, the survivors running to regroup at the centre of the field. The fighting became concentrated over to their left. The rim of the hollow was clear.

Eldareth gathered Tanthe's slender form in his arms and lifted her. Her head with its thick dark hair fell lifeless into the crook of his shoulder. He hadn't realised how strongly he felt for her until now. She could have been his daughter or sister, or something more, judging by the ache in his chest.

'Come on,' he said to the others. They ran.

Through the reeking fog he saw a handful of Kereyn's soldiers ahead, waiting to escort them. There was clear land in front. No *yrim* pursuing. Then he saw Helan and Mawrdreth ahead, and Kereyn herself. All of them were breathing hard, weapons gripped tight in their hands, faces flushed and savage.

'All present?' the older woman said gruffly. She glanced at Tanthe without comment. 'Onwards.'

Helan and Mawrdreth both looked at Tanthe, their eyes grave and questioning. Eldareth shook his head.

Behind them, the battle continued, but it was nearly over. Above, there was no sign of *ghelim*; their plan seemed to have worked, at great cost. They fled down a fold in the plain and into rougher country, stumbling along deer-trails, thorn bushes clawing their legs. Eldareth kept glancing back, seeing the action as a series of frozen moments. The Bhahdradomen holding their ground for a time, then thinning out and retreating; and gone at last, as if they'd vanished with the wisps of smoke that drifted over the battlefield. Exhausted soldiers stood with bowed heads, looking at the bodies of the fallen.

The path took them round the curve of a hill, and the scene was lost to sight.

Eldareth could feel no life in Tanthe's limp body. Auriel and Lahjaya walked on either side of him, blanched and silent. Then a sound came from her throat. He felt her ragged breath penetrating his jacket to warm his shoulder.

'She's breathing,' he said softly.

He turned to one of Kereyn's rebels, a strongly built man with corn-yellow hair and a weather-tanned face.

'How far before we can get her to a safe place?'

'Camp's a few miles yet,' said the man. 'Not too far, but we can't stay there long. Nowhere's safe on the border.'

By nightfall, they were installed at the camp to which Kereyn had brought them, in a valley they called Malachite Rift. There were scores of makeshift tents in rows on the banks of a stream, walled by hills veiled in dark green, thorny shrubs. The ground was dry and stone-scattered. The night felt warm; Helan heard insects chirruping in the darkness, while the three moons were all in the sky in various phases. Leaf Moon a half-shut green eye, Lily Moon three quarters full and piercingly bright, Rose Moon huge and lazy on the horizon. The night was beautiful, and deceptively peaceful. With a sigh, she ducked into the spacious tent of the commander.

Tanthe had been placed on a folding bed by one wall of the tent. She was still deeply unconscious. Her breathing was shallow and her forehead indented with lines, as if she was struggling against painful dreams. Lahjaya had cleansed and dressed the wound in her shoulder, but it went deep, the healer said. No one could rouse her.

Helan's party ate and drank around a table in the middle of the tent. Gloomy silence lay upon them. Lahjaya and Auriel looked devastated, Eldareth and Mawrdreth grave and worn out. As soon as Lahjaya had finished eating, she went and sat at Tanthe's side. Auriel was already there, gripping her hand as if to infuse his own life-force into her.

The others went in turn to look at Tanthe, returning to the table more restless than before. Helananthe leaned her head on her hands. She felt numb, as she had for months. Now there were tiny hooks snagging the nerveless edges of her dead spirit. It was a hideous feeling. Not exactly pain. Unbearable, tearing pressure that must break or kill her.

'Haven't we seen enough of our friends die at Garnelys's whim?' she said dully. 'Why must this go on and on? Tanthe didn't have to be with me, she bears no responsibility for Aventuria, she's just a citizen. I don't want to see my countrymen sacrificed and dying like this.'

'I don't think she'd agree with you,' Mawrdreth said. 'We all bear responsibility for Aventuria.'

Eldareth went and stood over Tanthe again. He seemed to be waiting anxiously for every jagged breath, afraid it might be her last. Helan hadn't realised how much they all cared for Tanthe. It had been too easy to take her bright presence for granted, until it was snuffed out.

'She saved my life,' said Lahjaya. 'I shall do my best to save hers.'

There were voices outside. The soldiers were returning from the battlefield.

The tent-flap was thrown back and Kereyn came in with a statuesque man at her side. His once-handsome face was creased with lines, his blond hair full of silver. He looked weary. Burns from Bhahdradomen weapons blackened his breast-plate and his right cheek-bone glowed with a livid, raised weal.

'Ma'am, sire, this is Karmensis, commander of the Paranian troops,' she said.

'Your majesties, my good friends,' said the man, bowing to Helananthe and Mawrdreth, dipping his head to the others. 'We won the day. The Eaters have retreated. It has been at great cost to us, but they're gone for now.'

Helan recognised him. He'd been an officer in Garnelys's army, one of the hated General Grannen's men.

'Karmensis?' she said. 'I know you. We met after Hethlas Rim, albeit briefly.'

'I remember it well. I'm at your service, ma'am.'

'You weren't exactly thrilled at the outcome, I seem to recall.'

There was a moment of tension, but his grey eyes on hers were honest and unwavering. 'Ma'am, I was loyal to Garnelys, as you know. Yes, I faced you across the battlefield on Hethlas Rim. Likewise, my troops and Kereyn's would have fought on opposing sides if we'd met. But those days are over. We're united now.'

'That's true, thank Nuth,' said Helan. 'You must know that the schism between humans was engineered by the Bhahdradomen in the first place?'

'Yes. So you'll believe my assurance that we're allies, and I thank Nuth and Anuth for it. Humans, Aventurians, we're all on the same side.'

'We work together, ma'am,' Kereyn added, sitting down with her strong arms crossed. 'Our efforts help to hold the border. Not that this was an attack upon Azura Maroc; only upon us.'

'I see.' Helananthe hardly knew what response to make. The hooks tore at her heart and throat. For months she had moved in a fog of self-loathing, hardly able to function. Despising herself for giving up the Sapphire Throne, breaking the Xauroma, failing. Yet here were these brave people, fighting on her behalf as if the thought of giving in could never occur to them.

Her numbness was being ripped apart like tearing flesh. She had so much to say she couldn't express any of it. 'You didn't listen to me.'

'Ma'am?' said Karmensis.

'When I stood on the walls of the Amber Citadel and told you all to stop fighting.'

'We knew it was the Devourers who made you say

that,' Kereyn said dismissively. 'Of course we didn't listen. Many fled the city, gathering up those who weren't wholly befuddled by the invaders' tricks. Then we began our campaign.'

'Even though the people of Paranios may suffer and die in punishment?'

Kereyn gave a dismissive *hmph*. 'We're all going to die sooner or later, ma'am. We're all suffering anyway. Surely the point is to deliver to our descendants a whole and healthy land – not a blasted wasteland and the stew of slavish superstition that the Eaters are brewing for us?'

Helan stared down at her hands, the long, strong fingers that had wielded swords and caressed her lovers' bodies and touched the red flame heart of the Xauroma. She feared that if she met their eyes she would fall to pieces in front of them.

'And the cost of this battle,' she said quietly, 'how great was it?'

'We lost over a hundred men and women today,' Karmensis answered. 'The Bhahdradomen have concentrated their troops on Parione and other key cities. They have little to spare for us, and not enough yet to launch a full-blown assault on Azura Maroc. However, although we outnumbered them five to one, it was a desperate and hard-won battle. Their weapons are superior to ours. They are harder to kill, and don't fall to wounds as we do. Unless we receive help from Azura Maroc, or some other source, we cannot hold our ground forever.'

Stiff and trembling, she couldn't speak for a while. At last the words came. 'You sit here and tell me these things as if I still matter, as if I am still your Queen. You expect commands, decisions, orders from me?'

'Yes, ma'am,' Karmensis answered. 'If you are willing to give them.'

'But I gave up the Sapphire Throne. I'm cut adrift from the Xauroma because the land no longer trusts me. Do you understand?'

She was aware of everyone in the tent staring at her, the tension of her husband and Eldareth and her friends fastened upon her, a palpable dread of what she was trying to say.

'We still trust you, ma'am,' Kereyn said firmly.

'We'll hold the border as long as we can,' said Karmensis. 'Vaurgroth's forces are concentrated on the capital. We don't know what he has in reserve, but there must be a limit to his strength, even if they've been hatching like flies in Vexor.'

'People are confused and terrified,' Kereyn added. 'They feel they've been let down, ma'am, it's true. This horror came upon us with so little warning. We're doing our best, but there are too few of us. We need a focus, someone to look to for hope, a leader. We need you.'

'You have me,' Helan said. It was hard to breathe. She pushed back her stool and stood up. 'You have shamed me today.'

'Ma'am?' Karmensis frowned. 'How?'

'You have opened my eyes. I've been like a sleepwalker, all my grief focused on that loss, not seeing . . .' She took a breath and made herself look at each of them in turn, meeting their anxious gazes. 'Queen or no, I will not forsake the land.' She felt tears running from her eyes, a fire of hope soaring up from the soles of her feet. It felt wonderful and terrible. Mawrdreth's hand was warm on her arm. 'Tell everyone that I will do everything humanly possible to deliver the Nine Realms from this hell. I haven't abandoned you and I never will. If I can't fight as Helananthe, monarch of the Nine Realms, well, then I shall fight as plain Helan, citizen of Aventuria.'

By evening the next day, they were on the move again. Tanthe was borne on a stretcher carried between two soldiers, her face bone-white against the brownish canvas. All night and all day, Eldareth and the others had taken it in turns to keep anxious watch over her. Her condition hadn't improved. She lay oblivious as Karmensis and Kereyn led them from the camp and several miles further on to the mouth of the Malachite Rift.

There an astonishing sight greeted them. Eldareth saw a pair of bright metal rails snaking into the darkness, and on them, a long wagon suspended on wood and metal wheels. Two huge dark chestnut horses were harnessed between its shafts.

'This is the wagon-rail that Garnelys built to take the Marocians up to the quarries,' said Kereyn. Lighter horses shifted in the shadows, their reins held by soldiers who were ghosts in the twilight.

'Same track we saw before, I take it,' said Eldareth.

'Yes. The northern part's in disrepair, but we've kept this stretch clear for our own use. There are stations along the way where you can change the horses, take on fresh water and food. There are barrels on a platform at the back; don't forget to refill 'em whenever you can. Water will be in short supply from here on.'

'Surely the rail doesn't go all the way to Lapiszul?' asked Helan.

'Alas, no, ma'am. Less than halfway. But it's the swiftest and least uncomfortable way for you to travel, at least across the worst of the red lands.'

'Will you come with us?'

'I shall do whatever you command,' Kereyn answered. 'Karmensis will send twenty of his best warriors with you as outriders to guard you. He has enough horses to mount most of them. And the Marocians will help you on your way, of course.'

'Thank you,' said Helan. 'Kereyn, much as I'd like you to come with us, I mustn't be selfish. I think you'll aid our cause best if you stay in Paranios. You know the territory and the people. There's no-one better able to rally them. Do you agree?'

From the look in Kereyn's eyes, Helan had made the decision she was hoping for. 'I do, ma'am. I'd go with you gladly, of course; but you're right, my heart is in Paranios.' She grinned. 'It's possible the rebels would falter without me to goad and bully them into some semblance of structure.'

'Then go, and all the goddesses and gods watch over you,' Helan responded, clasping the woman's hands.

Helan was her old self again, Eldareth noted with infinite relief. Extraordinary, the effect of her simple decision to shed her tortuous role as Queen and fight as a plain citizen. Somehow it enabled her to lead them as she used to.

'In that case, ma'am,' said Karmensis, 'I'll be coming with you.'

'Oh – are you sure? Who will command your troops?'

'My brother. He's capable, don't fear.'

'But I don't wish to take you away from your command . . .'

Karmensis's face creased in a smile. 'Ma'am, you must realise that our main concern is getting you to safety. Nothing's more important than that.'

'Well, if you insist . . . Thank you.'

A dark brown horse was brought to Karmensis and he mounted. He was going to lead the outriders. As the others said their farewells and climbed into the carriage, rain began to fall. Silver lines slanted down through the lamplight that spilled from inside.

'Enjoy this rain,' Kereyn said, looking up at the clotted sky. 'It's the last you'll see for many a day.' She raised her hand, and was lost to sight as the carriage door slammed shut.

Inside, lamps were lit and hung swaying from a wooden beam in the roof. Part of the bench along one side was made into a bed for Tanthe with a thin mattress, sheets and pillows. Carefully, they installed her upon it. Still unconscious, she lay white-faced under the covers. She didn't rouse even when the carriage lurched forward and began to trundle, creaking, into the night.

At least the carriage was warm, Eldareth reflected, as he stretched out his legs and tried to get comfortable on the hard bench. Cold played havoc with his travel-worn spine. A stove gave the interior a glow of dirty honey, and the air was thick with the scents of seasoned wood, old sweat, the tang of a privy bucket behind a screen in the rear corner. Next to him sat Helan and Mawrdreth, talking quietly to one another. Opposite, Auriel sat at Tanthe's head, stroking her hair. Lahjaya knelt beside her, fumbling in her pack for her instruments of healing.

Further down the carriage sat five of Karmensis's soldiers, three men and two women, seeming quiet and awkward in the royal party's presence. No doubt the ice would break eventually, Eldareth thought, but for now Tanthe's plight made lively conversation inappropriate.

Outside, he could hear the steady clop of hooves, and the lighter hoofbeats of the outriders. Soon, he knew, they would be entering the wilderness which ran for hundreds of miles with no tree cover. They were an all-too-visible caravan to the eyes of flying *ghelim* ... but what choice did they have, with Tanthe wounded? To abandon her?

The motion of the carriage lulled him to sleep, only to jolt him awake again at regular intervals. He gave up trying to rest and instead spent his time keeping watch through the forward-facing window. He exchanged a few words with the man who was driving the horses. The driver, a Marocian, sat hunched under a wide-brimmed hat. Occasionally, Eldareth caught a glimpse of an outrider in the darkness.

Just before dawn, the carriage rattled to a stop. They were at a village beside a small lake, in the midst of a dusky, nondescript no-man's land. Marocian villagers, who seemed to be expecting them, came out to change their horses for a fresh pair, to bring them food and pails of fresh water. Eldareth took the opportunity to alight from the wagon and stretch his legs.

As he did so, the sun rose to wash the landscape in

blazing rose-red light. A breathtaking vista was unveiled under a scrim of fire that hung shimmering from the heavens. Slowly, the glory spread inch by inch across the world. The village lay in shadow but the hills that cupped it were flame. All around lay an undulating stonescape, with pinnacles and great boulders standing upon it like trees, the paths scattered with sand like carnelian-dust. And all of it blazing scarlet and crimson, a desert of rubies.

Already he could feel the sun's heat. It would grow worse as they moved south.

'Where is this?' said Auriel, coming up beside him. His fine-boned, angelic face looked drawn and lustreless.

'The Ruby Plains,' Eldareth replied. 'You look exhausted, lad. You should get some sleep.'

'I can't, until I know Tanthe's recovering.'

Eldareth placed a hand on the young man's shoulder, to show he understood. There was no point in arguing. He couldn't rest either.

Climbing back into the carriage again, he found the others sharing breakfast and Lahjaya still bending over Tanthe. The healer's hands moved in smooth slow motions over Tanthe's body, lining up crystals from her throat to her abdomen, waving other gems over her as if describing arcane symbols.

'Is there anything I can do to help?' Eldareth asked.

'Just bring me some of that coffee I can smell, and something to eat,' Lahjaya replied.

He did as she asked. 'Is it pointless suggesting that you rest for a while?' he said.

'Don't fuss, my friend,' Lahjaya said briskly. 'When I am healing, time and energy move differently. I can do this for as long as it takes; only when it's finished, then you had better have a big soft bed ready for me.'

Tanthe moaned. She frowned and shifted in pain, but her eyes didn't open. Lahjaya lifted her head and held a cup of water to her lips. To Eldareth's relief, Tanthe took a sip or two; but she didn't respond to their voices, and as Lahjaya let her lie back, she seemed to sink back into delirium again.

'And do you know yet,' he said quietly, 'how long . . . ?'

'It's a hard one,' Lahjaya answered, her voice thin. 'She's somewhere very deep, and I can't reach her.'

All day, as the wagon rolled on deep into the red heart of Azura Maroc, Eldareth watched Lahjaya and Auriel leaning over Tanthe; the healer constantly moving crystals, the Aelyr touching Tanthe's head as if to feed energy into her. They seemed to be keeping her alive through pure force of will.

Outside, the Ruby Plains rolled past. Pillars of red sandstone had been holed and polished by the weather, making the stonescape an array of weird, twisted sculptures. A hot breeze blew eerie songs through these flutes. The sky burned blue. A few dra'a'ks sailed over, causing alarm. But these were true dra'a'ks – a small species as green as leaves – not *ghelim*. All that interested them was hunting lizards on the hot rock.

As dusk fell, Eldareth watched the lamplight moving on Lahjaya's hands. He recognised some of the blue-green stones she was using; pieces of turquoise, chrysocolla, malachite. And knurls of amber, like solidified light. The sight gave him a strange unease. Distant memories of his mother Elq'esq, always with crystals in her hands, always healing.

'I hadn't realised you were a *roth*-mage,' he said, as she paused to take a few bites of supper.

'You thought I was just a kitchen healer?' She gave a twisted grin.

'I try not to jump to conclusions about anyone.' Eldareth knelt down beside her. Auriel had fallen asleep where he sat. Tanthe looked no better. She was breathing steadily but looked shell-pale, a vertical line indenting her forehead. 'Will she live?'

'We're doing all we can.' Lahjaya's reply was short with

exhaustion. 'Auriel would make a fine healer, if he were not frightened of his own shadow.'

Eldareth paused, then asked, 'When you learned to be a healer . . . what did it involve?'

Lahjaya looked surprised at his question. 'A great deal of patience. You have to learn which stones work best for you. It's not easy, and it's not magic.'

'I know that,' he said. 'My mother was a healer, but I never asked her any questions. And now it's too late.'

Lahjaya regarded him, her round bright eyes seeming to learn more about him than he'd wanted her to know. She said, 'The body has an aura around it – an electrical field, the scholars of Lapiszul term it – like a shell of heat or, more accurately, a shell of energy. In health it has a clear structure.'

'I know a little about it,' he said. 'The structure is damaged by illness or injury and you try to make it whole again?'

'Your mother must have taught you something, then. The mage learns to channel the *roth* of crystals and stones, first to change that field in themselves, then to change it in others. We reconstruct the energy so that the body can heal itself.'

'I've seen my mother work,' he said. 'I know it is a long, hard process.'

She raised her eyebrows. 'Well, it's a shame you didn't follow in her footsteps. You would have been more use to Tanthe.'

'I had my reasons.' He was silent for a moment or two, then decided to go on. 'I've seen *roth*-mages use their skills for the opposite of healing, to the extent that the idea of dabbling with *roth* sickened me.'

'Such skills can be used for harm, in the wrong hands. If you can heal the aura, it follows that you can also disrupt it so violently that the person is injured, driven mad or killed.' She sighed, placing her copper-brown hands on Tanthe's chest. 'That's what the Bhahdradomen weapons do, I think. The little fire that made a hole in her shoulder has torn her life-energy so badly, I'm not sure I can reconstruct it. I pull the energy back into line and it skews away again.' Lahjaya drew breath and gave a short, tired sigh. 'That's why the shape-changers frighten us; because their *roth*-aura plays havoc with ours.'

'It was my father's fault I didn't follow my mother's path,' Eldareth said softly. 'Perhaps it's time I stopped blaming him. I cannot let him turn me aside from the path I should have been on.' To himself, then, he made a pact; if Lahjaya succeeded in healing Tanthe he, too, would become a *roth*-mage, whatever it took . . .

That was the moment when Tanthe started screaming.

She was deep, deep in some black place where the glimmer of the horizon was only a paler black than the ground. She tried to rise but the surface clung to her like tar. All existence was reduced to a dark plain under a small dome of sky, illusory mountains shouldering up on a horizon she would never reach; and all of this bleak dimension washed, soaked, saturated in despair.

She knew at once where she was. The *ezht*. A nightmare nothingness sandwiched in the cobweb-thin membrane between one reality and another. She'd been here before; Falthorn had sent her here as a punishment for attacking him. It had only been for a moment or two but those seconds had felt like a lifetime of loneliness, terror, despair.

Now the horror was clutching at her again. Her mind slipping away into a chasm.

Where am I how did I get here oh Goddess help me help me help me . . .

She clawed at the surface of the plain but it ran through her fingers like ink. It seemed to be tilting. She must cling on or she would fall. Misery rolled through her in an unendurable storm and she groaned, writhed, sobbed for mercy.

Falthorn let me out let me out let me come back please I'll do anything . . .

Somehow Tanthe managed to drag herself onto all fours. She began to crawl, shuddering, towards the mountains that would never come any closer. She couldn't remember how she'd come to be here. It was as if the Earth had been blasted by a huge fire at the end of time. All life and light had been extinguished and she was the last one left.

She knew it was only her consciousness here, not her physical form. If only she could find her body, slip back into it ... she shut her eyes, but the scene remained. Eyes open or closed, she couldn't block it out. Goddess, if this place was only in her mind, why did it feel so real, why did her body ache and shiver, why was there a fire in her shoulder that sent spears of pain through her?

Think, she told her disordered mind. This is the *ezht*. Poor Auriel has borne this a hundred times; if he bore it, so can I. Where's my body, what happened?

She couldn't remember at first. Then it came. She'd been on a battlefield, running for her life ... and then here.

Oh dear Nuth, am I dead? She knelt up and pressed her hands to her mouth. She was clothed in phantom flesh that felt almost real. I was killed ... does that mean I'm trapped here forever? Is this what being dead is? Rigours shook her. She was too horrified to cry. The possibility arched in front of her, bleak, infinite, unendurable.

But if I'm still alive ... ? she thought, staggering to her feet. Falthorn did this to me. He opened this gateway to the *ezht* in my mind, so now I fall into it at random and can't ever be free of it.

How can I know if I'm alive or dead? Last time, a few seconds felt like years. I may be here for years before I wake up and find I've only been here a moment or two. Years of this! I can't bear it, there must be a way out!

Her head swam. She felt drowsy, caught in a sticky web

of nightmare. She couldn't sleep, but neither could she wake up. And she was so cold, cold, cold.

'Tanth'riel?' said a voice.

She was standing on the same bleak plain, but now it was covered in strange sculptures, like wind-carved rocks. She felt horribly dizzy. She reached out to one of the rocks to steady herself, and it reached out to her in turn, and seized her.

She froze against the rock that imprisoned her in its glacial embrace. Stunned, she stopped struggling. There were no greater heights for her fear to reach, nor depths for her misery. She stared up at the featureless midnight of the sky and all the emotion rushed up through her and out of her, leaving her washed clean. The rock felt solid, comforting.

'It's not so bad if you are calm,' she said aloud. 'It can be borne. It's the fear that makes it unbearable, not the *ezht* itself. I can bear it.'

As she spoke, she found that it was not a rock holding her, but a living creature. A beautiful male Valahyr with long dark hair, his garments as black as the plain itself. He was similar to Falthorn but taller, harsher, as different as granite was to alabaster.

'Talthaliorn?' she said. 'Father?'

'If you can bear the *ezht* you are brave indeed.' She heard his words, yet his face remained as still as a statue's. 'We are trapped here.'

'You're an illusion,' she said, remembering what Auriel had told her, the first time this had happened. *You see things that aren't real.*

'No,' said a female voice. She turned and there was another sculpture behind her. A solemn woman with long dark red hair.

'Fiomir?' Tanthe said, her voice trembling. 'Tell me if you're real or not. I can't bear it.'

'Talanthyriel,' said the woman 'That is your true name, the name we gave you. I don't know if we are real. Nothing is real here. We've been here an eternity, alone.'

'My brother drove us here,' said Talthaliorn. His voice was strange and distant. 'Has he captured you too?'

'I don't know,' said Tanthe. 'I can't tell what's real, either. But Falthorn can't have trapped you here. He doesn't know where you are.'

'Does he not?' said her father.

She tried to order her thoughts and memories. It was hard. The *ezht* stirred everything into a cauldron, past and present. She spoke carefully. 'Last time I saw you, you said he had trapped you here. But he can't have done. He was using Auriel and me to find you; why would he do that if he knew you were here?'

'Ah,' said Fiomir. 'No. You are right. We came here . . . ourselves . . . did we not? I can't remember. I can't remember anything.'

Her distress pierced Tanthe. 'Try,' she said. 'Please tell me how to get you out!'

'No way back,' said Fiomir. 'We have tried for eternity. Once the fear fades, you stop trying. There's only the plain . . . Oh, my daughter, are you trapped here too? Then Falthorn has won. He may not possess us, but he has won!'

'No,' said Tanthe. 'No. Try to remember how you got here!'

'Searching,' said Talthaliorn. 'We were searching for answers . . .'

'The dark tower,' Fiomir sighed, clutching her, sending new threads of fear through her. 'Tanthe, please tell me you're not in the tower!'

'No,' she said, shaking her head. She couldn't be sure of anything. 'I don't know what you mean.'

'Falthorn was right,' said her father. 'We dared too much. We sought higher wisdom but it only led here, to nothingness.'

'I'm going to get you out,' Tanthe said desperately. 'Please tell me how.'

Their voices and forms rippled, like reflections in water. 'You can't.'

'Why not? You're not dead, are you? Where are your physical bodies?'

'In a tomb,' said Fiomir. 'In the dark spire. Don't go there, daughter.'

'No,' said Tanthe, despair fragmenting her. She couldn't stand their spectral forms any longer, couldn't bear to leave them, either.

'Tanth'riel, Tanthe.' Her mother's sweet, warm voice was fading. 'I am only dreaming you. This is a place of shadows and illusions. Am I dreaming Talthaliorn, too?'

Her father said nothing. He was no longer there.

'It costs us the most terrible effort even to glimpse each other. Do you know what that means? *We are each alone.* We're both trapped here, alone, wandering blind and without hope . . .'

Where her mother's voice had been there was only a faint, mourning wind. The last revelation speared Tanthe with anguish. Blue-white lightning burned her chest. She reached out to hold her parents, found only dumb pillars of stone under her hands. All the soft horror of the *ezht* blanketed her and she threw back her head and felt the white-hot pain come tearing up out of her throat. Far away from her, someone was screaming.

Jthery stared into the pure blue water, which was no colder than his heart. How blissful to wade into its chilly embrace once and for all, to escape the agonies wrought upon him by Falthorn. The merciful embrace of Eshte's arms.

For a long time after Falthorn had left him he stared at the lake and dreamed savagely of ending it all. How would Falthorn feel, to find him floating, dead, his hair a nimbus of water weed? Would he be distraught with regret, or would he just push the floating corpse with his foot, and laugh?

Jthery stood up. Blank-eyed, he waded into the water, not flinching at its coldness. When it came to his chest he stretched forward and floated with his face in the water, eyes open. He exhaled, his breath rushing up around his head in a flurry of silver bubbles. He waited, yet the need to take another breath didn't come. He stared down into the shadowy dark sapphire of the water without any sense of discomfort or faintness.

Then he realised, and despair surged through him. Of course he could not drown! Water was his element, and the elementals wouldn't let him. He grinned bitterly and water filled his mouth. A bolt of rage struck through him and he thought, No! I am not going to let Falthorn do this to me! I won't kill myself on his account! I'm not going to give up, I'm going to live and fight. Damn him. If he doesn't want me, he won't have me.

Instead, he concentrated on the water. Above him it was growing dark, but he saw the frost of Verdanholm starlight falling through the water. Suddenly it seemed the lake was infinite, threaded through with strands of jet, lapis and diamond. Strands that formed an interlocked web, vibrating around him and through him, connecting him through subtle *roth* to all the waters of Verdanholm and Earth. It was all one vast, interconnected organism.

Beautiful.

He could tug at the strands and change them. Change tides, and the flow of rivers, change the flow of *roth* through the silvery courses of the realms. Jthery laughed in silent exultation.

He saw a vision. A wide and glittering expanse of water, all charcoal and silvery grey but for the sparkle of light on the waves, and in the midst of it an island, and on the island a grey tower wrapped in mist and sea-spray.

The sight filled him with a haunting sense of awe. Suddenly he felt he was rising from the water and flying, hurtling faster and faster towards the mystical tower, destined to crash into its wall. In a panic he came out of the vision. He was spluttering for breath as he righted himself and pushed his sopping hair out of his face.

He coughed, suddenly feeling every inch human; frozen

to the bone and half-choked on water. As he swam back to shore he saw that the sky was velvet-black, the stars shining and singing like a billion chiming crystals.

Now what? he thought, drying himself as best he could and dragging his clothes onto his damp body. Do I go back to the house – back to Falthorn, like a scolded puppy? I don't have to. I could just walk away, or take Heron and ride.

He lingered by the lake for a while, undecided. He felt at peace here. Three moons climbed the sky in a graceful arc, lighting the valley to unearthly beauty. The hills were sheened with light, their reflections inverted in the mirror-surface of the lake.

Jthery felt calm. Whatever he decided to do, nothing could take away the change he had undergone. Whatever Falthorn did, he couldn't stop the power of water-*roth* flowing freely through Jthery's veins.

A movement startled him. He thought he was seeing things at first – but no, he was sure there was a shadow moving on the opposite bank. An animal? Or a small Aelyr, bent over and running from one covert to the next? The figure was making for the top of the lake. Curious, he rose and began to move softly along the shore, intending to intercept the creature there without it seeing him.

At the point of the lake, the shore gave into a tree-scattered meadow that swept up to the base of the hills. Jthery saw a dark little figure in a webby cloak skittering onto the hem of the slope, vanishing over a small ridge.

He felt warm now, and confident. He glanced around, saw no-one else. The creature, whatever it was, had no companions he could see. So he followed, and over the ridge found a narrow cave-mouth, hardly more than a slit in the ultramarine rock.

He paused there, feeling as if he had entered a dream. An eerie violet blush of enchantment lay on the valley. If he stepped into the cave he would enter the dark underworld of the Aelyr. Without fear, he began to walk into the fissure.

All that happened after that was a blur. The fissure tilted steeply down and there was a diffuse white glow coming from below. He saw the figure silhouetted against it. It looked neither Aelyr nor human. The next he knew, the creature had turned, and seen him, and was rushing at him.

Jthery cried out. It was Bhahdradomen, the thing rushing towards him, but of no kind he'd ever seen before. It was covered in dusty grey-black scales, with a membrane like the broken wings of a moth trailing from its shoulders. Its claws were outstretched, its eyes pointed like a chameleon's. Its face narrowed into a kind of beak, which came gouging at his face.

It leapt. As he fell into the dark well of unconsciousness, he heard a shriek that had not come from his own throat.

'Oh, Jey, what were you thinking of?'

He woke to find himself in silken sheets, and Falthorn looking down at him. Morning light gleamed through the interwoven living twigs of the shutters, filling the room with a soft gold glow. His head ached, his throat and shoulders felt sore. Raising a tentative hand he found several long, raw weals, coated in some kind of salve. He winced.

'Don't touch the wounds,' said Falthorn. 'You idiot, you almost got yourself killed!'

'Don't tell me you care,' Jthery said hoarsely.

'Would I have had you brought to my room and spent all night sitting beside you, if I didn't care? I thought you were going to die. Damned idiot!' Falthorn looked angry; did that mean he was genuinely upset? 'I don't suppose you remember what happened.'

Jthery shifted in the soft bed, trying to clear his thoughts. 'I saw a strange figure by the lake and followed it. I didn't realise or even suspect it was Bhahdradomen until it was too late.'

'Well, it was Ostarial and Alviath who saved your life.'

'What? I didn't see them.'

'No,' said Falthorn with a thin smile, 'you wouldn't. But they were following you. They heard you cry out. They reached you and slew the Eater just as it was about to tear your head off.'

Jthery shivered violently. 'I didn't know.'

'Well, you've done us a service; if not for you, we might not have realised the accursed *aghramen* was there.'

'What was it doing? The Bhahdradomen, *aghramen*, I mean?'

Falthorn paused, crossing his arms and looking down. Then his ice-grey eyes met Jthery's, candid and compelling. 'He was looking for the weapons. The Basilisks of Calabethron.'

'Would he have found them?'

Falthorn didn't answer. 'He was searching, spying, and that is crime enough. Now I am angry. In trying to steal the weapons, the Bhahdradomen have broken our agreement.'

There was an uncomfortable pause. As always, Falthorn gave the impression that his concerns were far above Jthery's head . . . but at least he was talking to him. Jthery asked, 'What are you going to do?'

'Oh, I have plans in reserve, don't fear. I knew they would do this. It was only a matter of time. I hoped that I was wrong for once, but no.'

Jthery waited for him to go on, but he didn't. 'And might I ask why Ostarial and Alviath were following me?' Falthorn tapped his fingers, said nothing. 'You sent them to spy on me, is that it?'

'Or could it be, if you would only give me the benefit of the doubt for once, that I was concerned about you? You didn't come back to the house. I sent them to look for you. A good job I did, isn't it?'

Jthery turned his head away. 'Too busy to look for me yourself, I suppose.'

'No, too proud,' Falthorn said lightly, with a quick grin and twitch of his eyebrows. 'Oh, foolish lover, how could I come and fetch you after what I'd said to you? I behaved appallingly.'

Jthery watched him through narrow eyes. Was this another of Falthorn's feints? Every time he seemed sincere, he proved otherwise . . . but the reverse was true, too. 'Yes, you did. All I've offered you is love, and all I get in return is contempt! Save your apologies, I can't believe a word you say!'

Falthorn's eyes glinted with anger. 'There's no point in me offering an apology, if you are going to throw it back in my face.'

'Is this how it's going to be?' Jthery said coldly. 'Seducing me then rejecting me, over and over again? I'm young but I'm not stupid. This is how you break people down, isn't it, like Auriel? You make people blind with love for you, then just when you've got them on their knees, you confuse them with rejection until they're ready to prostrate themselves, harm themselves, do *anything* to make you love them again! That's how you control them, isn't it – even your mother and father!'

'You're quite the philosopher, aren't you.'

His face was a cold storm, but Jthery ignored the danger. 'It didn't work on your brother, though, did it?'

'How dare you mention Talthaliorn? None of that is any of your business.'

'No, I forgot, I'm just your plaything! The gods forbid I should ask questions or have opinions!' Jthery raised himself off the pillow, projecting as much force as he could from his raw throat. 'Well, not any more. I have my own power now. What's the worst thing you can do to me? Come on then, do it. I'm not scared.'

Falthorn's eyes blazed with dangerous light. A force gathered between his eyes, a greenish egg of light that surged snake-like towards Jthery. As if time had stopped, he stared at the force poised between his skull and Falthorn's. He had no idea what it was but it filled him with irrational terror; the certainty of something worse than death.

It dissipated.

'No,' said Falthorn, all his rage vanishing in a sigh. 'You're right. Everything you said about me is true. I control my family. I control everything around me. It's a habit hard to break. Still, I never offer apologies unless I truly mean it.' He took Jthery's hand. 'I'm sorry. I want you with me of your own free will, not because you are terrified of me.'

Jthery was astonished. The pressure of Falthorn's hand felt exquisite. Jthery closed his eyes with a groan of twisted anger, frustration and relief. To hear Falthorn make such an admission. To know that Falthorn was manipulating him, and yet, behind the games, felt something real for him . . . It was all he'd wanted to know. Even though knowing it made it impossible for him to walk away. Anguish. He was a fly tangled in honey.

'You are a terrifying person, Falthorn,' he said softly, 'and you revel in it. You loved frightening Tanthe and Auriel. I think you only let them go so you could scare them even more when you recapture them.'

Falthorn gave a thin smile. 'Dear, I let them go because I don't need them. Not at present, anyway. You don't think I bear them any ill-will, do you?'

'I don't know. I think I know you, then it all changes.'

'You wouldn't find me half so interesting if I was predictable,' Falthorn said, accurately. 'Any more questions?'

'Yes. What about your brother and his wife? Have you given up trying to find them?'

'Talthaliorn and Fiomir. No. I have a suspicion . . . but I don't see how even they could have done something so impossible, and so stupid.'

'What do you mean?'

All at once, Falthorn was pale, distracted. Every glimpse of genuine feeling behind his lover's mask increased Jthery's confidence. 'I'll tell you one day. Not now. It's too tenuous.'

'Do you think you'll ever find them and make them come back?'

'I think Tanthe can. I am sure she will, all the better without me bullying her.'

'That's why you let her go!'

'And there you are again, assuming I want my brother for some nefarious reason.' He stroked Jthery's cheek. 'What if Tal and Fi were the ones who'd hatched some mad, destructive plan to the detriment of Earth or Verdanholm, and my only sin was trying to dissuade them?'

Jthery scowled. 'Is that what happened?'

'I hope that frown is because you are beginning to believe me.'

'Falthorn, I like you a lot better when you are honest with me. Just be honest. It might not hurt as much as you think it will.'

Falthorn gazed at Jthery with half-closed eyes, like a cat. 'All right. Put it this way; their refusal to help me may have put Verdanholm in mortal danger. I never thought I could do anything to solve the problem . . . until I met you.'

This sounded like a flash of truth, a wrung-out admission. Jthery laughed. 'You need me? That's it, that's why you behave so badly towards me – you can't admit that you need help!'

'Exactly,' Falthorn said. 'You see right through me.'

'But . . . what sort of help?' Jthery asked in a low voice.

Falthorn lifted Jthery's hands between his and kissed the fingertips. 'Your power, Jey. Your elemental *roth* power. I've watched it growing in you from the first day we met. It's the key to everything.' And before Jthery could voice any more questions, Falthorn bent down and silenced them with the firm and sensuous pressure of his mouth.

* * *

Tanthe crawled through darkness, mute under the weight of desolation. She was crawling towards something, or away from it; she no longer knew or remembered clearly. There was a spark of light; had it been there for a thousand years, or only a second? It was something to do with her, she knew. It was a spark, a seed, a child. *Her child.*

She changed direction and strove towards it. As she did so, there was a change. A faint glow appeared above her. Looking up, she saw spots of amber light floating over her, fireflies. Warmth flowed, sealing the hole through which her life was leaking out. The glow extended arms around her, pulled her gently upwards, out of the cold and dark, into a cocoon of sweet hazy fire.

Tanthe blinked. She was dazed; it took a while to realise she was no longer in the *ezht*. She was conscious, in a strange wooden room that jolted and swayed; and there were faces leaning over her. The pert brown face of Lahjaya, the unearthly white-amber features of Auriel. Their intent, anxious expressions alarmed her.

'Hello,' she said. 'Why are you staring at me like that?'

'Tanthe,' Auriel choked. He seized her hands and kissed them.

'Lady be praised, you're back with us,' said Lahjaya. She turned and snapped, 'Don't crowd her!' and Tanthe saw Eldareth, Helan and Mawrdreth looking down at her over Lahjaya's shoulder. 'At last.'

'What happened to me?' She tried to sit up, gasping as a dull fire tore at her left shoulder.

'You were shot in the battle,' said Lahjaya. 'You've been unconscious for three days and nights.'

She saw the lumps of golden amber in Lahjaya's hands, and understood. 'You saved my life,' she said, shivering.

'Well, you saved mine,' Lahjaya murmured.

'Did I? Oh . . .' The scene came back. She'd thrown herself across Lahjaya without a thought; it seemed to have happened only a few seconds ago. It must have looked brave to the others, but Tanthe hadn't considered that her split-second, selfless act might actually kill her. She swallowed hard. *Gods, am I really that vain, to think I'm immortal or something?*

'How is the pain now?'

'Just sore. I can't remember it hurting . . . though there was something about a shaft of lightning stuck through me . . .'

Auriel said, 'You were crying out as if you were in agony. It was terrible to hear.'

'Sorry,' she said. 'That wasn't pain, Auriel. I was in the *ezht*.'

He looked stricken. 'Oh, no.' He gripped her hand.

'It's all right.' She didn't want to upset him by describing the horror. 'It's fading now.'

'Did you see . . . anything this time?' His brown eyes were wide.

'I might have done.' She didn't want to distress him, didn't want to lie. 'I think I saw our parents there again.'

'What did they . . . say?'

She swallowed. Her mouth was arid. 'It was like talking to ghosts. They couldn't remember how they'd got there and insisted they couldn't leave. It was horrible.'

'You can't trust those visions!' he said fiercely. Again he was trying to deny it.

'Well, we'll see, shall we?' she said, holding his gaze. 'If they are there, we're going to find them and we are going to get them out.'

'They can't be there!'

'But if they are, we have to stop being scared!'

'That's enough,' Lahjaya said, pushing Tanthe back onto the pillow, pressing Auriel away with her other hand. 'I haven't made all this effort healing you, only for you to undo it by arguing.'

Tanthe resisted her for a moment, then relented. 'You're bossy.'

'For my patient's good,' Lahjaya agreed.

'You drew me out of the *ezht*. Both of you. Like hands

made of golden light, pulling me up into reality.' She frowned, looking around the strange, jolting carriage. 'Where are we, anyway?'

Smiling, Eldareth opened the wooden shutters that covered the opposite window. Tanthe stared at the scene in amazement.

A plain of red stone, with tors and pillars wind-sculpted into fantastical shapes. A hot breeze blew ruby dust into the forms of elementals that seemed to dance on the strange landscape. An apricot sun poured its heat from a dark-blue sky. It reminded her of the strange skies of Verdanholm. And the whole fantastical scene rolled slowly past the window, unveiling new wonders every moment.

'The Ruby Plains. Azura Maroc.'

Tanthe whistled. 'This is like going from one dream straight into another.'

There was a clatter of galloping hoofbeats alongside the wagon. A rider drew level with the window, his face flushed with exertion. 'Lord Eldareth!' he called gruffly. '*Ghelim* have been seen massing some miles behind us. It's certain they'll see us, if they haven't already. You must quit the carriage!'

Chapter Fourteen. The Wolf Mage

'I didn't mean to give you such a shock,' said Branq'elin.

'It's a good shock,' said Rufryd. 'I think.'

'I didn't mean it to happen, but now it has, I'm glad,' she said, stroking the girl's hair. 'We were a bit careless, I'm afraid. You had been gone for several weeks before I realised.'

'I – I can't take it in. Are you absolutely sure? Bran, I know I'm not the only man you've slept with . . .'

'But with the others, I took care,' she said with a touch of ice. 'And all the time I was with you, there was no-one else; you know that.'

'I just wanted to be sure,' he said lamely.

'I was distraught over my father's death, and not thinking as clearly as I usually should.' She smiled down at the child. 'Hence I neglected to avail myself of the benefits of the blessed arkh-wood tree. I was reckless.'

'I should have mentioned it myself,' Rufryd said uncomfortably. 'I didn't think. Sorry.'

'What for? Out of death comes life. Don't be sorry; I'm not.' She took his hand again. 'Look at her. She's the sweetest child in the world, Q'enartre's gift. And she is yours, Rufryd.'

'Got my good looks, definitely,' he said, beginning to smile.

'And she's my heir, of course.' Branq'elin was looking at him now with a warmth that was blatantly more than relief to see a friend. 'Your daughter is heir to the Dukedom of Thanmandrathor.'

Rufryd gave a quiet laugh of amazement. 'Is that allowed?'

'What do you mean?'

'Well, I'm a peasant. No royal blood, that I know of.'

Bran glared at him, her eyes vividly green. 'You should know that means nothing. Her father could have been a kitchen boy; she'd still be my heir. Besides, I can give you a title to befit your bravery..'

'How d'you know I'm brave?' He moved closer to her.

'You went to Vexor for me.'

Unable to hold back, he slipped his arms round her. 'You don't know what I did there,' he said, muffled, his mouth moving over her neck, her cheek, fastening on her lips. She responded hungrily, then pushed him away.

'Wait, wait,' she said. She leaned down and lifted the child out of the cot. The girl wrapped her arms around her mother's neck, still staring at Rufryd with large, curious eyes. 'Let me take Annuin to her nurse. Then you must tell me everything.'

Branq'elin carried the child across the main chamber and into another room on the far side. A smiling older woman took Annuin from her. Branq'elin vanished into the room for ten minutes or more; Rufryd waited. Then she came back, closed the door, and lit candles around the large bed.

She went to a window recess, where two chairs padded with green tapestry stood on either side of a small table. 'Sit down,' she said, pouring them each a glass of wine. 'Tell me what happened.'

Rufryd told her everything. How the queen-dra'a'k, Akarata, had carried him to Vexor, how he'd arrived there to find Vaurgroth ready to invade Aventuria, contemptuous of his arrival. And then Calathvahn.

Branq'elin showed no surprise at the first part of his story. But as he described the Order's attack on the village, her face drained of colour and she rose and stared out of the window, one hand crushing the edge of the velvet curtain.

'Are these people mad?' she said.

'I don't think so,' he replied, taking another mouthful of

wine. 'If you consider their beliefs to be real, as they do, they're behaving in a perfectly logical way. But from the outside, yes, they're barking.'

'The Bhahradomen are using them.'

'Yeah, I suppose they are. They're even more dangerous, in some ways. The Bhahradomen just want territory to live on, but the Order are on fire with these crazed ideas.'

'And they are going to attack Tasqabad?'

'That's what they said.'

Her slim, neat back was tense. He stood up behind her and rested his hands on her shoulders, half expecting her to shake him off, but she didn't. He gently kneaded the taut ridges of flesh until he felt her relax and soften against him. 'We have known this would come. We thought it would be Devourers attacking us, not humans.'

'The Bhahradomen aren't all bad, you know.'

'Not bad?' she flared. 'After what they did to my father?'

'I know, but . . . I lived among them. They're just different. Trying to survive.'

'And Vaurgroth, and their elite? Different? They are trying to destroy us! And we, also, are trying to survive.'

'Yes, I know,' he said, deciding that this was not a good time to explain about Vetru.

'This town and manor are ill-defended; we have no city wall, no fortifications. The house was built in a time of peace, when my ancestors thought war would not come again.' She cursed under her breath. 'My army is prepared. I can set them to building makeshift fortifications with stakes and moats. It will be better than nothing.'

'But leave us a path of escape, if you can,' he said. The scent of her hair and skin clouded his senses; he couldn't bear talking and thinking about war any longer. So long since he'd seen a woman, let alone caressed one. 'We don't want to be trapped in a siege.'

'No.' She bent her head, presenting him with the soft bronze curve of her neck. 'If we could get the townspeople away to somewhere safe in the forest, and just make a straight clean battle of it . . .'

Rufryd pressed his lips to her neck. His hands travelled over her breasts and over the slim curve of her abdomen to her hips. Bran turned in his arms and kissed him so sensuously that he, already hard against her, came perilously close to orgasm.

'Get undressed,' she said, pulling at his clothes, her eyes slitted and gleaming.

'I probably stink of horses.' He dragged impatiently at the laces of his shirt.

'I don't care. I want you. I like the smell of horses.'

'Yes, the stables, I remember . . .'

She pulled the green velvet dress over her head, then the cream shift she wore underneath, and stood naked before him. Her long slim form was washed in candlelight.

'Gods,' he groaned, closing his eyes as she helped remove the rest of his stubborn garments. They stood flesh to warm flesh. He lifted her, her legs around his hips, and bore her onto the bed. 'The er . . . arkh-charm?'

'It's done,' she whispered.

And with the next movement he impaled her, was inside her, somehow managing to control the excruciating urgency. Stretching out the delicate, hot pleasure until the sensation was nearly unbearable. Pushing gently and intently into her until she gasped and cried out and convulsed against him; and then at last his seed was bursting into her, so sweetly that he wept with the intensity of it.

The first time for so long. First time he'd held a woman for more than two years, and it was so exquisite to feel someone whole and warm and sacred in his arms instead of the bitter, life-denying nothingness of Calathvahn.

'I missed you,' Branq'elin said, arching against him and pressing her mouth to his.

'Q'enartre,' he whispered between kisses. 'Q'enartre.'

'That's the Goddess's name, not mine.'

'I know. You are the Goddess. I've been in a wasteland

for years with no sun, just the bone-freezing light of some god who doesn't even exist and this is like coming home where I belong, into the warmth again . . .'

'You're among friends, dearest,' she said, stroking his hair. 'Nothing to give each other but bad news, but at least we have love.'

'Bran,' he said, resting his hand across her sweat-damp waist, 'is there anyone else? This is a wonderful welcome, but for all I know you've got a husband hidden away somewhere with a big axe.'

She laughed. 'There's no-one, Rufryd. I've been on my own all this time, too. Well, not alone with Annuin, but there's no other man.'

'So, the Duchess of Thanmandrathor can make love to a peasant, but is she allowed to marry one?'

Her face and eyes became still, grave. 'Do you mean it?'

'I want to stay with you and Annuin.'

Bran spoke softly, stroking his cheek. 'The Duchess of Thanmandrathor can marry anyone she damned well pleases.'

For the first time in his life it seemed to Rufryd that it was possible to be happy and to belong somewhere. The next morning, when he went to the great hall to join Dawn and Mirias and Con, they greeted him with laughter and teased him relentlessly. He could only respond with a helpless grin.

'You bastards!' he cried. 'You knew, and you didn't tell me!'

'Come on, it was more fun finding out for yourself, wasn't it?' Mirias laughed. 'I wish I could have seen your face.'

Branq'elin did not join them for breakfast. She spent the morning closeted with the leaders of her army, but didn't ask Rufryd to join her. He was glad. Still aching and worn out from the journey, the last thing he wanted was to talk about fighting.

Under the pretext of checking on his horse, Rufryd slipped into the stable to see Vetru. The young *domen* was hardly visible in the dark; all Rufryd could see at first was the gleam of his small eyes. He was sitting in a corner alongside the door, while the big dun mare munched obliviously at a haynet. She was as placid as could be, but he'd told the stable hands she was unmanageable and must on no account be approached; he would look after her himself. Thus, he hoped, no one would discover Vetru.

'I brought you something to eat,' Rufryd said, offering the provisions he'd begged from the kitchens; a packet containing rye bread, pickled fish, a flat cake made with oats and dried fruits. Anything he thought Vetru might be able to eat.

Vetru picked suspiciously at the rye bread. 'Your food leaves me hungry,' he said.

'You're always hungry.'

'I need *graukhim* meat.'

'Well, I can't get you any,' Rufryd said, crouching down beside him. 'Can't you eat your arm, or something?'

'What?' The *domen* stared at him.

'It was a joke. You haven't eaten that stuff for weeks, anyway. If you are going to stay with me and be on our side, you can never eat *graukhim* again. You have to get used to our food. You must be able to adapt; other *domenim* have, I'm sure.'

'I try to adapt, and eat your food,' Vetru said acidly. 'I am on your side. Why then am I hiding in the stable and not allowed in the house?'

Rufryd groaned, pushing his hair back. It was growing long again. He was glad to get rid of the cropped style of Calathvahn. 'The mistress of the house is very sensitive. I have to introduce her to the idea gently. If I take you in now, the household will go mad and you'll end up with about ten swords through you. Please be patient.'

'I am patient,' Vetru said with cool dignity. 'I am good.'

'Yes, you are.'

'When will you tell them?'

'Look, I didn't ask you to come!' He shook his head; it was hopeless losing his temper with Vetru. 'I'll tell her today.' He rose. 'I have to go back now. Get some rest. I'll come back later.'

On his way back to the house, he found Halcyon in one of the other loose boxes. The lean blue roan stallion had been Lynden's, and then Rufryd's, until he'd given him to Con. Con was obviously looking after him well. He looked glossy and well-fed, whiffling at Rufryd's sleeve and flicking his big dark ears with intelligent interest. Rufryd scratched his neck and stroked the soft muzzle, suddenly overwhelmed by a mixture of sadness and optimism. His friends were waiting for him inside. His *family*.

He spent the afternoon playing with Annuin – or rather, staring at her while the nurse and Branq'elin's mother – also Annuin – kept her entertained. The child seemed to like him, even if she didn't yet understand who he was. She had a wooden horse on wheels and when she wanted someone to push her around the room on this steed, she insisted that only Rufryd would do. Still in a daze of disbelief, he obliged.

That evening, instead of them taking their meal in the great hall with the rest of the household, Branq'elin asked Rufryd, Con, Dawn and Mirias to eat supper in a private chamber. A fire blazed in the stone grate and tapestries of Thand'rathian landscapes softened the walls. They sat at a round table and Branq'elin's staff served them with food and wine.

Branq'elin, arriving last, looked stunning. She wore a simple dress of bronze velvet that hugged her body, and over it an open robe edged with gold. Her hair hung in loose ripples, full of gold from the firelight. She smiled at Rufryd. Even her smiles, he thought, looked dour on her cat-like face which was more usually serious and watchful.

Once her household staff had withdrawn, she said, 'Conawr has a story to relate that I'd prefer kept between the five of us. Much as it grieves me to confess it, when he first came back I had difficulty believing what he said had happened. But certain events, certain artefacts persuaded me he must be speaking the truth. Now that Rufryd's tale has confirmed much of what Con said, I know for certain. I'm sorry for doubting you, Con.'

'It's all right, my lady,' Con said solemnly. 'I didn't blame you.'

'Would you mind telling Rufryd the tale now? And I think the rest of us should hear it again, so we can best decide how to act upon it.'

'Of course.' He appeared pleased to be taken seriously.

Con had changed since Rufryd had last seen him. The flood that had separated them from Dawn and Mirias had carried Con into the claws of a hunting dragon-hawk, a huge queen possessed of ancient intelligence. Perceiving something unusual in Con, she'd spared him. Spared Rufryd, too, when he'd climbed up to rescue Con from her mountain eyrie. He'd been injured, so Rufryd had taken him to a farm at the foot of the mountain and left him in the care of the farmers.

Now Con had matured from a youth to a young man, and there was a watchful wisdom in his eyes that hadn't been there before. 'It seems a long time since you left me at the farm,' he said, looking at Rufyrd with steady green eyes.

'The farmers looked after you well, did they?'

'Yes, they were like a mother and father to me,' said Con. 'I was in bed for a couple of weeks, then hobbling around for a few weeks more. Once my back healed, they let me work for them. That got my strength back, until I was fit enough to ride Halcyon.'

'Then you came home?'

'It wasn't that simple,' said Con. He lowered his gaze. 'I wasn't going to return to Tasqabad. You know why.' There was an awkward pause; he was referring to Noli, his lost friend. 'I meant to follow you to Vexor. But the day I said goodbye and set off, Akarata was waiting for me.'

In the greyness of dawn, Q'enartre's Throne was a huge wall soaring into the mist, her peak lost in cloud. The dra'a'k loomed, a shadow on the greyness, her leathery wings creaking with each small movement, her breath steaming on the air. Her neck was gently arched towards him.

Con felt no fear as he went towards her. Her spell was on him. The claws of her feet and wings were terrible; her jaws could have sliced him in two. But he knew they were also capable of tenderness, of carrying a leathery egg without denting it, or of feeding slivers of meat to a dra'a'k-chick. She rumbled deep in her chest as he went to her.

Unexpectedly she seized him in her claws and rose. The breath shot out of him. His shout of terror was lost on the air. The ground fell away, the mountain came veering towards him. He hung in fog, caught in exhilaration as much as terror. Then they broke through the cloud layer and into a clear blue sky, gemmed with dawn stars. The peak of the mountain rose and rose in a breathtaking spire and they were ascending towards it.

Through a break in the clouds, for a few moments Con saw the land arrayed below him; a ragged patchwork of cloud-shadow floating over dark blue hills and forests. He saw the mysterious standing stone called Nilothphon's Finger, saw how it pointed firmly but enigmatically at the peak of Q'enartre's Throne. He saw the green eye that boiled on the side of the peak above him. An ancient Aelyr portal in the throes of self-destruction.

As he watched, the portal exploded.

The green vortex whirled faster and tighter, growing in brilliance until he could barely look at it. He held his breath, sensing what was about to happen, unable to escape because Akarata held him there, too close . . .

Leaf-green fire roared into the sky. The air shook. Con cried out, pressed his hands to his ears, felt the hot wind of *roth* howling past him.

He thought Akarata would wheel away but she hovered there, only a few hundred yards from eruption, swaying on the wind currents. Con hung in her claws, breathless, amazed. The explosion had a strange beauty, a fire-fountain expelling a billion green peridots. The clouds below reflected the colour, dancing and glowing.

It lasted for three or four minutes that seemed endless. The eruption was spent. An immense haunting silence followed. The old portal lay dark, cold, dead.

When it was over, Akarata flew down to the place where the green eye had been. She landed on the lip of a great crater that tilted steeply in the mountainside. Trembling, Con found his feet and stepped out of the embrace of her claws. He'd half-expected to see a black tunnel that led into nothingness; but no, the base of the hollow was blind rock.

He touched the rim cautiously. The rock was cold. The Aelyr portal had burned out as if it had never existed.

'What is it?' he asked the dra'a'k. 'What are you trying to show me?'

She had no words, he knew, so he tried to put the question in images. Her answer came as a series of pictures in his mind. He wasn't sure he understood. She showed him the lapis-blue pointing stone that stood far below.

Pointing like a finger at the crater. Warily he climbed over the lip and made his way down to the rugged stone of the floor. There he found one place that felt warm, and scattered over it shards of broken white rock, like alabaster, or quartz. He picked up some of the bigger fragments and put them in his pockets; they tingled against his fingertips. Then he found the bone.

It was a segment of animal thigh-bone, eight inches long; he knew as he touched it that it had come from a stag. It seemed to have been altered by a human hand, the cut ends capped with slices of polished bone. It felt warm. As soon as he held it in both hands and closed his eyes, it spoke to him.

Visions came rushing in. He was the animal from which it had come. He was a stag walking a younger, fresher Earth, and at his side was another animal, a great silver wolf.

Con saw the events of aeons past as if they were happening around him at great speed. He saw the portal newly made, a softly glowing jade-green gateway to the Aelyr realm through which Aelyr and humans walked freely. All was idyllic. Then he saw the two races separating into factions, arguing. The Aelyr were leaving the Earth, their lithe figures vanishing into the limpid glow of the portal. And when they'd gone, the portal changed. Its gentle glow became fierce. It transformed into a whirling fire, threatening any who tried to pass through with death.

Con in his stag-form walked on.

Now he saw humans gathered on a lone, round hill beneath the mountain.

Some were half naked, hauling ropes attached to a great blue stone. Others were dressed in green or ivory robes like priests, all of them wreathed in blue flowers. The great central stone was being raised into position, its lower half thrust deep into the earth, the upper portion pointing at the sky. One of the figures in ivory, a man, was directing them, showing the others how the stone must not be vertical but tilted to point at the far-off portal. To show future ages . . . what?

The silver wolf at his side turned to look at him and Con knew, with the natural intuition of the shamanic trance, that the wolf was the mage Nilothphon in animal form. He gazed at the stag with amber eyes and his voice echoed deeply in Con's skull, 'They act as I ordained.'

The scene changed again. Now he saw animals surging towards him through the majestic hills and forests of Thanmandrathor, leaving the land deserted. Deer and antelope, lynx and wolf, eagles and blue-doves, rats and green-wolves surging up from the lakes, all running or flying as if from a forest fire. Running, running until they fell dead in mid-stride or tumbled into the northern sea.

Even dra'a'ks were fleeing to escape the *ghelim* that mimicked them.

Surging in to replace not only dra'aks but all animals came the Bhahdradomen. Changing shape to resemble the animals they had driven out. Green-wolves with tiny eyes and clattering claws that could tear out a human heart.

And they changed shape with a sort of impassive fatalism, as if they couldn't help what they did; were simply driven to mimic, to supplant, to feed. But they fed so deeply, with such insatiable hunger, that the source could not renew itself.

Con knew he was seeing the future.

He tried to scream. His stag-self bellowed.

'Be still,' said the wolf-mage. His voice was deep, dry, ironic. 'Attend. Once there were many beautiful artefacts in the world, created by Aelyr *roth*-mages. *Silvenroth* mirrors with which people could speak at a distance, *liroth* crystals that could warn of danger, banded *zaharoth* agates the Seers use. When the Aelyr left the world they took these artefacts away. And humans destroyed the rest, refusing to make use of Aelyr wisdom. Alas, both races thus conceived their own destruction, for they lost many defences against the shape-changers. No longer could they speak at a distance, nor defend themselves with ease. But there were a group of Fhelethyr who foresaw this danger, and hid a cache of such items within the portal. And I, being of their number, left the clue, the pointing finger, so that in time of need some courageous intelligent human would brave the peak and the portal and find those items.'

'Where are they?'

'Destroyed,' said the wolf. 'Alas, it happens that one rises – among Aelyr as among humans as among Eaters – who is filled with wild ideas of greater glory. They upset the flow of *roth*. Now one of the Valahyr has kindled wars between his own folk and the Fhelethyr, set himself against humans and Aelyr alike. Too much *roth* power is concentrated in one place and this is the result . . .'

Con found himself in the crater of the dead portal again, still in stag-form.

'That Valahyr's ambitions have destroyed the portal and the last of the Aelyr weapons. I think that he did it deliberately. If you can find any still intact, take them.' The wolf turned away. 'The Wrothryr mourn, but are powerless. All my warnings lie in your hand; my dreams are done, and my lazurite finger points, like the finger of a skeleton, at nothing.'

The wolf trotted away and vanished into a mist.

Con came out of the vision, shuddering and sobbing. He was human again. A boy, staring at a piece of old bone. The vision had been so real, terrifying and yet so beautiful. He longed for the company of the dry-voiced, wise Nilothphon again. But it was over; the wolf was gone. Akarata was waiting. She showed him no more images, only dipped her long fierce head over him as if she understood and had seen everything.

'Then I came home,' said Con. 'I had to tell Lady Branq'elin.'

'You saw all that?' Rufryd said at last.

'Yes. I saw the portal die. You do believe me, don't you!' There was a flash of indignation in his eyes. 'You met Akarata yourself!'

'Of course I believe you. I wouldn't have got to Vexor without her. And that's the way she communicates. Shows you bits of the past, bits of the future. You have to piece it together yourself.'

'It was an extraordinary story,' said Branq'elin. 'It sounded like the result of fever; I've had to apologise to Con for doubting him at first. We've since heard many reports of the portal's death throes. We experienced it ourselves. The strange storms grew worse until there was one of such power we thought the world had ended; but it was over in a few minutes. Shortly afterwards, Con came back. And no more storms.'

'Can I see that piece of bone?' Rufryd asked.

'Here.' Con took the cylinder from around his neck, pulling the thong over his head. He passed it to Rufryd who weighed it in his hands, but saw no visions.

'That wolf – or Nilothphon, assuming you really met him – was talking about Falthorn, I should think.'

'Wasn't he the one Tanthe told us about, who forced her to have a child?' said Bran.

'Short of actually fathering it,' Rufryd said thinly. He examined the piece of bone as he spoke, turning it over and over. 'She said he was very powerful, and up to something sinister . . . The part about the animals speaks for itself. Akarata showed me something similar, though not as graphic. The long slow infiltration of Aventuria by the Devourers, until they've replaced every living thing. Turned into one big self-generating cycle. Maybe they'll start turning into plants as well, then they can really disappear up their own arses.'

He was glad of their shocked laughter. It lessened the tension, at least. 'I think that part of the message was aimed at Con. But the rest of it . . .' He tried to force a fingernail under one of the tightly sealed caps. To his surprise it came loose and shot onto the table before he could catch it.

'There's something inside,' he said, pushing in his little finger and drawing out a tightly rolled piece of paper.

'"All my warnings lie your hands,"' said Con. 'I didn't know what he meant.'

The paper, made of some yellowish woven reed, was covered in rune-like script. But it was in Paranian, and legible.

'"The secret of the Jewelfire is this",' he read, '"that it resides equally in Verdanholm and Earth. The substance of one is not more of the Jewelfire than the substance of the other; nor can the balance be pulled out of shape for long except that it snap back into its true place with terrible force.

'"You who read this know that the Earth is in peril. For

those that consume the Jewelfire are marching again, as they have marched before and will march again. And those that seem to be friends may become enemies and those that you thought enemies may turn to your side in the darkest hour of peril. So I say to you, fight not only their weapons but fight their thoughts. For it is their thoughts that will consume you. Their ideas that will destroy all love, all compassion, all sense, destroy even nature itself in their twisted reasoning. Their dreams that will lay waste to your dreams.

'"Whatever they tell you, with smiles and fiery words, hold to your own ideas. The spire of their terrible black tower leads nowhere."'

He stopped.

'Is that all?' said Branq'elin.

'That's all,' he said, passing it to her.

'Is it genuine?'

'I doubt it,' said Rufryd. 'The mage Nilothphon was meant to walking around at the dawn of time, wasn't he, taming the fires of the Earth so we could live on it? The Aelyr withdrawal from Earth took place thousands of years later.'

'Ah, but perhaps the portal was *opened* at the dawn of time, and that's when Nilothphon left the message,' Dawn said drily. 'These myths are so vague, there's no telling when anything really happened.'

'Or maybe Nilothphon lived to be thousands of years old,' Mirias said, half-serious. 'He was Aelyr, so they say.'

'Or appeared to someone like me, and got them to write it down,' said Con.

'Whoever wrote the message doesn't matter,' Rufryd said darkly. 'It's true. The real danger of Vaurgroth and the Order of Calathvahn is more than violence and conquest. Yes, that's bad enough, but this is worse. They'll never kill us all, no matter how hard they try. The real danger is their ideology, because that's what will destroy us. If people turn aside from the Earth and start believing all this mad stuff about the Ancestor instead, that will be the end of us.'

Silence followed his words. Branq'elin's face was drained and taut. 'I shall never let that happen,' she said at last.

'None of us will,' Mirias said firmly. He raised his goblet. 'I drink to life, to our Great Mother the Earth. I drink to Nepheter and Dyonis, the bringers of joy, and to Nuth, the beginning and the end. I pledge to defend them unto my death.'

Dawn stared solemnly at Mirias, her lover, and raised her own glass. Then in turn they all drank the toast and made their pledge. There was no need; they had all made it long ago in their hearts, but to affirm it aloud had a magical strength.

Presently Branq'elin excused herself, saying she must make her rounds of the kitchens and speak to her officers. As she left she leaned down to Rufryd's ear and said, 'Stay, talk to your friends; but come to my chamber later.'

Rufryd smiled. Comforted by wine, happiness and pleasant anticipation, he could forget the darkness outside. They hadn't yet told anyone of their plans.

Con and Mirias found a battered set of table skittles and began a noisy game on the other side of the room. Rufryd and Dawn stayed talking by the fire.

'How does it feel to be a father?' Dawn asked wryly.

'Weird,' he said. 'I still can't believe it. I'm no good with children, I don't know what you're supposed to do with them . . . but I look at her and I can see the young woman she'll become and it's breathtaking. What will the world be like then? What will she think of having this huge realm to look after? Will she love me?'

'I'm sure she'll adore you,' Dawn grinned, slurring a little. They had both drunk a great deal of wine. 'It's just like what happened to Tanthe.'

'How d'you mean?'

'Suddenly coming out of a magical trance to find she'd had a child.'

'I haven't been in a magical trance, Dawn.'

'I know, but the end result is the same.'

'This is nothing like that!'

'Isn't it? You've both ended up with a child you didn't expect; the difference is that she had hers taken away before she'd even seen it.'

'What are you trying to say?'

'Just that perhaps, if you had a second chance, you'd be a little more understanding with her.'

Rufryd felt a wrench of old but raw pain. 'Fuck it, Dawn, who appointed you to speak for my conscience? Yes, I was vile to her. I've regretted it every day since. You needn't think I haven't been punished.'

'How? By what happened in Vexor?'

'No, I mean by the fact that it made Tanthe hate me. That's all I achieved by getting angry with her; I made her despise me. She hated me so much she couldn't even say goodbye properly. No, it was worse than hatred; I could have dealt with that. She spoke to me like I was a stranger. I deserved it, but Anthar's balls, it hurt.'

'Okay.' Her voice was slurred, but her eyes were serious. 'So you know you were unfair?'

'Yeah, I know. I knew even while I was saying it, but it didn't stop me. I couldn't have reacted any other way at the time.'

'But you will apologise to her?'

He groaned. 'Dawn, even if I knew she was still alive, and we weren't thousands of miles apart, it wouldn't do any good. We both went too far, don't you get it? I think it's better for us both if we never meet again.'

She frowned. 'You don't mean it.'

He grinned sourly. 'Dawn, mate, I'm going to marry Branq'elin.'

Her blue eyes opened wide. '*Marry* her? Whose idea was that?'

'Mine, but she seems quite happy about it.'

Dawn looked seriously at him. 'Are you sure you know what you're doing? You don't know what she's like.'

'What d'you mean?'

'She's not the easiest person in the world to get on with. She's driven; all she thinks about is how to save Thanmandrathor, which is perfectly understandable, but it won't make her an ideal companion. We've all felt the sharp end of her temper, at one time or another.'

Rufryd shrugged. 'I don't see how she can be any worse than Tanthe.'

'Oh, Tanthe's got nothing on Bran, believe me.'

'You must love her, Bran I mean, or you would've left.'

'Yes, I do love her,' Dawn said quietly. 'She's completely pure-hearted.'

'Well, then. I know she's an awkward sod; so am I. Maybe that's why we get on so well.'

'Oh, Rufe.' Dawn smiled suddenly, and kissed his cheek. 'Congratulations. I'm happy for you. As long as you don't expect me to call you, "my lord" or, "your grace".'

'What?'

'This will make you Duke of Thanmandrathor.'

'Oh, fuck,' said Rufryd, nearly choking on his wine. 'I hadn't thought of that.'

'Rubbish. You must have done.'

'But I don't want that. I just want her. Bloody hell, isn't this what Eldareth and Helananthe broke up about?'

'I shouldn't worry about it,' Dawn said with a quick smile. 'She won't give away any of her power to you. She thinks that everything is her responsibility; the good of the realm is all down to her. Which it is, after all.'

'So you're saying it's not going to be easy.'

'Just so, my dear.'

'Oh well. No change there, then. My life never has been easy.'

'You do make a very beautiful couple. A threesome, rather.'

With a jolt, Rufryd remembered another child for whom he had responsibility. 'Er, Dawn, do you remember Noli?'

She paled slightly. 'Yes. I wish I could forget it.'

'I know how scary Bran can be. She joined in killing him, remember? We argued about it afterwards.'

'Why are you dragging this up again?'

'Well . . . I've got a really bad problem. Something I didn't mention when I told her about Calathvahn.'

Softly, so Con and Mirias would not overhear, he told her about Vetru. Dawn gaped at him as he explained, her freckled skin paling to greenish-white.

'Oh gods, Rufe, tell me this isn't true! You're hiding a *Bhahdradomen* in the stables?'

'Keep your voice down! I have to tell Bran.'

'You can't. She will go mad.'

'What else can I do? I can't just leave him there indefinitely.'

'You'll have to get rid of him somehow.'

'I've tried that. He won't go. Besides, he's been a good friend to me.'

'If you tell her, or somebody finds him, they'll kill him!'

'They aren't all bad, Dawn. He's harmless, and he's loyal.'

She was shaking her head, lost for words. 'Rufe . . .' She checked that Mirias and Con were immersed in their game, then leaned forward and whispered, 'Noli appeared to be harmless, too, and devoted to Con – but he was trying to poison Duke Tasq! Perhaps he didn't even realise what he was doing. Maybe a little signal goes off in whatever passes for their brains, and they start harming humans, like – I don't know – like cats kill mice. They just can't help it.'

'Vetru's different.'

'Is he?'

'Yes! Come and see him, if you don't believe me!'

She stiffened. 'No, thanks.'

'You're scared,' he said, his voice hardening. 'You're scared!'

'Who's scared?' Mirias said, returning to the table.

'I'm just challenging Dawn to an archery competition,' Rufryd said, not taking his eyes off her as he rose to leave.

'Great, can I take bets?' Mirias said, but they ignored him.

'You can't possibly win,' Dawn hissed at Rufryd. They glared at each other for a second or two, then he walked away.

In bed with Branq'elin, after they had made love, Rufryd said uneasily, 'Bran, there's something I need to talk to you about.'

'What is it?' she said drowsily, her head on his chest and her arm resting across his waist. 'Shake me if I fall asleep. I'm so tired.'

'Sorry, love, but it's important.'

She stirred, and propped herself up on a pillow. 'I'm awake. Go on.'

He took a breath, steeling himself. 'I left something out of my story. When I fled from the Order, someone came with me. A friend.'

She frowned, looking wide awake. 'A woman? Is that why you're being so evasive?'

'No, no, nothing like that. Someone who's looked after me and guided me for quite some time. I couldn't just leave him.'

'Well, where is he?'

'In the stables, looking after my horse.'

Her eyes were fierce. 'You left your friend in the stables? Why on Earth didn't you bring him into the house? What were you thinking?'

'Well, I wasn't sure he'd be welcome.'

'Gods, Rufe, you know we don't stand on ceremony here. I don't understand. Unless he's got the Grey Plague, I don't see why you thought . . .'

'So he'd be welcome here? He'd be as well-treated and safe as anyone else here?'

'Of course.'

'Promise?'

'I promise. What do you need me to promise for? Your guest is mine. Is he sleeping in the stables now?' Rufryd nodded, watching her closely. 'Go and bring him in, then. We'll soon find him a bed. Gods, I wish you'd told me earlier.'

He gave a fatalistic grin; now she was angry at him for being inhospitable.

'You must ask him in yourself,' he said.

'Why?'

'I want you to see him first. I don't want you to accuse me of deceiving you. But remember, you promised to treat him as you'd treat any other member of your household.'

Bran stared at him for a moment, then got up and slipped a robe over her head. He drank in a last glimpse of her body as the material fell. 'You're behaving very strangely,' she said. 'I like the way you wait until *after* we've had sex to tell me this.'

He grimaced. 'Yes, well, I'm not a complete idiot.'

The stable yard behind the house was in darkness, with only a few pools of light from lamps along the walls to guide their way. Rufryd took a lamp from the kitchen, and held it aloft for Bran to see her way.

As they reached the stable door she suddenly gasped. 'Oh.'

'What is it?'

'I don't know. I was dizzy for a moment.'

'It's all right,' Rufryd said firmly. He didn't notice Vetru's aura any more, and it had never been strong, but she had obviously sensed it. He raised the lantern high as he opened the stable door. He wanted Branq'elin to see Vetru clearly.

'Are you awake?' he called softly. 'It's only me. I brought someone to see you.'

The mare came snuffing at him but he gently pushed her away. Vetru was standing up, his back pressed to the side wall, his eyes gleaming warily. He looked almost human; like a smaller, shabbier, badly-fashioned version of Rufryd. But the unfinished transformation was clear in the dark scaly patterning across his cheeks, the mottled beige skin, the long, seven-fingered hands.

Branq'elin let out a sharp cry of pure, visceral horror. 'What is it?' she gasped.

'It's all right,' he said again, holding her tight with one arm round her shoulders. 'It's Vetru. The hatchling who guided me across Vexor.'

She moaned. He recognised the flash of irrational terror that he'd felt many times himself. But her fear flashed into rage and he felt her trembling, almost throbbing against him. 'You brought a Devourer to my house,' she breathed.

'It's just Vetru,' Rufryd said lightly. 'He's not even six years old.'

'But he looks like you! Q'enartre's breath, Rufryd! Why does he look like you?'

'He doesn't really. They can change shape, right? He made a pretty bad attempt at it and I told him to stop it. Imitation is the sincerest form of flattery, apparently.'

She was still shaking. He held onto her. His fear was for Vetru's safety, not hers. 'You promised,' he said again. 'You said he'd be treated like any other guest.'

'You didn't tell me he was . . .'

'That's why I brought you to see him. So you could say no, if you wanted. Bran, I understand how you feel but he's my friend. They're not all evil.'

She took a shuddering breath, said nothing. Rufryd said, 'Vetru, this is Lady Branq'elin. Say hello to her.'

Vetru said in a very quiet voice, 'Good evening, my lady.'

Branq'elin put her hand to her mouth. 'How can I possibly let him stay?'

'You promised. If he goes, I go.'

'Don't threaten me! You would put *him* above Annuin?'

The thought took him aback. 'No, no of course I wouldn't,' he said more gently. 'But you're asking me to abandon a friend, as if they're all the same as Vaurgroth. Don't threaten me into making a choice, either. He's done no harm. He's just a child, really.'

'So was Noli.' Her trembling lessened. 'You can let go of me. I'm not going to do anything.'

'He's not Noli,' Rufryd said. 'He's my friend. If anyone tried to hurt him, I'd defend him just as I'd defend Dawn, or Con . . . or you.' He let his hands fall. She didn't move.

'Rufryd,' she said evenly, 'I am not going to hurt him. Believe me, I never wish to lose control again as I did that night. Nor does anyone else here. Such brutality is for them, not for us. But how can you be certain of him?'

'I just am.'

'I am loyal,' Vetru put in. 'I left my *tzcement* for Rufryd and I follow him now.'

'Why?' Bran took a step towards the *domen*.

Vetru looked wary. 'Tsur tells me –' he corrected himself – 'told me to do so, and I obey. Rufryd is kind to me, like Tsur.'

'He's harmless, Bran,' Rufryd said. 'He's a bit annoying sometimes, but harmless. I can't abandon him. How would you feel if you were alone in Vexor, and no-one showed you any kindness? He saved my life, damn it.'

'No-one's going to be cruel to him,' she said. 'But still, I can't announce to my household that I'm allowing a Bhahdradomen to stay here, can I? He can stay in the stable, as long as he keeps out of sight.'

She was cold but unruffled. Rufryd breathed an inward sigh of relief. Dawn's dire warnings had been unfounded. 'Can't he at least have a decent room inside?'

'The stable is warm. The straw is soft,' Vetru said in a conciliatory tone.

Bran turned and stared at Rufryd, every inch the ice-flame he remembered. 'It's against my better judgement I let him stay at all. You've put me in an appalling position! How do you know he isn't a spy?'

'He isn't!'

'So you think. But can you say that you are absolutely, utterly *certain*? You can't, can you?'

With that, Branq'elin turned and strode away. Rufryd and Vetru looked at each other. Finally Rufryd said, 'Well, I think that went quite well, don't you?'

Branq'elin was sharp with him for several days, but she didn't ban him from her chambers or her bed, nor change her mind about the marriage. Rufryd realised that, despite her harsh demeanour, she loved him. And, more than that, trusted him.

'I'm not happy with what you've done,' she said. 'I wouldn't allow it from anyone but you. However, if you insist that Vetru is trustworthy, I can only take your word for it. But I warn you; he is your responsibility. If anything goes wrong, I shall hold you entirely to blame.'

'Fine,' Rufryd said. 'Nothing will go wrong. She likes the horse, doesn't she?'

He managed to deflect Bran's attention to their daughter who was happily urging her battered wooden mount around the chamber on its uneven wheels.

'It was Mawrdreth's,' said Bran, more gently. 'He adored it. That's why it's so worn out.'

'One thing I can't imagine is your brother as a small child.' She smiled, not looking at him. Rufryd added, 'Do you miss him?'

'Gods, I'd give anything for him to be here, or at least to know what's happened to him. I've sent messengers to Paranios but nothing comes back, except terrible news of the Devourers. I can only think the worst.'

'Don't,' Rufryd said, squeezing her hand. 'He's strong. I'd find him for you if I could.'

He looked at his daughter and thought, I've done one good thing in my life after all. Will I be any better at helping Bran to rule this realm than Eldareth was at helping Helan? Eld felt so unequal to the task, he bolted. No, not *ruling*, he corrected himself. Protecting it. And how to bring Annuin up so she's strong enough to take over?

The Order of Calathvahn was four weeks behind him. Branq'elin's scouts had reported them advancing from the south, white banners flying and a small legion of *yrim* in tow. They'd had almost four weeks of peace. Time to prepare; to evacuate children and mothers, the old and ill to farms up in the northern hills. To gather more Thand'rathian warriors and set them ready to defend the town.

Tension abraded the household. Dawn, Con and Mirias prepared to fight, their usual good cheer pared down to the occasional black joke. The Order were close, approaching the pleated skirt of meadows south of the town. The engagement would take place within a day or two. It was Branq'elin's intention that they would never even reach Tasqabad.

For it was a battle they were anticipating; not a secret infiltration of the house at night. Not a handful of invaders, threading their way mouse-quiet through the winding streets and orchards, evading patrols, creeping up through the kitchen gardens, penetrating a door from the stableyard, slitting the throats of household guards as they crept towards the heart of the house.

Rufryd woke abruptly, disturbed by an odd sound. It was too low-pitched for Annuin, who was in her cot in the nurse's room. More like muffled cries from outside their chambers. Then there was a fan of light, and Branq'elin exclaiming, 'Rufryd? Gods, what is that? *Vetru?*'

Rufryd sat up in bed, turning up the oil lamp. In its light he saw a figure in the doorway that he could have been his small, shadowy brother. Vetru swam into the room, his face lit eerily from beneath by lamplight.

'Rufryd, they're here,' he said, scared beyond clear speech. 'I followed them – couldn't stop them. They're here!'

'Get him out,' Bran said, leaping up and seizing her sword. Vetru fled.

Rufryd sprang out of bed and grabbed his Shaelahyr sword. Through the wide doorway he saw into the main chamber, which always had lamps burning. He realised there were figures moving around in there, their actions taut, quick, aggressive.

He recognised their voices.

Bran was running out ahead of him, all fearless rage, before he could stop her. They were both naked but there was no time to find clothes. He followed her into the chamber and saw them.

Herex. Three others from Calathvahn. And four *yrim* dressed in dark layers of blood-brown, their ghastly *roth*-whips seething like snakes in their hands. The door to the passage stood wide and he saw the bodies of their two guards outside.

Everything happened very slowly after that, as if some cruel god stretched out time to make him appreciate every split second. Herex looked up and met Rufryd's eyes. His pale gaze was manic with loathing. Then, in a calculated action, he attacked Bran, snapping his *tzirin* to wrap her wrist so she cried out and dropped her sword.

Rufryd launched himself between her and Herex. He felt the sting of the alien weapon, ignored it, and plunged his sword into Herex's abdomen.

In the same moment, he heard Bran cry out. It was the worst cry he'd ever heard. She bumped into him in her haste to get past him. And he saw clear through the door into the nurse's room where the cot stood. Saw the nurse already dead on the floor, grey plait uncoiled, her fists outstretched. Saw Annuin standing up silently in the cot, the dark figure of an *yrim* and the pale one of a brother reaching out for her. The few yards that lay between them might as well have been ten miles.

Bran was barely at the door, Rufryd still wrenching the sword from Herex's guts as he saw the Bhahdradomen lift his daughter in the air. The *yrim* held her, but it was the brother who wielded the knife. Casually, he slit her throat and threw her down onto the floor. She didn't make a sound. She was a crumpled doll.

With a hoarse scream, Rufryd flung himself across the chamber, through the door, past Bran, and severed the brother's throat to the spine. A heartbeat behind him, Bran was dispatching the *yrim*.

Panting, he turned, saw more of them thronging into the room.

Bran fell to her knees, shouting wordlessly as if in physical anguish. She plucked the little body from the floor and held her to her breast, but Rufryd already knew Annuin was dead. Her blood was everywhere, soaking Bran with gore, trailing the floor with red fingers.

Rufryd lifted his sword and went mad.

He barely remembered any of it afterwards; only the roar of blood in his ears, and the edge of the sword biting again and again into one enemy after another. Blood of humans, plasma of *domenim*, bodies falling everywhere. Feeling that he fought inside an impenetrable shield through which no weapon could touch him; not caring if one did.

He became aware of Dawn and Mirias in the doorway, horrified. He heard the dull uproar of the household as the alarm spread.

The intruders were dead. Rufryd's world was a dull gold roar in which nothing mattered but Annuin. People spoke to him but he couldn't hear them. He went back into the bedroom and began to dress for battle, seeing through two doorways the figure of Bran bending to place their child in her cot as if settling her for sleep.

He expected her to remain there but she came after him, moving like a wax puppet, green eyes mad. Without a word they dressed and armed urgently. They ran yelling like demons through the house and out into the paling night, rousing everyone to battle.

White rage drove them, catching the army in their wake and leading a charge like a torrent of bronze and viridian flame upon the Order of Calathvahn. Arax Vahan's little legion were taken wholly by surprise in the dawn. Overconfident, they'd thought nothing could stand against them. They'd thought the Will of the Ancestor and the strength of a thousand *yrim* would be enough; they hadn't been prepared for the weight of numbers, the ferocity, the sheer passion of the Thand'rathians.

They'd thought themselves invincible. Now their white banners fell and their white tabards turned red.

Rufryd's battle was a blur of noise, sweat, torn grass. Still he fought inside an impenetrable armour of cold fire. If a weapon felled him he wouldn't feel it, would care even less. All he wanted at this moment was death.

He found himself suddenly face to face with Arax Vahan. The Father had been unhorsed and was on foot, *sten* in hand like a sword. His face upon Rufryd was a blaze of contempt, pity, shock.

'My child.' The words rumbled with malice.

Rufryd's eyes narrowed. He was panting. 'Do you know what you did?'

'Of course. I sent them to prove to you the futility of life. Ancestor punishes those who turn aside from the light. His wrath is terrible.'

Rufryd bared his teeth. He saw Arax Vahan as if through a crystal veil. Everything was unnaturally sharp. His Order was falling around him yet he stood there as if nothing was wrong, a smiling figure of granite and unshakeable faith.

'You want to see wrath?' said Rufryd.

He swung his Aelyr sword two-handed. Arax Vahan tried to defend himself. He seemed astonished that Rufryd had dared to attack him. But Rufryd ignored the *sten* as if it were an insect sting and carried the stroke through, severing the Father's head. Blood flew.

The *sten* caught him flat across his side, cracked with lightning. The shock flung him to the ground. When he rose, half-stunned with pain, he saw the Father's head staring at him, still with that beatific, manic smile shining from the eyes. For a moment, he expected it to speak.

It was over. The survivors were fleeing, brothers and *yrim* mingling in disarray. The ravaged meadow lay stupefied.

Branq'elin stood like a statue, leaning on her sword as if it was all that held her up. Her exhausted warriors came dishevelled and bloodstained to group around her. With them were Mirias, Dawn and Con; they couldn't look at Rufryd, nor he at them.

After a long time, she spoke. 'So much for the Order of Calathvahn,' she said bitterly. 'My daughter is still dead.'

When they returned to the Hall, staff had taken all the bodies from the ducal chambers and done their best to clean up the blood. Only the body of the child remained, covered up in her cot. Bran and Rufryd stood and stared at her sleeping face. Neither spoke. At last Bran called servants to take the cot away to a chamber of state below.

As the door closed she turned towards him, her face yellow as wax.

'My daughter, too,' said Rufryd.

Her mouth opened, but no sound came out. Rufryd found he couldn't speak either. He couldn't cry, dreaded the feeling of starting and being unable to stop. Then for the first time Branq'elin looked at him, and her face was as rigid as his felt.

'You should have gone to her aid, not mine!' she hissed. 'If you had not wasted time slaying that man who attacked me!'

'And see *you* die?' he cried. 'What thankless bloody choice was it?'

'Better I died than her!'

'Blame me if you want! Go on!' Ice crawled over him. 'It *was* my fault. I drew Arax Vahan here. He must have found out I was with you and we had a child. He planned to assassinate us all.'

'I wish he had,' she breathed. She put her hands to her face. 'No, no, it's mine. Why didn't I send her with her nurse to the hills, with the other children? I was too selfish, I wanted her with me!'

'You were trying to protect her. She was safe until I came.'

She lashed a glare at him, then looked down. 'I don't blame you. Only those Goddess-forsaken, accursed bastards who slew her! Q'enartre curse them, Anketh blast them to cinders.'

'How did it get so easy to kill them?' Rufryd said. 'I remember the first time I killed someone; I thought the world was going to end. Now I don't feel anything at all.'

They went into her room but didn't touch each other, only sat in silence. Finally, to his relief, Branq'elin began to weep. He still daren't let himself go. He moved beside her and held her while she cried on his knees.

Was this harder to bear than Lynden's death? He'd only known the child such a short time, but still it was enough for that fine, exquisite bond to form and its severance to be as agonising. Pointless to compare one mass of unendurable pain to another. The gleaming strand of the future was cut.

Above Tasqabad, rags of purple cloud fled by, writhing and tearing. Birds raced as if hurled by the wind. Flying leaves filled the air, and the ground trembled as if in dread, or the beginning of its own death throes. Rufryd rode away through the gale, staring ahead with dead eyes, Vetru hunched beside him.

'It's not the end,' Con had said after the battle, with the voice of prophecy. '*Ghelim* will come. It was in the wolf-mage's vision.' Rufryd knew Tasqabad was still in danger, but he couldn't stay.

Branq'elin was again a stranger to him. All that had been between them was ash. They couldn't look at each other without being reminded, seeing that dreadful scene played out again and again.

'There is one who has not yet been punished for this,' Branq'elin had said. 'Vetru.' She'd said it days later, rising from the silence of grief like a raging dragon from a nest of ash.

'What?' said Rufryd in disbelief. 'What's he done?'

'He betrayed us. He must have let them into the house.'

'No!' Rufryd cried, alight with pain.

'How did he come into our chamber before them?'

'He slipped past them just as they were coming in. I've spoken to him! He knew nothing of it! They got in by stealth and killed every guard they met. He saw them breaking in from the stable yard. He was as scared as we were. Don't you realise how brave he was to follow them? He tried to warn us!'

'I want to believe you but I shall never, ever be certain he didn't betray us. Even if he's innocent, I can't bear him being here.'

'It was a human who killed Annuin.'

'While a Bhahdradomen held her.'

'Yes . . . but not Vetru.'

'All the same, you will respect my feelings on this matter. He must go. I can't understand your loyalty to such a creature!' He willed her to relent but her eyes were green acid. Suddenly he knew Dawn had spoken the truth with her warning.

'You're asking me to go, then.'

She looked at him for a few seconds, her eyes flickering with hesitation, pain. Her voice was stone. 'It might be for the best. Things can never again be as they were.'

'No,' he said. The mass of pain within him settled into a denser, colder shape under its own weight. 'Right. If you're determined to think the worst of him – of me – I'd better take him away from here.'

He couldn't accept her accusing Vetru. But he hadn't the will to argue because his feelings, too, were dead. Vetru was just a lever that enabled them to part.

'Where will you go?' she said later. A dry truce fell between them. She touched his arm. Their eyes met but the green light in hers was bleached, the remaining spirit as hard as iron, all tenderness stripped away.

'For the love there's been between us,' he said dully, 'I will try to find your brother Mawrdreth and send him home.'

Dawn and Mirias and Con said goodbye to him with tender kisses and tears, but he had no warm feelings to give in return. He turned aside their grief, their offers to travel with him. The only company he wanted was Vetru's. With the bruise-purple storm rolling around him and inside him, Rufryd rode away from Tasqabad.

Chapter Fifteen. Lord Sunstone

Tanthe never knew how she survived the next few days.

At the warning of *ghelim* they quit the carriage and fled to seek cover beneath a wind-sculpted poppy-red wave of rock. She felt faint and breathless as they ran. Her wound dragged her down with wires of pain. Keep going, she told herself. As long as I keep moving and don't pass out, I'll be all right. Lahjaya and Auriel were at her side, Helan and Mawrdreth in front, Eldareth behind. A handful of Karmensis's soldiers went with them, while the carriage and outriders continued as a decoy.

'My patient would have been safer to stay inside,' panted Lahjaya. 'We all would.'

'To start with,' Karmensis said briskly. 'Then it would have become a sitting target, a trap for the *ghelim* to hold us to siege. Best we scatter while we still can.'

'I implore Nuth to keep your comrades safe,' Helan whispered. 'I didn't want them to do this for me.'

Karmensis looked steadily at her. 'You must understand that we would all give our lives to preserve yours. You can't deny us that.'

'Since the reverse is also true, I cannot,' Helan said quietly.

From their hiding place they saw *ghelim* harrying the riders. A man and two *ghelim* fell. Then the rest of the shape-shifters arced away and vanished. The carriage rolled on, out of their sight.

Darkness draped the plain. The sky was midnight blue and burningly clear, gemmed with stars. No sign of *ghelim*. They began to walk.

'The track ends soon, in any case,' said Karmensis. 'We'll

go on in the dark and rest in the heat of the day. My riders will have to find fresh horses, or continue on foot. Sooner we hit the Vermeil Canyon, the better.'

The landscape through which they moved was haunting. Undulating masses of scarlet stone under their feet, sculpted pillars banded with rust-red and ruby lining their way. Glittering dust formed shapes that appeared sentient, and seemed to watch them before dissipating on the hot breeze. Elementals, Tanthe thought. The heat was growing harsher by the day, but the nights were chill.

The Ruby Plains were far from barren. Jewel-like flowers and plants whose leaves were fat with water clung in the most unpromising crevices. Most days they found a spring or waterhole to sustain them through the dry, thirsty days. Sometimes they shared the water with long-legged red birds, striped rodents, huge turquoise lizards.

The desert was beautiful. Tanthe tried not to hate it.

Thanks to her injury, the journey was fraught with excruciating fatigue, her rest stalked by nightmares of the *ezht*. It was as if the *uzrat* shot had bored a shaft of darkness through her and she was doomed to fall into it every time she slept. Images tormented her of her Aelyr parents trapped and lost, their identities slowly fragmenting. She wondered, If I threw myself on Falthorn's mercy and told him where they are, could he help them?

Only Lahjaya's friendship kept her going. That, and stern determination not to let her friends down.

Larger oases sometimes had villages around them, where dwellings had been made inside the fluted rock itself. The villagers welcomed them, as friendly as Lahjaya. They would send them on their way laden with supplies, and directions to the next water source.

One morning, some days into the journey, as the sun rose to chase away cold shadow, they rested in the shade of a curving crimson wall. The others were talking and eating but Tanthe, too exhausted to join in, sat apart with her head resting back against the rock. They'd walked all night. Her shoulder throbbed.

'How are you bearing up?' asked someone above her. It was Helan. She sat down next to Tanthe and passed her a flask of water.

'All right, thanks.' Tanthe's mouth was sticky. She drank deeply from the flask and passed it back.

Helan looked dusty, tired and travel-worn, the antithesis of a queen. Yet somehow more magnificent for it; a creature of the earth, her unbound hair a lion's mane, her face shiny with sweat. She sat with her feet apart, arms resting loosely on her raised knees. 'I've suffered all the lectures about eating and drinking to keep my strength up. Now it's my turn to lecture you.'

'Yes, ma'am.' Tanthe tried to smile. 'If you don't mind me pointing it out, you seem a lot happier . . . considering where we are.'

'Ridiculous, isn't it? Being happy where I'm supposed to be miserable.' She looked sideways at Tanthe, confiding. 'But this is paradise to me, no longer being trapped by enemies or by tradition. Being free to act. I feel like myself again. And you are changing the subject. Come on, this salty meat is delicious. All right, it's disgusting, but at least have an oatcake and some dried fruit.'

'Thanks,' Tanthe said, accepting the offering. 'I'll eat them in a bit. This soreness in my shoulder kind of turns my stomach.'

'You took a bad wound. We thought we were going to lose you.' Helan was really concerned, Tanthe realised, warming towards her. Only one thing stopped her loving her wholeheartedly, and that was her treatment of Ysomir.

'It's a good job it was me who got shot, and not Lahjaya. I couldn't have healed her like this. How much further have we to travel? It's months since I studied a map and I've no idea where we are.'

'Well, it's quite some way to Lapiszul,' Helan said. 'I

made this journey once with Eld, eight or nine years ago now. But we travelled the great Lapis Road, with good horses to ride and pleasant hostelries all the way.'

'I don't mean to complain, but I don't think I can stand much more of this desert.'

'You won't have to. The Vermeil Canyon cuts across our path to the south. The river angles down a little towards Lapiszul. Karmensis has sent some of the riders ahead to procure a boat for us so we can sail part of the way. Perilous, but our best bet.'

'Drifting along in a boat sounds blissful.' Tanthe tried to smile.

When she curled up to sleep she dreamed of Ysomir, Saphaeyender and Rufryd. They were all frozen pillars in the *ezht*, which had become as red as the Ruby Plains . . . She was woken suddenly, in the cold indigo of dusk, by Auriel shaking her.

'Fliyet? You were having a nightmare.'

'Oh.' She pulled herself upright. 'That's nothing new.'

Auriel frowned. He sat cross-legged, one hand caught in his long autumn hair, looking so other-worldly that she wouldn't have been surprised if he'd disappeared. 'What about?'

'The *ezht*, if you must know.'

The word made him blanch. 'Has it happened often?'

'Every night,' she said.

'Oh, no . . . Is that why you've been so quiet? I'm worried about you, Tanthe. I don't know what to do.'

'I know,' she said, taking his hand. 'That's why I didn't tell you. They're just bad dreams. Only I feel like I've got this black weight on my head, because I know our parents are there and I can't do anything to help them.' His fingers gripped hers so hard she winced with pain. 'Ow, Auriel!'

'Sorry,' he whispered. 'I can't bear to think it's true.'

'You never saw them when you . . . went there?'

A quick shake of his head. 'I can't bear to talk about this.'

'Neither can I, but we both need to face it. Our parents and our child, lost. Both of us nervous wrecks, thanks to Falthorn and Vaurgroth. Ymmi and Saph and Rufryd, Goddess knows where. All I've got is you.'

'And I'm no use.'

'I didn't say that.'

He was quiet, looking across the desert. 'You had another lover. Will you go back to him, if you can?'

'You mean Saphaeyender? I don't know. He asked me to marry him and I panicked and ran away.'

'Why?'

She sighed. 'Because he's a legend and I'm just me. I'm not up to creating the grand, mythical partnership he ought to have.'

Auriel looked at her in such amazement she almost laughed. 'Is *he*?'

'I never thought of it that way. He kept telling me he's only human, but I wouldn't believe him. Truth is, if I'd married him he wouldn't change; he'd just keep on seducing every pretty person who crossed his path, and I couldn't have stood it. I know the Goddess meant us to love freely, but there is a limit. Gods, Auriel, he'd love you. Remind me to keep you out of his way.'

She smiled but he looked away, his face like stone. 'He doesn't deserve you. You have an Aelyr spirit.'

She touched his arm. 'Would you be jealous?'

He was quiet. Then he said, 'I know you had a life before you found me. Your life is not mine. I don't think mine has even begun yet. I don't know where it will lead.'

'I'll always love you,' she said softly. 'It's impossible not to. I'm trying hard just to be your sister but I'll never forget how sweet it was between us . . .'

'Nor will I. But I'm not strong enough to be anyone's lover, Fliyet. Not with Falthorn's shadow over me.'

They sat in silence, looking out at the night, their arms only a hair's width apart so they could feel each other's warmth. She felt close to him, protective. Yet in spirit Auriel seemed so distant he was hardly there at all.

Her sudden longing for Rufryd was so intense it took her breath away. For all their arguments, he'd never been other than vigorously *present*. And because she'd known him all her life she'd never expected him to be perfect, then been disappointed. And he was no less beautiful than Auriel, in a darker, earthier way. His absence was a hole inside her like the *ezht*, and day by day she was falling through its unutterable loneliness.

The canyon split the red plain in half, a great rift that ran from one horizon to the other. The thunder of water stroked the air. Tanthe put a dusty hand to her forehead and squinted against the sunlight. There had been no water for a day or two and they'd had to ration their supplies. Just the thought of a river made her thirsty.

They reached the edge of the canyon as dusk fell. The scarlet rim was rugged and patched with succulents. Warm wet air rolled up to meet them, sifting up through lush ferns and foliage; further down, the vegetation became so dense that they couldn't see the river. The way down looked steep and perilous. The roar of the water made Tanthe's heart leap with apprehension.

Five riders came to meet them along a path just below the canyon edge, saluting Karmensis, bowing to Helan and Mawrdreth. There was good news; no further *ghelim* attacks. A couple of the riders dismounted, leaving their horses with their comrades, and began to lead Helan's party on foot along a path. It was a single-file track that ran parallel with the top of the canyon for a stretch before angling down towards the riverbank.

'Hurry,' said Karmensis. 'My scouts tell me there have been storms to the north-west, and the river's rising. They've found us a boat, but we must reach it and cast off as soon as possible.'

The way was steep and treacherous with ground-plants

creeping across their path. Lahjaya slipped, and would have tumbled into a chasm of greenery if Eldareth hadn't caught her.

'Thanks,' said Lahjaya, gasping for breath. 'This bloody country goes from one extreme to the other.'

'This is your country!' Tanthe exclaimed.

'So I'm allowed to curse it blind!' Lahjaya retorted.

Eldareth and Mawrdreth strode ahead to catch up with Karmensis. Steadily the canyon walls loomed higher. Through a break in the vegetation Tanthe saw the rushing black edge of the river. The far side was in shadow, hardly visible. The canyon felt deep, damp, echoey, full of rank scents and the cries of strange birds.

The first thing she noticed was that the bird-calls stopped. She looked up and saw purple-grey clouds clotting above the canyon, pressing on the air, sparking with electricity. The whole scene had an air of sombre malice. Then she felt a spot of heat against her hip-bone, knew what it was, tried to deny it.

'Auriel,' she said quickly, turning to him a few feet behind her. 'Your *mnelir*, is it getting hot?'

He hesitated, felt the little knife on his belt then drew it from its scabbard. It shone, the crystal sphere on its pommel glowing white. She drew her own and it was the same. Its heat burned her hand.

'Helan,' Tanthe called out, almost losing her voice. 'Helan, there may be Eaters nearby!'

The Queen, in front of Lahjaya, turned. She looked up, her face luminous in the gloom. Clouds massed above the red edge of the canyon with lightning flickering between them. The lightning grew more intense. The clouds swelled and broke, and out of the smoky tatters burst a score of shrieking *ghelim*.

'Eldareth!' Helan yelled, drawing her sword. 'Mawrdreth, Karmensis!'

On the path below, the men's faces turned towards them, small and pale. Tanthe flung herself flat against the side of the canyon as the first of the *ghelim* swooped over her. In the flare of lightning she glimpsed gnarled claws, tiny eyes behind long rows of teeth. The light slid blue-white over membranous wings. Their flapping blasted the stench of rotting meat over her. Her guts cramped with terror; her wound felt like a spear stuck through her.

'Only their aura disrupting yours,' Lahjaya gasped, telling herself as much as Tanthe. 'Remember. That's all it is.'

Arrows flew up from the men and women scattered along the path. The *ghelim* were untouched. With a chattering cry that sounded like laughter they swooped. Two soldiers fell to their claws and lashing tails.

All along the path a perilous fight began. The shape-shifters swooped easily out of the reach of swords and arrows. Tanthe held the *mnelir* in one hand, with the other drew the hated *tzirin*.

The edge of the canyon behind them was a thick, jagged crust of rock rearing against the sky. In the blaze of lightning, Tanthe saw a *ghelim* diving at Helan. The Queen swung her sword, half-severed its head. Tanthe let out a cry of relief.

Another was coming in its place. Wheeling on a wing-claw to sail straight at Tanthe. She lashed out with the *roth*-whip, caught it in mid-flight and brought it down. It crashed among the vegetation, jerking the whip out of her hand; she had to let go, or be dragged down after it.

Auriel was slashing out with his *mnelir*, carving a barrier of Aelyr light. The *ghelim* swerved to avoid it. Tanthe did the same, but this was only buying time.

'Get back against the side,' she hissed to him and Lahjaya. 'They can't fly at us without crashing into the canyon wall then.'

She was right; *ghelim* swooped within feet of them but couldn't touch them. But the attackers were tireless, relentless. She saw another figure fall further down the path, couldn't see who it was.

Below, she saw three men fighting wildly. Eldareth was hacking at *ghelim* with his sword, Mawrdreth wielding both *tzirin* and *sten*, both of them covering Karmensis as he dragged at a dark bulk. A body? They began to work their way back up the path. Other soldiers ran to defend them. She saw Mawrdreth throw his Bhahdradomen weapons down in disgust and help Karmensis with the burden instead.

They came toiling up the path, then diverted onto a steeper fork that took them above and to the right of Tanthe's group. Suddenly, in the confusing lightning-flares, she realised what they were carrying.

A net.

She saw the mesh of knotted rope as they stretched it out between them, realised Karmensis must have got it from the boat. Tanthe left the path and began to climb diagonally towards them, the *mnelir* hot in her palm. Her boots slipped on succulents and loose rock. 'Auriel, come with me!' she shouted.

As the next flight of *ghelim* reformed and came swooping over the canyon edge, Mawrdreth and Karmensis flung the net. They caught four, brought them down into a floundering mass on the ground. Their claws tore at the mesh, their jaws snapped. With rolling eyes they chattered their wrath, and their wings threatened to break the knotted ropes.

Without pausing, Tanthe lunged forward with the *mnelir* and took the first through an eye socket. It died instantly, as if it had turned to brittle paper. She took the second, Auriel the third; Eldareth severed the neck of the fourth with his sword.

They all stood back, sweating, panting for breath and sickened. The remaining *ghelim* reared back into the sky and circled; brooding, saurian silhouettes.

'Clever,' Helan panted, climbing the slope towards them. 'Whose idea was it?'

'Mine,' Mawrdreth said matter-of-factly. 'Get the bodies out of it and we can use it again.'

'Take too long,' said Eldareth. 'Let's get everyone down to the boat, and away.'

They almost made it. They crossed the path and cut down among the greenery. Eldareth in front, then Tanthe with Auriel and Lahjaya, Helan and Mawrdreth behind, Karmensis bringing up the rear. Vines caught at their clothes and slithered under their feet.

Hearts thumping and breath sawing with exertion, they emerged onto the riverbank. Seven of Karmensis's soldiers were there. Tanthe saw the dark shape of the boat, straining against its moorings as the river surged past. They ran towards it and one by one climbed on board, Helan and Mawrdreth helping them over the side as it swayed and bucked. Lightning danced on the roaring black water.

'Cast off!' Helan said, leaping on board.

Down swooped *ghelim* to harass the boat. Eldareth and Karmensis were struggling to release the knots. Mawrdreth swung his blade and brought one *ghelim* down into the current . . . but there were still scores of them coming. It was harder to fight from the boat, a small simple vessel in which they couldn't stand up without danger of capsizing.

Tanthe and Auriel slashed out with their *mnelir* as the shape-changers cleaved the air. She felt the blast of rank air from their wings, their relentless will. *Maybe they don't mean to kill us, only to wear us down until they can capture us*, she thought – *but who's commanding them?*

Suddenly, as if with Aelyr sight, she saw him on the riverbank.

Not a flying *ghelim* but a *domen* in unchanged form . . . no, not quite unchanged. He was like a ghost, camouflaged to invisibility against his background. Yet, for a few moments, a long break of lightning illuminated the contours of his fugitive shape.

A hideous figure in the storm light. A translucent gel of flesh draped on a hunched frame of bones, the skull-grin of a sadist. A staff in his hand, the fine layered-skin robes of a *bharu'grothrim*. She knew she'd seen him before. He'd been in the Sun Chamber when Vaurgroth took the Sapphire Throne. His name was . . . Gulzhur.

And before that, she'd glimpsed him near Riverwynde, leering as his *ghelim* attacked her friends and family. Grinning as they killed her uncle Ewain. Tanthe saw again her father weeping over his brother's body and she screamed, 'He's the one. Kill him!'

To her amazement, her shout made them all *see* him. Half a dozen arrows flew towards Gulzhur, missed or passed through his spectral flesh without harm. On impulse Tanthe threw her *mnelir*.

She threw well. The blade pierced his ribs. Gulzhur's expression turned from mirth to outrage. He roared, appeared to collapse, vanished. Her knife vanished with him.

Above, the *ghelim* ceased their attack and drifted on the air currents, confused. Then, one by one, they winked out of sight.

'Cast off,' Helan said again, her tone grim. The soldiers grabbed the oars, to no purpose. Then the mooring knots came free and the boat rushed, leaping and rearing, into the current.

'My *mnelir*,' Tanthe exclaimed.

'We're not going back for it,' Eldareth said firmly. 'If you've lost it, I'm sorry, but it was in a good cause.'

As the vessel lurched away she was certain she saw Gulzhur, standing high on the very lip of the canyon, a bruise-green apparition staring down in defeat and smouldering malice. But no, she was too far away to have seen such a thing. Overwrought imagination.

Then the force of the river took her breath away, and all her strength went into hanging on as the boat was borne along on a fierce current. Lightning receded. The Vermeil River sucked them down between its echoing walls, along its winding, mist-filled chasm of darkness.

* * *

'Where are we going?' said Jthery, picking his way along the narrow track.

'Wait and see,' said Falthorn. He was in a buoyant mood. In the star-brushed darkness he'd brought Jthery miles from the house. They were walking down a crease between two hills, following a path as faint as a deer-track. Here and there, stones nestled like azure toads in the grass.

The path took them alongside a stream. Presently stream and path ended in a magical glade, cupped by a wall of rock down which a waterfall surged. On either side the rock shone with moisture and the jewelled fronds of ferns.

'This is lovely,' said Jthery. 'Why didn't you show me this before?'

'Now, that's not the first time I've heard you say that.' Grinning, Falthorn stepped out of his robe and went to stand under the edge of the fall.

The water cascading down the rock was a sheet of jade. Light seemed to emanate from the rock itself to glow through it, translucent, glossy, alive with delicate luminosity. Falthorn was a shining icon beneath it. Throwing off his own robe, Jthery joined him.

The night was warm but the coldness made him gasp. His hair was immediately soaked. He pressed himself against Falthorn's wet chest and kissed him.

'Stop it,' Falthorn smiled. His hands slid over Jthery's back under the liquid jade.

'Why?'

'You're too distracting, Jey. We're here to work.'

He rolled his eyes. 'I might have known. Can't we work later?' He tried again, laughing as Falthorn made half-hearted attempts to fight him off.

'Starfire, you are beautiful,' Falthorn sighed, then he wrestled free and held his wrists. 'But we've things to learn tonight.'

Leaning over the pool's lip, he fumbled in his robe and brought out a sphere. It was dark blue but transparent, with stars trapped inside. 'This is the *anametris* sphere for this portal. The key. Some adepts can open portals without keys, and some portals can be opened without keys, and some may be opened by any key . . . but not this one.'

'Er . . .' Jthery pushed his wet hair back. 'What portal?'

Falthorn pointed to a place in the waterfall where it divided over a jutting rock. The two sides of the veil framed an arch of lapis shadow. 'Try it,' he said.

Jthery hesitated. Then he waded through the basin, under the fall, and warily pressed his hand to the rock behind it. It was deliciously dewy and mossy under his fingertips. 'Solid,' he said.

'Come away. Now watch.' Falthorn waded to his side, holding the blue sphere aloft. 'Move the *anametris*. Feel it pulling towards the *anaroth*, the energy . . . turn it, move it, until the sphere-shells inside start to rotate.'

'How can you tell what you're doing?'

'You get a feel for it.' Falthorn twisted his hand, concentrating. 'You'll feel the spheres go heavy and slide, like the tumblers in a lock . . . there. Now try. Don't go too far.'

Jthery felt static furring his face. The shadow had turned darker. It was black nothingness, rimmed by a cobalt glow. Splashing forward again he reached out and felt space under his hands. Cold air sighed through. A dark path tunnelled away before him. His foot suddenly went through into what felt like thin air and he scrabbled backwards, lost his footing and went under water.

Falthorn dragged him upright with one hand, laughing. Jthery spluttered.

'And to close it, do the same again . . . a slightly different sensation of weight . . .'

The tunnel was solid rock again. 'Does that . . . does that portal go through to Earth?' he asked, awed. He'd stepped through a portal only once before, to reach Verdanholm, and the idea amazed him.

'Ah . . . well yes, but I wouldn't recommend it. You'd

end up in the middle of a river. Not that that would worry you, my amethyst fish.' Falthorn grinned. 'Try it.'

Jthery took the sphere from him. Its weight was cold and sensuous in his palm. He waved it around, feeling nothing except slightly foolish. Falthorn sighed. 'Jey, feel for the *anaroth*. I know it's not the same as water-*roth* but you still have a sensitivity to it.'

He tried again. Closed his eyes, concentrated. He felt the surge of energies in the water itself, tried to tune those out and be aware only of the portal's subtler radiance. The sphere pulled in his hand. He nearly dropped it.

'Careful,' said Falthorn, steadying him. 'You have to resist it.'

Like pulling two magnets apart, Jthery thought. It took him long minutes of experimentation but at last he felt it. Something inside the sphere sliding into place. The frost-melt of the portal opening, like a sigh in the centre of his mind.

His eyes, then his mouth, came open. 'I did it.' The black misty tunnel yawned between the jade veils.

'Yes,' said Falthorn, taking the sphere from him. 'Now can you sense the *roth* of the water, both in this realm and Earth?'

There was something urgent, business-like in his tone. Jthery's lips thinned, but he immersed himself and closed his eyes. Threads of pale-green energy here ... strands of stars threaded on gossamer in the dark river on the other side ... 'Yes, easily.'

'I suppose it would not be so easy to direct a little of our energy through to Earth?'

He tried. *Roth* tangled like fishing line around his fingers. He tried it the other way, pulling instead of pushing. As he drew on the jade lines, he felt the star-strands rushing towards him as if joined to them. He almost panicked, trying to stem the flow. For a moment he was lost in a surge of glittering water and the arch was not a portal but a black tower above him . . . Flailing, he regained control. Eshte's tears, he thought, letting go of his breath. I could cause a torrent if I'm not careful.

Straightening up, he said, 'It's easier to pull the energy through this way.'

'I see,' Falthorn said neutrally. 'How easy?'

Jthery shrugged. 'Very.'

'*Very*?' His lovely dark eyebrows rose. 'Now you're just showing off. I can't do it. I only ever met one other person who could do it. And I have tried.'

'Why?'

'Healing.' Falthorn snapped the portal shut. 'The healing of realms.'

'Dangerous, though.'

'Not if we're careful.' Falthorn waded to the edge and gave Jthery a hand onto the bank. They sat side by side on the grass, letting the warm air dry them.

'Falthorn, believe me, it could be dangerous. I nearly let a torrent of *roth* through without even trying.'

Falthorn gave a satisfied, cat-like smile. He put his hand on Jthery's chest and pressed him back onto the grass. 'That's good. It's nothing to fear,' he breathed, rising over him. 'Work is over for tonight; you may continue distracting me . . .'

As they made love, Jthery had the vision again. Water surging around a thin dark tower. Two Aelyr figures hurrying towards it under twilight veils. That burning sense of urgency, the awful revelation about to break . . . He cried out, white light roaring through him.

'Jey?' Falthorn's voice brought him out of the trance; he was pinning him down with outstretched hands and feet, like two bright starfish welded together. Radiant face almost touching his. 'Are you seeing visions?'

He hesitated, disoriented and breathless. 'What . . . what made you ask that?'

'The way you cried out.'

'I should've thought the reason for that was obvious.'

Falthorn's grey eyes were huge, brooding, too perceptive. 'Mm. Well, that sounded like fear as much as pleasure. Your eyes were wide open but you weren't seeing me. I've been watching you.'

Jthery was unsettled. 'You are weird. You're supposed to be joining in, not taking notes.'

'It's quite usual for the Aelyr to give and receive visions, you know. Tell me what you saw.'

'I keep seeing a tower in the sea, like a lighthouse. And two Aelyr going towards it. It's meaningless but it has this awful, brooding aura over it that I can't even describe. Yet I keep feeling it has something to do with . . . Tanthe.'

'What colour is this tower?'

'Sort of grey, charcoal. Misty. What does it mean?'

Falthorn looked at him for a long time, pensive. Jthery had no idea what was going on behind those beautiful silver and black eyes. Finally he spoke, releasing warm breath on Jthery's neck. 'It may well not mean anything at all.'

Lapiszul.

Their first glimpse of the city was of gleaming golden roofs, jewel-coloured houses, greenery spilling between them laden with flowers of magenta, purple, blue. A pall of heat hung over the red cliffs that bore up this shining brocade.

'Look, you can see the palace,' Lahjaya said excitedly. 'There, up on the curve of the cliff! The Turquoise Court!'

The palace stood proudly overlooking the ocean in lines of bright blue walls and spires. It was as if the red rock of the cliff itself had been adorned with blue enamel. The walls folded along the cliff-face in tiers, glittering with windows. At the highest point a crystal dome flashed.

More than awe, Tanthe's main feeling was profound relief the journey was almost over. It seemed long in the past and dream-like now. The first violent surge along the river, which they and the boat had barely survived. Drifting, bruised and exhausted, into calmer waters. Days spent floating along the Vermeil Canyon, damp and uncomfortable and constantly bailing water. Camping on the banks, besieged by huge insects, snakes, frogs, all as bright as paint and dangerous as poison. And always the tunnel of greenery and the high red walls of the canyon soaring in majestic indifference around them.

At least they'd lost no-one else. All of them, including Karmensis and his seven soldiers, three women, four men, had survived bites, injury, heat exhaustion.

Eventually the Vermeil Canyon had flattened out into the plain and they'd disembarked at a town near the rivermouth. There they'd hired horses and ridden the rest of the way down the coast. The tough, graceful black horses went tirelessly along the baking scarlet roads. It seemed months to Tanthe since they'd escaped Parione. With the constant heat, she'd lost track of which festival fell due next. Midsummer . . . even Lunagh?

As they rode into the city, their view of the palace was obscured by buildings of white and gold, blue, red and green. Every surface was tile, enamel or mosaic. Tanthe wanted to reach out and stroke the walls, to feel their cool glassy surfaces cooling her hot skin. She saw porches and courtyards through archways, dark and lush with plants, enticing with the sound of playing water.

The streets that ran between the rows of dwellings were broad, dusty and paved with red slabs. There were water pumps or horse troughs scattered along the way, each one different and as beautifully embellished as a fountain. They stopped to water the horses, to drink and splash water on sweaty faces and necks.

Marocians came from their houses to watch the visitors. Their skin was like burnished walnut against the bright linen of their robes. Some came forward, smiling, to greet them openly and ask who they were, where from and where they were going? Lahjaya cheerfully tried to fend off their attention, without success. By the time they reached the avenue that led to the palace, they had gained an excited entourage.

The walls and spires of the palace spread back from the cliff-top to ramble into the city itself. Shafts of light fell along the avenue, and through these beams, as if through a rosy mist, the outer wall of the palace loomed. The wall was an imposing sweep of ultramarine with huge, half-moon bites cut out all along the top, and the point between each tipped with a spike of gold. The great gate at its centre was flanked by statues, twenty feet high; twin elongated hares with their noses pointing at the sky. Each was surfaced in tiny lapis-blue tiles with gold at the neck, ears and paws. They looked benign but aloof.

The gates stood open. They dismounted and went in, leading the horses. Within, they found a circle of sand-gold slabs, baking in the sun. Trees stood around the walls, dangling red trumpet flowers; in the centre towered a fountain tiled in dark blue, cobalt and turquoise. The splash of water was seductive. There were a few citizens about in this courtyard, strolling or sitting on the edge of the fountain. The scene was so tranquil it gave Tanthe a soporific desire to slip into the water and go to sleep, floating.

Lahjaya led them to a great gate of gold rails on the far side. Sea-serpents trailed their thick jewelled bodies over it. This gate was locked.

The guards who sauntered to meet them were dressed in loose green breeches and tunics, covered in surcoats of blue enamel disks. The delicate structures of wire and wings on their heads were more like stage headdresses than helmets.

Lahjaya, emboldened by her role as guide, strode forward to explain who they were. At once, the guards' easy demeanour vanished. A ripple went through them, sceptical amazement; but their leader, an older man, seemed to recognise the Queen.

'Her Majesty, Queen Helananthe of the Nine Realms, our sovereign!' he said, straightening up and making a quick, deep bow to Helananthe and her companions. Startled, the other guards hurriedly did the same. The gates swung open. The leader snapped an order. A handful of guards went sprinting towards the centre of the palace; others came to lead their horses away. The remaining guards deftly isolated Helan's party from the trail of Marocians, closed the gates, and led them towards a second gate in an inner wall.

'You are most welcome, ma'am, sire,' said the leader as they went. 'This is an immense honour. Duke Callais Jedraan is being informed of your arrival.'

'Thank you, Najan,' Helan said, and smiled at his startled expression. 'That is your name, isn't it? I remember you from the last time I was here.'

'Indeed, ma'am,' the leader gasped. 'I was part of the guard of honour on your previous visit. I'm amazed you remember me.'

'I have a good memory for faces. Alas, that visit was long ago and in much happier circumstances.'

Najan looked as if he was burning to ask more, but held his tongue in a professional manner. The second gate swung open to let them through. It was as magnificent as the first, flanked by two fantastical, stylised dra'a'ks which rested back on their wing-tips, jaws pointing at the sky. Inside was another courtyard; then a series of enclosed gardens, linked by archways that pierced the low curved buildings. Marocian men and women, moving gracefully through the gardens in jewel-bright robes, stopped and looked at them with cool interest as they passed.

Tanthe whispered to Lahjaya, 'Have you been here before?'

'To the outer parks and fountains, many times. But never inside the palace, no,' Lahjaya answered. She looked proud and nervous.

'Duke wotsisname should give you an award for helping to get us here in one piece,' Tanthe said, grinning.

'Callais Jedraan,' Lahjaya enunciated. 'He is also known less formally as Lord Sunstone.'

'What's he like?'

'I have only seen him from a distance. They say he's a great scholar.'

Tanthe felt more light of heart than she had for months. Elated to realise that it was true; Azura Maroc was still free from the Bhahdradomen. She smiled at Auriel and he gave her a ghost-smile back.

She caught the scent of the sea. They were standing in a formal garden of blue mosaic, edged by banks of flowers in all shades of ruby and sapphire glistening under sprinkler rain. Facing them was the front of the palace, a long, shining wall of lapis lazuli and gold mosaic, surmounted at the northern end by a crystal dome. The court of Duke Callais Jedraan.

Another guard came striding out and spoke quickly to Najan, who turned to Helan.

'Lord Sunstone asks if you would prefer to rest and refresh yourselves first, or to meet him immediately?'

Helan answered without pause. 'Let my companions go and rest. I'll see him now.' She raised a hand to halt Mawrdreth's protest. 'I need to see him alone.'

'My dear cousin,' said Jedraan, hurrying towards her and gripping both her hands. 'Oh, Lady of Tears, this is wonderful; I feared you were dead.'

They met in his main state room which was, in effect, a magnificent covered courtyard. It was a vast white and silver space on different levels, with fountains and man-made streams running through tiled channels. Plants dipped their pendulous leaves into the waters. The far wall was glass, dozens of thin bright windows like a veil of quartz. Most of the windows were open to cool the air, and the view of the ocean was magnificent. There were balconies edged in turquoise.

'I survived, as you see.'

Lord Sunstone's smile was as warm as it ever had been, and he looked just as she remembered. Older, of course, but he wasn't yet forty and looked in his prime. He was a little more solid than last time, but only a touch; he'd always been lean but seemed more imposing now, as if he'd filled out with experience and charisma. His long angular face was the colour of polished golden oak. He was completely bald – naturally, as far as she knew – his skull beautifully elongated like a burnished vessel.

Around them, various courtiers bowed to the Queen and stood in respectful silence. Some were in gorgeous robes of magenta, turquoise and indigo. Others were dressed more plainly in pale brownish-gold, with fine veils covering their faces. The veiled ones, she remembered, were the Duke's counsellors, philosophers and the like. Their veils denoted their academic status.

'My staff informed me of your arrival,' he went on, his Marocian accent round and velvety. 'This is most unexpected. You look . . . to be frank, dear cousin, you look . . .'

'A mess,' Helan finished, raking her dust-clogged hair out of her face. 'So would you, if you'd trekked hundreds of miles across occupied territory, got embroiled in a battle, travelled the length of the Ruby Plains, been attacked by *ghelim* and nearly dashed to pieces in the Vermeil Canyon. I apologise for making your court look untidy, but this really can't wait.'

Jedraan looked seriously at her, though a smile still hovered on his mobile lips. 'Are you sure you don't wish to rest?'

'No, really. But I'd appreciate a drink, and the chance to talk to you in *complete* privacy.'

'Of course.' He signalled to a servant, who hurried forward with a tray. The Duke poured them each a glass of pale liquid. Helan recognised the scent; it was a mildly alcoholic tincture flavoured with various Marocian herbs and flowers. She took a delicious mouthful, relished the cool effervescence fizzing in her dry mouth and throat.

'Now,' said Jedraan. He placed a hand on her upper back

and guided her to one side of the court, up some shallow steps and outside into a small courtyard. Creepers clung to the walls, laden with yellow flowers.

'I don't know what you've heard of Paranios,' she said as they walked.

'Terrible news,' Jedraan said gravely. 'Chaos on the Lapis Road, traders fleeing home in disarray with all manner of tales. It's been patchy, and impossible to tell how much of it is accurate, or how much we don't yet know. But yes, we heard that Vaurgroth invaded Parione and seized the Sapphire Throne. I truly feared you dead.'

They stopped by the inevitable fountain and sat on its lip. The basin was held by a highly stylised lion, the whole thing surfaced with tiny gold mosaic tiles. Falling water covered the sound of their voices. Helan told him everything. Jedraan sat and listened, his strong brown hand enclosing hers. The sun was setting by the time she finished, filling the courtyard with a subtle golden-red glow. Insects began to chirp.

'Paranios has fallen,' she concluded. 'You are our last hope, our only hope. Only with an army from Azura Maroc can we hope to reclaim Aventuria.'

Lord Sunstone went on smiling, nodding, his eyes fixed warmly on hers. And because his words were so at odds with his looks, she didn't realise for a few seconds what he was actually saying.

'I understand, dearest cousin. Your news has rent my heart, filled us all with grief. A counter-invasion would seem your only hope, if only I were able to command such a thing. Ah, dear . . .'

Her head jerked up. 'What do you mean, if only?'

'Azura Maroc cannot provide this army.'

Helan caught her breath. She said carefully, 'I hope you aren't refusing to help us. Be clear, before we misunderstand one another.'

'No, no, dear cousin, I shall help you in any and every way I can! My house is yours. The Turquoise Court shall be your safe refuge for as long as you wish. There is only one thing I cannot do for you, and that is to raise an army.'

He was still smiling. She stiffened, unable to look him. 'Why not?'

'I'm surprised you ask.' He stood up, and strolled a few feet away, his robe luminous in the twilight. 'Firstly, we do not forget the havoc Garnelys wrought upon us. He conscripted hundreds of my people to slavery, grossly abusing his sovereignty over my realm. And this when my people went so cheerfully at first, thinking to aid him! The Marocians will not countenance a second attempt. I can't ask it of them.'

'This is nothing like that!' Helan said fiercely. 'I am not conscripting anyone, I am asking for help. I'm not doing it to build a ludicrous monument, but to save the Nine Realms! Don't you see that if we do not stop the Bhahdradomen now, they will advance into this realm and find you utterly defenceless?'

Jedraan sighed. 'There is a limit to Vaurgroth's strength. I doubt that he is able to spread his forces that thin. If we don't antagonise them, they will leave us alone.'

Helan gasped in disbelief. 'You don't really believe that? Jedraan, you're being complacent. Dangerously so. To have this easy-going attitude is fine in time of peace, but to cling to it now could be fatal.'

Lord Sunstone's habitual good cheer was deceptive. It deflected attention from the stubborn steel of his character. He responded, 'What could be fatal is if I conscript my people into an army and send them to their deaths, thus drawing Vaurgroth's attention to us. *Then* he would invade us and find us defenceless.' The blue lights in his eyes were glacial.

'You're assuming we would lose.'

'It's a safe assumption. Helan, you know us. We're a lazy people. We love to talk and drink wine and ponder the nature of the universe. At fighting, however, we are shit.'

The last word snapped like a steel wire.

'Armies can be trained.'

'And thrown to their deaths against creatures with vicious supernatural weapons and no souls.'

Jedraan was right. But she saw her last hope trickling away like sand. 'You cannot refuse me!'

'Oh yes, I can, cousin,' he said gently. 'Hundreds of my people went to their deaths at Garnelys's hands. Now you are asking me to send thousands. It cannot be done. Stay with us, make your home here for the rest of your days if need be, and welcome. The one thing Azura Maroc will not give you – the only thing I *cannot* give you – is an army.'

Chapter Sixteen. Ink in the Skin

Vaurgroth's shadow haunted him around the chamber, crackling with sparks of *gauroth*.

'Lost them,' he said. 'Lost them?'

'Very nearly at the cost of my life, Master of Light,' Gulzhur replied, dropping the hated *mnelim* on the table between them. 'This thing almost pierced my heart. I was gravely wounded. It was only your power within me that preserved my life.'

Vaurgroth was nothing if not unpredictable. He could flash from warmth to fury in the snap of a *tzirin*. Gulzhur held himself taut, waiting. He wasn't given to fear, but still the anticipation was painful.

Vaurgroth eyed the Aelyr weapon with distaste. His *ghelim*-hound growled and cowered. Lesser *domenim* were terrified of such things, but adepts could overcome their fear enough to handle them, like venomous snakes, with caution. Zhoaah smiled at Gulzhur from the shadows as if to say, So this time you're the one in the mire.

Other figures were scattered around the chamber, watching. Every member of the inner circle had his own team of adept *bharu'grothrim* who in turn commanded lesser mages, *grothrim*, and they tended to emulate their masters. Rhazagramen's team were imperious little white vultures, Naghrur's polished steel scorpions. Gulzhur felt their impassive eyes on him. His own aides and Zhoaah's glowered at each other, in endless competition to rise in the hierarchy.

'It's only an old Aelyr trinket,' said Vaurgroth, poking at it without ill effect. 'Hardly a Basilisk, Enabler.'

'Still, a vicious little thorn,' said Zhoaah.

Gulzhur scowled at him. Facilitator smiled. Somehow he kept in favour regardless of the mistakes he made, slithering out of punishment time and again. Gulzhur, who lacked Zhoaah's charm, doubted that he'd be so lucky.

'Perhaps you are getting too old for this,' Vaurgroth said at last. His eyes glowed red against the milky skin. The look was ominous. Gulzhur felt a thread of pain trickle through him, that he should have served so long and skilfully only for the hated humans to bring his downfall . . .

'No, Master of Light,' Zhoaah put in. 'He was just unlucky. Being "too old" is a human weakness, not ours.'

Gulzhur gaped inwardly at Facilitator's cheek. His insides curdled with loathing. If his own failure wasn't humiliation enough, Zhoaah's pleading for him made it ten times worse. He felt himself shrivelling before the twin peril of Vaurgroth's stern warmth and the glacial threat of Naghrur behind him.

Then Vaurgroth lifted a hand. 'Yes, you were unlucky, Enabler. Facilitator speaks truly. You have never let me down before. And since you brought me such a rich tribute of their suffering – despite your wound – let us forget this. They'll come to light soon, whatever happens. However, if it comes to battle, as Bharamezht anticipates, I feel it desirable that you select the best of your *bharu'grothrim* to direct *ghelim* in the field, rather than taking the command yourself. I need you closer to home.'

Zhoaah grinned. So the humiliation had come after all. Gulzhur held himself rigid against betraying any trace of dismay. 'You are merciful, Greatlord,' he managed.

Vaurgroth made a dismissive gesture. 'It's Ancestor's Will that we triumph. What are a few setbacks? He was bound to place obstacles in our way, for what value is victory gained without opposition? He wills us to overcome adversity. Come, sit with me.'

Some of the human furniture had been kept, but the Amber Citadel was beginning to feel homely at last. Great cushions and bolsters of the finest *graukhim*-skin had been brought in to make eating circles or sleeping nests. The strips of skin left over made webs to mask out the glare of the tasteless coloured windows. The chambers smelled pleasantly musky, like a *tzcement*. The crackle of *gauroth* was energising.

They moved into the circle of *graukhim*-hide seats; Vaurgroth and Naghrur, Gulzhur and Zhoaah, Tzumezht and a handful of senior adepts. As they did so, Vaurgroth's hound, eager to follow its master, slipped in between them and almost tripped Tzumezht.

Prefigurer's charcoal face crimped with anger as he regained his balance. 'This *ghelim*, Greatlord, should be shut outside!' he grated. 'It has no place in our circle, it is a human conceit to—'

Vaurgroth's vermilion stare silenced his outburst. Naghrur said softly, 'You would do well to control yourself, Prefigurer Tzumezht. You are perilously close to insulting the Master of Light.'

Tzumezht's temper evaporated and he looked stricken. Gulzhur smiled. He had his uses but in truth, Prefigurer was an over-elevated, ill-mannered, common *domenim*.

'Forgive me, Greatlord,' he gasped. 'I meant no—'

'If you cannot appreciate a little subtle mockery of human habits, you had better keep silent, Prefigurer,' said Vaurgroth. His shape-changed hound flopped down in the centre of the circle, its scaly skin falling in folds. The atmosphere thrummed with danger, despite the Greatlord's emollient words. 'Now, let us anticipate better news. Grahzamen has sent *aghramen* on a secret mission to Verdanholm to discover the wherabouts of the Basilisks. The irritation that is Falthorn shall soon be flicked away. Meanwhile, our mages and scholars report ever more promising predictions of the Obsidian Tower. The forecast position has been calculated to within one hundred miles of a particular confluence of power.' His rich voice was dream-like, hypnotic. The chamber glimmered around him. His *bharu'grothrim* listened intently, *gauroth* light sliding like bloody jewels over their skin. Gulzhur was a religious doubter, but he believed completely in Vaurgroth himself. So if Master of Light promised it, then it must be true that the mythical Tower would reappear in this realm. 'Once we gain access to it, all wisdom shall be ours. The light of Ancestor shall pour freely upon us, bringing infinite power and blessing, an end to our dark struggle. Ancestor's own realm upon . . . Ah, here is the Theosopher himself!'

The door opened. *Vagharim* formed a corridor and Rhazagramen stalked in with a train of adepts. His wizened face split in a grin of triumph.

'Master of Light,' he said, bowing, his arid voice tremulous with emotion. 'The Obsidian Tower is manifest.'

Tangible joy broke on the atmosphere. Even Gulzhur's sore heart began to lift. Vaurgroth threw back his head with a shout of exultation. 'I was right! Our work with the Heliodor Tower has borne the fruit of its dark twin. Ancestor's Will be done!'

Helan found Mawrdreth and Eldareth, and told them what Jedraan had said. Their guest quarters were a rambling loop of rooms arranged about a central garden. Slender columns the colour of bluebells supported the gold-tiled roofs. There was no sign of Tanthe, Auriel or Lahjaya; Helan assumed they were asleep. She'd found the two men sitting by a carp pond, waiting for her. It was dark, but Leaf and Lily Moons shone through feathery branches to dapple their forms with silver and green.

Helan watched them as she explained what had happened. Eldareth's lined, angular face darkened more with resignation than anger. Mawrdreth, however, rose to his feet, his green eyes fervent.

'He cannot refuse to help us!'

'We have to consider why he's refused,' said Eldareth, folding his arms. 'To him, his reasons are perfectly valid.'

'Yes, he's a bloody coward!'

'Perhaps, but it's not helpful to pass such judgement on him.'

Mawrdreth gave an impatient laugh. 'Where would Thanmandrathor be if we'd said, "Oh, we are too lazy to fight Garnelys?" Only by fighting did we depose him. The Duke's stance is an outrage!'

Eldareth nodded, fixing the younger man with a firm stare. 'So, we must make him reconsider in a way that makes *him* believe he's doing the right thing.'

Mawrdreth only glared back at him, more fired up than ever. 'I haven't the patience for this. You are suggesting we treat him like a child. Such diplomacy will make us look weak; it will be our downfall!'

'Diplomacy is all that will save us,' Eldareth said grimly.

'Oh, stop it!' Helan exclaimed. 'If I'd known you were going to bicker like this, I wouldn't have told you. We have to think about things.'

'So, you're taking Eldareth's side?' Mawrdreth said, low and furious.

'We're all on the same side,' she began, but he wasn't listening.

'Anketh's teeth, I'll talk to the Duke myself! Someone has got to make him see sense!'

Mawrdreth went striding out of the garden, his hand on his sword hilt. Eldareth rose and made to go after him, but Helan stopped him. 'Let him go,' she said.

'All he'll do is antagonise Lord Sunstone and wreck any chance of him helping us.'

'Perhaps.' Helan sat down on the lip of the pond, profoundly tired. 'Let him find out for himself how stubborn Jedraan can be. Mawrdreth is my consort; I refuse to treat him like a child. He may be better than me at making Jedraan understand our urgency. If not, well, I can smooth things over later.'

Eldareth tutted. 'No, Helan. Mawrdreth losing his temper won't help. He's young and headstrong, he'll lead you to disaster through his lack of tact. Do you forever want to be smoothing over the trouble he's caused?'

'He's not that bad. He's a lot brighter than people give him credit for.'

'Doesn't always know when to keep his mouth shut, though.'

'Well, it might be more fitting to have someone calm, worldly-wise and diplomatic at my side,' Helan said acidly, 'but you refused.'

Eldareth tipped his head back to look at the sky. Moonlight silvered the grey in his fine black hair. 'I made the only decision I could.'

'You made the right decision. I see that now.' She stood up and glared into his eyes, losing patience. 'Don't you dare to criticise Mawrdreth! He's fearless, he's clear-minded and good-hearted, he's everything Aventuria needs. If he's volatile, it's for the right reasons. Calmness and wisdom will come with age. But not bitterness, I hope.'

'If you're suggesting I'm bitter, I have reason to be,' said Eldareth. 'I've lost the only woman I've ever loved, through my own failings.'

Helan felt a well of dread open inside her. As long as they stayed on a hard surface of anger, she could bear it. But if he strayed into the waters of regret . . . 'Well, then, your bitterness should be aimed at yourself, not my husband.'

'It is, believe me. We can't go on arguing like this.'

'I can't go on, caught between the two of you!' she exclaimed. 'It's unbearable! You compete for my attention, my approval, compete to prove which of you is best at protecting me, as if it's some deadly game – and I'm caught in the middle, Eld, because you're my friend and I cannot banish you from my life!'

He was quiet for a time. Then he asked, 'Do you still love me, Hel?'

'Eld, don't.'

'Do you?'

She felt moisture on her cheek, brushed it away. 'I've known you for far too long ever to stop loving you.'

He breathed out softly. 'Life would be simpler, wouldn't it, if your marriage was one of convenience?'

'But it isn't.'

'I know that. That's what makes this situation unbearable. Not that you married Mawrdreth, but that you love him.'

'I do,' she said. Feeling chilled, she stood up, hugging herself. Eldareth came close to her and stroked her cheek. 'He's loving and loyal.'

'Also young, strong and beautiful.' His mouth twisted wryly.

'Do you think I'm that shallow?' She laughed. 'Yes, he has many fine qualities . . . but you and I shared so much history . . .'

'So you can't choose between us.'

'No, I've made my choice,' she said. 'Yet I still can't seem to let you go.'

'You can't let me go – yet you're giving me no hope?'

'I'm sorry, but how can I?'

'Of course. You love your husband, and I let you down. I understand.'

'You sound angry.'

'No. No.' His hand moved into her hair and he leaned in and kissed her mouth, lightly and tenderly, which he had not done for a long time. She wanted to weep, and only controlled herself with an effort. 'I'm not angry, Hel. Only sorry. Good night.'

He kissed her again, and was gone.

When he left Helan, Eldareth went to his room briefly, just for long enough to write a short letter. He hoped it didn't sound self-pitying; that wasn't his frame of mind. But one of them must make a decision, and since she wouldn't do it, it had to be him.

Leaving the letter folded in clear view on the bed, he

went out into the garden again, found it deserted. He slipped across it and through the archway that led from their quarters into a larger courtyard. Working his way between palace buildings, he went north, parallel to the ocean, until he came to a place where wild rocks took over from cultivated gardens, and the wall was low enough for him to scramble over.

He found himself on the cliff-top, a stretch of rugged, fissured rock. He sat down in a hollow, with a small valley tilting away below him. He couldn't see the ocean from where he was but he could hear its unceasing, soothing roar. The sky was darkest blue satin, pricked with stars and adorned with the glowing spheres of Lily Moon and Leaf Moon. They looked huge in the southern sky.

Eldareth had no plan. He only felt that, as the cause of Helan's dilemma, he must remove himself and fight Vaurgroth in his own way. He must stop fleeing from the responsibilities that he'd shirked, in dread of becoming like his father, Mordraken.

After he had sat there for a time, he glimpsed movement in the darkness.

He caught his breath. All around him, the rocks were moving; humps of shadow catching the faintest grey sheen on their surfaces. He was instantly alert, staring through the darkness, straining his ears for the faintest sound . . .

A whispering. He sat forward, his hand on the hilt of his sword.

'Eldareth!'

He knew that voice. Couldn't place it. Not human.

'Who's there?' he said, turning quickly in the direction of the sound. Then he saw. They were not rocks, but small greyish figures creeping towards him. Zampherai.

'Eldareth,' the voice said again, closer. 'Mordraken Mordraken-son.'

He saw the figure clearly in the faint light of the moons. A wiry pewter man with thick black hair, huge light-hungry jet eyes. His head was on a level with Eldareth's mid-thigh, but his strength and presence made up for his tiny stature.

'Orque!' he exclaimed. 'My friend, what are you doing here?'

Now he saw the others clustering around Orque. The warrior Vranof, with blue streaks in his hair and crystals hanging from his throat and loins. Others he didn't know, silent half-seen presences. Denizens of the earth.

'We have waited a long time for you,' said Orque. 'Now you are ready, Eldareth.'

Although he knew Orque and Vranof – had known them a long time – they seemed different. Their manner was formal, almost sinister. As if this was something pre-ordained.

'Ready for what?' he asked softly.

'All your life you have rejected your parents' path. Even when we rescued you from Fortress Arabeth in Torith Mir, you were still not ready. But when Falthorn sold the Earth from under you . . . then you regretted your choice.'

Eldareth's heart began to pound. He knew what the Zampherai meant . . . though how Orque knew so much, he hardly dared ask.

He could have – *should* have – become a crystal-mage like his mother Elq'esq . . . but because of his father's brutality, his misuse of jewel-*roth* to make weapons, Eldareth had closed his mind to his parents' abilities. He'd made a conscious decision never to follow their path. And then regretted it, when he saw that Earthly weapons alone could not stop Falthorn, nor conquer the Bhahdradomen.

Regretted it even more when he'd watched Lahjaya healing Tanthe.

He stared at Orque. He knew the little man was right. And it was Lahjaya, in the end, who'd changed his mind.

'Yes,' he breathed. 'I'm ready. I will follow my mother's path.'

'Not just your mother's,' said Vranof. 'Mordraken's, too.'

Eldareth took a deep, shaky breath. 'Yes. His too.'

Orque held out his hand. 'Then come with us.'

And Eldareth went with them. Gave himself up to them as if to death, and let them lead him into a fissure in the rock, onwards through an endless tunnel, down and down into the darkest places of the earth.

'He wouldn't listen to me,' Mawrdreth said. His fire had spent itself into bewildered agitation. 'The more angry I got, the more calm Lord Sunstone was.'

He was pacing about the room. Helan sat and watched him from the bed. The last thing Mawrdreth wanted was any kind of consolation. Still less for her to say, 'I told you so.' She asked, 'Did he seem irritated, cold, anything like that?'

'No. He only smiled and kept saying, "As I have told Helan, I can give you no army." What does it matter if he was upset?'

'Only that it might make it harder to persuade him to our point of view.'

'If that's the case, I'm sorry. My sister always accused me of not knowing when to hold my tongue. But he was impervious!'

'Mawrdreth, come to bed. I'm so tired I can't see straight. Stop pacing about.'

'I can't rest,' he said, standing over her.

Kneeling up, she pulled the thong out of his plait and unravelled his hair over his shoulders. 'Then will you please put your energy into making love to me? We'll worry about this tomorrow.'

Days passed. At first, Tanthe was happy. It was the sheer relief of the journey being over, the luxury of being able to bathe, drink or eat whenever she wanted, sleeping in a soft silken bed, waking to warm glowing daylight and knowing she hadn't got to go anywhere . . . the pure physicality of it was delicious.

Her room, like the others, was large and airy, the walls

painted ivory and the bed hung with silken curtains that could be drawn to keep insects out at night. The floor was tiled with gold leaf, the table covered in a rich mosaic of green, red and blue. The bathroom was as fine as any she'd seen in Parione. Instead of white marble and classical statues, it had flowing blue mosaic like an underwater lagoon, with quirky Marocian animals to channel the water.

In the honeyed heat, she found it impossible to think of doing anything but lying about in the palace gardens or watching the ocean from the windows of the Turquoise Court. The thought of setting out again – probably to be killed in battle – was too far away and too horrible to contemplate.

So she spent the time relaxing with Lahjaya, recovering, exploring the palace. Jedraan was a friendly man who was happy to let them come and go as they wished, and always spared time to talk to them. Tanthe reserved judgement; she liked him, but she knew he was being difficult about helping the Queen. Lahjaya, though, seemed smitten.

'He's not married,' Lahjaya whispered, one afternoon when he had just left them. She had a fiercely hopeful light in her eyes.

'I wonder why not?' Tanthe said drily.

'Oh, you think he likes men? I've heard not. I think he's been waiting for me.'

When they had finished laughing, Tanthe said casually, 'I got the impression you were quite keen on Auriel.'

Lahjaya, to her surprise, looked affronted. 'What made you think that? I'm friendly to him, that's all. He seems lost. He is very pretty, but like gossamer, somehow. I like a man with more . . . how can I put it . . . strength of character.'

The last three words were accompanied by a suggestive action of her fist, making Tanthe laugh even harder. 'So, seduce Jedraan,' she whispered. 'Even if you don't end up Duchess Callais Lahjaya, Lady Sunstone, you'll have had a good time.'

Later, Tanthe reflected on Lahjaya's words about Auriel. Since they'd arrived in Lapiszul, he'd been quiet, almost reclusive. Each day Tanthe made sure he was well, and he assured her he was, making it plain by his demeanour that he wanted to be left alone. She felt puzzled, slightly hurt. She'd left him to his own devices . . . but now she wondered what he was thinking about, all those hours alone.

With time on her hands, she was dwelling more on her nightmares of the *ezht* and her Aelyr parents. I've got to find them, she thought, but I don't know where to start. It will mean going into the *ezht* again and that's too terrifying to contemplate. And Auriel knows I need his help but he's avoiding the issue, running away. She felt suddenly angry with him. Yes, that's what he's doing. But I can't know how or where to begin unless I break through to my Aelyr side. No one can help me do that but Auriel.

'Right,' she said out loud.

Tanthe found Auriel in his room. He was sitting on the low bed, half hidden by the curtains, reading. It was a book of poetry. Lady Amahlliah's reflections on the Aelyr, a work she'd loved herself, romantic but with a heart of disturbing mystery.

'Auriel?' He looked darkly up at her, plainly not welcoming the disturbance. The look made her hesitate. She became suddenly, deeply uneasy about what she was asking. 'I need to talk to you.'

'What is it?' he said, putting the book aside.

She sat beside him, put her hand on his knee. 'Do you remember, the first time we made love, the visions we saw?' He nodded warily. 'And you said it often happened, the Aelyr seeing visions when they make love to each other.'

He blinked at her, saying nothing, waiting for her to go on. 'Dear, there's no easy way to ask this. But I need to break through to the Aelyr side of my nature. I was so close, the first time; if I could find that place again, that complete transport into the Jewelfire, I could break through the veil this time and understand who I am. It's the only way I can learn how to deal with the *ezht*.'

'You should ask the Bhahdradomen about the *ezht*,' he said coldly. 'It's their place.'

She didn't know how to respond to this, so ignored it. 'I can't do it without you.' She smiled. 'I'm not asking you to do anything unpleasant. If it doesn't work . . . well it will be nice, anyway. You don't mind?'

Auriel was staring at her, lips parted. Then an extraordinary expression came into his eyes. Not anticipation, but a sort of wary passivity; a darkness. He didn't touch her but lay back on the bed so there was room for her to lie beside him. And there was something in the gesture that chilled her from head to toe.

'Auriel?' she said. 'What are you doing?'

'What you asked,' he said.

'By just lying there?' She stared at him for a few seconds, trying to swallow away the spasm in her throat. 'You look as if you're . . . obeying me.' He didn't speak. 'What is this? You don't have to *obey* me. I don't order you around like . . .' She choked on Falthorn's name. Horror transfixed her. 'If you don't want to do it, just tell me!'

To her shock, he leapt off the bed, his passivity vaporising into rage. She'd never seen him angry before; not like this. The change stunned her.

'No, I don't want to!' he cried. 'You're using me, as Falthorn used me! You saying, "Let us do this," is as bad as him saying it!'

'That's not fair!'

'Gods, Tanthe.' The flare faded as quickly as it had appeared. 'I love you. Of course it would be pleasurable, but that's not the point. You'd still be doing it for other reasons. Using me.'

He turned away from her. She stood looking at his back, so shocked she felt almost sick. The feeling that unfurled in her gut was unpleasant; self-loathing. At last she went to him. When she touched his shoulder he jumped like a wounded animal.

'D'you know what?' she said. 'You're absolutely right. I was trying to use you. I'm sorry.'

He wouldn't look at her. She couldn't tell whether he was weeping or not; if so, he didn't want her to see. 'I'm really sorry,' she said again. 'I didn't mean to be selfish. I didn't realise this would upset you so much.'

'We're too close,' he said gruffly. 'I see Falthorn in your face sometimes.'

'Oh, thanks.' She stepped back, feeling as if he'd hit her. 'We're both related to him, I can't help it.'

He turned round, stricken. 'Gods, I didn't mean to say that . . . It's just . . . I feel as if I've been in a dream and just started to wake up.'

'Well . . . why not talk to me about it, instead of shouting at me?'

'I didn't mean to shout at you,' he said wretchedly. 'But I can't help you. I just can't. Suppose you went into the *ezht* in this vision and took me with you? I couldn't stand it.'

'Why were you just going lie there and let it happen, then?'

'Habit,' he said bleakly. 'Life was easier if I didn't argue.'

Tanthe studied him. Her stomach was a lump of ice. So beautiful and serene, he'd seemed, when she'd first seen him, like a forest god . . . How disturbing to see the god-like Aelyr as helpless and tormented as humans. 'Auriel, I know Falthorn mistreated you,' she said, mouth dry. 'Are you saying that it included having sex with you?'

Auriel smiled. The expression was chilling. 'Now and then. It was beneath his dignity, really. He doesn't like losing control. I don't think I even pleased him particularly. It was just part of dominating me, so there was no part of me he hadn't invaded. But he used to say what you said – "You don't mind?" – and it was really a statement, not a question.'

'Oh, shit,' Tanthe breathed. 'I thought he just intimidated you. Well, that was really naive of me. You never said!'

'I was ashamed.'

'Why? It wasn't your fault.'

'I meant that I was ashamed because I thought I loved him for a while. But you can't go on loving someone who makes you live in fear every day of your life. I feel sorry for Jthery, but no one can help him.'

Cautiously she took his hand. He didn't try to evade her. 'But love, he's gone now. I didn't mean to remind you.'

'He's never gone. And it's not your fault, Fliy. I only acted like that because I was thinking about a lot of things I never dared to think about before. I feel as if I've woken up.'

'Sounds like I picked my moment, as usual,' she sighed. She gripped his hand. 'I don't want to go into the *ezht* again, any more than you do. But if we found the key to not being afraid, Falthorn would lose his power over us.'

'All the same, I can't make love to you for that reason. We had some wonderful times but that would ruin all we had. It would taint it forever.'

'It's okay, I wasn't talking about sex, I'm just saying . . .'

He went on as if he hadn't heard her. 'With you, that first time, it was sacred, beautiful – but all the time, I knew I was betraying you, doing it because Falthorn commanded me to. He was using us both. Now you're trying to use me. Everything – everything is tainted by coercion, hidden motives. I'm not what everyone seems to think I am.' He took his hand from hers. 'You don't know who you are? Well, neither do I!'

She looked at his beautiful, hurt face and felt hollow. She had the sinking feeling that they'd let each other down.

'We could just . . . meditate, like we did with Elrill. It would help us both.'

'No! No. Not even that. Tanthe, will you not accept that I just can't face it yet?'

'Could be too late if we leave it much longer,' she said

lightly. 'But no, sorry, if that's how you feel I'll have to find my way alone.'

He lowered his head, sighed, looking anguished. 'I should have gone with Elrill.'

'You don't mean it.' She folded her arms. 'I don't know whether to put my arms round you for being miserable, or hit you for feeling sorry for yourself! What is it you want, Auriel?'

'I want to go home,' he said bleakly, 'but I have no home.'

Days passed, and each one seemed to Tanthe longer, slower and more indolent than the one before. It felt as if the Lapiszul sun was thickening to toffee and holding time itself in its sticky golden strings.

After she'd seen Auriel, she met Helan, who placed the letter from Eldareth in her hands. 'I'm going to seek the path I should have found a long time ago,' he wrote. 'I'm not deserting you, I'm going to find the strength I need to help you.'

'Cryptic,' said Tanthe, still smarting from her encounter with Auriel. 'While everyone goes off to find themselves, what are we supposed to do?'

'I am really beginning to wonder,' Helan said thinly.

The strangest thing was that no-one got worked up about Eldareth's disappearance, nor about anything else. The air was a steamy bubble, thick with golden dust and midges. Everyone became languid, unable to stir themselves to action. Helan and Mawrdreth poured what little energy they had into arguing rather than making clear plans. Tanthe tried to talk to Mawrdreth a few times but he was preoccupied, hating inactivity but seemingly unable to change things.

Lahjaya was happy and soporific, spending most of her time asleep in the piles of silken cushions that were scattered about the main court. She confided a pleasant liaison with Jedraan to Tanthe, but Tanthe couldn't see that this was enough to cause such torpor. Unless there was a side to Lahjaya they'd never suspected.

The Turquoise Court surrounded them and cosseted them with its rich silks and jewel-colours, its fountains and tiled pools, delectable foods. There were exquisite gardens to walk in, museums to marvel at, libraries of books that would take a lifetime to read. Yet, Tanthe noticed, no-one ever seemed to do anything. It must be the climate, she thought. The Lapiszans appeared to walk around in a dream, the Duke included. He spent much of his day enthroned on a velvet couch, surrounded by admiring courtiers, talking of philosophy or art or fashion, with never a mention of what was going on elsewhere in the Nine Realms.

For the first few days, as Tanthe recovered from the journey, this tranquillity was a relief. Then it began to be unsettling. Perhaps the Duke only spoke of serious matters in private. Perhaps the beautiful men and women of his court, with their garnet-sheened hair and their blue-black eyes, only showed alert concern out of the public eye. Maybe the graceful counsellors actually put back their gossamer veils and offered some counsel. But all Tanthe saw, as the Duke beckoned his visitors to join his lazy circle each day, was high-minded frivolity.

As more time passed, it began to draw her in. Helan and Mawrdreth relaxed, and began to dress in robes of the Marocian style, rich red, blue or green with jewelled panels. They no longer talked about Parione, nor tried to persuade Lord Sunstone to help them. Maybe they did so in private, but Tanthe had the feeling that everything was being allowed to drift. And she drifted with it. It was so deliciously peaceful here. So easy to fall into long, dreamless sleeps, with nothing more arduous to do on waking than eat a peach and take a stroll through the gardens. Why leave, when they could stay here in peace and safety forever?

Only Auriel seemed unaffected. He kept to himself, and

was usually to be found in one of the Duke's libraries or reading under a tree. He was so different from the person Tanthe had first met. He'd grown aloof and serious.

'You've changed,' she said, flopping down beside him in the shade of a fig tree. 'I told you I'm sorry for my awful behaviour. Aren't you ever going to forgive me? I forgave you.'

'There's nothing to forgive,' he said, giving her the closed-away, guarded look that was all she saw in his face these days.

'Then why are you still angry with me?'

'I'm not,' he said. 'You are the one who's changed, not me.'

'What do you mean?'

'It's as if you're all asleep,' Auriel said tersely, looking at his book again. She saw the title printed at the top of the yellowing page, *Natural Philosophie of the Aelyryn: Rothanamir*. 'Do the Marocians live on some drug that causes euphoria? You all behave as if there's an Aelyr glamour upon you.'

'Nonsense.' Tanthe smiled.

'You don't even know it's happening, do you?'

She sat up straight. The movement felt slow, like moving through water. 'No, I do know what you mean, Auriel. I'm so tired. But it's just the heat.'

'Is it?'

'What are you getting at?'

'I don't know,' he said, meeting her eyes. 'I don't like it here. Something's wrong.'

The chill that fingered its way down her back shook her to awareness. 'Lend me your *mnelir*, will you? I lost mine, if you remember.'

He paused, then drew the small knife in its sheath from a fold in his sky-blue robe, and passed it to her. The crystal sphere on the pommel was cool against her hand.

'Take it,' he said. 'I don't think it will tell you anything.'

* * *

Tanthe prowled the court with the feeling she was going mad. Everything was the same; the Duke reclining with his entourage around him, sipping red wine and delicate liqueurs. Servants working huge fans made of green leaves, sitting with their eyes closed as if they too were half-asleep. The murmur of water and voices. Insects flitting in through a door that stood open to a balcony, and beyond that, the shifting, shimmering mass of the ocean.

If she went with the drugged feeling, all was well. If she tried to fight it, she felt disorientated. It was as if she'd wandered into some mad dream.

The *mnelir*, hidden inside her robe, remained cool against the skin of her waist. It throbbed no warning, yet her sense of something out of place grew stronger. Perhaps it's me who's lost my mind, she thought.

Lahjaya, sitting with Jedraan, raised a hand to wave lazily at Tanthe. Tanthe ignored them. She drifted on, saw a group of counsellors standing on the balcony. Impelled by curiosity she went on walking across the alabaster floor and stepped out onto the balcony among them.

They all stopped talking and turned to look at her. Still the *mnelir* didn't react, but a shiver went through her. She needed no outside aid to strip away the truth. Her own instinct, however wayward, was enough.

She could see their faces through the thin veils; men and women with copper-skinned faces and dark human eyes, staring at her. Nothing of the Aelyr or the Eaters about them . . . yet they all looked oddly similar.

'What is it?' said one in a low, husky voice. 'Why are you staring at us?'

'Nothing,' said Tanthe. 'I wanted some fresh air, that's all.'

The one who had spoken put back his veil. His face was nearly perfect; angular, gilt-skinned with human eyes. There was a strange dark mottling across the bridge of the nose, a slight scaliness around the eyelids. Nothing, really.

'What is that marking?' she asked.

'A tattoo,' said one of the others. 'We all have it. It marks our role and status, you see.'

'Yes,' she said. The mottling still looked like scales. 'It's very . . . good.'

And they all stared, stared at her from dark perfect eyes, willing her to see human, *human* in front of her. She felt the pressure on her mind, a blurring of her vision. But it was too late. She knew. The *mnelir* flashed hot, only for a half-second, and the heat sent trickles of sweat down her stomach. There was no scent to them, no fear-inducing aura. It was as if they were shielded even against the sensitive Aelyr weapon. Oh Goddess, they were good.

'The best I've seen,' she whispered, backing away. She was trying desperately to smile, not to let them see that she knew. She was so shaken she could barely hide it.

'It's only ink in the skin,' said the first, dropping his veil.

That was the worst shock of all. Realising that it wasn't just one *neshrim* cuckoo in the nest of counsellors, but all of them. All of them.

Chapter Seventeen. The Turquoise Court

A shadow moved across Ysomir's window. She'd been drowsing; shock brought her wide awake. She sat up, felt the *ethroths* bristling inside her.

'You seem to have exchanged one prison for another,' said a familiar voice.

She fumbled to light a candle. Zhoaah's bleached, smiling face floated into view.

'How did you get in here? How did you find me?' Terror fluttered through her; not for herself but for Saphaeyender, Eander's family, all the others in the household.

'I told you I'd watch you. I've always known where you are.' He moved closer and wrapped a thin white hand round her wrist. 'Ysomir, I know your friend the poet is here. Naghrur and Tzumezht are spitting blood with rage over his disappearance. I know that the lady of the house had already been in trouble with the authorities and if they find her harbouring you . . .'

His indrawn breath was a snake's hiss. Ysomir stared, tears of terror blurring her eyes. She felt the glow of power inside her stirring, pushing at Zhoaah.

As if he'd felt it too, he dropped her wrist and stepped back. She whispered, 'Have you told them?'

'Given you away? No.'

'Why not?'

He paused, the black worms of his eyes probing her. 'I'm reluctant to ease your fear, since I enjoy the feel of it so much. By the First Egg, my lady, you have so much to lose, have you not? If the *vagharim* were to descend upon this house and drag away all of your friends to be tortured and enslaved . . . *ahh* . . .'

Revulsion froze her. Green-gold light pulsed from her heart. 'Or I could kill you now,' she said.

'Quite.' His smile had an edge of tension. 'So be calm. Don't excite your spectral friends. I've come to set your mind at rest. Yes, I know where you are, but I shall ensure that the Bhahdradomen authorities never find out. There will be no *vagharim* searches, no visits from Protector Naghrur. This house is under my protection.'

She frowned, confused. 'Why? You must want something from me in return!'

Zhoaah's mouth was a small thin line. He blinked. 'Possibly.'

'What?' He didn't answer. She leaned forward. 'What, Zhoaah? Do you want to usurp Vaurgroth, is that it?'

'Keep your voice down!' he snapped. 'Of course not. I've served the Master of Light a long time, but . . .' He sat down on the edge of the bed and spoke as if to himself, sounding oddly weary, human. 'Vaurgroth is complacent. Mistakes have been made yet he is strangely unconcerned. He is too convinced that "Ancestor's Will" makes us invincible.'

'Don't you . . . believe it?'

'It's Vaurgroth's own *gauroth* skills that make us invincible. Does it make him a better, wiser leader to credit Ancestor rather than his own plentiful power? Or does it make him a fool? I am yet to decide.'

She crumpled the sheet between her fingers. 'What do you expect me to do about this?'

Zhoaah's head came up. 'Nothing. I was thinking aloud. There's no-one I could even whisper it to, except you. This alone makes your existence worth preserving.'

She gaped at him, incredulous. 'Are you saying you just want someone to talk to? Protecting the house seems an immense amount of trouble to go to, just for that. For Breyid's sake, there's no need to lie to me.'

'So, you assume I'm lying.' He sounded dangerously annoyed.

'I don't know! You helped me escape, you're protecting

Saphaeyender. I'm grateful, but I don't see why.' She folded her arms round herself. 'You must expect something in return. Tell me.'

He stood up, the sinister Facilitator again. 'You sit and look at me with such dread, convinced it's a price you cannot pay. You always think the worst of me. But what do you know about what I want, my lady?' He leaned down and brushed her shoulder. For a horrible moment she thought he was going to kiss her. 'Let us just say you owe me a favour,' he said softly. In a few whispering footsteps, he was gone.

'Helan, I must speak to you. It's urgent.'

Tanthe stood in the doorway to Helan and Mawrdreth's room, a shadow in the cool blue gloom. The day had ground on interminably and this was the first chance she'd had to find them in private. There was some muttering and slithering of sheets, then a lamp flared and they were sitting up in bed, regarding her. If she'd caught them about to make love, she didn't care. She closed the door and hurried to Helan's side of the bed.

'I thought of going straight to the Duke, but then I thought, what if he already knows? I had to tell you first. You must decide what to do, not me.'

'Tanthe, what on Earth are you talking about?' Helan said. She pushed her dishevelled hair away from her face.

Tanthe swallowed, took a breath, sat down on the edge of the bed. 'The Bhahdradomen are already here.'

They both gasped and protested. 'No, they're not,' Helan said. 'I think you must be suffering from heat-stroke, or something.'

She shook her head impatiently. 'I'm fine. You're the ones who've been in a dream! I need you to listen to me.'

Her sharp tone reached them. 'Go on,' Helan said, frowning.

'Haven't you noticed how passive and dreamy everyone

at court is? They give the impression of being bright with their endless talk about philosophy or whatever – but when do they talk about anything that's actually happening? Why don't they worry about the rise of Vaurgroth? And the longer we stay, the more we get like it too.'

'She's right,' Mawrdreth said. 'I've sometimes wondered if they're drugging us . . . then the thought fades, as if it doesn't matter.'

Helan hesitated. She folded her arms. 'I put it down to the heat. We aren't used to it. This is not proof of the Bhahdradomen being here, though. It's impossible.'

'No-one thought it was possible for Zhoaah to be in Garnelys's court,' Tanthe countered, 'but there he was.'

'Oh, gods . . .' Helan pushed the covers back, made to get up, then froze. 'Is it one of the counsellors again? Which one?'

'It's all of them,' said Tanthe.

Cries of denial. '*All?* This can't be!'

'I promise you,' Tanthe said in a low voice. 'I had a good look at them this afternoon. I could tell.'

Mawrdreth opened his palms on the bed-cover. 'But we've seen them every day. You can see their faces through their veils. They're Marocian men and women.'

'They're very good. They're much better than Zhoaah was. You really couldn't tell through their veils, or even without them. One of them lifted his and he was very convincing. But there were imperfections, dark scales on the skin, a bit of membrane across the corners of the eyes . . .'

'It's not proof,' Helan said, with less conviction.

'Helan . . . I'm sure I've seen him before. When they invaded the Sun Chamber. One of Vaurgroth's cronies?'

Mawrdreth groaned. He lowered his head, his brown hair falling loose on his shoulders. 'I'm thinking of that message Bran sent us. The boy at my father's house that we'd known for years. Noli. No-one realised he was Bhahdradomen, either. Even picturing him now, I can't see it.'

'If it's true . . .' The blood drained from Helan's cheeks. 'How could it have happened?'

'Perhaps they infiltrated one at a time, over a number of years,' Tanthe said. 'I think it's why everyone here is so complacent. It's an aura the Bhahdradomen are putting out. I could feel it when I was near them. Like they've adapted to cause euphoria instead of fear. And we've been sucked into it.'

'As people in Parione were pulled into Ancestor-worship,' murmured Helan.

'Tanthe's right,' said Mawrdreth. 'It's only when you see it from outside that you realise . . .'

Tanthe nodded. 'It was Auriel who made me wonder. As soon as I started actually *looking*, it seemed obvious.'

'That's an Aelyr trait,' Helan said, looking meaningfully at her.

'Humans can do it just as well, if they're sensitive. Remember Lynden?'

Helan nodded, her gaze falling. 'I wonder if this is why the Duke refused to help us? He can't be knowingly collaborating with these counsellors . . . can he?'

'I don't know.'

'So they play on the Marocians' natural inclinations,' said Helan. 'They encourage them to believe all is right with the world.'

'Then when Vaurgroth is ready to take Azura Maroc,' Mawrdreth added, 'the Bhahdradomen simply walk in and take over. No resistance.'

The three of them sat looking at each other in horror. Mawrdreth's green eyes were furious, Helan's alight with determination. Tanthe was unspeakably relieved that the news had woken them to their normal selves again. She'd feared that it might be impossible to reach them.

'Do the counsellors know you suspect them?' Helan asked.

'I hope not.' Tanthe shuddered. 'They asked why I was staring at them, but there was . . . how can I put it? A sort of arrogance about them, as if they thought no mere human could ever see through them.'

'And you've told no-one?'

'Only you.'

'Tanthe, I'm so grateful you came to us,' Helan said emphatically.

She grimaced. 'Well, I'd have made a right mess of things if I'd tried to deal with it myself. What will you do?'

'There's only one thing for it. I'll have to tell the Duke.'

'It's impossible,' said Jedraan, shaking his burnished head. 'Impossible.'

They were outside, on a cliff-top where warm salt-winds burned their skin and sea-birds wheeled above, mewing. Helan had insisted they speak here, where there was no possibility of being overheard. Mawrdreth had a surreptitious hand on his sword-hilt; but she was gambling everything on Jedraan's innocence.

'We have no proof,' she said carefully. 'But how well do you know your own counsellors? Do you speak to them often, know them intimately?'

'Naturally, I . . .' He broke off, still shaking his head. Light flashed on the brown skull. 'I can't remember.' He looked at Helan with an expression of horror. It was the first time she'd seen him stripped of the serene smile. 'I can't remember!'

'You must remember something.'

He put one hand to his head. The hand was trembling. 'Vague impressions. Yes, I remember endless days at court, conversations with chancellors and treasurers, the usual nonsense of ruling. Trying to deal with it as fast as I could in order to get back to the serious business of talking about the wonders of art or astronomy . . . I recall almost every word of those glorious conversations, but everything around me is vague. I'm not even sure who was there. Have they been drugging me?'

'I don't think so,' said Helan. 'I think it's a power

Vaurgroth's given them. An aura of *gauroth* that affects the mind. *Gauroth*'s an energy that's produced by—'

'I know what *gauroth* is. I haven't collected my libraries for nothing.'

'Sorry.'

'These counsellors ... I remember them whispering advice to me, but not the details. And when did they change from people I've known all my life, from my father's time, to these strangers? I have not the faintest recollection. Oh, by the Lady, what have they done to us?'

'It seems that the Bhahdradomen are more subtle than we gave them credit for,' Helan said. 'They were blatantly playing with people's minds in Parione. Here they've done it so discreetly that we didn't even notice. It's as if they've hypnotised everyone to walk through life in a dream, seeing no threat in Vaurgroth and no need to defend themselves against him. So when the Bhahdradomen decide to take Azura Maroc they just stroll in . . .'

'Take us, easily as plucking a ripe peach from the tree!' The horror in Jedraan's eyes hardened to rage. 'Gods, this is the worst possible nightmare.'

'No, it isn't,' Helan said, taking his arm. 'You don't know how afraid I was that you were already in their power. That you might turn around and have us all killed.'

'Cousin, that is not the case.'

'It could have been,' she said softly. 'If Tanthe hadn't found out in time.'

'So,' said Mawrdreth, 'they're spies here. They're not in charge; they're hidden. That makes them vulnerable.'

The Duke began to stride along the cliff-top, towards the lapis walls of the palace. 'I'll have them arrested at once. Let them answer for themselves!'

'Be careful,' Helan said, hurrying to keep up with him. 'Make sure they're all in one place and don't let them suspect.'

Suddenly his grin was back, but with a hard and wicked

edge. 'Oh, I can be as subtle as they, cousin, have no fear.'

Tanthe had been watching the nine counsellors all morning, as Helan had asked. They moved through the hot silvery air of the court among the unveiled courtiers, cooling themselves with golden fans, talking in corners with an official here, an attendant there. There was nothing out of the ordinary in their behaviour. Yet Tanthe saw the subtle signs that marked them as non-human.

It was in the way they moved, the way they interacted with each other; inclining their heads as if exchanging wordless signals. It was in the shape of their hands. These had the normal number of fingers yet were slightly misshapen, as if the extra digits had been removed. The clues were minimal, but they were there.

When they glanced in her direction, she pretended to be absorbed in her book. She had read the same page fifteen times. She was sure they knew she suspected, or suspected she knew . . . whatever, she'd drawn their attention. This waiting was unbearable. What if the Duke was knowingly in thrall to them?

The dent in her shoulder, where the *uzrat* missile had hit, itched and burned. She felt the darkness of the *ezht* pressing on the back of her eyes.

'Tanthe, what are you looking at?' said Lahjaya, lazing beside her.

'Nothing. Keep your voice down.'

'I'm whispering, I can't keep it any lower. You're sweating. Are you ill?'

'I think my gut is about to turn into the Vermeil River, that's all.'

'You should have said, I have herbs for it . . . Or is something going on?'

'No.'

'How long have we been friends? Tell me. Perhaps I can help.'

Tanthe hissed between her teeth, trying not to move her lips. 'Please, Lahjaya, no questions now. You can help by just acting naturally, all right?'

As she spoke, there was a whisper of movement in all the entrances to the court. The Duke's guards were coming in. Only a few at first, moving casually as if nothing was amiss. By the time the courtiers began to notice the unusual number of guards, all the entrances were blocked. More guards flowed into the chamber, forming a tight semi-circular wall. A couple of Lord Sunstone's men were moving along the glass wall, calling people in from the balconies then securing the great crystal doors. Startled and puzzled, the courtiers gathered near the central fountain. The counsellors kept in a group apart, expressionless behind their veils.

The centre of the rank loosened to let through the Duke, Helan and Mawrdreth. Tanthe dropped her book and stood up with a sigh of relief. Lahjaya rose beside her, murmuring, 'What in Hellaxis is going on?'

The Duke caught Tanthe's eye and gave a tilt of his head. She went to stand with him, Lahjaya at her side. 'Check them as they pass, will you?' he said. 'Just in case.'

She realised what he meant, and nodded. Helan gave her shoulder a squeeze.

'Your attention, my dear friends,' Jedraan began, his voice clear and powerful. He smiled as always but his eyes were grim. 'The court is secure. My veiled counsellors shall remain. The rest of you, however, may leave. This way, if you will . . .'

His human courtiers stared in astonishment, not moving. He beckoned. Jumping to life they hurriedly began to make their way towards him. The rank of guards spilt to allow them through one by one. As they went, with alarmed expressions, Tanthe looked carefully at each one in turn. Unless they were utterly faultless mimics, they were all unquestionably human. No more hidden *neshrim* among them.

Soon all the human courtiers were gone. The court was clear, but for the semi-circle of guards and the knot of figures under their dull gold silks.

'Put back your veils,' said the Duke.

There was a stirring of unease among the guards. This was an unprecedented breach of court etiquette. Tanthe guessed Jedraan hadn't told anyone, even the guards, why the counsellors were being arrested.

Nine slim copper-gold faces stared impassively at the Duke. Some were more mottled than others, but they all looked similar, as if they'd modelled themselves on a single human. They'd given an impression of being distinctly male or female before but now she knew the truth, they appeared to be neither. The illusion was tarnished.

The Duke stared at them for a long, long time. They stared back. He drew a hissing breath and let it go.

'My valued advisers. I thought I knew you. Now it seems I don't. You are impostors, are you not?'

The Bhahdradomen didn't speak.

'I suggest that you are worse than impostors. That you are not even human. How do you answer this charge?'

Still they were silent. Tanthe's nervous heartbeat grew faster.

'My friends, I am giving you the chance to defend yourselves. Your silence tends to condemn you. Speak! Explain what you are doing in my court!'

The counsellors remained as statues. The guards shifted uneasily; Helan and Mawrdreth exchanged glances.

'Very well.' Jedraan's tone was fiery with controlled anger. 'If you will not deny it I can only conclude that the accusation is true. You are Bhahdradomen.'

There was a distinct ripple of consternation among the guards. Lahjaya gripped Tanthe's elbow and whispered, 'I should have seen!'

'So should we all,' said the Duke, hearing her. He raised his voice again. 'You are under arrest. You will be imprisoned and questioned until you explain how you came to be here, who sent you, and what your intentions are. Is this clear?'

'Clear,' said one of the *neshrim*. It was the one who'd unveiled himself to Tanthe.

'I have seen him before,' Helan said suddenly. 'Tanthe was right. She raised her voice. 'I saw you with Vaurgroth! Your name is . . . Rhuaaku.'

The gilt face smiled. He said, 'As Ancestor wills it, so shall it be.' Then the nine figures began to move.

'Detain them!' Jedraan barked. The guards hesitated, transfixed.

The Bhahdradomen began what seemed a bizarre dance. Expressionless, they turned to each other and clasped hands as if exchanging a signal, which was then passed to the next partner, and the next.

'Wait!' The Duke raised his hand to stay the guards. 'What are they doing?'

No-one answered.

Tanthe began to see a pattern. Some of the Eaters appeared to shrink and darken, while others grew brighter. Suddenly the first of the weaker ones fell, while its partner glowed brighter. Three more fell, lifeless as air-dried birds. Those remaining formed pairs again, one drawing all the energy, the other dying.

'They're killing themselves,' Tanthe whispered.

'No!' the Duke cried. 'Stop them!'

But it was more than that. It was as if they were concentrating all their energy. There were three left, then two, then one; Rhuaaku. He glowed with a deep light, bloodshot gold speckled with black. Throbbing with *gauroth* he turned slowly to face his captors, smiling, beautiful as a Valahyr.

'You will never know our secrets,' he said.

Tanthe caught her breath. The guards were paralysed.

'Take him!' the Duke cried hoarsely.

'No!' roared a male voice, drowning Jedraan's.

It was Mawrdreth. He rushed forward, seized the glowing

neshrim in both hands and bore him backwards across the alabaster sweep of the court. Mawrdreth skimmed streams, scattered leaves in his wake. He was running straight at a closed window.

There was a crash as Mawrdreth thrust Rhuaaku through the pane.

Glass shattered. Rhuaaku shrieked. With shards raining around him, Mawrdreth flung him out into thin air, nearly falling after him, saving himself on the frame. The *neshrim* seemed to hang in the air for a moment, poised above the sheer wall of the cliff. Then he plummeted out of sight.

Tanthe and the others rushed to the windows to see the figure still falling far below. Down the cliff-face, bouncing off the rocks, vanishing into the wild silvery waves. And just as Rhuaaku hit the sea, he appeared to explode. His energy-swollen body vaporised into a ball of gold flame. Lightning spat within the sphere. Tanthe squinted against the brilliance. Gold faded to dull red and then to wisps of smoke. The sea steamed.

Further along the chamber, Jedraan was fumbling to unlock the doors to a balcony. They crowded onto it for a better view of what had happened; but there was nothing to be seen. Only foam breaking over the red rocks.

Speechless, they came back inside. Mawrdreth stood panting for breath, his big hands bloody from the broken glass.

'I saw what they were doing,' he said. 'Passing all their energy to their leader. He was going to destroy himself and take us all with him. That fireball would have been inside this chamber.'

'Lady of Tears,' the Duke said faintly. A hush fell on them. Trembling, they moved back into the court, where the guards were in disarray. They stood to attention as Jedraan re-entered.

'Mawrdreth, you have saved all our lives,' the Duke said hoarsely. He pointed at the corpses which lay in contorted poses on the floor, no more than skin stretched on bone.

They looked far from human now. 'Get rid of these,' he told the stunned guards. 'And make very sure they are dead!'

Jedraan was in a fire of activity for days afterwards. Every member of his court and staff was examined and questioned, even those he knew well, just in case they had been replaced by a subtle *neshrim* who could weave webs of illusion with his aura. Guards went out into the city, searching for more nests of Bhahdradomen. None were found. Then the atmosphere in the palace grew calmer, but Lord Sunstone's attitude had changed.

'When I told you that I would raise no army because of Garnelys's misdeeds, I meant it,' he told Helan. 'And when you told me I was complacent, you were right. Things are different now. I believed we were impervious to the Bhahdradomen because they had somehow encouraged me to believe it. Now I have no choice. I must defend my realm against them. And you, cousin, shall have your army.'

'I'm grateful,' Helan answered. 'I know you don't give it lightly. I never asked lightly. The cost may be terrible.'

'Not as terrible as losing Aventuria to the Eaters,' he said.

'You realise, don't you,' Tanthe said to Auriel, 'that you did this? Uncovered the spies?'

'I didn't do anything,' he said, dropping his gaze.

'Oh yes, you did. Don't ever again try to tell me you're useless.'

He wouldn't answer her. It was far from false modesty, Tanthe saw with foreboding. Falthorn had given Auriel to think he was worthless, and that was the darkness that lay on him now. And I can't help, she thought, because I was part of it.

'What will happen now?' he asked.

Tanthe looked around the garden, with its melting colours and the darting jewels that were humming birds and dragonflies. It was going to be hard to leave. 'Well, the Duke will raise an army, Helan and Mawrdreth and Karmensis will help train them . . .'

'How long will that take?'

'I don't know. Months, I should imagine.' Auriel was disturbing her, closed away yet needling her with questions. 'Don't let's think about it, because we'll be here for quite a while yet.'

Eldareth hadn't returned. Tanthe missed him. He'd been a reassuring presence, a father-figure to them all. She could only give offerings to Breyid and the Blue Lady of Azura Maroc, and ask that they keep him safe, wherever he was.

She wept about it, alone at night. All that had happened pressed her down with gigantic obsidian hands. She wept for Rufryd, certain now that he'd died in Vexor. How stupid their quarrel seemed now, set against the monstrous, unbearable knowledge that she would never see him again. Petty jealousy and wounded pride, ashes.

Time passed. As Tanthe had predicted, their stay in Lapiszul was to be a long one. It was no easy matter to raise and train an army from the leisure-loving populace, but Jedraan fired them to enthusiasm. Tanthe did her share, training recruits to fight in the Shaelahyr style she'd learned in Silverholm. Lahjaya was her normal brisk self again, teaching healers.

For a year or more, it was a different life. Tanthe missed the rhythm of the seasons; here there was nothing to differentiate summer from winter but subtle changes in heat, brief delicious spells of rain. With the sameness of the climate and the endless press of activity, the months raced and blurred into a single, golden cocoon.

Tanthe sometimes meditated as Elrill had taught them, trying to unlock her Aelyr side on her own. Her efforts brought only black-smoke visions of the *ezht*, fear, chaos; not enlightenment.

They stayed at the palace as Jedraan's guests, which

made their leisure time pleasant. Jedraan took a liking to Tanthe, recognising a curious soul with an interest in learning. He found her books to read, so they could talk about them afterwards. He took her and Auriel into his museum, high on the northern cliff beneath the crystal dome.

She fell in love with these airy rooms immediately. The walls held mosaic images of Azura Maroc's deities; the nameless Blue Lady, or Lady of Tears, goddess of rain. Mahan, the turquoise god of the sea, in the form of a sea-serpent. Definyah, their daughter, ruby-eyed snake goddess of the desert, who represented wisdom. Her brother Elahjah, a beautiful youth whose body was a constellation of stars. Both were also shown in their other aspect, twin lynxes. All the lesser pantheon of star, sea, rock and weather gods.

Beautiful artefacts stood in cases around the wall; carvings of jade and jasper, amber and carnelian, precious stones she'd never seen before in intricate forms that took her breath away.

'I wish Ysomir could see this,' she said. 'She loves carving. I thought she was good, until I saw these . . . Auriel, look!' She marvelled at a tall figure of the Blue Lady cut from chalcedony, so detailed and ice-perfect she couldn't believe human hands had made it. Auriel gave it a cursory glance, then returned his attention to the plainest artefact there. It was only a ball of quartz resting on a plinth of purple velvet, yet he seemed captivated by it. The label described it as an *anametris* sphere, believed to be seven hundred years old.

'Aelyr device,' said Jedraan. 'Pretty thing, isn't it? Would you like to go above and look at the view?'

Tanthe followed the Duke up a fragile staircase and onto a gallery that ran round the inside of the crystal dome. There were telescopes mounted at intervals. An observatory.

'It's best at night, when we observe the stars. Our

astronomers have been mapping the heavens for thousands of years. But come, the views are nice by day, too.'

Tanthe pressed her eye to the brass cup of a great telescope that faced out to sea. This reminded her of Lady Amitriya, the eccentric sister of the Duke of Sepheret. Eccentric? She'd been the only sane one in the family. How long ago it seemed now.

She glimpsed something out on the sea. A greyish tower, impossibly tall. It seemed to flicker and move about as she watched. Inexplicably, the sight filled her with dread, a nightmarish nebulous fear, the feeling of the *ezht*. She heard her mother's voice saying, 'Please don't tell me you are in the dark spire!'

She caught a sharp breath and jerked away.

'What is it?' asked Jedraan.

'What's that – that dark tower I can see out there? A lighthouse?'

The Duke put his eye to the brass cup for a time, then said, 'There's nothing there, Tanthe.'

Nervously she looked again. He was right. The ocean glittered pure and empty. Cold sweat ran down her spine and she felt vaguely ill. 'Great, I'm seeing things.'

Jedraan studied her, rubbing his chin. 'Our mystics hold visions in high regard. The Bhahdradomen are the ones with all the legends about a dark tower. I'll try to find the reference for you.'

She didn't know whether to be pleased or alarmed that he'd taken her seriously.

As they descended into the museum again, Auriel was still in the same place, gazing at the sphere on its velvet nest. She left him and went with Jedraan to the library, where he placed a thick, dust-scented volume in her hands.

It fell open and she found herself staring at an etching in fine black lines; a dark spire, sweeping from a broad base to a thin tip. A slight widening near the summit. It was on dry land, not the ocean, but otherwise it was an exact representation of what she'd seen. Elegant, sinister, enigmatic.

The caption read, 'The Obsidian Tower'.

There were many such interludes, relief from the tedium of training, the discomfort of sweat, dust and bruises. Sweet, cool escape. To Tanthe, their stay in Lapiszul had seemed eternal and dream-like. Then, suddenly, it was nearly over.

'We're leaving in a few days,' said Tanthe. She'd found Auriel in his room as usual, sitting at the desk Jedraan had given him. He looked for all the world like a Marocian scholar. His lovely brown eyes always seemed dark with preoccupation these days. She couldn't believe how long they'd been in Lapiszul. Time had flown. And soon they had a tedious march of months ahead of them again.

'Do you really have to go?' he asked.

He'd made it obvious he meant to stay in Lapiszul. No surprise, but she was disappointed. Relieved that he wouldn't be fighting, but still sad they had to part. Perhaps for the last time, if she didn't survive.

'Do you mean you'd miss me?'

'Well, of course,' he said. He looked upset. Tanthe felt awkward. 'I'd rather you stayed here. I feel safe with you here.'

'Auriel, don't.' She shook her head. 'Of course I have to go. I can't let Helan down. I must do my bit to fight the Bhahdradomen.'

'It's not really our war, is it?' he said softly.

'Not the Aelyr's, you mean? But I don't feel Aelyr. You decided – okay, we *both* decided – that it was a bad idea to explore, so don't blame me if I still feel human.'

He coloured. She went on, unable to hide how upset she was. 'You're staying here, I take it?'

'I have work to do.'

Tanthe laughed. 'What work?' Auriel didn't answer, but he looked suddenly, silently furious.

'I don't want you to go and get killed,' he said thinly.

'Well, you know what? I don't want you to get killed, either. I'm glad you're staying, Auriel. You'll be out of harm's way, at least.'

'It's not because I'm afraid,' he retorted.

'I didn't say you were.' She sat on the edge of the desk, unable to say goodbye to him. This was horrible. She always seemed to be saying goodbye to people she loved, with no hope of seeing them again. The thought of going voluntarily to fight the Bhahdradomen made her sick with dread, but it was the only choice she could make.

Tanthe noticed something shiny, not very well hidden under the cover of an open book. She closed the book and revealed a clear white sphere; several spheres, rather, one inside another, the divisions showing like the rainbow shells of bubbles.

'That looks exactly like the *anametris* in Duke's collection,' she said lightly.

Auriel met her gaze, looking guilty but defiant. 'You won't tell him, will you?'

'Auriel, did you take it?'

'Borrowed.'

'He'll go mad if he finds out! You seem to have an unfortunate habit of stealing things, don't you?'

'That's not fair. I only took the *mnelir* from Falthorn to help you.'

'Still, you can't just nick things wherever you go! What do you want with it, anyway? Or are you turning into a jackdaw?'

His eyes burned. She wasn't sure what had upset him more; telling him she was leaving, or accusing him of dishonesty. 'Ever since I set foot on Earth I've been useless. Well, now I'm trying to change – and all you can do is mock me for it? I don't want anyone's thanks, but I thought I might get some trust from my sister, at least.'

She drew back, her mouth turned down. 'Sorry. But

what *are* you doing? I know what these spheres are for. You're not trying to go back to Verdanholm, are you?'

'No, no!' He reached out and wrapped his long fingers round hers. 'It's much more than that.' She saw that the piece of paper in front of him was covered in odd diagrams; circles connected by lines, symbols she didn't recognise. Seeing her looking, he immediately covered it up. 'I don't know my Aelyr nature any better than you do. There's no miracle way to open it.'

'Not even making love?'

His eyes softened. 'We each have to find our own way, Fliyet.'

'Whatever you're doing, I hope it works.' She slid off the table and onto his knee. They held each other and she felt the strong, silken warmth of his body. They kissed.

'Don't go, Fliyet, please,' he said into her hair.

'I have to,' she said.

In Verdanholm, even the rain was different from that of Earth, fine and silvery, full of light and dancing with tiny elementals. Jthery could see them clearly. When he opened his hearing to them, they carried distant conversations to him.

Falthorn had a visitor.

Down in the garden, soaked to the skin, Jthery lifted his head and shivered. The elementals carried faint images of a flickering blue light, one perfect image in each raindrop. The *rothanamir* portal that stood on the far side of the house was active. The water conveyed the pulse of *roth* power and then a darker energy. The metal and blood taint of *gauroth*.

He heard Falthorn's voice, light and friendly, and then rounder tones answering, melodious yet laced with menace.

Vaurgroth.

The voices stopped. They'd gone inside the house.

Jthery ran up one of the spidery staircases that led from

the garden to the balconies above. Rain pattered on the leafy canopy above him as he crept along the balcony and peered through the lacework of leaves into the chamber beyond.

In the large, light room of silver-gold wood, Falthorn and Vaurgroth were facing each other with false smiles. Falthorn had a retinue of Valahyr behind him, while his parents and other members of his extensive family watched from the gallery above. He looked graceful and subtle, a contrast to Vaurgroth who was a garish figure in scarlet. He put Jthery in mind of a scorpion, the colour of blood and milk. Both he and Falthorn were replete with power and unshakeable confidence. A knot of *vagharim* stood behind Vaurgroth, the belts of their black and dark-green tunics bristling with weapons.

In contrast to the Bhahdradomen, Falthorn looked so elegant, dark hair flowing over the ebony of his robes, that Jthery's heart dissolved. My soul is nailed to him, he thought. He cannot do anything wicked enough to make me leave. I wonder if I'm going mad?

'It is most gracious of you to visit us, my lord,' Falthorn was saying.

'It is no trouble, Lord Falthorn. The *rothanamir* link between us is most convenient.'

'Indeed,' said Falthorn. 'Too convenient, some might say.'

There was a pause. The two leaders looked coolly at each other. Vaurgroth gave a minimal dip of his head, a tiny gesture of concession. 'I understand you have a complaint, my friend?'

'Complaint? I simply wish to point out that the Bhahdradomen are perilously close to breaching our agreement. One of your *aghramen* was caught, trying to steal the Basilisks of Calabethron.'

'This matter has been brought to my attention,' Vaurgroth said, his smile fixed. 'That is why I came here in person to reassure you that this unfortunate incident will not be repeated. Nor did it take place at my instigation.'

'Really?' Falthorn gave a quick laugh of surprise. 'Do you not have full control of your people?'

'I have absolute control of them, naturally. Alas, a small element sought to please me by acting on their own initiative. They thought they were helping our cause; and I must point out that they were only attempting to locate the weapons, not to steal them.'

'I wonder if they were rewarded or punished for their initiative?'

Vaurgroth looked at him with narrow, ruby eyes. 'One of them was killed by you. Empowerer Grahzamen was deeply distressed to lose a good *aghramen*.'

'One was killed, which is regrettable, but he attacked a member of my family. We know there were others, who fled.'

Jthery thought in amazement, does he consider me a member of his family now?

'They have been disciplined.'

'So, you are telling me that there was no official plot to steal the Basilisks? Our agreement stands?'

'Our agreement stands, my friend,' said Vaurgroth, nodding slowly.

'I'm glad to hear it.'

'However, since we are talking of threats to our treaty, you should look to yourself before you accuse us.'

Jthery felt himself becoming so tense his jaw ached. The flat stink of *gauroth*, Vaurgroth's deadly power and his appearance and everything about him was making him feel sick with dread. What if he got the better of Falthorn, had some vile trick up his sleeve?

'Meaning?'

'It was part of our agreement, was it not, that while the weapons are peace-bonded here, we should be allowed to inspect them at regular intervals. So far the first inspection has not taken place. You keep finding reasons to put it off.'

'Not at all. But surely the inspection is only necessary if you don't trust me.'

Vaurgroth's hairless eyebrows rose. 'It has nothing to do with trust. It was in our treaty that I might see the weapons, and since I am here with my *vagharim*, what better time to do it than now? You've no reason to deny me, surely?'

Falthorn's face took on the iced-granite look that masked fury. Jthery had learned to read him quite well. Then he seemed to relax, and opened his hands. 'Very well. On the condition that you come with me and my Valahyr alone. Unless, of course, you are afraid to do so.'

Some of Vaurgroth's retinue began to mutter in alarm. Turning to them, the Bhahdradomen leader spoke with them in their own language. Then he turned back to Falthorn.

'I have no fear of being alone with a good friend. My *vagharim* will wait for me at the portal. Lead on.'

As they left the room, Jthery slithered quickly down to ground level again. Presently Falthorn and Vaurgroth appeared at the edge of the garden, with a handful of Valahyr a few yards behind them. The two walked together like old friends out for a stroll.

Jthery waited for them to pass. Then he began to follow.

The rain had stopped, leaving the landscape saturated and gleaming. The wet clothes clinging to his skin connected him to the moisture lying on every leaf and grass blade. Verdanholm felt eerier than ever. Time passed strangely here, rushing forward, turning in little loops, standing still. Jthery had no idea how long he'd been here; if he returned to Earth to find a hundred years had passed, he wouldn't be at all surprised.

Falthorn took Vaurgroth beyond the garden, up a sloping hill and across meadows to the lake where Jthery liked to swim. They went to the head of the lake, Jthery slipping alongside them behind the cover of trees and bushes. There Falthorn told his guards to wait; he and Vaurgroth were going to view the weapons alone.

Hiding behind bushes and rocks, Jthery got past the guards and slipped into the narrow passageway that led into the cave. Falthorn and Vaurgroth were some yards in front of him. He clung to the rough wall, trying to keep out of their sight; but if they turned and saw him, so what? It would be Falthorn's responsibility to punish him, and Falthorn, Jthery felt, had already done his worst.

It wasn't the danger of being caught that frightened Jthery. It was everything else. The nature of the weapons. The ghastly tension that snarled and sparked between the two leaders. What Vaurgroth might do.

The passage led to a cavern which was filled with a greenish, dappled light. Its floor was flooded with a small oval lake, and in the centre of the lake rose a little island of blue rock. On the island stood a chest, bound with bright metal and glowing with an electric-white, crackling *roth*. The water was full of this light. It reflected ripples across the ceiling.

'There they are,' said Falthorn. 'The Basilisks.'

Vaurgroth's reaction surprised Jthery. He stopped well short of the lake's edge and seemed to draw back in distaste. 'All I see is a chest. What proof do I have that there's anything inside?'

Falthorn laughed. 'If you don't mind swimming, I'll show you everything you need to see.'

'Swimming?' Vaurgroth said in outright disgust. 'Are you insane?'

'Ah, I had forgotten how much the Bhahdradomen loathe water. Forgive me.'

'We do not loathe water. I thought you might at least keep a boat to avoid such ridiculous inconvenience.'

'I would, but a boat might provide too much of a temptation to the curious,' Falthorn replied softly. 'I wouldn't want the unwary to injure or kill themselves. The weapons are bonded with powerful *liroth*, as you can tell.'

Vaurgroth looked sour. 'This is a waste of time. You can't show me anything!'

'On the contrary, it's no inconvenience to me.'

Cheerfully, Falthorn threw off his loose black coat and blue robe and stood before Vaurgroth stark naked. Jthery gasped, putting his hand to his mouth to stop a laugh exploding from his throat. Vaurgroth looked thunderstruck.

Gods, what a shame his *vagharim* can't see his face! Jthery thought. What unbelievable bravado for Falthorn to make himself so vulnerable to a powerful enemy . . .

'If you would be patient, my lord,' Falthorn said, in a mockery of deference. He stepped into the lake and swam swiftly across to the island. Levering himself half out of the water, he made a few deft passes over the lid of the chest. The glow dimmed. Then he threw open the lid, and a brilliant white light spilled out. 'Behold, the Basilisks of Calabethron!'

Vaurgroth cursed, and turned away, shielding his eyes. Jthery started. He pressed himself back into the recess so the Bhahdradomen leader wouldn't see him.

'Enough!' Vaurgroth cried.

Falthorn closed the chest. He swam back, rose unhurriedly out of the water, and drew his garments back onto his gleaming, wet body without any sign of cold or discomfort. 'Don't you want to see each weapon individually?'

'I take your word for it that they are all there.' Vaurgroth folded his arms, adopting an arrogant posture.

'You could tell,' Falthorn said, his tone low. 'You're a great mage. You see through things.'

'Yes. I know the Basilisks are there. You didn't lie.'

'This seems to have disturbed you. I apologise.'

'I am not disturbed. Merely reminded that these obscenities destroyed my people and condemned them to miserable exile for two hundred and fifty years. It can never be allowed to happen again!'

'I agree,' said Falthorn. 'That's why they are here, with a promise that they will never be used, as long as the Bhahdradomen stay out of Verdanholm.'

Vaurgroth almost seemed to tremble, his eyes – or the one Jthery could see in profile – tiny blood drops. Red sparks crackled around him.

'And what of the other threat you made?'

'What threat would that be?' Falthorn asked, squeezing water out of his hair.

'Your story of a living Basilisk, a *roth*-mage so dangerous that it would not merely defeat us but annihilate us. Where is it?'

'My friend, it is but a child.' Falthorn's voice was low and patient.

'A child? Let me see it – if it exists.'

'It exists. It isn't here.'

'And where would you hide such a creature? The College of the Mediators?'

'Somewhere safe.'

'It seems to me,' said Vaurgroth, 'that for as long as you hold the Basilisks, it might be as well for you to put this child into our hands, a hostage to ensure your good will.'

Jthery gasped, but Falthorn answered smoothly, 'I'm considering it, if I can be sure you will not mistreat it.'

'We are not monsters. We cherish our hatchlings.'

'Mm. Especially the ones you send for meat, no doubt.'

For a terrible moment, Vaurgroth looked ready to kill Falthorn. 'Words, my lord. I dismiss this threat with the contempt it deserves – unless you show me clear proof.'

'That's not on today's agenda. Let us go back to the house and I'll escort you to the *rothanamir*. You must be eager to return to the Sapphire Throne before one of your underlings parks himself on it.'

'Don't think to mock us, Falthorn.' Vaurgroth pointed with a clawed hand; Jthery noticed how oddly-shaped the seven digits were, the thumb and first finger long and bony, the others increasingly stunted until the last two were hardly more than stumps. 'We are stronger than you know, with powers you can't imagine. This impasse is not eternal. I *will* have that child, and the Basilisks too. Verdanholm is safe . . . only for as long as Ancestor wills it.'

'I'll try to forget you made that threat,' Falthorn replied. 'It's only good manners to pretend not to notice that a guest is making a fool of himself.'

Vaurgroth laughed horribly. 'Perhaps I am a fool. It's safer than being too clever for my own good.'

Falthorn held out his hand, ushering Vaurgroth along the passageway. 'After you, Lord of Light.'

Later, when Vaurgroth and his retinue had taken their grim leave, Falthorn put his arm round Jthery's shoulders and said, 'Beloved friend, you are incorrigible.'

'What – what do you mean?' Jthery was alarmed. Falthorn could turn from nectar to poison in a moment.

'Following us this afternoon. Yes, I knew you were there. Why?'

'I – I was afraid for you, being alone with that—'

'How sweet,' Falthorn said, kissing his cheek. 'I'm glad you were there to witness it.'

'It was quite entertaining,' Jthery said, daring to smile. 'Especially the swimming part.'

'I enjoyed that. Do you know that the Eaters hate to be reminded that the Aelyr, like humans, are sexual beings? They hate it because they are jealous of us.'

'So that's why Vaurgroth looked so horrified?'

'And it had the added benefit, I hope, of whetting your appetite. Come to my room, Jey. The water in that lake was freezing. I need you to warm me.'

Falthorn smiled. Jthery could never resist him.

'You were heroic today,' Jthery whispered as they embraced and wrestled each other towards bliss, their bodies washed in the moist silvery light of Verdanholm's evening.

'Heroic? I don't think anyone's ever called me that before.'

'Nonsense. The Valahyr all see you as a hero for saving Verdanholm.'

'But how many times have I got to save it,' he said, his breath hot and fast on Jthery's neck, 'before it is truly safe for all time? They won't keep the agreement. It's already broken. Liars. But, a hero; I like that. I love it.'

When they lay apart, the sweat of passion cooling on their outstretched bodies, Jthery asked, 'Why did you refuse to let him see the child?'

'Because it isn't here.'

'Where is it, then?'

'Safe,' said Falthorn. He turned on his side and rested his arm across Jthery's chest. 'So many questions.'

'This is Tanthe's child you're talking about? Do you always call the child "it"?'

'"He," then. Safer to think of Mendyr as a commodity, then sentimentality can't take hold.'

'That's cold. How can you be so passionate, and then so cold?'

'I can be anything I need to be, dear,' Falthorn said. He closed his eyes, but Jthery stared at the rain-light on the ceiling. It reminded him of the light in the cave.

'You wouldn't really give the boy to Vaurgroth as a hostage, would you?'

'No, but I have to keep them guessing.'

'What will you do if Vaurgroth does attack you?'

'He won't,' Falthorn said sleepily. 'He's probably planning to. He must be sick to death of my insolence by now. But he'll be too late.'

'Will you use the Basilisks against him?'

'Oh, Jthery. Nothing so unsubtle. This is where you come in, you see. Why do you think I've been training you all these months? Or rather, letting you train yourself. You're completely at one with your element now.'

'Thanks,' said Jthery. 'I had to occupy my time somehow. Are you saying it was all part of your great plan?'

'Of course.' He ran his hand over Jthery's flank. 'You're a

roth-mage and don't even realise it. Naturally you've taught yourself better than I ever could. A natural, as she was.'

'Falthorn, what are you talking about?'

'Hush. Relax.' Falthorn stroked his hair, smiling. 'It will be beautiful. Remember what we did in the waterfall? Verdanholm needs energy, pure energy, Jewelfire, the fabric of the universe. The purest carrier of energy is water, is it not? Now you have the skills to make waters flow from one realm into another. You can charge the waters of Earth with *roth* and make them flow back into Verdanholm. That's the great thing we shall achieve together.'

'To what end?'

'To heal Verdanholm, of course. To repair the damage caused by the Eaters. To give us bountiful raw material so that we can go on endlessly creating and expanding our realm. The eternal creation of beauty.'

'So you're going to take energy from Earth to do that? *Steal* it?'

'Exactly. Thus solving all our problems. For as Verdanholm grows ever greater and stronger, so Earth will wither away. No more humans, no more Bhahdradomen to trouble us. Peace, Jey,' Falthorn sighed, falling asleep on his shoulder. 'Peace.'

Chapter Eighteen. Defiance

Jthery ran.

He'd left Falthorn sound asleep, seemingly exhausted by their love-making. In a cloud of panic and fear, he'd seized his old travelling clothes, quickly dressed on the balcony outside the room, then climbed down the living struts of the house into the garden. It wasn't hard to escape the house, and the Valahyr guards were all on the other side, watching the *rothanamir* portal.

He ran up through the garden he'd loved so much, breathless more from fear than exertion. At the top, between the golden-leaved trees and the flowered hedge of the field where the horses grazed, he stopped.

What am I to do? he thought. Falthorn means to steal the life out of Earth until it withers and dies, using me to do it? And, Eshte's eyes, he trusts me, thinks I'm so in his thrall I won't even argue? *What in cursed Hellaxis am I going to do?*

Jthery felt the breath shoot out of him as if he'd been kicked in the gut. Anguish, denial, cruel light of revelation; made worse because he could never claim this had come out of the blue.

This is all he wanted me for. *All along, this is all he ever wanted me for!*

The only possible course of action shone before him, bright and terrifying. He was frantic, yet his mind was clear. Pain stripped his thoughts down to acid clarity.

He thought of taking a horse, decided it would be easier without. He'd grabbed his old travelling pack but there was nothing in it, except an item he'd impulsively taken from among Falthorn's belongings. Food was the least of his concerns. He set off, tramping up the hill and across the rising meadows in silver-blue starlight. The night seemed as bright as day; Jthery felt he must be visible from miles around. A weird exhilaration took him and he laughed and wept. This was utterly insane. He was bound to be caught. He would probably be killed. But what did it matter? Falthorn had betrayed him. And all along, with wide-open eyes he had known this would happen and yet he'd still fallen for it.

I should have killed him, Jthery thought wretchedly. Found a knife and stabbed him where he lay. But I couldn't.

He reached the head of the lake and entered the narrow passage through the rock. It was dark at first and he felt his way along the wall. Then the glow grew and he could see clearly. He was staring at the mirror surface of the lake, and in the centre, the chest that contained the Basilisks of Calabethron, glowing bright and dangerous.

Jthery swallowed. He thought, is Falthorn complacent or confident, having no guards on this place? Maybe there are guards hidden, watching me. Or maybe the *liroth* around the chest is so deadly he doesn't need any other protection . . .

This is crazy. I'm going to touch the chest and be killed. He'll find me floating dead in the water and go mad . . . but then, at least then he will not be able to use me!

Jthery stripped off and slung the empty pack onto his shoulders. He waded into the lake.

No, wait. Wait, he told himself, as if his Goddess, Eshte, had spoken to him. *You aren't powerless. You have* roth *of your own*.

The surface began to move around him. Using his will to summon it, his hands to shape it, he surrounded himself in a shell of whirling, gleaming water. He swam to the island and hoisted himself onto the little table of rock with the water still coruscating over him, a shield.

The chest crackled menacingly. He stared at it, heart pounding. Between the silver strips there were panels of blue enamel, studded with jewels, the blueness hardly visible through the glare of *liroth*. Was his own power enough to protect him from Falthorn's? He remembered how Falthorn had moved his hands over the lid, pressing certain key points to dim the energy; the sequence had imprinted itself on his memory. But to do that he had to touch the chest . . .

Or . . .

He sent a finger of water pouring down on the chest, onto the point where Falthorn had first touched it. The chest fizzed angrily. He jumped. He felt the energy trying to leap into him through the water but he pushed it back, using the water's own muscular energy to deflect the *liroth*.

He formed another finger of water, and another. He held his breath. He could make the water twist into any shape, just by willing it. A ghostly hand took shape, moving lightly over the lid like an Aelyr hand over a musical instrument.

The glow dimmed. Shaking, Jthery reached out and lifted the lid. White light dazzled him. He tensed . . .

Nothing happened. There was no blast of energy. It was only light.

He found himself looking through the glow at five strangely formed objects. They looked nothing like weapons and were surprisingly small; he could have held each one across his two outstretched hands. Each was made of shiny white metal, inscribed with strange symbols and inset with small spheres of crystal and other jewels. A disc, a rod, a cube, a pyramid, and a horn that looked like a musical instrument.

Jthery forgot his fear and regarded the Basilisks in wonder. Magical objects. No, not magical, but made with a knowledge and arcane skill he couldn't imagine. Shaking, he began to lift them one by one out of the chest and place them into the bag. They felt cold, weird and heavy for their size; but he touched them without harm.

I'm a thief, he thought, smiling. Now Falthorn will know how Helan felt when she found the Basilisks missing!

He closed the lid. He wasn't sure how to bring the *liroth* shield back to life, so left it. The swim back was arduous, a struggle to keep the bag clear of the water while the weapons were a sack of rocks threatening drag him under. Panting for breath, arms aching, he hauled himself and his burden onto the rock-bank. There he wiped the worst of the water off himself with his jacket, got dressed, and hurried to the entrance.

Now, he thought, hands shaking as he strapped the lumpy sack onto his shoulders. Somehow I have to get back to Aventuria.

His mouth was dry. He considered the possibilities. The sheer audacity and hopelessness of what he intended to do stunned him. The *rothanamir* near the house led into the Heliodor Tower in Parione . . . but that way would be impossible. It was guarded on both sides; even if he managed to slip past the Valahyr, surely the Bhahdradomen in Parione would arrest him the moment he appeared? And, of course, the portal was not always active. It had to be opened . . . and Jthery had no means of opening it.

Or there was the portal he'd first come through with Elrill, Eldareth and Tanthe. It lay west of here . . . or was it east? That direction, anyway, he thought, looking towards the distant slopes of silvery grass and forested canyons that were ghostly grey in the night. Too far, even if he could find it again. They said the geography of Verdanholm shifted of its own volition, so it could never be accurately mapped. Even if he did find that stump of rock in the long grass, again he didn't know how to unlock it.

He fingered the corner of his pack, feeling the hard round shape through the canvas. It was the blue *anametris* sphere he'd taken from Falthorn's room. The thought of what he must do made his mouth dry with fear, but there was no alternative.

He began to walk fast, as close to a run as he could manage under the weight of the Basilisks. His shirt clung to him with dampness and his own sweat. His throat was parched.

'Goddess, what am I doing?' he muttered, remembering Falthorn's warning. *Not a good portal. A rabbit warren. You'd end up in a river* . . . 'Eshte, please be with me.'

He found the thin path lined with stones nestling in the grass. They seemed to watch him. He couldn't believe he'd reach the glade before Falthorn knew the Basilisks had gone. He had so many secret skills; Jthery was certain he had ways to observe events from a distance. His shoulderblades prickled with the anticipation of pursuit. Hoofbeats, voices, an arrow piercing him . . .

There was only the background hiss of the stars.

But if I do succeed, will I be condemning Verdanholm to destruction instead? How can I make this decision? I'll never get away with it. They'll catch me, then the decision will be out of my hands and it won't be my fault, but at least I will have tried, *tried* to save Earth.

And Falthorn will punish me and force me to help him anyway . . .

His fear writhed into terror. He'd betrayed Falthorn. Now all he could expect at his lover's hands was torment.

He found the place; the moist, cupped glade and the waterfall gushing in a sheet of jade down the lazurite wall. The water soothed him. He fumbled the sphere from his pack and weighed it in his palm. Fully clothed he jumped into the basin and began to wade towards the shadow that lay between the divided veil of the waterfall.

He spoke softly, calling Eshte and her elementals to help him.

Jthery felt the trance of power come upon him. He felt the currents and eddies of the stream as if it were flowing through his own veins. He reached the rock-face, gasping at the force of the falls dropping on either side of him. Began to weave and turn the *anametris* on the air, forcing himself to ignore his nerves and concentrate . . .

He felt the orb pull, dip, slide into place. The damp mossy wall was gone. He was looking into a gaping black tunnel. Icy mist breathed from it.

Trembling with cold, exertion and the worst terror he'd ever experienced, Jthery took one step after another through the roiling water. His feet found thin air. The dark tunnel sucked him in and he fell.

All the silvery lights of Verdanholm vanished. He landed with a crash in dark, fast-flowing water.

For a few moments all was choking confusion. He was neither floating nor sinking but falling in a torrent of water-*roth*.

This isn't Earth, he thought in panic. Not Earth. It was some other wild place where a hundred rushing streams of water met, branched, parted ways again and rushed off into a mysterious blue darkness in which there was no sky or ground, no reference point at all.

This was the nothingness between worlds that Falthorn had warned him about. Where all was pure *anaroth*, and all paths led everywhere and nowhere. And he was lost, drowning, being carried away in a dark swirling stream towards an infinite abyss.

Ysomir's days all ran into one, hidden in Eander's house. It was like being in prison again, she thought, only with a better view.

Amid the rich orchards below her window, she watched a herd of *graukhim* moving day by day. Dark scars began to appear, claw-wounds gouged in the grass. Leaves were stripped from the trees overnight, and now their fruit would never come. Death spread in merging cells. The great pale cattle chewed even the bark from the trunks, sucked the sap and ate the wood itself. The land sickened but the *graukhim* grew sleek and muscular. Sometimes, as they chewed, they looked up at the house with beady, expressionless eyes. Ysomir would stare back at them, wondering what they knew.

Viananthe, Eander's mother, sometimes wept at the devastation. Ysomir wished she wouldn't; it made her want to cry too and the pain of tears was too much to bear. It was easier to be alone, to close the curtains and lose herself in reading a book or writing down her thoughts. Trying to distract her mind from the chill anticipation of a visit from Zhoaah; half wanting to see him, half dreading it.

The house lay under a cloud of stoical tension. Ysomir could find no way to tell them that they were safe. If they knew about Zhoaah they would be horrified. Besides, she didn't fully trust him. If it suited him one day to betray them, he would.

Saphaeyender seemed to be suffering the most from their captivity. He was unfailingly gracious to Eander's family, but his face was shadowed with preoccupation and he was like a caged lynx. Ysomir noticed he was spending more and more time locked in his own chamber. Every day Eander would come in and spend hours talking to her, mostly about Saphaeyender.

'I'm worried about him,' he said. 'He locks himself away, not wanting to see anyone. Today he wouldn't even see me. It's as if I irritate him; I'm sure if we weren't trapped here, he'd be long gone. I can't stand this, Ymmi. If he doesn't want me, I don't know what I shall do.'

'Don't upset yourself,' she said gently. 'None of us can help it. Do you want me to go and speak to him?'

'Would you?' Eander said, looking at with desperately hopeful blue eyes. 'I'd be so grateful.'

She smiled. She liked Eander; he was gentle, as Lynden had been.

Ysomir left her small room and went along the narrow white corridor to the door at the end, Saphaeyender's chamber. The rooms in which they'd taken refuge were usually occupied by the household staff, isolated from the main body of the house. There were escape routes onto the hill beneath, in case the Bhahdradomen came searching.

She tapped on the door and said, 'Saph? It's me.'

There was a pause, then the poet opened the door and looked out with a weary, half-annoyed smile.

'Can I talk to you?'

'Er . . .' He ran his hand through his tangled hair. 'Of course, Ymmi. Come in.'

His room, like hers, was airy with simple white furnishings and touches of gold. His had a full-sized desk that was covered in disarrayed manuscripts. Every sheet, she noticed, was covered in energetic writing.

'We hardly see you these days,' she said, sitting on the edge of the bed.

Saphaeyender gave a vague smile, and spread his hands. 'I'm working.'

'That's wonderful, but . . .'

He sat down beside her and briefly clasped her shoulders. 'It's more than wonderful, Ymmi. It's an utter miracle.'

'More important than seeing your friends?'

He stood up, pushing his hair back again. He was restless, almost agitated. 'I'm sorry, but when I'm working it's almost impossible to think about anything else.'

'That's a shame, because some of us are still thinking about you.'

'You've come in here to lecture me. My dear, isn't it enough that you saved my life, without telling me how to live it as well?' She stared at him, shocked. He added, 'I never promised to be a good companion. It's nothing personal, but any of my old friends will tell you that I am no company at all when I'm busy. Don't be offended.'

'I'm not offended,' Ysomir said evenly. 'If I'd come here on my own behalf, I would have walked out by now. It's your lover you're upsetting, not me.'

He sighed; irritated, as Eander had suggested. 'So he asked you to come.'

'I'm worried about him.'

'There's no need. He knows I hate being disturbed when I'm at this stage.'

'No, he doesn't. He thinks you don't love him any more.'

Saphaeyender turned away. He said, '*Fuck*,' under his breath. Then he turned back and came slowly to Ysomir.

'The thing is, I . . . I'm fond of him, very fond. But he wasn't . . . I was lonely, Ymmi.'

'Missing Tanthe so much that you never mention her?'

Colour rose in his cheeks. 'You don't understand. You think I don't care. But it's because I do care that I can't stand to keep talking about . . . everything.'

'But if there's bad news, it will come whether we talk about it or not. And you can't raise the courage to tell Eander that it's over between you?'

'You've got a mind like one of Foul-gross's bloody *roth-swords*,' he said. 'It's like being impaled on a steel pin, talking to you.'

'You must tell him. You're hurting him.'

'How can I, when we're stuck in his parents' house together? Gods.'

'You can't expect me to tell him.'

'Don't tell him anything, Ymmi! Just say I'm busy.'

'But he will ask me what you said, Saph. I'm not going to lie.'

His handsome face frozen – almost gaunt, she thought – he went back to his desk. 'I don't mean to hurt anyone,' he said, 'but kindly remember that it is your fault I am still alive and thus causing you this annoyance. All I have to cling to is the fact that I can write again and there is so much, so much to write about! Don't you see, it's the only thing worth staying alive for! The only thing that gives me the remotest thread of hope for the future, while those mottled bastards cavort on the ruins of my theatre!'

She stiffened against his outburst. 'I know you're in pain. We all are. But don't you ever dare expect me to apologise for saving your life!'

'Sorry, Ymmi. I don't. You did what you thought best. All the same, it's hellishly more difficult being alive than dead.'

'Worth it, surely, as long as a good play comes out of it?' she said acidly.

'Oh, half a dozen plays. Classics. So, I implore you,

leave me to write. It's as good as letting blood out, don't you see?'

'Good. I understand.' With a grim smile she walked to the door, only to start as someone knocked.

Saphaeyender swore. 'Now what?'

Ysomir opened it. There stood Viananthe, and at her side another woman who looked dishevelled and worn out, the tell-tale scars of *sten* wounds on her forehead.

'We have a visitor,' said Viananthe. 'She wants to talk to you, Lord Saphaeyender.'

It took Ysomir a moment to recognise the woman. Then she realised it was Ariolne, the high priestess of Nuth.

She was in ordinary clothes – a grey long-sleeved robe over a plain blue dress of wool – and her hair was tied back. She was dressed like an artisan, but she still looked every inch the priestess. Nothing could diminish the authority of her features, the fierce eyes and hawkish nose. She had the look of an eagle in flight.

'Gods, we feared you were dead, good Mother,' said Saphaeyender. 'That first time in the temple, when the Eaters seized you . . .'

'Oh, they only beat me a little,' she said, striding in. She spoke matter-of-factly but Ysomir heard the strain in her voice. 'Then they placed all my priests and priestesses under house arrest in the temple. We were forced to witness Vaurgroth's minions turning it over to worship of their Ancestor. The clergy of Nuth can't be taken in by such delusions and we held out for all this time – until I realised that only by *pretending* to convert would we be released. So that's what we did. And here I am.'

She sat down on the edge of Saphaeyender's bed. A frown creased the high forehead. 'Ah, the humiliation was terrible. Vaurgroth is a subtle master of it. Still, at least it bought us our freedom.'

Saphaeyender looked at her. He swallowed, as if he had to force the words out. 'How are things in the city?'

'Bad,' said Ariolne. 'Terrible, and getting worse. People

usurped from their homes and sleeping on the streets until they are sent to the quarries. Those who've lost their minds to the Ancestor are at the throats of those who won't give up the old ways. Some try to carry on as usual with crafting and trading, and Vaurgroth holds them up as an example of human–Bhahdradomen co-operation! Tchah.'

'They're still working on the Heliodor Tower?' Ysomir asked warily. Helan had once brought Ariolne to visit her in her cell. She was in awe of her.

'It's rumoured that it's being constructed as some kind of offering to the Ancestor. A reconstruction of some sacred monument that stood in their own land, thousands of years ago. Even that this new tower will somehow call the old tower into being again.'

'Ah,' Saphaeyender put in. 'Sympathetic magic. Superstition.'

'I'm not sure,' Ariolne said thoughtfully. 'There's tremendous power in the Heliodor Tower. According to the Aelyr, the mysterious forces and realms around us, although they may not be tangible, are real enough to make superstition and religion unnecessary.'

'And you a priestess,' said the poet.

She glowered at him. 'You know Nuth deals in reality. It is reality we hold sacred, not false comfort. Now our reality is that we face starvation. *Graukhim* tear up our farmland. Vaurgroth's "mercy" is a foul lie. Ancestor-worship is a drug to keep them servile with false hope. I think that within a few years, Parione will be left a skeleton city, while the Bhahdradomen move onto the next rich pasture.'

Saphaeyender pushed at the papers on his desk. 'All this for nothing, then! There'll be no one left to give a fuck about literature.'

Ariolne sat forward and pinned him with her raptor eyes. 'It's not too late. My lord, there are rumours about you. It's said they found your house awash with blood, but no corpse. Many think you are dead, but I knew you weren't.'

Saphaeyender lifted his eyebrows. 'Nuth gives you privileged information, good Mother?'

'Call it common sense. If there was no body, there was a possibility you had left on your feet.'

'True.' He glanced at Ysomir, and they exchanged a smile.

'We need your help. Your eloquence, Saphaeyender, while we still have time. I need you to write pamphlets to be distributed secretly among the populace.'

'Saying what?'

'Something to give them hope, to let them know there's still a resistance. To explain why the Ancestor is false. To make them think for themselves again. To be angry, to be brave! You, of all people, can do this.'

Saphaeyender burst out laughing. 'Don't you realise why I tried to kill myself in the first place? Because the Bhahdradomen asked me to write propaganda for them! Oh, this is a wonderful irony, isn't it?'

Ariolne gave him a steely look. Lady Viananthe said, 'You may at least repay our hospitality by earning your keep, my lord.'

'As long as you're not too busy,' Ysomir added.

Saphaeyender threw up his hands, groaned. 'Yes, of course I'll do it,' he said. 'But what if they trace the pamphlets back to us?'

'I never said that resisting the Devourers would be without risk,' Ariolne replied.

'We'll make the risk as small as possible,' added Viananthe, 'and we'll take it.'

'And you,' said Ariolne, turning her aquiline glare onto Ysomir. 'You are the one who may help us most of all.'

'Me?' Ysomir's eyes widened.

'I came to visit you with Queen Helananthe, don't you remember?'

'Yes, I remember it vividly.'

'I know about your *ethroths*. They cling to you for a reason. You have power.'

Ysomir drew away. She felt cornered and intimidated again, as she had when Helan had done this to her, and Zhoaah and Vaurgroth. 'I can't control them.'

'You can learn. You must. It's your duty.'

'I don't mind helping Saphaeyender write leaflets . . .'

The priestess's expression became firmer; not unkind, but irresistibly demanding. 'And waste your true power? You've denied it for too long.' She rose and gripped Ysomir's shoulders. The familiar feeling of helpless horror ran through her. Ariolne seemed unaware of what she was doing, but to Ysomir it felt like being bullied, used, violated.

'Leave me alone,' she said faintly. She felt the *ethroths* gathering to defend her.

'When I come here next, we will talk of this again,' said Ariolne. And she dropped her hands just in time, never knowing what danger she'd been in.

As soon as the priestess had gone, Ysomir rushed to her own room and slammed the door. She was trembling with outrage. It wasn't that Ariolne was bad, she was only trying to save Parione; but why did everyone see her as an object to be used, her *ethroths* as public property?

A few minutes later, when she was beginning to calm down, there was a tap at her door. Eander came in.

Her heart sank. He looked so anxious and sweet, and so like Lynden even though he was blonder and had blue eyes, not brown . . . She had to keep reminding herself that he wasn't Lynden, all that was left of Lynden was inside her.

'Well? What did he say?'

'It got complicated. Ariolne arrived.'

'I know, but before that. He must have said something.'

She patted the bed beside her. Eander sat down. 'Look, there's no easy way to tell you. What you feared is true.'

'No.' The blond head shook vehemently.

'It should be Saph telling you this, not me. He said that

all he can think about is his work and he wants no lovers. It's over, Eander. I'm sorry.'

'No,' he said. 'No.' And he wept on her breast, while she held him and stroked his golden hair. She stared over his head, trying to feel nothing because she wasn't sure what she felt about anything. But, oh gods, it felt good to hold someone in her arms. It was so long since she'd been touched in love. No-one since Lynden and that was so long ago. And Eander felt so strong and male and warm in her arms . . .

He was talking, still in her arms, and she listened, not really hearing him. Her heart thumped in an insistent rhythm and she felt heat gathering between her thighs and a desire to touch him that was like ravenous hunger.

'It's all right,' she said, stroking his hair.

'Gods, Ymmi, I don't know what I would have done without you,' he said hoarsely. He sat up, still holding her arms, his face close to hers. She leaned in, thirsting for the kiss . . .

The next thing she knew, Eander was jumping away from her, almost falling over himself to get free. She stared up at him, startled, to see him already halfway to the door, staring back with alarmed eyes.

'No, oh hell, I'm sorry,' he gasped. 'I don't feel like that about women. I didn't realise you'd think – oh, gods, this is awful.'

Scarlet, he ran from the room.

Ysomir stayed where she was, her knees pressed together, her fists digging into the bed on either side of her. She stayed like that until all desire to scream, weep or throw something had subsided. And then she felt merely empty.

After Tanthe had gone with the Marocian army, Auriel was desolate.

He'd never really had to think for himself before. He remembered life with the Fhelethyr *eretru* who'd looked after him in childhood; a sweet and colourful dream, yet disturbing because they were always on the move and his mother and father weren't there. Then Falthorn had snatched him and the rest of his life had been lived on a knife edge, among people who were capriciously cruel or kind as the whim took them, always knowing he was a prisoner, a pawn.

Searching for Tanthe was the only thing that had motivated him, and Falthorn had even taken that away. And now he'd found his sister, and so completely let her down . . . what next?

Auriel had no idea who he was. His identity had been as Falthorn's captive. Now he was free, he'd lost all sense of self. How could he help Tanthe find her true self, when his own had been torn away?

There must be something.

The quartz sphere in the Duke's collection lured him, transfixed him. Shortly after he'd first seen it, he'd slipped into the museum alone and simply taken it.

He kept it hidden in his room. Each day he took out the glassy sphere and studied it, tried to attune with it. He read every morsel of information he could find in Jedraan's libraries. And one day, the spheres-within-spheres began to turn and sing in his palm.

He walked alone for hours, first around the palace grounds, then – growing more adventurous – through the city itself, and out along the cliffs and the thin road that wound along the coast. And there, for the first time, he found a small portal so ancient its *anaroth* smelled dusty with age. He opened it, closed it. He stood breathless with triumph.

He'd used power before, to communicate with Tanthe, to help his grandfather, Lord Valthiell, to open a portal. But he'd always denied his own gifts, even been afraid of them. Falthorn had poured scorn upon his small talents.

Now Auriel dared to explore his powers. He'd started long before Tanthe left; when she went, at least he still had this. He dedicated every day to study and experiment.

A day came when the full flowering of *anaroth* suddenly opened up to him in return. He stood on a scarlet cliff, the sphere shining in his hand. All at once he found himself staring at the glittering web of pathways that lit up around him, emanating from the central core of the *rothanamir* sphere.

His consciousness changed. The paths of *anaroth* leapt into life. He could see into other dimensions. The silver threads of the old roads ran through everything, a branching, elastic yet precise web. He recognised the maps he had plotted on parchment, brought to gleaming life.

Once he saw the web for the first time, it was always there. Day after day he studied it, learning it by heart. He plotted portals, doorways from Earth to Verdanholm. He found interstices, doorways that led from one place to another within Aventuria itself. It was as if he was at the centre of the web, seeing the whole picture as a mage might. It was a three-dimensional image laid lightly over the real world, dewed gossamer. Its beauty and complexity induced a constant rush of wonder.

This was what he could do. Not to create portals – they'd all been created by the ancients with powers long lost – but to find them, as a dowser might find water. To see what no one else could see.

He began to experiment more boldly, opening a portal, stepping through, returning. He found interstices everywhere, all along the coast of Azura Maroc. How could humans not know they were there, not make use of them?

Obvious. The pride of people like Falthorn, he thought. The Aelyr withdrew, humans rejected what was left of our skills. Thus they were lost.

Gaining courage, he discovered how to wander inside the web itself; a dark nothingness in which the unwary might be lost. He walked the silver threads and gradually began to get his bearings. He plotted their knots and nodes and followed them to their destination. And wondered why no one had ever told him that this was possible.

Perhaps, he thought one day, even Falthorn doesn't know. The thought pleased him. He was still savouring it when he heard a cry.

Auriel froze. He was standing on the very lip of a portal. The cry chilled him because it came not from the real world but from the web itself.

He'd found that if he closed his eyes, he could see the web better in his mind; it shut out the real world's interference. There was another web intermeshed with the first, harder to see because it was dark, like rushing streams of water instead of light. And in one of the streams a man was being swept along.

The web spread into an immensity of darkness. The tiny figure was being carried out of sight, into the abyss.

Without thinking, Auriel ran after him. The transition still made him dizzy; he was still a novice at navigating the silvery threads themselves. It was like floating in water, with no up or down, his only guide an insubstantial rope of silver fireflies. It was like dreaming.

He ran, slid, flew along the threads, following one branch then another as he tried to reach the man. In his hurry he didn't note which way he'd come.

'Come towards me!' Auriel cried.

The young man looked up and stared at him with huge, terrified eyes. Beyond speech, he uttered a brief scream. The watery *roth*-stream was carrying him away.

'Follow this thread of light!' Auriel called. The man couldn't reach it. A rucksack dragged on his shoulders as if filled with lead blocks.

Of course, take the thread to him. Auriel lifted the sphere, twisted it, and the path of light itself bent down to merge with the stream. The watery energy of the flow took his breath away. He reached out, caught the man's arm, and held on for dear life.

He felt the light-thread rising up again. The man came

with it. Their movements were blurred, as if time were moving in staccato rushes.

'Follow me,' Auriel said, hoarse with exhaustion.

If I can remember the way back, he thought.

He climbed, taking one fork then another by guesswork and instinct. His body ached, as if he were climbing a mountain. He hadn't realised how much stress this non-realm would place on them, human and Aelyr alike, for it wasn't meant to sustain life.

Fear grew in him. Everywhere looked the same. He glanced back, saw the man struggling, dropping back.

'Come on,' Auriel said, holding out his hand.

Panting for breath, the man took it.

Auriel looked forward again and saw the pattern he recognised. The confluence of several strands into a single, bright knot.

'There!' he said. 'The portal!'

Struggling, trembling, he reached it and pulled the man through. They tumbled out onto dry land as red as flame; the cliff top above the Lapis Ocean.

The man, bone-white, sat down where he stood as if his legs had given way. He slid the pack off his shoulders, pressed his hands to his flat, sodden hair and sat there shuddering. Auriel watched him for a minute, not wanting to admit to himself how close they'd been to disaster. I found the way back, he thought. I can do it!

Now that he was no longer thinking of the web, it vanished. The *anametris* was lifeless in his hand. He slipped it away into its pouch. Despite the man's blanched face and his half-drowned appearance, Auriel recognised him.

'You're Jthery, aren't you?'

'How did you know that?'

'I'm Auriel. Don't you remember me? We met at . . . at Falthorn's house.'

Then Jthery gave sour smile. 'Auriel. Of course you are; how could I forget you? And still working for him. Ah well, I knew I'd be finished. Take me to him; get it over.'

Auriel was horrified. 'No,' he said stiffly. 'I don't work for him. I have nothing to do with him any more. How do I know he hasn't sent you to us?'

Jthery shook his head painfully. His voice was fractured. 'I've just run away. I've done something so terrible. Eshte's eyes, what have I done?'

He let out a groan. Auriel could do nothing but put an awkward arm round his shoulders and hold him while he trembled.

'Come back with me, you're safe now,' he said. Jthery only moaned again. Frowning, Auriel asked softly, 'What *did* you do?'

Ysomir thought about all that had happened. She considered Saphaeyender's single-minded obsession with his work. Ariolne's insistence on using her. The jolting misery of so nearly giving herself to Eander only to find she was unwanted. Zhoaah's midnight visits.

There is nothing here for me, she thought coolly.

Ariolne is right; if there's power in me I must do something useful with it. But I'll do it in my own way, not hers.

In the middle of the night, Ysomir chose the warmest, most practical clothes she had, packed a few extras in a small pack that she slung on her shoulders. She pushed all her feelings into a compartment and sealed them there. She needed to be cool, fearless, dispassionate.

She left the house by one of the staff doors, the escape route they'd planned if *vagharim* came. It brought her onto the hillside above the ruined orchards. As she slipped down through the darkness, a voice beside her whispered, 'Where are you going?'

Zhoaah. She turned to face him, feeling the green-gold shield and the murmur of her *ethroths* encasing her.

'I'm leaving.'

The pale shadow exhaled displeasure. 'To go where?'

'I don't know.'

'But I only protected the house for you.'

The threat stopped her in her tracks. 'But you said you could find me wherever I go,' she whispered. 'What difference does it make whether I'm in the house or not?' She moved closer to him. To her surprise, he stepped back. 'What if I said to you, please protect the house for my sake?'

'You show unprecedented faith in my good nature,' he hissed.

'Well? Please, Zhoaah. If you still want to call in this favour, please keep them safe.'

All she could see of his face were two glaring spots of light. Then the spots narrowed into a smile. 'Very well,' he said. 'Since you ask so nicely. Besides, I think you will be considerably more interesting on the loose. Until we meet again?'

He inclined his hooded head. As Ysomir hurried away into the darkness, she could feel his gaze like two needles of fire in her back. She was free yet not free, full of dread but knowing she'd made the only choice she could. The night air filled her lungs with the fungal stench of *graukhim*.

Chapter Nineteen. Forest God and Dragonfly

The army made camp on a red plain, with the fertile arm of the Olivine River to sustain them, pouring its green waters into the sea only a few miles from their camp. They were near the northern rim of the Ruby Plains, due south of Parione but still not much over halfway there. And it had been a hard trek of months to come this far. Tanthe, like her companions, was worn out and dispirited.

Tanthe had been sorry to leave the beauty of Lapiszul. She made a pact with herself to return one day. She'd sit among those smiling copper-skinned folk, luxuriating in the lush hues of their clothing, the feast of mosaics and gold leaf, their pure love of speculation and knowledge. She'd see Auriel again . . . if he was still there by then. He seemed to have found a mysterious sense of purpose at Jedraan's court, so perhaps he would stay. If he confessed to taking the sphere, she had a feeling that Jedraan would be understanding.

There was a long sprawl of villages along the river that gladly billeted the soldiers. The dwellings were low and built of smooth red stone, a far cry from the glory of Lapiszul. The villagers irrigated and farmed strips of land along the riverbanks. As the army rested there for a few days, images burned themselves into Tanthe's mind. Flame-red stone against the intense green of the fields, the incandescent cobalt of the sky. Sunrise slanting through mist above the river, paling the fields to the colour of Ysomir's eyes. Sunsets of painted flame.

She and Lahjaya were billeted in a rambling, one-storey dwelling that was arranged in a half-circle around a sun-baked courtyard. The dwelling was empty so Helan had commandeered it, making sure her companions had decent rooms. On the far side of the courtyard, tents had been pitched, completing the circle. Each morning Tanthe would wake to sunlight glowing through the round unglazed window. She would rise and cross the bright red-gold circle of the courtyard to draw water from the well in the centre. Lahjaya would join her, and they'd share breakfast with Helan, Mawrdreth and Karmensis in the command tent. They would talk and make plans, turning over all the possibilities. Would the war be fought on the border? Could they hope to reach Parione itself? Would the Mediators negotiate again, as they had two hundred and fifty-three years ago?

'I don't think we can look to the Mediators for help this time,' Helan said grimly. 'The Bhahdradomen have wrecked that hope. We've had them abusing the Mediators by impersonating them, then murdering my friend Rathroem. So, if the Mediators retreat to their peaceful little enclave on the Serpent Isles and turn their backs on the world, we can hardly blame them.'

'It seems to me there are too many acting as if Aventuria's problems have nothing to do with them,' Mawrdreth said bitterly. 'The Aelyr don't want to know. Torith Mir's turned against us. Sucked in by Vaurgroth's false promises of power and ecstasy, no doubt.'

Helan looked grave. 'Oh, Viceroy Drathnen's so-called "neutrality" is no surprise. My father always said there'd be trouble from that quarter. Eldareth told me he was plotting to secede from the Nine Realms in his parents' day. He had Eldareth's father making *roth*-weapons to use against us. That came to nothing when Mordraken ... er, died, but Drathnen's never given up his ambition.'

'Siding with Vaurgroth's going to bring him nothing but disaster,' Tanthe put in. 'Torith Mir was already full of *ghelim* when we were there. Masquerading as greenwolves, the lot that attacked us.'

'There's a pleasant thought.' Lahjaya grimaced. 'All our animals replaced by *ghelim* ...'

Helan gave a barely perceptible shiver. 'I can only hope that my mother and brother are safe there, at least. What wouldn't I do for those *roth*-weapons now! But Vaurgroth's clever, conserving his military strength by offering bargains, wiping our minds with religious ecstasy or torpor. If he did that to Drathnen, he could do it with every Duke or Duchess of the Nine Realms. Serpeth, Dannion, Branq'elin . . .'

'Branq'elin won't fall for it!' Mawrdreth said heatedly. 'She's strong. But the others . . . Serpeth bends with the wind, Dannion's an old and frightened man. Duchess of Mithrain's a wily one but ancient, never had to defend her realm from an attack like this.'

Helan rubbed her furrowed forehead. 'The fact that the Deirlanders live mostly in tribes may save them. And the Devourers may not see the need to expand into Noreya yet . . . but Noreya is too far away to aid us.'

The discussions turned in circles around the unspoken hub; that they stood no hope of defeating Vaurgroth and were leading the Marocians to their deaths. No one would say it but the knowledge hung over every meeting, making them sharp and quarrelsome.

The rest of the day would be spent training, with a break for the hottest hours. Tanthe was glad to expend her frustration in physical exercise. The evenings, at least, were pleasant; cool dusks, spent sitting with Lahjaya on a bench in the courtyard, soothing their feet on the warm stone and drinking Marocian wine. There were always mundane chores, which were less tedious if tackled when slightly drunk.

'How long have we been here?' Lahjaya asked one day. They'd scrubbed some of their gear clean and were hanging it to dry on a line they'd rigged across the courtyard. It was late afternoon. The sinking sun flooded the area red-gold.

'About ten days, I think,' said Tanthe, passing her a shirt. 'Helan's muttering about moving on in a couple of days.'

Lahjaya pulled a face. 'Damn. I was getting quite settled here. This is so like the village I came from . . .'

'Well, don't,' Tanthe said brusquely. 'I'll be glad to move on. I'm so bored I could shoot myself.'

'Bored?' Lahjaya's thick eyebrows danced. 'You should count Definyah's blessings. D'you really want to swap a decent bed for sleeping on rock, getting bitten by flies – oh, and slaughtered by Devourers at the end of it?'

Tanthe gave a sour grin. 'I could do without the flies. I just want it to be over.'

'Me too.'

'You know, I'm really surprised you didn't stay at the Turquoise Court, Laya. No one forced you to come with us. And Jedraan seemed *extremely* fond of you.'

'Oh, Tanthe.' She gave a sad smile. 'I told you it was just a dalliance. A very pleasant one, but if he ever takes life seriously enough to marry, it won't be to a peasant like me. Besides, I couldn't let Helan down.'

'There's nothing wrong with being a peasant,' said Tanthe. 'I'm proud of where I come from, even though I couldn't wait to leave.'

'And we're both so heroic,' Lahjaya grinned, giving her arm a squeeze. 'Not ones to laze around drinking wine while others fight the battle for us, eh? Oh, look . . .'

Her grip tightened, make Tanthe exclaim with pain. Her gaze snapped over Tanthe's shoulder.

'Definyah's ruby eyes, who is *that*?' Lahjaya gasped. Her mouth fell open and her blue-black eyes looked close to springing out of their sockets. 'He is *gorgeous*.'

Tanthe turned, and saw what Lahjaya had seen. If her friend hadn't been there, she would have doubted her own eyes.

Walking towards them, across the sun-baked earth between the tents, came a lean, long-legged young man dressed in worn breeches and scuffed leather boots. His ragged green shirt was unlaced and stuck to his chest with sweat, sleeves rolled up, a bow slung over his shoulder. His hair, a thick chestnut tangle falling to his shoulders, looked as if it hadn't seen a comb for weeks but was still lustrous and full of bronze in the sun. Stubble shadowed his jaw. As he came closer, Tanthe saw haunted brown eyes that looked as if they had seen everything, yet survived.

Because he was the last person she was expecting to see, Tanthe didn't recognise him for a moment. Then when she did, she couldn't believe her eyes.

'Ohh,' she breathed. Breaking away from Lahjaya, she started towards him.

'Hey, I saw him first!' Lahjaya exclaimed – only half-joking, from the indignation in her tone.

'I know him,' Tanthe said over her shoulder, increasing her pace. 'Rufryd?'

He stared at her. They both broke into a run for the last few paces, and all but collided. Then she was in the air, being spun round in his arms, clasped so tight she couldn't breathe.

'Tan,' he said. 'I wasn't sure it was you. Goddess, I thought I'd never see you again.'

'I thought you were dead,' she choked. She wrapped her arms round him and they both held on as if they would crush each other. The pain was bliss. She was drowning in an ocean of relief. 'You're alive, you're here. I can't believe it.'

He began to kiss her hair, forehead, cheeks, lips. His eyes closed with the tension of needing to cry and not being able to. 'Tanthe, I'm sorry, I'm so sorry.'

'What for?'

'The stupid argument we had. All the foul things I said to you.'

'Oh, that. It's forgotten.'

'No, it isn't. I didn't mean any of it, I was just angry. It's no excuse, I'd give anything to take it back.'

'I know. I'm sorry I hurt you, too.' She'd forgotten how good the warmth of his body smelled, even when he was soaked in sweat with the earthy scent of horses on him.

Forgotten the delicious lean strength of his limbs. 'Haven't we got more important things to tell each other – like how on Earth you found me?'

'Yeah.' He pressed his cheek hard against her hair. 'But I promised myself the first thing I'd do was apologise for that stupid outburst.'

'It's all right. You're forgiven.'

'That easy?'

'I'm just so glad to see you.' She wiped tears off her cheeks. 'It's been so long. We thought you'd died in Vexor. Gods, Rufe, you don't know how glad I am to see you.'

'Are you, really?' He stroked her cheek with long, slightly calloused fingers. His eyes were serious, dark with suffering. Most expressive eyes she'd ever known. She'd seen everything between Rufryd's long dark lashes. Arrogance, contempt, anger, anguish, humour, tenderness, ecstasy. Now, an awful mix of wonder and pain.

'How can you doubt it?'

He exhaled. 'Gods, you mean it.' Behind them, Lahjaya cleared her throat, then huffed and walked away. They took no notice.

'Why is that a surprise?'

'I thought you hated me. You were so cold when we parted. I thought I'd poisoned everything between us.'

'You nearly did, Rufe, but no more than I did. Every day I've regretted it, would've given anything for you to be with us.'

'Really?' Hope glistened between his long eyelashes. He was still holding her so hard that her ribs ached.

'The things we quarrelled about were just smoke, compared to the thought of never seeing each other again.' She was crying. 'Weren't they?'

'Oh gods, yes. Yes.'

For a long time they stood holding onto each other. At last their grip eased and she asked, 'What's happened, how did you find us?'

He breathed out a soft, protracted groan that seemed

to come from the darkest core of him. 'Long, long story. I escaped from Vexor, went back to Tasqabad . . . left there and rode hundreds of bloody miles across Thanmandrathor then found the way blocked by Bhahdradomen troops when I got near Paranios. So I went down to the coast, got a ship. A band of Thand'rathian and Paranian fighters helped me. They said Azura Maroc was still free. Landed north of here, asked questions until we heard rumours of Helananthe and an army, then came down the coast until I found you. I didn't even know you were with them until I got here. I met Mawrdreth.' He hooked his thumb over his shoulder. 'He told me you were here and found someone to look after my horses and my, um, friend.'

'What's an "um" friend?'

'Well, that's quite hard to explain.'

'A woman?' She resisted his embrace, but he only tightened his.

'No, it's just, er . . . a boy I picked up.'

'This gets worse.'

He groaned. 'Tan, I'm so tired I can hardly string two words together. I'll explain later. It's so bloody hot here, isn't it? How have you not got a sun-tan?'

'You know I always stay pale. I think it's an Aelyr thing. You're quite weatherbeaten, aren't you? You look a bit rough, in fact.'

'Thanks. So I've travelled a couple of thousand miles to be told I look like shit at the end of it?'

She grinned. 'On the contrary, I was going to say it makes you even more attractive than I remember.'

'Sure.'

'You can't come all this way and not be teased.' She caressed his hair. 'Seriously, Rufe, you've obviously been dragged through a hedge backwards and yet . . . well, my friend Lahjaya there was about to jump on you.'

'But you held her back.' A trace of amusement came into his eyes. He didn't take his eyes off her to see who Lahjaya might be.

'Had to,' said Tanthe. She blotted a trickle of sweat on his chest with her fingertip.

'Well, you look just as good I remember, Tan. Like a goddess. Hell, I'm never going to get over you, am I?' His hands moved over her back, so warm and sensuous she couldn't let go of him. From the way he was pressing against her, he wasn't quite as tired as he made out.

'They never do,' she said. 'Come inside, I've got a room.'

At that he paused and gently released her. 'On your own?'

'Yes.'

'And all your lovers are . . . where?'

'All my lovers, honestly Rufe. There's no one. Come on. You can drink, eat, bathe, sleep. What would you like to do first?'

He slid a heavy arm over her shoulders and touched his lips to her ear. 'I think you know what I want to do first,' he said darkly.

They were kissing, pulling at each other's clothes even before she'd managed to close the door-curtain. The room was plain, not much more than a cell, but clean and red as a womb in the fading light. Tanthe fell onto the low bed and pulled Rufe after her. She tipped her face up to his and their mouths touched and opened to each other, hot and thirsty.

They struggled with boots and laces, swearing in impatience. At last they were naked, hands all over each other, sexual musk ripening the air. Tanthe was panting, almost sightless with desire. His hands moved over her breasts. His hair brushed down her stomach, unutterably delicate, and then his tongue and fingers were shaping wild sensations in the red temple of her vulva.

But she wanted him inside her. She pulled him up, tasted her own juices on his mouth, felt his prick hard and heavy and dewed with arousal in her palm. He gasped in pleasure.

'Tanthe, I don't think this is going to last long,' he said. 'Sorry, in advance, but it's been a long time . . .'

'It's all right,' she whispered, drawing him towards her. 'It's all right.'

He rose above her, parting her thighs, pressing forward.

Then he stopped. He rolled to one side and lay there, the length of his prick still pressing insistently into her thigh. 'I'm not sure I can do this.'

'What?' Empty, taken aback, she propped herself up on one elbow. His face was so troubled it cooled her own fire. She stroked his cheek. 'What's wrong?'

'I can't get this close to you and then watch you swanning off with some other man again, Tan. If it happens again I can't stand it.' His voice grew fierce. 'If you don't love me, it's all bloody pointless, isn't it!'

She was stunned. She stared at him open-mouthed while he hung his head, not looking at her. 'Rufe?' she said in a small voice.

He sighed, but didn't answer. His expression was so dark she couldn't bring herself to ask what had happened to him. She reached out, stroking his hair, his lean sides, his thighs. She kissed him. She felt him shiver with a mixture of desire and misery, but he didn't respond.

'Rufe, I don't know what to say. I've never stopped loving you. You don't know how I feel about you because you never bloody ask me! I do love you.'

'You said that before and still went off with . . .'

'Don't. We can't talk about this now. Rufe, please, just love me. I've missed you so much. I'd forgotten how good this felt.' A sob broke from her. She couldn't bear to see him wretched, but felt the more she tried to reassure him the less convincing it sounded to her own ears. 'Don't be sad, I do love you . . .'

He groaned. 'Gods, Tanthe . . . Don't cry.'

He slid his arms round her again and she lifted her thigh over his hip and gently, delicately began to impale herself upon him. They looked into each other's faces, lips parted, breath trembling and shallow. She'd never seen a face so shadowed with pain and yet so beautiful.

He gave himself up to her then, as she'd hoped. Closing his eyes he began to move inside her, slowly at first; now more urgently, shifting his weight on top of her, filling her, pleasuring her as he'd always done so wonderfully. She clasped him, her head falling back with joy. She was swollen, filled, stabs of pleasure shaking her. But just as her own sensations were building, he cried out sharply and thrust into her, his back arching with ecstasy.

His thrusts slowed. He embraced her loosely, resting his head on her shoulder. 'That was amazing,' he whispered. 'And I am sorry. I couldn't hold back.'

'That's all right,' Tanthe said through her teeth. 'Just don't even think of stopping. If you go to sleep now, I will kill you.'

He lifted his head and gave her a rueful smile. 'When have I ever fallen asleep on you?' His eyes were sleepy now, yet he began to move inside her again, still hard. She caught the rhythm again and the crimson stars of sensation flowered again, more intensely than before. She gasped in joy. She came.

The sensation sang through her body, a strong pure note held until her vision turned red and her whole body strained taut as a bowstring; then released in coruscating harmonies, throbbing, pulsing.

In that gap between the wordless held note and the release, Tanthe soared up and out of her body and along a loop of time, a path jewelled with stars.

She was floating in a milky light. All around her were tiny diamond points of light, and she knew that each of them was an Aelyr soul or essence, waiting to find expression in a living body. And she was one of those points of light. There was no time here, no true sense of waiting, no misery, no joy; only quiet serenity. And she was part of it. This was her Aelyr soul . . .

Rushing down through dark, starlit pathways. Sucked

in by the fusion of two cells, no, four cells, as if they were a dark carnivorous flower snapping shut upon an insect. She was trapped in the dark. Falling backwards into the dark . . .

It's true, she thought, feeling around her with senses that were endless gossamer tendrils. She wasn't afraid. She re-experienced her own birth with different eyes, with a solemn watchful consciousness that had always been there. She clearly saw the faces of her Aelyr mother and father, even though she had only seen them in visions; always turning, going away. She saw Auriel as a child, sweet red-haired beauty, being snatched from the Fhelethyr tribe by Valahyr raiders.

She touched his mind. *He always knew I existed. I knew nothing of him yet he always knew of me!*

She floated through veils of wonder, seeing different forms of *roth* as if they were visible lights, each with its own form; strands of smoke, gossamer spindles, hard shining eggs of light. Their variety was endless. She didn't fully understand what she was seeing yet she knew she was observing with Aelyr sight.

Jewelfire.

In a flash of revelation she understood how the Aelyr could create their own realm from raw Jewelfire, how the Bhahdradomen could drink it to feed only themselves. The knowledge was gone as swiftly as it came – but for one instant, she'd held it.

There was a greater battle hanging over this small, earth-bound conflict.

Rearing up in her vision – physically tearing up from the ground in front of her – was an immense jet black tower. Terror powered through her. The Obsidian Tower seemed the very opposite of the Jewelfire. Death against life.

But why fear death? said a booming voice, deep within her skull. *It is only peace. Nuth's dark wings.*

I am not afraid of death, Tanthe's Aelyr-self answered. *I am afraid of what I have to face while I am alive.*

The Tower was thundering towards her, dwarfing her. Panic and wonder whirled together. Everything stood in balance, anguish and ecstasy mixed, at one timeless point in the universe. She was at the centre, seeing all horrors and wonders at once. That was what it was to be Aelyr.

Her vision trembled as if her eyeballs would burst. The layer that was the sky behind the Tower peeled back and she saw a realm of dappled, dancing light; and framed against it, huge, sentient, undulating *roth* forms.

Their anger hit her in a tidal wall. *Do not dare to enter here. You have not the strength. That which you seek cannot be given!*

No, don't . . . A force flung her away from the pinnacle of the dread Tower. She jerked out of the trance with a yell, to find the last pulses of pleasure washing through her, and Rufryd looking at her with a tender, bemused expression.

'What was that?' he said. 'I've never heard you cry out like that before.'

'Oh,' she said, dazed and speechless. 'Oh Goddess . . . it was unbelievable.'

'I've got some hope then?'

'What?'

'Well, if I can do that to you every time, you might stay with me.'

'I'm with you now,' she said, slipping her arms around him. 'I'm not going anywhere.'

He hugged her and kissed her head. She lay with her eyes open, recalling the vision so vividly she couldn't turn it off. This was so strange, wanting to embrace Rufe and express her feelings for him . . . but because of the vision, she couldn't speak. It was like trying to be two people at once.

Of course, she thought. *So that's it. It didn't have to be with Auriel, because the memories were locked inside* me . . .

She thought Rufryd was falling asleep, so she wouldn't have to say anything. But after a few minutes, he stirred and said, 'Are you going to tell me what that was all about, then?'

'What?' she asked warily.

'Do you normally mutter things like, "No, don't," and, "I'm not afraid of death," at someone who is giving you what looked like an exceptionally long and intense orgasm?'

'Hell, did I say that out loud?'

'You were saying all sort of odd things.'

She put her fingers to her mouth in dismay. 'I wasn't saying them to you.'

His eyebrows rose. 'Oh, was there someone else in the room? It was like you weren't even seeing me. Thinking about someone else?'

'Rufe, I'm sorry. It's complicated. I wasn't thinking about anyone else. I was having a vision.'

'That's not much better, you know,' he said, hurt but making light of it. 'You were off somewhere else, not with me.'

'That's not true. The orgasm triggered the vision, I couldn't help it. The feelings sent me into a different level of consciousness. It was Aelyr stuff.'

He gazed thoughtfully at her. The Rufryd she remembered would probably have started an argument over this. The man she lay with now seemed more measured, less judgemental. 'Aelyr stuff. Okay. Would you like to tell me about it?'

She hesitated. 'Last time I told you about things like this, you called me a selfish little drama queen and stormed off.'

He flinched. 'I thought you said that was forgotten.'

'Yes, well. I'll tell you, but it may be stuff you'd rather not hear.'

'It's all right, Tan.' He spoke gently. 'I'm not going to storm off, whatever you tell me. Last thing I want is for you to feel you can't talk to me. I certainly don't want us to start arguing the moment we're together.'

'Why not? It's what we do best.' She shot him a grin. His expression was cautious, but receptive. 'All right, here goes. The first time I made love with Auriel—' she felt him tense slightly, but went on, 'I started having some really odd visions about being Aelyr. It's as if I was sealed off from those memories all my life, and they were trying to break through. Well, a while ago – when we first went down to Lapiszul – I had the idea that if Auriel and I made love again, I could break through the veil completely and understand it all.'

'You were in Lapiszul? What was Auriel doing there? I thought you hated him.'

'The second time we came back from Verdanholm, he came with us. I can see we've got a lot to tell each other. Anyway, no, I don't hate him, but we sort of . . . decided it was best if we were just brother and sister. Only I rather foolishly asked him if he would go to bed with me, just to see if I could have these visions again.'

'Did it work?' Rufryd said thinly.

'He refused to do it.'

'Proof he's an idiot.'

'Rufe, you don't know him. He was upset at being used by Falthorn; it was just the last straw, I suppose. I was wrong to ask. Anyway, I left it. But just now . . .'

'You started having these visions with me instead?' He frowned. 'Should I be flattered?'

She laughed. 'The thing is, it didn't absolutely have to be Auriel. The knowledge was inside me, all the time. I didn't realise.'

'That is flattering. Presumably a candle or your hand would have done the trick.'

'No, it wouldn't,' she growled. 'Apparently the trance of awareness could only be achieved with someone I love.'

He laughed, looking startled. 'You do love me, then.'

'I told you that.'

'But that was the first time you said it without trying to convince me.'

'Someone I love and trust,' she went on firmly. 'An energy to which I could utterly open myself. I'm sorry to lay this on you the moment you turn up, but I think it's happened. I've opened my mind to the Aelyr side.'

Now Rufryd looked concerned. 'This sounds amazing, but . . . what does it mean? Won't you be the Tanthe I know any more?'

'Considering the Tanthe you know always drove you crazy, you should be grateful. No, I think you're stuck with me. I don't understand it all yet.' She felt for his hand and wove her fingers with his. 'To be honest, I'm scared.'

'Why?' He caressed her neck with his free hand.

'I have to find my Aelyr parents and my child, the one Falthorn stole from me.'

His mouth twisted. 'Oh, how many others have you got?'

'Just the one that you went mad at me about. Anyway, I think I know how to do it now, or at least where to start. I must find a place called the Obsidian Tower.'

'What?' Rufryd cried, sitting bolt upright. 'Where the hell you did hear about the Obsidian Tower?'

She was startled. 'I keep seeing visions of it. I told someone, and he showed me a picture in a book, and there it was.'

'But it's – it's not a real place. It's a symbolic thing. You can't actually go there.'

She couldn't understand why he was agitated. 'What the blazes do you know about it?'

He opened his hands, speechless. 'We really have got a lot to talk about, Tanthe.'

'I have to find my child, Rufe, if it's the last thing I do.'

At that, he seemed to become utterly rigid. 'Don't. Just leave it alone.' She was looking at his back, so she didn't realise for a few moments that he was crying.

'Rufe?' she said, sitting up and placing her hand on his shoulders. She pushed his hair off his face and felt tears under her hand. His whole body began to shake with sobs. 'Rufe, don't.' Kneeling up, she put her arms round his neck and held him. Then he all but collapsed against her. 'Rufe, what is it? Tell me. It can't be that bad, can it?'

He wept for so long she feared he'd never stop. At last she skipped off the bed and brought him a cup of water. He drank it, and controlled himself, but when he looked up at her again his face was so desolate it broke her heart.

'What happened?'

'Oh, gods, I thought I was okay.'

'Tell me.'

He rubbed his face. He drew and released a long breath. 'I nearly got married when I was on my travels.'

She sat down heavily. That was a blow to the stomach. 'So much for my illusions that you were only thinking about me all this time. Who was she?'

'Er, Bran. Branq'elin, Mawrdreth's sister.'

'The scary one? Who is now . . . Duchess of . . .'

'We had an affair before I went to Vexor. I was stuck there over two years, and when I came back I found she'd had a little girl.'

'Yours?' It came out a croak. To her own horror, Tanthe found she was jealous. Jealous that he'd shared that with someone else.

'Definitely mine. We decided to get married, which would have made me Duke of Thanmandrathor. How insane is that?' He grinned horribly.

'Not handfasted, when you can change your mind after a year? Actually *married*?' He nodded. 'Were you in love with her?'

'I thought so. We got on well, considering what awkward sods we both are. I could have been happy with her, since I couldn't have you. That's what I thought my life would be, Bran and Annuin, and that house which is the only place that's ever felt like home.'

Her throat locked with the pain of imminent tears. She wanted him to stop. How selfish can I be, she thought, to be hurt that he found happiness with someone else, when it was my fault he left in the first place? But I am . . . And she sensed something terrible coming, and didn't want to hear it.

He went on, 'But then the . . . well, let's keep it simple and say the Bhahdradomen attacked the house. They came in the middle of the night. We woke up and they were in our chambers and they took the girl out of her cot and—'

His voice failed. He made a cutting motion with his finger across his throat. Tanthe was sobbing by now, tears flowing down her face.

'Bran blamed me, because I saved her instead of going to save Annuin. But what could I do? I couldn't make that choice. I was closer to Bran, so she was the one I defended.'

'I'm so sorry. I don't know what to say.'

Rufryd hooked his arm around her and they sat on the bed, pressed together, paralysed in a weird, speechless grief. 'Nothing you can say, love,' he said after a while. 'I wasn't even going to tell you.' He went on, telling how he and Branq'elin had parted, while she sat and shook against him.

'Rufe, you're not on your own. You've still got me. From now on, we'll stick together, right?'

He nodded, enfolding her hard against him. 'Yes,' he said with difficulty. 'It was worth coming back.'

'I've missed you like hell,' she said. 'I've never known anything like it. It was like having an arm torn off, or something.'

His hand, stroking her spine, came to a halt and probed there. 'Tan, what on Earth is this hole in your shoulder? The missing arm?'

'Oh, that. I got shot by an *uzrat* crossing the Paranian border. They shoot out these little balls of *gauroth* that—'

'I know what *uzrats* are, unfortunately,' he said. Leaning over, he groped for a flint and lit a candle. He investigated the scar, probing the hollow with his fingertip. 'It's healed quite well. They're usually lethal, you know.'

'I did very nearly die. Lahjaya saved me. And Auriel.'

He looked at her, shocked out of his own grief. 'Gods, and these . . . these awful red scars around your collarbone? I didn't notice them before.'

'Those were where Rhazagramen tortured me,' Tanthe said flatly. Self-consciously she put a hand over the worst of them.

'Oh, fuck. Rhazagramen? That wizened little bastard? I met him in Vexor!'

'He didn't even really get started. These were just a prologue. Mawrdreth and I managed to fight our way out before he went too far.' She shuddered. 'I still have nightmares about it. Not like yours, though, I know.'

'Don't let's start comparing nightmares,' Rufryd said, his voice rough. 'I should have been there. I would have stopped him.'

'I know you would. Hope you don't mind me a bit disfigured.'

He put his arms round her, kissed one of the scars. 'We're all disfigured, Tan. The point of what I was telling you is that although I only knew Annuin for a very short time, it was enough to love her, and for it to be worse than the torments of Hellaxis to lose her. If I'd never known her – say if Dawn or someone had told me about it afterwards – I would have been upset, but it wouldn't have been so real. It wouldn't have felt like being ripped to pieces with hot knives every time I think about it.'

'What are you saying?'

'Don't look for your child, Tan.'

'I've got to!' she gasped.

'But if things go wrong, I don't want to be sitting here comforting you instead.' He held her arms, suddenly fervent. 'I don't want you to feel like I do now! I wouldn't wish this on my worst enemy!' His voice fell. 'Please, Tan, don't do it. Be glad your child is still alive, and let him alone.'

* * *

Tanthe let the argument go, distressed but too tired to continue it. They slept.

She woke at dawn to find a Bhahdradomen staring down at her.

There was just enough light to reveal an almost-human face under a hood; unblinking deep-set eyes, a sheen of scaliness on the sharp cheekbones. He stood over her with the utter stillness that only the Devourers possessed.

She gave an involuntary yell, and felt for the *mnelir* under her pillow. Auriel had made her take it. The stone was hot against her knuckles as she gripped the hilt. She was about to strike when Rufryd seized her wrist and cried, 'No!'

Tanthe fought him in the panic of half-sleep. He got the knife out of her hand and she saw the figure backing away, staring with beady eyes at her and the *mnelir*.

'Devourer,' she gasped. What did this mean, had the camp been invaded? Her head was spinning. 'Give me the bloody—'

'Fuck,' Rufryd growled, putting the *mnelir* out of her reach and sprawling over her to light a candle. 'Vetru, you fucking idiot, what are you doing?'

'I came to look for you,' answered a soft voice.

The figure stood motionless by the window. Tanthe was sure she was having a nightmare. Then the flame flickered up, making the intruder hardly any less shadowy under the hooded rust-brown cloak.

Rufryd began to climb out of bed but she held him back. 'Rufe, he's Bhahdradomen, now give me my sodding knife back before it's too late!'

Weirdly, he didn't react as she expected. 'It's all right,' he said. 'It's Vetru.'

'What does that mean?'

'It's his name. He's the friend who came with me.'

She stared, feeling sick. He was *neshrim*, like the ones in Lapiszul, but not a very good one. All his human mimicry seemed to be modelled on Rufryd. The result was unsettling, if not grotesque. 'Didn't you realise he's . . .'

'Of course I did,' Rufryd said. 'He's come all the way from Vexor with me. I'm sorry, I should have told you last night. It went out of my mind. I didn't expect him to come in here and scare the hell out of you. Vetru, didn't I ask you to stay with the horses?'

'You are always asking me to stay with the horses. Perhaps I shall turn into one,' Vetru said tersely.

'You'd be a lot less blasted trouble. You know it's for your own safety! You walked through the camp, you came nosing about here and you were that far—' he held up his finger and thumb, pressed together – 'from being stabbed by Tanthe! Don't you understand that these people will kill you if they realise what you are? I might have done it myself, after what happened in Tasqabad!'

'I do them no harm. I just wanted to find you.'

'Anthar's prick and bollocks,' Rufryd sighed, putting his head in his hands. 'All right, you're here now. Sit down and we'll see if we can brew some tea, shall we?'

'I'll do it,' Vetru said, brightening. 'Show me where is the fire?'

'Tanthe?' Rufryd prompted.

She was still sitting with her mouth open, eyes gaping. 'It's . . . it's . . . along the corridor. There's a sort of kitchen area and a fire pit. I'd, er, keep your hood pulled up if I were you.'

Vetru scurried out of the room and she still couldn't speak or move. Her heart was racing.

'Don't look so shocked,' Rufyrd said, slipping an arm round her bare shoulders. 'I'm really sorry he scared you. He normally does what I tell him but he does have a mind of his own.'

'I can't believe it,' she said. 'After what they did to your child, you have one as a *friend*?'

'They're not all bad. He saved my life, more than once. I tried to leave him behind but he just wouldn't have it, so . . .' He shrugged. 'He's harmless, I promise. He's only a few years old, anyway; they grow up differently to us, but he's still pretty naive. Someone's got to look after him.'

'Do you trust him?'

'Yes.'

'Do you *like* him?'

Rufryd paused. 'Yes, I suppose I do, really. He's quite funny sometimes, usually unintentionally. He can be a bit irritating.'

'Ha.' Tanthe gave a twisted grin. 'Yes, that was pretty annoying, waking up to find him staring down at me. When our grandchildren ask us why we fought the great war against the Bhahdradomen, we can reply, "Oh, they were a bit irritating, dear."'

Rufryd laughed. 'Grandchildren, eh?'

'Figure of speech.'

'Are you upset with me?'

'No more than usual.'

'That's all right then.'

'As long as he's not expecting to live in here with us!' She shuddered. 'I can't make love to you with an audience.'

He slipped both arms round her, one hand travelling over her breasts and stomach. 'I'll make sure of that, don't worry. As long as you promise not to go off into a trance every time.'

'I don't think it'll happen again.' She kissed him, still amazed by his presence. So strange and wonderful that he was here after so long. Disturbing, though, to wonder what other darkness he'd passed through. 'You've completely stunned me, Rufe. Having one of the enemy as your friend. Caring about him.'

'Most *domenim* are no more dangerous than your average human. Less so, I'd say. They're quite passive, which is really their problem. It's their leaders we have to worry about. They're the ones who want to annihilate us, and they will, because all the *domenim* do exactly what they're told.'

'Eager to please?' Her eyes widened.

'Vetru's not that unusual. There's something for Helan and Mawrdreth to mull over.'

'But if you met the one who killed your daughter . . . you'd feel differently?'

'Oh, he lived all of ten seconds longer than she did,' Rufryd said grimly. 'And as many of the Order as I could take out with him.'

'What's the Order?'

'Ah . . . I've got a hell of a lot to tell you. I want to hear everything that's happened to you, as well.' He paused and added under his breath, 'The Goddess-forsaken bastard who actually killed little Annuin was human.'

They talked over breakfast, touching and kissing until they ended up back in bed; talked again afterwards as if the words would never stop flowing. Later they bathed together, sitting up to their necks in a tub of hot water, flesh to wet flesh.

Vetru had filled it for them. She was trying hard to get used to his presence, his obvious devotion to Rufryd.

Rufryd told her about the Order of Calathvahn, the massacre of the tiny village Mrenth. Tanthe described Vaurgroth's seizure of the Sapphire Throne, their escape and flight to Lapiszul, all her visions. Fear for Ysomir. The hopelessness of the counter-invasion.

'Perhaps we should just up and run away,' he said in her ear. 'Don't you think we've both been through enough?'

'Oh, I'd love to.' She stroked the strong brown arm that was locked around her stomach. 'Don't think I haven't thought of it. I was tempted to stay in Lapiszul. But I can't. I can't.'

'I know.'

Sadly she smiled up at him. He was as beautiful as the Earth with his dark chestnut hair, brown eyes gleaming under dark brows. His face seemed leaner. Awful that suffering had enhanced his beauty, but it was true. It seemed to have pared away all his volatile arrogance, traced something quieter and more watchful there instead. In a way he was a stranger. That was unnerving, fascinating.

'I dreamed about meeting you again,' he said, 'but I never expected you to be like this, so warm, so really genuinely thrilled to see me . . .'

'Oh, how did you expect me to be?'

'Cold, angry and indifferent, I suppose, like you were when I left. I dreaded it.'

'I thought you'd be like that as well. I thought I'd made you hate me.'

'I could never hate you, Tan. Then I saw you and it was all right.'

'So, you couldn't have been more wrong, could you?'

'This is wonderful,' he said gently, 'but what if you met Saphaeyender again? He was the lover of your dreams. Not me.'

'You think you're second-best?'

'Try third-best. Still, if it's like this, I can live with it.'

She bit her lip. 'Rufe, have you no idea what it's like to realise that your dream lovers, however delightful, have no clue how to cope with reality? You've no idea how much I missed you, how good it feels to see a familiar face, someone I can trust with my life, trust to the ends of the Earth . . .' She trailed off, crying. He hugged her, his breath suspended as if he hadn't realised.

When she could speak again, she said, 'The others were sweet and I still love them, but you're the one I've thought about and missed every day. Anyway, don't talk to me about third-best. I know that you wouldn't be here if your daughter hadn't died.'

He replied, quietly and darkly, 'This was meant to be, then.'

'Did we really have to go through so much to find out?'

'Hey, don't cry, Tan. You're making the water tepid.'

'You disappeared for three years on purpose, to make

me grovel. You just walk back in, looking like the sun, or Anthar strolling out of the forest . . .'

'Ah, you love me for making a dramatic entrance. My plan worked.'

'I love you because you're like a tree.'

'Thanks, I didn't realise I was that well-endowed.'

She hit him, scattering water. They fought, making the tub rock with their laughter. The floor was awash.

Someone cleared her throat. Tanthe looked up and saw Helan standing in the doorway, her face stern.

'Tanthe, I *was* going to ask why you didn't turn up for training today; I won't bother.' A smile hovered. 'Rufryd, I'm so glad to see you again that I can't find words to express it. However, I would appreciate your presence in the command tent. It seems to have slipped your memory that envoys returning from an official journey are required for immediate debriefing?'

'Sorry, ma'am,' Rufryd said helplessly. 'I got side-tracked.'

'So I see. I'll leave you to it. My tent, one hour, if you don't mind?'

Vetru stood before Helan. Rufryd stood behind him, holding his shoulders, like a father presenting his nervous son to a stern schoolmistress. Tanthe watched, hardly breathing.

'If it wasn't for Vetru, I wouldn't be here,' Rufryd said simply.

'I've considered everything you've told me about him,' Helan said, frowning. 'Can he speak on his own behalf?'

'Ma'am, I speak good Paranian,' Vetru said in a faint voice. 'I gave up my allegiance to Vaurgroth and Ancestor to go with Rufryd. I eat only human food, not *graukhim*. All I want is to serve Rufryd.'

Helan blew out a sigh through thinned lips. 'What can I say? You've left me completely speechless, Rufryd. Only you could have landed a thing like this on me! Sorry, Vetru, when I said "thing" I didn't mean . . . Anyway, I can't find any reason not to let him stay.'

'Thank you,' Rufryd said, and Vetru echoed, 'Thank you, ma'am.'

'Still, he mustn't be allowed anywhere he might overhear conversations.'

Rufryd laughed. 'He's not a spy.'

'How can you be sure?' said Mawrdreth.

'Who's he going to tell? We're in the middle of nowhere, miles from any Bhahdradomen troops!'

'It's said that their adepts can communicate through certain stones, as the Aelyr can. Who knows what else they can do?'

'I can do none of those things, sire,' said Vetru. He opened his spindly hands. 'If you don't believe me, behead me.'

They all stared at him. Helan looked as if her eyes would drop from her head. 'That won't be necessary. But Rufryd, I hold you responsible for him; it's up to you to keep him out of trouble.'

'Fine,' he said, patting Vetru's shoulder. 'He'll prove he's a good *domen*. You'll learn to love him.'

It was only when Rufryd had sorted out the business of Vetru that he submitted himself to Helan's questions. She interviewed him relentlessly for hours, several days in a row. Only Tanthe and Mawrdreth were allowed to be present and they sat listening, taut and uneasy, adding extra questions when they could get a word in. Mawrdreth was distraught by the news of his sister. He walked out at one stage and Tanthe followed him.

'Rufryd told me all about it,' she said, sitting beside him in the shade of an apricot tree. 'I'm sorry. But your sister is strong, isn't she?'

His green eyes were narrow, distant. 'Oh, Bran's a fighter. She'll die fighting. But she endured all that, and I wasn't there to help her! Lost a child to those . . . Yet now Rufryd is here and not with her!'

'Because she sent him to find you.'

'And what am I to do?' Mawrdreth said savagely. 'My

sister doesn't know I married Helan. She doesn't know that I am, or was, King of Aventuria. I can't abandon Helan – especially since Eldareth did that very thing. If I stay here, I am betraying Branq'elin, my own family. But if I go to her, I'm betraying Helan and all the vows I made to her and the Xauroma! What am I to do?'

'I think you know,' Tanthe said gently, putting her hand on his tense, resisting arm. 'You have to stay with Helan. It would take you months to reach Tasqabad, and we don't have months. The war could be all over by then. Your sister will understand, won't she?'

He sat unspeaking, his head lowered. Eventually he looked at her and said, 'You're right, Tanthe. My place is here. Rufryd has had a wasted journey.'

'No, he hasn't.'

Mawrdreth looked gravely at her. 'He seems to have forgotten my sister very quickly.'

Images knifed her heart. Rufryd happy with Branq'elin, still with her now if not for the *yrim* lifting the little girl from her cot and . . . She swallowed hard. 'Don't take it out on him,' she said. 'He's heart-broken.'

'It seems Vaurgroth has broken open all our hearts and sucked out the pain, an endless fountain of it. That's why he is so bloated with power.'

'The danger we face isn't just Vaurgroth's brute strength,' said Rufryd. 'It's the ideology of fanatics like the Order of Calathvahn. They want us to despise life, and especially to despise women as the source of life; can you imagine a greater obscenity? If it spreads, we'll turn round and destroy ourselves, and Vaurgroth won't have the agony of choosing which of his fourteen fingers to lift.'

Tanthe put in, 'You said you killed their leader . . . ?'

'But many of them escaped, and there were plenty left in Q'elethrios and Calathvahn. No guarantee we've put an end to them.'

'It's already started,' Helan said, paling. 'In Parione they were trying to seduce everyone into Ancestor worship. And it was working. People found some kind of addictive ecstasy in it.'

'Very nice escape, when real life is suddenly shit,' Tanthe said acidly.

'That's it.' Rufryd dropped his forehead onto the heel of his hand, rubbed his eyes. 'That's it, exactly. If that catches hold, we are fucked.'

'We're probably fucked already,' Helan said, clasping her elbows. 'We have an army of green warriors, armed with bows, spears and swords, against an array of pitiless *yrim* who have all sorts of *roth*-weapons we can't hope to recreate, and Vaurgroth's horrible mage-powers behind them. We're marching towards defeat and death, only because it's preferable to lying down and rolling over while those cold-eyed shape-shifting evil bastards trample all over us!'

The others were silent at this outburst. Rufryd felt for Tanthe's hand.

'And the Aelyr technology that might have helped us is all gone,' he said. He'd told them about Con's discovery on the mountain, and Nilothphon's message.

Tanthe growled in frustration. 'What is the use of knowing I'm Aelyr, seeing visions, when I can't make sense of what I'm seeing or do anything useful with it!'

Helan clasped her shoulder. 'Whether you're Aelyr or human, Tanthe, it's no good any single one of us thinking we can do it all alone. That's an easy road to madness; I should know, I've been down it. Don't the rest of you start.'

She moved towards the tent entrance. They'd been talking over Rufryd's news for days. 'We're tired,' said Helan. 'I'll send for refreshments, and we'll rest for a while.'

As she pulled back the flap, they heard a breathless voice calling outside, 'Helananthe! Ma'am!'

It was Lahjaya. She came into view in the triangle of

dusty golden light, panting for breath. 'Ma'am, someone's arrived. You'll want to see them. I can't believe it.'

'Eldareth?' said Helan.

Tanthe, Rufryd and Mawrdreth followed the Queen outside. Walking towards them between the tents came two figures, carrying a heavy-looking bag between them. Tanthe cried out in astonishment. This was as incredible as Rufryd arriving.

'Who are they?' said Rufryd.

'It's Auriel . . . gods, and I swear the other one is Jthery,' she said. 'But this is impossible. We left Auriel in Lapsizul. And Jthery was in Verdanholm! How can they be here?'

'Auriel?' Rufryd said in a tone of disgust, but she was already rushing forward to meet them, alongside Helan.

Auriel looked tired, his gold-tinged skin matt with dust, his dark auburn hair in rat's tails. He greeted Tanthe with a smile and they hugged briefly, then she stepped back to gape at him.

'How did you— ?'

Then she noticed how dreadful Jthery looked. His redgold hair was plastered back to his scalp, his face shellwhite. His grey eyes looked as if they'd seen legions of ghosts. Despite the heat, he was shivering. When he began to collapse, Helan and Lahjaya noticed just in time and caught him between them.

Auriel held up the *anametris* sphere, twirled it on his fingers. It caught the light. 'Stealing this wasn't fruitless, after all.'

'What's happened?' said Helan.

'I've got them, Hel,' Jthery said, his voice weak and fevered. He waved a pale hand at the bulky rucksack which was now lying on the ground. 'I've brought you the Basilisks of Calabethron.'

Everything changed then. Helananthe began to smile again. Although she didn't reveal the news beyond her closest circle, the whole camp picked up on her changed mood. Excitement charged the air. They had hope. They had the winning cards.

'Aren't they small?' Tanthe said, as Helan and Mawrdreth examined the five strange, pale objects. 'Do you know what to do with them?'

'Who appointed you awkward questions officer?' Helan said, grinning sourly. 'We'll work it out. I always had a feeling Jthery would come right in the end.'

Tanthe, though, had a feeling things were more complicated than that. Jthery himself had said very little. He seemed to be in shock and was in bed in a room near Tanthe's, being nursed by Lahjaya and her trainees. He didn't want to talk, that was plain – least of all about Falthorn – but from what Auriel said, he had very nearly died trying to escape back to Earth.

'I wasn't idle in Lapiszul,' Auriel told Tanthe later, sitting in the courtyard. 'I wasn't wasting my time.' His eyes were intent on Tanthe as he spoke, coaxing her approval. Rufryd's silent jealousy was like a weight on her back as he listened, and she knew that later she would have to reassure him yet again that her affair with Auriel was over. All the time they were talking, she was on edge, sensing that at any moment Rufryd might physically attack him. 'I knew there was some Aelyr gift I had, that Falthorn never let me discover.'

'There was a bit of a clue in the fact that you could make yourself appear, and communicate with me without a *silvenroth* mirror,' Tanthe said. 'It's not something all Aelyr can do at all, is it?'

Auriel shook his head, glowing with new-found power. She felt proud of him. 'I've found a web of paths and portals that's been lost for centuries. It's like a net, a complicated map. All connected. There are nodes everywhere. There's one not far from here –' he waved vaguely in the direction of the ocean – 'a conjunction of several strands, a place of power. I brought Jthery through after I'd rescued him. I thought he needed to rest first, but he insisted on coming straight to Helan, so . . .'

'Does this mean you can *make* portals?' Tanthe asked.

'No, they're set, like doors in and out of a house. But I can find them and open them. Even shift them slightly. I can see how they're all connected.' He glanced up into the air. 'I can see them now, if I want.'

She looked round, saw nothing but dusty blue sky, grinned. 'I'll take your word for it.'

'There's still a lot to learn.'

'This is just wonderful, Auriel,' she said, close to tears.

'I had to do something useful.'

'I have some news too,' she said, glancing at Rufryd. 'I found the way through to my Aelyr side.'

Auriel's eyes flashed warily. 'Without— ?'

'Never mind how I did it. I don't know everything yet. I've seen some disturbing things, but they're all linked. Something to do with a dark tower that we must find . . .'

'Tanthe,' said Rufryd.

'Anyway, we'll talk about it later.'

'I'll go and see how Jthery is,' said Auriel, planting his feet on the red stones and rising.

When he'd gone, and she was alone with Rufryd, she took a deep breath and steeled herself to face his jealousy. She turned on the bench, shoulders square. Rufryd was looking at her with one eyebrow raised.

'Auriel seems quite nice,' he said.

'*What*?'

'Your brother is a pleasant young man.'

'And?'

'That's it.'

Tanthe gave an astonished laugh. 'Aren't you going to go nuts?'

'What for?'

'I wouldn't be too pleased if one of your old girl-friends showed up. He is the person who tricked me into Verdanholm, seduced me, made me pregnant on Falthorn's behalf, basically lied to me from start to finish because he lacked the courage to defy Falthorn. And I still love him. I thought if you ever set eyes on him you'd kill him.'

'I've mellowed.' He gave a thin smile.

'Rufe?'

'Seriously,' he said, slipping his arms round her. 'At one stage, I would have killed him. It's hard to get out of the habit of being scared I'll lose you. It's like trying to hold onto a moth, you're always flying off to burn yourself on one flame or other. First Ysomir, then Saphaeyender, then Verdanholm, now this bloody tower which I keep telling you is not a real place . . . But that's all it is, fear. Whatever went on between you and him, I take it you're grown-up enough to have sorted it out for yourself.'

'Thanks. Goddess, you really have changed.'

'I hope so. After looking into the face of a truly evil bastard like Arax Vahan, believe me, I'd never dream of hurting a dragonfly like Auriel.'

The next day a dark line appeared on the horizon. It was moving, flowing towards the camp. Everyone went out to see, Helan and Mawrdreth leading them.

It was an army of Valahyr. They wore the flowing colours of night and their curved swords glinted with dark gems. At their head came Falthorn, riding the white stallion Nefri that had belonged to Elrill.

His face held the vast, controlled wrath of a god.

'Where's Jthery?' he demanded, Nefri dancing under him.

'Why?' said Helan.

'You know why.' Falthorn jumped down from the saddle and strode forward, his eyes menacing. 'The little traitor has stolen the Basilisks from me. I know he is here.' With a brisk gesture he indicated the graceful and terrible lines of Valahyr behind him. 'Now you will produce both him and the Basilisks – or else we shall take them by force.'

Chapter Twenty. Falthorn's Shadow

'Lord Falthorn,' Helan answered, 'Jthery is under my protection. You are the thief, not him. All he has done is return the Basilisks to their rightful owner.'

'Madam, I am not going to stand here arguing the rights and wrongs of it. I will have those weapons back. The safety of my realm depends upon it.'

Helan was fired with a rage to match his. 'You dare to make these demands of me, when you gave away my kingdom to Vaurgroth? What should I care for the safety of your realm? Your little force looks impressive but I have an army a hundred times that size. Do you really want to take us on?'

Falthorn hesitated. His gaze snapped to something over her shoulder.

'Jthery!' he shouted.

He strode straight past Helan. She spun round in indignation and saw, in dismay, Jthery a few yards behind her in a crumpled mauve robe. He was unsteady on his feet. Rufryd, Auriel, Tanthe and Lahjaya were with him. Both Jthery and Auriel looked aghast with terror as they saw Falthorn striding towards them, raven hair flowing and eyes like steel. The others clustered around Jthery; he stood defiantly in their midst, facing Falthorn as if confronting a ravening dra'a'k.

It was Mawrdreth who stepped into Falthorn's path and stopped him bodily before he reached his prey.

Falthorn stood braced against Mawrdreth's hands, ice-grey eyes blazing at the young lord. 'You fool!' he snarled. 'Have you any idea what you've done? What were you thinking?'

'You were using me!' Jthery yelled back. He lunged forward and it took both Rufryd and Tanthe to hold him back. 'You want me to tell them how? He's planning to bleed the whole Earth dry!'

'What does he mean?' said Helan.

'He's raving.' Falthorn took a breath, recovering some of his usual composure. 'He appears to have completely misunderstood something I said to him. More fool me for trusting him. I've no plans to destroy the Earth, I assure you. But I cannot let Verdanholm fall to Vaurgroth. I must have those weapons back.'

Some of Falthorn's soldiers had come to stand nearby, threatening. Their faces were pale-gold masks, their eyes cold diamonds.

'Give them back,' Falthorn said, low and intent. 'Give me the Basilisks and I'll take my army away.'

'Why do you threaten us with war?' Helan demanded. 'We have a far greater mutual enemy, do we not? Jthery intimated that things are far from friendly between you and Sour-breath.'

Falthorn's lips twitched in a grimace as she mocked the name. 'It's true I've only kept him sweet with threats, not brotherhood. That's why I need the Basilisks.'

'Why?' Tanthe put in. She came to face Falthorn, her arms folded. He looked icily at her. 'What's happened to my child, a weapon so terrible that he's worse than all the Basilisks put together? Did you give him to the Devourers?'

'That's not your concern.'

'Oh, yes it is. Jthery said you still have him, hidden somewhere.' Tanthe's face was cloud-pale against her dark hair, her eyes blue-green beams. Helan suddenly noticed a resemblance between them; faint, but there.

'Jthery has been talkative, hasn't he?' Falthorn said. 'Shame he couldn't find better uses for his mouth.'

Again Jthery jerked furiously against Rufryd's grip.

'My point is,' Tanthe persisted, 'why do you need the Basilisks if you've got our wondrous child?'

Falthorn's eyes narrowed. 'The Bhahdradomen have difficulty understanding what the child is, and therefore taking him seriously as a threat.'

'Crap,' she said. 'I think the child is a bluff, and they've seen through it. I doubt the poor little thing's got any powers at all. He's just a hostage, like Auriel was.'

'And if I offered the boy in exchange for the Basilisks?' Falthorn said without missing a beat.

Tanthe's face drained to white. Helan took her shoulders and gently eased her aside.

'Now, why would I consider exchanging my only hope of defeating the Bhahdradomen for someone else's – forgive me, Tanthe – someone else's child?'

'Perhaps, madam, you'd feel differently if I offered you your mother and brother too?'

Helan swallowed drily. 'Long ago my mother persuaded me that I must never again allow her to be used as a lever against me. She's strong; she would rather die. You can't play that counter twice.'

'Then I'll be frank with you. I did consider giving the boy to Vaurgroth as a hostage, so that while I held the weapons against him, he held the child against me, thus ensuring that neither of us broke our agreement. It was meant to keep the peace between us.'

'Why didn't you?' Tanthe asked.

'I was waiting for them to prove worthy of trust. Unfortunately, they have not. None have, who are not Valahyr.' He shot Jthery another savage look.

'No,' Tanthe said. 'The child was always a bluff, to trick them and torment me.'

Falthorn stepped closer to her. She flinched. 'Why are so many of my family such utter idiots? The last thing on my mind is tormenting anyone. But if you stand in the way of protecting Verdanholm, you will get hurt.'

Mawrdreth said, 'You should have asked us for help, instead of bringing an army to threaten us.'

'Ask humans for help?' he said contemptuously. He

gave Jthery another furious glance. 'You're no more to be trusted than the Eaters. Certainly not with *roth*-powers like the Basilisks.'

Helan said, 'I can see your advantage in having them back, but where is ours in taking the child in exchange? There can't be one. I think Tanthe's right, it's always been a bluff.'

'There is power in the child. However, the Basilisks are of more immediate practical use to me. They're a threat the Eaters understand.'

'Because the child, I assume, is too small to do any damage?' Helan threw back. 'What is he, an investment for the future? Of no use until he's grown – by which time you think you'll have found a way to take him away from us? And of course, you know he'll be safe in our care.'

Falthorn's face was so glacial, she suspected she'd hit on the truth. 'He could do greater harm now, before he's learned to control his powers. Madam, I can offer you the child in exchange, or I can use the child against you. Your choice.'

'Go back to Verdanholm,' Helan said thinly. 'Why should I help you, after what you did to me? To all of us?'

Falthorn laughed unpleasantly. 'Don't you find one enemy enough to contend with? You wish to take on the Valahyr, as well as the Bhahdradomen?'

'If you would help us instead of hindering us, we needn't be having this argument,' Helan said. Worth a try, but she saw from the contempt that flashed across Falthorn's face that he dismissed the suggestion out of hand. He would never help humans; even if he pretended to co-operate, he'd betray them at the first possible moment.

'I've outlined the options,' he said. 'I'm running out of patience. Decide!'

He was desperate, Helan saw, and that might give her the upper hand. 'It won't help either of us to lose patience. Why don't you ask your cohorts to sheathe their swords while you come in and talk to us?'

Jthery exclaimed, 'No, don't invite him in!'

'If it's going to cause such displeasure, I just might,' Falthorn said thinly. 'But I don't have that much time to waste.'

'We are not giving up the Basilisks,' Helan said firmly.

She felt a sudden shiver of dread. It was as if Falthorn's eyes locked onto hers and held them. An oval of greenish light was forming on his forehead like some deadly, unstoppable missile pointed from his mind to hers. She was frozen in its path, tasting for the first time the reason that Auriel, Jthery and Tanthe were so afraid of him. Involuntarily she tensed against it.

'At least show us the child!' Tanthe exclaimed. As she spoke, the light winked out and the tension vanished. Helan exhaled in relief. The others didn't seem to have noticed.

'What?' said Falthorn.

'We've seen no proof that he even exists! Let's see him!'

'Tanthe . . .' Helan began, but Tanthe held her arm.

'No, Hel, please. You can't make a decision until we've seen him. It might make a difference.'

'What difference?'

'I don't know, but how can we know unless— ?'

'All right,' Falthorn said, startling them. 'It's no trouble; not much, at any rate, since Auriel has done half the work for me. But Tanthe, have you considered whether this is a good idea?'

'What do you mean?'

'Seeing your son for the first time may have a dreadful effect upon you. I hope you are prepared.'

'I'll risk it,' Tanthe retorted, but Helan felt her breathing fast, shaking. She put a reassuring arm round her. Falthorn always did this; let you think you'd got your own way, then turned it back upon you.

'Very well,' said Helan. 'Show us.'

'Follow me,' said Falthorn, turning casually in a swirl of

blue-black fabric. 'It's quite a confluence of power Auriel has uncovered, and only a short walk from here. Anyone who wishes to come, be my guest.'

Tanthe's heart butted its way into her throat and stuck there as Falthorn led them across the scarlet plain. He was heading north and east, leaving the green fringe of the Olivine River behind them. A handful of Helan's soldiers and Valahyr went with them to guard each party. Rufryd was beside her, holding her hand, Helan and Mawrdreth walking alongside. Auriel and Lahjaya walked a few yards behind with Jthery. He had hung back at first then changed his mind. Glancing back, Tanthe saw that he and Auriel were walking close together, both washed out with fear and helpless anger. It's brave of them to go anywhere near Falthorn voluntarily, she thought. Me, too.

'Why are you all so scared of him?' Rufryd whispered.

Tanthe paused. 'Imagine the most terrifying nightmare you've ever had, and not being able to wake up from it. Ever. That feeling of being completely hysterical with terror and not even knowing why?'

'Er . . . yes, that's happened.'

'He can do that to you. There's a place called the *ezht*; not a place but a kind of psychic dimension that the Bhahdradomen use. He can send your mind into it and that's what it's like. You come back after a few minutes feeling like you've been there for years. I can't describe it. I feel sick just thinking about it. You come back and it's like all the spirit's been sucked out of you. You never feel safe again.'

Rufryd looked at her, horrified. 'That's how he broke Auriel, you see,' she added. 'He's probably done it to Jthery, too. And I think my Aelyr parents are trapped there. And maybe my child, too, I'm not sure.'

'Are you sure about doing this?' Rufryd said after a minute.

'Yes.'

'He won't give you this infant, you know. It's got to be another trick.'

'I don't care. I just want to see him.'

Rufryd sighed, shaking his head. Falthorn looked round at them, as if he'd heard every word. He fell into step beside Tanthe and said, 'He's been well-looked after, you know.' As before, she couldn't tell if the hint of friendliness in his manner was real or faked. Falthorn sounded utterly sincere when he wanted to.

'But where's he been all this time?'

'In a safe place.' To her surprise, Falthorn expanded. 'He has his own little realm within Verdanholm.'

'A pocket like the one you kept Princess Ghiseyma and her son in?'

'Along those lines, but on a larger scale. Not just a room but a glade for him to play in, sheltering woods, a fresh stream. A very pretty place.'

'It sounds lovely, but he's a baby, not a fawn.'

'He wasn't alone, obviously. He has been in the care of the Laefrohyr.'

'Who?'

'The Laefrohyr are a small, shy *eretru* who keep themselves hidden. They are biddable, however, and have been most helpful to me. A couple called Artis and Sehnya have been looking after him.'

Tanthe's heart was beating so fast she thought she might faint. She sensed Falthorn was telling the truth. 'I would have looked after him.'

'Better you never saw him at all, never even knew he existed,' Falthorn said, off-hand. 'Still, the best laid plans go awry. I didn't come this far without being ready for the most unlikely contingencies.'

They came to the edge of the plain. It fell away beneath them into sheer red cliffs that curved away on either side. Beyond, the ocean crashed green and silver against the coast. Fingers of rock ran out into the foam, rising here and there into little spires and islands.

At once, Tanthe sensed power about the place. There was a wide, oval platform of rock that stood a few inches proud of the flat cliff-top. It was polished ruby-smooth, its edges rounded. Suspended above it was a rippling knot of heat-haze. The more she looked, the clearer it became. It was like a pursed mouth of air. Then she began to see that it had a silvery glow, tiny sparks dancing within it like fireflies. Falthorn held up a hand, stopping them before it.

'Look!' she whispered to Rufryd.

'I can't see anything.'

'Well, I can.' Tanthe glanced at Auriel, who gave her a quick, wary smile. 'I'm seeing it with Aelyr sight. Weird.'

'It's as bright as Lily Moon to me,' said Auriel. 'Can't you see the strands coming off it, like threads of glass? Each one is a path.'

'No,' Tanthe admitted. 'Not yet.'

'Lord Falthorn,' said Helan, 'I can't allow my people to be taken through any portals. You may well be acting honestly, for a change, but I'm not risking it.'

'No one has to leave this spot.' Falthorn took out an *anametris* sphere, palest green. 'Simply watch. If you decide to agree to our bargain – which you will – I can go through and fetch the child myself.'

He began to turn the sphere in his hand with short twisting jerks, as if unlocking a puzzle. The node of silvery air glowed brighter.

Rufryd clutched Tanthe's arm. 'I can see something!'

Tanthe said, 'Auriel, what's happening?'

'He is opening one portal after another . . . I can't keep track of the pathways he's following . . . but they're all interconnected, like following a map. There's no real space or time between them so he can draw the realm-pocket to us.' Auriel was staring intently at Falthorn, who appeared oblivious to them. A good time to take him by surprise and stab him to death, Tanthe thought – except that if she did she would never see her baby. 'I didn't know this was possible.' He sounded annoyed. 'I hoped Falthorn didn't know about the web, but he was bound to, I suppose.'

'Could you do it?' she asked.

'I think so,' said Auriel. 'Now I've seen what he's doing.'

'Lost arts of the Aelyr,' Rufryd said bitterly. 'Loves to show off, doesn't he?'

'Watch,' Falthorn said with a flourish.

Above the platform shimmered a scene, hazy but so real Tanthe felt she could have stepped into it. A forest glade with the look of Verdanholm about it, a silvery cast to its lush greens. She saw a winding stream, trees, a stump of blue rock. The glade was empty, but after a few seconds two figures appeared.

They were a male and a female, obviously Aelyr but of an *eretru* she'd never seen before. Their skin was pale green, their hair silver, their features long and eldritch. They came hurrying into the glade with their garments floating like many-layered insect-wings.

Tanthe guessed they'd come in response to the portal opening. She trembled, straining for a first glimpse of her elusive son.

Falthorn stepped forward and appeared to stand both on Earth and in the glade at the same time. The two Laefrohyr stared at him.

'Good day to you, my Lady Sehnya, my Lord Artis. I wish to see the child.'

The green-skinned Aelyr looked distressed. Tanthe felt dread tainting her excitement. 'Many days have passed in this realm since you last enquired after Mendyr,' said the woman. Her voice sounded tinny, far away.

Mendyr, Tanthe mouthed. Is that what they called him?

'Alas that you didn't enquire after him more often,' said the man. 'That you confined us here so that we could not tell you!'

They were more than distressed. They were frightened. 'Where is he?' Falthorn said furiously. He stepped forward and was in the glade.

'The Wrothryr came and took him, as they threatened.'

Tanthe saw the wave of disbelief and rage shake Falthorn's form. 'But I secured this realm against them!'

'We warned you,' said Sehnya, 'that nowhere would remain secure against them forever. You mocked our fears!'

'They came – and you did not stop them?'

'We tried!' said Artis. 'We were helpless against them!'

'Fools,' Falthorn snarled. 'Craven idiots!'

Artis and Sehnya looked as terrified as Auriel had, but faced him bravely. 'How could you think to create a being like that and not attract their wrath?' said Sehnya. 'We could do nothing to stop them! He is only a tool to you but he was flesh and blood to us!'

Falthorn let out a roar of pure frustration. He raised his hands and the two Laefrohyr fell, crying out as if he'd shot arrows into them. Tanthe gasped, wanting to help them, impotent. Falthorn stepped back. The glade whirled and was sucked away into its own realm.

As it vanished, Tanthe's head swam with the currents of power. She felt her Aelyr awareness opening, a painful flower of light. Staring across the platform, out over the cliff-edge, she saw another, greater apparition looming upon the sea; shimmering and, for a few seconds, vividly real. The Tower, the dreadful Obsidian Tower that did not exist.

Beings of light were whispering warnings all around her, *Do not enter here. Stay away, for your strength will not suffice. That which you seek cannot be given.*

Tanthe stood petrified, with all the breath knocked out of her, unaware of Rufryd's and Auriel's hands on her. Cheated, empty, bereft.

'This changes things,' said Helan. With folded arms she faced Falthorn across the table. His retinue sat around him, including Ostarial and Alviath and others whose names she didn't know, looking as grim as their leader.

Lamps cast a tarnished bronze light inside the tent. She had Mawrdreth, Karmensis and a handful of her officers around her. Tanthe had collapsed on the way back, so Rufryd, Auriel and Lahjaya had taken her to her room. 'You appear to have lost all your bargaining counters and hostages.'

'Which is unfortunate for you,' Falthorn retorted, 'since, unless you will give me the Basilisks, I shall take them by force. I warn you not to underestimate the power of highly skilled Valahyr warriors and my own *roth* powers.'

'We've more cause to declare war upon *you*,' said Mawrdreth. He looked as stern and inflexible as Falthorn himself. 'You are the one who usurped the Queen from her throne, and sold Aventuria from under us! You are no less grasping, devious and evil than Vaurgroth himself!'

Falthorn jerked his icy gaze at the tent-roof. 'Don't let us descend into a simplistic discussion of the nature of evil. I must protect my realm. To me, that is the ultimate good. Vaurgroth doubtless holds the welfare of his *domenim* dear to his heart. And humans think they have a Goddess-given right to all the resources and territory of Aventuria.' He tapped his long, hard fingers on the table-top. 'We are all "good" people in our own way. All we have here is a fatal conflict of interest.'

Helan said, 'If you want to make war upon us, go ahead. We're ready. If we defeat you and keep the Basilisks, we still have hope. If we lose, then we may as well surrender to Foul-gross and all throw ourselves into the sea.'

'Very well,' said Falthorn, rising, his garments midnight-black in the dull light. Oily rainbows of power glimmered around him, bronze, blue, violet. 'If you want a fight, you shall have it.'

'*Gauroth*,' Helan breathed, realising. 'That's why you're so powerful.'

'It is the greatest *roth* of all, madam, in the right hands.'

'It destroyed my grandfather.'

'It only destroys fools.'

'Do all the Aelyr *eretrue* want to be saved by someone so utterly unscrupulous?' she said. 'Lord Elrill will never thank you. The Fhelethyr will never be your friends.'

'I am grateful, since thanks and friends only make people weak. Now, I ask you one last time, will you give me the Basilisks and Jthery?'

She felt he was hypnotising her. Again she saw that slow missile of light forming between his eyes. If he attacked her here in the tent with *gauroth* she was powerless. Mawrdreth and Karmensis rose at her side, their hands on their sword hilts, realising something was happening.

'No,' she said. 'Since you seem so intent on avoiding battle, I can only conclude that you have the most to fear from it.' Although she spoke coolly, her chest was one solid lump of dread.

'Conclusions are the death of enquiry,' Falthorn said softly.

Their gazes locked in a frozen moment of hostility. Then, as Falthorn broke the contact, the tent-flap opened and a pale figure stood against the light.

It was Jthery.

'Helan?' he said, his voice faint. 'Tanthe told me what happened.'

'Go away,' she said.

Instead, he came nervously into the tent. 'I know what's happening. I've been listening. Let – let me talk to him.'

Both Helan and Falthorn turned to stare at Jthery.

'Don't be stupid,' Helan said. 'There's no reason for you to be anywhere near him. Let us deal with this.'

Jthery looked at Falthorn. He looked a good deal better than when he'd first arrived; his apricot hair was washed and silky and he'd found a Marocian robe in a colour he liked, watery blue, but he still appeared terrified of his tormentor. He fiddled nervously with the carved amethyst carp that hung round his neck.

'Falthorn, if I go with you, will you leave Helan alone?'

'Jthery!' she cried. 'Don't you even think about it!'

'Can I talk to you, at least?'

'Very well,' said Falthorn, moving towards him. 'As long as it's alone.'

'I can't allow that,' Helan began to say, but Jthery cut across her.

'No, Helan, it's all right. I'm not afraid of him.'

'I warned you,' said Rufryd. 'Tan, this is going to tear you to pieces!'

She sat on the bed, pallid but composed. Rufryd couldn't stand seeing her like this. He wanted the spirited, bright, sarcastic Tanthe that he knew. She looked so alluring languishing there, one knee raised, her flesh like ivory and her sable hair in disarray, that he wanted to send the others out and caress her . . . but her eyes were cold blue-green seas, limpid with distance. This Aelyr business made her seem unattainable. Maybe that was why she'd always seemed above him, somehow, though he'd done his best to bring her back to earth. He felt, painfully, that however many times he poured himself into her body, he would never truly know what it was to be inside *her*.

Auriel and Lahjaya sat around the bed. Vetru hovered like a shadow in one corner. Jthery had been to see her, leaning so close he seemed to be kissing her. Rufryd had almost put out a hand to stop him, until he realised that Jthery was actually whispering something in her ear. Tanthe went paler. Jthery left.

'At least the child's not in Falthorn's control any more,' Tanthe said at last. 'I think it will be even harder to get him back from those who've taken him, though.'

'What are you talking about?' said Rufryd.

'The Laefrohyr said that something called the "Wrothryr" had taken the child. I've heard that name before. I'm not sure what they are but I think I've seen them. Rufe, when we – er, when I had that vision, I saw beings made of light, pure *roth*.'

'But Tanthe, visions aren't real.'

She fixed him with her startling eyes. 'This, after all that stuff you told me about Akarata?'

'Well, that was . . .'

'No, don't tell me it was different! I keep seeing the Obsidian Tower, more and more real. My mother – Fiomir, I mean – said something about a dark spire. She warned me not to go there. The Wrothryr – if that's what they were – gave me the same warning.'

'Perhaps it's worth listening to them,' Rufryd put in hopelessly.

'Just now, on the cliff, I saw the Tower and the Wrothryr again.'

'How do you know you weren't hallucinating?'

'She wasn't,' said Auriel. 'I saw it too.' She looked at him, eyes quick and bright with hope.

Rufryd groaned. 'Why are you encouraging her?'

'I'm not,' Auriel said, giving him a look. 'I'm saying what I saw. It's my child too, in case you'd forgotten.'

'I can't forget, unfortunately,' Rufryd said, as mildly as he could.

'Rufe,' Tanthe muttered.

'And I've heard of the Wrothryr,' Auriel added. 'Falthorn mentioned them to me once or twice, in unguarded moments. They are *roth*-beings. They are to the Aelyr as Aelyr are to humans.'

'So you're scared of them?' Rufryd asked.

Auriel shrugged. 'I suppose so, but they're never seen. They have nothing to do with us. Until now.'

'I feel that the Obsidian Tower is the key to rescuing our parents and finding out where . . . where Mendyr is,' Tanthe went on. 'I must find it.'

Rufryd was becoming exasperated. 'Look, Tanthe. The Obsidian Tower stood in Hellaxis, which is either right on the other side of the world or in another realm entirely, depending on which myth you listen to. It no longer exists. It's a symbol to the Bhahdradomen. It represents the long hard climb through darkness to reach the light of

Ancestor's wisdom, or something like that – Arax Vahan talked so much crap I've tried to forget most of it. But it's just a symbol.'

Tanthe folded her arms. 'All right then, would you like to hear what Jthery just told me? He's had visions of the Tower as well. He said that he kept seeing two figures going towards it. Not only did he know they were Aelyr, he knew they were my parents. Our parents.' She looked at Auriel; his eyes were huge.

'Still,' said Rufryd, 'he may have been elaborating on things you told him.'

'No. There were things he couldn't have known.'

'Tan, did nothing I told you have the slightest impression on you? You want to find a place that doesn't exist, to look for a needle in a haystack, and probably get your heart torn to pieces in the process?'

Colour burned in her cheeks. 'Whatever it takes, I am going to find my son.'

Rufryd had tried to be calm, but her stubbornness enraged him. The prospect of her rushing headlong into another inferno of danger was unbearable.

'You're on your bloody own, then,' he exclaimed. 'If you won't listen to sense, I can't support you on this stupid wild-goose chase! I can't pick up any more pieces. I've had enough.'

Everyone stared at him. Lahjaya said, 'If you're going to shout at my patient, you'd better leave.'

'It's all right, he always shouts at me,' Tanthe said sourly. 'I'm used to it.' They both sat with folded arms, refusing to look at each other.

'Well, if he won't go with you, I will,' Auriel said, taking her hand. 'They're our parents and he's our son. I'm not scared any more.'

'Well?' said Falthorn, as distant and intimidating as he'd ever been. 'Are you going to explain what the hell you were thinking of?'

He and Jthery were walking by the river, where ferny trees edged green strips of farmland. 'I had to do it.' Jthery could find no strength in his voice. He was shaking from head to foot. There was a distinct danger that Falthorn might kill him, but he'd insisted Helan send no guards with him. 'You told me you were going to use me to drain all the *roth* out of the Earth . . .'

'You didn't tell them how, did you?'

'Not yet, but I could.'

'You bloody little traitor. I trusted you. I thought you were on my side and believed in Verdanholm as I did.'

'No, I was just infatuated with you,' Jthery said.

Falthorn seized him, grabbed the cord that held the amethyst fish round his neck and tightened it until it cut into the skin. 'I should kill you for what you've done!'

'But you won't,' Jthery choked. 'You can't use my powers if you kill me!'

The Valahyr lord let him go. Jthery rubbed his neck, gasping. 'I'm angry enough to kill you, but anger is an emotion of chaos suited only to children and humans. You've wrecked my plans. Now Vaurgroth can walk into Verdanholm and there's nothing to stop him.'

'He doesn't know where the Basilisks are.'

'He'll find out, sooner or later – especially if the humans start using them against his forces. Damn you to Hellaxis, you weak-minded little idiot, do you have the faintest idea of what you've done?'

'Yes. Given Aventuria a chance.'

'I thought you loved me.'

'I can't love someone who uses me as you were doing. What did you expect? I am heir to Mithrain, I had to try at least to save my own realm!' Jthery opened his palms wide. 'Water is sacred to us, how can I use water against my own land? It's obscene!'

Falthorn was quiet for a time. 'I was wrong about you. I thought you were weak, even a bit simple. Seems you have some fire inside you after all.'

'Thought I was simple?' Jthery hissed. 'You just hate anyone who won't bow down to you.'

'On the contrary. Servility disgusts me.'

'Falthorn, please listen to me. Don't do this to Helan. Give her a fighting chance against the Eaters.'

'Why should I?'

'If you let her keep the Basilisks, I'll come back with you. If you make war on her, though, I'll kill myself – then you'll never have the use of my powers, will you?'

Falthorn turned to Jthery, placed his hands on his shoulders, glared at him. 'You're a clever little boy, aren't you?'

'I know what you used to do to Auriel,' Jthery said, his voice steady now. 'Send me into the *ezht* and I'll stay there. Or if I come back, you'll be left either with a cowering fool, or else with someone who despises you for eternity. Is that what you want? I don't suppose you care, since you have a lump of granite for a heart.'

'Don't you despise me already?' His dark brows indented; he looked less sure of himself.

'Not as much as I should. Not as much as I will. You've been making ultimatums all day; here is mine. Fight them and I'll kill myself. Let them keep the Basilisks and I'll let you use my powers, although I will hate you for it.'

'This is not much of a choice.' Falthorn's eyelids fell; he looked troubled, disheartened suddenly.

'Or . . .' Jthery tilted his head. 'You could just throw in your lot with Helananthe. If you join forces against the Bhahdradomen, you'll be so much stronger. You may actually defeat them, instead of being forced to make these fragile, humiliating bargains with them.'

Falthorn swallowed, very nearly gagged against the idea. He stared at the river, winding its slow way through the red and emerald landscape. 'Join forces with the humans. And then what shall I get from you in return?'

'Not my powers. They're only for me, and Mithrain. You will just get a lover.'

Falthorn turned away. Jthery's heart sank. It had always been the most hopeless of gambles. He braced himself for the Valahyr's scorn, didn't even care any more.

'What is that greatest of human insults?' Falthorn said quietly. 'Tanthe was always throwing it at me. You Goddess-forsaken, motherless bastard, Jey.'

'I loved you. But love wears a bit thin when you realise you are just being used.'

'You bastard,' Falthorn said again, still gazing at the river.

Jthery turned and began to walk away.

Helan and Mawrdreth had refreshments brought for the waiting Valahyr. Tanthe, Rufryd and Auriel came in to join them and the two parties had even begun to talk to each other. Most of the conversation consisted of them needling each other, but their animosity was half-hearted.

At last the tent-flap was flung back. Jthery came in first, followed by Falthorn. They both had oddly blank expressions that gave nothing away; Helan was simply relieved to see Jthery in one piece and no longer distressed.

'Jthery and I have had a most interesting talk,' Falthorn said brusquely. 'As a result, ma'am, I wish to make you a rather less unpalatable offer. Keep the Basilisks. The Valahyr are going to fight alongside you.'

'What?' Helan spluttered on the wine she was sipping.

'Is it too late for us to become allies?' he said, looking at her, his gaze clear and steady.

She glanced round the faces of the Valahyr. They looked startled, but relieved if anything. Her own side appeared stunned.

'No, of course not. I couldn't have wished for better news.'

Mawrdreth added, 'As long as this isn't another deception.'

Falthorn's face stiffened. 'It is not. I can assure you,

sire, this is the most difficult decision I have ever had to make.' His gaze rested lightly on Auriel, Tanthe and Rufryd in turn. They stared back in a mixture of suspicion and amazement.

'Since you've had the grace to make this offer, we shall have the grace to take it at face value,' said Helan.

Falthorn held out his hand. Cautiously she took it, and they shook hands in wary friendship. 'You won't regret this,' she said.

'I trust not.' He inclined his head. 'Our first task should be to get the Basilisks into action. By the way, you may take whatever precautions you think fit to assure yourselves that I am not trying to steal them.'

'If you help Earth, we shall do our utmost to help Verdanholm in turn. This is the most wonderful turn of events.' Helan smiled. 'Jthery, what on Earth did you say to him?'

Her cousin's lips curved in a small, inward smile. 'That shall remain between us and the river.'

'What *did* you say to him?' Tanthe asked later, catching Jthery on his own and slipping her arm round his waist. He had the amethyst fish with its moon and teardrop in his hand and was polishing it with the sleeve of his robe. 'Come on, you can tell me.'

Jthery grinned. 'All right, well ... He treated me so bizarrely at times, and told me things he shouldn't have told me, that I began to suspect he had actually fallen in love with me.'

'Has he?'

'The first time he saw me, apparently. Only he'd rather cut his own tongue out than admit it, especially to himself.'

'But you made him?'

'After he'd cursed me blind. That's all; he's helping us because he loves me. Because he would have lost me, otherwise. He's doing it because I asked him to.'

'Oh, Jey. Please be careful. Do you really believe him?'

He was sombre. 'This time, yes. You've no idea how difficult it was for him to say it. He doesn't want a soul to know, either.'

'I'll make sure everyone does, then.'

He laughed. 'They will, anyway.'

'But do you really want to be in love with someone as cruel as he can be?'

'I had no choice, and neither did he. Don't you think people can change for the better?'

'Yes, but in Falthorn's case it would be a bloody miracle.'

'I don't need a miracle.' He threw the amethyst fish high in the air and caught it triumphantly. 'I'm the one with the power now.'

The army broke camp and marched on. The landscape changed abruptly as the red plain gave way to dry hills patched with tough grass, scrubby bushes, ground plants with tiny crimson flowers. From the coast, a mile or so to the east, the sea roared softly. They were perhaps two hundred miles south of the border with Paranios.

The hillside on which they chose to make camp was dark with loam and lichens, the sunset on fire behind it. As they were pitching tents and settling in, two of Helan's scouts came rushing to her, scarlet with exertion.

'Ma'am, the Bhahdradomen are camped three miles to the north, above the Almandine Vale.'

'How many?'

'An army. Eight, ten thousand. Perhaps more.'

'More?' She and Mawrdreth exchanged grim, shocked looks. So soon, she thought. We weren't expecting to face them for days or weeks yet. More than ten thousand? We have only seven. Still, we have the Basilisks now . . .

'That's our best guess, since we didn't have time to count them all. The camp is huge, and making ready for war.'

A blend of dread, resolution and peace settled on her. 'Well,' she said calmly, 'go and inform the officers. It looks as if they've come to meet us.'

An hour later, the Bhahdradomen commander himself arrived at the camp amid a retinue of elite *vagharim*. They were carrying a banner, Helan saw in shock. That was a human tradition they'd copied. And it looked as if the banner had been taken from the Amber Citadel; it was rich royal blue with the eight-spoked emblem on it in gold, but in place of the Tree of Life, the image of a tall black tower had been superimposed.

She stared at the banner in complete outrage. How dare they!

The Bhahdradomen commander was bigger than *domen* usually were and made her think of a bull. He had a look of *graukhim* about him, a thick-shouldered solidity and a fierce, heavy head, as if he'd made a partial change into something other. His face was all scaly furrows, his eyes copper pinpricks under a jutting brow.

His aides announced him as Lord Thunderer Bharamezht.

Helan stood with Mawrdreth and Karmensis on either side, her guards around her. The Valahyr were keeping out of sight; Falthorn didn't want Vaurgroth to find out any sooner than necessary that he was on her side now.

The air smouldered with *gauroth* latent in the Bhahdradomen weapons. It made her feel weak and slightly faint, as if she could never fully harden herself to it. Behind her, a score of human bows and crossbows were trained on the Bhahdradomen party. A dozen, much deadlier *uzrats* were trained on her. The two sides met under the flaming bowl of the sky.

'My lady,' said Bharamezht, 'if your army advances any further than the southern rim of the Almandine Vale, it will be considered an act of aggression.'

'Consider it an act of justice,' Helananthe replied. 'We are coming to reclaim what was stolen from us.'

'If you advance, you will be destroyed. Our Master of Light's arm is long and lethal.'

'Don't be too confident. I ask you courteously, Lord

Thunderer, let my army pass. Let Vaurgroth be warned to give up his false authority before we take it from him by force.'

Bharamezht gave a low grumble, more a purr than a laugh. 'I see no force.'

'Your eyes deceive you more than you can imagine. Unless you desire a repeat of the Silver Plains, let us pass.'

The copper pin-pricks dulled with suspicion. 'You don't possess the Basilisks. They are in safekeeping.'

'Are you certain of that?'

'Of course.' Bharamezht looked angry.

'Then you are willing to take a terrible risk. We may not have the Basilisks, but we may have something more deadly.'

'Vaurgroth's good legions never shrink from risk,' he replied. 'Your bluff is hollow. Whatever weapons you have, bring them on; we have worse!'

The Bhahdradomen party retreated, the offensive banner snapping arrogantly on the air. With a heavy breath, Helan turned to her companions. Falthorn, who had concealed himself in a nearby tent, came out and looked gravely at her.

'He's spoiling for a fight,' she said. 'They're so blown up with power now, I think that even if we stuck the Basilisks under his nose, he wouldn't care.'

Mawrdreth's face was dark with anger. 'He will regret it.'

'Now we had better move fast,' said Falthorn, 'before word reaches Sour-breath that Verdanholm is undefended.'

'Yes, but – damn it – we needed more time than this to get the Basilisks working!' Helan growled. 'If we haven't learned how to use them by morning, we're buggered.'

'Then we had better get on with it,' said Falthorn.

They withdrew to a hollow, south of the camp; Helan and Mawrdreth, Tanthe and Rufryd, Lahjaya, Falthorn, Jthery,

Karmensis and a handful of her senior officers. The light was still good. With careful reverence, Helan unwrapped each of the Basilisks and set them on a square of linen.

Tanthe looked at them in awe. She had been a finger's length away from them herself, the first time she'd been in Verdanholm. When she'd touched the chest, white light had thrown her across the room. She guessed she was lucky to have survived.

None of the weapons was bigger than eighteen inches across. They were compact, but they had a deadly, unearthly quality that set her teeth on edge. Shiny white metal and crystal cast into inscrutable shapes; they looked sleek, whimsical, alien.

'I've pieced together as much as I can from the slabs Mawrdreth and I transcribed,' said Helan. 'But the fact is that even those slabs didn't contain all we need to know. I think I know what each is for, but not how to make them work.'

'That, unfortunately, is as far as I had got,' said Falthorn.

'I thought you would have made yourself an expert on them long ago,' Helan said harshly.

'They were intended to be a deterrent.' Falthorn gave her a flinty stare. Tanthe still didn't trust him. She never would. 'I never expected to use them. The Eaters fear them, but are wholly ignorant of the ease or otherwise of deploying them.'

Helan touched the one nearest to her, a disc set with a large central sphere and a ring of smaller spheres around it. 'This one I believe is referred to as "Sunfire", designed to dazzle the Bhahdradomen on the battlefield. To cast nets of light, as the histories put it. This . . .' She indicated a horn with a curly stem like a giant sea-shell. 'This is "Calabethron's Song." It produces a note that deafens them . . .'

'More than deafens them,' Falthorn put in. 'Liquefies their brains, if used correctly. It's a modification of a common Aelyr tactic, the voice as a weapon. Calabethron designed it to produce *roth*-energies harmful only to the Bhahdradomen.'

'This one's more prosaic, then.' Helan touched the third, a slender pyramid surmounted by a long, tapering nozzle. The shaft could be angled on a spherical joint of crystal. 'The famous "Dragon" which, unsurprisingly, sends out blasts of fire. Now these other two. The cube, I'm pretty sure, is the "Swallower"; instead of sending out *roth*, it absorbs it, thus disabling their mages and hopefully most of their weapons too. That leaves the rod.' She picked it up; it hummed faintly as she turned it. Just a simple white shaft with a clear ball at either end, and three thick rings of crystal around it. 'This is the "Pin of Time." Meant to take *ghelim* out of the air.'

Mawrdreth added, 'We learned from the slabs that certain flying *ghelim*, under the direction of an adept, can fold time in a small way and seem to appear from nowhere. The Pin of Time disturbs whatever it is within their minds that enables them to do it.'

'Pin, as in the sort that would fasten a butterfly to a card,' said Falthorn. He was on his knees, examining each of the weapons in turn. 'It disrupts whatever it is in their small brain that senses direction. Without it they can neither jump through time nor fly.' Tanthe watched him closely, but he appeared to be absorbed. Not about to do anything devious.

'How do they work?' she asked.

Helan said, 'We know from the accounts of the time that mages took these weapons into battle. Only they had probably worked with them for months, if not actually manufactured them under Calabethron's supervision. But Mawrdreth and I aren't *roth*-mages. We didn't even have the chance to finish transcribing the slabs, let alone fully to understand them. Too much knowledge has been lost.'

Falthorn looked disdainful. 'Do you have no mages at all among you?'

'Lahjaya is a healer. I don't know whether she'd have the right skills for this, though. I really couldn't speak for Tanthe and Auriel.'

He shook his head. 'No, no, they're fledglings, hopeless for this. I believe most of the mages that helped King Maharoth were Aelyr of long experience and great skill. So, there's only me.'

Falthorn and Helan looked at each other. 'I can't expect you to do this for us.'

'I wouldn't *trust* you to do it for us,' Tanthe added.

Falthorn gave her an indifferent glance. 'The tragedy of this is that, used purely as a threat, the Basilisks were highly effective. In the field, without mages who know what they're doing – which may involve feeding *roth* into them – they're all but useless.'

He raised the horn to his lips and blew. All that came out of it was a dull rasp; unpleasant enough to make them wince, but lacking force.

Falthorn lowered the instrument and gazed at it, frowning. 'I have worse news for you,' he said at last. 'Even *roth* weapons suffer the ravages of time.'

'What?' said Helan.

'Look closely. There is a degree of corrosion on most of them. There, around the sockets that hold the crystals. Rust, if you will. It will impede the *roth* flow.'

'Oh, Dyon's balls,' Helan said under her breath. Her face was stiff, trying not to reveal despair. 'Does this mean they're unusable?'

'Possibly not. The Pin . . .' Falthorn weighed the rod in his palms. 'I can feel life in this. And there's no sign of corrosion on it. But the others are ailing, if not actually dead.'

'Can they be repaired?'

'I doubt it,' Falthorn said flatly. 'Even a small amount of decay in the metal means the whole housing must be replaced, and we lack the time, materials and knowledge to do it. I doubt that even Calabethron anticipated rust.'

Falthorn jumped to his feet, lifting the heavy disc of the

Sunfire. 'Let me try and coax some life from this one. Stay there.'

He carried the Sunfire to a smooth, flat area of grass, some twenty yards away. They all rose to their feet to watch him, caught anxiously between suspicion and the need to trust him. There Falthorn set the weapon down and bent over it, moving his fingertips over the crystals as if attuning to them.

Rufryd slipped his arm round Tanthe and held her. Silence lay on Helan's party. The air was thick with apprehension. Tanthe jumped, feeling the sudden throb of *roth* power before the others did. Aelyr sense. She suddenly felt that her human senses had been quite enough.

The disc gave off a faint glow of palest yellow. It seemed a pure power, not blood-tainted like *gauroth*. The weapon emitted a faint hum. Falthorn was a statue, fixed in concentration, his fingers in play on the spheres.

The hum began to waver. It grew louder, rougher. The delicate glow grew harsh. Tanthe caught her breath and clung hard to Rufryd.

The Sunfire exploded.

There was a blaze of dazzling light, brighter than the sun it seemed. It made them gasp and shield their eyes. Falthorn was hurled backwards. When the glare faded, Tanthe saw him lying on the ground, yards from where he'd been.

'Falthorn!' Jthery yelled, anguished. 'No!'

He was already running towards the fallen Valahyr, reaching him ahead of the others. He fell to his knees. By the time the others reached the pair, Jthery was lifting him up, and Tanthe saw Falthorn moving, flailing his arms. He wasn't dead; she wasn't sure whether to be glad or not.

Her heart raced in gathering horror. Falthorn was rising to his knees, then his feet, like a corpse climbing out of a grave. His hands clawed at the air. As they reached him he turned slowly towards the sound and she saw his eyes; staring black pits swimming with blood.

'I can't see, Jey,' he said, quiet and hoarse. 'I can't see.'

Chapter Twenty-one. The Dark Spire

Jthery was sitting beside the makeshift bed on which they'd placed Falthorn, his head drooping with tiredness and misery, Falthorn's hand grasped tight in his. In the dull light of the lantern, Lahjaya knelt over the injured Valahyr. Ostarial and Alviath were sitting silently at the foot of the bed, looking despondent.

Tanthe took in the scene as she and Auriel came cautiously into the tent. Auriel had missed the incident. When she'd told him about it afterwards, he'd reacted with a laugh. She couldn't blame him, after all Falthorn had put him through. Yet his first reflex of delight had quickly turned to the same sad confusion as hers.

'Er . . . how is he?' Tanthe asked.

'*He* can still hear and reason, Tanthe,' Falthorn said savagely.

'Sorry. We just wanted to know.'

Lahjaya sat back from her patient and looked up. Her usually merry eyes were serious. 'There are certain things I cannot cure. This is one of them. All I can do is ease the pain.'

With that blunt statement, she rose to her feet and busied herself with an array of herbs, tinctures and crystals on a small folding table. Tanthe and Auriel went closer to Falthorn. She put a hand on Jthery's shoulder but he shrugged her off, beyond being comforted.

Falthorn's eyes were terrible. The pupils were fixed open, two black holes in rings of silver. The whites were full of blood, the lids swollen, leaking floods of tears. His once-lethal gaze twitched without purpose.

She could still see an after-image of the flash herself.

Falthorn had caught its full intensity. She swallowed. She didn't know what to say.

'Speak,' the Valahyr lord said brusquely. 'I can only imagine the gloating smiles on your faces.'

'No!' said Auriel, sounding dismayed. 'I thought I'd feel joyful if you were ever punished for all you did. But I'm not.'

'Well. Well.' Falthorn groped with his free hand, found Auriel's arm. 'I'm touched, nephew. Be assured, at least, that I am beyond doing you any further harm.'

'You're no fun now, are you?' Tanthe said sardonically. 'How can we hate you while you're lying here so pathetically?'

Falthorn let out a bark of laughter. 'Ah, I'm glad of you, Tanthe. A refreshing change from the miseries who surround me.'

'What are going to do?' she said.

'Whatever it is, I can no longer help you.'

'But we still have an army of Bhahdradomen three miles away, ready to slaughter us.'

Falthorn tensed and gasped, tears streaming down his cheeks. The sight of him in pain was unutterably disturbing. He'd always been so strong. Jthery gripped his hand tighter until the spasm passed.

Falthorn spoke, trying to minimise the pain in his voice. 'The Basilisks are all but useless, as you saw. Age has damaged them, their delicate attunements have been lost. They might be used as crude explosives, no more than that.' He gave a *tchah* of frustration. 'For all my careful planning, I did not foresee this. I should have studied them more closely, but they were always to be a deterrent, never to be deployed . . . Soon, Vaurgroth is going to know that we are virtually defenceless.'

'What can we do?'

'You had better go and retrieve the child, hadn't you?'

She hesitated. Her stomach turned with a thrill of fear. 'I don't want to find him, only for him to be used. Maybe Rufe was right.'

'But Mendyr is your only hope now. It won't be easy, but if anyone can do it, it's you, Tanthe. If you succeed, you have my word that I won't take him from you. I know what you think of me and it's fully deserved, but grant me a little leniency. I am on your side, since this friend of yours –' he lifted Jthery's hand – 'has breached the shell of my better judgement. Siding with Aventuria is now my only hope of protecting Verdanholm. And I am in no position to deceive you. So find the child, if you can.'

'Any idea how to start?'

'The realm of the Wrothryr is a non-physical one; or rather, it exists in a very different form from Earth or Verdanholm. I don't know whether it's possible for them to have taken the boy's physical form there, or only his consciousness . . .'

'Then how am I to get into it?'

His swimming eyes seemed full of terrible glee, a threat. 'Through the *ezht*,' he said.

She flinched, terror rising in her stomach. She felt Auriel's hand gripping her arm. She thought for a moment that Falthorn was going to hurl them into it, there and then. 'No, wait . . .'

He smiled. 'Don't fear, I shan't send you there myself; I can only do so for a few seconds, and it's not enough. Our minds enter the shallows, and snap out again. For the purpose of this quest, the trance would have to be deep and sustained. There is only one way to do that, unfortunately.'

Fear made her annoyed. 'I don't understand.'

'That is the problem,' Falthorn said thoughtfully. 'Humans and Aelyr alike tend to become lost in the *ezht*. The Bhahdradomen adepts use it to communicate with each other, but even they cannot break through the first layer. The *ezht* is not of itself evil; we find it terrifying only because it is so inimical to us. A reminder of how utterly alone we are.'

'Falthorn,' Tanthe said warily, 'there's something I need

to ask. I still don't know if I can trust you, but here goes. When you sent me into the *ezht*, I saw Fiomir and Talthaliorn.' She was aware of Auriel behind her, hardly breathing. 'I'm sure I didn't imagine it. Is there any chance they could be trapped there?'

Her uncle's reaction surprised her. He groaned. 'Oh yes, I'd suspected it. Damned idiot, my brother . . .'

'They seemed to think it was your fault. Did you do it?'

'No, I did not. I pursued them ruthlessly for years, it's true. Often we were so close to capturing them . . . until, a handful of years ago, they vanished altogether. I began to suspect, though I could find no proof. I couldn't believe that Talthaliorn had chanced so much, let alone succeeded . . .'

'What do you mean?' She leaned closer to him. 'Is this something to do with Jthery's vision about the Obsidian Tower?'

'Ah, he told you.'

'And he told you as well, obviously.' She shot a glare at Jthery, displeased that he might have given Falthorn a clue to finding her parents. Not that it mattered now. 'He saw a recurring image of Fiomir and Talthaliorn going towards a mysterious Tower. And I keep seeing it too. Last time it was so real I could have touched it!'

'Ahh,' Falthorn breathed. Her reached out and took her hand; she winced at the contact, but endured it. 'Then it's clear what you're meant to do. I'll try to explain; what little I know, at least. The Obsidian Tower is a place of power, a legend to mystics who spend their lives searching for it and never find it.'

'I thought it was a Bhahdradomen legend. That's what it said in the book Jedraan showed me.'

'Not so, they only appropriated it into their own mythology. Some say it was created by an ancient race who sought to contact the Wrothryr; others, by the Wrothryr themselves, as a test for us. That is part of its delightful mystery. It's real, but elusive. It moves in and out of other dimensions. Enter it and you will enter the *ezht*.'

Tanthe gave a short laugh. 'Why would anyone do that voluntarily?'

'Because it is the way into the higher realms. As I said, the *ezht* is not evil; that's only the way we experience it. It is just the first step, the threshold, the entrance hall. It's said that even the greatest adepts are in danger of being stranded forever at that elementary stage. It's a trial to weed out the unworthy.'

'Have you been there?'

Falthorn smiled. 'I have not had time, nor any wish to devote myself to such a thankless pilgrimage. Talthaliorn spoke to me of it once. He wasn't pleased that I poured scorn upon his ambition.'

'And he'd want to go there . . . why?'

'I imagine to gain wisdom from the higher realms, in order to protect himself from me. Sadly, it appears he failed. Now if he and Fiomir *are* in the Obsidian Tower, I have no idea how they found it. The Bhahdradomen, however, have a firm conviction that if they raise enough power and devote themselves in the right way, they can cause the Tower to manifest itself. They think it will connect them to their Ancestor's light, which will give them boundless power, or some such.'

'Oh.' Tanthe had to force herself to keep breathing. 'So if I've seen it, and assuming what I saw was real . . . it's not because I've got some amazing talent. It's because the Bhahdradomen have manifested it themselves?'

'It would seem so.'

The dark spire loomed in her mind, forbidding. 'Will I find my parents there? Mendyr?'

'I don't know,' Falthorn said. His voice, for once, sounded kind, sad, regretful. 'You can but try.'

Dry-mouthed, she asked, 'Why *did* the Wrothryr take Mendyr?'

'You would have to ask them, but apparently they think

he is dangerous and they would be right. That did not give them the right to take him. Interfering . . .' There was a hint of his old fire in his voice.

'Tell me honestly,' she said, 'do you really think I stand a chance? Or are you just throwing me into this in the vague hope that I might restore my parents or Mendyr into your clutches? You made it fairly obvious I'm dispensable.'

His face was still. His sightless eyes quivered. 'You'll go, anyway. I know you.'

'Yes, I'm predictable like that.' She jerked her hand out of his, but he reached out and touched her forearm.

'Tanthe, I am proud to count you among the Valahyr. You deserve greater respect from me than I've shown you, it's true. If you cannot endure the trials of the Obsidian Tower, then no-one can.'

Tanthe ducked under the tent-flap and stood in the gathering darkness, shaking.

A movement in the shadows made her jump.

'It's only me,' said Rufryd. 'Are you okay?'

'Not really.'

'How's his lordship?'

'Blind. Helpless. I thought I'd be glad to see him brought down like this, but I'm not.'

'Hey, don't shed any tears for him.'

'I'm not, but when you've been struggling against someone and they're not there to fight any more . . . it's really hard not to feel sorry for him. He was trying to help us. He didn't blind himself on purpose!'

She made to walk away, but he caught her arm. 'Where are you going?'

'I'm going to find the Obsidian Tower. Helan's going to be pissed off, but I have to leave now or it will be too late. I'll just tell her, then I'll get ready and go.'

He opened his mouth to protest, but she lifted her hands to avoid his touch,. 'Please, Rufe, I know what you're going to say. You don't want me to look for my son, because you don't want me to get hurt. I understand, I'm not annoyed with you, I love you more than you'll ever know, but I have to do this.'

'Not on your own.'

'I won't be on my own, Auriel's going with me.'

She walked away quickly, hugging herself, struggling not to cry. Hard as she tried to sympathise with Rufryd's viewpoint, she felt let down. She hurried through the darkness towards Helan's tent. I am going to be strong, she told herself. I'm going to do this and shut my mind to anyone who won't help me ...

She was alone for a few moments. Then there were footfalls behind her, and Rufryd caught her arm.

'What are you doing?' she said, exasperated. 'I'm not arguing about this any more.'

'Neither am I, you pig-headed bugger,' said Rufryd. 'I'm coming with you.'

The sun rose gloriously over the sea, revealing the Lapis Ocean rolling in majesty against the red cliffs. Tanthe, Rufryd and Auriel sat on horseback on the cliff-top. They shielded their eyes against the glittering light of dawn, but Tanthe could see no shadow of the Tower against the waves.

'I've seen it in different places,' she said. 'Ever since we were in Lapiszul. I know it's out there somewhere.'

Rufryd said nothing. He was being very, very good for holding back his usual cynical comments, Tanthe observed. Or he'd grown out of the need to mock everything.

'I'm sure it's connected to the *rothanamir* where we saw the Laefrohyr,' Auriel said. 'It's manifesting there most strongly because it's a confluence of paths. We must go further south yet.'

All night they had ridden back towards the Olivine River, which they'd left a couple of days earlier. Unhindered by the slow march of the army, they'd made swift progress. Rufryd was on the golden dun Thand'rathian mare he'd ridden from Tasqabad, Tanthe and Auriel on wiry black Marocian horses. They had brought arms, enough provisions for a few days' travel, lanterns.

To Tanthe's relief, Helan had been understanding. She'd expected her to insist they couldn't be spared from the battle. Instead she said, 'If you can find this child, and it is what Falthorn claims, it may be our only hope. Of course you must go. We'll always be grateful for your bravery.'

The words were heartfelt, but ominous. Tanthe felt fairly calm, until they rounded the gentle curve of the coast and Auriel said, 'There's the portal; can you see it?'

She felt the thrum of power, saw a rippling patch of air a couple of hundred yards away. Auriel's *anametris* sphere was bright, its inner shells whirling. As they drew closer, she saw a faint outline on the sea, like a refraction that could only be seen from a certain angle.

'Look!' Tanthe cried.

It was a mirage; a ghost Tower sketched on the sky, appearing and vanishing. For a fleeting second it would harden into focus, then fade again. As they reached the dais of ruby-red stone, where the portal hung like a diamond suspended, it shone clearly in lines of silver ink.

'I can't see anything,' said Rufryd.

'I'm not imagining it.'

'No, I see it too,' said Auriel. 'But it's not fully manifested in this realm.'

Rufryd exhaled. 'How are we going to get into an invisible Tower, then?' He unstoppered his water flask and passed it round.

Tanthe jumped down from the saddle to ease her horse's back. Her own was sore and stiff. 'I'm hoping Auriel's going to help with that.'

Auriel was silent. Dismounting, he went to the cliff-edge, his hair streaming back on the breeze. The *anametris* gleamed and flashed in his palm, like a tiny sibling of the *xauroth* sphere.

While he worked, Tanthe and Rufryd went inland and

found a crevasse, with shade for the horses under an overhanging rock, and some scrubby grasses. Vetru had wanted to come with them but Rufryd had made him stay at the camp under Lahjaya's watchful eye. Now, Tanthe thought, it might had been an idea if Vetru had come. *There would have been someone to take care of the horses if we don't come back . . . Perhaps the villagers will find them. What am I thinking, of course we'll come back!*

A black bar of cloud crossed the sun. She shivered.

'I don't see why the Tower should be "manifesting" anywhere,' Rufryd said as they walked back. 'Are you sure it's not wishful thinking between you and Auriel?'

'No, it isn't. I can't explain. It feels like different forces, all converging. I had a long talk with Falthorn about it. And I think Fiomir has been trying desperately to give me clues.'

'Fiomir . . . your Aelyr mother?'

'Well remembered.'

'I was just thinking of Riverwynde, how you drove us mad wanting to live a life of high culture in Parione. Didn't foresee any of this, did you?'

She took his hand. 'I'm glad I didn't or I would have gone mad. Parione seems so far away now. I should've known the reality could never be like the dream; it was better, in some ways, but it wasn't *me*.'

When they reached the cliff-top, Auriel greeted them with bright, anxious eyes. 'I've found the way in,' he said.

'What?' said Rufryd. 'I still can't see anything.'

'There's a small path that leads from the confluence to the place in which the Tower is physical. It's not a separate realm, it's part of this world, but slightly skewed from reality so you can't enter it unless you know what you're doing.'

'Or not, in our case,' said Rufryd.

'It's only a short way, like walking out onto the shore,' said Auriel. 'But you have to step into the portal to get there. I shall have to stay here, to keep the way open for you.'

'All right,' said Tanthe. She rested her hand on Auriel's shoulder, met his hopeful gaze. She hadn't expected or wanted him to enter the *ezht* with her. 'Rufryd and I will go.'

Rufryd was settling his bow and arrows on his back, adjusting the scabbard of his sword, and the sinister-looking *sten* and *tzirin*. He looked nervous. 'I've never done this before. Gone through a portal, I mean.'

'Don't worry,' said Tanthe. 'You might go dizzy or even forget who you are for a few moments.' She grinned. 'Just hang onto me until it passes.'

'Wait,' said Auriel as she pulled Rufryd towards the confluence. It hung scintillating before them, inviting and fearsome. 'When you go into it, it's like a labyrinth. You need to go straight ahead. Look for a little patch of daylight, like a window in the portal's fabric, the same as here. You must enter that or you'll be lost.' He smiled ruefully. 'I don't want to have to rescue you, like I did Jthery.'

Tanthe nodded. She stepped in boldly, holding Rufryd's hand. At once, silvery corridors snaked off in every direction, hanging in nothingness. She held steady against panic, kept her eyes fixed forward – and there it was, a slot of daylight; red cliffs, blue sky, silver ocean.

When they stepped through, they appeared to be on the same cliff looking at the same ocean. Only it was not the same. Auriel had vanished. And there was the Obsidian Tower, rearing above them in all its monolithic glory.

'Anthar's balls,' Rufryd gasped, gripping her arm. 'It's real. It looks exactly like the image I saw in Vexor!'

The Tower stood some way out from the shore on a plug of crimson rock. The way to it was a causeway of stone, narrow, jagged and red as sunset. The tide was out, so the causeway stood proud of a shining beach.

'Come on,' she said.

They hurried to the cliff-edge and found a steep path to

scramble down. The beach was rose coloured and smelled of salt, fish, seaweed. Their boots made wet prints in the sand. This place was utterly real, no different to the real world – except for the monumental presence of the Obsidian Tower. The closer they came to it, the more immense it seemed.

It rose from a broad base, tapering gracefully into a spire that was encircled by a broader pod of rock. Its height was terrifying. She didn't see how the island could support its weight, nor how it could stand at all. It was so black that it looked flat against the sky, swallowing all light that dared to fall upon it. Watching rags of cloud drifting past the pinnacle, she went dizzy.

'Goddess, it's real. It's real,' Rufryd breathed.

Tanthe opened her own water flask and wetted her dry mouth, then passed it to him. 'Should have put some whisky in this,' she murmured.

'Yeah. So ... do we go in? What did your visions tell you?'

'Not much. There were strange beings warning me not to come here.'

'Great. So these were fairly stupid beings, then?'

She grinned. 'Good point. Or very bright ones who knew I'd do the opposite of what they told me.'

'So, we just go in?'

'I suppose so.' They began to walk slowly to the beginning of the causeway. Fingers of vermilion rock thrust in lines out of the sand. 'Looks like the tide's well out.'

'Hope we can do whatever we need to before it comes in again,' Rufryd said. 'This ocean is well and truly real.'

Flooded sand shone on either side of them. The Tower loomed. They were climbing, the causeway rising from a flat path to a thin ridge now some twenty feet above the beach. At one point it dipped and became so precarious that they crossed it only with difficulty. Tanthe slipped, just saving herself from a fall onto the rocks below.

Presently they reached the edge of the island. The base

of the Tower dominated it, leaving only a thin path around it, which was impassable since parts of it had fallen away into the ocean.

They stood there, catching their breath and staring up at its unbelievable height.

'There's no way in,' said Rufryd.

So black was the fabric of the Tower that Tanthe couldn't see an entrance. There was nothing to focus on. The Tower disturbed the eyes as well as the mind. Then she saw the faintest line of greyness and realised it was the edge of an aperture; a tall, tapering arch that mimicked the shape of the Tower itself.

'There,' she said. 'Right in front of us.'

Rufryd frowned. 'Bloody hell, you're right.'

'Don't invoke Hellaxis here,' she said. 'What are you doing?'

'Lighting the lanterns.' Cursing, he got the wicks to catch and shut the glass doors on them.

'Oh, good idea.'

'You do the metaphysical stuff. I'll just try to keep us in one piece.'

Inside the Obsidian Tower there was – nothing.

Only the black circle of the walls, soaring up and up into darkness. The walls were glass-smooth and had a slight sheen where the lamplight caught them. The air was icy. The sense of utter emptiness plucked a thread of fear inside her. The note resonated and swelled, joined by harmonics of dread, despair, an awareness of cosmic indifference too vast to encompass.

'There's nothing here,' Rufryd said. His voice echoed.

'No . . . look.'

She saw a faint line winding upwards around the wall. Going closer, she saw that it was a narrow stairway, barely two feet wide, with nothing to protect a climber from the abyss beneath.

'You're not going up there?' he said, looking as uneasy as she felt.

'There's nowhere else to go.'

'What if you fall?'

'I break every bone in my body, presumably.' She found the bottom step and began the cautious ascent, one slow careful step after another.

'You're not going up on your own,' he said, following her.

The stairs were uneven yet smooth as soap. Tanthe climbed in trepidation, keeping her right hand on the wall, trying not to look down. The higher she went, the more uncomfortably aware she was of the long, lightless maw yawning on her left.

'The long hard climb through darkness to the light of wisdom,' Rufryd said behind her. His voice shook. 'Didn't think they meant it so literally. I wish Arax Vahan could see me now. Demented bastard would probably be beside himself with envy. I can think of better ways to spend the morning.'

'I can't see any light up there, can you?' Tanthe said. She felt she'd been climbing forever. It took perhaps twenty minutes, enough to give her a taste of eternity.

They reached the top, shaking with tension as much as weariness. The stairwell brought them onto a walkway that appeared to ring the spire. It was enclosed, without any window that she could see. Only their lamps gave them light. Tanthe felt sick with claustrophobia. She thought of the long drop below them, and felt the Tower swaying. The wind moaned outside.

'Well?' Rufryd said. 'Seems to be a chamber through there . . .'

She turned and saw a tapering archway. It was small and she had to duck to see into the room beyond. She entered cautiously, holding out her lamp, aware that this chamber was in the core of the Tower and might contain a long drop back to the base.

No, a solid floor. Her lantern glimmered on obsidian.

She gulped a breath of shock. 'Rufryd!'

'What is it?'

He pressed into the archway beside her. She stared. The room was a plain black dome but she felt its darkness infiltrating her, whispering. It had the atmosphere of the *ezht*. All it contained was a circle of twelve stone couches. Each was shaped so that a human could lie on it with their torso raised and knees bent.

Ten were empty. Two had occupants. A man and a woman, lying in the moulded stone like corpses upon biers.

'Fuck, who are they?' Rufryd whispered.

Tanthe crept into the room. She was trembling with a dread she couldn't voice, a whisker away from screaming and fleeing the Tower in panic. Perhaps that was the test. Give way to fear and you'd slip on the precarious stairs and fall . . .

She looked at the first body. It was a man, a tall Valahyr with a grave, carven face and long black hair. She knew what the other would look like before she even turned. It was no surprise, but still a visceral shock. A woman, as pale as herself, with dark-red hair like Auriel's.

A sob broke out of her. 'They're my parents,' she said.

'Are you sure?' Rufryd leaned out of the archway. 'Are they dead?'

'I don't know.' She pressed a hand to her mother's shoulder. Her own breath cut into her throat like ice. Gods, to touch them like this in the flesh, to find them at last, too late . . .

She felt her mother's chest rise and fall in a long, slow breath. Tanthe snatched her hand away. Then stillness again.

'No . . . no, I don't think they are.' Cautiously she gave Fiomir's shoulder a gentle shake. It seemed sacrilegious. 'Fiomir? Mother?' She did the same to Talthaliorn. No response. Apart from an occasional sigh of breath, they were lifeless. Too deep in trance for her to reach. Her hand moved to the curved stone of the couch and she felt a deep slow pulse of *roth* move through it. And she began to understand.

'Then what . . . ?'

'Rufe, don't come in. This place is a way into the *ezht*. That's where their minds are. I can feel it, can't you?'

'No, it just feels like a cold miserable chamber to me. If we get them out of here, will they be all right?'

'I don't think so. If we take them off the couches, they may die. I don't think they can come out of the *ezht* unless I go in and fetch them.'

'I don't like this. Come out!'

'No, I have to stay here. I must go after them and find them.'

'Tanthe, I'm warning you, come out of there now. This place has a bad feeling about it.'

'I know.' She looked at the empty couch next to her mother and moved towards it. Already she could feel the *ezht* pulling at her mind. The dark chamber was losing its boundaries and turning into the dark plain. 'But this is what I came here to do.'

'You're not going to—' He stared at the deathly forms of Fiomir and Talthaliorn.

'The couches are like huge *roth* crystals,' she said. 'They lead your mind into the *ezht* and keep your physical body alive.'

Rufryd's form and voice seemed unreal. Frightened, she tried to hold them steady.

'Let me come with you, then.'

He started towards her but she held up her hands and said, 'No! I need you to watch over us, while I'm . . . wherever.'

'Oh, Goddess . . .' He put a shaking hand to his forehead, looking as terrified as she felt. And she really didn't know what she was doing. 'All right. I'll be here.'

She began to lower herself onto the couch. At that his eyes widened in alarm. 'Do you *have* to do this?'

She nodded. She couldn't speak. The couch was surprisingly comfortable. It moulded perfectly to her body and its fabric felt warm and spongy, not like stone at all. Its energy began to pulse through her like a heartbeat, hypnotic. A sleep paralysis was dragging at her body. Her eyes closed as her physical form slipped away. Her unconscious mind was already staring across the soul-draining nothingness of the *ezht*.

Lines of Bhahdradomen smothered the landscape like a presage of night. All living colour was swamped as if by hordes of ants, a swaying mass of lichen hues, punctuated by the green and black of *vagharim* and the bronze of officers. The crackle of *gauroth* weapons hung in the air.

Helan, commanding her troops from a high point to the west, sensed the unease that lay on the humans. The collective aura of the Devourers sapped their courage and spirit. As vigorously as she and Mawrdreth had tried all morning to inspire them, she had a growing suspicion that if the Bhahdradomen attacked first, the Marocians would simply turn and flee.

The Bhahdradomen waited. The humans waited. Silence rolled like storm-clouds over the bowl of the Almandine Vale.

Rufryd stared at Tanthe's insensible form in the closest he'd come to panic since Annuin had died. 'Tanthe?' he said. No response. *You don't know what you're doing, do you?* he shouted silently at her. *Go rushing into the worst of dangers with never a thought of how you're going to get out of it!*

When, after ten minutes or so, she still hadn't stirred, his fear reached its nadir. Fighting the Order had never terrified him as this dreadful place did. He wasn't sure he had the courage to negotiate the stairs on his own, if she didn't come back. How long was he to wait? A day, a year? He struck the wall, cursing.

After that he calmed down, and resigned himself to waiting. He went back onto the walkway and leaned against the chamber wall, arms folded, trying to go with the swing of the Tower and ignore the fear that it was falling every time the wind caught it.

Presently he made a circuit of the walkway, discovering that it encircled the chamber as he'd thought. On the far side, though, he found a narrow chink in the outside wall, no more than an eye-slit. It seemed intentional, not a fault in the fabric.

He pressed his eye to it and was glad to see a view of the shore. There was the beach and the red cliffs from which they'd come. He even thought he could see the shimmer of the portal. He rested there, soothed beyond words to see the outside world, albeit in a skewed reality. Already he hated the Obsidian Tower with a passion that went far beyond his first stirrings of unease in Calathvahn.

The view was serene, disturbed by nothing but the soft roar of waves and the cry of sea-birds. The tide was still out. He knew little about the sea but had heard that, according to the scholars of Lapiszul, the three moons pulled the ocean into capricious shapes. When we get back to Parione, he thought, I'll try to learn something instead of mocking Tanthe for caring . . .

His thought stopped mid-flow. There were figures on the beach. Dozens, coming from the direction of the cliffs, pausing to stare up at the Tower. They were far away but he could tell from the way they moved that they were Bhahdradomen.

His heart surged into his throat, setting up a fierce rhythm. Maybe the rumours were true. Vaurgroth's power had summoned the Tower into being. Now they were coming to claim their glorious, sacred prize.

Without a thought for danger, Rufryd launched himself into the stairwell and went full-tilt all the way down, round, round, round, to the bottom. He didn't want to fight them on the stairs. He didn't want them entering the Tower at all, if he could help it.

Rushing out of the archway onto the scarlet rock, dazzled, he saw the figures coming towards him through the glare. They were picking their way in single file along the thin walkway. And leading them – his head rearing back to stare at Rufryd with a naked blend of disbelief and contempt – came Rhazagramen.

Helananthe cast her gaze over her troops, arrayed under a darkening sky. Her archers were poised in front, her small cavalry on the flanks, line upon line of infantry with their spears and hurriedly forged swords glinting dully. She sensed their restless fear. Mawrdreth and Karmensis were tall, heroic figures beside her, but their eyes were narrow with apprehension. Around her, a selection of officers and messengers waited in growing tension. Their horses fidgeted as the wind stirred their manes, blowing the strange metallic scent of *gauroth* over them.

She felt no better equipped now than when she'd faced her own grandfather's army. True, she had a much greater force, fully equipped and better trained than the assortment she'd led the first time. All she and Mawrdreth had learned in their battles against Garnelys had been added to their armoury. Yet what her first army had lacked in skill they'd made up for in passion and daring, not like these Marocians who truly didn't want to be here. Who were facing a far deadlier foe than Garnelys, and knew it. And this time, there was no Lord Serpeth waiting in the wings to switch sides at the crucial moment.

She tried to shake off her foreboding. That, too, was an emanation from the Bhahdradomen, deliberately meant to sap their will. At least they had the Valahyr in reserve, waiting to surprise the enemy.

'What are they waiting for?' said Mawrdreth.

Helan tightened her hands on the reins. 'Us to attack first. Why should they start it, when they've got more to lose? Berenys!'

The herald she'd summoned, a stocky young man with

spiky hair and amber eyes, rode forward nervously. 'Ma'am?'

'Take a message to Bharamezht. Tell him that we have the Basilisks of Calabethron and demand his surrender.'

'Yes, ma'am.'

As Berenys turned his horse and galloped away – a small retinue of riders following to guard him – Mawrdreth turned to her, his green eyes luminous. 'Helan? You know we can't use them.'

'Bharamezht doesn't know that. Vaurgroth doesn't know it, either. We may not win a battle but we might just win a game of bluffs.'

They waited as the figure of Berenys and his guards dwindled to specks on the far side of the valley. The Almandine Vale had a reddish sheen from the cover of ground plants with tiny blood-red flowers. Rain spat from a purple sky. Something rumbled on the far hills, out of their sight. An uneasy murmur of voices from the troops grew louder, until Mawrdreth sent officers down to silence them.

Presently Berenys returned, his face deathly grey and sheened with sweat. His horse was blowing hard. He gasped, 'Ma'am, Bharamezht replied –' he paused for breath – 'that they don't care. They have *this*.'

'What?' Helan snapped.

'You will see it.' He slumped forward over the front of his saddle and began to sob. 'Oh, ma'am . . .'

'Go back to the camp,' she said firmly. 'This day is over for you.'

The herald rode away, unmanned. His fear had shaken them all. They watched the dark shifting mass of the Bhahdradomen forces, saw a stir begin in the midst. The mass began to part, and between the two edges rolled a great and terrible engine.

Green and bronze, it gleamed like some squat, poisonous toad rising from a swamp with marsh-fires slithering over its surface.

Mawrdreth hissed a curse between his teeth. 'What in hell have they made?'

Helan put her telescope to her eye. Karmensis and the other officers did the same. The beast leapt towards her in detail; a great contraption trundling on a wide base of wheels. It was armoured like a gigantic beetle, and the plated sides sweated *gauroth*. Six long barrels protruded from its blunt face like insect eyes, and each muzzle dripped fire.

The machine came to rest on a flat part of the hill, with a score of Bhahdradomen on either side. It looked unwieldy. Plainly they couldn't move it far or fast, but the barrels swivelled this way and that as if scenting the air.

Helan had barely lowered the telescope from her eye, when fiery *roth* came spewing from one of the muzzles. It travelled with incredible speed, a tongue of liquid white fire lashing towards them. The blast slammed into the front line of her archers and they fell, screaming, the ones around them scrambling for their lives. The whole formation disintegrated into chaos. The grass where the archers had stood was a lake of black oil, scattered with charred bodies.

A stench of burnt flesh and alien, volatile oils choked the air. People were coughing, retching, screaming. Helan turned away, eyes streaming, her hand pressed to her mouth. Mawrdreth's face was a death mask.

'Retreat,' said Helan. She straightened up and shouted, putting all the desperate force she could into her voice. 'Retreat!'

Karmensis and the other officers were riding down the hill, yelling for order and calm. Even as the troops began to pull back, another blast came, and another, cutting long streaks of death through their ranks. White-heat, stench, panic. Helan's horse reared and screamed its fear beneath her. As she brought it under control she saw Mawrdreth with his teeth bared and his sword in his hand, turning as if to charge the Bhahdradomen alone.

'No!' she yelled, catching his arm.

'What have we to lose?' he shouted back.

'Our lives! Retreat, regroup!'

'Drag it out for how long? Better to end it now!'

He stared at her wildly, but the madness that nearly sent him rushing into the teeth of the fire passed. He sheathed the sword, stayed alongside her. She turned to see if they were out of the war-engine's range yet.

The next blast unhorsed them both.

The tongue of fire passed within twenty feet of them, causing their horses and all those around them to rear and plunge in terror. Helan found herself on the ground with hooves thundering around her head, people yelling, the sickening oily stink of the fire-*roth* strangling her.

Someone helped her up. It was Karmensis. She saw Mawrdreth lying motionless and her heart nearly stopped; but a moment later he was struggling to his feet.

'Ma'am, we can't evade this fire, even over the hill,' said Karmensis. 'It follows the contours of the ground. And the machine's on the move again.'

She looked across the wide bowl of the Vale and saw the mindless, malevolent crawl of the engine trundling closer. 'Then we have to move the troops beyond a piece of ground that it cannot pass,' she said, panting. She felt bruised all over. 'Jagged rocks, a river, anything.'

Even as she spoke, she knew it was hopeless. The ground for miles was undulating but smooth. Her troops would all be scattered or dead before they reached a safe place. The ground between her and the Bhahdradomen was scorched by hard black lines. She coughed and it became a sob. She straightened up, half hoping the next blast would take her. In all her worst fears she'd never dreamed it would be over so quickly.

Mawrdreth came up beside her and gripped her shoulders. 'Those bastards, those Goddess-forsaken bastards . . .'

The ground shook, nearly throwing them off their feet.

'Ma'am, sire, get down,' Karmensis said, pulling them unceremoniously behind a rock. The Devourer's war engine was silent but it inched forward, dripping oily fires on the ground as it came. *Vagharim* walked impassively alongside it.

The ground shook again. The machine stopped.

'What's happening now?' Helan said. Fumbling, she managed to find her telescope and pressed it to her eye. Across the valley, the Devourers accompanying the war-engine appeared to be in a state of consternation. They were casting about them, testing the ground with their gnarled feet. Above, the stormy bowl of the sky flickered with lightning. It was as if the world itself had been roused to fury by the war.

'That's why she broke the Xauroma,' Helan said to herself.

'Helan?' said Mawrdreth.

'It wasn't just me who broke the vow. Earth herself wanted to break the bonds so that she was released from the obligation to nurture us. Set herself free to be angry and destroy all who damage her, not just the Devourers. Humans too. Earth blames us for letting the Devourers in.'

'Don't talk about this now,' Mawrdreth said unevenly. 'Pass me the spyglass, I've lost mine.'

'Wait . . .'

Down on the plain something was happening. It looked as if the ground itself was bubbling. Like molehills forming . . . but these were rising to twenty feet or more high. She couldn't comprehend what she was seeing.

Neither could the Bhahdradomen, from the way they were staring and backing away. She saw Bharamezht among them, lured from his command post.

Then from the earth-hills emerged figures. A dozen or more lumbering giants that appeared to be made of stone. Her mouth dropped open. Mawrdreth wrestled the telescope from her but she could still gain an impression of what was happening.

'Umbaroths,' she breathed.

It was as if the rock bed had torn itself up into great,

shambling, living forms. One rose beneath the engine itself and tilted it up like a stranded turtle. Fires burst from it. *Yrim* scattered.

Then it was lost to sight as more Umbaroths rose from the earth. They settled in a chain, forming a barrier around the engine and the Bhahdradomen troops. As they settled it was as if they turned back into stone. A great, curving wall stood there. Along its top were shapes that resembled huge, blunt heads and now and then one of those heads would turn a little.

Cries of amazement made her realise that not all her troops had fled. A scattering were still around here. They'd seen it too.

'That barrier must be twenty-five, thirty feet high,' said Karmensis. 'Umbaroths, what are they?'

'Zampherai lore,' Helan said. 'They're creatures of stone that the Subterraneans can command. The Zampherai . . . when have they ever loved us?'

The war-engine roared into life again. The *yrim* must have righted it. Gouts of fire struck the top of the wall, exploding like waves into millions of flaming droplets. One of the impassive stone heads crumbled in brief avalanche. The Bhahdradomen were trying to destroy the wall.

The dry storm overhead became more intense. All the world had turned to fire and thunder; shaking, roaring, flickering.

'We had better retreat and regroup our forces,' said Mawrdreth. 'That wall won't hold them forever.'

'Hang on,' said Helan, snatching the telescope from him again.

She'd seen a small figure darting towards them across the plain. Tiny compared to the Umbaroths, so it must be Bhahdradomen . . . no, it didn't move as they did.

She caught the figure in the disk of the lens and kept pace with it. Human, definitely . . . impossible . . .

'Put down your bows,' she said through her teeth. She'd

heard both Mawrdreth and Karmensis setting arrows to strings. 'Look!'

The figure came closer and now there was no doubt. She threw down the spyglass and rose to her feet, arms open.

It was Eldareth running towards her. Eldareth with his hair wild and a long silver-speckled black beard and a gleam of desperate joy in his eyes. Eldareth, the same yet transmogrified.

They met on the bleak hillside in a hard, wordless hug. She forgot Mawrdreth and Karmensis standing behind her, even forgot, for a moment, the Bhahdradomen.

'Where have you been?' she cried.

He looked at her with a distant light in his face. 'In another realm,' he said.

'Did you have something to do with . . . ?'

He followed her gaze towards the long stone bulk of the barrier.

'I had everything to do with it,' he said.

Rhazagramen and his cronies had not expected to meet Rufryd, standing square on the highest part of the path. They halted and fumbled for their weapons, so he had time to loose his arrows, picking off four of them in quick succession. With grim satisfaction he watched them tumble onto the sea-soaked rocks far below. He loosed one at Rhazagramen but it lodged in the *bharu'grothrim*'s shoulder and he jerked it out, barely flinching.

Rufryd cursed. He aimed again, had to duck as blue-white comets came whizzing at him. He straightened up, at the risk of making himself an even easier target. Held his breath and let the arrow fly. It struck the wrist of the one wielding the *uzrat*. The weapon whirled away onto the shore, spitting fire as it fell.

With an unseemly scramble, Rhazagramen got himself behind the others and was barking orders at them in their own language, not realising Rufryd could understand. He'd learned a lot from Vetru.

His last arrow gone, he threw the bow aside and drew his *sten*. Rhazagramen stared in disbelief and rage. 'Where did the filthy crawling vermin steal that?' he hissed in Bhahdradomen.

'The filthy crawling vermin was given it by your mate, Arax Vahan,' Rufryd replied in the same tongue.

Rhazagramen looked close to exploding with shock and rage. 'What are you doing here?' he rasped, switching to Paranian.

Tzirin and *sten* came lashing at him, but the *vagharim* were having to attack upwards and couldn't quite reach him. 'Pissing you off, I hope.'

'You have no right. This place is sacred! You are defiling the holy ground of the Ancestor. Surrender or die.'

'I don't think so,' Rufryd panted. He caught his attacker through the throat. The Order of Calathvahn had trained him well. The *sten* crackled with power and *gauroth* killed the being instantly. It fell like a nestling from an eyrie. Another was immediately there to replace it. He couldn't let Tanthe down, but he knew he'd begin to tire soon and they were tireless . . .

'Take him, you idiots,' snapped Rhazagramen. 'You're fighting like humans. Kill him!'

At that the attackers seemed to overcome their hesitancy. He found himself fighting twice as hard and then a *tzirin* came snaking out and ripped the *sten* from his hand. The shock went right through his body and all he could see was Rhazagramen's red eyes boring into him, two beams of loathing, and the weirdly glittering sky swimming across his vision.

'There wasn't time to explain,' said Eldareth. 'The Zampherai came for me. I had to go with them, then and there. I could only hope you'd forgive me.'

Under the louring dome of the sky they had regrouped their forces. For the time being, at least, a wall of Umbaroths encircled the Bhahdradomen army, effectively imprisoning them. They were slow, blunt beings, Eldareth explained. Directed to fight the shape-changers, they would only crush a few with their weighty fists while the rest swarmed between the pillars of their legs.

Now the air shook with the dull booms of the war-engine as it tried to blast its way through the wall. Helan let her troops rest and eat – those that could eat, after what had happened. She listened to Eldareth without ever taking her eyes off the sky.

'What do you mean, the Zampherai came for you?' she asked.

'My friends Orque and Vranof. They took me with them into their own realm, beneath the earth.' The wonder in his voice struck a chord in her. She'd been in that realm too, dipping her hand into the red flame core of the Xauroma.

'Why, Eld?' she whispered.

'I've been running away from myself for too long. They seemed to know it better than I did.' He let out a heavy sigh. 'I was always meant to be a *roth*-mage, Helan, like my mother. The *roth* of stones is inside me. Still I kept running away, denying it because of my father's misuse. Until at last I realised that the only way to help you was to become what I should have been from the beginning. My Zampherai friends have been waiting a long time, they said, for light to dawn.'

'So they took you under the earth . . . ?'

'Down through crevasses and deep potholes, along subterranean rivers, into caves of wonder. Forests of crystal, purple and gold and white. And there they taught me the lore of gems, the subtle *roth* of every stone, the ice of crystallised Jewelfire. And it was as if I already knew it.'

'Weren't you afraid?' she asked.

He smiled. 'Do I look as if I was afraid? Bloody terrified, at the start. But that fades.'

'How did you not starve?'

'The Zampherai brought me food.' He shrugged. 'I can't even remember. Food didn't matter.'

She sat wordless, studying him. 'You've really changed, Eld.'

'Yes,' he said. 'More than you can imagine. When you've touched the pure Jewelfire in quartz, in diamond, all the stones the Aelyr love, you learn to stop hungering. You let go of love, hate, desire, hope, despair. Instead there is a wonderful calm silence. That's what it is to be a mage.'

'Let go of love?'

'I don't mean that I don't love you. But I no longer want or need to wrest you from Mawrdreth, nor hate myself for failing.'

'You don't need me any more?' A pang.

'I don't need anyone or anything. There's no need, no hunger any more.'

And Eldareth smiled, so serene and distant that he might have been a total stranger. Helan gazed at him, aware of the slow faint wrench in her chest that was her heart breaking, so gently it barely even hurt.

'The Eldareth I knew is gone, then,' she said.

He touched her hand, but his fingers were stone cold. 'This is the Eldareth I should have been, all along.'

'I liked the old one better.'

'I didn't. Now, I can help you make *roth*-weapons to rival those of Vaurgroth.'

'There isn't time,' she said, jumping to her feet.

Here came the moment she'd been dreading. The clouds above them boiled, dipped and split open like smoky pods, disgorging scores of winged creatures with snapping fanged jaws, claws like sharpened bone, eyes burning with death.

'*Ghelim!*' she yelled. The cry was taken up all across the battlefield as her soldiers leapt up. 'To arms! *Ghelim!*'

Chapter Twenty-two. The Eye of the Sun

Tanthe was cold, colder than she'd ever been. She was standing in the centre of the *ezht*, the plain a perfect circle holding her at its lifeless core. But every point on the *ezht* was the centre, for it had no boundaries. The knowledge possessed a terrible significance that made her want to weep with despair.

No, I won't give in, she thought, hugging herself. Her body felt real. Terror welled, unconquerable because the *ezht* unravelled clear thought. What if I am trapped here forever and never find a soul? Even if my physical self dies within weeks or days, it will seem to me like centuries . . .

Cold seeped through her like the press of clammy stone. She was hurrying along a pallid path that bisected the plain. All at once she felt she'd been doing this for years, suddenly returning to awareness after losing a long tract of memory. Where am I going? Why am I fleeing?

She had no answer. Panic rioted through her. No landmarks, no memories, nothing but utter desolation all around her. The faintly luminous black limbo of the sky arched above her. The path beneath her feet had no substance. It was a solid glow, a line leading nowhere.

Then, a short way in front of her, she saw figures moving. They were ghostly and hunched with malevolent power. They drifted in a strange dance, meeting, whispering, parting. Bhahdradomen adepts.

She recognised them. Gulzhur, Zhoaah, Tzumezht . . . Vaurgroth.

That struck her memory to life. She realised, sharply, where and who she was, the danger she was in, the reason she was here. Everything. She halted and stared at the spectral forms of the adepts engaged in their mystical and sinister transaction.

Vaurgroth turned and looked straight at her.

She stood petrified under his excoriating gaze. Did he recognise her astral form? She couldn't move, felt she'd literally turned to stone, like her Aelyr parents.

Leave the path, said a tiny voice at her feet. Tanthe looked down and saw a minuscule human figure, hardly four inches tall. It shone like a diamond. *Follow me.*

Stunned, Tanthe turned her leaden feet and followed the glowing mote off the path. She caught her breath and ran, didn't stop until the shadow of a rock rose out of the plain. Hiding behind it she looked back. There was no sign of the Bhahdradomen. Her terror subsided to a background level.

Follow me. I'll guide you.

Mesmerised, Tanthe watched the little beacon trotting in front. She let it lead her across the plain, towards the dark slopes she remembered with dread. Mountains in some bleak other-world that had been scoured of life and lain desolate under the black sky for millions of years. She remembered the stone-forms of her parents, trapped there, so alone they could not even touch each other.

'My mother and father,' she said anxiously.

Her guide seemed to have grown, but she couldn't make out detail. Blurred by its diamond glow, it was a vague, pale faerie-child. *Yes, this way*, it said.

The thought was a bird swooping inside her. Could this be my son? She daren't voice the question. She let the child lead her, trusting. The plain stopped abruptly in a ledge that reared above a boundless black sea. In horror, she tried to halt the rush of her feet, failed. Some outside momentum carried her on and over the ledge.

'No!' she cried. 'No, my mother and father!'

Too late. She plunged into the water. She sank down, down through black currents. Every nightmare she'd ever had of drowning, suffocating, being pulled under the earth, came to claim her. Her lungs heaved and her heart thundered and this was so real she had no doubt she was physically here and dying.

All she could see was the marsh-light of her guide, its shine silvering the bubbles that poured from her mouth. She had been tricked into death.

An aeon passed. Tanthe became aware that she was lying at the bottom of the ocean. Sand gleamed colourless beneath her. Arches of black stone rose around her, ghostly in the rippling water. Sea-serpents undulated through the ruins. They came to investigate her, tickling her face with curious tendrils. Each had a jewel of glorious colour in its forehead; turquoise, ruby, amber.

She realised that she no longer needed to breathe. She saw her guide floating with its back to her, a little naked merchild. It was much bigger now, perhaps eighteen inches tall. It seemed to be waiting.

On either side of Tanthe was a statue, crusted with coral and barnacles. She stretched out her hands and her wrists were caught by ropes of seaweed. She hung outstretched between the statues, floating in the gentle currents.

'Who are you?' said her mother's voice, muffled by water, eerie.

'It's Tanthe,' she said in shock. They'd always known her before. 'Talanthyriel.'

'Tanth'riel?'

'Yes, your daughter.' She mouthed the words, but they came from her mind.

'Daughter,' two voices echoed. 'Our daughter has come again.'

'Yes, I've come to take you home.'

Silence. Foreboding gripped her. She felt weak and drowsy. The forms of her parents seemed ancient, as if they'd fallen into the sea from some crumbling mansion in a lost time. They barely seemed to know her any more.

'Mother? Fiomir?'

'This is our home,' sighed the voice at last. 'We can never leave here. But your self will begin to fade after a century or two.'

'Your self no longer matters,' came her father's voice,

deep and distant. 'You will become part of the *ezht*, as rocks are part of a landscape. The fear fades, then there is peace.'

'No,' said Tanthe, trying to wrench herself out of the seaweed grasp. 'This isn't peace, it's forgetfulness. You've got to remember who you are! Fiomir, Talthaliorn. Your bodies are in the Obsidian Tower. I'm there too!'

'Then we are all trapped here,' Fiomir said sadly. 'One with the darkness.'

Tanthe felt herself drifting into the same trance state. As fear faded, so did hope. So did the will to escape.

'No!' she cried. With a monumental effort she jerked her hands free. 'We're Aelyr! We're strong, we see through things, we know who we are!'

She launched herself at Fiomir's stone-form and pushed it, hard. It was like pushing a small Umbaroth. Pain shuddered through Tanthe's hands and arms, and she saw the pain crackling around her in red lines on the darkness.

'Look,' she panted, holding up her hand in front of her mother's face. 'Feelings become physical energy here! If you want to escape, you can!'

From Talthaliorn came a deep eerie groan. 'To be free of feeling is to be free of despair.'

'But it's despair that's trapping you here!' She ran at him, trying to shake the shell-encrusted pillar. 'We're all in the Obsidian Tower. Don't you remember?'

'I remember,' Fiomir said, a trace of curiosity awakening in her voice. 'But you were not with us.'

'Well, I am now. I found you. The *ezht* has sucked you into itself, it's trapped you here, but it's an illusion! Father, don't you remember, you wanted to go into the higher realms? The Wrothryr?'

Talthaliorn gave a long exhalation, *ahhh* . . . Tanthe looked imploringly at her guide. 'Please help me,' she said. 'I don't know how to wake them.'

Don't speak to them of higher realms, answered the creature, shell-pale, its hair a floating halo. *Remind them of reality.*

Her parents seemed oblivious to her faerie guide. 'Remember the real world,' Tanthe said desperately. 'Grass and water, sunlight, rain. You have a son, Auriel. He's out there waiting for you too. Remember my human parents, who were your lovers? What were their names?' No answer. 'Aynie and Eodwyth. Think of Falthorn, for Goddess's sake! Why did you quarrel with him?'

'Eodwyth?' said Fiomir. 'Aynie?'

'Yes,' said Tanthe. Her tears leaked into the sea. 'Think of their faces, their kindness. If not for them, I wouldn't exist and I wouldn't be here now, breaking my hands and my heart trying to make you listen to me!'

'Falthorn,' said her father. And both statues began to move. Coral shattered and fell away in fragments. Like sea creatures emerging from egg-cases, her mother and father pushed their way out of the stone and floated before her, new-born. Tanthe gazed at them in wonder.

'Yes . . .' Talthaliorn said as if to himself. 'We went into the Obsidian Tower, searching . . . Starfire, what were we looking for?'

'Ah, Tanth'riel,' said Fiomir. 'We know you. But we are all still trapped deep in the *ezht*.'

Tanthe looked to her smiling companion. Her parents still seemed oblivious to it. The creature had grown again, nearly reaching her chest now, yet she couldn't tell whether it was male or female through the light. 'What do I do now?'

You know what to do. The figure dived through the ruins and appeared to snatch a jewel from the forehead of an iridescent green-blue sea-serpent. Tanthe stared. She thought of the mosaic in Lapiszul, Mahan the turquoise god of the sea . . . When the being swam back to her, it seemed to have threaded a cord through the jewel. Tanthe saw that it was a flat disc of amber, pierced by a hole. The guide leaned forward and placed it over her head, saying, *This is the Eye of the Sun*.

As she received the gift, Tanthe realised that she did know what to do. She reached out and clasped hands with her parents.

'We have the essence of the Jewelfire in us,' she said. 'We must call it out of ourselves. Hold onto me and each other. Keep thinking of the real world, the higher realms, the child I need to find . . .'

Fiomir and Talthaliorn joined hands as if they'd only just seen each other. Their faces were vague in the dark water, glazed with bewilderment. Tanthe knew she must work hard or lose them again.

'Imagine the Jewelfire as three dots of white light, one coming out of each of us to form a greater dot, and the dot flaring and whirling to become circle, rising in a cone around us.'

Tanthe visualised hard. At first nothing happened; the seabed remained dark, dreamy. Then she felt heat in her body, saw a white glow spring from her own forehead. Three white ovals hung in the air between them, merging into one. In the light she clearly saw her parents' faces, and they were just like the faces in the Tower, strong and gaunt and beautiful.

The egg of Jewelfire began to whirl, chasing its own tail. It fountained upwards, cloaking them in a cone of light. Fiomir gasped. Tanthe felt the power growing stronger, hotter. She trembled with exhilaration as it rushed through her. Only fear had held it back. That was all. To pass though fear to what lay on the other side, that was the key . . . The cone began to rise through the sea, lifting them.

The waters grew bright above them. The tip of the cone pierced the surface. The dark skin of the *ezht* peeled back and delivered them into a realm of dazzling light.

The glow softened. They were floating in a sea of glittering blue-green light. It looked like water but felt dry and buoyant. Above them was a mass of pale, golden radiance with ethereal figures floating against it, forming and reforming.

'The realm of the Wrothryr!' said Talthaliorn. 'This is the place we sought!'

'Yes,' said Tanthe. 'Yes.'

The scene changed subtly. The surface of the sea tilted and became a mountainside, a slope of gleaming gossamer that swept down to an endless sparkling landscape. Its ghostly substance made Verdanholm seem as solid as Earth. It was Verdanholm taken to the extreme, a realm of pure Jewelfire.

Tanthe saw that her guide was still with them, a figure of light now the same size as her. Disappointment touched her as she realised that this could not be her son. She wondered if it was Wrothryr . . . Looking at her parents and herself, she saw that they were all made of light. Pure Aelyr essence.

Two *roth*-forms drifted down and floated just above them. One was pale green, with many flame-like limbs undulating from a central torso. The other was rose-coloured and flowed constantly from one shape to another; sphere, knot, oval.

You were told not to come, they said. *You were warned that what you seek cannot be given.*

'I know what you said,' Tanthe replied, 'but I want my son.'

She felt her parents' hands tighten on hers, Fiomir on her left, Talthaliorn on her right. In this altered state, it seemed she was the protector and they the children.

Your son should never have come into physical form, said the green-flame Wrothryr.

'Why not?'

His is not an Aelyr soul. He is a renegade spark of ours. Dangerous, too dangerous to let such a being roam the Earth in solid form, human or Aelyr.

'Dangerous, in what way?'

The battle you fight on Earth is only a shadow of a greater conflict. There are those who disrupt the balance of energies through the different realms. If roth *is drained from one realm to another, all realms will wither, from drought or flooding of Jewelfire. That is our concern.*

'Are you gods?' Tanthe asked, then felt foolish for asking.

The rose one pulsed amusement. *No, we are not gods. We didn't create you, we don't rule you. We simply are. Our concern is the flow of roth.*

'What has this to do with my son?'

Of all the dangers wrought upon the Earth, he would be the greatest of all. He has unfettered power to cause unimaginable disruption. Better he dwells here with us. For your protection, more than our own.

Incorporeal or not, her throat ached. 'Can he come back, or have you killed him?'

We do not kill. His flesh is manifest.

'Then he's still my child. I can't believe he's dangerous. I want him.'

We have answered you. You are foolish to endanger the world.

Uneasy, she looked from Fiomir to Talthaliorn. 'Are they speaking the truth?'

Her father said, 'Falthorn used you to create a being he knew would have dreadful power. He was cruel and irresponsible. However, there is nothing to say that the child's power is uncontrollable. What's done is done.'

Tanthe looked at the Wrothryr again. 'My father's right. I gave birth to him. I must insist on seeing him, at least.'

He wishes to see you, also.

As the green one spoke, a ball of white light appeared between the larger forms. The shock nearly sent her reeling.

I am here, said the light. *You say you are the mother of my earthly form?*

'Er . . . yes. Mendyr?' Tanthe stammered. This all seemed mad. How could a being of Jewelfire need a mother? Perhaps I'm just being selfish, she thought. Meddling with what I don't understand out of earthly instincts which have no meaning here. But her guide whispered, *No, it's all right. You have the Eye of the Sun.*

The sphere of light said, *I remember you. I knew you'd find me.*

It drifted towards her. Out of it radiated a powerful emotion that hauled like a chain on her soul. 'Do you want to come back to Earth with me, as a physical child? Do you know what that means?'

I had begun to know, said the child. *Yes, I want to come with you.*

She looked at the Wrothryr. 'He wants to leave. So, you can only keep him if you do it by force.'

We will not imprison him. If he insists on leaving, we must let him. But you have been foolish to do this. If you would be wise you will go, leave him here.

'It's up to him,' she said firmly. And still she didn't know if she was doing the right thing. Was he really dangerous, or was there yet another secret agenda behind the Wrothryr's warnings? 'Mendyr, do you want to come to Earth with me and your father, or stay here?'

In answer, the white light drifted closer and closer to her. She saw that it was taking on the form of a small, pale human; Jewelfire blazing from its skull. It came close until it nestled into her, its head on her shoulder, weightless. A mixture of amazement and alarm filled her, but it was too late now.

I will come home with you, Mother, said the child. *I wish to experience my physical being.*

The Wrothryr throbbed with anger. *Then if you will take him, all responsibility rests with you!*

She hesitated. If they were right and she was doing something incalculably stupid . . . No, they had no proof to give her, and she had no choice. 'Of course,' she said. 'I won't let him disrupt anything, if I can possibly help it.'

The Wrothryr vanished. The slender ethereal form of her faerie guide moved in front of Tanthe, smiling in triumph. And Tanthe found herself looking into her own face. The blue-green eyes looked knowingly into hers for a moment, and winked. Then she passed inside Tanthe, and was one with her.

Mendyr touched his hand to the amber disc round her neck. Tanthe was filled with a warm red energy. She could see every point in the universe at once, and step into any reality she chose. Clasping the hands of Fiomir and Talthaliorn, and with her son clinging round her shoulders, she rose, turned, stepped forward, and fell out of the light into a rushing cold throat of darkness.

The Almandine Vale exploded into battle. All across the field, *ghelim* dived out of nowhere, harrying, attacking, vanishing, reappearing to swoop again.

Helan and Mawrdreth were fighting desperately. They wielded swords two-handed above their heads in a wild attempt to bring down the shape-shifters. Claws like bone daggers came lashing at them. Jaws gaped, dripping venomous saliva. Above, the sky boiled and lightning flickered behind monstrous green clouds. The endless pounding of the war-engine against the wall of Umbaroths made the ground shake.

Flock after flock of *ghelim* poured from nowhere. The metallic trumpet of their cries was deafening. They swooped with tiny passionless eyes, pitiless as the hunters whose shapes they'd copied and far deadlier. They were soaked in Vaurgroth's loathing. Claws ripped at skulls, wings sent swords flying from broken arms, venom fell scalding into soldiers' upraised eyes.

A claw ripped across Helan's upper arm, cutting through her sleeve and deep into her flesh. Blood flowed. She tried to ignore it and fight on. The next she knew she was on the ground, dizzy, with Mawrdreth, Eldareth and Karmensis crouching anxiously over her.

'Ma'am,' gasped Karmensis, as their attackers wheeled away to spread chaos elsewhere. 'We must get you back to camp.'

'No,' Helan gasped. 'I'm not leaving while the attack lasts.'

'You can't stop it single handed!' Mawrdreth exclaimed. 'You're wounded. Come on!'

Mawrdreth and Eldareth half-carried Helan across the field of battle, with a handful of guards to defend them from *ghelim* as they went. She saw Valahyr among the Marocians, fighting valiantly against the screeching *ghelim*, severing heads with their curved swords. But they were tiring, and couldn't hold out forever. The forays were unpredictable, relentless. Beyond the worst of the battle, they caught a couple of stray horses and rode the rest of the way, heads down on the terrified horses' necks.

In the midst of it, Helan remembered the Basilisk, the one Basilisk that still might work. She urged her horse on, ignoring faintness from the throbbing pain in her arm.

'Helan, what are you doing?' Mawrdreth demanded as she threw herself off the horse and ran into the command tent. Four Marocian soldiers stood to shocked attention; she still kept a guard on the remaining Basilisks, just in case Falthorn or someone else should have a devious change of heart. There was the Pin of Time, a pristine rod with its glacial spheres and rings of crystal. She seized it and ran into Falthorn's tent, Eldareth following her. They seemed to have lost Mawrdreth.

Jthery was there, as usual, but Lahjaya was busy elsewhere with the wounded. There were also a handful of Valahyr who had just run in from the battlefield, from the look of them. She ignored them, and strode up to the invalid.

'This,' she said, 'how does it work?'

Falthorn, who was lying motionless on the low bed, turned his sightless eyes towards her. 'If I could read your mind I would answer you,' he said caustically.

'Sorry,' said Helan. She went to him and placed the weapon in his hands. 'The Time Pin.'

Falthorn weighed the cold shaft in his palms. He pressed his fingers to the spheres, concentrating as if he was tuning a musical instrument. Eldareth watched closely. 'Now it is active, I believe. It needs to be taken among the enemy and placed somewhere in the vicinity of the adepts who are directing the *ghelim*.'

She gasped at the fire in her arm, pushed the pain away. 'Great, how can we get someone that close without them being noticed? Must it be taken among them?'

'Ideally. It produces a field that interferes with whatever mechanism in their brains enables them to fly, to leap through time and operate as one mind. But it's only fully effective if it disables the adepts themselves, preventing them from sending instructions. I see the difficulty. Only an Eater is likely to get close enough without being stopped.'

She sighed through her teeth. 'Well, there's only Vetru, and I can't send him.'

'Why not?'

'He's hardly more than a child, so Rufryd says.'

'Still, we are in dire straits,' Falthorn said grimly. Eldareth turned and left the tent. 'My people and yours. My comrades here tell me it goes ill.'

'They're right.' Helan sat down on a stool, dizzy.

'You are wounded,' said Falthorn. 'I can smell blood.'

'I'll live,' she said shortly.

Eldareth returned within a minute, accompanied by a puzzled Vetru. Mawrdreth followed with Lahjaya, and Helan realised he'd been to fetch the healer for her. Business-like, Lahjaya began examining, cleansing and bandaging her arm. Helan did her best to ignore the process, despite the pain.

The young *neshrim* stood nervously in front of Helan, his head twitching as if he was unsure whether or not to bow.

'You have asked to see me, ma'am?' Vetru said.

Helan sat and looked at him, trying not to flinch as Lahjaya worked. 'Vetru, you've sworn your loyalty, both to Rufryd and to me. Now there is a battle raging between your people and mine. Does your loyalty stretch as far as helping us against them?'

'If Rufryd asked me, I would do it.'

'Rufryd isn't here.' She held out the Pin of Time in her

good hand. 'This needs to be taken among the enemy lines across the valley. It will stop the *ghelim* attacking us. You stand more chance than the rest of us of passing among them ignored. If you do get caught, though, they will probably kill you.'

Vetru looked at her with deep, unwavering eyes. 'I would die to preserve my *tzcement*,' he said. 'This is my *tzcement* now.'

'No-one will make you.' She felt exhausted from blood-loss, pain and struggle. 'If you don't want to do it, I'll find a human volunteer instead.'

'But if I go, the fighting will stop?'

'For a while, at least.' She sighed. She felt no animosity towards Vetru. Rather, she felt sympathy for him.

'Then I will go,' Vetru said firmly. 'Rufryd would want me to go.'

Helan and Mawrdreth rode along the right-hand edge of the battlefield and watched Vetru set off on his hopeless trek to the far side of the Almandine Vale. Camouflaged in a brown tunic, in which he wouldn't be remarkable among the lowest *yrim* of the Devourer forces, he was soon lost to sight on the sweep of the plain. The Basilisk was hidden in a pouch against his skin.

Around them the battle raged on. The metallic squawk and plunge of *ghelim*, the cries and yells, the swish of swords through empty air. Her warriors were tiring, but the *ghelim* could go on forever. Bharamezht might well be telling his officers, 'They have no Basilisks. They have nothing worse to throw against us than dumb stone. The day is ours!'

Her bandaged arm ached like heartbreak. She watched Vetru until she couldn't see him any more, still went on watching. Her throat hurt. He won't make it back, she thought, and how is Rufryd going to feel when he finds out?

'Helan, you must come back to camp,' Mawrdreth said at last. 'You can't fight any more today.'

'But today may be our last stand,' she said hoarsely.

Thirty yards away, she saw two Marocian women fall dead, cut down by *ghelim* claws, their blood spraying everywhere. Helan cried out. Mawrdreth charged forward, yelling, his sword flashing to bring one of the creatures down. The other wheeled out of his reach, shrieking triumphantly. Pain and dread filled her whole body. A third *ghelim* was dropping towards her husband and he hadn't seen it.

'Mawrdreth,' she called, her voice failing. She rode towards him and it was like wading through a turbid swamp. '*Mawrdreth!*'

The monster was an arm's length from him before he turned, too late. Helpless she watched the jaws scissoring, the death lunge—

At that instant, the *ghelim* vanished.

All over the battlefield, *ghelim* were winking out of reality. Others veered and crashed to the ground, where they lay thrashing until soldiers ran in to finish them. All fighting stopped. A shocked hush fell over the battlefield. Warriors stared at the sky, exclaimed, sat down where they were standing and leaned in breathless relief on their swords.

Vetru had made it.

Rufryd swayed but didn't fall. He drew his last remaining weapon, his silver-white sword, which had no power but the pure skill of the maker and the Shaelahyr who'd trained him to use it. He was aware of the deep relentless roar of the sea behind him, its breathing, glittering mass. Brine-scent filled his head like the odour of a living entity.

He fought on, hand to hand, deflecting every lashing blow of *gauroth* that might have killed him. He was exhausted, but drew reserves of strength he couldn't believe he possessed. All the time the roar of the sea grew louder. To protect Tanthe, he'd go on fighting even after he was dead, a living corpse to match Rhazagramen.

His lips peeled back in a savage grin at the thought. His smile seemed to enrage Rhazagramen further.

'Take him, you useless hatchlings!' the *bharu'grothrim* bellowed.

The ocean was rising at Rufryd's back, implacable jade and silver. Its vast, cold immensity made even the Obsidian Tower seem tiny and fragile. He tasted salt and felt exhilarating fear.

'The tide, the tide!' cried the *vagharim*.

Waves began to gush around the narrow ridge on which they fought, rich with the rank scents of brine and seaweed. Tide was coming in fast. Veils of foam and explosions of spray soaked the rocks. Soon the little island on which the Obsidian Tower stood would be stranded.

The Bhahdradomen began to glance nervously at the waves, losing concentration. Seizing his chance, Rufryd swung his sword and half-severed his attacker's neck. The body plunged into the foam below. The *gauroth* weapon spluttered and gave off smoke as it hit the water.

Rhazagramen looked panicky now. It was true they hated the sea, then. Anthar's horns, how they hated it!

'Come on!' Rufryd said in their language, hefting the sword. He felt the sea's terrible, elemental power and loved it.

Waves broke on the rock, splashing them all. The tide was only inches below the lowest part of the ridge, where they must place themselves to fight him. The four remaining *vagharim* lost their nerve, looked around them in horror, and tried to run back towards the shore while they still could. But Rhazagramen stood furiously barring their way. Panicking, they clung to each other. A wave roared up, broke, and washed them off the causeway. The spray hit his face. He heard their unhuman cries as they were swept away. Saw dark limbs flailing, vanishing beneath hills of green and silver.

Now only Rhazagramen was left, scrabbling to keep his feet on the narrow ridge. Seawater rushed in and covered the dip that lay between them.

'Come on, you cowardly bastard,' said Rufryd, making a

figure of eight with the sword-tip. 'Scared of a bit of water? You kicked me in the guts and left me to die. You tortured Tanthe, you wizened piece of shit. But look, we're still here. Still alive, laughing, copulating and all the things you hate about us.'

The pale mage stood seething, glaring at the tide, his red eyes shooting hatred at Rufryd. Then, to his astonishment, Rhazagramen made a rush at him. With one hand he lifted the edge of his robe as his gnarled feet splashed along the dip of the path. The water was nearly up to the first long joint of his legs. In the other hand he held a glowing, crackling knife.

Rufryd swung and twisted the sword. Rhazagramen's knife went flying into the sea, his seven fingers still furled around it. He stared at the oozing stump of his arm in disbelief. Then Rufryd brought the blade around in a second swift arc, divorcing the white prune of a head from its scaly neck.

Rhazagramen's body went tumbling into the waves after his minions.

Rufryd stood leaning on his sword, sobbing for breath. He couldn't believe it was over. Water lapped at his feet. Waves broke on the crimson rocks. The tide was well and truly in now; at least it made them safe from further attacks, but it also meant they were stranded until it went out again. He wiped the sword and sheathed it. The sea surged and purred.

Then Rufyrd began the long perilous climb up the interior of the Tower for a second time. His legs shook with exhaustion. Reaching the top, he pushed his hair off his salt- and sweat-grimed face, and ducked cautiously through the arch into the inner chamber.

'Tanthe?' he whispered.

She lay where he had left her, alongside the Aelyr man and woman she called her parents. She looked . . . His heart now thick with dread he went softly into the chamber and knelt beside her. Gods, her skin felt stone cold.

'Tanthe. Tanthe!' he shouted, growing desperate. No response. Her face was slack. He couldn't find her pulse nor detect her breath.

She was dead. All this struggle and the pointlessness, the hopelessness of it all. Rufryd crumpled to his knees beside the stone couch and began to sob. This last blow, this was the one he truly could not bear. He held her and wept, hoping the *ezht* would take him, wishing Rhazagramen had killed him, hoping for nothing now but to sink into death after her.

In Thanmandrathor, Branq'elin looked up at the skies and despaired. From stormy purple clouds *ghelim* poured thick as flies. Her warriors fought bravely amid the folded hills and dark green forests, but for every *ghelim* they took down there were three to avenge it.

Other *ghelim* came on all fours, disguised as black bears, wolves, wild cats. Their shape-changing was warped and grotesque, a mockery of the animals they mimicked. It was as if all nature had turned upon them. All as the ancient dra'a'k, Akarata, and the mage, Nilothphon, had warned.

She fought furiously with Mirias, Dawn and Con alongside her. Rain fell, making the grass slick and vision difficult. They were battling desperately now, in a narrow valley with a pine forest giving some cover on their left. The cruel silhouettes came veering out of nowhere, blurred in the dark silvery light.

Branq'elin's army had been well-prepared. After the stealthy attack on the house she was determined not to be taken unawares again. Yet they had little defence against an attack from the sky, the sheer numbers of them.

Bran had put the refugees from Tasqabad into the heart of the forest while she and her army defended the edge. They'd tried taking cover under the canopy, but the winged ones would fly in among the trees without regard for themselves. The close quarters of the forest only made them lethal.

They will weaken us with *ghelim*, she thought, then send legions of accursed *yrim* to finish us. And what help has Helananthe sent us, after all our trouble, our petitioning? None! Not even my brother.

There was a brief respite. The knot of shape-changers attacking them wheeled away. Dawn lowered her sword and turned to Bran, her copper hair plastered to her face with sweat.

'If this goes on, we're finished,' she said in her gentle Parionian accent.

'If you want to rest, go into the forest,' Bran said, resting a hand on her arm. 'It's all right.'

'Yes, go on,' said Mirias. He looked ready to drop. He had changed more drastically than Dawn since she'd first met them. His clear, handsome face was traced with lines of worry. His bravery was worn down to its very essence of thin, unbreakable toughness.

Bran knew the change had begun the day that Mirias – but not Dawn – had helped to kill the wretched impostor Noli. Now Bran was filled with a pure fierce hatred of the Bhahdradomen. For planting a changeling among them to prove that humans were no better than Devourers themselves. For killing her father. For destroying all she had with Rufryd. For turning the world to chaos, taking away her brother, causing this hopeless conflict and misery. And, beyond all, for murdering her daughter.

'Don't be ridiculous,' Dawn was saying. 'As if I could rest while you lot carry on fighting! None of you looks any better than I feel.'

'My lady, wait,' Con said suddenly. He caught Bran'qelin's arm and guided her into the edge of the trees, then let her go in embarrassment. 'Forgive me, I didn't mean to be disrespectful, but . . .'

'There's no point in standing on ceremony,' she said briskly. 'What?'

Con was taller than her now. He'd changed from a youth to a man very quickly. He gazed at her with dark-green eyes that were full of life, passion, concern. Bran stared back grimly. She couldn't bear to see him, and all the other young men and women like him, cut down and destroyed by Vaurgroth.

'I'd like to try . . . I have this bond with animals, if I can only reach them, ask them to help us . . . Will you give me permission to try?'

Bran wasn't entirely sure what he was asking, but she trusted him with her life. She glanced out, saw her soldiers arrayed across the valley, *ghelim* swooping implacably through the rain. Blood and mud smeared the grass. Purple clouds rolled ever lower and darker, like a manifestation of Vaurgroth's hatred bent on extinguishing them.

'Do whatever you can.'

Con seated himself on a fallen tree. He closed his eyes. Presently his head fell back and he cried out, 'Akarata!'

And he was answered. Branq'elin looked up in astonishment. Down through the clouds dra'a'ks came gliding, true dra'a'ks and not the horrific mockeries that were *ghelim*. They began to fight the *ghelim* in the air.

Con came out of the trance and regarded Bran with a mixture of amazement and relief.

'Draw your sword,' she said harshly. 'The dra'a'ks are few and the *ghelim* are many. It's not over yet.'

She ran out into battle again. Overhead a strange aerial battle raged, winged creatures tearing and slashing at each other. The dra'a'ks were helping . . . but now she saw something more terrible.

Lines of *yrim* gathering on the hill opposite. Watching, preparing to end what the *ghelim* had only started. Her soul quailed. Her Thand'rathians could not have fought more valiantly but they had nothing left.

Dawn screamed.

Bran spun round, saw too late what was happening.

A *ghelim* had taken Mirias, raking great hooked claws through his breastplate. It still had him, lifting him clean off his feet and high into the air. Then it dropped him and he hit the ground like a stone, breath grunting out.

Bran, Con and Dawn took the *ghelim* down between them, with an arrow and two sword-swipes.

Then they rushed to Mirias. The rain was pouring in earnest now, even putting the *ghelim* and dra'a'ks off their sky-battle. Dawn crouched down on the grass. Her lover, Mirias, lay in a pool of watered blood, silent.

Branq'elin saw at once that he was dead.

Dawn began to weep, soft and relentless. Above, thunder rolled and lightning flickered like the wrath of the gods themselves; dra'a'ks wheeled away in defeat and *ghelim* honked in triumph; and on the hill the Devourers waited to sweep down, to purge the last of Thanmandrathor, to make an end of everything.

It seemed appropriate to Rufryd that everything ended here, in the loathsome Obsidian Tower that had been the bane of his life ever since he'd entered Calathvahn. Arax Vahan was mocking him with images of the Tower, telling him how much happier he'd be if he gave himself up to the dark, lonely, tomb-cold climb. How much happier he'd be without Tanthe.

And now the Tower had killed her. She couldn't stop, couldn't ever stop rushing into danger until it was the death of her. It was as if Arax Vahan had known all along and had been cruelly taunting him.

'You stupid, mad fool,' he said, rocking her lifeless form against him, weeping. 'Just fuck off into another realm, leave me a corpse, leave me with a mystery, and I've got myself nearly killed so you could do this . . . Tanthe, Tanthe, please come back . . .'

'Rufryd?'

For a moment he was in a different place. He was standing on a road in the dark and there was Tanthe staring at him, a pale child hanging round her neck, a man and a woman with her.

'No, you can't be here!' she said.

A jolt and he was back in the chamber. 'Rufe?' said a voice.

He suddenly realised that the lifeless form in his arms was moving. She was breathing with difficulty, struggling feebly as if she'd forgotten how to move. Then her arms tightened around him. Rufryd wept harder.

'What are you crying for?' said Tanthe.

'I thought you were dead.'

'Why? I told you this would happen.'

He shook his head. Couldn't speak. 'Hey, don't,' she said gently, kissing him. 'I'm all right. I just saw you in the *ezht*; you nearly got lost in there yourself, you idiot. Help me off this couch.'

As she disentangled herself from him, he looked round to see the other two bodies beginning to move. The man clenched his fists and opened his eyes. The woman gave a sigh, then struggled to sit up. Tanthe went to help her.

'Mother,' she said, with tears in her eyes.

That was when Rufryd saw that a fourth couch contained a body that hadn't been there before. It was a child. An odd glow shivered around it, like a portal closing. The others were still too dazed to have noticed.

As the mist of light cleared, he saw that it was a boy of about eight. The boy uncurled and sat up in the dip of the couch, blinking, apparently as solid and real as the rest of them.

'Er, Tanthe,' said Rufryd, 'where did he come from?'

'We commend the dead of our *tzcement* to the light of the Ancestor,' Vaurgroth intoned. 'Uryzht, Enlightener, savagely murdered by the unenlightened. Rhuaaku, Shadower, who sacrificed himself to preserve the secrecy of the circle. Rhazagramen –' his voice almost broke on the last name – 'Theosopher, Counsellor, lost seeking the ultimate wisdom.'

Gulzhur stood with head bowed. He never thought he could feel grief for Rhazagramen, but the loss was fresh and the old adept had seemed immortal. Vaurgroth had gleaned the news only minutes ago from vibrations of the *ezht*; the details weren't yet known.

Vaurgroth's voice echoed off the walls. He'd chosen a simple place for the ceremony, the roof of a small round watchtower rising from the Amber Citadel, one of his cells of power, a secret meeting place for his inner circle. Mist drizzled down from the sky in lines of spider silk. Lamplight gleamed, reflecting off the power-stones at their feet; haematite, bournonite, pyrites. Small doorways to the *ezht*.

The circle was much reduced. Three were lost. Bharamezht was in the Almandine Vale, preparing to defeat the humans as if flicking away a fly. Now there were only Gulzhur and Zhoaah, Tzumezht and Grahzamen. And the ever-present Naghrur, a sinister, inscrutable presence at Vaurgroth's shoulder.

'We commend them to the light of the Ancestor,' the *bharu'grothrim* murmured in unison. They stood in silence for a few moments. Then Vaurgroth raised his head. His face was composed but his eyes were fire-rimmed.

'We do them the greatest honour by building upon their work. Now let us exchange other news, the better to consolidate our strength.'

Gulzhur cleared his throat uneasily. Vaurgroth had already heard what he had to say but he felt a powerful compulsion to pick his words carefully. 'Thunderer Bharamezht prepares for an easy defeat of the Marocians – despite minor setbacks.'

'Setbacks?' said Tzumezht. His eyes, in the long, charred-wood oblong of his face, looked as yellow as his teeth. He'd taken the news about Rhazagramen badly.

Gulzhur waved a dismissive claw. 'That the Basilisks fell back into human hands and one has been used.' He'd been resentful that he hadn't been assigned to direct the *ghelim* in the Vale, feeling that Vaurgroth no longer trusted him. Now he was glad. At least he couldn't be blamed for the debacle. 'It is rumoured that the rest are useless.'

Vaurgroth laid a hand on Grahzamen's shoulder. The webby *aghramen* tilted his beaked head in deference. 'Soon, Grahzamen. Falthorn's violation of our agreement – albeit despicable and predictable in equal measure – at least gives us leave to invade Verdanholm freely and drink our fill there.'

Grahzamen's grey membranes rustled with anticipation. Vaurgroth's hand, as he removed it from the *aghramen*'s shoulder, shook a little. He plucked at the end of his white braid. A haematite bead came loose and he rolled it between his fingers.

'As for the Obsidian Tower, Rhazagramen's failure is not the end of the world. The Tower is still there, thanks to our efforts. Once the battle is won I shall go there myself. Channel the light of our Ancestor through the tip of the spire and an unending flow of his power shall be ours.' Vaurgroth tilted his face to the sky, his mouth stretched in a grimace. 'All opposition shall be swept away! All lesser life consumed by the fire of His light! The Bhahdradomen shall inherit their birthright and Ancestor's kingdom shall be manifest here on Earth. All is going well. All is going as Ancestor wills it.'

Gulzhur looked sideways at Zhoaah, whose face was bland and serene. 'As Ancestor wills it,' they repeated.

Then Tzumezht spoke, his voice crow-harsh in comparison to the Greatlord's. 'Might I venture to suggest, Master of Light, that all is not going so well?'

Vaugroth turned to him, his face an angry winter dawn. 'What?'

Prefigurer stood like a charred tree, his taciturn lack of grace only too obvious. A common *domen*, Gulzhur sneered to himself, who never should have been so elevated. 'We *bharu'grothrim* are smoothing things over to appease you, Greatlord. Naghrur and Rhazagramen mislay an alarming number of prisoners who then gave Gulzhur the slip. Rhuaaku is lost in Lapiszul. Falthorn breaks our treaty,

Rhazagramen is lost on the very threshold of the Obsidian Tower. None of this can be construed as good news! The city is full of evil propaganda against us, whose source cannot be discovered. There is open mockery of Ancestor in temples, secret meetings of Goddess-worshippers, raiders killing our *graukhim* . . .'

Vaurgroth's face was as blank as Zhoaah's, but Gulzhur saw dangerous rage building behind his red eyes. 'What are you trying to do, Prefigurer?'

'To make us all face the truth,' said Tzumezht. 'I am sick of these platitudes we mouth. Even you, Master of Light! We are not hatchlings! Unless we admit the truth and face up to our failures, we will lose!'

The haematite bead burst into fragments between Vaurgroth's fingers. 'You deny Ancestor's Will?'

'No, but . . .'

'Then, since you expose these small setbacks in such a harsh light, you will not mind letting the blame for all of them settle upon your shoulders.'

The furrows of Tzumezht's face went rigid. 'I don't claim to be spotless, Master, I have made mistakes of my own, but—'

Vaurgroth crooked a finger. Protector Naghrur stepped forward, a pillar of gleaming mica. Expressionless, he seized Tzumezht and pressed him back against the watchtower wall. A long grey spike shone in his hand, fizzing with *gauroth*. Business-like, Naghrur slipped this spike first into Tzumezht's left eye then his right.

His gargling shrieks tore their ears. The noise made Gulzhur tremble with a frisson of excitement and dread. Then Naghrur's spike slid through Tzumezht's throat and cut off the sound. The blood-sweet odour of plasma pervaded the air.

Naghrur threw down the body in the centre of the circle and stepped back as if nothing had happened.

'Now all our failures are cleansed,' Vaurgroth said thinly. 'Would anyone else care to question Ancestor's Will?'

Chapter Twenty-three. Reunion

Tanthe felt like a rag doll weighted with lead as her consciousness eased back into her body. Her chest heaved with the effort of breathing. Somehow she hauled the leaden weight out of Rufryd's warm arms and across to the stone couch where her mother lay.

Tanthe clasped Fiomir's cold hands, helped her to sit up. Fiomir seemed dazed; she'd lain there, her life suspended, for long seasons. To touch her and hold her was unbelievable. She was familiar, yet a stranger; the pale glow of her skin and the long delicate features marked her unquestionably as Fhelethyr. Her dark-red hair, the same colour as Auriel's, spilled over Tanthe's hands. She looked up at Tanthe and smiled.

'Tanth'riel,' she whispered.

From the corner of her eye Tanthe saw Talthaliorn stirring. She was about to look at him when Rufryd said, 'Er, Tanthe, where did he come from?'

On a couch that had been empty sat a child.

Tanthe nearly yelped her shock out loud, just managed to stop herself. Incredulous, she watched as he rose and stood looking around the chamber. Meeting him in the realm of the Wrothryr and seeing him in reality were two utterly different things. It was as if he'd been part of a dream that, on waking, she'd half forgotten. She gaped.

He wasn't what she'd expected. Her mind reeled. One glimpse she'd had of him, as the Valahyr delivered him and took him away; pearly skin glowing through streaks of birth-blood. Falthorn had clouded her memory and that was the only fragment she'd retained. Since then, she'd seen him only as an apparition in the *ezht*, a shining entity that might well have sprung from her imagination.

Mendyr should have been no more than three. She'd always thought of him as a baby, forced herself to accept that by this time he would be a walking, babbling toddler. This child, however, looked nearer to eight, and he regarded her from still blue-green eyes that seemed to know far more than she did.

He was tall and straight, with dark hair and pale skin like hers. He was in a simple green robe with short sleeves. He looked so like her – so like Talthaliorn, too – that she didn't for a moment doubt he was hers. Yet how could he be this age?

'Breyid help us,' Tanthe breathed. It seemed Verdanholm's capricious time had played tricks upon them again. Leaving her mother's embrace she went warily towards him. 'Are you . . . Mendyr?'

'That's what they called me,' said the boy in a voice clear as a bird-call.

'Do you know who we are?'

'You're my birth-mother. You fetched me from the Wrothryr. I recognise you.'

'How?'

He blinked, as if the answer was obvious. 'I saw you when I was born.'

Tanthe felt tears coming. She held them down, for the child's sake. 'These are your grandparents, Fiomir and Talthaliorn. This is my friend Rufryd. I'm Tanthe,' she said, reaching out to him. He placed his small cool hand in hers. 'I'm so sorry I wasn't there to look after you. People took you away from me. Things happened that I couldn't help. It's taken me all this time to find you.'

It was only as she leaned down to him that she realised the amber disc was still hanging round her neck. Real. Mendyr examined it briefly, frowning. 'It has taken you a very long time,' he agreed.

'We're going to keep you with us now.' She hugged

him, but he felt like marble in her arms and the embrace was awkward. Drawing back she added, 'We're going to Earth.'

'I thought I wasn't allowed on Earth,' he said, stiff and cool, like a tiny version of Talthaliorn. 'Sehnya always looked after me . . .'

She sensed confusion behind his oddly composed exterior. Gods, she thought, what have I done? He must see Sehnya as his mother, not me, and I haven't a motherly bone in my body . . . She felt shocked and dizzy at the import of it all. The dream of finding her son had been far easier than the reality.

While she was talking to the boy, Fiomir came to her side. She looked like a newly woken sleepwalker.

'Tanthr'iel, is this really you?' she said faintly. 'You came here . . . for all of us?'

Tanthe nodded. It was hard to speak. Rufryd was helping Talthaliorn as he rose stiffly to his feet. Tanthe looked up at the forbidding figure of her father and shivered. He looked like an older, more serious version of Falthorn, his face harsher and less beautiful than she'd expected, but still breathtaking. She had a feeling he wouldn't be easy to get on with.

Yet he smiled, and took both Tanthe and his wife in a wordless, enveloping hug.

'Daughter,' he said hoarsely. 'We were lost indeed . . . I can't believe you found us.'

'We have a lot to talk about,' Tanthe said as the embrace ended, 'and it's cold and dark in here, so let's leave.'

'Are you sure you're all right to tackle those stairs?' said Rufryd, raising the lantern.

'Yes, I think so.' They moved out of the chamber and onto the walkway that circled it, Tanthe holding the boy's hand. Rufryd passed his water flask round. Fiomir and Talthaliorn gratefully accepted a drink. Tanthe had hardly noticed their garments before but now she saw they were both in travelling clothes of blue-black Valahyr silks, and over that they had Fhelethyr cloaks like layers of grey-violet gossamer.

Handing back the flask, Mendyr asked, 'Are you my father?'

Rufryd looked at Tanthe, eyebrows lifted. 'No,' he said. 'I wish I was, but I'm not.'

'I want to get out of here,' Tanthe said. She looked into the maw of the stairwell, and shivered. 'I hate this place. Do you want to lead the way, Rufe? Then I'll follow with Mendyr and Fiomir . . .'

'I'll carry him,' said Talthaliorn. He raised the boy into his arms with a swift, strong motion. Mendyr didn't seem to mind. 'We know the peril of the stairs, having ascended them some time ago.'

'We'll just go slowly.' Tanthe gave them both a quick, wary glance. Her father, her son. Total strangers to her.

'Well, there's no hurry, anyway,' Rufryd said off-handedly. 'Tide's in.'

'Oh, no!'

'Hey, don't complain. It saved our lives.'

'What do you . . . ?' Looking more closely at him, she realised how dishevelled and weary he looked. 'Gods, Rufe, what happened? You look awful!'

'Well.' He drew a breath and looked from her to the others. 'We're not the only ones interested in the Obsidian Tower, it seems. Couple of dozen Bhahdradomen turned up, led by that bastard Rhazagramen. I had to keep them out. If the tide hadn't come in when it did, they would have finished me.'

'Oh, Rufe.' Tanthe leaned her head on his shoulder, eyes squeezed shut.

'It's all right,' he said stroking her hair. 'I'm still here.'

'Auriel!' she cried, catching her breath on a rush of horrific realisation. 'They must have come through the portal where we left Auriel!'

By the time they'd completed the long, dizzying descent of

the Obsidian Tower, the tide was beginning to withdraw again. The light was dazzling after so long in darkness. The sky shone cream and silver above the red cliffs of the shore.

She heard the slow, breathing rush of the sea. They were stranded for a time. Anxiously they watched the waves throwing long curves of lace across the distant beach. When the water level receded enough to reveal the causeway, Tanthe saw the corpses of Bhahdradomen lying like driftwood on the sand. The sight shook her.

If she'd won her parents' and her child's freedom at the expense of Auriel's life – had it been worth such a terrible price? She daren't even think of it. She went first, at a near-run on the treacherous narrow path, and nearly lost her footing on the wet rock.

'For Breyid's sake, be careful,' Rufryd shouted.

She reached the beach yards ahead of them, had to force herself to stop and wait. Fiomir and Talthaliorn were slow, uneasy in their bodies after so long in the *ezht*, and Rufryd was half-dead on his feet. As soon as they caught her up, she drew her sword and began to climb up the cliff-path.

'Auriel?' she called, reaching the top. Where the portal had shimmered there was empty air. The smooth dais was deserted; no portal, no-one waiting. '*Auriel!*'

The edges of the landscape were blurred. Tanthe was suddenly, horribly aware that although this dimension shared the fabric of the real world, it was somehow separate. The insights of her Aelyr senses were still new and shocking to her. Dismay clawed her heart. *If we've been through all this, only to be trapped here!*

'Auriel!' she gasped, running full tilt towards the closed portal.

Nothing . . .

Then she saw him. He appeared as if from nowhere, unfolding from the ground some twenty yards away. As he came running towards her, she saw the *anametris* sphere glinting in his hand, and the portal whirled into life again.

'Thank gods, you're all right!' She threw her arms round him, laughing and crying with overwhelming relief. 'Rufryd said Bhahdradomen came through, I was so afraid . . .'

Auriel laughed into her hair. He was shaking. 'I saw them coming on the other side. I jumped through the portal, ran and hid in a crevasse over there. Not very brave of me.'

'Don't be an idiot. Who cares, as long as it saved your life?'

'I was terrified.' His golden face was sombre with anxiety. 'I saw where they were going but there was nothing I could do to warn you. I thought they'd killed you. I was going to try trapping them in the portal, but they didn't come back.'

'That's because they're all floating about in the sea,' she said, swallowing drily. 'They met Rufryd.'

'And he's all right?' Auriel's eyes were large and worried.

'Look,' said Tanthe, turning.

Over the cliff-edge came Rufryd, his weary gait only making his long-legged, lean silhouette more magnificent. Then came Fiomir and Talthaliorn, graceful as a queen and king walking out of some ancient tapestry, with the glory of the sky outlining their statuesque forms and the dark flames of their hair. And in Talthaliorn's arms, clear-eyed and calm, was the boy; their son.

Auriel stared, his eyes huge with disbelief. Tanthe could guess what he was feeling. She slid an empathic arm through his and thought, how miraculous this is, and what a mess. Parents who are strangers to us. A child who doesn't seem to be anything to do with us. And if only Rufryd was his father – or if Auriel had been my one true love and not my brother – but instead it's all a mess and what if Mendyr is full of dangerous powers as the Wrothryr warned and I have done something insanely irresponsible?

'Well, we made it,' she said.

* * *

The cliff-top seemed little different when they stepped through the portal. The air lost its strange shimmer and the far reaches of the landscape came into clear focus; otherwise the scarlet cliffs were the same, desolate and peaceful. But as they looked back towards the ocean, the Obsidian Tower had vanished. The jagged island of rock on which it had stood was still there, washed silver by the waves; but there was no dark spire upon it, not even a ghost against the sky. Tanthe felt only relief. She never wanted to see it again.

Rufryd had gone to fetch the horses from their hiding place. Now her Aelyr parents were embracing Auriel, who seemed more stunned than joyful. He at least had a vague memory of them, but it had been years. She wondered if Fiomir and Talthaliorn had pictured him as a small red-haired Aelyr child, not a man. Everything seemed fraught with awkwardness

Tanthe crouched down to Mendyr and said, 'He is your father.'

'I know,' said the child in his steady, piping voice. 'As soon as I saw him, I knew.'

'It's a very long, complicated story. We'll try to explain, but you may not understand until you're older.'

A frown creased the pale, high forehead. 'I expect you're right. I don't understand much at all.' He said it as an adult might, recognising his limitations.

Auriel and Mendyr looked at each other. There was a sort of nervous recognition in their faces, but no instinctive bond. Tanthe took a short painful breath. The Aelyr were so strange at times. It was as if they remembered each other as specks of Jewelfire in a milk-white sea, and so felt the bonds of blood less keenly. Or was it just that Auriel seemed barely an adult himself?

It was difficult to believe Mendyr belonged to anyone. He seemed to have sprung out of the ether, complete in himself.

'You're much older than I expected,' Auriel said.

'I don't know how old I am,' said Mendyr, 'so how could you know . . . Father?'

A tentative smile pulled the corner of Auriel's mouth. Tanthe said, 'That's Verdanholm time for you. More time passed when you were with the Laefrohyr than it has for us. Perhaps Falthorn meant that to happen, so you'd grow up faster.'

She stopped. It was too soon to delve into that darkness.

Rufryd reappeared, leading the horses. Mendyr, to Tanthe's surprise, looked horrified; he went rigid from head to foot, then ran and hid behind her. 'They're only horses,' she said, turning to him. 'Haven't you seen them before?'

'No,' the child said, wide-eyed. 'What are they?'

'Large friendly animals. They won't hurt you. We sit on their backs and they carry us around.'

'Aelyr don't need to be carried around,' Mendyr said stiffly.

Tanthe sighed. 'Come and meet them, anyway. You'll see how friendly they are.'

Reluctantly, Mendyr allowed her and Auriel to introduce him to the horses. He began to relax. Touching their soft muzzles, he even gave a smile. Tanthe found his nervousness reassuring; it meant there was something normal about him, at least.

Rufryd handed the reins to Auriel. 'Things okay?' he said, coming to Tanthe and putting his arm round her.

'I've got absolutely no idea,' Tanthe said with a dry laugh. 'Here they are, my family. At least you know I wasn't making it all up.'

In answer he hugged her closer. 'I never thought that.' He stroked the amber disc, which was nearly the size of his palm. 'How long have you had this amulet?' he said. 'I don't remember seeing it before.'

'It's the Eye of the Sun.'

'It's what?'

Tanthe winked. 'It was a sort of gift from the *ezht*. No-one could've been more surprised than I was when it came into the real world with me.'

'What does it do?'

She stroked its matt golden surface. 'I think it's just a symbol. Wisdom, or something. It represents the secret of the *ezht*.'

'Which is what?'

'Be guided by the inner wisdom of your own soul, and you won't get lost.'

She grinned, remembering; Rufryd looked bewildered. 'Okay, I'll take your word for it. One day I'll even understand you.' He raised his voice to address the others. 'We're all tired. I suggest we find somewhere inland to eat and rest, then go on in the morning.'

'Back to the camp?' said Tanthe.

'I suppose so. Where else would we go?'

'I was only wondering if there was somewhere safe we could take Mendyr.'

'Unless Helan's had a miraculous victory while we've been away, nowhere will be safe.'

'Are things on Earth so bad?' asked Fiomir, pulling her twilight cloak around her.

'I'm afraid so, my lady,' said Rufryd. 'Our Queen Helananthe's got her army camped a day or two's ride north of here and all our friends are there. Whether Vaurgroth's forces have attacked yet, I don't know.'

'We'll go with you, anyway,' said Talthaliorn. 'However, a rest would be welcome. Our bodies have lost their strength after so long in the *ezht*. And we have much to talk about.'

'By the way,' said Tanthe as they set off, all on foot except Mendyr, whom they had perched on the saddle of Rufryd's golden mare. 'I think you should know that Falthorn is at the camp.'

Talthaliorn turned to her, his face thunderous, even more intimidating than Falthorn himself. '*What?*'

'He's come over to our side, so he claims,' Tanthe went

on, trying not to let him unnerve her. 'I think he means it, but you can never quite tell with him. I can't absolutely promise that he hasn't used Auriel and me purely to find you two and Mendyr and deliver you to him.'

Talthaliorn and Fiomir both stopped in their tracks, looking stricken. Their obvious fear and shock alarmed Tanthe. 'Without question, he's done exactly that,' said Fiomir.

'Well, if it's true, I'm sorry,' Tanthe said tightly. 'But before you go mad at me, I've got something else to say. First, isn't it time we all stopped being terrified of him? And second, he's blind.'

'Blind?' they said together, their attention now fixed wholly upon her. For the first time she was aware of their power, a pearly energy like *silvenroth* radiating from them. Tanthe explained as succinctly as she could about the Basilisks.

When she finished, Fiomir looked stunned; Talthaliorn's sculptural visage was harsh and introverted, showing no relief or joy, only distress. *'Blind,'* he repeated softly to himself. And it was the last word he spoke for hours.

'Should I call you Mother and Father?' Tanthe asked later, as they made camp beside a clear, tree-shaded pool. They'd shared out their provisions, keeping some back for breakfast. Mendyr ate hungrily but Talthaliorn touched barely anything and now sat like a statue, gazing into the heart of the pool. Rufryd and Auriel were entertaining Mendyr with a game, using stones for dice. Tanthe wasn't sure how much the child understood. He was strange, difficult to know, like an ancient spirit staring out of youthful eyes. Yet, in other ways, he was as child-like as her little brother Feryn had been at that age.

Tanthe and Fiomir were sitting apart from the others. It was the first chance they'd had to speak to each other properly. 'It seems so weird. It's all right for Auriel, he at least knew you when he was small. But Aynie and Eodwyth are my mum and dad.'

'Call us whatever you like,' said Fiomir. 'Fi and Tal, as our friends used to.'

'That seems too familiar.'

'I hope we'll become familiar enough for it not to matter.' Fiomir smiled. Tanthe couldn't stop looking at her. Couldn't believe she was real. Tanthe had met Fhelethyr before and could see that her mother was of that *eretru*, with their pale grace and quick movements, their mysterious quietness. She looked hardly any older than Tanthe herself. Her face wasn't pretty, exactly, but it was striking in that not-quite-human way of the Aelyr. She was gentle but had a sharpness to her, a stinging wit that could, occasionally, be barbed. At least she seemed open. On the journey she had talked to Tanthe and Auriel a lot, and touched them, sometimes with a kind of sorrowing fervour, as if it gave her as much pain as happiness.

'I'll call you Fiomir and Talthaliorn for now,' Tanthe said. 'I hope you'll become so familiar that I can be as rude to you as I am to Rufryd.'

Fiomir grinned. 'You are very forgiving, Tanth'riel.'

'Would you just call me Tanthe? I'm not used to . . .'

'Talanthyriel. An old Fhelethyr name that can be shortened into any form that pleases you; Talanthe, Tanth'riel . . .'

'Maybe Aynie couldn't remember it, because all I got was Tanthe. It's a lovely name, though; I'll use it if I ever become famous.'

'As you wish, Tanthe.' Fiomir sounded sad.

'How am I being forgiving, though?'

'Since we abandoned you for so long.'

'I was all right. Auriel's the one who really suffered.'

'Ah, you are angry with us for that. So am I; angry with myself, and with Falthorn.'

'Do you know what he did to us? He captured Auriel from the Fhelethyr, used him to lure me to Verdanholm, then got him to seduce me. That's where Mendyr came from. Falthorn forced the child on me then stole him, and I was never even supposed to know he'd been born. Only my uncle's methods of suppressing my memory weren't quite effective enough so I forced Auriel to tell me what had happened and that's when I found out that Falthorn had treated him so abysmally he was scared of his own shadow . . .'

Her voice was rising with emotion. She had to stop and fight for breath. She'd longed for years to have the chance to shout at her Aelyr parents, *'Where were you?'* and now they were here she could hardly find the words.

Fiomir's face was a mask. Her eyes turned blue with tears. Neither of them could speak and the wordless tension went on so long it became excruciating; then Fiomir broke it at last.

'Please forgive us,' she said remotely. 'We thought Auriel was safe. We would have come to you, if only it had been possible. You don't know how ruthless Falthorn was. Talthaliorn thought the only way to outwit him was to gain higher knowledge from the Wrothryr.'

'How did you get into the Obsidian Tower?' Tanthe put in. 'Falthorn said even great mages couldn't find it.'

Fiomir gave her husband a lingering glance. 'Talthaliorn is very determined. It took years of searching, following arcane clues. We were lost in a labyrinth of paths and portals. Many times we wished we hadn't begun, but there was no turning back. When at last we found our way in . . . you saw how it was. We became utterly lost . . .' Her eyes glazed with hideous memories. 'Foolish, to think we were superior to the dangers. I wish I knew how you did what you did.'

Tanthe laughed. 'I must have my father's determination.'

'Even in the *ezht*, we knew the child had come into existence, because we saw his essence there.' She placed a hand on Tanthe's shoulder. 'We knew he was from you and Auriel, and that Falthorn must have got his way. He'd been obsessed for a long time with bringing a child of power into being . . .' Fiomir broke down. 'I'm sorry. Being with you doesn't seem real.'

'I know.' Again Tanthe fought the spasm of her throat. 'Fiomir, why *did* you quarrel with Falthorn?'

'Didn't Auriel tell you?'

'He told me it was because the Valahyr disapproved of Talthaliorn marrying a woman of a different *eretru*. To be honest, I always thought it was more than that.'

'What did you think?' Fiomir asked gently.

Tanthe shrugged. 'That Falthorn was in love with you himself and jealous of Talthaliorn?'

Fiomir gave a sharp laugh. 'Hardly.'

'Yes, well, I realise now that it was unlikely. But it could have been. I also heard that Talthaliorn and Falthorn disagreed about how to vanquish the Eaters. You wanted to fight with the humans, Falthorn wanted to use more devious methods.'

'That's true, but they disagreed about much more than that. I have a certain empathy . . .' She leaned down and touched the surface of the water, and in doing so she looked like Jthery.

'Ohh . . .' Tanthe began.

'A certain form of power that Falthorn thought he could harness. That was the core of it. He wanted to use me, and Tal, naturally, was furious.'

'Water *roth*,' said Tanthe.

Fiomir stared at her, he head making tiny movements like a bird's, as if to see her daughter from every possible angle. 'How did you know that?'

'Because he's found someone else with that power. It all starts to make sense.'

'Someone else?' Fiomir looked alarmed. 'What happened?'

'I'm not sure. Nothing yet, because . . .' Tanthe was out of her depth, unsure how much to say. Perhaps it was never safe to trust Aelyr, even those who had given her life.

'Do you think his accident has destroyed his power?'

'I don't know, but this person with the *roth* power,

Jthery, he seems to have persuaded Falthorn to help us . . . I don't know what to believe.'

'You're very human,' said Fiomir. 'The way you speak, the things you hide, your mannerisms.'

'Sorry if I've disappointed you.'

'No, I don't mean it like that. I can see Eodwyth and Aynie in you, and we were so fond of them. I like the way you are so warm and impulsive. And brave beyond dreams.'

'I'm really not brave. Impulsive, definitely.'

'Did you have human brothers or sisters?'

'One sister, who proves that being weird is not the prerogative of the Aelyr. One brother, who was a daft little kid when I left and will probably be a middle-aged grumbling farmer by the time I see him again.'

'You love them?'

'Of course, why?'

'Love can be more terrible than hate, when it goes to extremes. Don't think that Falthorn hated Talthaliorn; it was the opposite, in truth. He loved him, worshipped him, wanted to *be* him, was jealous of him.' Fiomir gazed at the water, speaking more to herself than Tanthe.

'I can't imagine Falthorn being jealous of anyone.'

'Ah, he was. If anything, it was me he hated for taking Tal away from him. Tal can seem cold; Falthorn is very passionate, and Tal's coldness drove him mad. Worse than mad, when he saw how warm his brother was with me.' Fiomir smiled to herself. Tanthe felt, uncomfortably, that she was learning more than she wanted to. 'However, Falthorn had great plans for the three of us. We would do so much with our combined powers. But his plans . . .' She shook her head. 'He saw them as full of glory, but to us they were terrible, unconscionable. We tried to persuade him to our point of view but the quarrels between us only grew worse. He knew he would never have my powers at his disposal except by force. The ultimate quarrel between us ended with his warriors trying to capture us. We had no choice but to flee.

'Tal and I had made a great mistake. We hadn't realised how powerful Falthorn had become, nor that he'd got all his family and the whole Valahyr *eretru* on his side. He'd done all that behind our backs. We thought we were equals, who might persuade him with reasoned argument. How wrong could we be! He tried to imprison us, he threatened our lives and those of our children, and when we escaped he sent his forces to pursue us. He had become, out of years of frustration, ruthless.'

'I know he's ruthless,' Tanthe put in.

'We had to hide our children and flee. And I had to watch Talthaliorn become afraid of the brother who had once adored him.'

'Talthaliorn doesn't look like he's afraid of anything.' Tanthe looked along the bank to where Rufryd and Auriel were entertaining Mendyr, the dark Valahyr lord looking on.

'Don't be fooled,' said Fiomir. 'I don't know anyone who isn't afraid of Falthorn. Even his own parents.'

'Lord Valthiell and Lady Cielemne. I met them.' Tanthe pulled a face. 'I can't say I liked them very much, though they did try to help me in small ways. I got the impression they were too much in thrall to their precious son to do more.'

Fiomir laughed. 'If it's any consolation, I didn't like them either. They would have preferred a noble Valahyr woman for Tal; not one of the Fhelethyr, who are only noted for singing, time-wasting, and running away.'

Tanthe's jaw dropped. 'Oh, singing piercingly enough to make your foes fall over on the battlefield? Time-wasting by weaving Jewelfire into new pockets of Verdanholm? Running away, to avoid the Eaters destroying you? I've met the Fhelethyr. I liked them a lot better than the Valahyr.'

Fiomir sat upright, gazing intently at her. 'You met them in Verdanholm? My family?'

'No. I met someone who knew someone who thought they might have heard of your family, but Falthorn intervened before we got there.'

Fiomir's taut posture loosened with disappointment. 'Ah.'

'Falthorn was making war on the Fhelethyr.'

'No. Oh no.' She tensed again, eyes flashing dismay.

'It didn't last long, because he won quite easily. He's made himself, to all intents and purposes, Verdanholm's leader.'

'This is terrible news.'

'Well, all the Aelyr were acclaiming him as their saviour. What he did to me was the least of it. The story of how he saved Verdanholm from the Eaters is an interesting one; he did it by selling Aventuria from underneath us.'

'Stop.' Fiomir rose to her feet, seeming unnerved by Tanthe's tone. 'Talthaliorn should hear this. I must speak to him first.'

Later, when Mendyr was asleep with his head on Auriel's thigh, she and Rufryd and Auriel told Fiomir and Talthaliorn all that had happened on Earth while they had been trapped in the *ezht*. They listened in grave silence. Above, clouds were massing and the air pressed down like a clammy hand.

'Everything we feared about Falthorn is coming true,' said Fiomir at last. 'I never dreamed he would end up in league with the Bhahdradomen.'

'Not any more,' said Rufryd. 'He's with us, and not up to doing anything – unless this is his biggest con trick yet.'

Talthaliorn gave a sudden laugh. 'You might say my brother has always been blind; blinded by love for Verdanholm. He could never see the wrong in any of his schemes; for as long as they benefited Verdanholm, they must be pure and desirable. And he called me the traitor, for saying, "This will harm others!"'

'What about Mendyr?' Tanthe said softly. 'Why did

Falthorn need him so badly? What might he do that's so dangerous?'

'I don't know, my daughter.' Talthaliorn gave a quick light caress to the back of her head. Her scalp tingled where he had touched her, a thrill of delight that he'd shown her that small sign of affection. 'How could Falthorn get the better of us if he told us all his secrets?'

Tanthe looked at Mendyr, tousled and sound asleep on Auriel's knee. He was sweet, yet she felt no more of a maternal bond to him than she would to any other child. Perhaps it would come, if he wanted it. 'He doesn't look a bit dangerous at the moment, does he?'

They decided to take the trip gently back to the camp. They rested often, and took it in turns to ride the three horses, or to lead them when they were tired. As they went, Tanthe and Auriel talked endlessly to their mother and father about all that had happened. Rufryd listened, but when the conversation turned to Aelyr matters, much of it went over his head. He felt mildly envious that Tanthe suddenly had a complete family around her, and another back in Riverwynde. All I've got left is a father who can't stand me, he thought.

Yet there was no real bitterness in the thought. At night, he was the one who curled up with Tanthe under their cloaks. That was what mattered.

Mendyr seemed to spend most of the journey asleep, nodding in the saddle in front of Tanthe or Rufryd or Auriel. Poor little bugger's exhausted, Rufryd thought, feeling a sneaking sympathy for him. Wish I could just drop off to sleep with Tanthe to hold me in the saddle. Doesn't know how lucky he is.

The weather worsened as they rode north. He recognised the taint of *gauroth* in the air and knew the lightning that flickered among the clouds was caused by Vaurgroth's power. The clouds were thick with smoke. Rufryd's heart sank.

As they came in sight of the camp, moans filled the air. Rufryd and Tanthe looked gravely at each other but said nothing.

The camp was busy, they found, as they rode towards its heart. The moans came from the wounded. They lay everywhere, inside tents and outside, tended by healers who were bathing and bandaging wounds, giving herbal infusions, manipulating crystals over their ravaged bodies.

'Looks like they started without us,' Rufryd said drily.

To hear soldiers sobbing in terror was more disturbing than moans of pain. The travellers passed quietly through the camp, too shocked to speak. Lahjaya raised a weary hand to Tanthe in passing, obviously too preoccupied to bother being surprised.

As they reached the command tent, Helan came out to meet them, looking worn to the bone. Her honey curls were scraped back and dark with dirt, her garments grimy and blood-spattered. Mawrdreth beside her looked no better. *Doesn't look like they want to hear any tales of heroism from us,* he thought. Then from the tent came a third figure, someone Rufryd hadn't seen for years.

'Eldareth!' he shouted, leaping off his horse and rushing to embrace the older man.

Tanthe followed, exclaiming, 'Where the hell did you disappear to?'

'I might ask the same of you,' Eldareth said, hugging them both, then regarding them at arm's length. 'It's good to see you.'

Eldareth had changed, Rufryd saw. Not necessarily for the better, he thought; there was a distant look in his eyes that hadn't been there before.

'Helan, we found them,' Tanthe said, holding out a hand to usher her parents and her child forward. 'Lady Fiomir, Lord Talthaliorn, and, er, Mendyr. Their Majesties Queen Helananthe and King Mawrdreth of Aventuria.'

'You're very welcome.' Without ceremony, Helan shook their hands. 'You don't find us at our best. To be honest I'm amazed to see you. Not that I doubted Tanthe's resourcefulness, but I'm so relieved . . . Come in, come in.' She held up the flap of her tent for them. 'So you're Mendyr. Well, you're a lot taller and more grown-up than we thought you'd be.'

'Ma'am, I understand my brother Lord Falthorn is here?' said Talthaliorn. 'I would like to see him.'

Rufryd was looking around the dusty maze of paths between the tents. The figure he'd expected to greet him wasn't there. 'Where's Vetru?' he said.

'Ah, Rufe, I'm sorry,' said Eldareth. Placing a hand on his shoulder he drew him aside. 'Your, er, young friend has done something exceedingly heroic for us. He took the Pin of Time in among enemy lines. It was all that stopped the *ghelim* massacring us.'

'*What?*' Rufryd was horrified. 'Where is he?'

Eldareth spoke gently, not seeming to notice the level of his distress. 'Well, it was never expected he would come back. He knew that, and accepted it.'

Rufryd stood open-mouthed, unable to breathe. 'You bastards,' he managed at last.

'Rufe?' Eldareth frowned. 'Please . . .'

'How could you make him do that? You thought, just because he was Bhahdradomen, he was worthless?'

He sensed the others staring at him. Tanthe slipped a hand through his arm. 'We didn't make him,' said Eldareth. 'He volunteered.'

'I don't believe you. I knew I should have taken him with me! I knew I should never have trusted him to your care!'

'I'm sorry,' Eldareth said, with a pity that made Rufryd want to hit him. 'We had no idea you'd feel so badly about it.'

'Neither did I,' Rufryd said savagely. 'Neither did I!'

Tanthe held him. He was beyond weeping, only stood there shuddering, not understanding why this hurt nearly as badly as Annuin's death. Yet it did. And he was so furious he didn't trust himself to speak to anyone.

'Rufe, Rufe,' she whispered, clinging tight to him.

After a while he calmed down. 'I think I've had enough,' he said, pushing his hair out of his eyes. 'When we were in the Tower, I thought you were dead. First Lynden, then Annuin, now this. Is the Ancestor having some vile joke at my expense for sticking two fingers up to him, or what?'

'Love, I wasn't dead, I'm still here. Not much consolation, I know.'

'You know what would be the sickest joke of all?' he said bleakly. 'If we went through all this and still lost in the end.'

Jthery jerked from a half-sleep to find the tent-flap flung back, and an imposing Valahyr silhouetted against the gloomy daylight. There were others behind him; an Aelyr woman, Auriel and Tanthe. But they stayed outside while the stranger came striding into the tent. Ostarial and Alviath shot to their feet, swords swishing from scabbards.

He didn't say a word, just stood glaring down at Falthorn. Jthery sat stunned. Falthorn's sightless eyes flickered, and all at once he smiled.

'Talthaliorn,' he said.

'So it's true,' said the man. 'They told me you were blind; I didn't believe them.'

'Then this is a wondrous shock for both of us,' Falthorn said, propping himself up on pillows. Jthery hurried to help him.

'How did you know it was me?'

'I still recognise your footfall, the sound of your breath, the way you move,' Falthorn said. He looked, Jthery thought, demonically thrilled. 'Is Fiomir there too? Tanthe, the whole happy band?'

'Tanthe freed us from the *ezht*,' said Talthaliorn. Jthery studied him, mesmerised. No question they were brothers.

'And how astoundingly foolish for you to have got stuck there, and then try to blame me for your folly.'

Talthaliorn ignored the remark. 'My daughter said, quite wisely, that it was time for us to stop fleeing from you.'

'Well, as you can see, I'm in no position to pursue you.' Falthorn's smile vanished. He looked sad. 'Sheath your swords,' he said to his guards. 'I don't think my brother has come to assassinate me. Find him a chair, Jthery, please. Tal, I'm actually glad to see you – or, rather, I would be, if I *could* see you.'

Uneasy, Talthaliorn sat down in the chair Jthery had vacated. 'Of course, this might be your most elaborate trap yet.'

'It might be,' Falthorn said with an edge. 'Yet you were prepared to risk it. I'm touched. Did you find the missing child, by any chance?'

Talthaliorn paused. 'He is with us, but in our care. You will never have control of him again.'

'That is unfortunate.'

The Aelyr woman with dark-red hair came softly into the tent, with Tanthe beside her. Jthery looked questioningly at Tanthe, but she only shrugged. He felt fiercely protective of Falthorn, who could no longer defend himself.

'Unfortunate, why?' said the woman.

'Ah, Fiomir,' said Falthorn. 'So pleasant of you to visit me. I mean that it's unfortunate for you, since you lack the remotest idea of how to guide him.'

'The Wrothryr didn't consider you fit to look after him, either,' Tanthe said in annoyance. 'Why don't you just tell us what his powers are? You're in no position to play games with us now, are you?'

Falthorn sat up, his gazed fixed on the direction of her voice, as if he could see her. The look was terrible, even to Jthery. Tanthe flinched. 'Didn't the Wrothryr tell you?' he said. 'Haven't you worked it out?'

'Not yet.'

'Well, why don't you just ask him? Go on. Bring him in here and ask him.'

Tanthe hesitated. Then she said, 'Right,' and marched out of the tent.

'It's a shame,' Falthorn went on, lying back again, 'that you have utterly wasted the past twenty or so years, when you could have been doing so much to help Verdanholm.'

'No-one wasted those years but you,' Talthaliorn said bitterly. 'It grieves me to see you reduced to this.'

'Only my eyes are damaged. Not the rest of me. As soon as that jewel among healers, Lahjaya, permits me to rise, I shall.'

'Then what?' said Fiomir. 'Nothing can be as it was before. Tanthe and Auriel found us, which I expect is what you planned. But you will never control us, never use us.'

'Fiomir, darling.' Falthorn reached out and caught her hand; she stiffened. 'I don't need you any more. I found someone who has all your talent, and more, besides being a highly imaginative lover and utterly devoted to me.'

Fiomir fixed Jthery with a hard, knowing glare. Her eyes seem to lance right inside him. He wasn't expecting it and his heart leapt in astonishment; then he sensed, with the weirdest thrill of recognition, the deep blue waters that lay behind her eyes, the elementals whispering like shadowy fish through her soul. Light dawned. This was the woman Falthorn had meant when he said those mysterious words, *'You're a* roth-*mage and don't realise it . . . a natural, as she was.'*

'Lord Jthery, you're a fool,' she said crisply. 'He's using you as he tried to use me. My friendly advice to you would be to leave him, before it's too late.'

Jthery glared at Falthorn, annoyed with him for saying anything, forgetting for a moment that he couldn't see him. 'My lady, I appreciate your advice but I should tell you that I know exactly what a devious swine Falthorn is since he's demonstrated it to me in a score of interesting ways. You could say we've reached an understanding.'

'Jey!' Falthorn exclaimed.

He sounded amused, but Fiomir looked furious. 'He has threatened our lives, imprisoned and tormented my son, abused my daughter. Sold the Earth to Vaurgroth and he lies there laughing at us! He would use us to suck the last drop of power out of every living and moving thing, so you had better pray to Eshte that you know what you are doing!'

'Losing my sight hasn't won me any sympathy,' Falthorn said drily. 'Perhaps I should arrange to have all my limbs blown off next time.'

Fiomir's outburst made Jthery recoil. He rallied, folding his arms. 'My lady, don't you think that people can repent and admit they were mistaken?'

'Not him,' she said. 'I shall never forgive what he did to my son and daughter. Never.'

'Tanthe and Auriel might regard my influence as character-forming.'

For a moment Fiomir looked ready to attack Falthorn. Jthery was so afraid she would that he put his hands on her to stop her. She stood frozen. Talthaliorn whispered something into her ear and it was only then that the tension went out of her, and she gave Jthery a glare of such imperious rage that he snatched his hands from her immediately.

'Might I point out,' Falthorn said, 'that I sustained these injuries trying to get those wretched geriatric weapons working in order to help the humans? Jthery is speaking the truth. He has prevailed upon my better nature where you, Tal, could not.'

'How?' said Talthaliorn.

'I should have thought that was obvious. You see before you a reformed character, a spent force.'

Jthery clasped his hand. He knew that Falthorn's ambiguous, joking tone was only a front; a convincing one, but fragile.

The tent-flap stirred, and Tanthe came in with the child, Auriel anxiously following them. Half the camp seemed to be standing outside, eavesdropping. The porcelain-skinned, dark-haired child stood shyly against Tanthe for a moment. Then he ran forward, and as he did so, Jthery saw the blood drain out of Tanthe's face, and Auriel's.

'Uncle Falthorn!' said Mendyr, rushing to his bedside and throwing one arm over him. 'Are you ill?'

Falthorn gave the child a brief hug. 'I've had a slight accident, that's all. How are you?'

'Very well, thank you.' The boy showed no fear of his erstwhile guardian. Jthery saw Tanthe standing aghast with her fingers pressed to her open mouth. He felt almost sick with sympathy for her. She had no idea, he thought, that Falthorn had any kind of relationship with the child, let along an affectionate one. *He didn't even tell me.*

'It's a long time since I saw you,' Mendyr was saying.

'I'm sorry. Business kept me away. If I'd known sooner that the Wrothryr had taken you from Sehnya, I would have come looking for you.'

Tanthe and Auriel pressed close together, their faces taut as they watched the encounter. Talthaliorn and Fiomir looked no less worried. Their fear shook Jthery; what did they think Falthorn was going to do? Only Mendyr was calm.

'It's all right, Uncle. I wasn't frightened. I sort of remembered them from before I was born . . . but I was confused. I'd got used to being a Valahyr boy. I knew I didn't belong with Laefrohyr or Wrothryr. Then Tanthe and the others came . . .' A neat frown indented the porcelain forehead. 'I'm still not sure where I belong.'

Tanthe gave a quiet, anguished, 'Ohhh . . .' When Jthery looked round, her face was hidden on Auriel's shoulder. Everyone was silent.

'Perhaps you belong with me?' asked Falthorn.

The boy considered. 'I don't know.'

'It's because you're so young,' Falthorn said, with a tenderness that seemed to hypnotise everyone. 'When you grow older, you'll know. Until then, these people are going to look after you. Will you like that?'

Mendyr thought, then nodded. 'Oh, yes.'

'Good,' said Falthorn. 'Now it must seem to you that you have had a very unsettled life, but there is a reason. Do you know what it is?'

'No.'

Falthorn sighed. 'Of course you do, we've talked about it before. Your special power, which you will learn to use when you are older . . . ?'

Mendyr shrugged. 'It can't be special if it's so easy. Everyone can do it if they try, surely? Actually you have to stop yourself, not *try* to do it.'

'Oh no, I promise you they can't,' he answered with a laugh. 'I can't. Talthaliorn can't. Fiomir can't. Even your talented father Auriel can't.'

'Some of the Wrothryr could, but they told me I must never, ever, do it. It's dangerous, they said. It was why I mustn't go to Earth. I don't see why, but . . .' His small shoulders rose and fell.

'It's all right. Just tell Tanthe what it is. She would like to know.'

Mendyr turned, his small face tilted towards her. 'I can't explain it in words. I don't really know what it's for.'

'Try.' Her voice was shaky. 'If we don't understand, I'm sure Falthorn will explain.'

'Oh,' said the boy. 'Well, all right . . . I can do this.'

He held his hands up in front of his chest, a foot apart as if he were holding an invisible sphere. Jthery couldn't tell what he was doing. A black pin-prick appeared in the centre of his vision. He tried to focus on it until his eyes hurt and he concluded there was something wrong with his own sight.

Then he felt a faint sense of disorientation as if the earth was moving slightly, the air itself bending in towards the pin-prick. The spot grew larger. Jthery frowned, physically uncomfortable but not understanding. The others stared, puzzled.

Then Falthorn yelled, '*No!*'

The spot vanished. The deformed air sprang back into shape. Mendyr looked startled and ready to cry.

'No, don't,' Falthorn said again. 'Not here, not now. Not until you are old enough to know what you are doing!'

'But Tanthe asked . . .'

Talthaliorn rose to his feet, towering furiously over Falthorn. 'You fool, you arrogant, irresponsible fool! Stars above us, I never dreamed you would do something this insane! Falthorn, you knew – you've brought this soul into flesh who should have stayed among the Wrothryr, knowing full well he might destroy everything! Now I know there is no limit to your madness!'

Falthorn actually flinched before his onslaught.

Tanthe said in a small voice, 'Would someone mind telling me what you are talking about?' Mendyr was now half-hiding behind her. She placed a protective arm around him.

'He's a maker of gates,' Talthaliorn said brusquely. 'He doesn't open existing portals. He can actually create them. And not only simple *rothanamir* between Verdanholm and Earth but gates between other worlds, even the stars themselves. If he acts irresponsibly he could turn the world, Verdanholm, any realm he chooses, into lacework.'

'It's obviously a talent that runs in the family,' Falthorn put in. 'Auriel has a gift for finding portals. Mendyr can actually create them. Rather elegant.'

'You are a madman,' Talthaliorn said, leaning menacingly over his brother. 'I know why you've done this! The same reason you tried to use Fiomir and Jthery! You thought to make gateways to other realms, other universes, and suck all their *roth* power for Verdanholm's use!'

Falthorn sat up, edging away, his sightless eyes flickering. 'And your point is?'

'That the opposite would happen. You accursed lunatic!' He caught Falthorn by the neck of his robe. Jthery tried to intercede, only to be flung aside by a chopping motion of Talthaliorn's fist. There was a struggle; it took

Fiomir, Ostarial, Jthery and Alviath to hold Talthaliorn back, while Falthorn flinched against the canvas, looking truly alarmed.

At last, Talthaliorn stood still in their hands, breathing hard. Mendyr was hiding his face against Tanthe, crying now.

'You are quite right, Tal,' Falthorn said savagely. 'That is why I wanted him. I knew it was a risk, but still; if he was properly looked after, properly trained, he would do everything I wanted, draw all the Jewelfire Verdanholm needed to endure forever.'

'Steal it!' said Fiomir.

'Steal it, yes, to save us and suck the Bhahdradomen into oblivion. I would have used Mendyr's powers responsibly. However, you have chosen to intervene and there you are. The child exists. What is done cannot be undone. What are you going to do, kill him?'

'Of course not!' Talthaliorn cried.

'That's just as well. If you did, the seed of Jewelfire that powers his soul would destroy a sizeable part of the world; it would certainly have done for the Eaters if they'd harmed him. So, since you insist on keeping him, I suggest you look after him well.'

And Falthorn lay back on his pillow, hands cupped loosely behind his head, grinning.

Mendyr sobbed for nearly an hour, while Tanthe watched over him, her heart breaking. Auriel and Fiomir stayed too, in the dismal gloom of her tent, hugging the boy and stroking his hair. Talthaliorn and Rufryd came and went, restless and upset.

Presently Lahjaya came in and sat next to Tanthe, putting an arm round her. 'You found him; doesn't look too happy, does he? What's happened?'

'I'll tell you later. I expect you'll hear soon, anyway. Poor little bugger; he didn't ask to be born.'

After a time, Mendyr stopped crying. He sat up, blew his

nose on a piece of cloth Rufryd offered, and drank the milk Lahjaya had brought for him. He was composed and eerily grown-up again.

'I'm not going to destroy the world,' he said. 'I don't want to destroy anything. I don't want this power.'

'I know,' Tanthe said. 'I'm sorry.'

'I don't believe Uncle Falthorn only wanted me to use me,' he said stiffly. 'I don't believe it!'

'He's obviously fond of you,' she said lamely.

'Because he was the only one who ever wanted me,' Mendyr said forlornly. 'I know that you didn't want me!'

Tanthe didn't answer. She couldn't. His words were a spear through her heart and at that moment she wished they could have been a real spear. Her son fell asleep and she sat staring at him, seeing only a hurt little stranger whom she couldn't reach or help. Auriel looked as distressed as she felt, yet they couldn't talk to each other.

When Mendyr was asleep she put her head in her hands. 'I had no idea that he and Falthorn might be actually fond of each other. Never occurred to me. How many more knives has Falthorn got to stick into us?' No-one answered her.

Helan came in, followed by Mawrdreth and Eldareth. The Queen's face was sheened with sweat, the strain of impossible burdens. 'We heard most of what happened,' she said, touching Tanthe's arm. 'Can I talk to you?'

'No,' said Tanthe, standing up, knowing she had to escape for a while or go mad. 'There he is, the last and greatest Basilisk, only he's just a little boy. Are you going to carry him into battle on the front of your saddle or shall I?'

'Tanthe, don't,' Helan said gently. 'No-one's going to do anything like that.'

She was furious. 'But you'd like to. Our only hope. How bloody inconvenient, that he's a child and not a lump of metal!'

* * *

As evening fell, Eldareth took Tanthe and Rufryd, Fiomir and Talthaliorn up onto a ridge to the east of the camp. From here they had a clear view across the Almandine Vale to the enemy. Clouds of smoke black as tar boiled there, shot through with flashes of red flame. The stink that drifted to them was foul.

Tanthe was calm now, but waxen-faced and reluctant to speak to anyone. Rufryd had never dreamed a living child could cause such pain, but he knew better than to say, 'I warned you.' He was glad she'd agreed to leave the boy in Auriel's care. It was a relief to escape the camp, even for this.

'I can't see a thing,' said Rufyrd. 'What's happening?'

Eldareth gave a thin smile. 'The Zampherai and their pupil have been at work.'

'Pupil?' Tanthe said sharply. 'You?'

'I have been deep in the underworld,' Eldareth said. 'I've learned much that I should have learned years ago. But not enough yet to do more than delay Vaurgroth's forces by a day or two.'

As they watched, a gust of wind rolled back the smoke, and Rufryd saw the wall of jagged rock piled high across the far hillside. He heard the thunder of some great engine or battering ram pounding at it from behind. The air trembled with shock waves; crimson sparks and black energies hissed on the air.

'What the hell is that?' he said.

'We called Umbaroths from deep in the rock beds. They rose, and took living shape, and set themselves all around the Bhahdradomen, effectively walling them in.'

'You did that?' Rufryd exclaimed. 'Gods, Eld, you are a marvel.'

'Not so,' Eldareth said ruefully. 'We didn't realise that Vaurgroth had built such a powerful engine. The Umbaroths can't prevail forever.'

'They're letting themselves be dismembered,' Tanthe said quietly.

Eldareth shook his head. 'No. They were animated by the *roth*-spirit of the rock that we called into them; they aren't sentient as we are. It's a slow-moving but sensitive energy. The attack upon the Umbaroths will have sent the spirit fleeing deep into the earth, almost as soon as it began. So all you see is dumb stone being reduced to rubble. With better foreknowledge we would have destroyed the engine itself . . .'

'There's something moving down there,' Rufryd said suddenly.

He saw a figure, just a shadow-sketch on the dark background, visible only because he saw it flitting from one scrubby bush to the next. It was working its way along the edge of the valley to his right, scampering close to the ground, stopping, running again.

Talthaliorn and Tanthe both began to draw their swords, but he said, 'No!'

He rode a little way down the slope. Now there was no doubt. The figure saw him and dropped behind a rock, plainly not realising who he was.

'It's Vetru,' he called back to the others. 'Vetru!'

He leapt off the mare and ran to the rock, his heart racing with relief. 'Vetru, it's me. I didn't meant to scare you. Come out.'

The *neshrim* rose from his hiding place and stood trembling, his mottled almost-human face a picture of dread.

'Nuth and Breyid be praised, you're all right!' Rufryd seized Vetru and hugged him tight. 'I thought you were dead. Gods, you made it! How did you get out?'

He began to lead Vetru and the mare up the hill towards the others. Vetru seemed too shaken to speak, but eventually he said, 'I climbed over the wall, the same way I got in.'

'What happened? You took the Basilisk, they said.' They had reached the others now. Vetru went on speaking to Rufryd as if he hadn't noticed them.

'Yes, in a pouch. I went through their lines and no-one

stopped me; they were all too busy with their *gauroth*-engine, trying to destroy the wall. I went close to where Lord Bharamezht was with all his *vagharim* and mages and did as the Queen told me; buried the Pin of Time in the ground between some rocks so they wouldn't find it.' He shook his head. 'I was glad to leave it. I can still hear it.'

'How d'you mean?'

'A whining noise. It made me dizzy. The air, the ground around us was suddenly full of *ghelim*, wheeling about and falling like humans when they're drunk. Hundreds of them. I was frightened. One of them knocked me over and I crawled away but I saw Bharamezht, all his officers and adepts going mad with rage.'

'Did they know what had happened?'

'I heard them speak of Basilisks. They ordered a search. I was trying to hide, so afraid I daren't move. I think they saw me, but they were looking for human, not *domen*. And so they ignored me.'

Vetru was shaking from head to foot. Rufryd gave him a drink of water from his flask. 'Come on, you're safe now.'

'No, no, we're not safe. *Yrim* start climbing over the walls. The engine is too strong. The wall is crumbling and when it breaks they will attack us again . . .' Vetru all but collapsed into Rufryd's arms. He hauled the thin figure up and slung him over the mare's saddle.

'Better go and warn Helan,' said Eldareth. 'She showed me the Basilisks. Cursed ill-fortune that they're all but useless . . .'

'Oh, I don't know,' said Rufryd. 'Falthorn nearly got his head blown off; I call that a result.'

As he spoke, there was a roar of flame, a billow of smoke. Across the valley, the untenanted remains of the Umbaroths collapsed at last. As the smoke lifted, a wide smoking gap was revealed in the wall; and through it came rumbling the huge *gauroth*-engine, and then thousands of Bhahdradomen ground-troops, like a swarm of ants.

* * *

'There's no need for you to fight,' Helan told Talthaliorn, Fiomir and Rufryd. 'You're all exhausted. Stay back at the camp with Auriel; make sure Tanthe and the boy are safe.' None of them argued, not even Rufryd, for once.

Then she touched Vetru on the shoulder. 'I can't thank you enough for what you did,' she said awkwardly. 'To work for us, even though it meant acting against your own people; it was an act of the highest bravery.'

Vetru said nothing, only dipped his head in embarrassment.

'Don't think you'll be idle,' said Lahjaya. 'You can help the healers. We are going to be very busy, I fear.'

Helan waited until they'd left her tent. Then she leaned on the table, ignoring the attendant who was lacing her breastplate. Despair settled on her like black, fiery tar. They were going to fight, they were going to lose; she knew this in her bones. Mawrdreth was grim and short-tempered, striding outside to bark orders at Karmensis and the Marocian officers; she'd never seen him like that before. The war corroded even his gentle temperament.

Eldareth was oddly calm, anxious but resigned. His detachment unnerved her. He wasn't the Eldareth she remembered.

'Tanthe's right about me, you know,' said Helan. 'The longer this fight goes on, the more ruthless I become. I did curse that child for being little and vulnerable. For two pins I *would* take him into battle and hurl him at Bharamezht. One life, to save so many!'

'You could never be cruel,' said Eldareth. He spoke to her more like a Seer or a Mediator than a friend. 'You will know what to do. So will we all, when the time comes.'

'You've changed so much,' she said, stroking his cheek as she made her way outside.

'I had to,' he said, catching her fingers briefly and kissing them. 'We both know that.'

One of her officers was outside with her horse. She mounted. Her limbs felt liquid with dread, but she couldn't afford weakness now. Mawrdreth, Karmensis and her attendants were ready. They rode up onto the high promontory from which she could view and direct the whole field. Eldareth followed. Talthaliorn joined the party, even though Helan had suggested he stay behind.

She saw the endless lines of Bhahdradomen troops, arrayed before the ruins of the Umbaroth wall. They looked implacable, fierce, burning with Vaurgroth's power and the certainty that their victory was Ancestor's Will. She saw the dreadful war-engine in their midst, like a gigantic scorpion, steam and fire wreathing from beneath its oily bronze plating.

Helan was suddenly, seethingly furious. 'We have arrows, crossbows, spears and swords against *that*!' She pointed a taut finger at the *gauroth*-engine. 'Like trying to subdue a volcano with twigs and pins! And it is the fault of your people, Talthaliorn; for if we'd had Aelyr help, Aelyr weapons, we might have stood some chance of surviving!'

She thought for a moment that Talthaliorn's stony visage was about to explode in fury. Instead he only regarded her harshly, then turned his face aside. 'You are right, ma'am. And for agreeing with you, and arguing that we should indeed be helping you – fighting the Eaters instead of making vile bargains with them – Fiomir and I have been persecuted and driven from Verdanholm. And I am ashamed of my own people, my *eretru*, my very family. Ashamed!'

He turned his horse and rode away. Helan barely noticed that Eldareth had slipped away after him. She stared at the terrible machine and her whole being convulsed with despair.

'I cannot throw human beings against that,' she said. 'Bharamezht knows that I can't initiate this attack! He's mocking us.'

The Bhahdradomen lines waited, shifting slightly, as if they could wait for all time. The engine steamed and brooded.

'Whether we initiate the attack or not,' Mawrdreth said, 'sooner or later, that monstrous weapon will be launched against us.'

Falthorn grinned; but as soon as Talthaliorn and the others left, his smile vanished and he looked, to Jthery's eyes, desperately sad. He'd sent Ostarial and Alviath to command the Valahyr. They were alone.

'Falthorn?' Jthery said softly.

'Jey,' he breathed, drawing Jthery onto his chest and stroking the long red-gold skeins of his hair. 'None of this is as I would have wished it. I can't accept being blind. I can't accept being powerless. If I believed in your gods I might conclude that they were revenging themselves on me for the harm I have done the Earth. But I don't, so what am I to conclude?'

'This is all my fault,' Jthery said wretchedly. 'If I hadn't taken the Basilisks . . .'

'No, you did the right thing. All that my brother said about me is true. I conclude, therefore, that I must have been wrong. I did my utmost for Verdanholm but I over-reached myself; one last thing I would like to do and that is to take Greatlord Vaurgroth firmly by the throat and strangle the smug life out of him.'

'What do you mean, one last thing?'

'I'm not sure I can go on in this state, Jey. There is nothing wrong with my legs. I could get up now – but I am afraid, so afraid to walk out into a world that is permanently dark. I cannot bear it.'

'Don't you dare think like that!' Jthery said fiercely. 'I'm here, I'll always be here, I'll see for you and protect you.'

'Eshte bless you for that,' Falthorn's arms tightened around him. 'No, I shan't die, since it would mean leaving you. So will you get under the covers with me and make me forget all this?'

'I thought you'd never ask,' said Jthery.

Recklessness possessed him as he slid into Falthorn's

arms, alabaster flesh to honey flesh. Their love-making was feverish, tender, savage. When Falthorn bit him, he bit back. Always the Valahyr had entered him, controlled him, but now Jthery gave him no quarter. For the first time he rose above Falthorn and pierced him. Pressed his mouth to his to stifle his struggles and indignation until at last he gave in to bliss. Then Jthery smiled. Visions played behind his eyelids, golden-sharp as ecstasy, but he let them go. He didn't want power. Only the delicious victory of knowing that Falthorn was so in thrall, he would let him do anything.

'No-one ever—' Falthorn said through his teeth afterwards, mock-angry.

'You seemed to enjoy it,' Jthery retorted.

'That is not the point,' he said. But his voice and smile were languid. He played with Jthery's hair. 'I would give anything to see the beautiful, smug expression that I can sense upon your face, Jey.'

Jthery kissed him. 'I should get dressed. So should you. You're obviously malingering.'

'Must you?' Falthorn said darkly. 'What wonderful perversity, that we should lie here making love while outside these thin walls people are fighting and dying . . .'

'You are perverse.' Jthery struggled out of his lover's embrace, rose and dressed and made them both a concoction of hot spiced tea laced with Serpent Isles whisky. As they sat drinking it, Talthaliorn came into the tent alone. He brought the chill scent of the battlefield with him.

Jthery stood up, ready to intercede, but the Valahyr only raised a conciliatory hand. 'It's all right. I only wish to talk to my brother. Would you leave us?'

'He stays,' said Falthorn, catching Jthery's hand.

'As you prefer.' Talthaliorn sat down on a stool and leaned close to his brother. 'I haven't come to argue with you.'

'I'm glad to hear it.'

'Vaurgroth's forces are half a mile away, threatening

the humans with annihilation. And I'm led to believe that Ostarial will lead the Valahyr into battle on the humans' behalf. That this young man has persuaded you to turn your back upon your ambitions.'

'It's true. I didn't do it willingly, as he will tell you, but since it was the only way to keep him . . .'

'Then we've really nothing left to argue about.'

'I'm sure we can think of something.'

'There is this,' said Talthaliorn. 'You planned to ravage Earth in order to feed Verdanholm. But Verdanholm cannot exist without Earth. One is a reflection of the other. It would be like an infant in the womb sucking all the life-force from its mother; once her life was gone, the infant too would die. This is the mistake the Aelyr have made, in withdrawing from Earth, failing to guard her. In order to protect Verdanholm we must cherish the Earth. The Jewelfire runs through everything.'

'This war is about far more than who controls Aventuria, and always has been,' said Falthorn. 'It is a struggle to control the Jewelfire itself.'

'But that is where you and the humans and the Eaters are so mistaken. It isn't our business to control it! I'll admit I didn't gain the revelation or power I sought from the Wrothryr, but I learned this much from them. If you had flooded Verdanholm with Jewelfire, our realm would have drowned like an overwatered plant, even as Earth starved. Use Mendyr to open gates to other worlds and you will begin a chain of destruction that you can't even imagine. The Wrothryr are beings of sentient Jewelfire. Their concern is to maintain a natural balance that requires no adjustment from us. This I always knew but lacked the armour of knowledge to persuade you.'

Falthorn was quiet for a time. 'You could never have persuaded me, Tal. An army of Wrothryr could not have persuaded me. Only Jey.'

Talthaliorn exhaled through his teeth. 'I thought you

were the last person to resist logic yet be swayed by a pretty face.'

'Don't insult my companion,' Falthorn said thinly. 'Much as it pains me to say it, Tal, you are right. I know it. I was mad; blind with dreams, if you like. Altogether too hot to prove myself as great or greater than you, in some twisted way.'

His brother answered so quietly that Jthery could barely hear him. 'I assure you, Thorn, that any qualities you perceive or envy in me are entirely a product of your own imagination.'

Falthorn turned his head away, not responding. 'Still, I love the Valahyr and I would rather they did not throw themselves into this suicidal battle on anyone's behalf, even their own.'

'It's too late. We were always going to have to fight the Bhahdradomen sooner or later – with arms and human comrades, not with tricks. I told you that years ago and you wouldn't listen.'

'This is nice. Losing my eyesight so I can't see my beloved brother's face as he says, "I told you so".'

'I'm not smiling. For all the anguish you have caused us, you are still my brother.'

'Do you think I hated you?' Falthorn said with a spurt of fire. 'You could not be more wrong.'

Talthaliorn reached for his brother's hand and they clasped each other's wrists. Jthery felt uncomfortable, wishing he had left the tent after all. He sat scowling at Talthaliorn but the Valahyr ignored him. His strong face was turned to Falthorn and his expression was regretful, grim, tender, all at once. 'Then can we stop fighting each other?'

'Do I look in any position to fight you? Yes, it's over, Tal.'

'I want to lead the Valahyr into battle.'

'What?' Falthorn sat up. 'Why? Ostarial and Alviath are ready to do it. They won't follow you.'

'They will,' Talthaliorn said gravely. 'You're their leader. They will if you command it.'

Falthorn pushed the covers back. 'And what do Tanthe and Fiomir say to this?'

'They won't know until it's over, for good or ill.'

Falthorn began to get up. Jthery helped him; he was shaky at first, more from days of inactivity than any real injury. Then he seemed to gather his strength, and dressed himself as Jthery passed him the appropriate garments.

'Jey, ask someone to bring me my horse.'

'Your horse?'

'Elrill's blasted horse, then. Bring Nefri. I shall endure the indignity of being led along like a child on a pony.'

Helan had arrayed her troops in two main blocks, one to either side of the hill. That way the war-engine had only a swathe of empty space in front of it. She had seen that it could turn, slow and cumbersome, but if it did so it would leave one flank of her troops free, at least. Her spirit, as she gazed across the blood-hued Vale, was calm obsidian, with the tiniest red flame burning at its core. The Xauroma had broken, the spirit of the Earth withdrawn from her and buried itself deeper even than the realms of the Zampherai; but she still had a tiny spark of it left within herself. Her last hope.

Mawrdreth placed his gloved hand on hers. They exchanged a swift, desperate look. 'I love you,' he whispered and she echoed it back to him, wishing it did not sound like goodbye.

'Look,' he said.

The Valahyr troops were embedded in the eastern flank just to their left, lines of light-footed men and women with javelins, bows and curved, gemmed swords. She saw the stolen white stallion Nefri, and on his back Falthorn, being led along by Jthery. Beside him, Talthaliorn rode a black Marocian stallion.

Falthorn's voice drifted up to them, lacking the strength it had once had, but still clear and confident.

'All enmity between my brother and myself is ended,' he announced. 'The only way to preserve Verdanholm is to preserve the Earth. On this we're agreed. I wish you to welcome Lord Talthaliorn among you as your noble Valahyr brother!'

A cheer rang from the Valahyr, more a song, so loud the Bhahdradomen must have heard it. Perhaps it was that – a noise of exuberant defiance – that made Bharamezht decide it was time to act.

'Were I not indisposed, I'd lead you into battle myself,' Falthorn continued. 'Instead I give you my brother. These noble gracious cousins shall lead you; Lord Ostarial, Lady Alviath, Lord Talthaliorn!' His voice rose. 'The light of Verdanholm against the darkness of Hellaxis!'

Another wild song broke out. Nefri reared. Falthorn looked magnificent in that moment. Helan's heart quickened with inspiration. She and Mawrdreth watched as Talthaliorn guided his prancing black mount into the forefront of the Valahyr. Falthorn turned Nefri and rode away, Jthery hurrying to catch up and guide them. Soon the white stallion was lost to sight.

When she looked across at the enemy again, her heart leapt with dread. The *gauroth*-engine was on the move. It inched slowly across the landscape like a giant blind beetle. It quested to the west, sending out a thread of fire that missed her western flank by only a few yards. Then it rotated clumsily towards the east. And she knew that wherever she deployed her forces, however nimbly they ran, the *gauroth*-machine would destroy them in the end . . .

It crawled forward, wreathed in steam and oily fires. She heard voices murmuring in fear, anger, panic. They'd already taken too much punishment from the *ghelim*. She must rally them or they'd break and flee.

Helan put her telescope to her eye, saw a small figure

darting towards the engine from the side. She adjusted the focus. Too far away to make out his face, but he was obviously human. *Yrim* were trying to stop him. He battled, ran, battled again, made a last desperate rush at the monster's side. He ducked under its prehensile, fire-dripping muzzles and seemed to be climbing onto its plated back . . .

'No,' she gasped, dropping the telescope.

And then the *gauroth*-engine exploded.

The explosion shook the sky and the ground. Fire licked the clouds. Torn metal flew screaming in all directions; scores of Bhahdradomen were caught in the blast and thrown through the billows of smoke.

The smoke cleared to reveal a scene of devastation. Where the machine had been there was a blackened crater, filled with mangled metal and the corpses of Eaters. A deafening cheer rose from the human and Aelyr ranks.

Helan's horse stood on its hind legs but she kept her seat, sitting like a rock as it reared and plunged. Horror paralysed her. She knew what had happened.

'Eldareth,' she breathed. She gathered up the reins.

'Helan?' said Mawrdreth.

'Sound the advance,' she said woodenly. She heard the horns blaring behind her but she was already moving, urging her horse at a blind gallop down the hill, straight towards the heart of the enemy, the scream tearing itself from her throat, '*Eldareth!*'

Chapter Twenty-four. Beyond the Almandine Vale

Eldareth knew, as soon as he touched the Basilisks, that Helan had spoken the truth about them. He was alone in the semi-darkness of the command tent, having persuaded the guards that he was here at her instruction. The horn, Calabethron's Song, was dead, its delicate crystal reeds broken. The remaining two held possibilities. The cube, Swallower, no longer had the integrity to hold onto the power it absorbed; he could tell that as he stroked the crystal spheres set into its casing, sensing the broken and weakened flows of *roth*. Yet it might absorb enough, and hold it long enough, to cause a violent explosion as it destabilised. And the Dragon, too, might be shaken into a last brief burst of life.

Eldareth told no-one of his intention. He wanted no arguments, no plans and counter-plans. This could only work if he went now, alone.

His long training in the realm of the Zampherai had taught him to work alone. He felt no fear as he set out down the long curve of the Almandine Vale, his dark clothes giving him camouflage as he slipped from bush to rock. The two Basilisks hung heavy in a sack on his shoulder, chilly and inert. No fear, no emotion; he'd left all that behind, and with it all tender feelings as well. His love for Helan was a cool fact, not an experienced feeling. His fondness for Tanthe and Rufryd was a rock set in a landscape; merely there. He moved clear-minded towards his goal without any need to look back, to hesitate or waste time with pointless farewells.

He guessed that once he had planted the Basilisks on the *gauroth*-engine, he had a few seconds to make his escape.

The machine reared hideous against the purple-black sky, sweating steam. Oily patterns of green and bronze swirled on its thick turtle-plates. He must cross open ground to reach it. He drew his sword.

The first attack came unexpectedly from behind. He felt the bow-wave of *gauroth* before he even heard them; turned to find five *yrim* closing upon him. Sweat broke out on his back. *Gods, I am getting too old for this . . .*

He steadied his breath, called on the skills he'd learned. Kept his own aura intact against theirs. Used it to deflect the sting of *sten* and *tzirin* that lashed at him. His blade swung in an arc of light, took two down before the others retreated in fear. '*Grothrim!*' they cried as they went. They'd recognised him as a mage.

Ducking, Eldareth ran towards the great bulk of the machine. More *yrim* and *vagharim* walked alongside it. He was gasping for breath, his throat sore and sticky. To keep himself alive just long enough . . .

A second attack. Bhahdradomen peeled away from the side of the engine and converged upon him. Need gave him strength and agility to compare with Rufryd's. He swung the sword, his mind on a higher level even as his body dodged and laboured. His attackers had left the side of the engine undefended and all he had to do was break through them . . .

A *sten* blow took him down. Without his mage-skills to deflect it, it would have killed him. Instead he rolled down into a dip, struck up to pierce a *vagharim* through the heart. Then he leapt up and ran.

The engine loomed, a steaming giant. He darted in under the fire-nozzles before any more Bhahdradomen could stop him. Those who were walking some distance behind seemed not to notice him – or if they had, they were too late to stop him leaping onto its side, finding footholds where its curved plates overlapped. Its harsh hot stink overwhelmed him. He felt echoes of the human pain, anguish and emotion on which *gauroth* fed and grew. He sensed undertones; the rage of the Zampherai at the way Vaurgroth's adepts had scooped smoky quartz and oily haematite from the ground and filled it with their own dark powers . . .

Eldareth's hands shook, despite his calm. He drew out the two weapons. The strange cube, the pyramid with its nozzle like a miniature version of the monstrous engine. He set them into niches on the engine's armoured back. The hot metal was scorching his hands and knees. Quickly he pressed the crystal spheres and the Basilisks began to whine, their unstable energies running wild. And he realised, too late, that he did not have seconds in which to escape.

Half a second, it took, for Swallower to turn crimson, purple, black with swelling *gauroth*. It throbbed like a heart. The Dragon screamed. Eldareth saw it happening before he had time even to blink; but this had been the risk, he'd known that. His mind was the eye of the storm. And then the world turned into a roar of hot light.

The battle raged around Helan as she reached the lip of the crater. Showers of arrows rained onto the advancing Devourers, but few died. Unless they were taken through a vital organ they simply wrenched out the shaft and marched on. Their faces were terrible with cold hatred, mottled things out of nightmares. On her left, Marocians fought furiously, their swords and shields poor defence against the lash of *tzirin* and crackling death-sting of *sten*. On her right, the Valahyr had better fortune; but still she saw them fall, one after another, taken down by the bolts of blue fire from the Bhahdradomen *uzrat*, the deadliest weapons of all.

Helan flung herself off her horse to avoid the lethal shots. She crawled on hands and knees. And there on the lip of the crater she found his body.

Eldareth.

His torso and head were still intact but his left arm was

gone and the right leg ended at the knee. She stared at the gore of the shredded stumps and couldn't breathe, couldn't scream, couldn't retch.

'You bastard!' she cried on the last rasp of her breath. *'Bastard!'*

She crumpled to her knees and struck him in the chest with both fists. A deep hoarse moan ripped itself from her throat. She sank down until her head rested against his waxen cheek and his blood matted her hair. She cradled him, groaning until her chest hurt because she still could not draw breath.

Who told you to sacrifice yourself? Who? How dare you do this, you miserable bloody martyr? Eldareth, Eldareth, you cannot end it like this, not like this . . .

A hand landed on her shoulder. Mawrdreth. 'Helan, come back, you'll get yourself killed!' he said savagely. She looked up blankly; and behind him, perhaps ten yards away, she saw Talthaliorn fall. His black stallion went down with a hole in his chest, crimson staining the perfect jet silk of his coat. Helan gave a dry moan of despair.

A massacre.

That was what she saw as she rose shakily, letting Mawrdreth help her up. In dark snaking lines the Bhahradomen moved easily over the ground, ignoring the wreckage of their great engine. A shock-wave of terror passed over the human lines. Swords and spears could not prevail against the cruel fires of the Devourers. They saw their comrades falling all around them. Saw the nightmare flowing easily among their ranks like shoals of dark fish through water.

Terror overwhelmed Helan's army. Helpless, she watched it happen. Soldier after soldier turned – his or her face ghastly with fear – and ran. Human and Valahyr alike. The Valahyr lasted longer and took more of the Eaters down before they gave way; but in the end, it was the same.

Her army was in full flight. The Bhahradomen followed,

shooting and hacking them down from behind. Heading now for the camp.

Mawrdreth clung to Helan. She wondered for a brief wild moment if they should kill each other, escape the misery before it was too late. The world shuddered and moaned.

Suddenly out of the smoke came Commander Bharamezht, surrounded by his officers, swollen with power.

'Stop!' she screamed at him. 'They're fleeing, you can't kill them while they're fleeing!'

'I'm not sure you've suffered enough yet. You have inflicted considerable damage upon us. Not enough, however. The more you suffer, the stronger we grow.'

'*Gauroth* will turn on you in the end,' Mawrdreth growled. 'The Earth itself will turn on you!'

'Make them stop,' Helan hissed.

'There is a way to stop this, my lady,' said Bharamezht in a calm, velvety voice. 'Surrender. Give yourselves up to me as prisoners. Then the punishment may end.'

'Do what you want.' She held herself straight, arms open in a gesture of defeat. Mawrdreth's tall frame drooped with despair beside her, his head touching hers. 'Take us. We surrender. Only make your army stop killing my people!'

'It shall be done at once,' he said, giving her a stare of loathing. 'We are not monsters, my lady.'

The camp's illusion of peace and safety was soon shattered.

Rufryd went twice to the rim of the Almandine Vale to see what was happening in the valley. The first time, after the explosion had shaken the camp, he went to see the wreckage of the engine then ran back to tell the others the good news. Soon after, Lahjaya came into their tent, grey-faced and exhausted, to tell them there were so many casualties they couldn't treat them all; scores more lying on the battlefield, beyond reach of help.

Rufryd went out a second time, and came back at a sprint.

'Okay, that's it, I suggest we make a run for it. Right now.' They all stared at him in dismay. 'Move!' he cried. 'The fucking Bhahdradomen are winning! They're going to be all over the camp in about twenty minutes!'

At that, they leapt to their feet and began to get themselves into panicky order, Tanthe helping Mendyr on with boots, filling water flasks. Fiomir said quietly, 'I can't go until I've found Talthaliorn.'

'Mother!' Tanthe cried, without thinking.

'I know he has gone into battle!' she exclaimed. 'And I can't forgive him – but I'm not leaving until I find him! You go, take Mendyr. Keep him safe.'

Tanthe stood pale and stunned as Fiomir gave her, then Auriel, a quick kiss before she hurried out of the tent.

While Tanthe, Rufryd and Vetru continued scavenging for what provisions they could find, Auriel stood frozen. Tanthe marched up to him and shook him. 'Auriel, don't just stand there! Help us.'

'I can't,' he said, staring at her. 'I'm sorry, Tanthe. I have to go after Fiomir, I can't let her go alone.'

'What?'

'Sorry.' He backed away from her, turned and ran out.

'Auriel!' She went after him. 'Auriel, you've got to come with us! Don't do this to me!'

'Great,' Rufryd groaned, and followed them both. Auriel had already vanished between the tents. He saw Tanthe collide with Jthery.

'What's going on?' Jthery asked, looking white.

'Eaters're on their way,' she said brusquely. 'We're off.' She glared angrily at Jthery, then her expression softened. 'Well, you'd better grab your true love and be back here in two minutes if you want to come with us.'

'Great, why don't we go in a bunch of about a hundred?' Rufryd said, striding up to them. 'That will really make it hard for the Eaters to find us. Tanthe, don't you dare go after Auriel. We can't afford to split up. We have to think about Mendyr.'

'That's who I am thinking of,' she flared. 'Where are you going?'

'To get the mare. One horse between six of us won't be much use, but I'm not leaving her for the Devourers to slaughter.'

'We could take more.'

'Take too long, make us more visible – especially Nefri,' he said over his shoulder. 'I'll just untie them and hope they escape on their own.'

When Rufryd returned to the tent a few minutes later, he found Tanthe trying to persuade Lahjaya to go with them, Lahjaya arguing that the wounded would still need her, even if the Eaters did come. 'And if any of us get hurt or wounded?' Tanthe said. 'Mendyr isn't well, for a start.'

'All right,' said Lahjaya. 'All right! Only for my best friend.'

Rufryd looked round the tent. Falthorn and Jthery were there, with cloaks and packs, arguing.

'Where is Ostarial, Nialorn, my brother?' Falthorn was saying. Rufryd had never seen him so ashen, distraught. Perhaps there was a trace of humanity in the cold Valahyr heart after all. 'I cannot leave my *eretru* . . .'

'You've got to,' Jthery growled, gripping his arm. 'You can't save them, all you'll do is get us both killed!'

'Auriel and Fiomir still not come back?' Rufryd asked. Shaking of heads. Tanthe was flushed with distress.

'Well, we can't hang about waiting for them. They'll have to catch us up. Come on!' His tone made them start, and hurry to comply. Rufryd gritted his teeth. He had to be forceful with them or they'd never make it.

They set off on foot, with Mendyr sitting on the golden mare's back and Vetru leading her. The child seemed calm but he was snuffling with a cold and looked tired and pasty. Hardly a creature to destroy the world. Vaurgroth's making a fine job of that himself, Rufryd thought, without any help from a small child. Ahead, the landscape was misty with smoke that had drifted over from the battlefield. Rufryd could still hear the horrific noises of the battle. All along, this had seemed inevitable. He wished, now, that they'd fled from the Obsidian Tower and never come back.

'What news of the Valahyr?' said Falthorn. He looked ashen and frankly not well enough to be walking. Even with Jthery to guide him, he kept stumbling on the uneven ground.

'They didn't look in much better shape than our lot,' Rufryd said. 'But they were still fighting.'

'I knew that this would be disaster.' They'd rarely heard such unguarded emotion in Falthorn's voice. 'I should never have listened to humans, or to Talthaliorn!'

Rufryd turned on him. 'Oh, and what makes you so special to escape all this? Easy beating the crap out of the Fhelethyr, not so easy against a real enemy?'

'Leave him alone!' said Jthery.

'It's all right,' Falthorn sighed. 'Losing my eyesight hasn't deprived me of the ability to conduct an argument.'

Rufryd shook his head, too tired and preoccupied to bother. 'Anyone got any bright ideas about where to go?'

'Back to the portal where I showed you the Laefrohyr,' Falthorn said. 'You can reach Verdanholm from there. However, I can't leave Earth until I know what's happened to my *eretru*.'

'I can't either,' Tanthe said. 'How can I go through a blasted portal, when I don't know what's happened to Fiomir and Talthaliorn – not to mention Auriel?'

Rufryd caught up with her and slipped his hand through her arm. 'Tanthe, might I point out that Fiomir's first thought was Talthaliorn – not you? She left her son, daughter and grandchild behind, to look for him. Doesn't that tell you something?'

'What do you mean?'

He exhaled through his teeth. 'She's a grown woman, she can look after herself and Auriel. We've got to think of Mendyr now. And Vetru. Have you any idea what the Devourers will do to him if they catch him with us?'

She looked sideways at him with troubled eyes. 'I can imagine.'

'So keep that pulled up,' Rufryd said, turning to Vetru and drawing the edge of his hood well over his head. 'We'll make out you're my younger brother.'

'They won't believe that for a moment,' Vetru said wretchedly.

'Then we'll make out we captured you. Tell them how cruel we've been.'

'But if they see I'm partly *neshrim* – without permission – that I'm not an adept—'

'Stop it,' said Tanthe. 'They're not going to find us!'

They walked and walked until it was all they could do to stand. Even Falthorn, whom Rufryd had expected to flag first, kept going with icy determination. Rufryd guided them along shallow ravines that wrinkled the edge of the Ruby Plains, trying to keep them hidden in this bleak, hot landscape that was now becoming tediously familiar. Looking up once or twice he saw *ghelim* floating overhead. Or were they just dra'a'ks? If they were *ghelim* it meant the Bhahdradomen had found the Pin of Time, destroyed it, or simply moved out of its range.

'We must stop,' said Lahjaya at last. 'Have pity on the poor physician, her legs are only half the length of yours.' She lifted Mendyr down from the mare's back. He'd been nodding in the saddle and now fell asleep on her shoulder.

'Here's as good a place as any,' Rufryd said.

They settled down in a narrow, overhung valley, with a few scrubby bushes to shelter them. It was still quite light, but the light had a strange frosted quality and it was turning cold. A pall of dread lay on everyone. Tanthe looked dreadful, her face so pale it was almost luminous, and Rufryd knew she was worried sick about her Aelyr family. To find them then lose them so soon . . .

She and Jthery passed round the bread, salted meat and oatcakes they'd seized from the camp. It was a dry, unpleasant meal. Rufryd kept watch as best he could but he could see little in the gloom and dare not light a lantern. Vetru, next to him, sat silently with his strangely jointed legs drawn up under him and his head bowed, deep under the hood.

Mendyr slept, curled up beside Falthorn. Falthorn sat with his back resting against a rock, utterly still as if in some secret meditation. He made Rufryd uneasy. His ruined eyes scanned ahead of him as if they could, after all, see something the others could not.

Lahjaya sat beside Tanthe and reclined across her, the back of her head nestling between Tanthe's breasts. Rufryd compressed his lips, feeling vaguely envious of Lahjaya's head. Tanthe put her arms loosely around the healer, who smiled and said, 'Don't look so sad, dear.'

'Can't help it,' said Tanthe. 'All those people around us, Helan and Mawrdreth, Eld, my parents and Auriel. One minute they were there, the next they're gone. I can't believe it.'

'No good us fretting over what we can't control,' said Lahjaya. 'Ah, look at all the things I have failed to achieve. I didn't marry Duke Jedraan. I missed my chance to poison Foul-gross while I was in the Citadel kitchens.'

'He probably eats poison for breakfast.'

'I couldn't save every single soldier who fell today.'

'So you're not superhuman,' Tanthe said quietly, kissing the top of her head. 'We still love you.'

Rufryd's eyelids flickered. He fell asleep, only for half a second, and was woken by Falthorn's voice, low but sharp with warning.

'Rufryd.'

He looked up and saw that they were surrounded by Bhahdradomen *yrim*. They'd materialised out of the shadows. He was befuddled, knowing that he'd only dropped off for a split second. He could tell, because no-one else had moved. And yet none of them had heard the stealthy approach of the Devourers. Only Falthorn, perhaps.

His heart leapt with panic, dismay. Then he only felt dull

resignation. With Bharamezht's troops swarming everywhere it had never been likely they'd make it.

'Give yourselves up quietly,' said a cloaked figure, stepping forward, 'and you won't be harmed.'

They all stared at him, paralysed.

'Do you not understand your own language? You are being taken prisoner. Rise. Throw down your weapons.'

Tanthe said softly, 'Fuck, that's Gulzhur! I thought I'd killed him!'

'No, you didn't kill me,' said the figure, turning his skull-face to stare at her. He was hideous; greenish translucent flesh slicked over bones, vessels snaking over the dome of his skull, a staff held in a vulturine hand. His skin-cloak changed to blend with the background. He looked spectral. An avatar of death. 'I am very much alive. Master of Light is very much victorious.'

'How did you find us?'

Gulzhur sneered. 'You think you are the only creatures that walk through portals, or the paper-thin dimensions squeezed between worlds? The Bhahdradomen have forgotten more than you'll ever know.' He flicked a hand, and two of his minions stalked confidently towards Mendyr. The child woke up and blinked at them with bleary eyes. Tanthe shot to her feet, crying, 'What are you doing?'

'We need the hatchling.'

Tanthe threw herself across Mendyr. Rufryd's hand was on his own sword hilt when a scaly seven-fingered hand shot round his chest like steel wire and jerked him backwards. In open-mouthed horror he saw one of the *yrim* raising its *sten*. In the same instant, Lahjaya threw herself between Tanthe and the weapon, shouting savagely, 'Don't you dare!'

The *yrim* slashed out with the *sten*. The cruel black blade sliced through Lahjaya's throat. She toppled and hit the rock with a sickening smack. Blood pumped from the wound. Her eyes stared at the sky and her fingers trembled.

Tanthe let out a single horse scream of anguish. And suddenly she had hold of Mendyr, and her *mnelir* pressed to his small pale throat.

'Have you got any idea what will happen if I kill him?' she yelled at Gulzhur.

Mendyr began to struggle, plainly terrified. Tanthe held him hard, her teeth bared. Vetru, Falthorn and Jthery were all on their feet now, frozen. Falthorn groped for Jthery's shoulder, but seemed to know or sense exactly what was happening.

Gulzhur stared furiously at Tanthe. His aura pulsed over them, bringing heavy waves of fear. There was a long, hostile pause.

'In case you don't know,' Falthorn's voice fell coolly into the silence, 'the resultant unleashing of Jewelfire will kill us and all life within a considerable radius.'

'So you told Vaurgroth,' Gulzhur said in a thin drawl that dripped malice, 'you treacherous piece of excrement.' He turned back to Tanthe. 'Very well. Take your knife from his tender little throat; you're frightening him. Sheath it. And don't think to use it against us; we are not peasant *domenim* to be frightened by such a thing.'

Tanthe didn't move. Mendyr whimpered.

'You won't kill your own son,' sneered Gulzhur. 'Give that toy to me. Do as I say and you can keep the hatchling among you for now. Continue with this foolishness and you can watch the rest of your friends cut down one by one!'

Gulzhur was nervous, Rufryd saw that. But he was also in control. The taut lines of Tanthe's body slumped with despair and she gave up the *mnelir*, whispering, 'Sorry,' into the boy's ear. Tears were streaming down her face. Her friend, Lahjaya, lay dead, all her warmth and dreams gone forever, like Annuin's, like Lynden's.

'Good,' said Gulzhur, and his minions closed in to lead them away.

* * *

Helan strained against her bonds, more in an attempt to relieve the ache in her arms than in hope of escape. The Bhahdradomen tent was a dome-shaped darkness, rank with the smell of *graukhim*-hide and some eye-watering herbs that their guards were burning.

They'd had their weapons taken away, then been made to march all day, surrounded by the Commander Bharamezht's *vagharim*. When the Eaters set up camp, she and Mawrdreth had been thrown in here, and their ankles shackled.

By then, all Helan could hope for was rest and oblivion. It wasn't to be. Bharamezht came in with two companions – mage-adepts from their garb of ivory, black and red – who held crackling *sten*.

'The child,' said the Commander. 'Where is the child?'

'I don't know what you're talking about,' she said.

The tip of a rod kissed her forehead. Blazing red pain gripped her skull and branched right through her body. She convulsed, tasting acid.

Mawrdreth cried out in helpless rage, struggling, only to be knocked sideways to the ground by the second *grothrim*.

'You know which child we mean. The Basilisk. Vaurgroth knows of its powers and he knows it is in your possession.'

Helan coughed and tried to spit the fizzing taste of *gauroth* out of her mouth. 'There's no child in my possession. I don't know what it is or where it is!'

The torture continued at a leisurely pace for hours. Never quite enough to make either her or Mawrdreth fall insensible. Always just enough respite for them to recover before the next wave.

The relentless sizzling caress of the *sten* rendered her speechless, her body in a tight ball, knotted around its pain. She couldn't even think, let alone speak. And she was glad. At least it stopped her blurting out the truth about Mendyr. And the longer they kept on, the more chance there was that her friends had escaped.

Shortly before dawn the torment ceased. She and Mawrdreth lay on their sides on the damp ground, arms bound behind their backs. Every bone, every tiny joint ached. Her throat was raw, her tongue swollen, her mouth so thick she couldn't swallow. Neither of them could speak, even to each other.

She slept briefly, but as soon as she dropped off, the image of Eldareth leapt at her and she awoke with a hoarse scream. Dry sobs shook her chest. Mawrdreth's fingers, constrained by thongs, brushed numbly against hers.

When day broke, their leg shackles were removed and they were again forced – without even a sip of water to revive them – to march all day. Mawrdreth was doing everything in his power to protect her, which was little; he could only try to shield her with his body, defend her verbally, watch her to make sure she wasn't about to collapse. His brave efforts moved her unbearably. All the time her thoughts were haunted by Eldareth, Eldareth; and yet she realised now, how very much worse it would have been to find Mawrdreth lying there instead . . .

They were moving north, Helan realised. The fact that Bharamezht hadn't had them killed must mean they were being taken to Vaurgroth.

That night, the same routine was repeated. Mawrdreth and Helan were shackled, and in came the two quiet, conscientious adepts with their *gauroth*-weapons shining and fiery, as if fresh from the forge.

Our pain is feeding them, Helan realised, her whole being recoiling with disgust. The more they hurt us, the more powerful they become.

'Why don't you just kill us?' Mawrdreth's voice was rough and hoarse.

'Because you are more use to us alive. Because Vaurgroth wants to speak to you about the trouble you have caused him.'

'We're no fun if we're dead,' said Helan.

'Exactly,' said Bharamezht. 'Now, where were we? The child?'

Mercifully, at last, she lost consciousness.

When she came round, there was a small fire burning red in a pot in the centre of the tent, and an *yrim* was holding a *graukhim*-hide goblet full of water to her lips. She sipped it thirstily, despite the leathery taint. The scene had changed; the torturers had gone. Bharamezht was still there, but nearer to the tent's entrance, as if he'd been away and come in again.

'Good news,' he said thinly. 'You can rest. The child has been found.'

Helan and Mawrdreth groaned. Their heads drooped to rest together in silent, complete despair.

The journey north was slow, grinding and wretched. It was the worst time Tanthe had ever known. Gulzhur commanded a troop of two hundred *yrim* who kept them hemmed in at all times, moving at a steady relentless march with never enough rest or food. They'd left the mare behind so Rufryd, Tanthe, Jthery and Falthorn took turns to bear Mendyr on their backs. There was no more physical brutality, but that was the only concession. What food and water they were given was stale, disgusting. They were all ill, one after another, with stomach pains and fevers, yet the Bhahdradomen wouldn't let them rest.

First they passed the remains of the camp. It was hard to see much, because they passed at a distance and the *yrim* were all around them. Tanthe glimpsed scores of Marocians, a scattering of Valahyr. Impossible to recognise Fiomir or Talthaliorn among them. It seemed the Bhahdradomen had rounded them up as prisoners of war.

It didn't appear they'd yet made a full invasion of Azura Maroc, but Vaurgroth had all the time in the world for that.

When they crossed the Almandine Vale itself, there were bodies everywhere. Tanthe wept until she didn't even know she was weeping any more. Sobbing became an unconscious reflex. Again and again she thought of Lahjaya's warm body soft and friendly against her, and seconds later bleeding to death.

Tanthe was in shock. So much had been torn away in a few brief seconds of confusion. Her brother, her parents when she'd barely begun to know them, her best friend. Mendyr seemed more forlorn than ever. The fact that he plainly felt safest in Falthorn's company, despite all Falthorn had said and done, was another burning wound.

As they passed the wreckage of the war-engine, Gulzhur told them about Eldareth, caustically praising his heroism.

'I don't believe you,' Tanthe cried. 'Not Eldareth.'

'He should think himself lucky he's dead,' said Gulzhur. 'The cost of the weapon he destroyed, in materials, labour and skill, was astronomical. If he'd lived, Vaurgroth would never have let him stop paying for it.'

Tanthe had to hold Rufryd back then, or he would have got himself killed, too. She hung onto him until she felt his rage subside to despair. 'It may not be true,' she said. 'It might just be Gulzhur tormenting us.'

'Tanthe,' said Falthorn, 'I'm afraid he's probably telling the truth. Eldareth asked me many questions about the Basilisks, how they worked and so forth.'

'And you told him?'

'I had no reason not to. I suspected he planned something like this.'

'Why didn't you try to stop him?'

'Why would I?' Falthorn said coolly. 'If he wanted to make a magnificent gesture, that was his prerogative. Human sentimentality, which would save a single life at the expense of thousands, is what will get us all destroyed.'

She felt too hollow to be angry. 'I'd like to see you say that if it had been Jthery's life.'

'But then, the fact that he'd gone in a glorious blaze of sacrifice would at least give some meaning to the loss.'

Tanthe glowered at Falthorn, forgetting he couldn't see her. It was Jthery's miserable eye she caught.

'I'm sorry,' said Jthery. 'I admired Eldareth. I can't believe it either.'

'He was always there,' Rufryd said so quietly she could hardly hear him. 'I thought he was indestructible. Stupid.'

Tanthe was already so distraught she couldn't cry any more. Neither could Rufryd. He wrapped his arm round her as they stumbled over the blood-soaked ground. Another fibre of her soul torn out to leave a raw, stinging wound where she thought there couldn't possibly be any more pain. And Gulzhur – it took her a while to realise, but now she knew – Gulzhur was lapping up their anguish like cream.

Beyond the battlefield they came into the Bhahdradomen camp, and there joined a long retinue of *yrim* heading north to Paranios. Rufryd struck up conversations with the guards in their own language, but could divine no news of Helan, Mawrdreth or her parents.

Tanthe managed to keep Mendyr with them, but only at a cost. She'd frightened him so much with the *mnelir* he no longer trusted her. She'd tried to explain, afterwards, why she'd done it; said, 'Sorry, I didn't meant to frighten you, it was the only way.' Mendyr had nodded seriously and assured her he understood. Yet there was still wariness in his eyes when she went near him, and he flinched when she went to touch him. She stopped trying.

Poor soul, she thought. All he's known is a peaceful life with the Laefrohyr in a safe little pocket of woodland. Then torn into the realm of the Wrothryr, and seized from that only to be thrown into this nightmare. Seen Lahjaya slaughtered in front of him and had his own mother stick a knife to his throat. And there's nothing I can do to comfort him.

As soon as they began to travel within the main body of Vaurgroth's troops, the Bhahdradomen came and took

Vetru away. Rufryd was sick with worry, certain they'd torture and kill him for consorting with humans. But a day or two later, to everyone's astonishment, Vetru was returned to them.

'What happened?' Rufryd asked. They'd made camp and were resting, encircled as always by *yrim*. He took Vetru to one side so the others couldn't hear.

Vetru didn't reply for a long time.

'Come on, please tell me. Did they hurt you?'

'No,' Vetru said at last. 'They were kind to me, like Tsur. But I was afraid.'

'Why?'

'They asked me a lot of questions. About humans. I told them things . . .'

'Hey, it's all right. I shouldn't think there's much Vaurgroth doesn't already know. He's won, anyway, so what does it matter?'

'No, I mean, I only told them things that didn't matter, or weren't true.'

'Well, good for you.' He put his arm round Vetru's narrow back. 'I suppose you're here spying on us now, in case we start hatching plots or discussing secrets?'

Vetru nodded. 'I didn't mean this to happen, Rufryd. I can't help it.'

'It was inevitable, really, wasn't it? Don't worry. We'll concoct some rubbish for you to tell them.'

The young *domen* rocked slightly, looking distressed. 'We are not bad *domenim*. I don't understand why we are doing these terrible things. We are not bad!'

'I know, I know. Humans are the same. We can be as nice as anything until a bit of a war starts, then we all start carrying on like complete arseholes.'

'I could have told them much more. I didn't.'

'What, things about Mendyr?'

'No, no, nothing to do with him.' His voice fell to a whisper. 'Something I learned from the Bhahdradomen in Q'elethrios. It is something terrible, Rufryd.'

'Terrible, how?'

'It is sacrilege,' Vetru breathed. 'They shouldn't have told me. They only did it to upset me. I wanted to tell you but I couldn't speak of it . . .' Rufryd racked his memory, recalled Vetru murmuring something about 'bad things' he'd heard in the Q'elethrios *tzcement*. 'I wanted to tell the *yrim*, but they would have killed me if I had. I don't even know if it's true, but if it is, *domenim* should know. *Someone* should know, in case something happens to me, but I dare not tell the *yrim* . . .' Vetru looked up with pleading eyes. He was trembling. 'Rufryd, you are my friend. Can I tell you?'

To enter Paranios again, after a tedious journey of weeks, was more bitter than sweet for Helan. She recognised the familiar, beloved landscapes, but now their sweet greenness was scarred with the ravages of *graukhim*. Ugly *tzcements* clustered on the hills. There were grimmer buildings too, foundries that stank of hot metal and *gauroth*, forging Vaurgroth's terrible weapons.

The damage was far worse than it had been when they'd fled, more than three years ago. Helan regarded the changing scene blankly. What she felt was too great to bear.

'Why is it that every tiny bit of this rests on me?' she whispered to Mawrdreth as they walked.

'It doesn't,' he said. 'It rests on all of us.'

'I was once proud to be Queen of the Nine Realms. But no single person should have to bear this. Eldareth gave his life to save us – yet his sacrifice achieved precisely nothing.'

'That's not true. He saved probably hundreds of lives. He gave us a chance, even if we lost in the end.' Mawrdreth was silent for a time. Eventually he said, 'If I could have died in his place, to make you happier, I would have done so.'

'No,' she gasped, taking his bound hands in hers and pressing them to her face. 'No, no, Mawr. It would have been even worse, because Eldareth was the past and you are the future. And I love you as much as I ever loved him, if not more. But to die just when he had found his own future, his own strength, just when he knew where he was going . . .'

'Perhaps that's the best time,' Mawrdreth said. A smile ghosted across his face; first time she'd seen him smile since they were in Lapiszul. 'Better to die fulfilled and happy, than when you're still lost and raging against the world.'

'Aren't you the philosopher? You should tell Saphaeyender that thought . . . If he's still alive to appreciate it.'

Rufryd pondered what Vetru had told him, but told no-one, not even Tanthe. It made a horrible kind of sense. He wondered if poor old Aazhoth had known.

'What is this?' Tanthe said, poking suspiciously at the strips of pinkish meat the *yrim* had brought them for their evening meal.

'It's *graukhim*,' said Rufryd. She stared at him in sheer horror as he took a bite of it. The raw-chicken sliminess made him feel faintly ill, as it always had in Vexor. He grimaced, but was rewarded by her expression of stunned revulsion.

'Rufe, do you know what *graukhim* are? They're actual Bhahdradomen, shape-changed to . . .'

'I know,' he said. 'I only puked the first time I tried it.'

'You ate this?' Her blanched complexion took on a green tinge.

'I had to. There was virtually nothing else. Unfortunately, we can't digest it properly; it fills you up but goes straight through, like eating . . . I don't know, paper or something.'

She put the meat in its leaf-wrapping on the ground. 'Well, I'm not eating it. Mendyr certainly isn't.'

'Nor am I,' said Vetru. 'I do not eat *graukhim* any more. I only eat human food.'

'You speak for us all,' said Falthorn, his voice sour with distaste.

'I must admit, it tastes better cooked.' Rufryd jumped to his feet and strolled over to the nearest *yrim*, who were sitting on the ground eating their own meagre supper. The others watched him in trepidation, but he was long past being frightened of them. They turned their round, lichen-mottled faces to him. He asked, in their own language, if there was anything else to eat.

'If you find something, you can have our *graukhim* in exchange,' he said.

The *yrim* obliged, five of them coming back with grain-cakes and some sad-looking berries, olives and wizened apples. Along with the food, they exchanged a few, not unfriendly, remarks in a mixture of Bhahdradomen and halting Paranian. To the alarm of his companions, Rufryd said, 'You may as well sit and eat with us.'

After that, it became routine for some of the *yrim* to sit and share food with the humans in the morning and evening – at least when their officers weren't watching. The *yrim* relaxed, became less taciturn. Sometimes they even found the same things funny.

Eventually Tanthe said, surprised, 'They're really not that bad, are they, when you get to know them? Not that different to Vetru.'

'I told you Vetru wasn't unusual,' Rufryd said gravely. 'They aren't all hateful. Like the Aelyr, they're more similar to us than they are different.'

When they made camp that night, Helan knew they were perhaps only sixty or so miles south of Parione. The thought of entering the Amber Citadel – being dragged in front of Vaurgroth in defeat and humiliation, yet again – was sickening. Every moment she went on living was a torment. She had let down Aventuria so completely it seemed an obscenity she should still be alive . . . and yet she'd tried, gods, she'd tried.

The interior of the tent was dark, dimly lit with red lamps, and rank with the stench of ill-cured *graukhim*-hide. Helan's throat tightened against nausea. The Bhahdradomen who moved around the tent had a dark iridescence, as if their skin and garments gleamed with oil. It was the shine of *gauroth* and easy confidence. In the stifling heat she felt close to passing out. Commander Bharamezht came towards them, his face harsh and malign like a furious bull.

'The child,' he said.

'What about it?'

'We have it, but Vaurgroth requires information concerning the extent and nature of its powers.'

'Vaurgroth isn't frightened, is he?' she said thickly.

'Vaurgroth fears nothing.' Bharamezht put leaden emphasis on each word. 'He requires knowledge.'

Forward came the *grothrim* adepts again, with their shining *sten*. Helan's whole being quailed with revulsion. If they came one step nearer she would vomit.

All the lamp-flames flickered in a sudden breeze. She couldn't see where it had come from since the tent-flaps were sealed. Yet there was a definite stirring of the air. Wind outside, flapping the hide walls, causing a weird whispering that sounded almost human. The Commander looked up, the thick grey folds of his forehead creasing.

Suddenly the temperature fell dramatically. The air turned clammy, chilling. Helan glanced at Mawrdreth but he only gave a small shrug. There must have been a drastic change in the weather to make the Bhahdradomen so uneasy.

With a deep tearing sound one side of tent ripped and flapped open to the air.

Into the tent came pouring . . . ghosts.

Helan started back, as far as she could in her bonds. She saw a whirl of light, figures moving within it. Only the hint of a face here and there, phantom hands wielding swords and spears, flickering too fast and vague to see clearly . . .

yet her brain seemed to fill in what was missing. It was as if a small army came storming in with the cloud of light.

They were real enough to the Bhahdradomen. Some of them fell to the phantom swords as if to *gauroth* bolts. The rest fled. The whole tent tore up from its moorings and ballooned out for a moment before keeling over on itself, collapsing. Helan and Mawrdreth both hit the ground by instinct. Chaos of booming hide and spectral battle whirled around them. Then it was over; five Bhahradomen lay dead while others could be heard crying out as they fled.

Helan and Mawrdreth found themselves in the open air. Looking up, Helan saw no ghostly warriors. Only a young woman with dishevelled tawny hair looking down at them. She was breathing hard. A faint yellow aura surrounded her.

'Ysomir!' Helan gasped.

'Quickly, your majesties,' Ysomir said, fumbling with a small knife to undo their bonds. 'Come away, before they recapture you. The resistance is nearby. Kereyn's group. You know her, don't you?'

'We do,' said Helan, as they ran into the darkness. Wincing with pain she dragged the last strands of rope from her sore wrists. 'How did you . . . ?'

'Kereyn received intelligence that human prisoners had been brought here,' Ysomir said coolly. 'I was the one who stood the best chance of getting you out.'

'And what about the . . .'

'The *ethroths*?'

'Save the questions until later,' Mawrdreth said, glancing back. 'There are lights behind us.'

'It's all right,' said Ysomir. 'If I put myself in danger, they will defend me.'

'What d'you mean?' he said. 'If they catch up, you intend to turn round and face them? Are you mad?'

'So most people think,' Ysomir replied lightly. 'Come down this way.' She diverted from the forest path onto a thin track that plunged down between dense bushes.

'They won't catch us. I trust my spirits more than I trust the living.'

Ysomir brought Helan and Mawrdreth to Kereyn's small camp, concealed in a steep ravine with dark trees to hide them and a stream trickling along the valley floor. There were no tents, only woven roofs of branches slung between the trees to make shelters which would be invisible to flying *ghelim*. Kereyn greeted them with expressions of joy and relief, sat them down to rest on the grass beneath a branch shelter. Her officers brought them water, wine and food. All the time, Helan watched Ysomir in wary amazement.

Ysomir took no notice of her. She went about her business – helping to prepare food, repairing a torn jacket, sharpening weapons – as if the Queen who had once imprisoned and intimidated her wasn't there.

Presently Kereyn came and sat cross-legged by Helan and Mawrdreth. She looked rougher and more desperate than she had the last time Helan had seen her. Her grey hair stuck out like a bird's nest as if she'd impatiently hacked it short with a knife, and her face was deeply lined granite. All her city polish had been weathered away, except from her precise, authoritative voice. She still appeared robust and vigorous.

'Ma'am,' Kereyn said after a time, 'we hear that things went badly in the south.'

Then Helan found that she couldn't speak. Exhaustion, grief and the black haunting taste of torture overwhelmed her. Mawrdreth, his arm resting heavily over her shoulders, answered instead.

'We raised an army from Azura Maroc, but it wasn't enough.' His voice was strained. 'Our weapons were no match for Vaurgroth's, that's the simple reality. We had to surrender, to prevent a massacre.'

'What of Karmensis?'

'He fought bravely, but we were separated from him. I can only hope he survived.'

Kereyn was silent. Her powerful stocky form drooped fractionally and her gaze fell to the ground. Then she nodded, and raised her chin. 'We have fought a persistent guerrilla war against them, but our numbers have been devastated. The few hundred people you see in this valley are all there is left of the Paranian resistence. Perhaps it's not our destiny to be victorious; maybe it's for another generation, a century in the future, to purge this plague and take Aventuria back into the light. However, I will never accept it. I will go into the darkness fighting, fighting to my last breath.'

'You are brave.' said Mawrdreth, sounding close to tears. 'There's been so much darkness, the past few weeks, that I fear you're right.'

'I'll leave you to rest. The Bhahdradomen have used you ill, that's obvious.'

As she got to her feet, Mawrdreth asked, 'Why did you rescue us?'

Her grey eyebrows shot up. 'I should have thought that was obvious, sire,' she said, somewhat brusquely. 'However dark things are, I never, *ever*, give up hope. I trust that you haven't, either.'

For two days, Helan didn't speak. All she could do was eat, sleep, stare numbly at the valley walls. She needed time to think. Eldareth haunted her dreams, but each one was less painful than the last. She realised that the last time she'd seen him, he had been saying goodbye. No, the Eldareth she'd known had said goodbye in Lapiszul . . . said goodbye the day he'd refused to be her King.

And Mawrdreth was still alive, damaged, but strong and beautiful beside her.

On the third day, Helan felt her strength beginning to return. She rose to her feet and went to find Ysomir. The young woman was seated on a rock, carving an arrow-head. As Helan approached she stopped work and looked up.

'We ought to talk,' Helan said, sitting on the ground and dragging her tangled hair back with her fingers.

'If you want,' Ysomir said mildly. She, too, seemed harder. Definitely not afraid of me any more, Helan thought with a strange kind of relief.

'It was the last thing I expected, being rescued by you.' Ysomir said nothing. 'How did you escape from the Amber Citadel?'

'Someone helped me.'

Her cat-green eyes with their gold spokes were cool and guarded. Helan sensed she had no intention of revealing her secrets. 'I – I'm glad you got out.'

Ysomir blinked. 'Really? You, who would have kept me in there for the rest of my life?'

'Everything's changed. You killed Garnelys in passion, I imprisoned you in passion. I was angry, but my anger is long gone.'

'Mine is, too,' Ysomir said quietly.

Helan felt uncomfortable. She couldn't bring herself actually to utter an apology – neither could Ysomir – but a truce would be enough. 'You felt I bullied you, didn't you? All my questions about your *ethroths*?'

'I know why you did it. I hope you realise why I couldn't help you.'

'I think so.'

'I had to escape, because Vaurgroth wanted to use me, as you did. It was no different.'

No different. Helan shivered. 'Ysomir, I . . . I hold no ill-will towards you. We've all done desperate things. You saved my life, and Mawrdreth's.'

Ysomir's gaze held hers, steady and unassailable. 'As long as you understand that you cannot use me, I bear no grudge towards you either, ma'am.'

'Call me Helan.' Cautiously she reached out and took Ysomir's hand. Ysomir didn't try to pull away. She returned the conciliatory caress.

'Helan,' she said, long lashes sweeping down over the brilliant irises. 'I couldn't help you then, because I had to discover my own abilities in my own time. You're right, I should use whatever power I have to help Aventuria. And now I shall; but of my own free will, not because others made me.'

Helan nodded. 'I appreciate that. Now I want to ask you questions, but I don't want you to think I'm interrogating you again.'

'I don't mind,' she said guardedly, 'if it's as a friend.'

'I think that's understood.' Helan was startled to find how hard it was to smile, but she managed it. 'Can I fetch Mawrdreth? I've done a lot of thinking, the past two days.'

'Of course,' Ysomir said, her expression softening.

Helan came back with Mawrdreth and a flagon of elderberry wine. He poured three measures into leather cups, and passed them round. The three of them sat cross-legged on the grass, with Paranian oaks towering over them, pipers singing their fluting song high in the canopy.

'I've been thinking about Vaurgroth and his circle,' said Helan. 'They feed on our fear and pain.'

'Also on our land,' said Mawrdreth.

'Yes, but that's just food. It's not the source of their power and confidence. Our anguish is.'

'And that disgusting religious ecstasy they stirred up,' he said.

'But even that was only another kind of fear. It came from our desperation to believe there was some hope in the darkness, some purpose in what had happened. It was denying the situation. That is fear.' Helan stared up at the sky. Leaves moving against the grey with such vibrant green life. She knew she must make one last stand. 'I've been such a fool!' she exclaimed, making the others start. 'We were never going to defeat them in battle! We have to do what Vaurgroth did to us. Trick him, force him to give up of his own accord.'

'He'll never do that in a million years,' Mawrdreth said heavily.

'How much power has he, without his *gauroth*? It's a

self-perpetuating circle. In the beginning he gathered a small amount of power to himself – perhaps by torturing and killing a few of his own *domenim*; I wouldn't be at all surprised, since that's how Garnelys did it – then used the stolen energy to generate more fear and horror in others. He fed a little of the power to his supporters, sent them off to generate some terror of their own, which they then fed back to him. And all the time storing the excess in whatever crystals will absorb *gauroth* energies, using them to make weapons to spread the horror even further. We need to cut off the source of *gauroth*.'

'Are you saying that if we stop fearing him, we'll defeat him?' Mawrdreth put in. 'Come on, Helan. It will take far more than that.'

'I know. But it would be a start. What do you think, Ysomir?'

'Mawrdreth's right, it will take a lot. But until we let go of fear, we're paralysed.'

'I get the impression you already have,' Helan said, meeting and holding her gaze.

'I missed my chance to harm Vaurgroth, because I was frightened. I ran away. But now I'd do it; or I'd try, even if his power tore me to pieces.' Ysomir smiled. 'There is a small piece of good news, Helan. The clergy of Nuth have been hard at work in Parione, undermining the Bhahdradomen.'

'Any success?'

'So we've heard. Saphaeyender's been writing a lot of the material. Pointing out the falsehood of the Ancestor, reminding people who they are. It's had a big effect. Whatever power Vaurgroth drew from Ancestor-worship must be waning.'

'But they have the child,' Helan muttered, more to herself than the others. 'They're taking him to Vaurgroth.'

'What child?' said Ysomir.

Now her face was anxious. Helan said gravely, 'The child Tanthe had taken from her. Didn't she tell you?'

'Yes, of course, but it was so long ago. I've heard nothing since. When . . . when did you last see her?' Ysomir's composure was gone. She was white with distress.

'Shortly before the battle. She'd just found him then. His name's Mendyr. An extraordinary boy. His powers are alarming, or will be, if he learns to wield them. Unfortunately, Bharamezht told me the Bhahdradomen have captured him.'

'And Tanthe?'

'I'm sorry, I don't know. She didn't take part in the battle. We can only hope the Eaters took her alive.'

'I think I would know if she was dead,' Ysomir said pensively. 'So, if she isn't, she must be their prisoner too. And what does Vaurgroth mean to do with the boy . . . Mendyr?'

'The obvious, I should think. First, to stop us using his powers against him. Second, to see if he can bend the boy's power to his own ends.'

Mawrdreth said, 'So, we take Kereyn's men, find the *yrim* division that's holding our friends captive, and fight to free them.'

'Or . . .' began Helan. 'I think we'll have to be more subtle and more direct than that. We must enter the Amber Citadel.'

Mawrdreth snorted. 'That will be impossible! The only way would be to give ourselves up to Bharamezht again, which would defeat the point of everything!'

They were silent for a time. Then Ysomir said quietly, 'I can get us in. I know someone who will help.'

The trek to Parione took several arduous and miserable weeks. Tanthe felt worn to nothing by it, constantly hungry and aching, and so tried by the need to ensure Mendyr wasn't suffering that she could think of nothing else. Only Rufryd kept her sane. He was always there, like a rock, befriending the *yrim* to make the ordeal less onerous than it could have been. At night, though, the Bhahradomen made them sleep separately. That was the worst thing. She would have done anything to sleep in Rufryd's arms. Instead she lay on the cold ground alone, while Mendyr preferred to sleep near Falthorn.

They had joined the Lapis Road. When it took them at long last into the outskirts of Parione, she felt only relief. It would all be over soon. When they came in sight of the Amber Citadel, she wept.

Rufryd asked her why, but she couldn't speak. It looked the same, with its glorious, vaunting tiers of honey-golden stone. Only she'd hoped to see it in happier circumstances, not in this bleak despair.

The city had an air of ruin about it. Gardens were overgrown, the streets filthy, buildings neglected or blackened with the smokes of whatever sinister industry was taking place inside. There were Bhahdradomen everywhere; *vagharim* in their leathery uniforms of black and green, adepts and officials strutting in fancier garb, common *domenim* in plain grey or brown. Even the *domenim* moved with pride and confidence through the crumbling streets. They looked sleek and well-fed. There were humans, too, but they scurried like vermin eager to avoid their conquerors' attention. How different they were from the handsome, ebullient citizens she'd known. These people were thin and their clothes were old and patched.

They were taken into the south gate of the Citadel, which had changed. The filigree gates had been replaced by iron. The arches of golden stone had been plastered with cement into which grey stones had been pressed. The stones were like eyes, winking with oily power. A heavy storm-grey force hummed in the air.

One after another, the gates slammed shut behind them. Outer and inner walls, then the entrance to the palace itself. It was dark inside. The gorgeous windows of stained glass had been hung with webs to keep out the light. The air smelled thickly of old earth, mildew, leather, blood, and the crackling metal-scent of *gauroth*.

Then a handful of Vaurgroth's adepts came, along with ten of Vaurgroth's *vagharim*, to receive them from the *yrim*. She recognised Naghrur as he came to greet Gulzhur. Even Gulzhur was less intimidating that the watchful, ice-cold blade that was Protector Naghrur. The *yrim* had seemed like kind friends in comparison.

In a light, emotionless tone, Protector congratulated Gulzhur on his prize. His eyes were steel orbs, taking in everything. Even Gulzhur, Tanthe noticed, seemed nervous of him.

They walked in procession, Jthery guiding Falthorn in front, then Mendyr beside Tanthe, Rufryd behind them keeping the frightened Vetru close at his side. Tanthe tried to take Mendyr's hand but he evaded her.

I am going to be punished for killing Uryzht, she thought suddenly. Rufryd for Rhazagramen. And poor Vetru, just for being with us. We are not ever going to leave here. A glacial horror passed through her but she couldn't connect with it. She felt numb. She held onto Rufryd's hand but they had no hope to offer each other.

Tanthe saw that Jthery was weeping softly as they were led through the broad, high corridors. She touched his shoulder. He remembered the palace's glory, too.

Mendyr began to shiver. His teeth were chattering. Yet it wasn't cold.

'Are you all right?' Tanthe said. 'Rufe, give him your jacket. I think he's got that fever again.'

'No, I haven't,' said Mendyr. 'I don't like this place. There's a cold power here. It's too heavy . . .'

His knees buckled. Tanthe grabbed him before he fell.

'It's like the Obsidian Tower!' the child wailed. 'It's crushing me!'

'No, it isn't,' Tanthe said anxiously. 'It's all right, we're with you. Don't be scared.'

'Silence!' snapped the *vagharim* officer. 'Keep moving!'

Mendyr quickly regained control of himself, refused Rufryd's offer of a jacket or being carried, and walked on.

In the ante-room to the Sun Chamber, all the portraits of Aventuria's monarchs had been taken down and stacked against a wall. The space felt bare and deserted.

Then the great gilden-oak doors opened onto the throne room. Tanthe caught her breath. It was the Sun Chamber no more. All its golden energy was gone and instead it had become a vast, sighing grey space, desolate as the *ezht*. The Sapphire Throne faced them from the far end, a shadow beneath the web-veiled window. The air felt furry with power. Static brushed unpleasantly over their skin as they entered. A dozen of Vaurgroth's counsellors stared down their thin noses at them from the dais.

'Sit,' said Gulzhur. He guided them to the side of the chamber, indicating the first tier of seating where the Council of the Sun Chamber used to sit. 'Refreshments will be brought. Vaurgroth wishes to interview you.'

Naghrur added, 'When the Master of Light enters, you will fall to your knees and place your foreheads upon the floor. Remain like that until you are told to get up.'

'I'll do it backwards and stick my arse in his face,' Rufryd hissed, but Tanthe seized his arm and shushed him. Naghrur only gave them an expressionless look and glided away. Tanthe saw him exchanging glances with the adepts who stood near the throne dais. They seemed to pass information without words, in the strange way they did.

'I hope you're pleased with yourself, Uncle,' Tanthe said bitterly. 'This is all your doing.' She'd dreaded Falthorn's powers; now she resented him for the fact that all his *roth*-power seemed to have vanished with his sight. What use was he on their side, helpless?

Falthorn said nothing. There seemed to be no spirit or personality left in him. In that moment he was no longer Falthorn, just a shell that resembled him. Jthery's eyes were red with pain. She looked away.

A guard brought them water, tea, some grainy cakes that weren't too unpleasant, and a sinister-looking yellow liqueur which Rufryd assured them was not as bad as it tasted. He and Vetru had a sip, but the others declined.

'Mendyr, come and sit by me,' Falthorn said suddenly. The boy obeyed. 'They are going to ask you questions. What will you tell them?'

'The truth.'

Falthorn tutted. 'Now, that's not the way I brought you up, is it? You must confound Vaurgroth. Make him believe your powers are mysterious and many. Flatter him. Charm him.'

Mendyr stared at Falthorn, looking faintly outraged. 'Why?'

'Because, my dear,' his voice fell to a whisper, 'it is quite likely that we are all going to be slaughtered in front of you. Then the Bhahdradomen will bring you up among themselves. They will do this because they want to use your power. So it's just as well to be friendly to Vaurgroth.'

Mendyr's face was stiff with denial. His lower lip trembled.

'What on Earth are you telling him?' Tanthe said angrily. 'Stop it!'

'I'm being realistic. Mendyr needs to face reality if he's to survive. So look, if we are taken away from you, or if they cut us down in front of you, you're not to mind, even if there is a lot of blood. Be nice to Vaurgroth. Lull him. Later you can make a gate which will suck them all into oblivion.'

'No,' Mendyr said, shaking his head frantically. 'Everyone told me I'm not to use my power.'

'But it will be all right to destroy the Bhahdradomen, you see. Make a nice dark gate to nowhere for them.'

'You're sick!' Tanthe hissed. 'Don't talk to him like that!'

Falthorn turned his face to her. His unseeing eyes looked huge, liquid and mad. 'He's not the child you think he is. If they destroy us, they're coming with us.'

There was a stirring in the ante-room. A score of *vagharim* strode into the chamber and formed an avenue. Tanthe felt a thrill of nightmare terror, as if a cold finger had lanced her brain. Jthery jumped and gasped out loud.

Attendants preceded him. First his elite personal *vagharim*, then a gaggle of adepts and court officials, arrogant little figures in their black and cream finery, bloated with importance. The scaled *ghelim* hound, trotting with its head high, like some enamelled automaton. And then, trailing an entourage of minions, *he* came; a slow-moving whirlwind of thunderous power, and at its heart the spidery red figure of Vaurgroth.

Ysomir's 'friend' came to meet them in a wood just outside Parione. They were waiting in the shadow of an earth bank clasped by tree roots. Part of the bank had fallen away to reveal a broken chalk-boulder, white and soft as fresh curds. As pale as the chalk, he came gliding soundlessly between the trees towards them and Helan's heart almost stopped. In his light-grey cloak she thought it was her friend Rathroem.

Rathroem, though, was dead. Surely this couldn't be a Mediator. They'd withdrawn from Aventuria, refused to help.

'It's all right,' Ysomir said, not sounding too sure.

The figure put back its hood. Helan and Mawrdreth both stepped back, hands on sword-hilts. It was a pale, human-looking Bhahdradomen with amused black eyes. Zhoaah.

'Ysomir, we've been tricked,' she said.

'No,' Ysomir said in the same oddly calm tone. 'We must trust him.'

The world swayed. Helan's first thought was that she'd made a fatal mistake in trusting Ysomir. All along she'd meant to lead them into a trap. '*You've* tricked us!'

'No!' said Ysomir more fiercely. 'Please, believe me! It was Zhoaah who got me out of the Citadel!'

'It is true, ma'am,' Zhoaah said, with a slight and mocking bow. 'And I can get you back in.'

'He protected me while I was in hiding,' she added. 'And my friends.'

'Why?' Helan frowned. She pointed her sword-tip at the *neshrim*, touching his throat. Mawrdreth moved behind him. Trapped between them, Zhoaah looked uneasy. Of course, he might be faking it. You could never tell with these creatures. 'This is Zhoaah, also known as Laphaeome, who corrupted my grandfather, encouraged him to torture and kill his own subjects. Zhoaah who built the Heliodor Tower. Who promised my throne to Lord Poel then stood laughing as Vaurgroth knifed him!'

'I didn't know about Lord Poel,' Ysomir said awkwardly. 'But I knew the rest. I still think I trust him.'

'You *think*? What's led you to this tenuous conclusion?'

'He's had every opportunity to kill or betray me and my friends, but he hasn't.'

'Then he can only be saving you for some even direr purpose. Gods, Ysomir, what have you done?'

'I don't know, but I think he's changed. He's protected me. He helped me.'

'With what motive?' Helan exclaimed. 'This is completely incredible.'

'May I speak?' Zhoaah said, pushing the tip of her blade aside with a thin finger. 'Ysomir is telling the truth. I have helped her, for the sole reason that I like her. She has touched some soft spot within me that I didn't know was there.'

'I don't believe a word of this.'

'The truth!' said Mawrdreth. 'Don't think you're indestructible. We know how to take the life out of your gristly little body.'

'I'm sure you do,' Zhoaah said, pulling a face. 'Very well. I took Ysomir out of the Citadel because I thought she was a threat to Vaurgroth's life. And now I am taking her back in because . . . ?' He nodded expectantly, prompting Helan.

'You tell us!'

'Think about it. We are not called shape-shifters for nothing. There is more to this, ma'am, than you can ever realise.'

'Are you trying to say that you've come over to our side?'

'Not that, no. Still, I am prepared to help you. It's only fair to warn you that, if any of you do try to attack the Master of Light, it is far more likely *he* will kill *you*. However, if you want to take the risk, it's up to you. It will be easy to take you back into the Citadel as my prisoners. They are *quite* upset that you escaped; the phrase "headless chickens" leaps to mind. I shall say I've recaptured you.'

'Fine,' said Mawrdreth, 'but what's in it for you? Are you planning to usurp Vaurgroth? Or just to win favour by delivering us to him?'

'I shall win no favours by delivering Ysomir, since I told him she was dead. I'll have to think my way around that.' His inky eyes narrowed. 'I have no desire to usurp him. He's far too powerful.'

'What, then?'

Zhoaah grinned. 'Let us just say that I am bored. The court of Vaurgroth is so tedious that I am ready to poke my own eyes out with a *sten* for entertainment. Victory is dull, dull. I like chaos.'

Helan exhaled heavily. Finally, he had said something that rang true. 'Then you had better take us to the Citadel, Zhoaah.'

Vaurgroth sat on the Sapphire Throne, resting an elbow on one of the arms and his chin on his hand. Rufryd and the others stood in a tight group below him, waiting for him to speak. His reptilian hound curled at his feet.

They waited, waited. He was a brooding presence staring down at them. The weight of his power flowed over them in wave after deadly wave. It was hard even to look at him properly; he was dark, light, crimson. His eyes were winter suns. His breathing was a razor whispering back and forth across their senses.

Rufryd knew that Mendyr wasn't going to save them. He hadn't a clue how to manipulate his own power and even if he opened a gate there and then, it would swallow them all and no-one would have won. Vetru crouched on the marble tiles, his head pressed to them as if he was trying to make himself as small as possible. For all Rufryd felt like shaking him, he sympathised. He didn't blame Vetru for being utterly terrified.

Again, he thought about what Vetru had told him during the journey. No, no, it was plainly impossible. A lie, a sacrilegious rumour.

The mottled, serene faces of the *bharu'grothrim* and their acolytes stared down. Gulzhur, Naghrur, others whose names he didn't know. There was a mass of grey webby beings, others like younger versions of Rhazagramen or less hideous mimics of Gulzhur, a scattering of smiling *neshrim* who weren't that much more convincing than Vetru. Naghrur's minions reminded him of shiny poisonous snakes. They were hungry for the final humiliation of their enemies.

Rufryd was gratified that the hated Rhazagramen was gone, at least.

'Lord Falthorn,' Vaurgroth said at last. His rich voice resonated. 'You have betrayed the trust between us in the most shameful and heinous manner. I can't say I didn't expect it. That is why I've had Lord Empowerer Grahzamen and his *aghramen* poised to return to Verdanholm the moment you failed me.'

Falthorn stiffened with fury. '*I* betrayed it? *You* are the ones who plotted to steal the Basilisks in direct contravention of our agreement. Furthermore, you planned to do so from the beginning.'

'Yet it was not we who stole them,' Vaurgroth said with smooth amusement. 'My sources inform me that your human friend, Lord Jthery here, was the culprit. Alas, the folly of trusting humans, my lord.'

'And yet, it was my human friend, Jthery, who made me understand the folly of trusting you,' Falthorn retorted.

'You disgust me.' Vaurgroth leaned forward. 'Is it not enough that you are all split in half, male and female, and rut against each other in your pathetic attempts to rejoin? So degraded are you, my lord, that you cannot tell male from female!'

'You're only jealous,' said Falthorn.

'Jealous, never. I pity you all, human and Aelyr alike. Still, I am not a cruel *domen*.' He referred to himself as one of the common people; nice touch, Rufryd thought. 'It was Ancestor's Will that you tried to fight me. It was Ancestor's way of proving to you that we cannot be defeated. He is a just god. You will all be dealt with in a manner that befits the degree of your foolishness. Jthery, you deserve leniency; your actions have helped more than hindered us.'

'What?' Jthery said under his breath. He shook his head vehemently. 'No, I didn't help you!' Falthorn gripped his arm and he subsided.

Vaurgroth continued. 'Vetru, child, I am sure there is hope for you, away from the corruption of these split beings.' Vetru flinched and tried to make himself even smaller. 'Rufryd, erstwhile ambassador, your crimes are many and serious indeed. Tanthe, you have made certain needling blows against us but, as the mother of this mystifying hatchling, I shall grant you clemency, if you will explain his powers to me.'

There was a long pause. 'Well?' snapped Vaurgroth.

Tanthe looked stricken. 'He's just a little boy. Falthorn was bluffing. He has no power.'

'Bluffing, indeed. No power? Then we may as well kill him where he stands.'

He raised a deformed hand. A *vagharim* started forward. 'No!' Tanthe cried.

'I can make gates,' Mendyr piped. 'It's nothing.'

'Gates? To keep in sheep? I take it you mean *rothanamir*. That is a useful talent, but not especially dangerous. You are all liars.' Vaurgroth's crimson gaze crawled over them. 'You will regret treating me as a fool. The boy shall be taken away and questioned on his own. The rest of you, I think, shall be privileged to sample some new methods of torment devised by Rhazagramen before his untimely end. Naghrur cannot wait.'

'You sound desperate, Lord Vaurgroth,' Rufryd said. 'I know why your minions were at the Obsidian Tower.'

The colourless face flushed red. 'You can't be expected to comprehend our spiritual quests.'

'Spiritual, my arse. You thought you were going to channel masses of power through it. You were thwarted. So, not as powerful as you make out, then?'

Vaurgroth glared at him, but with the glare came a burst of heavy *roth* power that made his whole body burn. Rufryd jerked and fell to his knees.

Tanthe cried out. She bent down to him and held him until the agony subsided. The moment he could move again he staggered back to his feet. She helped him and kept her arm tight round his waist. He was badly shaken. This was the beginning of the end, he knew. No amount of insolence was going to save them from dying in long drawn-out anguish.

Vaurgroth's attention had drifted beyond them, to his relief. There was movement in the entrance to Sun Chamber. Vaurgroth tensed, and a warm, delighted smile split his milky face. 'Facilitator! You found them! Ah, this completes a wonderful day.'

Rufryd, hurting from head to foot, looked round with difficulty. His heart leapt and sank as he saw Helan and Mawrdreth being brought towards the throne. So they'd survived the battle, only to be captured.

With them came Zhoaah and another, an old woman who walked with a stoop. Her hair was dusty grey and caught back in a bun, her face a map of greyish lines and shadows.

Vaurgroth's hand curved a greeting in the air. 'Lady Helananthe, Lord Mawrdreth, my commander Lord Thunderer Bharamezht wishes to commend you on conducting the most inefficient campaign we could have hoped for. I've a mind to let you live as thanks for the amusement you've afforded us. Who is this with you?'

'Just some crone who was guiding them through the woods,' said Zhoaah. He brought Helan, Mawrdreth and the old woman to stand alongside the others. Tanthe and Rufryd glanced at each other in puzzlement, for the old woman looked weirdly familiar.

'We realise our mistake,' said Helan. She looked a wreck, her clothes dirty and her hair wild. Her face, though, was calm, her voice strong and confident. Rufryd gripped Tanthe's hand. Something was happening. 'We were wrong to confront you in battle.'

'I'm glad you realise it,' said Vaurgroth. 'The Almandine Vale was never going to be your Silver Plains.'

'No. You took the Sapphire Throne from me by using hostages. Well, we have hostages of our own now.'

'What is this idle nonsense?' Vaurgroth said, tilting his head like a schoolmaster. 'You lost. I'm prepared to make peace with your subjects, but as their leaders you will be executed. You hasten your own deaths by irritating me.'

Helan didn't seem to be listening to him. She touched the old woman then watched her intently. The crone's stooped form straightened. Her hair scattered chalk dust. The lines on her face, Rufryd realised, had been drawn on with ash or charcoal. She threw back her head and a glow began to burn green-gold round her.

'Seize her!' Vaurgroth barked. A thread of red lightning shot from him and would have killed her – if it were not for the aura that sprang out of her to deflect it. Red fire broke on the golden shield and slithered off like bloody water.

Vaurgroth rose to his feet. His hound sat up and bared its fangs. His *grothrim* stirred; the *vagharim* drew their weapons.

'Facilitator, did you not know this was a *roth*-mage?'

'I did not, Master of Light,' Zhoaah said silkily.

'You idiot, get her out of here!'

'Ymmi?' said Tanthe, her voice faint with shock.

As the *vagharim* converged on Ysomir, the glow grew stronger. She stood like stone. Ghost-figures chattered in the aura. In their hands were weapons that looked like insubstantial swords and spears. Ghosts can do nothing . . . Even as Rufryd thought it, the swords of light struck out and lashed the guards with sizzling *roth* energy, deadly as lightning.

Two of the *vagharim* fell dead. Rufryd and his companions jumped or pulled each other out of the way by reflex. The other guards hesitated, disoriented by Ysomir's bright, inimical force.

Some of Vaurgroth's mages, led by Gulzhur, hurried onto the lower steps of the dais and added their energy to his. Together they projected a stream of red-black force against Ysomir. She staggered, but the *gauroth* only surged over her light-shield and took down two of the guards who were behind the group.

The shock-wave shook the whole chamber. As it subsided, Ysomir's leaf-gold aura expanded to surround the group of humans. Ghostly figures wove in and out of it, amorphous. Electric tension shone in the air.

Vaurgroth stood very still, as if pondering what to do. His adepts were whispering to him. Meanwhile Rufryd saw Naghrur on the move, muttering to a group of *grothrim* who'd hung back. His steely form glided like a snake behind them. Most were greyish ones like him but there were others mixed in. They were planning something. Didn't react like humans at all, no panic, only this cold calculation. The only one who seemed panicky was Vaurgroth himself. He was staring at Ysomir in open-mouthed rage.

'Facilitator, this is the female you told me was dead!' he roared.

'I seem to have been mistaken,' said Zhoaah. He was edging back towards the doors, until guards moved behind him and stopped him.

'You told me you disposed of the body yourself. You lied!'

Zhoaah's face was set in a soft smile that didn't quite conceal his fear. There was a sense that Vaurgroth had lost his iron grip. Rufryd was looking for a moment to seize, but there wasn't one. Protect Tanthe and the boy, that was all he could do.

While Vaurgroth was shouting at Zhoaah, Helan whispered, 'Join hands so we're all linked. All of you, do it!'

In a moment it was done. Rufryd was clasping Ysomir's right hand, Tanthe her left, then Mendyr, Falthorn, Jthery, Helan, Mawrdreth, and back to Rufryd. Vetru remained on the floor in the middle. As soon as they joined, the aura glowed more brightly. It seemed too delicate to destroy Bhahdradomen power.

Helan threw back her head and cried out, 'We invoke the guardians of the land and the spirits of Aventuria. Come, beloved dead, and calm all fear, extinguish all *gauroth*!'

Ysomir's eyes rolled back in her head and her lips parted. Her voice was strange and terrible. 'I call out of me the eight spirits that have dwelled within me. I am King Maharoth. I am Queen Hetys. I am Calabethron. Silana. Garnelys. Namane. Serenis. Lynden.'

Her voice broke on the last name. The amorphous figures separated into distinct entities, eight men and women shaped from topaz and peridot light. Rufryd nearly choked. Which one was Lynden? He couldn't tell, their shapes were too vague. They hung shining above the group of humans and Aelyr, one spectre above each of them. Then the beings sank down gently to fill and surround each person in a caul of light.

Rufryd felt a rushing, electric warmth all through him. The sensation transfixed him. All the Bhahdradomen seemed to be frozen – trapped outside the circle of power as if it was a wall of glass. Is this Lynden surrounding me? But no. Lynden would be with Ysomir, of course.

Hetys, fool. The words echoed through him in a shockwave. A strong, dra'a'k-faced, sensual queen who had died fighting the Bhahdradomen, leaving her son Maharoth to win victory. He felt a surge of relief, terror, awesome ecstatic power.

At the same time he saw a glittering light pouring from Falthorn's forehead. So, he'd been faking helplessness, Rufryd saw without surprise. Out of him came a pure white stream of Jewelfire to chain the circle into a cone of power. Then it seemed the other Aelyr realised they could follow his lead. The same light began to unspool from Tanthe, and an even brighter stream out of Mendyr. For a moment Rufryd feared the boy would get carried away and create a portal without meaning to. He didn't. The others stabilised him.

He became aware that *vagharim* were trying to attack them, Vaurgroth and his mages pulsing waves of *gauroth* at them, but nothing could break through the shield. Bright, throbbing *roth*-power filled the chamber. No one in the circle was without power; Helan and Mawrdreth had touched the Xauroma, Jthery his water elementals. Even I must have something, Rufryd thought.

The will to live life, murmured a voice in his head. It was Lynden, not Hetys. *The gift of Nuth, most powerful of all.*

Enflaming the strength of the living was the essence of those who'd built the Amber Citadel, fought for it, defied the Bhahdradomen, suffered at their hands. An overflowing of will, implacable determination, love. Garnelys's agony shimmered in the chamber, a counterpoint to the simple bravery of Serenis and Lynden, his victims.

It was a cone of pure *ethroth*, spirit. And it obliterated all *gauroth* from the chamber like a spring wind blasting away the smoky stale air of a winter-bound hovel.

A booming, tremulous voice rang out, louder than Vaurgroth's. Deafening. Ysomir's lips moved with it, yet it wasn't coming from her throat.

'I am the mage Calabethron. My Basilisks were my greatest creation and my greatest mistake. I designed them to fail, for never should such devastation be wreaked upon one race by another. They were for Maharoth only; not for his descendants.' The towering figure above Mendyr pointed at Helananthe. *'If they gave you false hope it is because you did not translate the tablets correctly. All the clues were there. Find the wiser way!'*

Ysomir let out a long, anguished cry. All the spirits shot upwards like a fountain. They swirled, filling the Sun Chamber in glittering light. They merged, blazed, dissipated in chains of sparkling motes. Vanished.

Ysomir collapsed. Tanthe knelt down and hugged her sister.

A lesser shield of light cocooned them still, mainly emanating from Falthorn now, enough to protect them from retaliation. Some of the *vagharim* had legged it, Rufryd noticed. The various adepts and officials around the dais looked stricken; Gulzhur was almost hopping with frustrated rage. The others, Naghrur's cronies, were moving into odd little groups, as if performing some esoteric dance. Rufryd sensed counter-attack.

Vaurgroth was sprawled on the Sapphire Throne. He appeared to be having a fit. He looked tiny. His face had flushed as red as the cobweb map on his skull and he was twitching. His *ghelim*-hound whined.

The *gauroth* in the chamber was gone. Even Rufryd, not the most sensitive of people, could feel the difference, the clarity of the air. And that meant that Vaurgroth – if only temporarily – was powerless.

He glanced around. 'Still nothing to stop them physically killing us, of course,' he said, addressing Helan. 'Those *sten* are bloody sharp, even without any extra power in them.'

Naghrur had left his cronies and was crossing the dais to help Vaurgroth.

'The Master of Light has been taken ill,' he said. Waving the other adepts back, he bent over the twitching form. 'Greatlord, can you hear me?'

'Arrest them,' Gulzhur shrieked at the remaining *vagharim*, pointing a gnarled finger at Helan's party. 'Lock them up! Their power is spent!'

'No,' Naghrur's voice rang out. 'Don't touch them.'

He appeared to have more authority than Gulzhur. His face was grey ice, expressionless. As Rufryd watched him tending Vaurgroth, wiping foam from his mouth and helping him to sit up, he went suddenly cold all over. What if, all along, Vaurgroth had been a puppet, and Naghrur was the real power behind him?

'No, *your* power is spent,' said Helan. They'd broken the circle but their combined energy still sparkled in the air. 'Look at your Master of Light!' she said, turning to the Bhahdradomen. 'He's nothing without his power. Just an evil little man.'

'How dare you insult the Chosen of the Ancestor like this?' Gulzhur came stalking towards her. He and Naghrur were the only ones who still had some menace about them, but Rufryd sensed they'd been drastically wrong-footed. An air of chaos was growing.

Vetru was tugging at Rufryd's knee. He grabbed Vetru under the arms and hauled him to his feet. 'Stand up, stop cowering.'

'Tell them,' Vetru whispered urgently. 'Tell them what I told you.'

'Now?'

'Yes. They should be told.'

'You said it was sacrilege.'

'Only if it isn't true. But Rufryd, I think it is true . . .'

'You tell them, then. It was your story.'

'No, I can't! You speak better than me and you're

not afraid.' Vetru's tone intensified. 'If you want to get Vaurgroth off the Throne, you must make his *domenim* throw him off themselves. Tell them now, Rufryd!'

'Gods. All right, I'll try.' He drew a breath and thought, Okay, if I'm going to do this let's make it as impressive as possible . . .

Vaurgroth seemed to have recovered somewhat. With Naghrur supporting him, he rose trembling to his feet. 'You've proved nothing with your conjuring tricks. There is always more *gauroth*. You are still my prisoners. You will regret the day you so insulted me!'

'Calling you evil, or little?' Mawrdreth said contemptuously.

'I think he means the "man" part,' said Rufryd. He stepped forward, folding his arms. Vaurgroth glared, but it was still Naghrur who seemed the truly dangerous one.

'He's a bit sensitive about that,' Rufryd went on, raising his voice so everyone in the chamber heard. 'There's something you should know about your Master of Light, your supreme Bhahdradomen leader. He's human.'

Rufryd had no idea whether what he was saying was true or not. It was a rumour Vetru had heard in the Q'elethrios *tzcement*, one so scurrilous and offensive that he'd never dared repeat it to another Bhahdradomen. Still, Rufryd spoke with conviction and his words had the desired effect. Most of the Bhahdradomen in the chamber gaped. He repeated it clearly in their own tongue, to make sure they got it.

'Liar!' cried Gulzhur.

'Vaurgroth sprang from a human settlement of Ancestor-worshippers in Vexor, the Order of Calathvahn. A damaged human boy named Sebreth from a village called Mrenth entered Calathvahn. Thirty years later he emerged as Vaurgroth. It's a long story but I've got all day.'

'This is an outrageous falsehood!' cried Vaurgroth. 'I forbid you to listen to him!'

His own fervency more or less gave him away on the

spot. Many of the adepts were plainly horrified, but others showed no reaction beyond sideways looks at one another. Rufryd happened to glance at Naghrur and saw his mouth flex in a smile.

He knew! Rufryd laughed in silent astonishment. Naghrur knew all along – and he wasn't the only one, from the look of them.

'Alas, it was only a matter of time until this was revealed,' Naghrur said softly, looking benignly over Vaurgroth's shoulder. He addressed all the *vagharim*, counsellors, mages, aides. 'I've suspected it for a long time. I tried to protect you from this, you his loyal adherents, while his power was still holding this frail empire together. It was inevitable you'd find out.'

'Naghrur, you traitor!' Vaurgroth snarled. He struggled, found himself held tight by Protector's steel hands. 'You are under arrest!'

'Who is going to arrest me?' said Naghrur. 'Some of your inner circle know your little secret and have chosen to ignore it. To most of your people, however, it's come as a great shock. You had better step down before all *domenim* learn the unpalatable truth.'

Rufryd and the others watched in amazed horror. The adepts to whom Naghrur was speaking earlier and over half the *vagharim* in the chamber began to separate out and form a distinct band.

'This is a coup,' Helan whispered. 'Look. Naghrur must have been planning this for months and we've just handed it to him!'

Vaurgroth stared in disbelief at his *domenim*; half of them openly supporting Naghrur, the others staring at him in blatant fury. They looked betrayed, each like a child who had just been told his beloved father was not his father. Rufryd felt sympathy for them. 'Don't listen to Naghrur and these human fools! Have I not led you to victory and riches? Have I not directed you always in Ancestor's light, Ancestor's Will? This is a conspiracy! You elected me your leader. Support me now or damn yourselves to Vexor!'

Naghrur let Vaurgroth go and opened his grey hands. 'Decide,' he said. 'Do we want a human to lead us?'

'No,' the Bhahdradomen called, their voices rising in volume. '*Nech! Nech!*'

'You ungrateful spawn of *graukhim*!' Vaurgroth yelled over them. 'I have given everything to you! Given my whole life! I was not hatched like you but I became *domenim*, I became more Bhahdradomen than you are! Depose me and you damn yourselves to Vexor for eternity! It was Ancestor's Will I lead you, Ancestor chose *me*!'

Rufryd felt very nearly sorry for him them. The chamber threatened to erupt into chaos; the humans were forgotten. Mawrdreth began to edge them aside. Tanthe helped Ysomir, who was on her feet but dazed.

'Hell, I never dreamed this would happen,' Helan said.

'It's wonderful,' said Falthorn. 'I only wish I could see the spectacle as well as hear it.'

'Is it just me, or don't you realise Naghrur will be worse?' Helan retorted. 'Even the Bhahdradomen are frightened of him, and we haven't won yet!'

As she spoke, an *yrim* messenger came scuttling into the chamber, unnoticed at first. He struggled through the jostling ranks of *vagharim* and skidded to a crouch in front of the dais, where he choked out a message in his own language. Silence froze the chamber. Rufryd laughed.

'What?' said Helan. 'What did he say?'

'He said, "Master of Light, the city is under attack from the Shaelahyr. We cannot hold them back."'

'Elrill!' cried Tanthe.

Into the silence, Naghrur's voice fell crisp as ice. 'In the light of this news, my Lord Vaurgroth, might I suggest you step down gracefully before you are forced? You'll be well-treated. Retirement with honours.'

Face flushed scarlet, eyes dripping blood, hands clawed

with despair, Vaurgroth removed himself from the Sapphire Throne and strode quickly to the corner of the dais. No one followed him, not even the mages who had apparently known his secret and still supported him. Only his *ghelim*-hound slunk at his heels.

Vaurgroth had barely set foot on the first step down when Gulzhur came towards him and stopped him with one hand to his shoulder. It seemed a friendly gesture. Then Rufryd saw that Gulzhur had a knife glinting in his skeletal hand. The blade flashed. It looked like Tanthe's lost *mnelir*.

'Liar,' said Gulzhur, his voice as sour as that of a betrayed lover. He, who'd been Vaurgroth's ardent lieutenant. 'Deceiver!'

With those words he thrust the knife in and up. Vaurgroth doubled over the hand. Gulzhur wrenched the blade free. Bright arterial blood followed it. Still on his feet, Vaurgroth staggered. He looked confounded, lost, pitiful; he was the one betrayed, not Gulzhur. His hound sprang at Enabler, only to be dispatched with a careless swipe of the blade. Grief flooded Vaurgroth's face as he saw his pet fall. Then he pitched headlong down the steps and lay with his life pulsing out, scarlet against the flame of his robe.

Not plasma. Red human blood.

Gulzhur continued along the top of the dais towards Naghrur. Rufryd saw clearly that it was the *mnelir* in his hand, as dangerous as any sharp blade to humans, but pulsing with *liroth* that was terrifying and lethal to Bhahdradomen. Enabler pointed the shining blade at Naghrur. Discomforted for the first time, Naghrur drew back.

'I see,' said Mendyr. Before anyone could stop him or protest, he raised his hands with the palms facing each other, his small face intent. It was over in three seconds.

A black dot formed on the air. The scene around it distorted, pulled inwards. The dot expanded into a disc of dark nothingness edged with a corona of silver. The disc flared, rotated, swallowed Gulzhur and shrank again to a black dot.

The mote winked out. Naghrur was still there, staring at the place where it had been, his steely eyes crimped with astonishment. His would-be assassin had vanished.

Chapter Twenty-five. Heliodor and Obsidian

The last of Branq'elin's army fought valiantly, but all was over. Dra'a'ks battled fiercely in the sky but were routed. *Ghelim* swooped victorious across the churning clouds. Rain fell red with the blood washed from *ghelim* claws and teeth. Branq'elin crouched over Dawn and Mirias, as if that could protect her friends from the last savage blows of their enemies.

'No,' Dawn whispered and bent her head on Mirias's chest, sobbing. Rain trickled down his pale, still face and watered the blood that stained his shirt. His eyes were half-closed, as if he were still looking tenderly at Dawn.

Branq'elin gave a long, shuddering sigh.

Beside her, Con stared up at the sky. There was no fear left in their faces, only bleak resignation. She put one arm around Dawn, reached behind her and took Con's hand. They were all injured. There was nothing to do but wait, a hopeless rain-soaked tableau.

She heard the sharp metallic voices of the Bhahdradomen some distance away, closing in. The whole world was storm-torn, bloody, weeping with grief. She thought of her little daughter and a wave crested through her chest. At least Annuin was spared this . . .

Presently she realised that the noises had stopped. There was silence around them.

Con breathed, 'My lady?'

Slowly, to spare her aching shoulders, she looked up and saw that the sky was empty.

The *ghelim* were gone. She saw the last one vanish in a vapour-wisp as if sucked back into its own dark world. The clouds themselves were boiling away to nothing, leaving only the white, high streaks of mares' tails above. Of the *yrim* there was no sign. They'd melted away like shades into the landscape.

Con stood up, cautiously unfolding his stiff limbs. 'They're gone,' he said.

Branq'elin rose beside him. She looked all around her. Everywhere she saw her own soldiers – those that were still standing – dazed and disbelieving, with no enemies to fight.

'It's over,' said Con. 'What happened?'

'Q'enartre sent us a miracle,' said Branq'elin. Tears ran down her face and the next she knew, she and Con were hugging, looking joyfully into each other's eyes. Their mouths met in a deep kiss, cold with rain, hot with tears and blood.

Dawn, meanwhile, hadn't looked up from Mirias's body. The miracle was not enough to bring the fallen back to life.

'Dawn,' Branq'elin said softly. 'The Bhahdradomen are gone.'

'Too late for him,' Dawn whispered.

Branq'elin kissed her too. She embraced her, held onto her until at last she was ready to be helped up and led away from her dead lover.

'Come on,' Bran said gently. 'Come home with us. You're not alone.'

Dawn turned to her, eyes wild with grief, and put her arms round Bran's neck.

Slow, stumbling, bedraggled, with their arms wrapped tight around each other, Con and Dawn and Branq'elin began to make their way back to Tasqabad.

'I *can* control it.' Mendyr's light voice pierced the silence. Naghrur stared at the child, but Mendyr ignored him, turning to his human companions with an air of contained revelation. 'I know what to do now.'

'Good, wonderful,' Helan said, pulling the child into their

midst. She was sure her heart would fail if this day went on any longer. 'Please don't ever do that again without us discussing it first!'

'He was going to kill the grey one,' said Mendyr.

'It might have been better you'd let him,' said Tanthe.

'No.' The child spoke with eerie certainty.

'You did well, Mendyr,' Helan said, putting a hand on his shoulder. 'Can you do it again, if you need to?'

'Yes, ma'am,' he said politely.

Helananthe left them and went to confront Naghrur. 'You've seen what this child is capable of,' she said with all the force and confidence she could muster. 'Vaurgroth gave up the Sapphire Throne and now he's dead. You've seen that my friends are *roth*-mages. Your power is diminished, the Shaelahyr have invaded the city. If you do not admit defeat and remove yourselves from the Amber Citadel forthwith, the child will create gates to suck each and every one of you into oblivion.'

Naghrur stood above her like a steel blade, his hands folded precisely in front of his lean abdomen. He looked deadly. Yet when he spoke, his voice was unexpectedly soft.

'My lady, can I speak to you in private?'

She was startled. She'd been expecting more histrionics. 'If you wish. Not without my husband and friends, though.'

'Of course.' Naghrur uttered a few sharp orders in his own language, then came down the steps towards her. The Bhahdradomen began to leave the chamber, murmuring to one another. Some of the elite were seized by Naghrur's *vagharim* but went without struggling. Others – Naghrur's cronies – lifted Vaurgroth's body and carried it away.

Zhoaah was nowhere to be seen.

'I've ordered them to gather in a lower chamber,' said Naghrur, 'where I shall address them later, once we've decided how to proceed.'

Naghrur took them to the Serpentine Chamber, a council

room that lay off the Sun Chamber. The walls were green amber, the chairs set with malachite, moss agate, emerald, the table an oval of blond marble inlaid with serpentine. Helan bristled at the ease with which he conducted them around her palace, but said nothing. At least there was a couch for Ysomir to rest on. She lay silent, rubbing off the charcoal and chalk with which they'd fooled Vaurgroth, at least for long enough to get near him.

Mendyr sat on the floor, leaning against the couch. Ysomir's hand drifted down to caress his hair; Helan noticed he didn't duck away, as he usually did from Tanthe. Tanthe noticed too, judging by her grim expression. Vetru sat down beside the boy. The rest of them went to sit in the high-backed chairs around the table. Jthery guided Falthorn as usual. Tanthe gave Ysomir a kiss before she sat down next to Rufryd. Mawrdreth was a strong quiet presence beside Helan, his arm encircling the back of her chair. The room looked as if it hadn't been cleaned for three years, but at least the Bhahdradomen didn't seem to have made much use of it. It was dusty but unchanged. The three moon windows gleamed through curtains like sagging webs.

'Things aren't looking good for you, Protector Naghrur,' Helan said. 'I cannot force you to surrender, since I have no army. But we have Mendyr. And if the Shaelahyr prevail, you seem to have usurped Vaurgroth to no purpose.'

'Don't make assumptions about the reasons for which I usurped Vaurgroth.' Naghrur's Paranian was as precise as that of a cultured citizen of Parione. 'I wish to explain.'

The door opened, and one of his acolytes came in with a tray of glasses and a sealed glass flagon of wine from her own cellar. The dust was thick on it. Naghrur said nothing, but Helan sensed a message; a sealed, dusty bottle was unlikely to have been tampered with. He was trying to reassure her that he meant them no harm.

Vetru jumped up to help. He wiped the bottle, unsealed it and poured wine for them all. He kept looking nervously at Naghrur. When he turned to resume his position at Ysomir's feet, though, Naghrur said, 'Come and sit beside me, hatchling.'

Looking both wary and pleased, Vetru obeyed. Helan took a long drink of her wine. Sour plums and spice. Goddess, how good it tasted!

'It's true I have planned to depose Vaurgroth almost from the beginning,' Naghrur began. 'I could do so only by appearing to be the closest and most ruthless of his lieutenants. I have worked hard to make all of them – Gulzhur, Rhazagramen, the whole sorry band – more afraid of me than they were of Vaurgroth. Easing certain key players, *bharu'grothrim*, *grothrim* and *vahgarim* to my side, without them ever betraying me, has been a difficult task, requiring more twists and turns than an eel. I didn't intend it to happen quite when it did, but I must thank you for precipitating events. I doubt, in fact, that I would ever have reached a position to achieve it without you.'

'Don't thank us,' said Helan. 'We didn't set out to help you. You're obviously a very clever man – sorry, *domen* – but I don't see what you've gained. Why destroy your source of power, the leader who gained this great victory for you? It seems a hell of a sacrifice to make, just because you despise humans.'

'I do not despise humans,' said Naghrur. 'What I despised was Vaurgroth's philosophy. However, I must play upon my *domenim*'s natural distaste for humans by displaying Vaurgroth's body for their inspection, in order to encourage them to support me instead. I need them to hate him. To turn against everything he stood for.'

'But he was an inspiring leader,' said Rufryd. 'He got you out of miserable Vexor, he gave you everything you wanted.'

Naghrur tapped his long thin fingertips on the table. 'The Order of Calathvahn. A collection of male humans who, for their own reasons, have become embittered against their own species and decided that our Ancestor offers something better. No-one is more enthusiastic than a convert, apparently. They have turned Ancestor-worship into something it never was, and was never meant to be. Our *Ancestor* is only that. A symbol of our origins, a representative of all our dead forebears whom we entreat for ancient wisdom. He is our identity, that's all. Not a god. This idea of Ancestor as the one Great God, a white light in whose name we must worship and conquer, is an invention of the Order. It is false. Vaurgroth and his followers brought this fabricated belief into Zhahgrament and infected us with it. I am sworn to purge it.'

Helan sat back, breathing out in surprise. 'Well, this is quite a revelation. Still, those beliefs, however false they were, got him in control of Aventuria again. I don't see what you had to gain by destroying him. You don't look power-crazed.'

'I am not power-crazed, my lady,' Naghrur said, icily soft. 'Do you think that is all we care about? Destroying, tormenting?'

'That's what our history books tell us. That's what Vaurgroth has done to us, and I haven't much else to go on.'

He exhaled sharply. 'Well, your ignorance is our misfortune. If you doubt what I am telling you, ask yourselves how you escaped from the Amber Citadel. When we searched the palace, I knew full well you were in the bedchamber of Princess Ghiseyma. I knew you were hiding in the kitchens. I let you escape.'

Helan gasped. They all stared at him. He went on, 'It was I who arranged for your mother and brother to be taken to Torith Mir, so that they could no longer be used against you. I require no gratitude, only for you to understand.'

'I am speechless, Lord Naghrur. Go on.'

'In some ways, Vaurgroth's heart was in the right place. He had a passionate sense of injustice. He wanted the Bhahdradomen to be released from Vexor and live freely; he didn't especially wish to torment humans, though some of his underlings did. He had a fantasy of appearing a benevolent conqueror, adored by *domenim* and humans alike. His idea was to let humans live and share the wonder of the Ancestor. They would be rewarded for bowing down to him with ecstasy and illusions of power; they'd fall happily into slavery, believing it was Ancestor's Will. He believed his own lies. The reality was, naturally, that he was as brutal as any such conqueror. Our way of life alone was bound to destroy humans in the end. Still, Vaurgroth had some extraordinary ideas. You heard how they came about?'

'No,' said Helan. 'When Rufryd came out with it in the Sun Chamber, that was the first I'd heard of it. What was this story about Vaurgroth?'

'Oh.' Rufryd took a swig of wine. 'According to what Vetru heard in Q'elethrios, the truth about Vaurgroth was well-known, but no-one dared to speak it out loud. He was born in Mrenth in Thanmandrathor, a strange little albino boy called Sebreth who had the misfortune to be born with extra fingers. His mother died, his father abandoned him; he was passed around the village because no-one really wanted him. An outsider. A changeling, they thought. All through his childhood he was taunted and rejected for those extra fingers and his weedy pale body, accused of being Bhahdradomen. And I've seen how some Thand'rathians feel about the Eaters. One day some boys thought it might solve the problem to push him into a bonfire.

'Sebreth survived, but he came out scarred and angry. He fled; how could he go back to the village after that? So he wandered miserably in the wilderness for a long time and eventually stumbled into Q'elethrios harbour, where the brother-Order took him in and looked after him.

'He'd found people who didn't reject him, something he could belong to. Soon after that he was delivered to Calathvahn and became the most devoted disciple they'd ever had. This scarred boy decided that if people were going to call him Bhahdradomen, he would *become* Bhahdradomen, and so consummately that even the Eaters themselves would never realise. During his time in Calathvahn he trained himself to become a *gauroth*-mage and discovered he had a virtually limitless gift for it. Enough to transform himself, depose Aazhoth, fill everyone around him with power. He forged himself into everything the poor exiled *domenim* had dreamed of. Their saviour. Seems a bit ironic, really, that they could turn against him just for being human, after all the effort he put in.'

'Don't start feeling sorry for him,' said Tanthe.

'Oh, I don't. Now I know why Mrenth was the first place the Order attacked. Vaurgroth's revenge.'

'The story Vetru heard is true,' said Naghrur. 'I knew it. It's understood that he even physically mutilated himself to appear more like us. A handful of us knew, but chose to go along with his pretence. I'm surprised Vetru heard it at all, though, because Vaurgroth went to great lengths to suppress such rumours. He'd kill anyone who whispered them.'

'I was told I'd be killed, if I ever repeated it,' Vetru said quietly.

'Not any more,' Naghrur said, and patted his shoulder.

'You say he had extraordinary ideas,' said Helan, 'but what are yours?'

'I don't believe that Bhahdradomen and humans can co-exist. I don't believe we should even try. It gives me no pleasure to see your land stripped bare by our *graukhim*, not even out of revenge. That is the most pitiful motive of all.'

'If you have anything to suggest, I'm prepared to listen.'

'That's magnanimous of you, considering you might have wished to slaughter us all.'

'I'm not vengeful,' said Helan. 'I want a peace that lasts, not an endless cycle of defeat and revenge.'

'We're in accord, then,' said Naghrur. 'We came from another land in another realm – attached to the Earth, as

Verdanholm is – called Hellaxis. Humans believe we left it because we stripped it bare and sought other lands to consume. That is not true. The Obsidian Tower stood in Hellaxis, the legacy of a vanished race far older than us. It had become a symbol of our unity, our oneness with the world. But the Obsidian Tower fell. It fell for prosaic reasons; it had been built upon the crater of an ancient volcano, which erupted. But greater spiritual resonances were read into this, and who am I to say they were wrong? They said it had not fallen but vanished when the volcano woke. *Domen* believed this meant doom, spiritual schisms and disaster, and so they made their prophecy self-fulfilling. Bitter wars and struggles broke out. Certain groups of Bhahdradomen migrated to escape them, and always upon a quest to find the Obsidian Tower again.' His voice became even softer and more reflective. 'Vaurgroth almost succeeded. It is a real place of real power, and perhaps it holds answers for us.'

Helan looked at Tanthe, but she sat with her lips firmly closed upon her secrets.

'I hope that I shall see it one day,' Naghrur went on. 'Rhazagramen and Vaurgroth, however, would only have violated it in their thirst for power. To go with a fixed and false idea of what they would find there would have led to disaster. It's just as well that it vanishes again. We don't deserve it yet. However . . . it is thousands of years since we left our land. I believe that Hellaxis is still there and that we should go back.'

'Do you know how?' said Helan.

Naghrur shook his head. 'We have been stranded here. Whatever gate we first came through has long been closed and lost.' He looked at Mendyr for so long that the boy got up and came to the table. 'I have long dreamed of finding a mage who could actually create such a gate . . .'

'Hold on,' said Tanthe. 'You can't use him like that. He's a child, he's untrained. Can't you let him grow up first?'

'There isn't time,' said Naghrur. Helan agreed.

'I can do it,' said the boy. 'I can see into the spaces. It's easy.'

Tanthe put her head in her hands.

'If we make such a gate, I can't promise that every single Bhahdradomen will return with me,' said Naghrur. 'A few may prefer to stay in Aventuria. You will have to deal with them as you see fit. But many, many will come with me. Enough to deliver Aventuria back into human hands.'

Falthorn said, 'And does this agreement include the Bhahdradomen abandoning another invasion of Verdanholm?'

'Yes,' answered Naghrur. 'If you find any still there, again you must deal with them in your own way. Most will prefer a chance of going home, I assure you.'

The Valahyr lord let out a long breath. 'At last. In that case, I shall help and advise Mendyr as best I can in the creation of this gate. All I have ever wanted is freedom for my own realm, yet for this I have been painted as the blackest villain under the three moons.'

'I wonder why,' said Tanthe.

'I must go and address the *tzcement*,' said Naghrur, rising. 'I thank you for your co-operation. You are free to leave – or to stay, of course. And would you ask your Shaelahyr friends to cease their attack? We shall lay down our arms. The war is over.'

'So, poor old Aazhoth got his way after all,' Rufryd said.

Naghrur turned and fixed him with his gimlet stare. 'You know of Aazhoth?'

'I met him in Calathvahn, in the dungeon where Vaurgroth had thrown him. He told me about the false beliefs. I don't think even he knew Vaurgroth's secret, unless he was too horrified to tell me.'

Sadness passed over Naghrur's face. 'He was a well-intentioned *domen* but lacked the strength to uphold our old beliefs in the face of Vaurgroth's fervour. We had no idea he was still alive.'

'I was with him when he died,' Rufryd said, his voice low. 'Sorry. I quite liked him. At least he didn't die alone.'

Outside, Parione was in chaos. Tanthe, Ysomir and Rufryd stood on the stone walkway that ran behind the top of the outermost wall, looking down at the scene in the great square below. Hordes of *domenim* milled around the walls of the Amber Citadel, civilians mingling with nervous *yrim* whose officers had fled and whose *gauroth* weapons had lost their power. There were a few humans on the fringes, looking confused. Tanthe kept her arm tight around Ysomir.

Helan and Mawrdreth were still inside, with Falthorn, Jthery, Mendyr and Vetru, but Tanthe had wanted to escape for a while. If only to test the truth of Naghrur's words, 'You are free to leave or to stay.'

She looked out over the city she loved. Close at hand, the neglect and dirt made her want to weep. Further away, though, it looked no different; still the same graceful roofs set among the cloudy treetops. The dome of Nepheter's temple on one hill, the stump of the Heliodor Tower on the other. She saw that the tower was a little taller than before. So they'd gone on building it. Her heart sank with resignation. The evanescent hope they'd received lay like a ground mist over her sorrow. She felt numb relief but no joy. They'd lost too much.

'How are you, Ymmi?' Tanthe said, hugging her sister. 'You've hardly said a word. I'm so glad to see you.'

'I'm all right.' Ysomir's voice was tired and pensive. She still had smudges of her crone-disguise on her face, and chalk stuck in her less-than-clean hair, turning it powdery grey. 'Shaken up, that's all. Finding it hard to speak. All the *ethroths* are gone now. When I called them out of me, they didn't come back in. I'm glad, in a way; but I feel sort of empty.'

'Lynden, too?' said Rufryd.

'Lynden . . .' Her voice cracked. 'He's still here, but at

peace now. So quiet I can't hear him any more. I can't hang onto him forever. I think I should take him home.'

Nodding, Rufryd moved close to the wall and looked over, so they couldn't see his face. He wanted to be left alone, Tanthe saw. She took Ysomir aside and spoke quietly to her.

'Does this mean all your power's gone?'

Ysomir shrugged. 'For now, at least. I shall never be the same as I was; you know that, don't you?'

'Oh, yes. None of us will.'

'I don't know what will happen in the future, but for now I'm glad to have a rest. It's quiet.'

'It won't be with us around.' Tanthe grinned. 'Have you, er, heard anything of Saphaeyender?'

'I was in hiding with him, until a few months ago. As far as I know he's safe.'

'Thank the Goddess.'

'Tanthe, I did something rather stupid . . .'

Tanthe put her hand to her mouth. She'd always dreaded this and felt a pang of possessive jealousy, even though she'd left Saphaeyender long ago. 'Don't tell me. You've been sleeping with him. He's in love with you. Or he's broken your heart, like he does. Oh hell, Ymmi . . .'

'No, no!' Ysomir looked stunned. 'The stupid thing was that when I fled from prison, I forgot to take the *silvenroth* mirror with me. If I'd taken it, I might have found a way to let you know we were all right. I like him, Tan, but not in that way. He's too self-centred.'

'Oh.'

'He did have someone else, though.'

'Right. I shouldn't be surprised. I shouldn't mind, either. Who was it?'

'A boy called Eander.' Ysomir swallowed. 'It was his family's house we hid in. Saphaeyender dropped poor Eander and spent most of the time shut in his room, writing.'

'Writing? That's wonderful.'

'Not for the rest of us, especially Eander. Guess who was left trying to patch things up.'

'But how did you come to be with Helan and Mawrdreth?'

'Ran away and joined the rebels. We rescued them from the Bhahdradomen.'

'You're mad!' Tanthe exclaimed, horrified but thrilled at her sister's bravery. 'Why leave a safe house?'

'You could say I decided to stop reacting and start acting,' Ysomir said with ghostly smile.

'You seem so much older. You look as if you've been to Hellaxis and back.'

'So do you, Tan.' They looked into each other's eyes.

'Shall we take bets on which one of us is going to start crying first?' said Tanthe.

Rufryd called suddenly, 'You two, look!'

They rushed to the parapet. Along the avenue that led into the square the Shaelahyr were coming. Some rode ice-white horses, others were on foot, a procession like a river of snow. They moved with the exhaustion of battle and the proud, relaxed stride of victory. Elrill led them, mounted on a pale grey. The Bhahdradomen scattered out of their way.

There were darker figures riding with him too, Aelyr of a different *eretru*. Valahyr scattered among the Shaelahyr.

'Ymmi, look, it's . . .'

Not finishing, Tanthe rushed away and took the steps down from the walkway at a precipitous run. Ysomir followed. They reached the courtyard inside the main gate just as Elrill was riding in. Sitting behind him on the saddle was Auriel. And beside them, together on a tall cream mare, were Talthaliorn and Fiomir.

Tanthe opened her arms and let out a yell of joy. Moments later her brother and her parents were sweeping her into their embrace. Elrill stood holding the horses, smiling.

'I don't understand,' Tanthe said, trying to get her breath back. 'I was so scared I was never going to see you again. What are you doing with Elrill?'

'I found Talthaliorn wounded on the battlefield,' Fiomir said in a tone of disapproval. 'His horse had been killed and Tal was unconscious. I revived him and we were on our way back to the camp when Auriel came to meet us and said we should flee before we were taken prisoner. We gathered up as many of the Valahyr as we could and made straight for the coast.'

'I took them to the portal,' Auriel added. He looked radiant, auburn hair shining on his shoulders. He produced the gleaming *anametris* sphere, spun it on one finger, slipped it away again. 'We came out north of the city and found Elrill's army there. It was meant to be.'

'I'm so glad to see you all, I can't speak,' said Tanthe. 'We've got a thousand things to tell you.' She remembered what close friends Elrill had been with Eldareth; she knew she'd have to take him somewhere alone to break the news.

'How is Falthorn?' Talthaliorn asked, looking at her with intent concern.

'On form,' said Tanthe. 'Don't worry, he's fine. Did you hear what's happening?'

'Messengers reached us,' said Elrill, 'but the fighting was as good as done by then. Their weapons went dead and they were finished. We're not sure why.'

Tanthe turned to Ysomir and smiled. 'I think we can enlighten you. Oh,' she added, pulling Ymmi forward and presenting her. 'Sorry, I left my manners in the Almandine Vale. Fiomir, Talthaliorn, Elrill, Auriel. This chalk-covered apparition is my little sister, Ysomir. She only won the war for us.'

When Tanthe and Ysomir had gone, Rufryd remained on the wall to see what was happening in the square. There was activity.

Outside the main gate, almost directly below him, a bier had been placed. As he watched, a group of *vagharim* had come from the Citadel and were placing the scrawny white corpse of Vaurgroth upon it, spreadeagled. One of Naghrur's supporters stood beside the bier, announcing the shameful secret for all to hear.

Something puzzled Rufryd. He frowned, couldn't see clearly. Morbid curiosity propelled him down the stairs, out through the main gate and into the seething throng of *domenim*. They were filing past the bier, groaning, chattering, wailing their disbelief, but he pushed through them as if they weren't there.

There lay their leader in pathetic indignity. He was naked, his rope of white hair dangling off one end of the bier and dried blood crusting his pale skin. It was obvious from the blood alone that he wasn't *domen*. Human knees and elbows must have made him look deformed in their sight. He'd hid it well under his robes but now it was undeniable. Yet in the blond shadow between his thighs he appeared to have no male genitals.

That was the puzzle he'd glimpsed. Vaurgroth was female? Surely not. Rufryd moved so close that he could smell the gory body and was jostled against it by *yrim*. Then he saw the stark truth. Where the penis and balls should have been was a purplish mass of scar tissue.

So, Naghrur was right, he thought, his throat sour with loathing. Vaurgroth took the beliefs of Calathvahn to the absolute limit. So intent was he on despising humans and becoming Bhahdradomen, he had castrated himself.

Mendyr created the gate inside the Heliodor Tower. He chose the place himself, telling the others that the energy of the *rothanamir* that had been opened inside would make his task easier. It was already a place of power. Falthorn, Auriel and Naghrur went to guide him – and Tanthe with Fiomir and Talthaliorn to keep an eye on him – but he hardly seemed to need anyone's guidance. He needed no *anametris* sphere. The boy worked with his eyes closed and his face intent, shaping power on the air with his hands.

Tanthe watched anxiously through a narrow archway into the tower. A bright-edged black dot appeared, rotating as it grew. Unnerving pressures pulled at the air. Soon the embryonic gate grew into a cone of blackness that looked flat from every angle, an arched doorway into nowhere.

It struck her that it might be quite easy to trick the Bhahdradomen and send them into nothingness, as Helan had threatened. Yet Mendyr had a pure integrity about him; Tanthe knew by instinct that he would never do that. He had a wise, Wrothryr soul and no mischief in him. Naghrur deserved integrity, at least.

Watching her son, she felt a sense of awe that made the earth sway around her. He seemed to have nothing to do with her. Surely he'd been dropped onto the earth from a higher realm, not come from her body.

Within the archway, a scene glimmered. A landscape; low dark hills, a sky streaked with thin bands of violet and silver, the empty crater of a volcano.

Naghrur sent one of his adepts through. The adept returned and collapsed to the ground at Naghrur's feet – overcome with joy, Tanthe assumed. For Naghrur turned and touched Mendyr's head and said, 'You are blessed by Ancestor's wisdom.'

Helan had ordered the entire hill and the streets around it to be cleared of inhabitants while the gate was made. She'd feared Mendyr might lose control and swallow half the city. She had been far more worried than she would admit, but the boy had, as far as Tanthe could see, perfect control of what he was doing.

That was what made him so disturbing. She could guess what terrible things he'd be able to do, if he had the motive. Turn the Earth into a lacework of gates or draw something dreadful through from another, unimagined place . . .

And I'm supposed to look after him? she thought. She felt more agonisingly than ever that she was never going to be a true mother to him . . . Thanks, Falthorn, she thought bitterly. Thanks so much.

Later, in the drizzly light of late morning, Naghrur's exodus began.

The human populace of Parione lined the route at the base of the hill, watching in disbelief the slow, steady procession of Bhahdradomen towards the tower. The humans had a grey, cowed look about them, the result of living for several wretched years under Vaurgroth. Tanthe silently entreated Nepheter and Dyonis to fill them again with energy, to put light in their eyes and the urge to dance into their feet. It would take time, but it would happen.

The exodus went on for hours. There were *yrim* and *ghelim*, peasants and *graukhim*, hordes of ordinary *domenim*. Tanthe stood with her family around her, Helan and Mawrdreth nearby. The procession hypnotised them. Naghrur and a couple of his adepts stood a short distance from Helan, watching without emotion. Many of the humans grew exhausted and wandered away before it was over – perhaps to reclaim their homes and their lives – but Tanthe felt she must stay to the bitter end.

Vetru was with Rufryd. He seemed twitchy and restless, like a colt in a field watching a herd of wild horses galloping past.

Mendyr stood near Tanthe, watching the tower. From this position they could just see the entrance as a tiny black slit. The procession, passing in and vanishing.

'Mendyr,' said Tanthe, 'what happens when they've all gone? Do you have to go up and close the gate?'

'No,' he answered, moving away to stand with Falthorn. 'The gate will close itself.'

How does he know so much? she wondered.

'He's such a beautiful child,' Ysomir said in her ear. 'He looks so like you. I can hardly believe he's yours.'

'Neither can I,' Tanthe said drily. 'I look at him and feel completely inadequate. I don't know how to treat him. I never had a problem with the children at home, but I treat him like a child and he cuts me dead. So I talk to him like an adult and he's suddenly eight-going-on-four again. I don't think he likes me very much. I feel no connection with him.'

'It'll come,' said Ysomir.

'Will it? He's not a normal child. Falthorn manufactured him. He probably thinks I abandoned him. He's got some strange alien soul inside him, and Aelyr for parents, with a tiny sprinkling of human just to fuck him up completely. He's had the weirdest upbringing, and his soul is about a thousand years old, trapped in a child's body and mind ... how can he hope to be normal?'

'I don't know. Just love him. I do.'

Tanthe hugged her. 'You're such an optimist, Ymmi. What shall we do after?'

'What do you mean?'

'It's almost over. Aventuria can heal now, and you're free. Do you want to stay in Parione?'

Ysomir paled. 'I hadn't thought about it. It will depend on what you and the others do, of course. But I think that I should really like to go home to Riverwynde and see Mum and Dad.'

'You know something?' Tanthe said, realising for the first time. 'I'd like that, too. When spring comes, that's what we'll do.'

The procession was tailing off to nothing. Presently it ceased. Naghrur turned to Helananthe and bowed his head in a respectful gesture to her. 'Now it is time for me to go after my *domen*,' he said in his precise voice. 'Mendyr has made a very generous promise that when he is older he will travel Aventuria and help other *domenim* he meets to return to Hellaxis also. I regret the enmity there has been between us. We are forever grateful for the clemency you've shown us.'

Helan nodded, as if she couldn't find any words. Naghrur

and his companions began to walk away. Vetru jumped on the spot as if someone had kicked him.

'Rufryd, I wish to go with them,' he said in a rush.

Rufryd looked stunned. Upset, Tanthe realised. 'Oh?'

'They're my *domenim*. I belong with them.'

'Yes, I know. But if you go, it's unlikely you'll be able to come back. We'll never meet again.'

Vetru hesitated, his face displaying an anguished indecision that was wholly human. 'I know, but I want to be where I belong. With Naghrur. I guided you in Vexor. You guided me to this.'

Rufryd nodded. 'Go on, then,' he said hoarsely. 'Be happy.'

Vetru briefly clasped his hands, and darted away up the road. Naghrur was already looking round, as if he'd been waiting for Vetru all along. Rufryd watched with one hand pressed to his mouth, eyes glittering. Tanthe slipped her hand through his arm and they watched, in silence, the last of the Bhahdradomen entering the Heliodor Tower. There was a long pause. It was over.

'That's it, then,' said Helan, turning. 'I suggest we go back to the Citadel and get very drunk. Tomorrow we have to start cleaning up this mess.'

'I didn't see Zhoaah go in, did you?' said Mawrdreth. 'Haven't seen him at all since he took us to Vaurgroth.'

'I am much too tired to care about Zhoaah,' said Helan. 'Let's hope he got all the chaos he wanted.'

The party turned to walk back towards the Amber Citadel. The ground trembled. A noise began behind them, a sliding roar that grew rapidly in volume.

They swung back and stared up at the hill, Falthorn demanding Jthery tell him what was happening. Thunder shook the air. The ground convulsed as if bombarded by an avalanche. Dark against the red sky, the Heliodor Tower was falling.

Stone by stone at first; then the whole structure was swaying, splitting, collapsing under its own monumental weight. Slowly, gracefully it went down, taking trees and houses with it. A great cloud of dust rose. The rumbling fall of stones went on for long moments.

Abruptly the world was still again. The Heliodor Tower was gone.

'I didn't mean that to happen,' said Mendyr.

They stood in astonishment for minutes. Tanthe guessed they felt, as she did, relief rather than sorrow. 'I doubt it was your fault, child,' said Talthaliorn. 'The structure couldn't sustain its own weight.'

Helan gasped, 'Oh, thank Great Nuth I had the hill evacuated!'

'You were saying,' Mawrdreth said drily, 'about having a mess to clear up tomorrow?'

Winter in Parione passed in subdued peace. Rains came to cleanse the streets and wash the seeds of autumn into the soil. Then snow and frost arrived to glitter on every surface, turning the city to a fantastical ice sculpture. Food was in short supply, the palace cold and draughty, but they survived.

Falthorn and Jthery departed almost immediately for Verdanholm, with all the Valahyr who'd survived the battle. By then Falthorn had reached some kind of truce with both Elrill and Talthaliorn. They'd also had long discussions with Helan. In future, the Aelyr would work in friendship with humans.

'The ancient schism between us was the weak point that allowed the Bhahdradomen in,' said Elrill. 'We must never let that happen again.'

Falthorn and Jthery left in the chill of a silver-blue morning, wrapped in indigo travelling cloaks, Jthery guiding his companion as always. The portal in the tower had been destroyed by the creation of the gate, so they were going into the Serpentines to seek another. They looked magnificent, their hair flowing around them in veils of black and rose-gold.

Tanthe was there with her Aelyr family to say a rather stiff farewell. Although Falthorn's accident had subdued his ruthless fire – or Jthery had softened it – he seemed to have acquired serenity rather than bitterness. She was glad. She would never like Falthorn, never truly forgive him, but she didn't want revenge.

At that moment she was simply, desperately glad that Mendyr hadn't asked to go with him.

'We will meet again,' said Falthorn, giving the boy's head a meaningful caress. His unseeing gaze drifted across Tanthe, Auriel, Fiomir, Talthaliorn. 'Look after him well. It is a great responsibility you've taken on.' A cool smile flickered on his perfect lips. 'We shall all meet again.'

To Tanthe's surprise, Rufryd agreed that they should return to Riverwynde in the spring. 'I don't know why I want to go back,' he said. 'I can't take Lynden home. All I've got there is a father who hates me, and will hate me even more bitterly when he knows I failed to save Lynden's life. But I belong where you are, Tan; that's all there is to it.'

'More than that,' she said. 'I think you need to go home and face Arthryn.'

Rufryd was quiet for a long time. Eventually he said, 'I know.'

Meanwhile there were many tasks to occupy them through the long months of Holly and Bronia. Reclaiming the Amber Citadel, cleaning the streets of the city, restoring people to their homes and farmers to their ravaged lands. Even Fiomir and Talthaliorn helped, to Tanthe's delight. The damage would take long, slow healing.

Tanthe cosseted her sister. Ysomir had always been quiet but now she seemed positively introverted, keeping to her own chamber and avoiding company. She denied any distress, but Tanthe saw she wasn't herself. Delayed grieving over Lynden, the shock of possessing and losing the *ethroths*, memories of Garnelys, the desire for the isolation she'd welcomed in her prison cell . . . she had all that and more to bear. Her eyes were haunted. Tanthe knew she'd gone through experiences that she couldn't even describe.

Still, Tanthe persisted. What drew Ysomir out of isolation, in the end, was the need to educate Mendyr. The child couldn't read, so Tanthe persuaded Ysomir to help her teach him. And then had to endure the quiet pain of seeing Mendyr's blatant preference for her sister. He'd taken an instant liking to her. Whatever they were doing, it was Ysomir he wanted beside him, Ysomir he turned to first with his questions. There was nothing Tanthe could do but bite her tongue and bear it.

Day after day, Auriel watched Tanthe and Ysomir teaching Mendyr to read, encouraging him to draw or to help them with tasks. The child wasn't one for games; he was too serious, always worried about his power, asking questions. Auriel found he got on best with the boy when they were alone. Then they talked freely about *rothanamir*, Verdanholm, the Wrothryr; anything, for hours and hours. When the others were there, though, Auriel tended to fall into the background. Legacy of his time with the Valahyr, when he'd always felt an outsider. It was bad enough with Tanthe, because he was aware of the pain she must feel every time Mendyr turned to her sister. With Ysomir, though, it was worse.

She rendered him utterly tongue-tied. She had the same piercing stare as Tanthe, like the sun shining through two jewels, but where Tanthe's gaze was tempered by humour or affection, Ysomir's was cold enough to scorch. He couldn't read her at all. She frightened him, and because of that – because she was so different to the sweet-natured creature Tanthe had described – she obsessed him.

He found himself watching her as she taught the boy. She was smaller and curvier in build than Tanthe, hauntingly pretty; not in the cold sculptured way of the Aelyr but with a human, rosy glow. She looked, really, nothing like

Tanthe. Her sister, he thought, but not mine . . . He studied her hair flowing over her neat upright shoulders, the colour of tawny beech leaves in autumn, glossed with gold. Her long white hands turning the pages.

He saw her warmth while her attention was on Mendyr; but if ever she caught Auriel's eye, she was like a book closing. The few times he gathered courage to speak to her, she would cut him off with that icy leaf-green stare and turn away. Auriel knew that she must hate him for what he had done to Tanthe. Tanthe had forgiven him, but Ysomir couldn't; it was as simple as that. He desperately wanted her forgiveness but couldn't ask for it. She rendered him speechless.

'Tanthe?' She was alone on a balcony, looking out over the roofs and treetops of Parione, when Auriel found her. Gazing at Theatre Hill with its glaze of ruins and Temple Hill . . . where Saphaeyender lived. 'Tan, I've been talking to our parents.'

'That still sounds so weird,' she said as he came to her side and leaned on the parapet beside her. '"Our parents." I know I should be used to it by now.'

'You know you said you were going back to Riverwynde when the good weather comes?'

'Mm?'

'Would it be all right if we come with you?'

A startled laugh shot out of her. 'Of course! More than all right! I was going to ask, but I didn't think you'd want to.'

He smiled, his long auburn hair half-hiding his face. 'Fiomir and Talthaliorn say they would like to meet your human parents again.'

The thought gave her a shiver. 'Oh?'

'And I don't want to be left behind. Now I've found my parents and Mendyr, I want to stay with them,' he went on. 'And you, of course. After it's taken so long to find you all, I'm not letting you out of my sight.'

'It would be wonderful,' Tanthe said, thrilled. 'I thought you'd all vanish off to Verdanholm, with or without Falthorn. It's an awful journey to Sepheret, though, it will take from spring until autumn even with horses.'

'It needn't,' Auriel said with a grin. 'I'll find a portal for us to go through. A path, I mean, a short cut.'

She laughed. 'Yes, that was so obvious I didn't think of it. Oh, that would make life so much easier.'

He looked sideways at her, worried. 'The only thing is, will your sister mind me coming?'

Tanthe was startled. 'Of course not, why should she mind?'

'Because she doesn't seem to like me at all. Has she said anything to you? Is it because of . . . ?'

She placed her hand over his. 'I explained everything, and she knows it's all sorted out and forgiven and wasn't really your fault anyway. I don't know what it is. She never used to be like this . . . but she's been through a lot, Auriel, and needs time to get over it. She only said . . .'

'What?'

'That she liked being in the cell because no-one could see her. She doesn't like being watched, it makes her uncomfortable.' Tanthe folded her arms and looked candidly at him. 'So, you've got a good reason for staring at her, have you?'

She'd never seen him blush so vividly before. 'She scares me.'

'She's not Falthorn. Just my little sister.'

'Not like that.'

'What, then?' No answer. 'Look, Auriel, just let her be and stop feeling guilty. You can't make everyone like you. My advice on this is the same as what I told you about the *ezht*. Follow your inner wisdom.'

Tanthe heard that Saphaeyender was still in the house of Eander's family, and refusing to see anyone. She put off going to find him. It was so long since they'd seen each other and she wasn't sure what she expected from the encounter. She didn't want to meet the prickly, obsessed person Ysomir suggested he'd become. Better to remember him as he was the first time they'd met; her radiant hero, a god.

As the weather grew milder and spring flowers began to poke through the earth, news came that Saphaeyender was returning to his villa on Temple Hill.

'If you want to see him, go,' said Rufryd as they lay in bed together.

'Not if it will upset you. Not if you're going to hit him in the face and try to strangle him again.'

Rufryd sighed. 'I was another person when I did that. From what I've heard, I feel a bit sorry for him.'

'Aren't you afraid that if I see him again, I'll go back to him?'

'I think *you're* afraid that might happen,' he said gravely. 'If it does, there's nothing I can do. He is the great legend, your dream lover. I'm just the boy you grew up with.'

He smiled as he spoke, looking so desirable with his dark-brown hair tangled around his face and shoulders that she wanted to devour him. 'Rufe, who went into Vexor all alone? Who defended the Obsidian Tower against the Devourers and saved my life? Not Saphaeyender. You. What will make you love yourself?'

He answered simply, 'If I'm good enough for you to love.'

There was activity at the villa when Tanthe arrived. The courtyard was a mass of winter-browned weeds, the fountain dead. In the living area the palms and ferns drooped yellow in their pots and the couches were thick with dust. A slim young man with yellow hair was dragging a trunk into the centre of the marble floor, making white trails in the grey. She could hear Saphaeyender's voice from another room, '. . . that is if Meritus & Heyma are still there, and there is still such a thing as printing ink, and anyone actually cares to watch a play about the horrors they've just undergone. Gods, how can the place have attracted all this dirt? I know the Eaters were living here, I can smell them. Have they no idea how to use a duster or broom? For Dyon's sake, let's get these windows open.'

Meanwhile the young man had straightened up and was scowling at Tanthe.

'You must be Eander,' she said.

'And who must you be?'

Saphaeyender came into the room in a tattered ivory robe, wiping his hands on a cloth. He stared at her. He looked harassed and exhausted. The distinctive streaks of white at his temples had thickened to invade the black. Yet he still looked like a god. She didn't think his strong radiant face would ever lose its beauty.

'Oh, Tanthe,' he said, throwing the cloth aside and coming forward. His embrace lifted her off her feet. 'I'd almost given up hope of ever seeing you again.'

'I'll leave you to it,' Eander said sourly. Saphaeyender led her to a padded couch and flung the dust cover off it; underneath, the ivory silk was reasonably clean.

'Sit down,' he said, pulling her onto his knee. 'I want to hold you for a few minutes. You look wonderful.'

This felt wonderful. His warmth and his arms around her, her face against his long black and silver hair. 'I wasn't expecting this,' she said. 'Ysomir said you'd turned into a right misery.'

'I am a right misery,' he said lightly. 'That's what I'm like when I'm working. How is she? She just vanished, we were worried.'

'You didn't go and find her, though.'

'You know I'm no hero,' he said quietly. 'All I can do is that thing you first loved me for; playing with words. She protected me, not the other way round.'

'She practically saved Aventuria, Saph,' Tanthe said, not meaning to needle him about his shortcomings. 'Did you hear?'

'All manner of garbled stories. You can tell me the facts later. For now, we're just glad they've gone. I can't believe it. It went on so long I can't feel joyful about it; I just feel bloody tired, and dead inside. Life might seem worth living if you'd come back and live with me . . .'

She sighed. She had to tell the truth. 'Saph, I can't. I'm with Rufryd again.'

'Ah.' He paused. 'I always had a feeling that would happen. He's not lying in wait for me with a bow and arrow, is he?'

'Of course not. He's changed. He's been through worse things than any of us yet somehow managed to turn out better at the end of it.'

Saphaeyender gave a rueful smile. 'I'd like to see him. You must come for dinner, when we've got the place in order . . . The best man won, obviously. What was his secret?'

Tanthe stroked his cheek. 'Oh, Saph, meeting you was the most exciting thing that ever happened to me. But you could never give me your whole self, we both know it. Rufryd can. He's always there, like an oak. I took him for granted because we grew up together. I had to go off and do wayward things in order to learn where I really belonged.'

He exhaled slowly. 'I'm glad for him.'

'We're going home. Not this moment, but soon.'

Saphaeyender was quiet for a time, holding her. 'I hoped you would stay. But I think I knew you were going to tell me this.'

'I have to see my family again, find out what's happened at home.'

'It's such a long way. Will you ever come back?'

Her throat hurt. 'I doubt it.'

'Oh, don't go, Tanthe.'

'Saph, don't,' she said, struggling against tears. 'You have no idea how torn I've been. But the idea of living with you was always a dream. What I desired was the enchantment of the first time we met; I know that couldn't last forever. I think I'd disappear if I stayed with you. I'd be second to your work, your friends, your theatre, your lovers, your worshippers . . .'

'So the fact that Rufryd is extremely good-looking, athletic and half my age has got nothing to do with it?'

'Honestly.' She bit her lip. 'The fact that you are so unutterably ancient never even occurred to me. Still, I do have far more in common with him, and I know the difference between dreams and reality.'

'Indeed, you do.' He smiled sadly. 'Well, I never lied; I told you I'm only human. Now my honesty comes back to haunt me. I'm vain, selfish, obsessive and so fragile I can't live without the constant attention of audiences and lovers.'

Tanthe smiled back. 'I know about Eander. He knows about me, judging by the filthy looks he was giving me. He looks a lot like Lynden, doesn't he, only blonder?'

'I hadn't noticed.'

'Liar. And you embraced me in front of him.'

'It's over, he's just my assistant. He knows that.'

'I don't think he does. He looked heartbroken to me.'

'You both know I am faithless, cruel and vacillating,' Saphaeyender said melodramatically.

'Not cruel. Just a bit hopeless,' she said gently. 'You're also one of the kindest people I've ever met.'

'H'm, well, I must have some redeeming virtues.'

'I'll never forget how good you were to me when I came back from Verdanholm after Falthorn had misused me.'

'I heard something about you finding the child . . . is that true?'

'Yes.'

'There is no chance, is there, that you were mistaken about his father? That you might have already been pregnant before you went to Verdanholm?'

She went rigid, her mouth opening. She thought about it carefully. Let go of her breath at last. 'No, Saph, I'm sorry.

I know what you're getting at but there is no way Mendyr could have been yours.'

'It was just a thought.'

'You seem so lonely. I wish I knew what to do.'

'I'm fine,' he said, smiling. 'Just tired and sad. Eldareth will never again walk in through that door to greet me. The woman I wanted to marry is leaving me.'

'Who?'

'You, you fool.'

On impulse, Tanthe kissed him. Saphaeyender nearly pulled away in surprise, then responded. His mouth, opening to hers, was still as sweet and warm as she remembered. And she touched the Aelyr side of her soul, the door to Jewelfire, and let that sparkling milky flow of energy pour through her and into him.

The kiss ended. His head fell back and he blinked at her. 'What did you do?'

'What does it feel like?'

'As if . . .' He pressed the fingers of one hand to his forehead, and laughed. 'As if you blew light and energy back into me. The black cloud's gone. Life could feel like fireflies and nectar, instead of crashing hammer blows. It was wonderful.'

They hugged, and she knew suddenly that it was all right. This felt friendly, comfortable. She couldn't have everything she'd dreamed of, but she could bear it. 'Now will you show some of your kindness to Eander? He obviously adores you. Stop treating him like a servant. Love him.'

She tried to slip off his knee, but he held her there. 'I'm afraid I'll lose him.'

'Take a risk.'

'But I'm losing you.'

'Give me something to remember you by. Do you have a copy of your children's poems I can have for Mendyr?'

He looked at her with narrowed eyes. 'Yes, but you'll have to bring it back.'

'Nice try,' she said softly. 'Give me a copy he can keep, and I will come back and visit you.'

'For that you can have the pick of my library.' He spread his arms and exclaimed, 'Why must these things be all or nothing? We can always be friends. We can always be lovers, if you want. I know you have to leave, but I lay an obligation upon you to return. My door will always be open to you, lamps burning to welcome you, ruby-red wines waiting for the caress of your lips and tongue . . .'

'You really are incorrigible.'

'I don't want you to be sad. You won't disappear, Tanthe. I'll make certain the world doesn't forget you. I've been writing about you.'

'Oh, you can still talk, too.'

'I'm not joking. You've been so special to me. Perhaps it's your Aelyr blood.'

The corner of her mouth twisted. 'More likely my sheer cussedness.'

'Oh, that will go into the plays and poems too.'

'Plays? Poems?' she exclaimed. 'Gods, Saph, what are you planning?'

'You'll just have to come back and see.'

The day that Helananthe conducted the healing ceremony was the first warm day of spring. The Estrae sun warmed the foothills of the Serpentines and illuminated a colourful mass of her subjects who had gathered from the Nine Realms. The atmosphere was sombre yet optimistic. They had suffered. Many had died. Yet now Aventuria had a future again.

She'd chosen to hold the ceremony not inside the Amber Citadel but here, on the ancient site called Silana's Mound. Here it was said the first ever Xauroma, the covenant between monarch and land, had been made. Helan and Mawrdreth, however, had already remade it in private.

They had come here last night, hurrying from the Citadel disguised in drab cloaks like young lovers running away.

Here on the damp grass they had thrown off their cloaks and made love like animals, fingers wet with dew, bodies slicked with moisture and grass stains and soil. The three moons smiled down at them from a vast pathway of stars as they caressed and laughed.

'I feel I've done nothing,' Mawrdreth said, while their love-making was still slow and languorous. 'I stood beside Branq'elin, stood beside you, but did nothing to help.'

'But that was everything,' Helan breathed. 'To know you were there, like a wall protecting me, a guardian stone; I could have done nothing without you there. Mawrdreth, every single person has contributed to our achieving peace. Not one of us could have prevailed without the others. You got us out of Vaurgroth's hands. You were and are everything to me. And Eldareth refusing to be King – it was as if he knew that he must make way for you. I'm grateful to him now, for his wisdom, his unselfishness.'

'As am I,' whispered Mawrdreth, his breath quickening, 'and I honour him, but now let us think only of each other . . .'

'We remake the covenant here, now,' Helan said fervently. 'There is time later for underground chambers, temples, thrones. This is what's real.'

And Mawrdreth was one with her, his carven bronze face and long green eyes shining with a joy she hadn't seen in them for years. His long umber hair rippled around her and he was all heat, muscle, arousal, an animal-god. 'Now our lives can begin,' he said.

'And everything will be shared fully between us. No inequality because I am born to the throne and you married to it. We are Queen and King . . .'

'Goddess and god . . .'

'Guardians of the heart of the flame. The power of earth flows through us both . . .'

They blazed together in green light, and fell through the darkness of earth to bathe in the red flame at its core. It was simpler and far more powerful than the tentative rituals she'd been through when she was first crowned. This was real. When the Eaters came, the *roth* of Earth had recoiled and left them in darkness, testing them. Now it leapt hungrily to embrace them. They writhed to the pulsing beat of the land, the throb of its deep red heart.

When Helan and Mawrdreth came out of the vision, they lay laughing and drained, as if washed up by the sea. She felt suddenly that Eldareth had given her this. He'd sacrificed himself to the earth to make this possible.

'Now we are one,' Helan said. They looked into each other's eyes.

'Part of each other,' said Mawrdreth. 'Now I understand.'

'I'm happy,' she said, beginning to laugh uncontrollably. 'It's only just started to sink in. We prevailed. Now we can make Aventuria everything she should be and our children will inherit this wonder. I am so happy.'

Returning to the Citadel later, they had slipped into the chilly underground chamber, and found the *xauroth* sphere alive again. It rotated lazily, like an otter turning in a stream. In colour it was palest green and as clear as water.

The public ceremony was rather more decorous, but Helan smiled to recall the previous night. Mawrdreth kept catching her eye and grinning. She could only imagine what her guests would think if they knew what their King and Queen had been doing on this very spot the previous night.

There were representatives from seven realms. Lord Pheilan from Sepheret, tribal leaders from Deirland, Jthery's grandmother from Mithrain. Lord Serpeth was there from Eisilion, making valiant attempts to seduce the tall blonde noblewoman who represented Noreya, Callais Jedraan from Azura Maroc. From Thanmandrathor, Branq'elin had come with Conawr and Dawn.

Bran and Mawrdreth had worked out between them that the moment the *ghelim* stopped attacking Tasqabad was the moment that Vaurgroth had died.

Helan herself represented Paranios. The only realm that had sent no-one was Torith Mir. She knew that her mother and brother were on their way home so she could only assume that the representative was travelling with them. It might even be Viceroy Drathnen himself, though she had no wish to deal with the man who had tried to execute Eldareth. They were late, however, and there was no word from them. She couldn't delay the ceremony forever. Meanwhile, an ambassador from Torith Mir – a slim, grey-eyed man – was to stand in until the official representative arrived.

Helan, Mawrdreth, Ariolne and trusted members of the Sun Chamber Council had talked for hours, days and weeks about this moment. And the visiting leaders knew what was going to happen, but no-one knew what their decisions would be.

The ceremony began with Ariolne and other priests and priestesses leading a chant, calling the blessing of Nuth, Nepheter and other deities upon them. Then Helananthe, standing on a green mound in the centre of the circle, raised the crown of nine jewels above her head.

'I give you a choice,' she said. 'The bond of the Nine Realms has brought prosperity and strength, but it has also occasioned dissent. Some of you have sought your independence. To become kingdoms in your own right and no longer be subjugated to the Crown of Paranios. Each jewel in the crown represents one of the Nine Realms. I give them to you now as a symbol of your choice of freedom. Dukes shall become kings, duchesses queens. Take the jewel as a symbol, not of power, but of love for your country and a covenant of the eternal bond of friendship between us.'

Helan was shaking from head to foot as she spoke. This was the most momentous decision she'd ever had to take. Yet she felt it was the right one.

The rulers of the other realms began to come forward, one by one, each to receive his or her jewel from her hands.

Branq'elin came last, and she looked for a long time into her brother's eyes as she took the topaz that symbolised Thanmandrathor.

Sombre emotion washed through Helan as she looked at them, no longer her subjects but her equals. The empty crown felt weightless in her hands. They stood looking solemnly back at her, a different emotion burning in each face.

Then, to her absolute disbelief, they began to come to her again, one at a time, each bowing as he or she raised the jewel and pressed it back into its place in the crown.

'Your majesty, you are the Xauroma,' they told her. 'We wish the realms to remain intact, and you our monarch.'

Helan couldn't refrain from weeping then. Pure, astonished happiness. 'I must have done something right,' she said sideways to Mawrdreth.

All but two. Branq'elin kept her jewel tight in her palm, her eyes calm and defiant upon her brother. So, Queen Branq'elin now. They'd given her the choice, so had to accept it with good grace. And the grey man from Torith Mir. He would have to wait until someone came from that realm with the authority to make a decision, but she doubted Drathnen would give it back. It might be for the best. Perhaps, granted freedom, that realm would be friendlier from now on.

'This is a joyful day, indeed,' Helan said. 'The shadow is lifted, thanks be to Nuth and Anuth and all the gods. They would wish us to celebrate!'

She threw the crown up in the air and caught it again. Wild cheers rang out. The musicians struck up a rousing song to close the ceremony.

'Look, we have company,' said Mawrdreth.

A party of riders was making its way up the hill towards the mound. The crowd parted to let them through. Helan caught Mawrdreth's arm and cried out with joy. There were riders from Torith Mir, a couple of Valahyr, and in their midst the beloved faces she hadn't seen for so long.

Princess Ghiseyma, her grey head held high, a beaming smile on her face. And her brother Venirryen, grown so tall and strong he looked closer to eighteen than fifteen.

'Mother! Veny!' Helan called out. She managed to retain some dignity befitting the occasion by staying where she was and not rushing down the hill towards them. At last, her family could come home and live in freedom. Priestesses of Nepheter began strewing spring flowers before them.

'Darling,' called her mother, waving.

Veny looked calmly at her as they came close. He appeared to have matured mentally as well as physically. She smiled at him. Not taking his eyes off her, he reached his hand inside his cloak and brought it out again.

The last thing Helan saw was the crossbow he was aiming at her heart, and the quick jerk and *thack* as he fired.

Chapter Twenty-six. Blood Sunset

'I didn't know. I didn't know,' said Princess Ghiseyma, over and over again. She sat on a couch in Helan's office chamber, not so much sobbing as fighting for her life against her own dry convulsive breaths.

Mawrdreth sat at the desk with his head in his hands. There were a handful of others in the room; his sister, Lord Derione, a couple of his aides. All of them stood around like manikins, dumb with shock.

'If I had known he planned this, I would never, ever have countenanced bringing him home,' Ghiseyma gasped. 'He never gave the smallest indication he would do this terrible thing. The idea must have eaten at him, and I didn't know. His own sister . . .'

'I disagree,' said Mawrdreth, rising to his feet. 'Helan knew full well he was jealous of her and imagined himself more fit to take the throne! He must have spoken of it to you!'

Ghiseyma flinched at loudness of his voice. 'Veny spoke often of his resentment that she was the older. He thought she had mismanaged the war and given the Sapphire Throne away. He was young, he couldn't see the complexities! But I never imagined in my wildest nightmares he would do this. To kill his own sister!'

She collapsed, struggling for breath. Mawrdreth signalled to the aides. 'Take the princess to a bed-chamber and get a physician.'

They obeyed, easing the princess to her feet and helping her out of the room.

'All of you, go!' Mawrdreth yelled at the rest. Stunned, they obeyed; all except Branq'elin. She knew he hadn't meant her. He sank back into his chair again, weighed down with a grief so immense he doubted it could ever emerge as tears. His voice was the dry skeleton of a leaf. 'How much more sorrow must this family bear?'

Branq'elin came behind him and placed her hands on his shoulders. 'You must be strong now,' she said. 'The moment you capture that vile little stoat, you must have him killed on the spot.'

In the shocked moment after Helan had fallen, Prince Venirryen had turned his horse, a fast Torish racer, and fled. Mawrdreth now had men all over the Serpentines hunting for him.

'He is her brother. I am only her husband. In theory, he is now King.'

No,' she said. The fire that had always been in her eyes had hardened to something glittering, fervent, implacable. 'In practice, he is despicable little murderer. You are the King, Mawrdreth, and you must remain so. Hold the Sapphire Throne now, or everything Helan achieved will be lost!'

He reached up and gripped her hand. He knew she was right. He must hold on, or Aventuria would explode in chaos. 'I never foresaw this,' he said. 'I thought we would have years. Beautiful children to take our place. This is so unfair!'

'Be strong. There are things more important than our own fires of grief, and we must cleave to them. Think. I am Queen of Thanmandrathor. You are King of Paranios – of Seven Realms, still. We still have each other, Mawr. Think of all we can achieve if we hold firm now!'

He let out a long, raw sigh. 'Some time ago, Helan and I talked about how much better it would be to die fulfilled than empty. She was so happy the day of the ceremony. How much worse it would have been if she'd died in battle, thinking that all was lost!'

'And she knew that you were beside her, of one heart and mind. She would want you to be King. Aventuria needs stability.'

'Yes.' He raised his head, dry-eyed and determined. 'I will be strong, Bran. I shall remain on the Sapphire Throne, whatever it takes, for Helan's sake.'

Later, when the immediate rawness of emotion had subsided and Mawrdreth could think calmly again, he summoned Rufryd, Tanthe and all those who'd helped win back the land, including High Priestess Ariolne and the rebel leader Kereyn. With them came Derione and other councillors and staff from whom he must build a new court.

'Helan was insistent that I be her equal and enter fully into the Xauroma. She wanted to instil in me that I am as much King as she was Queen,' Mawrdreth said.

'Are you suggesting she knew that this would happen?' said Ariolne.

'No, of course not. However, she clearly wanted me to be ready in case something *did* happen to her. She willed me to remain monarch in my own right, even though I am not the heir by blood. I need to know that I have your support.'

'The heir by blood has forfeited all claim with this heinous act,' Ariolne said. 'All of Paranios will support you, sire.'

'I know what Venirryen plans. Since Helan and I have no heirs – since he has robbed us of that chance! – he thinks himself the legitimate heir to the Sapphire Throne. He thinks to set himself against me, and take the Nine Realms under his control again – by violence, as he made only too obvious. I shall have him executed the moment he is captured. And he *will* be captured.'

'We want you, Mawrdreth,' Tanthe said, reaching across the desk to place her hand over his. 'Aventuria needs a monarch who is strong and benevolent, not a vicious, warped little boy. There isn't a man, woman or child in Aventuria who would support the prince after this.'

'Except Drathnen of Torith Mir,' said Mawrdreth, brooding. 'The last thing I want is another war.'

'Can I say something?' Tanthe asked, her face intent. 'Aventuria was peaceful for years. Its people were kind and gentle. But witness how quickly we were corrupted when Garnelys started all this. How easy people found it to become cruel and violent, turn their backs on the Earth, take up the twisted beliefs of Vaurgroth or the Order of Calathvahn.'

'It was a form of madness,' Derione put in, looking ashamed. 'Terrible.'

'We're not as strong as we should be,' Tanthe continued. 'We're still in danger. We're part of the way there, but still stumbling in the dark. Unless we give ourselves completely to Nuth, to the Earth, to the Xauroma and each other, this will happen again.'

'Well said,' Ariolne put in. 'Tanthe speaks the truth. It's not enough to pay lip service to goddesses and gods. We need to learn that reality itself must be held sacred. It is only knowledge and self-knowledge that will make Aventuria truly inviolable.'

Mawrdreth gazed at their passionate faces and felt hope firming inside him. 'That shall be our work, then. With your support, I am sworn to remain King and to maintain this hard-won peace. Everything that Helan planned for the future, I shall carry out. I shall not let all the good she won be lost! Make this pledge with me!'

And they all pledged him their support. Some were weeping by then; but Mawrdreth felt, at last, that he could go on. The golden *ethroth* of Helan would be watching over him.

'Some of you are going back to Sepheret, I understand,' he said, taking Rufryd, Tanthe and Ysomir aside.

'If it's all right,' Tanthe said. 'We'll stay if you need us.'

'I shall manage perfectly well,' he said with a grim smile. 'But I hope you will return one day. Helan intended to give you a gift before you left. Now it has fallen to me to give you this myself.'

He presented Tanthe with a scroll of thick parchment, heavy with gold-leaf script and seals. 'What is it?'

'Deeds to a very beautiful estate on the border of Mithrain and Azura Maroc, for you and your descendants. Titles to honour your role in the war. There will also be an award of ten thousand ralds each. From now on you are Lady Tanthe, Lord Rufryd, Lady Ysomir of Celestios.'

'Lord Rufryd of Celestios,' Rufe said later, grinning. 'Give me a break.' They were in their chamber, making ready to leave as soon as the funeral was over.

'Do you think there's a palace there?' said Tanthe. 'Shall we build one?'

'Yeah, right. The most ambitious thing I've ever built is a goat pen.'

'We wouldn't have to do it ourselves, idiot. We've so much money we could tile the floor with it.'

They pulled faces at each other, became sombre again. The titles and ralds weren't real, didn't matter. 'I'd rather we still had Helan,' he said.

'By the way, did you . . . speak to . . . Branq'elin?'

'Briefly.' He flinched. 'It was awkward. She was polite enough but it was plain she didn't want anything to do with me. History.'

She took his hand. 'I'm sorry, Rufe. Were you . . . I mean, do you still have feelings for her?'

'Are you jealous?' he said, looking hard into her eyes.

'Yes, I was so jealous when I saw her that I wanted to kill her. How unworthy is that, after all she's been through? I don't hate her, I like her . . . It was just the thought of what you shared with her. Sorry, I know I'm a monster.'

'Not as monstrous as I've been, sometimes.' He slid warm, hard arms round her. 'I won't forget her, any more than you'll forget Saphaeyender or Auriel. But it's long over. Ashes. You're the only one I've ever really wanted, and you know it.'

She exhaled her relief. 'How was Dawn?'

Rufryd's face darkened. 'All right. Surviving without Mirias, poor bastard. She's strong. At least she and Bran have each other . . .'

'Oh?'

'I always knew there was something going on between them,' he said wryly. 'So, Dawn tells me they have each other . . . and Con.'

Her eyebrows rose. 'The dark-haired lad? The three of them—?'

'I really didn't like to ask too many questions.' Rufryd chuckled. 'Still, we can go home safe in the knowledge that life at Tasqabad Hall must be very interesting indeed.'

Auriel found their *anaroth* path, but there was still travelling to be done. First, two days' walk along the Meiondras Road and a diversion through the woods that lay south of it, heading for a long-untouched site nestled amid ancient trees.

Travelling through interstices was not necessarily an easy option, Tanthe thought, as she pulled her cloak free of long, spiny thorns. They were inaccessible. They must be long disused for a reason. And the thought of stepping through any kind of portal was about as comfortable as the idea of stepping off a cliff.

Her companions – Rufryd and Ysomir, Auriel and Mendyr, Fiomir and Talthaliorn – were subdued by what had happened in Parione. Tanthe still couldn't believe it. To have had to attend such a funeral . . . She'd hoped this journey would be cheerful, but there were too many hooks in her soul, pulling her this way and that.

Relations between her and Mendyr had grown more difficult, if anything. Maybe he sensed she was in awe of him and it made him uncomfortable. Perhaps he would never forget she'd pressed a knife to his throat. The memory of fear was stronger than his rational knowledge that she'd been trying to protect him. Or it might be that he simply didn't like her; there was never any guarantee that children would like their parents, or parents their children. Whatever, it was always Auriel, Fiomir or Ysomir he turned to first.

Ysomir had expressed concern, asking Tanthe if she wasn't hurt.

'It would be childish of me to be hurt,' she'd answered. 'I'm here for him if he needs me, but I can't make him love me. I don't possess him. He's a separate being who just happened to pass through me on his way to earth.'

Secretly, she was wounded, of course; couldn't help it. Yet what she'd told Ysomir, she felt to be true.

Something else Tanthe was learning about Talthaliorn and Fiomir. They were obsessed with one another. It was as if they were wrapped up in a fiery, almost mythological love affair that was wonderful for them, but left little room for others, not even Tanthe and Auriel.

That must have made it easier for them to abandon us, Tanthe thought. They love us, I know, but not as they love each other . . .

She was learning things that she would rather never have known. Because Rufryd was there – warm and down-to-earth, making sardonic jokes, always touching and kissing her – she could bear it. For Auriel, though, it was hard. He had hoped for so much more than just a brief caress from Fiomir as she passed him, again, on her way to Talthaliorn's side.

'Can I sit beside you?'

Ysomir looked up and found Auriel standing over her. They'd stopped to rest and eat in a green glade, deep in the fold of an old, ferny arkh-wood forest. A waterfall trickled down a rock wall that was green with moss. The pool below was obsidian.

'If you like,' she said reluctantly. She moved up to make room on the small grassy bank on which she'd perched herself.

Despite all the time they'd spent in the Amber Citadel,

they'd barely spoken. Everything about him made her uneasy. The fact that he was Aelyr, knowing what had happened between him and Tanthe, his own shyness, the way he stared at her sometimes but was so easily put off daring to speak to her. His Aelyr radiance, palest gold and dark autumn red . . .

The long auburn ripples of his hair half-hid his face, and he looked down at the waterfall pool as he spoke. 'I know you don't like me and I don't blame you,' he said, sounding nervous.

Ysomir frowned. 'I don't dislike you. I don't know you.' Usually her abruptness would have been enough to make him retreat, relieving her of his paralysing scrutiny. This time, though, he persisted.

'Tanthe must have told you what happened in Verdanholm. The first part, I mean, where the Valahyr trapped her, and I . . . Falthorn made me . . . no, it's not fair to say he *made* me, but . . .'

'Auriel, don't tell me about it!' she said, recoiling. 'Yes, of course she told me. She was distraught, scared and hurt. She said she hated you at the time.'

He nodded, looking unhappy. She felt compelled to add, 'Since then she's told me that it's all sorted out. Obviously you wouldn't still be friends otherwise.'

'Oh. Good. I wasn't sure if you understood that.'

'Why?'

'Because you . . . you avoid me and ignore me as if you still think I'm some demon who hurt your sister.'

Ysomir laughed softly. 'You don't look like a demon, Auriel. I'm not avoiding you. I just don't see what we have to talk about. You seem scared of me. The first time we met I was a right sight, dressed in rags with my hair all grey with chalk and ash on my face; I must have frightened you half to death.'

'It washed off.' He nearly smiled. 'I am scared of you, but not for that reason.'

'Why, then?'

He hesitated, colouring. 'You're a *roth*-mage . . .'

'No, I'm not,' she said firmly. 'I'm not. Something strange happened to me in Parione, but it's gone now. I'm only human. I didn't mean to be unfriendly, I just couldn't . . .' She stopped and swallowed hard. She didn't know how to begin explaining that she was cold because she'd grown so used to being alone; that, after losing Lynden and killing Garnelys, she'd forgotten how to be warm; that when she'd made a first tentative effort, with Eander, she'd met painful rejection. It would be a long time before she was ready to take that risk again, and not with Auriel. He was the last person she would encourage to kick her when she was down.

'Have *you* forgiven me, though?' he asked. 'For what happened with Tanthe?'

'Is that what this conversation is about?' she said flatly, annoyed. 'Salving your conscience?'

'No.' He drew away from her, looking flustered and more nervous than ever. 'I was just trying to . . . make friends.'

'Well, don't!' she cried.

'I know what you must think of me. I can't change what happened. Sorry.' He jumped abruptly, gracefully to his feet. She tried not to notice the lean strength of his legs in forest-green breeches or the silkiness of his bare forearms as he rose. 'We should go now.'

'Where?'

He pointed to the cleft in the mossy rock, behind the ribbon of falling water. 'The interstice is there. It's better to eat and rest before going through. Saves feeling so light-headed on the other side.'

Saphaeyender felt sad after Tanthe had left Parione, much as he fought the feeling. He felt empty, restless. He'd imagined the companionship of a wife, perhaps a child or two, but it wasn't to be. He doubted now that it ever would be, since he couldn't imagine another woman to take Tanthe's place. And maybe she was right. Since he would never be able to give his whole self to one person, it wasn't his destiny.

He wandered the avenues of Parione, waving at people he knew but avoiding conversation. The day was exquisite, softly golden. The air smelled dusty, rich with the scent of broken stone and new vegetation. So many friends gone – Eldareth, Saliole, Lynden, Helan – but with Mawrdreth as King there was still, after all, hope. If I'm not careful, he thought, I might even let myself fall in love with Eander.

He was walking up Theatre Hill towards the ruins of the tower. His heart lifted and he quickened his pace. It was a scene of devastation, tumbled rocks everywhere, broken trees poking from the ruins. Yet he was filled with exultation.

A soldier in a blue tunic was standing looking at the ruins with his hands planted on his hips. Seeing Saphaeyender, he came towards him.

'Don't go any further, sir. It's dangerous.'

'Not any more,' Saphaeyender replied. He walked straight past the soldier and began to climb up the huge blocks of broken stone until he reached the very summit of the hill.

There he stood, gasping for breath, his heart overflowing with hope.

'I am going to rebuild the royal theatre,' he said out loud. 'However long it takes, however much it costs, if it's the last thing I do – my theatre will stand here again!'

Opening his arms and throwing back his head, Saphaeyender shouted his exultation to the sky.

They stepped out of the interstice into another forest. This one was different, Ysomir noticed at once. The trees were taller, darker, more widely spaced. The air was cool and fresh.

'This feels like Sepheret to me,' said Rufryd.

'It is,' said Auriel, turning the *anametris* sphere until

the wavering green column of light from which they'd emerged had vanished. 'Don't you trust me?'

'You're a bloody Aelyr, of course I don't trust you,' said Rufryd, giving him a friendly slap on the back. 'We may still have a few days' walk but I think we're on the right side of the Torland Moors, thank Breyid.'

They walked on. Instead of the ferns, thorns and exotic flowers of Paranios, the vegetation here was simpler; birch and hawthorn, the familiar plants and scents and landscapes that Ysomir had missed for so long. No sign of *graukhim* damage. Out of the forest it was warmer; the sun was shining. Presently it bathed the early evening in a rosy aureate haze.

They decided to make camp in an oak-wood, on the bank of a small, still lake. The waters glowed blood-red and golden from the sky, dappled with reflections of trees. After they'd eaten, Ysomir moved well away from the others and sat on the edge of the shore, gazing across the serene glassy surface. She was so overwhelmed to be going home that she was close to weeping. She didn't want the others to see her break down.

When Auriel followed her and sat a couple of feet away from her, she cursed. Now she'd have to control herself.

'I've had glimpses of Sepheret before,' he said, 'when I was trying to reach Tanthe.'

'I saw you once,' she said, trying to swallow away the ache in her throat. 'We both thought how gorgeous you were.'

The words were out before she could stop herself. She put her chin on her drawn-up knees. She was going to cry, there was nothing she could do about it.

'Ysomir?' he said. 'Are you all right?'

Now she couldn't speak. Warily he came closer and knelt beside her, watching her. Then, hesitantly, he put his arms round her. 'What's wrong?'

She shook with quiet sobs. She didn't push him away, but shrank into herself under the weight of his arms. It was the last thing she wanted, to be touched by him in pity. 'Please tell me,' he said. He must have felt her flinching; he let go, and sat beside her instead.

'I've been alone for so long,' Ysomir said, pushing back her hair. 'It's all I know now. Even in Riverwynde, I felt alone, because I was different to everyone else, saw things they didn't. I feel my natural state is to be on my own. I miss Lynden, I miss seeing him and touching him, but I've learned to live with it. That's the only reason I wasn't friendly to you, Auriel. I've had to accept being alone. I don't want pity, it's just a fact.'

'Then my life has been the same as yours,' he said. He was looking at her, his dark eyes fixed on hers. 'I've always been alone, even with my Valahyr family. Never more alone than with them. I know what it's like in the *ezht*, the bleakest place that could possibly exist. That was always Falthorn's punishment, the threat of the *ezht*. I had no-one to help me, until Tanthe came.'

Her hand slid into his; she hardly noticed it happening, but it felt warm, natural. 'Do you love Tanthe?' she asked.

'Yes, always, but we can't be together. It's not meant to be.'

'Are you sorry?'

'Yes and no. I love her as my sister. I'm not sorry we were lovers but it was bound to end. I know that. But I feel . . . desolate, dead inside.' He sounded anguished. She'd never dreamed that he might feel the same as her. 'Falthorn used me, and left me ruined for ever finding someone who can love me.'

She was stunned. 'Why do you think no-one can love you?'

'Because of what Falthorn made me. Weak, scared . . . All I trust in myself is the gift for finding *rothanamir*. People unnerve me. You terrify me. I shouldn't be talking to you like this, Ymmi. I know you could never feel anything for me; you, least of all, being Tanthe's sister.'

Her mouth had gone dry. 'Why do you think I couldn't?'

'You're strong. You see people for what they are.'

'Oh, you don't think I've ever felt helpless, like you did? Garnelys used me, then Helan used me, then Zhoaah, Vaurgroth, Ariolne. I dealt with it by pretending nothing mattered. I discovered that you must learn to what extent you're *allowing* it to happen. Only then can you decide whether or not you want it to stop.'

Auriel's eyes widened, froze. 'Perhaps I didn't want it to stop,' he whispered.

'Because Falthorn was all you had.' She touched his shoulder. 'It wasn't your fault. You *have* stopped it. You're learning to be strong, Auriel. Look how much you've done to help everyone! Falthorn knows he can never control you again.'

'You don't think I'm completely beyond hope, then?'

She let out a short sigh. 'You know you're not. I don't know why you want my approval.'

His lovely eyes glittered. Then he dropped his gaze again, under long dark eyelashes. 'I'm being idiotic,' he said softly. 'I can't do this, Ymmi. It's too painful.'

'Can't do what?' He didn't answer. Tears stung her eyes. They were both strung rigid with tension.

Eventually she made herself say what she was thinking, even though she knew she was going to regret it. 'I wish I looked as beautiful to you as you do to me,' she said. 'I am trying very, very hard not to notice how attractive you are. I've been trying all winter. I've been so envious of Tanthe . . . Don't you realise I'm scared of you, too? You completely unravel me and don't even know it, and it is killing me to know you would recoil in embarrassment if I tried to kiss you.'

'*Oh*,' said Auriel.

He didn't move. There was a long silence. 'I shouldn't have said that,' she murmured.

'No – you should, it's just – I can't believe it. We're both sitting here thinking the same thing. I don't know what gave you the idea I don't think you're beautiful. Why do you think I was looking at you all the time? I didn't mean it to upset you, but I couldn't take my eyes off you.'

'Oh.' The ground jolted under her.

'I thought *you*'d be horrified if I tried to kiss you. I thought you hated me,' He dragged his hand through his hair. 'I am really, completely hopeless at this. Unless someone throws themself at me, I don't know what to do.'

A sound between sob and laugh escaped from her throat. 'I'm not as forward as my sister, but I think we both have a perfectly good idea of what to do. Unless the Aelyr do it very differently to humans?'

'We don't.' He smiled. 'We don't.' They were touching now, hips and thighs and shoulders pressed together. Their hands entwined more deeply, fingers laced. 'Should we, though?'

'A kiss probably won't hurt,' she said. His long fingers traced her cheek, slid into her tawny hair. Ysomir raised her face to his. Auriel's expression was a reflection of hers; hopeful, rapt with desire, nervous.

'Do you think that we must both go on being alone?' he asked softly.

'I don't see why.' Her heart was beating so hard it shook her whole body.

A subtle tilt of their heads and their mouths touched. Auriel kissed her with amazing gentleness and Ysomir, who had not kissed anyone for so long, was suffused with a fire of relief and amazement. It was like sucking nectar from a flower after starving in the desert for years. The more she tasted him, the more she wanted.

Then she knew why he'd said, 'Should we?' They both knew it was not going to stop at a kiss. That was just a flame touched to a torrent of oil. They pulled each other down on the grass and made love in a tangle of half-shed clothes, silken hair brushing each other's skin. Pleasure intense as pain, a slow arc of release as crimson and wordless as the sunset melting into the lake . . . then holding each other, gasping, laughing.

'But what are they doing?' said a small voice on the bank above them.

Ysomir looked up, just in time to see Rufryd grabbing Mendyr and sweeping him in a half-circle to face back the way he came.

'Being very, very friendly,' said Rufryd. 'Go back to your grandma.'

Ysomir felt herself turning crimson, but Rufryd only grinned and put his hands on his hips. 'Spirit of Anthar got into you at last?' he called cheerfully. 'Gods, it took you long enough.'

Auriel hardly even noticed them. The world was glazed with a shimmering veil the colour of Ysomir's hair. The weight of her breasts rested softly against his fingers. He was sightless with happiness; all he could see were her willow-green and golden eyes upon his, as fervent as they had once been cold. Her breathless amazed smile.

'Just a kiss?' she said. 'You know Rufryd's going to tell everyone, don't you?'

'I don't care.' He kissed her again, trembling. 'My life has just begun.'

Tears filled her eyes. 'And mine,' she said, burying her hands in his hair. 'And mine.'

By the time they reached Riverwynde, the whole party knew about Ysomir and Auriel.

To her own surprise, Tanthe experienced only the faintest reflex of possessiveness when Rufryd told her. Then it was gone, replaced by pure relief and joy.

'Are you sure you're all right about this?' Rufryd asked worriedly. 'I know you still have feelings for him, there's no point in denying it.'

'Rufe, I am fine. He's my brother. I thought he would go off and find some Fhelethyr maiden; that would have been hard. I would rather a thousand times over he was with Ymmi. I knew he liked her months ago; she only cold-shouldered him because she didn't want to get hurt. You feel like banging their heads together sometimes, don't you? Anyway, are you all right about it? You know . . . Lynden.'

'Well, if she'd dumped Lynden to go off with him, I wouldn't have been, but she didn't, so . . . yeah, it's just too adorable for words.'

She gave him a gentle punch. 'Don't you dare give them a hard time.'

'Come on, they've got to be teased.'

'Well . . . just a little. They've both been so lonely and miserable, the gods know they deserve to be happy at last.'

What Talthaliorn and Fiomir made of it was hard to say. They said little, seemed mildly pleased. The last thing Tanthe wanted was for them to disapprove of their son and daughter falling in love with humans; she only wished they would seem more interested.

A bend in the path revealed the village, lying peaceful amid green meadows with pearly mountains rising up in the background, as it seemed to have done for all time. Tanthe's heart bounded.

'The Bhahdradomen didn't reach Riverwynde,' she said.

'You know why,' said Rufryd. There was no pride in his voice, only awe – tempered by horror at what might have happened if they'd failed. 'We stopped them.'

'Another year or two, they would have been here.'

'D'you think they know? The villagers, I mean?'

Tanthe didn't answer. Her heart was jumping to an anxious beat. Who was still alive, whom would she find sick or dead? She broke into a run along the path that wound between the cottages, with Ysomir close behind her.

The door to their parents' cottage stood open, as it always had. Smoke skeined out of the chimney. A boy of about twelve or thirteen stood stripped to the waist, chopping logs on the grass outside. Tanthe realised it was their brother, Feryn.

'Oi, you!' she yelled. 'Have you got a licence for that axe?'

He looked round indignantly, wiping sweat off his brow. His face lengthened. He flung the axe aside and cried, 'Mum, come out here!'

Aynie appeared from the kitchen, looking just as Tanthe remembered, her amber hair floating untidily over her shoulders. Her face was more sombre than before and she was thinner; otherwise the same. Seeing her daughters, she froze. Then she flung her arms wide with a yell of joy and rushed into their embrace.

Ysomir seemed to be doing the crying for all of them. Tanthe couldn't stop laughing. They danced like children. She saw her father, Eodwyth, appear in the doorway and stand like a lean shadow, watching. He'd never been demonstrative but the smile that lit his face told Tanthe everything.

'I dreamed, hoped, made offerings, everything,' Aynie said, pressing her hands to her apple-cheeked face, catching their hands again. 'We never gave up hope you'd come home. Never.'

'I never gave up hope either,' said Ysomir, tears running down her face.

'I kept looking in the *silvenroth* mirror but you were never there. We were so worried.'

Ysomir groaned. 'My fault. I left mine . . . somewhere. Even now it's still there. Stupid of me.'

'Doesn't matter now,' said Aynie. 'What happened? We want to know everything.'

Tanthe and Ysomir looked at each other. Ymmi laughed. 'Have you got from now until Darkeve, Mum?'

'Ymmi married King Garnelys and wrote a book about it,' said Tanthe, grinning. 'I gave birth to a magical child. We defeated the Bhahdradomen and all got made Lords and Ladies for our heroism.'

'Yeah, right,' said Feryn. 'Tell us what *really* happened.'

Eodwyth and Feryn came to hug them, in their awkward but affectionate way. A crowd was gathering. The village always turned out to stare at newcomers; nothing had changed. 'We've brought some people to see you,' Tanthe said. 'Rufryd's with us.'

'But not Lynden?' said Aynie, her smile vanishing. Ysomir shook her head, fresh tears falling from her eyes. Eodwyth thrust a handkerchief into her hand, put his arm round her. Now they were all crying. Aynie went on, 'When you spoke to me through that mirror, I was never entirely sure whether I dreamed it or not.'

'You didn't, Mum,' said Tanthe. 'So no, you didn't dream telling me about my Aelyr parents, either.'

'Oh.' Aynie coloured.

'In fact, they're, er . . .'

Rufryd and the rest of the party came into view on the curving path. He was in front, Auriel and Mendyr just behind, then Fiomir and Talthaliorn. They looked, despite weariness from their long walk, magnificent. Twilight cloaks billowing.

Aynie's hand flew to her mouth. Even Eodwyth looked stunned. Oh, Goddess, Tanthe thought, they're embarrassed! What have I done?

'This is Auriel, my, er, my Aelyr brother, and this is Mendyr, the magical child I just mentioned,' Tanthe informed her startled family. 'And, er, I think you already know Talthaliorn and Fiomir . . .'

'Aynie, Eodwyth,' Fiomir said as she reached them. Her tone was warm. 'It is wonderful to see you again. We wish to thank you for taking such loving care of Tanthe. We can't thank you enough.'

'She was never any trouble,' croaked Eodwyth, at which Rufryd gave a derisive laugh.

'Oh, Rufryd,' Aynie said, 'your father will want to see you.' She frowned. 'I told him about Lynden; said I couldn't be absolutely sure it was true, but I thought he should know . . . It might have been better if I hadn't, though. He's been ill ever since.'

Rufryd's smile vanished. He sighed. 'Is he still—?' He tilted his head towards Riverwynde's only large house.

'He still lives there, yes, but he's not village leader now. That ended the day he let Garnelys's soldiers take Ymmi. Helwyn let him stay when she took over.'

'Right,' said Rufyrd. He looked grey. 'I'd better go and see him then. See you later.'

'I'll come with you,' Tanthe said. 'I want to see Helwyn and Osforn.'

'Osforn . . .' Aynie said, shaking her head. Tanthe took the news in. So her grandfather was dead, her grandmother still alive. Illusion to think Riverwynde hadn't changed; there would be more reunions, more shocks, before the day was over.

'Well, come in then,' Eodwyth said to the others, prosaic as ever. 'Ale all right for everyone?'

Later, as evening bathed the village in slanting light, Tanthe watched her four parents sitting together in the herb garden beside the cottage. The boys were in Feryn's room; Feryn seemed to have taken Mendyr under his wing, and the younger boy had taken an instant liking to him, which pleased Tanthe. Ysomir and Auriel had gone for a supposed walk. Now Tanthe was alone with her two mothers and her two fathers, feeling ridiculously uncomfortable. As she edged away towards the garden wall, she turned back and saw them, caught like a tableau in the liquid light.

Aynie petite, sun-tanned and smiling, Eodwyth tall and wiry, handsome in a weather-worn way, his dark hair now sprinkled with silver. Humans, warm and earthy and imperfect. And the Aelyr, like mysterious figures out of myths, with their sculpted faces and haunted eyes. The dark-red curve of Fiomir's hair against her sapphire garments, Talthaliorn, a statue of alabaster and midnight silk. They were so different, so impossibly different.

Tanthe tried not to, but she couldn't help remembering, again and again, Aynie's description of how she'd been conceived. *'We all made love. All four of us. But this was sorcery as well as sex. Somehow Talthaliorn put his essence into me and into Eodwyth, and Fiomir put hers into Eodwyth and me. We all loved each other. So really, you were part of all four of us. I don't know how it worked, love. It was a magical force that created you. Don't be angry with us.'*

I'm not angry, Mum, she thought. Just . . . she sighed to herself. Just horrendously embarrassed. Whatever was passing between them now, she didn't want to know.

'Hello,' said Rufryd from the other side of the garden wall. 'Fancy a walk?'

She hopped up on the wall, swung her legs over and jumped down beside him. 'Love to. How did it go with your father?'

He looked faintly bemused. 'It was fine, actually. I thought I was going to meet this snarling, raging, grief-stricken man who would rise from his sickbed to deliver every curse under the three moons at me, then drive me from his room with a cane. But it wasn't like that at all. He was in a chair, nodding by fire. When I went in, he hugged me. He's never done that before.' Rufryd rubbed the heel of his hand across his eyes. 'I said I was sorry about Lynden and he said it was all his fault, and he was just glad I was still alive. We both cried. It was all a bit awkward, really. But it was all right.'

She squeezed his arm. 'I told you he loved you really.'

'He's pretty ill, Tan. Helwyn doesn't think he'll last much longer. She thinks he was just waiting for me to come back.'

'So you could both say what needed to be said.'

'Something like that. Anyway.' He shook back his hair. 'They've got a ton of wine in the storeroom, said we could help ourselves . . . What do you think?'

'Oh, yes. Anything that will stop me imagining Talthaliorn putting his essence into my father.'

'I beg your pardon?'

'Nothing. We could go up into the woods. As long as we don't trip over Ymmi and Auriel up there.'

'Are you trying to get me drunk and have your wicked way with me?' he said, turning and kissing her. One hand slid gently to her breast.

'Yes.' She pressed harder against him, breathing his warmth and the arousing scent of his body. 'Goddess, it's good to be home,' she sighed. 'But what are going to do with ourselves here, Rufe?'

'I want us to have so much sex we can't walk.' His breath was hot on her neck. 'I want to wander round all the places we used to be nasty to each other and kiss each other instead. I want us to lie in the meadows with a flagon of wine and get very, very drunk under the stars. How about you?'

'I want to make love to you in my little forest grove where I used to make love to myself,' said Tanthe, pressing a fingertip to his chest.

'I'll get the wine,' said Rufryd.

And it was there, in Tanthe's forest grove, that Rufryd shared her visions for the first time. Bodies pressed together, spiced with heat and moisture, limbs entwined, joined, soaring, falling. He rose through the rhythm of his own thundering heartbeat and hung there in the most extreme ecstasy he'd ever known. Saw the living energy that ran through everything, vibrating in the smallest crystal, roaring in the great infernos of the sun and stars. Running in glittering lines through water, through boiling red rivers of lava. He swam through the milky sea that birthed the Aelyr. Saw the glowing forms of the Wrothryr, and knew that it pulsed through all of them, Wrothryr, Aelyr, human . . . Bhahdradomen. All swam out of the same sentient ocean of *roth* and flowed back into it. It took a million forms but all were ultimately one. Jewelfire. He felt the green *xauroth* flame of the earth, grass and leaves like jewel-flakes against his skin. And curving down in the arc to where it had begun; the pulsing ruby energy of Tanthe surrounding him, loving him. Her body, her being. Her flushed face and rosy mouth and her eyes shining with the secrets they shared ... Sacred.

Tanthe knew, almost as soon as Talthaliorn and Fiomir entered Riverwynde, that they would not stay. They seemed so out of place there. They were restless, their eyes on other landscapes that only they could see. A few days after they'd arrived, Fiomir came to Tanthe and slipped a hand through her arm.

'Tal and I must leave soon,' she said gently. 'Verdanholm calls us, and the realms of the Fhelethyr, which we haven't seen for so long. Don't be sad. We will meet again.'

'It's all right,' Tanthe said, wiping her eyes. 'I don't know why I'm crying. I hardly know you.'

'We owe everything to you. You saved us, you gave us back our lives and freedom, you and Auriel; but we are wanderers.'

'Fiomir,' Tanthe said, sounding calmer than she felt. 'Mother. I know that you and Talthaliorn love each other more than anything else, even us. It's all right. You more than compensated by giving me a perfectly good set of real parents.'

The remark wasn't meant to be barbed, but it was. Fiomir lowered her gaze and nodded. 'You're right. Perhaps Tal and I should never have had children, but we had no choice. Your soul and Auriel's demanded to come into flesh through us and here you are, beautiful and whole and free. We gave you all that we could.'

Tanthe looked into Fiomir's warm yet alien eyes, and knew she spoke the truth. It might not be a comfortable or human truth, but it was an Aelyr one.

'How will you . . . ?'

'There are ways up in the forests there, old Fhelethyr

ways. We'll find one. Don't come to say goodbye. We're saying it now.'

By evening, Talthaliorn and Fiomir had vanished. Tanthe didn't even know whether they'd said a proper farewell to Auriel or Mendyr; they simply slipped away. All evening, she and Aynie were restless, and everyone else in the household seemed to have vanished too. Eodwyth said he was off to see Helwyn; Feryn and Mendyr were in bed; yet the atmosphere was eerie, electric.

Tanthe and Aynie looked at each other. The next they knew, they were tramping across the meadows, heading up to the woodlands by the light of Rose Moon. And there they witnessed the wonder that Aynie had described, a wonder that Tanthe had once been a part of, in a different place: a procession of Fhelethyr.

Faerie figures moving within a silvery, sparkling glow. Grey as dew, glittering with elusive rainbows, soundless but for the faintest strain of music that might have played only in human imagination. Tanthe had seen beneath those grey robes to the vibrant hues of auburn, bronze and chrysocolla beneath. And knowing she was linked to this *eretru* only heightened the awe she felt.

She couldn't see Fiomir and Talthaliorn among the others. They were all veiled. She sensed they were there, but even if she'd recognised them, she would only have watched, and said nothing.

So easily she could leave Aynie and blend in among them . . . she could hear the music vividly now, clear and plangent, and she only had to open the door to her Aelyr nature to be swallowed by the rapturous energy of Jewelfire . . .

She yearned on the spot as Vetru had, watching Naghrur go towards the tower. Yet she stayed. The procession was gone, leaving a slow-fading silvery light.

'Mum,' said Tanthe, 'What did you and Dad talk about with Fiomir and Tal?'

'Oh, nothing.'

'Come on.'

'Really,' Aynie laughed sadly. 'To be honest with you, it wasn't a magical reunion. It was all a bit stilted. Embarrassing, even. Eodwyth made it plain he didn't want any rekindling of what happened before, and neither did they. They just wanted to thank us for looking after you so wonderfully.'

Tanthe laughed. 'And that's all?'

'They seemed to feel quite awkward about it.'

'And now they've buggered off again. Mum, don't you feel as if they used you?'

'I know they used us.'

'Aren't you annoyed?'

Aynie laughed softly and hugged her daughter. 'I wouldn't have missed it for the world. Any of it.'

They were turning for home when they heard a cry, and footfalls on the forest path. Ysomir came rushing towards them and threw herself on Tanthe's neck.

'Auriel!' she cried. 'Auriel went with them!'

Ysomir was sobbing bitterly. She was usually so controlled – too controlled – and when she broke it was a flash-flood. Tanthe and Aynie held her, Tanthe thinking, I can't believe he'd do this to her, but I should have known. Feckless, the bloody Fhelethyr; tricksters, the lot of them. Maybe it was an act all along, little-boy-lost with the long fluttering eyelashes . . .

'Ymmi, love, don't.'

'I can't bear it. Not after Lynden. Not again.'

'Shh. I nearly went with them too. Perhaps he just got drawn in and didn't mean to . . .' Oh what's the use? Tanthe thought, hugging Ysomir's slim, rounded form with all the strength she had. How the hell are we going to get her over this?

Aynie tugged Tanthe's sleeve. Over Ysomir's shoulder, Tanthe saw Auriel walking towards them. He was barefoot on the leafy path, his hair flowing; a vision.

'Er, Ymmi. You've completely soaked my shirt for nothing.'

Her sister pulled away, wiping her eyes, and turned round. 'You bastard!' she cried, rushing at Auriel. 'I thought you'd gone with them!'

Auriel looked stunned. 'No, I was just saying goodbye to my mother and father.'

'You vanished! I couldn't find you anywhere!'

He put his arms round her. 'I'm sorry, I didn't realise. I went a little way with them, that's all. It was hard to let them go. But I would never leave you and Mendyr.'

And that was it. Ysomir, Auriel – and Mendyr.

'What are we going to do?' said Tanthe. She and Rufe sat on the wall of the herb garden, kicking their heels. They had been home not long after Estrae and now it was past Midsummer. Arthryn had passed away peacefully in Rufryd's arms, ten days after they'd got home.

'What do you want to do?' said Rufryd.

'It's been lovely staying here,' she said hesitantly. 'A wonderful, healing rest. But . . .'

'It's too quiet,' he said, meeting her eyes. 'Nothing ever happens. We're bored.'

She let her breath go in a rush. 'Exactly.'

'So come on, Tan, name ninety-three things that would make you feel guilty about leaving.'

'Just the one.'

'I know.' He put his arm round her and she leaned in to him. 'Mendyr will be fine here. There couldn't be anywhere better for him. He's got Ymmi and Auriel, your parents, Feryn, the whole village to look after him. And when he needs help understanding these powers he's got, Auriel will help him find it.'

'I know that,' she said painfully. 'He wants to be with Auriel, and Auriel's his father, so that's fine. He loves Ymmi. He's made it perfectly plain who he wants to be with and I know he'll be like a foal in clover with them, but . . . He's my son. Why couldn't we love each other, Rufe?'

'I don't know, love.'

'I don't think I should have any more children. I'm complete rubbish as a mother.'

'But standard for an Aelyr parent?' Rufryd said, raising his eyebrows.

'I'm sure they're not all the same. Anyway.'

Rufryd held her face between his hands. 'Guilt is a human emotion. You are Aelyr. You and I will follow our hearts, like the Fhelethyr. Shall we go and inspect our estates at Celestios?'

She threw her head back. 'And if that's too, too boring, we shall go on to Lapiszul and taste the delights of the Turquoise Court of Lord Sunstone.'

'We can go anywhere we damn well please,' said Rufryd, grinning.

Saying goodbye was difficult, but not as hard as Tanthe had feared. She'd hardly begun to tap into her Aelyr nature; there was no reason why she couldn't learn to find and open portals, as Auriel could, in time. There was so much to learn.

'That's why we're leaving,' she told her family. 'We will come back, though I can't say when. We may come back to tell you we've built a magnificent mansion in Celestios and you can all come and live in it.' They smiled at her indulgently. 'And don't think I'm joking.'

It was hardest saying goodbye to Mendyr. If he'd burst into tears and begged her to stay, she would have relented immediately, but he didn't. He was so formal, yet smiled sweetly at her as if she were a favourite aunt. That was progress. She took the amber disc from around her neck and placed the cord over his head.

'You'd better have this,' she said. 'It's the Eye of the Sun. You probably know more about it than I do. You're going to need all the inner wisdom you can find.'

He nodded and said, 'Thank you, Tanthe.'

She kissed his cheek. She managed not to cry.

Just as she and Rufryd were ready to leave – on the edge of the village, with a crowd to see them off – Auriel suddenly came and took her on one side. Of all her family, strangely, he seemed the most concerned that she was leaving. His eyes were dark.

'Hey, don't be upset,' she said. 'We won't be gone forever—'

He cut her off. 'I know. There's something I need to say.'

'Go on.'

'We both love humans, but we are Aelyr,' Auriel said, soft and intent. 'We may outlive them by many years. If a day comes when they are gone and we are both still here . . .'

He looked meaningfully at her, as alluring and graceful as first time she'd seen him. She understood. She nodded, and couldn't speak.

'We will meet again, won't we?' he said. 'We shall still have each other, Fliyet.'

'Always,' she said with difficulty. She held his face gently between her hands. 'Go and love Ysomir.'

'What was all that about?' Rufryd asked as she came back to him and hefted her rucksack onto her shoulder.

'Oh . . . nothing. Just saying goodbye.'

The Fhelethyr never came to reclaim the house, so Falthorn and Jthery stayed there. It was in their nature, Falthorn said, to move on.

Falthorn chose to recuperate by spending a good deal of time in the garden, sitting beside one of the sapphire pools in the shade of blue-green foliage. The music of rills and waterfalls sang constantly in the background. Jthery enjoyed these quiet times. It was a pleasure to be alone in Falthorn's company. He would read to him, or they'd talk, or just sit in pleasant silence.

The casualties the Valahyr had taken on the Almandine Vale had been light, compared to the humans. There was sorrow, but not enough for the Valahyr to turn against Falthorn. They saw the battle as necessary and noble. He had the gift, Jthery saw, of making his own exploits seem heroic. He still had the Valahyr in the palm of his hand, which meant there were dozens of *eretru* members happy to wait on him hand and foot. Jthery had to admire his nerve.

'I shall have to go back to Mithrain eventually,' Jthery said one golden afternoon.

'I thought there were a dozen of your vigorous relatives to get through the dukedom before it fell to you.'

'Three, but I should still take an interest. Anyway, by the time I take the seat I'll be an old, old man and you'll have long since stopped desiring me.'

'Even the Aelyr get old eventually,' said Falthorn, 'and I have a head-start on you. We can become decrepit together. But you needn't wait that long . . .'

'Stop it,' said Jthery. 'Just stop!'

'A boating accident, parent, grand and great-grand all at once, such a tragedy.'

'Falthorn, I swear I'll throw you in the pond if you don't stop.'

'Still, you do realise that unless you can bring yourself to copulate with a human woman, you'll die without heirs?'

Jthery winced. 'For Eshte's sake, Fal, what's got into you?'

'It's called foresight. Considering all permutations. Suppose we were to take a Valahyr child and pass it off as yours . . .'

'Then you'd be in control of one of the Nine Realms. Surely you're not still trying to think of ways of controlling the Earth!'

'No,' Falthorn said with a mischievous smile. 'I'm just checking that you're awake. I may have made mistakes but that doesn't mean I should go into a decline and brood upon them for the rest of my days. Would you want me to?'

'It wouldn't be you if you did.' He laughed.

'What's so amusing?'

'I'm just thinking of a warning my Goddess, Eshte, gave me. *"Beware, Jthery. There are different kinds of love waiting for you. One is true, the other is false and lethal."* I didn't realise they were both with the same person.'

'Touching. And both on the same day, sometimes,' Falthorn said, raising an eyebrow. 'You need encouragement to think in a more creative way. Not to assume one way is all bad, another all good. Now we have a new mood of co-operation between human and Aelyr, a Valahyr influence on Mithrain might be no bad thing.'

'Falthorn, I'm all for co-operation, but certain things are unquestionably wrong. *Gauroth*, for example.'

'You prove my point! You mustn't think that *gauroth* is intrinsically evil. It is a wild, chaotic energy that can destroy or corrupt its wielder – but under control, it is a powerful force for change.'

'Yet it comes from fear and pain . . .'

'Fear and pain, though, are not in themselves evil or even undesirable. If we didn't feel them, we wouldn't survive. Our ancestors would all have leapt off cliffs to see if they could fly, or set fire to themselves to create living art. Powerful emotion, traumatic events in nature, all these set *gauroth* free. I never had to torture anyone to find it. It is like a hot spice; a little goes a long way. Too much and you burn yourself from inside out, as Vaurgroth did.'

'Perhaps we should agree to differ,' Jthery said, running a fingertip along the back of Falthorn's hand.

'Jthery,' Falthorn said suddenly, 'are you wearing a silver robe?'

'Er, yes. Yes I am.'

'There's some violet embroidery on the shoulder. And you have a leaf stuck in your hair.'

Falthorn reached out and dislodged the leaf. Jthery gaped at him. 'Your sight's coming back. This is wonderful. How much can you see?'

'Just shadows, shapes, colours. It's blurred, but . . .' There was genuine, unfettered joy in his face. 'If this is all I ever see, it's wonderful enough. But there's hope it will improve. Aelyr bodies have a way of healing themselves. Jewelfire, it is so good to see your face again.'

Jthery studied him, thrilled but suddenly wary. Falthorn seemed happy, but he didn't seem overly surprised. 'Wait a minute. How long have you known your sight was coming back? Was it really just now? Or did it happen before and you didn't tell me?'

Falthorn was affronted. 'Why would I do that?'

'So you could play being blind for all you were worth! I know you, Falthorn. You might have been seeing for weeks for all I know!'

'Jey, you are most unfair.' Falthorn caressed his head. 'I'd forgotten what a beautiful colour your hair is. Don't be such a cynic. It's only just happened.'

Jthery sighed. 'I want to believe you.'

'Believe me, then.' Falthorn smiled. 'When have I ever lied to you?'

Acknowledgements

For their endless encouragement, moral support and love throughout the writing of The Jewelfire Trilogy, I especially wish to thank Mike Llewellyn, Justina Robson, and my Mum and Dad. Thanks are also due to my steadfast agent, John Richard Parker, my incomparable editor, John Jarrold, and to my dear friends Storm Constantine, Anne Gay, Chris Baker, Rachel Baker, Chris Roe, Lolita Soares and Jay 'Alice' Cooper . . . not to mention the Brum Writers' Group, who have helped me through many an awkward chapter. Blessings also upon the Dark Angels of the Nottingham Vampyre Group, for all the fun and good times. Last but not least I salute Vikki Lee France and the Prophets – past, present and future – who know my innermost secrets yet who, amazingly, are still friends with me . . . Thank you for being there, all.

Freda Warrington's web site can be found at:
http://members.aol.com/FredaMike/index.html

EARTHLIGHT

A SELECTED LIST OF FANTASY TITLES AVAILABLE FROM EARTHLIGHT

THE PRICES SHOWN BELOW WERE CORRECT AT THE TIME OF GOING TO PRESS. HOWEVER EARTHLIGHT RESERVE THE RIGHT TO SHOW NEW RETAIL PRICES ON COVERS WHICH MAY DIFFER FROM THOSE PREVIOUSLY ADVERTISED IN THE TEXT OR ELSEWHERE.

☐	0 7434 0893 4	Talisker	Miller Lau	£6.99
☐	0 6848 6036 8	Cettika	Robert Holdstock	£16.99
☐	0 6710 2261 X	The Sum Of All Men	David Farland	£6.99
☐	0 7434 0827 6	Brotherhood of the Wolf	David Farland	£6.99
☐	0 6848 6061 9	Wizardborn	David Farland	£10.00
☐	0 6710 1785 3	The Royal Changeling	John Whitbourn	£5.99
☐	0 6710 3300 X	Downs-Lord Dawn	John Whitbourn	£5.99
☐	0 6710 2193 1	Sailing to Sarantium	Guy Gavriel Kay	£6.99
☐	0 7434 0825 X	Lord of Emperors	Guy Gavriel Kay	£6.99
☐	0 6848 6131 3	The Dreamthief's Daughter	Michael Moorcock	£16.99
☐	0 6848 6670 6	Silverheart	Michael Moorcock & Storm Constantine	£16.99
☐	0 6710 2190 7	The Amber Citadel	Freda Warrington	£5.99
☐	0 7484 0826 8	The Sapphire Throne	Harry Turtledove	£5.99
☐	0 6710 2282 2	Into The Darkness	Harry Turtledove	£5.99
☐	0 6710 3305 0	Darkness Descending	Harry Turtledove	£6.99
☐	0 6848 6007 4	Through the Darkness	Harry Turtledove	£10.00
☐	0 6710 2189 3	The Siege of Arrandin	Marcus Herniman	£5.99

All Earthlight titles are available by post from:

Book Service By Post, P.O. Box 29, Douglas, Isle of Man IM99 1BQ

Credit cards accepted. Please telephone 01624 675137, fax 01624 670923, Internet http://www.bookpost.co.uk or e-mail: bookshop@enterprise.net for details.

Free postage and packing in the UK. Overseas customers allow £1 per book (paperbacks) and £3 per book (hardbacks).